PAUL SCOTT

A Division
of the Spoils

arrow books

Published by Arrow Books in 2005

16

First published in Great Britain in 1975 by
William Heinemann
Random House 20 Vauxhall Bridge Road,
London SW1V 2SA

www.randomhouse.co.uk

Addresses for companies within The Random House Group Limited
can be found at:
www.randomhouse.co.uk/offices.htm

The Random House Group Limited Reg. No. 954009

A CIP catalogue record for this book
is available from the British Library

ISBN 9780099478836

Penguin Random House is committed to a sustainable future for
our business, our readers and our planet. This book is made from
Forest Stewardship Council® certified paper.

MIX
Paper from
responsible sources
FSC® C018179

Printed and bound in Great Britain by Clays Ltd, St Ives plc

To Doreen Marston
With my love and regard

CONTENTS

BOOK ONE 1945

An Evening at the Maharanee's

I

Hitler was dead, the peace in Europe almost a month old; only the Japanese remained to be dealt with. In June the Viceroy left London, flew back to Delhi, said nothing in public for nearly two weeks and then announced a conference of Indian leaders at Simla to discuss proposals which he hoped would ease the political situation, hasten final victory and advance the country towards her goal of full self-government. To enable all the leaders to be there he had to issue several orders of release from imprisonment.

The conference opened on June 25 and did not break down until July 14, an unexpectedly long time in the opinion of many English officials for Congress and Muslim League views on the composition of a new Indianised Executive Council or interim government to prove irreconcilable. The Viceroy, Lord Wavell, admitting failure, blamed himself and begged that there should be no recriminations. Subsequently, in press conference, the leader of the All-India Congress Party, a Muslim, blamed the leader of the Muslim League for the unbending nature of his claim for the League's right to nominate all Muslim members of the proposed Executive Council and blamed the British Government for not having foreseen that the conference would break down if one party were given the right of veto on nominations and therefore the opportunity to hold up the country's progress to autonomy. The leader of the Muslim League spoke disapprovingly of a combination of Hindu interests supported by the 'latest exponent of geographical unity' – the Viceroy – whose plan in his opinion was a snare for Muslim interests. Mr Nehru described the Muslim League as mediaeval in conception, and warned that the real problem facing a free India would not be

3

communal and religious differences but economic backwardness.

The members of the conference then left Simla to consider the situation .in private. Among the first to go was Mr Mohammed Ali Kasim, a Muslim Congressman and ex-chief minister of the pre-war government of the province of Ranpur, who, if Jinnah had his way, could expect no portfolio in the higher council. Like several other prominent Congress politicians Mr Kasim had not been seen in public for nearly three years. Guarded from reporters by a small but efficient entourage headed by his younger son Ahmed, he ignored the questions shouted at him as he left the Cecil Hotel and concentrated on helping Ahmed to support a frail old man later identified by onlookers as his aged and ailing secretary – Mr Mahsood. Safe in his car at last he snubbed the young man from the *Civil and Military Gazette* who got close enough to the window to say, 'Minister, is Pakistan now inevitable?' by commanding Ahmed to put up the glass and pull down the blinds.

The lowering of the blinds caught the imagination of an Indian cartoonist who portrayed the car (identified as that of the ex-chief minister by the initials MAK on one of its doors) with all its windows, including the driver's, shuttered and making off at high speed (smoke-rings from the exhaust) from a once imposing but now crumbling portal inscribed 'Congress' towards a distant horizon with a sun marked 'Hopes of Office' rising behind a broken-down bungalow on whose rickety verandah the leader of the Muslim League, Mr Jinnah, could be seen conferring with several of his associates.

The cartoon annoyed adherents of Congress. They objected both to the inference that Mr Kasim was about to betray them and join the League and to the representation of their party as a derelict doorway with nothing behind it. Similarly, Muslim Leaguers objected to the portrayal of the Qaid-e-Azam as the occupier of a squalid little property such as the one depicted.

By the time the cartoon appeared (two days after the end of the conference) the liberals and middle-of-the-road men in Indian politics – who might have protested at the lampooning of a man whose legal skills and political integrity had commanded wide respect for a quarter of a century – could not

4

help wondering whether Mr Kasim had after all shown himself as capable as men of lesser merit of acting with an eye to the main chance. What else, they asked, but an intention to shift his allegiance to the League, in the hope of securing his political future with a party that had grown strong enough to wreck a viceregal conference, could better explain his subsequent mysterious behaviour?

Between Delhi and Ranpur Mr Kasim seemed to have succeeded not only in evading the journalists but in disappearing together with his entire entourage. He was not on the train when it arrived in Ranpur and he never turned up at the old Kasim house on the Kandipat road. This house had been closed since Mr Kasim's wife (and then Mr Mahsood) had left it in the middle of 1944 to join him after his release from the Fort at Premanagar in the protective custody of his distant kinsman, the Nawab of Mirat. The reason given for that release had been Mr Kasim's reported ill-health, but it was Mrs Kasim who, some six months later, died.

The journalists who waited outside the still-locked gates of the house on the Kandipat road to greet the distinguished Muslim Congressman on his return home after three years detention and restriction, found themselves joined, towards evening, by colleagues who had waited just as uselessly at the station, and then by a growing crowd of spectators who eventually tangled with a truck-load of police sent to disperse them. A running battle developed between the lathi-armed constables and the quicker-tempered of Mr Kasim's admirers (students). The peaceful pleasures of families taking the air in the Sir Ahmed Kasim Memorial Gardens opposite were disturbed. A number of arrests were made and rumours then spread through the Koti bazaar and out to the suburb of Kandipat that Mr Kasim had been arrested by the British on the train from Delhi, had been abducted by Hindu extremists, had been murdered by the communists, had succumbed to poison administered by agents of the Viceroy. The shop of an unpopular merchant, a Hindu who gave short weight, was broken into and looted and that of another, a Muslim, ransacked in retaliation. The following day students of the Ranpur Government College demonstrated in the area of the Civil Lines carrying placards asking 'Where is MAK?' and hartal was observed in the Koti bazaar by Hindus and Muslims alike for fear of riot, arson and the consequent loss of profits.

At this stage it was discreetly leaked by the Inspector-General of Police to the Municipal Board that Mr Kasim was alive and well and back in the Nawab of Mirat's summer palace in the Nanoora Hills, and this information was simultaneously confirmed by a telephone call from a correspondent in Mirat to his editor in Ranpur. It seemed that Mr Kasim and his party had left the Delhi-Ranpur train at a wayside halt some miles outside the provincial capital and had then been driven to another wayside halt where the Nawab's private train awaited him and carried him back to the scene of his protective custody, although in this case it had to be assumed that his return was voluntary and caused by nothing more sinister than the need to sort out the detritus of the year he had spent there under government restriction.

The news inspired the same cartoonist to a further interpretation of Mr Kasim's evasive behaviour. Mirat was a princely state whose territory was contiguous to the province, whose inhabitants were predominantly Hindu but whose ruler was of the Islamic faith. In the new cartoon MAK was shown sitting cross-legged at a low table in the company of the Nawab and Mr Jinnah. The table, heavily spread with a feast, was labelled 'Islam'. Beneath it, only head and arms visible, was the struggling body of Free India. From behind a pillar the puckish face of Winston Churchill peered, the head sporting a Jinnah-shaped fez to depict the English leader's alleged preference for Muslims and sympathy with their aspirations, the face smoothed by an expression of satisfaction at the thought that the Princes, those loyal Indian supporters of the Crown in two world wars, and the Muslim League which had refused to have anything to do with the non-co-operation tactics of the Congress Party, would together – for whatever different reasons – now so bedevil every move the Congress made to force the issue of Indian independence to a conclusion favourable to themselves that British rule could comfortably be extended far enough into the future for the phrase 'indefinitely if not in perpetuity' not to seem inappropriate. Another cartoon on the following day depicted Mr Churchill receiving an ovation from a moronic (or badly drawn) and adoring British public, to whom he was about to appeal for re-election, holding in one arm a baby labelled 'Victory in Europe', with the other arm extended presenting its hand in giant perspective and the famous V-sign, but with the two fingers raised the wrong way round. One of these fingers was labelled 'Jinnah' and the other 'Princely India'. Clenched in the curled fist below the fingers was a limp body representing Indian unity and nationalism. Thereafter, as a result of a visit to the editor's office by a representative of the CID no cartoons by this particular artist appeared in this or any other newspaper for some time.

The news that Mr Kasim had gone back to Mirat caused a similar influx of journalists into Nanoora to that of the previous year when he had been let out of the Fort; but although there were now presumably no restrictions on his movements or activities the journalists again failed to obtain an interview and this time did not even receive official messages of regret from court officials that Mr Kasim had no statement to make. Several abortive attempts were made to enter the grounds of the summer palace; a costly business since it involved bribing servants and officials, and a dangerous one because there was the risk of arrest for trespass, even (it was said) of summary imprisonment in one of the Nawab's dungeons. One by one the journalists departed, filing imaginative copy, until only a handful remained in the rambling little hill town, drinking in the coffee and liquor shops, discussing the interesting rumour about Mr Kasim's elder son Sayed, which their editors dared not yet print, and visiting the brothels, for private entertainment but also in the hope of meeting Mr Kasim's younger son, Ahmed, who was said to be a drunkard and a lecher, an incorrigible wastrel who had come near to breaking his father's heart before being packed off to Mirat in the Nawab's service, to womanize and drink himself to death if he wished.

But there was no sign of Ahmed Kasim either. A story that he was being treated for venereal disease in a room in the private residence of Dr Habbibullah, chief physician to the Nawab, sent the remaining journalists from the Nanoora Hills down to the city of Mirat and then a rumour that MAK

7

had initiated the story of his younger son's illness to get rid of the press and leave Nanoora unnoticed sent some of them rushing back and others out of the State altogether, back to Ranpur and British India. The latter found the Kasim house on the Kandipat road still closed and the former were no more successful than hitherto in establishing through the evidence of their own eyes whether the elusive Congressman was in fact in residence at the summer palace.

Journalists in other parts of India thought they detected in the attitude of members of the Congress high command more pious hopes than firm convictions of Mr Kasim's continuing allegiance to the twin cause of freedom and unity which he had supported throughout his political life, and a characteristically enigmatic comment by the Mahatma (not spoken, but written down, it being his day of silence) did little to remove the suspicion that during the Simla conference there had been private differences of opinion between MAK and his distinguished colleagues. Asked if he could throw any light on Mr Kasim's apparently self-imposed security screen, Mr Gandhi wrote: 'God alone throws light on any matter and in this light we may from time to time perceive the truth.'

With this the two journalists had to be content because the Mahatma indicated that the interview was over. They departed, leaving him to bathe and have his massage.

A few days later public interest in Mr Kasim's political intentions was temporarily extinguished by the unexpected news that the British electorate had voted overwhelmingly for the Socialists and, in doing so, relegated the arch-imperialist, Mr Churchill, at the moment of his triumph, to the post of Leader of His Majesty's now numerically harmless Tory Opposition.

*

The story that three senior members of the Bengal Club promptly died of apoplexy, although not without a certain macabre charm, proved to have no foundation in fact; but there was no doubt that for several days relations between many British officers and the rank and file of conscript British soldiers serving their time in India, who had voted by post and proxy, were a little distant, and in one reported case demonstrably strained and only saved from escalating to the point where they would have formed the basis of a very serious affair of conduct prejudicial to good order and military discipline by the presence-of-mind of a sergeant-major who stood between his captain and a lance-corporal who had admitted 'voting for old Clem' on the railway station at Poona and said, 'Sir, I think we have a little touch of the sun.' It was raining at the time.

The rifle company of which this captain was in command formed part of a British infantry battalion that was on its way to Kalyan, near Bombay, to join the forces gathering there for the invasion and liberation of Malaya, in an operation known as Zipper. The battalion reached Kalyan on July 30 and settled itself in to a section of an immense hutted encampment that looked and proved dreary. The wet monsoon was at its peak. The Churchillian officer and most of his colleagues managed to travel frequently by jeep to find solace in Bombay, in whose roads part of the invasion force of shipping had already anchored in preparation for the embarkation of the troops, but the rank and file were less fortunate.

There was Housey-Housey, a camp cinema, and Indian prostitutes who were cheap but out-of-bounds. There was mud. It was a bleak terrain that it took some effort of imagination to see as once having been part of the background to the romantic and exotic affairs of the Mahratta kings in whom a fair-haired and well-spoken British Field Security sergeant – with a degree in history from Cambridge – attempted to interest a bored and restive group of captive Cockney, Welsh, Midlands and Northern Englishmen who had to be forgiven for wondering what they were doing in Kalyan getting kitted up for the Far East when the real war (the one in Europe) was over and the lights had actually gone up in London, in every sense. Accounts received from home of VE night celebrations had already eroded what little sense of India's attractions they had acquired and since this had in any case never been lively enough to nourish in them any kind of curiosity about her history or her future, the Field Security sergeant, whose name was Perron, was soon left in little

9

doubt of his audience's indifference to the political machinations and territorial ambitions of Mahdaji and Daulat Rao
Sindia. Since he had embarked on the lecture with neither
enthusiasm nor optimism, the audible appeal to wrap it up for
****** sake caused him no surprise and scarcely a pang. His
closing description of a lady-warrior said to have reduced her
male rivals to a state of military impotence, by admitting
them to her chamber one after the other on the night before a
battle, brought the lecture to an end in an atmosphere of near-
hysteria. 'Bring 'er on,' the same voice cried, and the room
then resounded to whistling and the stamping of hundreds of
ammunition boots – a noise that greeted the Welfare Officer
as he arrived to see how Sergeant Perron was getting on and
which seemed to encourage him in a belief that such lectures
were a good thing; a belief of which Sergeant Perron did not
disabuse him because he had decided quite early in his
military service that for life to be supportable officers had to
be protected from anything that might shatter their illusion
that they knew what the men were thinking.

Knowing himself incapable of reaching the required standard of self-deception in this, and other matters that came
under the heading 'Leadership', and believing that life in the
ranks would provide him with a far greater measure of
freedom and better opportunities to study in depth human
behaviour during an interesting period of history, he had
politely but stubbornly resisted every attempt made to
commission him. Only one set of the batch of uncles and
aunts who had taken it in turns to bring him up thought this
short-sighted. The others approved of his decision. They
thought it agreeably eccentric, quite in keeping with the
radical upper-class tradition which they liked to feel distinguished them as a family.

'It obviously went down well,' the Welfare Officer said,
toning down his North Country accent and matily accompanying Perron from the lecture hall. 'I must say I had doubts,
but a chap who really knows his subject is more likely to pass
some of his enthusiasm on than not. You must do some more,
sergeant.'

'A good idea, sir.'

'These waiting periods are damned difficult. There's a

batch of airborne blokes due in soon. Now that the show in Germany's over they'll be itching to get started and give the Jap a knock. They'll be a handful to keep occupied and entertained. I know you've got your own special security job to do but I'd be grateful if you'd spare half-an-hour to talk to them one morning on this Indian history thing of yours. I'll try and come myself. Learn a bit too. Extend my range beyond the Black Hole. Never too late for that, eh?'

Perron said, 'Actually, if you don't mind, sir, I think they're more relaxed without an officer present.'

Captain Strang looked relieved. To reassure the officer that his interest was appreciated but that his friendliness would not be taken advantage of and made an excuse for slack behaviour, Perron slapped up a particularly smart one when they parted and would have stamped his feet had they not been standing in a puddle. Perron had cultivated a formidable parade-ground style and soldierly manner not only to preserve that encouraging image of discipline and efficiency which heartened officers but also (after a tiresome experience with a Seaforth Highlander captain in the map-room of a camp on Salisbury Plain) to minimize the risk of his BBC accent (as fellow-NCOS called it) and his cultural interests giving them the impression that he was a pansy.

*

The sight of the armada gathering off Bombay – a city to which Sergeant Perron's field security duties now began to take him fairly regularly – appearing, disappearing and reappearing as the curtains of monsoon rain and mist rose and fell with sinister effect, did not usually depress him. In four years of service he had learned to look upon the entire war as an under-rehearsed and over-directed amateur production badly in need of cutting. In this light the low grey shapes of the troopships and escorts could be seen as figments of the imagination of an unknown but persistent operational planning staff whose directives had caused them to appear. The same imagination could just as easily dispel them. Nothing in the army was absolutely sure until it happened and he did not

11

intend to worry about Zipper or the danger he might be in until the ships weighed anchor with himself on one of them.

But on the afternoon of Sunday August 5 as he drove past the Taj Mahal Hotel in a brand new jeep that had been lent in temporary exchange for the motor-cycle he had left at the motor-pool for water-proofing for the sea-borne landings in Malaya, he observed that the armada had increased in size since his view of it a couple of days before. Perhaps it was the sense of futility lingering from his previous day's lecture on the Mahrattas that chiefly contributed to his unusual feeling of disquiet, of there being something in the air that boded no good and moved him to nostalgic thoughts of a world where peace and common sense prevailed.

Being early for his appointment with a Major Beamish he stopped the jeep and gazed at the brown-grey waste of Bombay water. Without ever having taken any other personal avoiding action than that of co-operating cheerfully over the deferment of his call-up to enable him to sit his finals and obtain his degree, he had managed to get through the war so far without coming any closer to a violent end than half-a-mile away from a bomb off-loaded by a Heinkel over Torbay after a night visit to Bristol. But he had always assumed that his turn for danger would come. Posted to India in 1943 he had expected it to come quite soon but, of course, any apprehension that he felt in regard to that was combined with the excitement of finding himself after several years' scholarly absorption in Britain's imperial history actually in the country in which so much of it had originated.

In the first six months the luck of the draw of postings had given him opportunities to visit Cawnpore, Lucknow, Fort St George, Calcutta, Seringapatam, Hyderabad, Jaipur and Agra, and if he had felt some disappointment in these places as relics of old confrontations he had always managed to suppress it before it grew strong enough to undermine his academic confidence. 'India' he wrote in his notebook, 'turns out to be curiously immune to the pressures of one's knowledge of its history. I have never been in a country where the sense of the present is so strong, where the future seems so unimaginable (unlikely even) and where the past impinges so little. Even the famous monuments look as if they were built only yesterday and the ruined ones appear really to have been ruined from the start, and that but recently.'

Occasionally he was tempted to blame the war for his inability to relate the country he saw to what he knew of its past and at such times he thought how interesting it would be to come back or stay on when the war was over, to examine India undisturbed. But this afternoon, looking at the unfriendly vista of the Arabian Sea which as a boy he had thought the most romantically named ocean in the world, he felt more strongly than ever how perilously close to losing confidence the actual experience of being in India had brought him; and he wanted to go home – not (like the men to whom he had lectured) merely for home's sake or to enjoy the first fruits of a new political dispensation (for which he too had posted his vote by proxy through his Aunt Charlotte) – but so that he could regain lucidity and the calm rhythms of logical thought. These, he knew, depended upon a continuing belief in one's grasp of every issue relevant to one's subject and India seemed to be the last place to be if one wanted to retain a sense of historical proportion about it.

He got out his notebook with the intention of writing something down that might clarify his thoughts and expose as baseless his nagging doubts about the value of work he intended to do in pursuit of certain ineluctable truths but just as there seemed to be no connection between the India he was in and the India that was in his head there was no connection either between paper and pencil and the page remained ominously blank. This depressed him so much that he wrote out in a determined hand: 'Tell Aunt Charlotte that Bunbury is deteriorating rapidly?'

*

'This is Captain Purvis, sergeant,' Major Beamish said, indicating a thin-faced, mousy-haired, ill-looking man who was dosing himself with brown pills which he washed down with water without quite choking. 'You an' 'e are goin' this evenin' to a party.' Beamish, like so many elderly regular officers, spoke a kind of upper-crust cockney.

'Yes, sir,' Perron said, keeping his thumbs in line with the seams of his trousers.

Beamish was in a bad temper, either as a result of a thick Saturday night or of lingering resentment at being made to work on a Sunday. He said, 'Fer God's sake sit down. It's too bloody hot fer parade-ground manners.'

Perron, who stood over six feet in his socks, chose the deepest of three available chairs in deference to Major Beamish whose trunk was short in proportion to his legs and who therefore sat lower at his desk than seemed either fair or suitable for a man of his domineering temperament. Satisfied that his eye-level was now a flattering few inches below Beamish's, Perron met the officer's gaze with soldierly frankness.

'D'yer have yer civvies with yer?'

Before Perron could answer, the other officer – who was now sitting with his eyes closed and his arms folded broke in. 'Shouldn't advise civvies in this case.'

'I have my Army Education Corps gear, sir,' Perron said.

'Those'll do,' Purvis said.

'You fill 'im in, Purvis, or shall I?'

'Would you? I'll interrupt if I don't think you've got it right. Could we have that fan on more?'

Perron got up and went to the board of switches and turned up the dial that regulated the ceiling fan. Irritably, Beamish re-allocated weights to keep the papers moored to the desk top, then lit a cigarette but did not offer the tin.

'It's about security fer Zipper and loose talk here in Bombay,' he began. Perron listened attentively for the ten seconds it took Beamish to pass from the informative to the opinionative mood and then tried to tune in what he called his other ear: the one that caught the nuances of time and history flowing softly through the room, a flow arrested neither by Beamish's concerns nor his own sense of obligation to further them by putting himself at Beamish's disposal. Glancing at Purvis he wondered whether that officer also heard the whisper of the perpetually moving stream or whether the expression of concentration was due to the compelling effect of the brown pills. When Purvis's brows suddenly contracted he decided it must be the latter.

'Are yer still with us, sergeant?'

'Yes, sir.'

'Right. Tell 'im about the party, Purvis.'

For a moment Purvis neither spoke nor moved. Then he opened his eyes.

'God!' he said, got up and went out of the room.

'Feller's got squitters,' Beamish explained.

'Who is Captain Purvis, sir?'

'Damned if I know. Brig didn't say. Never met 'im in me life till half-an-hour ago. Seems a bit of a wash-out ter me. Chap should be able to keep 'imself fitter than that!'

A chaprassi came in with a foot-high pile of folders tied up in pink tape and put them by the side of a similar pile on the In side of Major Beamish's desk. There was a single file in the Out tray. The chaprassi took this with him when he went. Beamish poured himself a glass of water then took the top folder from the nearest of the two piles.

'Smoke if yer want ter,' he said. 'While we're waitin'.'

Perron murmured his thanks but did not do so. Beamish read the note in the file, initialled it, flung the folder in the Out tray and reached for the next.

Ten minutes later Purvis came back. Beamish was reading the minute in the last folder of the second pile. Without glancing up he said, 'Feelin' better?'

'Frankly, no. I think the sergeant will have to come back to my billet. I'll put him in the picture there. In any case he'll need somewhere to change and freshen up for this evening.'

'All right, sergeant, get along with Captain Purvis. Are yer goin' back ter Kalyan ternight?'

'That was my intention, sir.'

'Ring me from there in the mornin'. We'll decide if there's anything ter follow up.'

Perron stood, put his cap on, stamped to attention and saluted. As he turned he caught the tail end of a wince on Captain Purvis's face.

'Shoes, sergeant! Have you got *shoes*?' Purvis asked.

'In my pack, sir. With the uniform.'

'Thank God for that. What are you on, a motor-bike?'

'I've got a jeep today, sir.'

'We'll dump it at my office.'

15

Outside in the corridor Purvis maintained his distance a couple of paces ahead. They passed a long bench on which a line of chaprassis dozed, like figures on a frieze in bas-relief, awaiting employment. The building – currently at the disposal of the army and navy – belonged to the port authority and smelt of rope, gunny sacks and the dust on old bills of lading. Through the immense windows in the main corridor into which they turned came that other pervasive dockyard smell of oily water: Bombay, Bom-Bahia, an island swamp, part of the dowry brought by Catherine of Braganza to Charles II which it took the British five years to persuade the Portuguese Viceroy actually to hand over. Perron stemmed the stream of thought before it could disorient him; apart from which Purvis walked very fast and Perron didn't want to run the risk of losing him in the labyrinth. He concentrated on Purvis's back and noticed that the officer's shoulders were hunched – probably against the ringing sound of Perron's studded boots on the stone floor.

Descending by a broad stone staircase they reached the main entrance hall on whose marble flags stood a profusion of poles on heavy plinths which bore directional signs. None of the officers and NCOs passing to and fro glanced at the signs and Perron wondered how long it would take for the place to be reduced to a state of hopeless confusion if someone ever took it into his head to move the signs round. Perhaps no one would ever notice.

He smiled and at that moment Purvis stopped and faced him. They nearly bumped into one another. Whatever Purvis had intended to say he forgot.

'Something amusing you, sergeant?'

'No, sir.'

'I mean if there is, do *share* it.'

Perron told him his thought about the signs. Purvis glanced at them. Without another word he led the way into the open: a fore-court normally crammed with vehicles but today fairly empty. In the minute or so since they had left Beamish's office the sun had come out. The heat struck Perron's eyelids.

'Where's this jeep of yours, then?'

Perron indicated it.

'No driver?'

'Only me, sir.'

Purvis went down the steps. 'Mine's that fifteen hundred-weight Chevvy. Follow me and for God's sake keep up. Right?'

Jeep-borne, Perron followed the truck through the archway which was blocked at night by a white pole but at present open to all comers and goers under the eye of a stick-guard who was supposed to inspect identity cards but was taking people on trust. They drove along a road parallel to the docks. At the end of it Purvis's truck turned left. Caught in the midst of Bombay's traffic – buses, cyclists, hooting taxis, overladen trucks, horse-drawn doolies and jay-walking pedestrians – Perron concentrated on not losing contact. The truck braked sharply to avoid an obstacle Perron couldn't see. He slammed on his own brakes and stopped a foot or two short of an impact that might have snapped the tether Purvis seemed to be near the end of. Possibly the nest of spies, fifth-columnists and loose-talkers Perron gathered Purvis thought he'd uncovered was totally illusory. Driving on, but allowing more distance (and noting that the cause of the abrupt halt had been a handcart piled high with crates of live fowl, hauled by a half-naked coolie) Perron decided that so long as Purvis wasn't at his elbow the entire evening, hissing warnings, the party might be supportable; or even enjoyable.

*

Purvis's billet turned out to be a flat in one of the modern blocks opposite the Oval – that elegant, coconut-palm fringed rectangle of open, grassed, space; or *maidan*; brilliantly green at this wet time of year. They reached the block in Purvis's truck, having left Perron's jeep in the courtyard of a house several streets away which was guarded by sentries but otherwise unidentifiable as a military office. Purvis had instructed the guard-commander that Sergeant Perron was to be re-admitted on production of his identity card at whatever time of night he returned, in whatever kind of clothing or uniform, and be allowed to collect and take away his jeep; but – short though the journey was – the route then taken from Purvis's office to Purvis's billet seemed to Perron, in the back

17

of the truck, so complicated that he had doubts about finding his way back to his jeep unaccompanied. This had not bothered him much because he assumed they would go to the party in the fifteen hundredweight and be brought back from it by the same means, after which he would be taken to retrieve the jeep; but when they dismounted in Queen's Road Purvis signed the driver's log book and dismissed him until morning.

'Is the party being given nearby, sir?' Perron asked as they approached the entrance to the block of flats. Purvis didn't answer. He was in a hurry. Reaching the two steps that led to the open doorway and a dark hall he stumbled up them, bumped into and almost knocked down a servant who was coming out ahead of a young English woman.

'For God's sake look where you're going!' Purvis shouted.

If he was aware of the girl he gave no sign of it. He brushed past the two of them and disappeared into the dark.

'I do beg your pardon,' Perron said to the girl.

'Why?' she asked.

'I'm afraid the officer isn't well. He couldn't have seen you.'

She studied his uniform briefly, taking everything in at a glance as young English women in India were trained to.

'It wasn't me he bumped into, it was Nazimuddin. But thank you for apologizing for him.'

He waited for her to add ' –sergeant', but she smiled instead, an ordinary friendly smile, then put on the hat she had been carrying. The movement released a little wave of delicate scent. She came down the two steps and made for the pavement and the road where the ill-used bearer was flagging down a cruising taxi. She was a bit thin, a bit bony, but she walked well. He judged her to be in her early twenties but found it difficult to place her. Accent, style of dress, forthrightness: these proclaimed her a daughter of the *raj*, but her manner had lacked that quality – elusive in definition – which Perron had come to associate with young memsahibs: a compound of self-absorption, surface self-confidence and, beneath, a frightening innocence and attendant uncertainty about the true nature of the alien world they lived in. They were born only to breathe that rarified, oxygen-starved air of the upper slopes and peaks, and so seemed to gaze down, from

18

a height, with the touching look of girls who had been brought up to know everybody's place and were consequently determined to have everybody recognize their own.

Waiting until she had completed that movement – charming in a girl, especially in her – of climbing into the taxi, he shouldered the pack containing his Army Education Corps disguise, went into the building and through the gloom to an inner only slightly better lighted hall where there was a lift shaft and a flight of stone steps leading up. A notice, askew on a piece of string suspended from the handle of the trellis-work gate, informed him that the lift was out of order, but in any case he would not have known which floor to go to. There was no sound from above of Purvis climbing. The door of the flat immediately to his right had a dark-stained strip of wood above the bell with gold-lettering on it saying Mr B. S. V. Desai. To the left a similar notice read H. Tractorwallah. Both these doors seemed unlikely ones for Purvis to be on the other side of and neither had the look of having been opened recently.

Perron ascended. On the next floor the two flats were occupied respectively by a Lieut.-Col. A. Grace and a Major Rajendra Singh of the Indian Medical Service. The Indian medical officer's name seemed to have been painted on its strip of wood longer ago than Colonel Grace's. Perron hesitated, but then, deciding that if Purvis was billeted on this floor one of the two doors would have been left open, started on the next leg up and as he did so heard a voice above call, 'Sahib?'

Purvis's servant, he supposed. The man salaamed, stood back as Perron reached the next landing, and indicated the open door of the flat above Rajendra Singh's. As he entered he heard a groan. The servant closed the door and went quickly down a corridor to a curtained doorway. The groan was repeated. A tap was turned on. Perron put his pack down, went in the opposite direction to the one the servant had taken and entered a dining-area. This was separated from a living-room by a wide uncurtained arch. The living-room was elegantly furnished, filled with aqueous light of sunshine filtered through a set of louvred shutters. On a wall behind a long settee hung a series of what looked like paintings from the Moghul period, which upon close inspection Perron identified as genuine. He was still admiring them when the servant came in and invited him to go along to Captain Purvis's room.

This room, although large, was barrack-like by comparison. Apart from an almirah and a wooden table littered with books, papers and some discarded shirts, there was nothing else in it except a rush-seated chair and the camp-bed on which Purvis was lying, one hand over his eyes, the other hanging free, almost touching the floor. But an open door afforded a glimpse of a well-appointed green-tiled bathroom.

Purvis said, 'I'm not going to be able to make it, sergeant. You'll have to go by yourself or forget the whole thing. I wish to God I'd kept my mouth shut. It's all an utter waste of time. Every bloody civilian in Bombay knows where Zipper's going and why it's going and how it's going. We're the exceptions. We know where. But they know where better. They can even name the damned beaches. It'll be a shambles, a complete and unholy utter bloody cocked-up shambles.'

Suddenly Purvis uncovered his eyes and stared wildly at Perron.

'You *are* Field Security?'

'Yes, sir.'

'Beamish isn't. What the hell is he?'

'He has certain responsibilities for liaison between intelligence and operations.'

'But he's not your officer?'

'No, sir. My officer is in Poona at the moment.'

Purvis shut his eyes.

'Poona,' he said, almost under his breath. 'It scarcely seems possible.'

'Poona, sir? Or that my officer is there?'

But Purvis didn't say. Outside the barred but open window there was a sudden piercing contest of crows and then a human voice below in the courtyard raised in what to an untutored ear must sound like a protracted cry of pain but which Perron knew was only the call of an itinerant tradesman. Purvis groaned and turned on his side, the side away from the window. At that moment the sun went in and the sluice-gates of the wet monsoon re-opened. Purvis's lips began to move but Perron could hear nothing above the noise of the rainstorm.

The bearer parted the curtains and came in with a tray of tea for two. Perron assisted by clearing a space on the table and when the bearer had gone he looked at Purvis intending to say, 'Shall I be mother, sir?' but the officer's eyes were open, fixed and unreceptive – in fact, glazed. For a moment Perron thought he was dead, extinguished by the single clap of thunder that had heralded the arrival of the tea.

*

Refreshed, bathed and now disguised as a sergeant in education, Perron walked – shoe- instead of boot-shod – along the tiled passage to the living-room where he found Purvis standing on a balcony that had been revealed by the folding back of shutters and windows. It was now a beautiful evening with a sky the colour of pale turquoise. The coconut palms framed a view of the Law Courts and clock tower on the other side of the *maidan*.

'I appreciated the bath, sir. I'm afraid I used some of your Cuticura talcum.'

Purvis had a glass in the hand that rested on the balustrade.

'Help yourself to a drink, sergeant. You'll find everything on the tray.'

There was, if not everything, a generous selection: Gin, whisky, rum, several bottles of Murree beer and various squashes and cordials. The spirits were country-distilled so Perron – not caring much for rum of any kind – chose the gin which he found more palatable than Indian versions of Scotch. He added lemon-squash and – luxury for him – a cube of ice from a zinc-lined container.

'Cheers, sir.'

'I'm an economist,' Purvis said, irrelevantly to everything except his private train of thought. 'It's enough to send you round the bloody bend.'

He came in from the balcony, refilled his glass with rum and lime and sat on the long settee under the priceless paintings. After drinking a stout measure he shuddered, closed his eyes and put his head back.

21

'Can you guess how long I've been ill, sergeant?'

'No, sir.'

'Since I got off the boat. And that's three months, two weeks and four days ago.'

'Bad luck, sir.'

Purvis raised his eyelids a fraction and looked at him. Perron was standing with his feet apart, one hand behind his back, the other at waist level holding the tumbler steady.

'How long have you been in this bloody country?'

'Since 'forty-three, sir.'

'And in the army?'

'Since 'forty-one, sir.'

'Before that?'

'Cambridge, sir.'

'Doing what?'

'I rowed a bit. And read history.'

'What was your school?'

'Chillingborough, sir.'

'How the hell have you avoided getting a commission?'

'By always saying no, sir.'

Purvis shut his eyes again. His face began to contort.

'I'm sorry,' he said, 'but that is extremely funny.' He did not say why but took another long drink, set the glass on a low table in front of the settee then leant back with his hands clasped behind his head.

'The party,' he said, changing the subject and ploughing straight into the new one, 'is in the apartment of an Indian lady living on the Marine Drive. I'll write her a note, so you'll have the address on the envelope. There should be no difficulty about your going in my place. I was there the other night and she doesn't seem to care how many people turn up or whether she knows them or not. You'll see what I mean when you get there. Judging from the other day there'll be a lot of non-commissioned men so you won't feel out of place. The fact is, it seems to be the kind of flat where officers and men fraternize, not to mention white, black and in-between. Sexually I'd say some of the company was on the ambivalent side.'

'Yes, sir.'

'Will that worry you?'

22

'I don't think so, sir.'

'You may even be taken for a special sort of friend of mine.'

'I think I shall be able to cope in the event of a misunderstanding arising, sir.'

'Not that I care a fig about my own reputation. I shan't go there again. In any case you'll find lots of girls, if you can sort out the ones who're only interested in men.'

Perron finished his drink but retained his glass.

'Apart from unambivalent girls, sir, what precisely should I look out for? Any special person or group of people?'

'So far as I'm concerned, sergeant, you can just go there and get stoned or laid, as our American allies so picturesquely put it. I *told* you. The whole thing's an utter waste of time. You're not going to arrest anybody. At least, not for spying.'

'Major Beamish seemed to think otherwise about it being a waste of time, sir.'

'Think? Think? He's a professional soldier. They're all alike and worse out here than back home. Totally automatic. Touch a button by accident and they go into action. I'll tell you, Perron –'

Perron was surprised to find that his name had registered.

' – how this bloody farce you're up to the neck in started.'

Three days ago Purvis had encountered, in circumstances not clear, an old friend – obviously a breezy, hectic sort of man – who had whisked him up from whatever he'd been doing, dined him at the Taj and taken him off to the apartment in Marine Drive which Purvis's friend had described as 'always good for a lark', as indeed it had proved, in so far as an uninterrupted flow of drink, food and merrymaking was concerned. Although Purvis did not say so, Perron understood that the larkiness had been infectious enough to make Purvis forget his chronic internal disorder and become expansive with his hostess to whom in a weak but hospitable moment he had promised one of two remaining bottles of whisky he'd managed to get hold of in England and bring out to India for personal consolation. She had declined but he'd insisted and then been invited to come to another party with or without the bottle on the evening of August 5.

'I could have forgotten the whole damned thing,' Purvis said, 'if I hadn't stupidly made a casual remark next day to the

23

bloody fool officer I work with about the amount of careless talk going on in Bombay. He said – where for instance? And instead of shutting up I said "Well, take this odd party I was at last night where the Indian civilians were actually telling *us* that the Zipper invasion fleet wouldn't sail for Malaya until the end of August because of the tides on the beaches around Port Swettenham," and the next thing I knew the bloody man had reported it and I was hauled in front of that Brigadier Whatsit and congratulated on keeping my ears open. When he heard I'd been invited to the same flat tonight he was like a cat with two tails and before I knew where I was I was under strict security routine and told to say nothing more until I had instructions, and that was this morning when I was ordered to report to this Beamish fellow of yours. When Beamish told me I had to go to the party with a Field Security chap in disguise I thought he was joking. I tried to tell him you can hear that kind of talk anywhere in Bombay but he wouldn't *listen*.'

Perron put his empty glass on the drinks table.

'Are we landing on beaches near Port Swettenham, sir?'

'How the hell do I know? I've got no personal interest in Zipper. I'm not going, thank God. Are you?'

'Yes, sir.'

'Oh.'

Purvis noticed Perron's drink was finished. He said, 'Help yourself, sergeant.'

'Thank you, sir. But I think a clear head might be advisable this evening.'

'Advisable? In this country?'

Purvis became restless and Perron momentarily allowed himself to stop thinking of him as an officer with an officer's responsibilities for getting the war over and done with and think of him as a man, one whom in other circumstances he might even like.

'Well if you're *on* Zipper,' Purvis said, 'I suppose you have to take all this incredible lack of security seriously. I don't suppose you want to be shot out of the water by the Japanese before you've even set foot in the damned country, especially at this stage in the war.'

'I should prefer not to be, sir.'

'Does it bore you to call people sir?'

24

'No, sir.'

Purvis got up. He refilled his glass.

'What is your actual job, sir, if I may ask?'

'You may well ask. I've given up asking. I've even given up asking myself. Three times in my life the phone's rung and the fellow on the other end has said, "Can you get down to see me, Purvis? I've got something special for you." And each time it's ended like this, with me wondering not what's special about it but what it *is*. The first time was 'thirty-nine. I'd done a few papers that were well thought of. I'd got a good lectureship. And then the war started and the phone rang. "Purvis," this fellow said, "if you can get here in twenty minutes I've got something that will interest you." I was there with three minutes to spare and an hour to wait. And that led to a folding chair behind a deal-table in an attic without heating and a telephone that never rang. I thought I was supposed to contribute some original thinking to the problems of distribution of goods and services as between high and low priority demand sectors, or in layman's terms, the problems of trying to stop the army wasting what could be saved and what the civil population could bloody well make use of. I even drafted a paper and this chap rang up cock-a-hoop and said it was just what he wanted but if that was so I must have been under a misapprehension about what he wanted it for. I was in that attic for eighteen months. Then the phone rang again. Same chap, "Purvis," he said, "I've got something I think will get you out of that dead-end you're in." I arrived half-an-hour late, deliberately, which put him in a filthy temper because he'd promised to ring this colonel chap that very morning and tell him if I was interested. He sent me off to one of those anonymous areas somewhere near Stanmore which always strike me as vaguely sinister. When I saw the colonel he struck me as sinister too. He said, "We've read your paper" but hedged when I said I'd done several and which did he mean.

'The trouble is, Perron, I used to be the sort of man who couldn't bear to embarrass another by making it plain I saw through him and knew he was talking cock. So I let it go and just concentrated on trying to find out what I was supposed to *do*. I never did from him. But then they sent for me from the

War House. This time it was a mere major. Awfully pleasant chap. He'd actually read my paper on high and low priority demand sectors. I don't say he'd understood it. But he'd read it. And he called me *Mr* Purvis. He was even articulate about the job. Wrong. But articulate. He made me feel the inspiration for the special joint services advisory staff that he said was being got together to liaise with the various ministries and industry had been my paper and that I'd be one of its kingpins. "One thing," he said, "we'd want you in uniform. An immediate commission, naturally." '

Purvis's complexion suddenly went grey, either as a result of acute recollection or of acute physical discomfort. He downed the rest of his rum and poured another.

'I said I couldn't see what use a commission was. I'd signed the official secrets thing when I went to the attic. Well, as I said, he was an awfully pleasant chap. We didn't argue, and I went back to the attic and waited. I waited three weeks. When the summons came it wasn't to the War House but to the office of my benefactor. He congratulated me on making such a good impression on the people he'd recommended me to. He described my new job as the opportunity I'd been waiting for to exercise my talents as an economist for the country's benefit, an opportunity not to be thrown away on the totally irrelevant issue of what style of dress I exercised them in. I said, "You're right. Irrelevant is the word. So why the fuss? The army isn't me. Neither is officer status." '

Purvis sat down; he'd got up to get more lime-juice. He sat crouched, elbows on knees, head lowered and eyes hidden by his free hand. His shoulders began to shake.

'I'm sorry, sergeant, but it's so bloody funny. What you said about always saying no to a commission brought it all back.'

He straightened up.

'I'll tell you what this fellow said. "Purvis," he said, "in this country only a man born and bred *in* the officer-class can decline a commission without running the risk of having his integrity and future usefulness doubted." '

'Was that some kind of threat, sir?'

'Threat? It was a bloody ultimatum. Get into uniform or get out of the department. Not just out of the department but out of line for anything half-decent going after the war. Not to mention the immediate danger of ceasing a reserved occupation, getting called up and wasting the rest of the war as a highly inefficient and underemployed squaddie.'

'And subsequently, sir? Were your experiences as an officer on the advisory staff as unsatisfactory as those in the attic?'

'Oh no. No, I couldn't say that. Not unsatisfactory. Nor satisfactory. You see, Perron, there never was an advisory staff. I mean there was never *that* one. Plenty of others. It took me several weeks to realize that ours didn't actually exist. I used to go to these meetings. At first I thought I'd missed something important about its inauguration, because of the Gas course.'

'Gas course?'

'The day I reported to the War House disguised as an acting captain and war substantive lieutenant, the nice major said, "Oh, Purvis" – he'd dropped the mister, you see. "Purvis," he said, "d'you mind awfully, there's this boring gas thing come up, but I suppose you might just as well learn how to use a WD mask since you've now got to carry one." So I went down to Salisbury Plain.'

'An interesting part of the country, sir.'

Purvis looked at him, as though testing for sincerity.

'I didn't find it so. I expect you had some rudimentary military training at that public school of yours. Isn't it one of those places with a long record of turning out the future soldiers and administrators of Empire?'

'I wasn't in OTC, sir. It wasn't compulsory.'

'Well I had no military training whatsoever. My progress to my current distinction was from elementary via secondary to grammar school and to the earnest heights of the London School of Economics. Walking about with three pips up and no faintest notion of how to salute let alone whom to salute can be a highly embarrassing experience. I was glad when I got back to the War House and they sent me to this quaint little establishment off the Marylebone High Street where a retired Guards sergeant-major taught a batch of poor fellows like me how to dissemble sufficiently to avoid being put under close arrest as nuns parachuted in from Stuttgart. I almost wished, Perron, yes almost wished I'd scrubbed the whole career thing, been called up and gone into intellectual hibernation

27

for the duration. There was something soothing about Sergeant-Major Bracegirdle. He was so pleased with us when we got anything *right*. In a way nothing is more restful than to stand in the ranks and do what the man says. The whole thing is definitely erotic, a sort of communal wet-dream without the discomfort but with that same sublimated asexual quality of purely involuntary obedience to a dominant force.'

Purvis caught his breath, placed one hand on the left side of his abdomen and then slowly breathed out. Inflammation of the colon, Perron decided. Amoebic in origin, almost certainly. Perron had become interested in the effects of tropical environment on temper and character. At home Purvis might well have been, as he had intimated, the most mild-mannered and considerate of men. Of strong constitution himself, Perron – who had not maintained his health in India without an almost valetudinarian attention to the medicinal needs of his body – had even so not been free of the shortness of temper that was one of the side-effects of an overworked and easily discouraged digestive system. The insight this had given him into the possibly important part played in Anglo-Indian history by an incipient, intermittent or chronic diarrhoea in the bowels of the *raj* was one of the few definite academic advantages he felt he had gained by coming to India.

'Shall I freshen your drink, sir?'

'Oh, God, would you?'

Perron did so. Purvis now sat back, one arm stretched along the top edge of the settee, his face turned towards the window and the view – now fading – of the coconut palms.

'Have you ever felt it too, Perron? That the only way to survive a war is to treat it as totally unreal?'

'The thought has struck me, sir.'

'But have you ever succeeded?'

'From time to time.'

Purvis was silent for a moment.

'I envy you,' he said. 'I've tried. But I don't seem to have the capacity to pretend.' He looked at Perron. 'Six years! Six years criminal waste of the world's natural resources and human skills. History, you said?'

Perron nodded.

'Seriously, or just as a way of spending the years of gilded youth?'

'I intend to continue.'

'Well, it's different for you, Perron. If you make a study of history you make one of human folly. But sometimes I believe I simply shall never be able to *forgive* it. I had a breakdown, you know.'

'I'm sorry to hear that, sir.'

'They sent me to this place full of human wrecks like myself, but I did my own therapy. Bloody fool me. I'd had a lot of spare time in the three years I was on the non-existent advisory staff. I'd been thinking about the long-term deleterious effect of imperial possessions on the economic viability and creative drive of the country that held them. Now I really got down to it. I did a paper and sent it to a chap I knew who published it. But how my benefactor in Whitehall got hold of it, God knows. I suppose he still received the journal it came out in and read it because my name was under it. Otherwise he'd given up serious reading in 1938, I should say. Incidentally, he's probably right now in the process of landing himself a plum job with Attlee's crowd. He was a Marxist when I first knew him, a Liberal Edenite anti-Municheer under Chamberlain, a high Tory under Winston, so why not a milk-and-water Socialist under Clem? But that's by the way. Let me tell you what happened.'

'The phone rang again, sir?'

'Same man, of course. "You've had a raw deal, Purvis," he said, "no one knows it better than I but it wasn't my fault. When you're out of that place come and see me. I think I can really help you this time if you make it soon." Has it ever struck you, Perron, that there is nothing more gullible in the whole animal world than a human being? One has this hysterical belief in the non-recurrence of the abysmal, I suppose. One always imagines one has reached the nadir and that the only possible next move is up and out. And then, of course, there was the magic formula – third time lucky. Why not? I placed the most inordinate confidence in that third ring of the telephone, so much so that the trick-cyclists thought I'd had an unprecedented overnight recovery and con-gratulated themselves no end. Directly I got down to London I

29

rang this fellow and arranged to meet him. This time it was lunch at the club he'd been bucking to get into for years. He was already veering left again because he didn't see Churchill lasting long after the war. He introduced me to some of his new friends – I knew one or two of them myself and there was one in particular I respected. I thought, God, something's going to be done at last. I was right, but wrong about what. Something was being done. Von Rundstedt's attempt in the Ardennes had collapsed and all the signs were that the Germans were on their last legs. What was happening was people sniffing the peace and jockeying for position, but I was too stupid to see it like that at the time. I swallowed the whole line this fellow shot, about things now swinging the way of what he called "our sort of people" and how necessary it was to spike the guns of the old reactionary gang who'd be happy to let the war with Japan drag on and on and how our sort of people were determined that shouldn't happen. I ought to have seen through it when he started waffling about the Singapore-mentality that had come within an inch of bringing us to our knees in '42 and still existed out East in spite of all the efforts of men like Slim and Mountbatten to blow the cobwebs off the whole imperial-military apparatus. But I didn't. I just said, "Where's all this leading?" He said, "You mean what's in it for you?" That's the way he thought. "I'll tell you," he said, "that Indian paper of yours. It's really made an impression." I'd never thought of it as an Indian paper and I told him so. I told him it was a paper dealing in philosophical terms with an aspect of imperial economies and India came into it simply as an example, which didn't make me an expert on India. I shouldn't have said that. It gave him the line he needed. "But Purvis, experts on India are the last thing we want in India. We only want clear thinkers who'll help men like Bill and Dickie cut through the Singapore mentality and put ginger up the backsides of all those curry-colonels sitting in the Bengal Club in Calcutta and living in the nineteenth century." So I said, "Is that where you're sending me?" And he said it would be more likely Delhi where the real damage was done because GHQ India was still a vital link in Mountbatten's chain, *the* vital link, upon which the whole thing depended logistically, from the supply of men, arms and ammunition to the last piece of string and bamboo. Moreover, he said, if I wasn't an expert on India now I would be within a few months, at any rate in my own specialized field, and since the Indian empire was simply not going to survive in the kind of post-war world he knew he and I both hoped to see, my personal experience of it should prove invaluable to whatever government had the intricate job of transferring power to the Indians and advising them during a period of transition. "And that, Purvis," he said, "is the kind of little tree on which CBES grow for the plucking. After which you can pretty well write your own ticket. Continue in public life or retire, suitably rewarded, to the blessed groves of Academe." '

A flash of monsoon lightning lit the darkling flat.

'Has he risen much himself, sir?'

'Oh yes. You mean since '39? Immeasurably. He might with questionable luck for the nation be a future Chancellor of the Exchequer. He wasn't permanent establishment. I shouldn't be surprised to hear he's resigned his appointment and contested and won a safe Labour seat in the recent election.'

For a while Purvis sat without speaking or moving. Then he said, 'I must admit that as a man who can see the way things are and the way they are going, he's always left me standing. Academically it was the other way round and I don't expect he's ever forgiven me for that. People don't, do they? Inside every successful man there's often a disappointed and envious one, wouldn't you say? Moaning and groaning and plotting and planning. You see, Perron, I know the score now. He's got me out of the way deliberately. So that no nice little plum should fall in my lap.' Purvis again suffered a spasm of pain. 'I suppose you wouldn't be so kind as to give me another refill, sergeant? I have an idea it would be dangerous for me to move.'

Perron again performed this duty. While he did so the servant padded barefoot into the dining-room area where he clicked two or three switches which turned on some of the wall lights in the living-room and a well-shaded table lamp. The effect was pleasant.

The bearer told Purvis his bath was ready.

Purvis waved him away. The bearer went.

31

'Is the entire flat yours, sir?' Perron asked, handing Purvis the refilled glass.

'No. Thank you, sergeant. No, I wish it were. I'm only billeted here. It belongs to a senior British bank official, his ghastly wife and his beastly simpering daughter. They're on leave in what they call Ooty, which I gather is Anglo-Indian for Ootacamund. As you can imagine, he and I don't get on. We don't see eye to eye on the subject of the creation and distribution of wealth. He thinks England has just committed suicide and thinks I'm mad when I point out that it's not a socialist government but capitalist, simply substituting labour for finance. He tells people I'm a communist. Politically he's a bloody fool.'

'Are those paintings his, sir?'

'What paintings?'

'Those eighteenth-century paintings in the Guler-Basohli style. Behind you.'

Purvis didn't look. 'They may be part of the fixtures and fittings belonging to the bank for all I know.'

'I wonder whether he realizes their value.'

'Are they valuable?'

'Yes, sir.'

'Then obviously he doesn't. His lady-wife locked up all the Sheffield plate before going to Ooty. Frankly, I personally wouldn't know a work of art from a bee's arse and I fail to see any valid reason why one bit of pigment-daubed paper or canvas should be worth thousands and another worth sod-all, unless you fix the value of such things on the comparative basis of size of canvas and amount of paint actually expended.'

Perron stopped thinking of Purvis as a man and concentrated on the image of Purvis as an officer. Apart from inflammation of the colon, Purvis was suffering from paranoia. The man ought to be treated.

'What do the doctors say about your illness, sir?'

'I haven't seen any doctors.'

'Do you think that wise, sir?'

'Yes, I do.'

'You were taking some pills in Major Beamish's office, sir.'

'Oh, those. Our banker friend's lady-wife recommended them when I first arrived and she saw I'd already got the trots.

32

They're supposed to cement you up. Sometimes they do. Sometimes they don't. The only thing that really helps is liquor. No wonder the sahibs have always gone around half-cut. If I report to the army doctors they'll either prescribe the same treatment or send me into dock for a check-up and I can't afford to be in dock, Perron. Not for a day. Not for an hour.'

'Why, sir? You gave me the impression that your duties here aren't onerous.'

'That's because I'm not even supposed to *be* here. I'm supposed to be in New Delhi. We're all supposed to be in New Delhi.'

'All?'

'The six of us who formed the para-military mission sent out to liaise with and advise the Indian Government, heads of services, and the Government at home, on – I quote – "all matters relevant to the anticipated increase of military forces requiring to be based in India as a consequence of a cessation of hostilities in Europe and the continuance thereof in South-East Asia, with special reference to the supply/demand factor as it will affect the existing ratio between civilian and military claims on the Indian economy." End of quote.'

'It sounds very distinguished, sir.'

'Quite. I should have smelt a rat. And I should have smelt another when I saw the names of two of my fellow missionaries, including that of the head, and another when we were sent out before the war in Europe was quite over, although in the latter case I could be forgiven for noticing no alarming odour, except that of uncharacteristic forethought.'

'Where are the other five members of the mission?'

'Disposed, singly, by the cunning Indian Government to various parts of the country. Only the head of the mission has managed to get to Delhi. So you see, Perron, why I must stay on my feet. I must be where the head of the mission knows where to find me. I must be instantly available to join him.'

'Have you heard from him recently, sir?'

'No.' Purvis again shut his eyes. 'No. *No*. I can't bear to let myself think it but I believe he's ratted on us. I believe he's comfortably esconced in some niche he's found that just fits him and no one else. I used to send him reports. I suppose the others still do. But when I began to suspect that he was collating them, falsifying them, and sending them back to Whitehall as an account of the mission's collective activities, I stopped. Childish, I suppose, but necessary, to flush him out or persuade him to flush *me* out. And, of course, I've nothing to report except a state of total chaos far worse than ever I encountered at home.'

He opened his eyes again but only for as long as it took him to drink the rest of his rum and lime.

'I used to think, Perron, that on the day we started handing the colonies back to the bloody natives we'd all be able to look the twentieth century in the face at last. But if India's an example the only way we'll be able to do that and stay sane is by wearing blinkers and dark glasses and forgetting such places actually exist, and leave them to stew in their own juice except during their inevitable periods of acute financial crisis when we'll have to pour money into them to stop a chain reaction of bankruptcy bringing any half-civilized economy to its knees.'

'What makes you think that, sir?'

'For heavens' sake, sergeant! You've been in India for what's it, two years? It's taken me no more than three months to write it off as a wasted asset, a place irrevocably ruined by the interaction of a conservative and tradition-bound population and an indolent, bone-headed and utterly uneducated administration, an elitist bureaucracy so out of touch with the social and economic thinking of even just the past hundred years that you honestly wonder where they've come from. Not England, surely?'

'Perhaps it's the enervating effect of the climate, sir.'

'It's nothing to do with the bloody climate. The fact is places like this have always been a magnet for our throwbacks. Reactionary, unco-operative bloody well expendable buggers from the upper and middle-classes who can't and won't pull their weight at home but prefer to throw it about in countries like this which they've always made sure would remain fit places for them to live in. They've succeeded only too well. The most sensible thing for us to do is get rid of it fast to the first bidder before it becomes an intolerable burden.'

'Wouldn't that be rather unfair, sir? Historically, we have a moral obligation, surely?'

'I couldn't disagree more. Moral obligation! What next? It's disastrous *ever* to feel a moral obligation for other people's mistakes.'

It was in Perron's mind to say that he'd always been under the impression that certain material benefits had flowed from the imperial possession, enriching Britain if not demonstrably impoverishing India (but somehow widening the gap in the two standards of living?) and that moral considerations could surely not be totally ignored by economists and accountants. But he thought it better not to aggravate Purvis who in any case would almost certainly be a member of the school of thought which held that the flow of benefit had petered out several years ago and a law of diminishing returns set in so that now the flow was operating in reverse. He compromised.

'All the same, sir, and though I do appreciate what you say, I should hope to see the transfer of power accompanied by some indication of our continuing interest and concern.'

'I'm sure you'll be gratified then, sergeant. The demission will certainly be accompanied by such pious assurances. But they won't mean what it will be hoped they're thought to mean. Labour capitalism is no more generous than finance capitalism. Incidentally, we talk about transfer of power, demission of power, getting rid of it, whatever phrase you prefer, but that's going to be easier talked about than done.'

'Do you think so, sir? Some people say that once it's appreciated that we sincerely mean to go the Indians will sink their differences and agree how to work together.'

'Then personally I think some people are absolutely wrong because the Indians are utterly demoralized at the very thought of having to take the ghastly mess over and run it themselves. We'll have the devil's own job off-loading it. And, God! one says "it" as if it's a single transferable package which it isn't, never has been and now never will be.'

'A fact for which we're partly to blame, sir?'

'We? Don't sell me that divide and rule stuff. The bloody place was divided when the sahibs first came and will be divided when the stupid sods go because they've always been

35

content to sit on their bums in their bloody clubs and interfere only when the revenues were slow coming in. The place is still *feudal*, Perron. And so far as I can see the only man of influence who's worried about that is whatever the chap's name is, Nehru, but he's a Brahmin aristocrat and can hardly speak any language but English, and against him you have to set the Mahatma and his bloody spinning wheel. Spinning wheel! In 1945. For God's sake, what's the man *at*? In the past twenty-five years he's done as much to keep the country stuck in the mud with his village-industry fixation as the whole bloody *raj* put together.'

Stung as much by his feeling that there was something in what Purvis said as by the sense of the unfairness of such casual elimination of any consideration that didn't automatically fall within the economist's habitual terms of reference, Perron said:

'Your sponsor in Whitehall was right, sir. You've become an expert on India in a very short time.'

Purvis stared at him.

'Most Indian economists I've met happen to agree with me.'

'Yes I see, sir. Then perhaps that is a reason for optimism.'

'I doubt it, sergeant. It is in the Indian character to complain, but not to contest if a job depends on a posture of acquiescence. I'd better write you that letter. Bearer!'

While the letter was being written, Perron waited on the balcony and gazed across the Oval to the dark bulk of the Law Courts. For a moment – perhaps under the influence of that symbol of the one thing the British could point to if asked in what way and by what means they had unified the country, the single rule of law – he felt a pressure, as soft and close to his cheek as a sigh: the combined sigh of countless unknown Indians and of past and present members of the glittering insufferable *raj*; all disposable to make the world safe for Purvis. And other men like Purvis. (And, I suppose – Perron thought – for men like me.)

Purvis called him over and handed him an envelope. It was addressed to a Maharanee. Perron glanced at Purvis, mildly surprised, but the man was leaning back again, eyes closed. To Purvis, Maharanees were probably two a penny.

II

At seven-thirty Perron arrived by taxi at a block on the Marine
Drive which according to the address on the envelope bore the
name Sea Breezes. The driver he had flagged down in the
Queen's Road translated this after several movements of
uncertainty as Ishshee Brizhish, a place known to him.
Armed with the envelope and a square package which
contained the bottle of whisky, Perron entered the building
and went up in the lift to the floor indicated by the board
which gave flat numbers and the names of the occupants.

The décor in hall and landings was reminiscent of that in
houses and apartments built in the ultra-modern style of the
late 'twenties and early 'thirties, but it achieved a severe and
bleak rather than a severe and functional effect. The cream-
painted walls were dingy and the chromium rails bore the
patina of years of contact with the human hand. The door of
the flat at which he now stood was peagreen like those he had
seen at successive stages through the latticework iron gates of
the lift shaft and was well finger-marked round the keyhole.

He pressed the bell. No comforting sound of having got it to
ring reached him and no hum of party conversation either. He
wondered whether Purvis had the date right and then whether
someone had tipped the Maharanee off about Security's
interest in her circle of friends so that she had cancelled the
party and would be found curled up with a good book.
Wondering this he next considered the possibility that she
had taken a fancy to Purvis and planned to lure him back to
the flat with or without the bottle of whisky on a night when
she knew they could be alone together. He could not assess
the power of Purvis's sexual attraction. In such matters
women had their own unassailable scale of values and
judgment. But, having arrived at this possible explanation he
now wondered how old she was and, if young, how well-
favoured. The evening suddenly seemed full of an unexpected
kind of potential.

The door was opened abruptly by a young Indian girl of
gazellelike charm. 'Hello,' she said. Clearly she had none of
that creature's timidity.

'Hello. I've got a note and a package.'

'For me?'

He gave her the envelope. Her beautifully architectured eyebrows contracted. 'Oh, it's for Auntie. What a jolly shame. But do come in.'

'Thank you.'

Perron stepped inside and let her close the door. Her scent was too cloying for his taste but welcome after the smell on the night breeze blowing in from the Bombay foreshore which Perron was convinced was used as a lavatory. Indian insistence that it was just the smell of the sea and the seaweed had not yet made him change his mind.

In the hall – the top end of a long wide passage with doors leading off from either side of it and cluttered with solid but poorly assorted furniture, including an ornately carved black Chinese settle upholstered with velvet cushions – the girl took the package from him and put it together with the envelope on an ebony table on which a heavy and thick-ankled Shiva danced in his petrified ring of fire. She said, 'Come and have a drink why not?' and led the way into a living-room.

Around the walls sofas and chairs were set in the solemn and rather hostile manner of the segregational East. The tiled floor was uncarpeted – perhaps for dancing. There was no balcony but the windows were wide open. The lighting was less successful than in Purvis's flat. From the centre of the ceiling hung a cluster of bulbs in a cruciform wooden chandelier of the kind that at home was *de rigueur* in rooms that sported fake beams and parchment lampshades with galleons stencilled on them. But these bulbs were unshaded. A few wall-lights in glass and chromium brackets added to the glare but did nothing to eliminate the harsh shadows. Near the window was a cocktail cabinet of impressive vulgarity, and to this the girl had gone. She turned round.

'You're a sergeant, aren't you? Auntie says all sergeants drink beer but there was one the other night who asked for a White Lady.'

'Were you able to oblige him?'

'One of the officers got it for him but it took them ages because of the glass having to be put in the refrigerator.'

'A straightforward gin and lemon squash would suit this

38

sergeant very well. Shall I make it myself and get you a drink too?'

'Oh, no. I'm supposed to do this sort of thing. Auntie says it's good for me because it helps me not to be shy. I used to be very shy. But if you like to hold the bottle and help to pour it would be nice because I find the bottles so heavy, and once I dropped one and Auntie trod on a piece of the glass and was very cross.'

Perron joined her at the Wurlitzer-style cabinet. At a rough estimate he thought there were about fifty glasses of different shapes set ready, none of them as clean as they might have been. Gravely he uncapped a bottle of Carew's and held it above the glass she presented. She put her hand on his and canted.

'Is that enough?'

'More than generous.'

'May I leave you to do the rest? I must take Auntie the letter and parcel. Oh –' She half-ran to an occasional table and returned with a cigarette box and a lighter. After he had taken a cigarette he had to hold the box because she insisted on lighting the cigarette for him and needed two hands to produce a flame.

'There. Please excuse me now. There are plenty of ash-trays.' At the door she again remembered something impor- tant. 'What is your name? If there were a lot of people it wouldn't matter but since there's only you it would look rude not to tell Auntie who it is, wouldn't it?'

He told her, and added, 'But I'm sure it's mentioned in the note.'

After she had gone Perron went to the window. For all his doubts about its present source he had long since learned to appreciate the sensuousness of the warm smell of the East and how it could set mind and body at ease. He enjoyed a sensation almost of tranquillity and continued to enjoy it for some time, in fact until he became aware of the riding lights of a section of the anchored Zipper-destined flotilla out in the roads. And then a ludicrous but slightly worrying image presented itself, of the Maharanee standing at this very window, observing the scene in daylight through a telescope and dictating notes for the girl to record (in invisible ink)

39

about the class and tonnage of each ship as it arrived and dropped anchor.

'Auntie says will you come through?'

The girl was standing in the open doorway. He stubbed his cigarette and followed her into the long passage and down to a door at the end which, if closed before, now stood half-open upon a room so dark that at first he thought there was no light on at all and hesitated to enter when the girl indicated that he should do so.

'It's all right. Auntie has been resting but she's finished now.' Inside, he saw that there was a light, but this was from a table lamp in the far corner of the room whose shade was draped with a square of what looked like heavy crimson velvet. A hand, in silhouette, crept over the cloth and removed it; and in the now brighter but still deep rosy glow of the lamp the Maharanee was revealed, recumbent on a Récamier couch. Her saree was also red, but of what shade and intensity Perron could not easily judge because the material obviously took colour from the lamp shade. She seemed like an ember that might at any moment pulse brilliantly and dangerously into life. She wore no jewelry. Her skin was pale but darker than that of the Parsee ladies of Bombay. Her hair, cut and set in a style that obviously owed more to what she thought suited her than it did to any fashion of the day, was black, unoiled, parted in the middle, and fell, in corrugations of the kind obtained by using hot tongs, just short of her shoulders, framing a classic Rajput face of prominent cheekbones, full red lips, a hawklike but beautifully proportioned nose, and eyes whose luminosity was accentuated by cunningly applied kohl. Between her black brows she had painted a red tika one-quarter inch in diameter. She looked about thirty and was probably forty. She wore no choli and both arms, one shoulder and part of her midriff were bare. Perron, half-convinced he also saw the thrust and outline of a nipple, found her seductively handsome.

'Auntie,' the girl said from behind him. 'This is Sergeant Perrer. Sergeant Perrer, this is my Auntie Aimee.'

Perron bowed.

'Have you come to my party?' the Maharanee asked in a high-pitched but slightly hoarse voice. 'I'm afraid you're on

the early side. Aneila opened the door to you because all the
servants are resting. I make them rest because sometimes my
parties go on for a day or two. Aneila, what is wrong with you?
Why is our visitor still standing?'

'I'm sorry, Auntie.'

Perron turned to help her but the chair she chose was very
small and presumably almost weightless. She managed it
easily, placing it two feet from the couch.

'Now you had better go to start rousing everybody.'

'Yes, Auntie.'

'Tell them the guests are beginning to arrive. Do sit down.
Have we met before?'

'I've not had that pleasure, Your Highness.'

'Please call me Aimee. Pandy and I are divorced. I keep the
title because it is useful and servants and shop people like it
and Pandy's new wife doesn't. Are you a friend of someone I
know?'

Perron explained his mission and drew her attention to the
package and envelope which were on the table, propped
against the lamp where Aneila had presumably left them.

'Captain Purvis?' she asked, reaching for the letter. 'He
must be one of Jimmy's friends. When Jimmy is in Bombay he
brings so many people.' She opened the letter. The paper it
was written on seemed to displease her. She held it between
the tips of two fingers whose nails were elegantly manicured
and varnished. 'Leonard?' she said. 'Leonard Purvis?' And
presently, 'Whisky?' The note although short called for
concentration. 'Chillingborough and Cambridge? Why does
he tell me this? Why shouldn't you have studied at Chillingborough and Cambridge? So many Englishmen do. Who is
Leonard Purvis?'

'A member of an economic advisory mission to the Government of India.'

'Are you also in this mission?'

'No, I'm concerned with army education.'

'What does the mission do?'

'I don't think it does anything.'

'And what do you do?'

'Very little.'

41

'What a relief. People are always dashing about. What is your first name?'

'Guy.'

'Have you another?'

'Lancelot.'

She frowned.

'There's also Percival,' he said, and added, 'but I'm not keen on it.'

'Names are a terrible problem. It is best to make them up. Will you stay to my party? It may be boring but it is difficult to tell in advance. It depends on who comes. If it is too tedious I just come back to my room and tell the servants to lock up the drinks and go to bed. It is the only way to get rid of people. Anyway tonight I will be optimistic because it has begun well. Where are you staying?'

'In a place called Kalyan.'

'Oh, then you are on Zipper. Nearly all the military people who come here nowadays are on Zipper.'

He thought it wiser to let this pass.

He said, 'It's very kind of you to invite me to stay and I do have an evening off duty. But if I'm too early shall I come back later?'

'Oh, no. Other people will be here in a minute. If not ask Aneila to entertain you. Ask her to play the gramophone, and then you can dance. She is a very good dancer but needs practice with men. She loves it when I bring her to Bombay. Her mother is so strict with her. Her mother is my sister, the one who married that business man and has become very serious as a result. Before you go would you be so kind as to ring the bell?'

Perron stood up, touched the button on the wall which she had indicated, murmured his thanks and took his leave. On his way out he had an urge to turn back and explain who he was and why he was there. He had never enjoyed the part of his job which involved deceiving people and tonight deception seemed irrational. He believed that if he confessed his true identity and purpose to the Maharanee she would probably be amused, for the few seconds it took her to forget and concentrate again on her own affairs. But, leaving the room, closing the door and facing the long cluttered passage of more closed doorways he re-accommodated himself to the masquerade because Aneila was in the act of greeting more guests, let in this time by a servant. Again there had been no sound of a bell. A woman servant was hastening down the corridor to the Maharanee's room. Perron wondered whether he was going deaf or whether the bells rang on a note that only members of the household had learned to detect; but before he could become more than passingly interested in the subject his attention was taken by something of potentially more serious consequence.

Among the new arrivals – the only one he automatically took notice of – was a girl, an English girl; but not just an English girl, *the* English girl; the one to whom he had had to apologize for Purvis's discourteous behaviour at the entrance to the block of flats on the Oval. Remembering the penetrating glance she had given him he could scarcely doubt that she would recognize him when they came face to face. The question was whether she would notice his miraculous change of employment or whether the fact that he was in off-duty khaki drill and not in jungle green would be sufficient to distract her from any previous impression she had gained that education was not at all his line. The other question, of course, was whether if she recognized that a transformation had taken place she would thoughtlessly comment on it to him in the hearing of others, or sensibly put two and two together and keep mum.

There was only ten yards distance between them and no way of lengthening it. In fact it was already shortening because Aneila had waved the men in the party towards the living-room and was now bringing the girl to a room in which presumably women-guests could make themselves comfortable. This room turned out to be the one against whose door Perron was standing. No confrontation could have been more direct.

He stepped aside, smiled at Aneila and then at the girl. He thought it best to take the initiative. 'Good evening. We meet again.'

'Oh,' Aneila said. 'Do you know each other? I'm awfully glad because if not I would have to introduce you and I'm so bad at remembering names.'

43

'Perron,' Perron said, to both of them.

'Sarah Layton,' the girl said. Rather shrewdly, he thought, she said it to Aneila.

'Please join the guests in the living-room, Mr Perrer. Auntie says men can always introduce themselves if there is no one around to do it and I must show Miss –'

'Layton.'

' –Miss Layton where to powder her nose.' She opened the door. Sarah Layton nodded and started to go through. He caught the moment of hesitation, the slight frown, that followed the brief fall of her glance upon his left shoulder tab. Expecting the glance then to be redirected upwards to meet his he prepared to meet it as frankly as possible, but she followed Aneila into the room without looking at him again.

He continued along the passage and re-entered the living-room where a bearer was presiding over the cocktail cabinet and where he had another and rather more devastating shock.

*

Perron had been stationed in the Bombay Presidency for nearly three months but before becoming involved in operation Zipper he had visited the city only once. The reason for that visit, made in the company of his officer, had been the arrival of a ship that had sailed from Bordeaux in June bringing several hundred Indian soldiers, ex-prisoners of war captured in North Africa, who had succumbed to the temptation to secure their release from prison-camp by joining a Free India Force which its leader, the revolutionary ex-Congressman, Subhas Chandra Bose, at that time in Berlin after escaping police surveillance in India, had hoped to put into the field to fight alongside the Germans.

In England, Perron had learnt quite a lot about this embryo army and its failure to cohere into a fighting force. Details of it had been among items of classified information it had been his job to study but say nothing about. Because of the tremendous pride the British had always taken in the loyalty of their Indian soldiers, and in the Indian Army's apolitical nature, this evidence of a flaw in its structure had interested him, both then and later when he heard of the numerically far greater and infinitely more serious defection among Indian soldiers taken prisoner by the Japanese. They, it seemed, had formed themselves into operational fighting formations, at first under an Indian King's commissioned officer and then under Subhas Chandra Bose (translated by submarine from Berlin to Tokyo) and had accompanied the Japanese in their attempt in 1944 to invade the sub-continent through Manipur. Some of these, recaptured in the recent successful British campaign in Burma, had, he understood, already arrived in India and were being held in special camps where presumably the contingent from Europe would join them. Many more would follow after the end of the war in Malaya and the Far East.

His duties in regard to the boat load of disgraced Indian officers, NCOS and sepoys from Bordeaux had not been exacting. Neither he nor his officer was sure where their responsibility began or ended. So far as they could tell their main job was to keep an ear to the ground and report to the military and civil authorities anything that might give cause for suspicion that a popular movement was afoot in Bombay to storm the docks and whisk the prisoners from under the noses of those in charge of them off into the bazaars or into the hills where in the past many a band of irregular Mahratta horsemen had melted away to live on and fight again. But of this there had been no sign at all. Bombay went about its business and the military quietly got on with the job of transferring the boatload by trainloads to a destination Perron understood to be in the vicinity of Delhi and the Red Fort.

On only one occasion had he had the opportunity to observe the process, and this was at dead of night when he found himself standing with a group of military police on the dockside at a point where a file of the men in question straggled past, in oddly assorted uniforms, in the imperfect lighting of well-spaced and high-pitched arc-lights which left him with no more than an impression of the vacuity that falls upon the human face when a peak of incomprehension has been reached. That they were home at last they could not doubt. The smell of home must have been unmistakable. But what this might mean to them they obviously could not judge. After the last man in the batch had gone by and the cordon of armed military police had closed in and hidden them from view, Perron had found it difficult to assess the significance of what he had just seen. There was, on this scale, surely no parallel to the situation in the whole of Anglo-Indian history? No such gathering of Indian soldiers (and the present one represented no more than the tip of the iceberg) had surely ever gone abroad across the black water to fight in the Sahibs' wars and come back as the Sahibs' prisoners?

He was still testing the situation to find a weakness in his estimate of it as one that was historically unique when his officer sent a message calling him over to the shed from which the security side of the operation was being conducted and there introduced him to a British officer, a major in the Punjab Regiment whose face had been burnt badly, on the left side. The left arm had been damaged too, although it had taken Perron rather longer to realize this and to appreciate that the glove hid an artificial hand. Several ribbons decorated the officer's chest, the foremost that of the DSO.

Perron was introduced by his own officer as 'the sergeant I was telling you about'.

'You'll appreciate this, sergeant,' he said and began a story he said he'd heard earlier that evening. Perron assumed he'd already told it to the Punjab officer because the man glanced at a wrist-watch which he wore with the face on the inner side of his right wrist and then turned his attention to a wall-map of the dock area. The story was about the boatload of prisoners. In Bordeaux, hearing that they were to be shipped *en masse* back to India in a boat reserved exclusively for them, they decided it was the British intention to take them out to sea, disembark the crew and scuttle the ship. They refused to go until a sufficient complement of British soldiers had been taken on board to insure against the execution of such a diabolical plan.

'Don't you think that's rich? I mean you have to give them full marks for an undiminished sense of self-preservation, don't you?'

The Punjab officer broke in.

'I'm told you speak fluent Urdu, Perron. Will you be able to follow a brief interrogation in that language?'

'Yes, sir.'

'Good. I have a few questions to ask one of the prisoners, none of special importance but I prefer to have independent witnesses in case the man says anything I consider valuable. If he does I shall tell you what it was and you will then treat it as restricted and highly confidential information.'

'Yes, sir.'

'Whatever he pretends, this man will be very apprehensive at being singled out for immediate questioning. The MPS who'll bring him will remain in the room but they're British and won't understand what is said. I want you to place yourself behind my chair and keep your eyes fixed on him, for the psychological effect. It would help if you could manage to look not in the least sympathetic.' He turned to Perron's officer. 'I should like you to sit at the table with me. Have you a file you could be looking at?'

'A file?'

'Or an official-looking book. It's always helpful if the man sitting next to the one asking the questions appears to be absorbed in some task of his own which the prisoner finds it difficult to connect with the proceedings.'

Perron's officer laughed nervously. 'I could always play patience.'

'A file or a book preferably.'

'Why is it helpful?'

'It increases the prisoner's sense of isolation and weakens whatever resolve he may have to withhold information from the one man in the room who is speaking to him. He should be here any moment. Shall we take up positions?'

They did so. The table at which the two officers sat was the ordinary trestle type, covered by an ink-stained army blanket. It had been cleared of the papers and trays that were on it when Perron visited the hut earlier. A briefcase, a spare glove, a swagger cane, marked the Punjab officer's place. One-handed he opened the case and withdrew a file of papers and a fountain-pen. Perron's officer, having rummaged about on another table, now joined him, bringing with him a notebook and a thick folder of assorted cyclostyled memoranda.

The room was the inner one of the two into which the hut was divided. It was poorly lit by a single electric bulb. The trestle table faced the connecting door through which the prisoner would have to come after passing through the outer room which was used by MPs and dock police but at this hour of the night, morning rather, occupied by just one sleepy corporal. It was this corporal who presently knocked on the door, looked in and announced the arrival of prisoner and escort.

They came in in file. The MP in front, a burly sergeant, halted about three paces from the desk, saluted, put a folded note on the desk, took a pace to his right and one to the rear, while the MP at the back took one to his left and then a pace forward, a manoeuvre that revealed the man they guarded; a thin, stoop-shouldered Indian in denim fatigue trousers the bottoms of which flopped over ill-fitting looking boots, a long-sleeved khaki pullover and, beneath it, a khaki shirt whose shoulder tabs were thrust through the slots made for them in the pullover. The man wore no belt. On his head there was a forage cap without a badge. The taller of the two MPs removed this roughly enough to jerk the prisoner's head to one side. There was nothing on his sleeve to denote rank. The clothes had obviously been issued in Europe, perhaps in Bordeaux. He appeared not to have shaved for a couple of days. His thick black hair was over-long. A strand of it lay across his forehead. He stared from one officer to the other and finally at Perron who had been shocked to see that the prisoner's hands were manacled. It was as if everything had been done to make him look and feel unworthy of any uniform whatsoever.

The Punjab officer asked the escort to remain in the room but to retire to the door. So far he did not seem to have looked at the prisoner but when he spoke to the MPs the man looked at him with close attention and took no notice when the two policemen moved. The Punjab officer (again so far as Perron could tell, having his eyes more or less dutifully fixed on the prisoner) still did not look up. After a while, perhaps as long as ten seconds, the prisoner glanced at Perron's officer who was uselessly busy with pencil, note-book and the folder of papers, but almost immediately had his attention taken again by something the Punjab major was doing.

Perron glanced down. One-handed, the major had taken out a tin of cigarettes and a lighter. He opened the tin, selected a cigarette, lit it, closed the tin and then with the good hand

48

reached across to the left arm which hung straight, grasped the wrist of the gloved artificial hand, raised it and placed it on the table. Having taken a draw on the cigarette he inserted it between two of the gloved fingers and left it there: an erect white tube with smoke curling from the tip.

As Perron switched his glance back to the prisoner he caught the burly MP's eye. The MP winked.

'Tumara nam kya hai?' the Punjab officer asked suddenly in a low voice. The prisoner put his head on one side as a man might who recognized a language but could not identify it beyond doubt. *What is your name?*

Without waiting longer for an answer the officer continued, again in Urdu –

It says in this paper that your name is Karim Muzzafir Khan. Havildar Karim Muzzafir Khan, 1st Pankot Rifles, captured in North Africa with the other survivors of his battalion. With his comrades. With his leaders. Colonel Sahib himself also being captured. Is this so? It says so in this paper. You recognize the emblem on the paper? Does the Sircar make mistakes?

The man seemed bewildered. He looked at Perron, as if for help. Perron stared at the bridge of the man's nose. The man looked down again at the officer.

Well?

Yes, Sahib.

Yes, Sahib? Yes? What is the meaning of this answer?

Karim Muzzafir Khan, Sahib.

Karim Muzzafir Khan, Havildar, 1st Pankot Rifles?

Yes, Sahib.

Karim Muzzafir Khan, Havildar? Captured with his battalion in North Africa?

Sahib.

Karim Muzzafir Khan, Havildar. Son of the late Subedar Muzzafir Khan Bahadur, also of the 1st Pankot Rifles?

Sahib.

Subedar Muzzafir Khan Bahadur? VC?

Perron was aware of his own officer looking up, alerted.

Well?

Sahib.

The Punjab officer removed the smoking cigarette, drew on

it, tapped the ash into a tray, slowly exhaled and replaced it between the rigid gloved fingers. He turned a page of the file. The prisoner's head was lowered. He was staring at the cigarette and the artificial hand as though they exerted for him the special fascination of an object or arrangement of objects which, properly interpreted, might help him to understand precisely what it was that was happening to him. Perhaps this was what the Punjab officer intended. He continued to study the new page in the file. He was in no hurry. Perron kept glancing at the cigarette. If left to burn right down would the artificial fingers react? Unexpectedly the officer removed his cap and sat back. The prisoner stared at the scarred face, then looked away at the other officer's busy pencil and then at Perron and after a moment shut his eyes.

Are you fatigued?

The prisoner opened his eyes.

Sahib.

You are not getting good sleep?

No answer.

Why? Why are you not getting good sleep?

No answer.

Something troubles you? What? What will happen? This troubles you? What will happen to you? What will happen to your wife and children? You have a wife and children?

The man nodded.

What they will say? That this is a matter of great shame? Is that what troubles you? What your wife and children will say? What the people in your village will say to your wife and children? Is that what you are thinking? That your wife will not hold up her head? That this will be so because of all the men in the battalion who were not killed but captured only Havildar Karim Muzzafir Khan was not true to the salt? Only Havildar Karim Muzzafir Khan listened to the lies of his captors and of the enemies of the King-Emperor whose father rewarded his father with the most coveted decoration of all? Only Havildar Karim Muzzafir Khan brought shame to his regiment and sorrow to the heart of Colonel Sahib?

A pause.

How long is it since you saw Colonel Sahib?

No answer.

Where do you think he is? At home in comfort? You think perhaps on the day he and the other officers were released from prison-camp in Germany that he got into an aeroplane and flew home to his family in India? This is not so. It is you who are in India first, ahead of him, ahead of all your comrades of the 1st Pankots. Like you they had not seen Colonel Sahib since the day of their capture when the officer sahibs were taken to one camp and the men to another. But on the day Colonel Sahib was released he said, now let me go to my men. I shall not go back to India without them. Come, let us find the men, let us go to the prison-camp where the men are. Let us go to the camp and collect all the men together. Let us wait in Germany until every man who was still alive after the battle and was taken prisoner has been accounted for and then let us sail back to our families in India, as a regiment. And so it has been. And only one man of the 1st Pankots has not been accounted for, one man who was not killed but who was not in any prison-camp. He had deserted his comrades to fight alongside the enemy. We do not know why. We shall find out why. Where you are going you will be asked many questions. You will be asked many questions by many officers. You will see me again also. I also shall ask you many more questions. Tonight I am not asking questions of this kind. I speak to you only of the shame and sorrow you have brought to Colonel Sahib. I do not know Colonel Sahib but I know Colonel Memsahib and I know the two young memsahibs. Susan Mem and Sarah Mem. I was in Pankot four weeks ago. They had a letter from Colonel Sahib. Be patient, he wrote. I am making arrangements about the men. So, they are patient. All Pankot is patient, awaiting the regiment's return from across the black water. In Pankot they do not yet know the story of Havildar Karim Muzzafir Khan who let himself believe in the lies of Subhas Chandra Bose. But soon they will know. And they will be dumb with shame and sorrow. The wild dogs in the hills will be silent and your wife will not raise her head.

The Punjab officer spoke a resonant classic Urdu. It was a language that lent itself to poetic imagery but Perron had heard few Englishmen use it so flexibly, so effectively, or to such a purpose. Throughout the speech the prisoner's eyes

51

had grown brighter, moister. Perron thought he might break down. He believed this was the officer's intention and he was appalled. He would have understood better if the officer and the prisoner were of the same regiment because by tradition a regiment was a family and the harshest rebuke might then be ameliorated by the context of purely family concern in which it could be delivered and received. Then, if the man wept, it would be with regret and shame. If he wept now it would be from humiliation at the hands of a stranger.

But he managed not to weep. Perhaps the years in Europe had eroded his capacity to be moved – as Indians could be – by rhetoric. Perhaps he suddenly realized that nothing except full bellies would keep the wild dogs of the hills silent, and was astonished that a British officer should use such high-flown language. Perron thought that for a second or two a flash of contempt was discernible in the moist eyes. Certainly, they dried, and were directed again at the burning cigarette.

There was silence for perhaps as long as a minute. 'I have finished with this man,' the officer said suddenly. Karim Muzzafir Khan understood English. He drew in a deep breath and glanced round, awaiting the MPS who, put off their stroke by the abruptness with which the interview had ended, made a somewhat patchy job of coming forward, saluting and leading the prisoner out.

When the door shut, the officer picked the cigarette out of the artificial hand and sat smoking and making notes on the file. The episode, to Perron, seemed pointless. His own officer obviously thought the same because he pushed away the file he'd pretended to work on, leant forward, rested his forehead on his right hand and watched the other man's note-taking, clearly inviting comment.

At last the Punjab officer spoke.

'I wonder whether your sergeant would ask the corporal next door to get hold of my driver and tell him I'll be ready in about five minutes? The corporal will know where to find him.'

'Oh, I'll do that myself. I need to take a leak.'

Perron's officer got up and went into the other room. He left the door ajar. Perron collected the notebook and folder and took them back to the other table. The Punjab officer stubbed the cigarette and began to repack his briefcase.

'Were you able to follow every word?'

'Yes, sir.'

'What did you make of him?'

'He looked fairly harmless, sir.'

The officer closed the briefcase. He leant back and looked at Perron. 'His name has cropped up several times in depositions made in Germany in connection with the coercion of sepoy prisoners-of-war who were unwilling to join the Frei Hind force. In fact it has been linked with that of an Indian lieutenant suspected of causing the death of a sepoy in Königsberg.' A pause. 'But I grant you the harmless look, and, of course, he may be innocent of anything like that because a lot of these fellows are going to be only too ready to accuse each other to save their own skins.'

He put his cap on.

'Incidentally, your officer was singing your praises before you arrived. I gather you have a degree in history and are particularly interested in the history of this country. Have you studied Oriental languages too? I mean, systematically?'

'Not awfully systematically, sir. Naturally I became interested in Urdu and learned some during vacations and had some practice in conversation with a fellow-student during term.'

'An Indian fellow-student, at university?'

'Yes, sir.'

'If you followed every word you've become very proficient. Have you taken Higher Standard out here?'

'Yes, sir.'

'It's not much use, of course, except in the army. It's nice to be able to speak it. In my old job I generally had to use a mixture of bazaar Hindi and the local dialect of whatever district I happened to be in.'

'What job was that, sir?'

'The Indian Police.'

Perron was surprised. Neither the ics nor the police had been in the least co-operative over pleas from their officers to join the armed forces. Recruiting to these services had lapsed at the beginning of the war and the men had been needed

53

where they were, administering the law, collecting the revenues, keeping order, preserving the civil peace. Perron judged the officer to be in his middle thirties. At that age he would normally have held a senior post in the police, which would have made a wartime transfer to the army even more difficult to arrange.

The officer got up. He tucked the briefcase under the left arm which he then adjusted until it was clamped to his waist. The arm must have been amputated above the elbow. He took the spare glove and swagger cane in his right hand.

'By the way, sergeant. I gather from your officer that you were at school at Chillingborough. When, exactly?'

Perron told him and after a moment added, 'Were you there as well, sir?'

The officer paused before replying. 'Hardly. I had quite other grounds for asking. Presumably you would know an Indian boy there, who called himself Harry Coomer. Actually Hari Kumar.'

'Harry Coomer? Yes, I remember him, sir.'

'He would have been a year or two your junior, I suppose? Did you know him closely? Closely enough to have learned much about his attitudes and interests?'

Perron was thinking back, attempting an image of the young Indian. The way Coomer came into focus was in white flannels making one of those sweeps to leg which even Perron who had been bored by cricket and played it badly recognized as elegant. The boy's actual presence was otherwise misty. Only an ambiance remained; and a detail or two.

'Actually,' Perron said, 'I don't remember him being interested in anything much except cricket.'

He was about to add, Why, sir? Do you know him? But the answer was self-evident.

Perron had not thought of Coomer for years. He realized he had not even thought of him when he came out to India, perhaps because at school he had never really thought of Coomer in connection with any place but Chillingborough. Only a brown skin had distinguished him from the several hundred other boys undergoing the Chillingborough experience. Everything else, manners, behaviour, had so far as Perron could remember been utterly commonplace. Perron could not even recall Coomer speaking English with an Indian accent. What he did recall was asking Coomer a question about the difference between karma and dharma and being told politely that Coomer was afraid he didn't know because although born in India he had grown up in England and couldn't remember a thing about it and didn't know anything about its peculiar customs and odd ideas.

'Cricket,' the officer said, smiling at last. 'I'm afraid that his range of interests began to extend beyond cricket once he got back to this country. That expensive education turned out to be pretty much a waste. As so often happens in such cases. Did you know anything of his background?'

'Nothing at all, sir. Nothing I can remember.'

'No, well, I suppose you wouldn't. Not being a close friend of his.'

Perron's officer came back.

'We've unearthed your driver,' he said. 'He's waiting outside. I'm trying to whistle up some char. Would you like a mug before you tootle off?'

'No, thank you. And thank you for your help this evening. I'm sorry the havildar was so unforthcoming. It would have been more interesting for you if he'd been one of the talkative ones. But the object of the exercise was achieved from my point of view.' He seemed about to say goodnight and go but then stood his ground, as if thinking something out.

'It's interesting,' he began, and turned to Perron. 'There you have the havildar, whose father got a posthumous vc in the last war, and who I dare say was brought up to have his father's example rammed down his throat day after day. One thing it will be worth finding out is how he behaved in action, when it came to it. My guess is he showed up badly and couldn't face being shut in behind barbed wire for the rest of the war with men who'd seen how frightened he was. What do you think, sergeant? Psychologically, could it work that way?'

'I think it could, sir.'

'Well Kumar couldn't face it either. I mean face the fact that he wasn't what his father tried to make him and had led him to believe he was. You know nothing of this?'

'Nothing, sir.'

'When did you reach India?'

55

'In 1943, sir.'

'Ah well. It happened the year before. But I'm glad he wasn't a close friend of yours. He kept pretty poor company out here. He and five of his disreputable friends were arrested in '42 on a very serious criminal charge. They wriggled out of that, but we got them under the Defence of India Rules and locked them up as political detenus.'

As he spoke the officer kept his eyes firmly on Perron. And now continued so, as though demanding a comment or a question. The only thing Perron could think of to say was: 'Was it you who arrested him, sir?'

'Yes. It was. It was indeed.'

He nodded at Perron, and saluted Perron's officer by touching his cap with the swagger cane, and went.

Perron returned his officer's glance. He said, 'Who was that, sir?'

'Name's Merrick. Described himself as involved at a high level with this INA tamasha. Frosty sort of bugger, wasn't he?'

It was this man whom Perron saw first on re-entering the Maharanee's living-room.

*

He was, however, under observation by three. As well as the one-armed Punjab officer there was a tall elderly white man in white ducks who leant on an ebony cane and whose left eye was hidden by a black patch secured by a strip of elastic round his head, and – the only man of the three not suffering from any physical disability – a good-looking young Indian in well-cut civilian clothes.

Sometimes, since the night on the docks, in the moment before sleeping, the last conscious image in the blackness behind his lids had been of Coomer, driving, sweeping, cutting or blocking a rapid and relentless stream of deliveries from an invisible bowler, in an empty field that was green, sunstruck and elm-shaded, devoid of sound. The boy's face was never clear. The images conveyed little except a melancholy idea that they were a reproach of some kind, and by morning he had usually forgotten them. But the sight of the young Indian, combined with the shock of coming face to face

56

with the Punjab officer, brought them back and for an instant he had an absurd notion that the young Indian was Coomer.

His hesitation on entering had been marked enough to be interpreted by the elderly man in the white ducks as shyness. The man smiled and said, 'Come in.'

Approaching them, avoiding a direct glance at the Punjab officer, Perron said good-evening and then, 'I'm afraid I'm an interloper. An officer sent me with a package for the Maharanee and she's very kindly invited me to stay for the party. My name's Perron. Sergeant Perron.'

'Perron? Perron? That is a most interesting name. Any ancient connection with the Sergeant Perron who became a general and Governor of Hindustan under Daulat Rao Sindia?'

Perron smiled. It was rarely that the question was asked.

'No, sir. In any case the Perron who served under Daulat Rao was really Pierre-Cuiller. Perron was his nickname.'

'That I either did not know or have forgotten. Anyway, Mr Perron, at Aimee's parties what you call interlopers are the rule rather than the exception. For instance I am the only one of us here with a personal invitation. But Aimee likes one to bring people along.' The accent was un-English but Perron could not place it.

'So let me initiate introductions,' the man continued. He placed a skeletal hand on his breast, indicating himself and bowing slightly. 'Dmitri Bronowsky. This is Mr Ronald Merrick, actually of the Indian Police but at the moment as you see employed as a major in the Punjab Regiment. And this is my secretary, Mr Ahmed Kasim, younger son of Mr Mohammed Ali Kasim, of whom you may have heard.' Bronowsky put a hand on Perron's shoulder, turned him round an inch or two, to read the shoulder tab. 'Ah, now what does this mean, A E C?'

'Army Education Corps, sir.'

The slight twisting of his shoulder enabled him to look directly at Major Merrick. In this harsh light the scar-tissue that disfigured the left side of the man's face was revealed more unkindly than it had been in the shed on the docks, and the blue of the eyes – now recollected – was intensified. The look Perron got in return gave nothing away.

Bronowsky's hand was still on Perron's shoulder. Letting him free now he said, 'How does one educate an army?'

'It's not so much a case of educating it, sir, but of finding ways of stopping it being bored.'

'Nevertheless, you need teaching qualifications?'

'Not always, sir.'

'But you have such qualifications?'

'Yes, sir.'

'A degree?'

'Yes, sir.'

Bronowsky asked in what subject. Perron told him. The bearer entered their midst with a tray of drinks but this did not halt the old man's catechism. Which university? Which college? Before that what school had he attended?

'A place called Chillingborough, sir.'

'Indeed?' Bronowsky hesitated. 'How interesting. And what will you do after the war, Mr Perron? Go on to a course of post-graduate studies?'

Perron nodded. But the flow of questions could not be stemmed. In what subject? What aspect of Indian history? Why that one? Perron attempted to deflect the question and open the conversation out with a general comment about the narrowing range and increasingly esoteric nature of study in the post-graduate field but Bronowsky was not to be put off.

'That is its charm and logic, surely. I expect you have found that being in India has encouraged you in your choice. Have you thought of staying on for a while after the war?'

'Not really, sir. One tends to lose ground so quickly. The academic world is as competitive as any other.'

'That is so. But one should perhaps sometimes ignore the professional competition and arrange matters in a way most advantageous to the scholar in oneself. You would easily find a temporary post in a university here and have plenty of opportunity to do original research. Either in a university or in one of the colleges. Our own college in the little state of Mirat is always short of well qualified teachers. In history, for instance.'

'Are you its principal, sir?'

Major Merrick interrupted.

'Count Bronowsky is Chief Minister to the ruler, the Nawab of Mirat.'

'But emotionally I'm very attached to the college and always anxious to foster its interests because it was one of my first innovations. When I went to Mirat to advise Nawab Sahib, nearly a quarter of a century ago, there was no place of higher education in the state where clever young Hindus could go. There was only the Muslim Academy which taught boys to pray and recite the Koran and which turned out tax-collectors – if Ahmed here will forgive me for saying so, although he did not personally undergo such a traditional Islamic training, did you, Ahmed?'

'What?'

'Incorrigible!' Bronowsky exclaimed, but laughed and put three fingers of the hand that held the ebony cane on the young man's shoulder. 'He seldom listens to conversations. He comes to parties only to drink as much whisky as he can and to make up to the prettiest girls. That apart, as a secretary he is quite efficient. And here are two very pretty girls. Aneila, my dear, was I in error in supposing your aunt said seven-thirty on? Are we as conspicuously early as we feel?'

'Oh, no. Auntie's parties begin when the first people arrive. Have I omitted anything? Auntie will be very cross if I have, so please tell me. Oh! Nobody is smoking! What a bad beginning. Please help yourselves. I will tell Auntie to hurry.'

She ran out, and in the passage called instructions presumably to some of the servants. Perron, the only guest who knew without looking where the cigarettes were, picked up the box and went first to Miss Layton who was now standing next to Major Merrick. He arrived at her side a few seconds behind the bearer with the tray of drinks. He noted the gleam of her unfussily set fair hair and then her dress which was not the one she had on when they met outside the block of flats on the Oval, but was not obviously labelled 'party only'. A bag hung in the crook of her arm. The left hand was raised. She wore no engagement ring. She chose a gimlet and then, seeing the box, smiled at him and shook her head.

'Thank you, not just now.'

Merrick declined too. He made no attempt at an introduction. Perron passed on to Bronowsky. 'I always smoke these,'

Bronowsky said, opening a gold case and showing the contents: a row of oval-shaped pink gold-tipped cigarettes.

'But only in the evening,' Miss Layton said, from behind Perron.

'Ah, so you remember my little anecdote. By the way you know Mr Perron of the Education Corps?'

'Yes,' came her voice, 'we introduced ourselves in the hall.'

Perron offered the box to Ahmed Kasim but he declined. Bronowsky moved across to Miss Layton and Major Merrick, Perron put the box down, retrieved his drink and set about trying to make conversation with the young Indian.

'Your father must be the Congress statesman, MAK.'

Kasim nodded, then reapplied himself to his glass of whisky. So far as Perron knew it was the first time he had spoken to an Indian whose father had been imprisoned by the *raj*. He did not know quite what to say to him. He could hardly apologize. He would have liked to ask what truth there had been in newspaper reports that Mr Kasim senior was realigning himself politically, abandoning Congress in favour of the League and Jinnah's mad, divisive dream of a separate state for Muslims: Pakistan; but that was a tricky subject too. He wondered what on earth a son of a politician like MAK was doing acting as secretary to the Chief Minister to the Nawab of Mirat. There was generally no love lost between Congress and the autocratic rulers of the Princely states. But he could not ask that question either. He fell back on small talk.

'Are you in Bombay for long?'

'A few days.'

'It must be interesting working for a Nawab's Chief Minister.'

Ahmed Kasim nodded, but his attention was elsewhere. Hearing voices Perron glanced round. A group of English officers had come in, but they were obviously not the object of Mr Kasim's study. A stunningly attractive Eurasian girl and two pretty Indian girls had come in too and were talking excitedly to Aneila. Two more bearers joined the one already in the room. After a few seconds Perron turned back to Kasim.

'Is Mirat in relationship with the Crown through a Resident or through a provincial government?'

'A Resident. Except that he isn't.'

60

'A non-resident Resident.'

'It used to be through the provincial government but all that was altered some time ago.'

'Generally, or just in Mirat's case?'

'I think generally. Something to do with the federal scheme. But that's fallen through. Things do in this country.'

'Where does the non-resident Resident reside?'

'In Gopalakand.'

'Is that far from Mirat?'

'Far enough.'

'Is that a good thing, then?'

Mr Kasim looked into his glass.

'I'm sorry,' Perron said. 'Undiplomatic question. Is Count Bronowsky what we used to call a White Russian? A member of the emigration from the revolution?'

'Yes.'

'A soldier?'

'No, I don't think so.'

'I wondered about his loss of an eye.'

'He says his carriage was blown up by a revolutionary when he was on his way to the Winter Palace in St Petersburg. He's lame in the left leg for the same reason.'

'He mentioned being in Mirat for twenty-five years. Was he Chief Minister from the beginning?'

'Not officially. Not until the Political Department was mollified.'

'How was it mollified?'

'I believe when they saw he was a good influence on the Nawab. Then they allowed the appointment. Dmitri says that nowadays some of the senior members of the Political Department behave as if they invented him themselves. Before he came the state was quite feudal.'

'Does Miss Layton have any connection with Mirat? She and the Count seem quite old friends.'

'She visited once. Her sister got married there. They stayed at the Palace guest house'.

'She lives in Bombay?'

'No, in Pankot.'

'Pankot?'

'You know it?'

'Of it. Anyway, of its regiment, the Pankot Rifles.'

'Her father was CO of the 1st battalion. She's in Bombay to meet him. He's been a prisoner-of-war in Germany.'

Perron moved so that he could see her. Her back was to him. She stood in a group consisting of Count Bronowsky, two of the English officers, and Merrick. Merrick was watching him, still with that expression of giving nothing away although Perron fancied he now read into it an understanding that Miss Layton's name had just been mentioned and a warning to give nothing away himself, as if they both had something to hide: Perron his real identity and Merrick – what? Just the fact that they had met before or, primarily, the circumstances of that meeting? The interrogation of the Pankot Rifles havildar? Sarah Layton was one of Colonel Sahib's daughters. Although he now recognized the name Sarah in this connection he could not remember the name of the other daughter – the one presumably married in Mirat. Merrick had referred to them both when questioning the havildar. Sarah mem and — mem.

He turned back to Kasim.

'Is Colonel Layton back in India yet?'

Mr Kasim had to incline his head and ask him to repeat the question, but before he could do so there was a cry, 'Ahmed, darling!' and an elderly Indian woman in a green and gold saree brushed them apart to embrace the young man. 'What are you doing in Bombay? Is your father here? I wrote to him after the Simla fiasco but he never replied.'

Perron stood back to give them more room. She ignored him. 'Is it true what Lodi told me about your poor brother Sayed?' she shouted. Perron moved away and did not hear Kasim's reply. Gramophone music started up and the stunning Eurasian girl began dancing with one of the two Indian girls who had come in with her. The other rather reluctantly accepted a young English officer as a partner but talked to the Eurasian girl as they moved round in the limited space available. So far the services were represented entirely by officers. Perron was the only non-commissioned man in the room. Four Indian women, neither young nor handsome, had settled themselves on a long settee and were in conversation of the kind that did not invite interruption. The servants had multiplied and the room was quite full. There was still no sign of the Maharanee.

He made his way through the room towards the hall. At the door he stood aside to let in a middle-aged, portly, red-faced English civilian in open-necked shirt, white duck trousers and black cummerbund. The civilian said, 'Hello, Sergeant, where's the bloody bar, then?' and looked ready to talk but Perron, indicating the direction, went through. There were more people in the hall. A servant stood at the front door staring at the wall above it where there was what looked like a bell-box, which in a sense it turned out to be because an orange bulb inside it suddenly lit up and the servant promptly opened the door and admitted two more guests. Perhaps the same sort of signal was given in the servants' quarters. Perhaps there was a bell-light watcher on the staff. Perhaps the Maharanee didn't like the sound of bells ringing. He was glad to have the question basically cleared up.

'Hey, Sarge, what d'you reckon, then?'

The speaker was a REME corporal. He was standing against a wall with an AB of the Royal Navy.

'Reckon?'

'To all this.'

'Are you on your own?'

'No, with him.' The corporal nodded at the sailor then looked at Perron's glass. 'What they rush you for the booze?'

'They don't. It's free. It usually is at parties.'

'Parties? Isn't it Amy's?'

'Well the hostess's first name is Aimee.'

'Hostess?'

'The lady giving the party.'

Perron recited the Maharanee's full title. The corporal looked at his mate. The sailor said, 'The rotten sods.' The corporal felt in a pocket and produced a grubby piece of paper. He looked at it and then showed it to Perron. On it was written: 'Amy's', the address and flat number and a note at the bottom saying: 'Six chips.' Perron handed the paper back. He shook his head. 'I think someone's played a practical joke on you. It's not that kind of place. What did you say when the bearer opened the door?'

'I just said, "Amy's?" He didn't ask for names or nothing so it looked okay. At least it did until we saw the company. I mean, *women* –coming *in*. We'd better blow before we get chucked out.'

'I don't think you would be.'

'But we don't know anyone and from the look of this lot we aren't likely to.'

'Hey, have a dekko at that,' the sailor said. He nudged the corporal in the ribs. Perron turned round. Aneila was flowing down the corridor to her aunt's room.

'Yeah, that's better. Who's she, Sarge?'

'The Maharanee's niece.'

'Any more like her inside?'

'Yes, several.'

'Who are you with, Sarge?'

'No one in particular.'

'If anyone asks can we say we're with you?'

'You'd better say you're friends of Captain Purvis, but he hasn't turned up yet.'

'Suppose he does turn up?'

'He won't. He's ill in bed.' A bearer came by with a loaded tray. Perron stopped him. 'Have a drink anyway, then you won't look conspicuous. There's beer too if you want it. You only have to ask.'

The two lads gingerly took glasses from the tray.

'Okay?'

'Yeah, thanks. Thanks, Sarge. Captain *Purvis*?'

'Leonard Purvis. The economist.'

The corporal nodded, abstractedly.

'See you, corporal,' Perron said and turned away. Major Merrick had come out of the room and was waiting for him.

'I'd like a word.'

They moved to an uncluttered part of the passage.

'Are you on duty?'

'Yes, sir.'

'Are you expecting your officer?'

'No, sir.'

'I take it this disguise is permitted?'

'In certain circumstances, yes, sir.'

'Always a bit risky though, isn't it? However slight the chances of coming across someone who knows you. For instance, Miss Layton has just told me about your meeting earlier this afternoon. In your other uniform.'

'Not in anyone else's hearing I hope, sir.'

'No. But quite properly she thought I ought to know.'

'Did you tell her you knew already, sir?'

'Without going into detail, yes. This officer – Captain Purvis? Is he in your department too?'

'No, sir.'

'Are you going back to his flat?'

'I shall have to, sir. To change.'

For a while Merrick stared at him without speaking. In the living-room another record was put on and there was some loud laughter. Eventually Merrick said, 'What time do you expect to leave?'

'I'm not sure, sir.'

Merrick glanced at the other people in the passage. Three young Indian women sat on the settee chattering and giggling. The corporal and the sailor were now being talked to by the middle-aged Englishman in the cummerbund. Merrick continued: 'I've been thinking about making our excuses and taking Miss Layton home. Everything considered and in view of what you know, would you think that justified, to save her possible embarrassment?'

A movement near the doorway into the living-room caught his eye. The middle-aged civilian was shepherding the corporal and the sailor in. He gave the sailor an encouraging pat, low enough on the spine to rank as a slap on the buttocks. Perron returned his attention and saw that the gesture had not gone unnoticed by Merrick. Perron assumed as blank an expression as he could manage.

'I simply can't say, sir. It should be quite easy to slip away, I imagine, without giving offence.'

'Giving offence wouldn't bother me. What I'm asking you to tell me is whether in your view the reasons for your own presence here are likely to become apparent, through some kind of general or particular unpleasantness.'

'I'm not sure I understand you, sir,' Perron said. 'It's all fairly routine from my point of view.'

Merrick looked across Perron's shoulder in the direction of the settee where the three Indian girls were.

'Routine?' he said.

Perron lowered his voice although with no one in easy earshot there was no need. 'The reason for my presence, sir.'

Merrick continued staring at the girls on the carved sofa and then looked in the opposite direction at the main door of the flat which the bearer had just opened. Two tall white girls, exaggeratedly made up and wearing sarees, came in ahead of a couple of Air Force officers, an Englishman and an American. The taller of the girls, who seemed familiar with the flat, led her companion down the passage towards the room set aside for women. As she went by she gave Perron a dazzling smile. But heavy make-up – and pungent scents – had never much appealed to him, neither for that matter had white women in sarees. Their bones were usually too big – as in this case. He watched them go into the women's room. Apparently the three Indian girls thought them as incongruous as he did; they lowered their heads, covered their faces and laughed.

'I sympathize with you then, sergeant, if this is routine.'

'I don't mean the party, sir. The reason for my being at it.'

'You see nothing odd about the party, though? Nothing that would encourage you seriously to consider leaving if you were in my shoes and had Miss Layton to think of? Or even if you were by yourself and had no special reason for staying?'

'I suppose it is a bit noisy, sir. And of course it does have its unusual aspect.'

'What is that, in your opinion?'

'Other ranks mixing with officers, sir. But of course I knew beforehand, otherwise I should have had to come in civilian clothes and that leads to so many awkward questions; who does one work for, what does one do. A sergeant is more anonymous.'

'And better bait. Well, I won't ask you what you expect to hook but if you're thinking of this as routine I should advise you to be careful where and how you cast. In fact, although I think you're being less than frank with me I'll give you the benefit of the doubt and a friendly warning. I have a much longer experience of this country and its peculiarities, on most levels of its society. In Indian terms you may think this an example of the top level because the hostess is a Maharanee. That is as may be. But it's at the top you find the scum, isn't it? You can certainly see plenty of it here. I must give Count Bronowsky the benefit of the doubt too and assume he had no idea the particular kind of party the Maharanee is giving this evening. I shall know better about that in a moment when I go back in and tell him I intend to take Miss Layton home before things get worse.'

'Worse, sir?'

'Worse.' Merrick studied him. 'I begin to wonder about your powers of observation, sergeant. The two white girls in sarees who have just gone into the ladies' room – one of whom made a pass at you – are boys, probably airmen. The three Indian girls giggling on the sofa there are also boys, not professional transvestites, which as you may know is a special kind of Indian sect, and all right in its place, but not I assure you all right here. They will undoubtedly dance for the company later in the evening and manage to make it clear what they are, and what they are offering.'

Perron looked at the three figures on the settee. He studied their covered breasts, their ringed fingers and bare forearms, the sandalled feet and bangled ankles; the shapes of jaws, joints and noses. Because he had been told, he saw.

He turned back to Merrick.

'Yes, I see.'

'I'm glad to hear it. The English boys' get-up is very good but crude in comparison. That's why the Indian boys laughed at them. Tell me at least one thing. Are the REME corporal and the AB you were talking to also on duty, like you?'

'No, sir. Certainly not to my knowledge.'

'Do you know who they're with?'

'They're just with each other, sir. But the party's a bit of a surprise to them. They were expecting something rather different.'

'Meaning?'

'A place called Amy's at a cost of six rupees.'

'They weren't far wrong. Would you say that an ageing teaplanter wasn't what they hoped to find?'

'I should think it highly unlikely that they did, sir.'

'In that case, sergeant, I think your duties might conceivably extend to ordering them to leave, for their own good.'

Perron felt a twitch of irritation.

'I don't think I need interfere, sir.'

'Then you misjudge the degree of temptation.'

They broke off. The two white men in sarees had come out of the women's room. This time Perron got a smile from both of them. They wore wigs. Now that he had been told, the masquerade was obvious. When they had gone by he glanced up the corridor where the two officers they had come with were waiting for them, holding drinks ready. The draped hips swung rhythmically. As the men reached their escorts Perron caught the American officer's eye: a beefy-looking fellow, who winked at him.

He looked back at Merrick, thinking of the map room.

'Do I, sir? Misjudge the degree of temptation?'

'I think you do. A corporal and a sailor can't have found it easy to scrape together six rupees each for a visit to a prostitute. Some flattering attention, a taste of what they think of as the high life, an offer of a handsome tip or a present that they can sell in the bazaar aren't necessarily inadequate or unacceptable payment to very young fellows like that. Alternatively, the tea-planter might find himself badly beaten up and his money gone and there could then be two more young men who've discovered a way of making easy money and will end up in serious trouble. Either consequence is one it seems sensible to avoid.'

'I do see that point of view, sir. But I couldn't risk it.'

'Risk it?'

'Risk doing what you suggest. They might not go quietly.'

'They would if you took them on one side and dealt with it tactfully but firmly.'

'I'm sorry, sir.'

Merrick paused, but never let his glance fall.

'Have you a proper identity card with you?'

'Yes, sir.'

'Then you could show it to them on the quiet.'

'No, sir.'

'Why not?'

Perron's irritation was gone and his temper roused.

'You must know why not, sir.'

'Would you show it to me if I asked to see it?'

'No, sir.'

'If I ordered you to?'

'No, sir.'

'Let me put a hypothetical case, sergeant. I have seen you in one place, in one *persona*, apparently bona fide, but here I find you in another and in the most unsavoury surroundings. I have suspicions about your true identity. I order you to show me the card. You refuse. I call another officer to ring for the military police. What then?'

'Presumably I would be arrested, sir.'

'And then?'

'And then, sir, we should see.'

Suddenly Merrick smiled.

'Your officer was right.'

'Right about what, sir?'

'About your being a tough nut to crack. I think I told you he was singing your praises. But I wanted to find out how easy it would be to force you to act against your better judgment and the security of the job you're doing. I agree it would be quite absurd to risk drawing attention to yourself by warning those fellows off. If I'd looked like succeeding in browbeating you into it I'd have had to stop you. I was only testing you out.'

'May I ask why, sir?'

'I can't tell you here. But if it's not too late when you get back to Queen's Road and have collected your things from Captain Purvis, ring the bell at Lieutenant-Colonel Grace's door on your way down and ask for me. Colonel Grace is Miss Layton's uncle. You know, of course, who her father is.'

'Do I, sir?'

'Weren't you pumping young Kasim? I could have sworn you were.'

'Yes, I know who her father is.'

'Well, if you call you may meet him. They're going back to Pankot tomorrow. I should want you to say nothing about Havildar Karim Muzzafir Khan, either to him or to Miss Layton. In fact nothing at all about the circumstances in which we met before. The other taboo subject, at least in front of Miss Layton, is the subject of Hari Kumar. It might conceivably crop up because Colonel Layton is an old Chillingburian too.'

Merrick broke off. The door of the Maharanee's room had

69

opened and Aneila was coming hastily towards them. Seeing Perron she ran to him and grasped his arm.

'Oh thank goodness you are still here, Auntie is asking for you. Please come quickly. She is in a terrible temper and won't come out to her party. It is so embarrassing with all these people here.'

Still holding his arm she turned back towards the room so that Perron was forced to follow. As he went Merrick said, 'We shall be here for another few minutes, I expect.'

Directly Aneila entered the room the Maharanee cried, 'Shut the door! I cannot stand it! Why do they hang around in the corridor when there are all the rooms to use? Why don't you organize things better? How am I going to rest for my party with all this noise going on?'

'Oh, Auntie, please don't shout, people will hear!'

'How can they hear? I cannot even hear myself speak!'

But it no longer mattered. Aneila had shut the door and stood, visibly trembling, leaning against it.

The Maharanee was still on the couch but by its side now was a small table holding a tray, the bottle of whisky and a glass.'

Pointing at the bottle she said, 'Taste it! Taste it! What is this Purvis creature trying to do? Poison me?'

Perron went across to the couch and picked up the bottle. It was nearly a quarter empty. He glanced at the Maharanee and then at the label. Surprised, he put the uncapped top near his nose and sniffed. The label was genuine. He wondered where Purvis had managed to get hold of it. He hadn't seen a bottle since 1939. He had first tasted the particular brand of whisky it contained at the age of eighteen when it had had an elaborately erotic effect on him. He looked at the Maharanee again, warily.

'You see!' she shouted. 'It is disgusting! Taste it! The taste is even more disgusting than the smell. Aneila, why are you standing there doing nothing? Get Mr Perron a glass.'

Aneila ran into the adjoining bathroom.

'Actually, Your Highness, it's a very fine and rare old malt whisky, an acquired taste perhaps, admittedly –'

'It is disgusting! What is keeping you, Aneila? I said bring Mr Perron a glass.'

70

'I'm bringing it, Auntie.'

She ran in with a tumbler. It was wet from running water from the tap under which it had been rinsed.

'Pour him one!'

But Perron took the glass and reverently poured the whisky himself. It was too precious to waste. He sipped.

'Well? Is it not disgusting?'

'Not to my way of thinking, Your Highness. On first acquaintance it could seem a little smoky but that's part of its charm to people who like it.'

'They must be depraved then. Who but people with depraved tastes could drink such disgusting stuff?'

'There's a very interesting story about it. They said it wasn't until the English learnt to drink and appreciate it that they managed to subdue the Scots.'

'Scots, English, what is the difference? You are all barbarians. Are there many of you at my party?'

'Yes, I'm afraid so.'

'Who else? Aneila is hopeless. She remembers nobody's name.'

'So far I've talked to only a few. I think you know one of them – Count Bronowsky.'

She waved a hand impatiently. 'Yes, I know. Even Aneila can tell me that. But why is he here? Why is Dmitri here tonight? I told him any time except tonight. Who is with him?'

'The secretary who's a son of Mr Mohammed Ali Kasim.'

'Politics!' she exclaimed. 'It is too boring.'

'And a Major Merrick with a charming girl called Sarah Layton. Count Bronowsky brought them.'

'He is mad! And how can Sarah Layton be charming? With a name like that she must be English. I detest English girls. They are always so stupid and rude. They come out here because in England they are nobody and wouldn't be looked at twice. It is impossible. The party is cancelled, Aneila. Tell the servants to lock up the drinks and stop preparing the food. Tell them to go to bed. I am ill. Poisoned by this Purvis creature. I wish to see no one, not even Mira if she arrives. We shall leave Bombay tomorrow. It is too full of spongers and hangers-on. I am tired of it. Tired of it.'

71

'Oh, Auntie, Auntie!'

'Is that all you can say? Is coming to Bombay and having a good time all you can think of nowadays? Isn't it time to consider my feelings in the matter?'

'Auntie, what can I *say* to everybody?'

'Why should you say anything? What right have they to an explanation? Do as *I* say and then go to bed. They will soon get fed up.'

She looked at Perron and indicated the bottle.

'Please return it to the Purvis creature or better still since you seem to like it drink it yourself and then you will not have come all this way for nothing. Only take it. I cannot bear even the smell.'

Perron bowed, retrieved the cap from the table, put it on the bottle. The paper in which the bottle had been wrapped was on the floor. He stooped and picked it up. As he did so the Maharanee reached across to the table on which the lamp stood and recovered the shade with the piece of crimson velvet. She went out like an illuminated picture that had been switched off.

'Goodnight, Your Highness,' Perron said. 'I regret being in any way the cause of your indisposition.'

'Goodnight, Mr Perron. You must visit me again when I come back to Bombay and give my next party. Some of my parties are very nice and go on for a day or two.'

He groped his way back to the door. Somewhere in the darkened room Aneila was crying quietly to herself.

*

There was ample room on the back seat of the limousine for Miss Layton, Major Merrick and Count Bronowsky, and for Perron and Mr Kasim on the bench that was let down to face it. Separated from the passengers by panes of glass set in panels of upholstery and figured walnut rode a chauffeur and a footman wearing what Perron assumed to be the livery of the Nawab of Mirat. The limousine had been waiting outside Ishshee Brizhish and now glided along Marine Drive towards the Oval.

'Mr Perron, may I thank you for your thoughtful tactic in

tipping us off?' Count Bronowsky said, breaking a rather strained silence. 'It means I have a little less to apologize for to Miss Layton and Major Merrick. We were able to come away in fairly reasonable order.'

'Why *have* we come away?' Miss Layton asked. She seemed perfectly composed. She just wanted to know. He thought her behaviour admirable. When he came out of the Maharanee's room, found Merrick and warned him that the party was over it had been obvious that Merrick hadn't yet suggested leaving. Perron was surprised that during the time it had taken them to get away from the flat Merrick hadn't found an opportunity to tell her what had happened. It was a better excuse than the one he might have had to invent.

He waited for Merrick to tell her now but still the man said nothing. Street-lighting alternately illuminated the left and right sides of his face and it was not until the car turned a corner and a brief but total exposure of the whole head was made that it occurred to Perron that the disfigurement of the left side in a curious way reflected something otherwise inexpressible about the right. Realizing that an explanation was being left to him, he said, 'I have an unhappy feeling that a certain Captain Purvis is to blame.'

He told the story of the whisky.

'What's wrong with the whisky?' Miss Layton asked.

'In my opinion, nothing.' He mentioned its official name. She said, 'The genuine thing?'

He unwrapped the bottle sufficiently to expose the label.

'But it's extraordinary,' she said.

'You know it?'

'Great-grandfather had some in his cellar. My father was talking about it only the other day. He said great-grandfather had the sense to keep going until the last bottle was finished. Then he died.'

Perron wondered whether Miss Layton's great-grandfather had referred, as his own Uncle Charles always had, to this particular brand as Old Sporran. He said, 'The Maharanee called it a drink for barbarians but she'd had a glass or two before she decided to complain. I think the whisky was just an excuse to end a party she'd decided she didn't want to give after all.'

'A shrewd assessment,' Bronowsky said. 'Poor Aimee has never made up her mind what she wants in life. But perhaps the whisky was a blessing.' He turned to Merrick and Miss Layton. 'I was beginning to have doubts about the wisdom of having taken you along. May I in addition to most abject apologies for the failure of the first part of the evening offer some entertainment for what is left of it? For instance the supper I misled you to expect at the party?'

'That's very civil of you,' Merrick said, 'but Miss Layton has a tiring journey ahead of her tomorrow and all things considered an early night now would be a good thing.'

'I understand. Quite. So we have met again merely to part. But better briefly than not at all. What about you, Mr Perron?'

Unprepared for the invitation Perron hesitated. He would have liked the opportunity to talk to the old *wazir*.

'Well, thank you, sir, but ...'

'What the sergeant means, Count,' Merrick interrupted, 'is that he hadn't expected to be asked to stay at the Maharanee's and he's been worried about getting back to his billet because he has no late pass. Isn't that what you were rather delicately avoiding telling me in so many words when we were talking in the corridor?'

Perron admired Merrick's inventiveness, but resented becoming the victim of it. He said, 'More or less, sir.'

Bronowsky was smiling. He said, 'I had no idea that in the education you were so regimented. Is the place where you suggested being dropped the most convenient or should we first deliver Miss Layton and Major Merrick at Queen's Road and drive you on? We have plenty of time.'

Merrick interrupted again. 'I'm afraid the sergeant is quartered quite a distance away but I think I can lay on transport for him. If that's all right by you, sergeant?'

'Thank you, sir.'

'At the same time you could take a document for me to the Major Beamish I mentioned. There'd be no need to deliver it until morning, but I'll give you a note as well if you like to satisfy anyone who might try to get you into trouble for being out late without permission.'

Beamish's name, so casually used, presumably served a double-purpose: to lend credibility to what was a complete fiction, and to alert him to the fact that Merrick had an intimate knowledge of that department. He said, 'It's very good of you, sir. I don't think a note will be necessary.'

'We'll see.' He turned to Miss Layton. 'It's all right if the sergeant comes in for a moment, I hope? The document's in the case I left.'

'Of course.'

Perron again offered his thanks. Merrick said, 'A lift back to camp seems the least we can do. Your warning saved Miss Layton the embarrassment of finding the drinks locked up under her nose and all the servants gone to bed, it seems. I find it quite inexplicable.'

After a moment Bronowsky said, 'It is India.' He stirred, as if to ease his lame leg and turned his face fully to Merrick who had the seat next to him.

'I hope you are not plagued still by incidents such as arose when you were in Mirat, Major Merrick? Has all that sort of thing died down?'

'Yes, thank you.'

'I'm glad. We for our part have not been revisited by the venerable Pandit who was using the boy's aunt on that occasion. You never met the girl's aunt, did you?'

'No.'

'Because I had that pleasure – perhaps I should say melancholy pleasure – last November in Gopalakand. She was staying, in a sense incognito, with the Resident, Sir Robert Conway, an old friend apparently. We didn't, of course, refer in any way to Mayapore. In fact our conversation was confined almost entirely to the safe subjects of the weather and the historical and architectural interest of the Residency. I did gather however that she had spent most of the recent hot weather in Pankot, but in what she called the seclusion of the unfashionable side. So I don't suppose any of you were aware of her presence, Miss Layton?'

Merrick moved abruptly as if trying to identify the stretch of road they were on. Miss Layton spoke across him:

'Are you talking about Lady Manners, Count Bronowsky?'

'Yes, the girl's aunt.'

'Actually she signed the book at Flagstaff House when she arrived.'

'Indeed?'

'And again when she left. She didn't write in an address.'

'How strange. I mean, signing the book. Does one interpret it as a gesture of submission or defiance, or simply an ironic observance of hill-station convention?'

'I don't know,' Miss Layton said.

'Strange. Very strange. But how interesting. And talking of this,' Bronowsky said, attracting Perron's attention by lightly touching Perron's right shin with the tip of the ebony cane, 'when you were at that school of yours you must have known a boy called Kumar.'

'Kumar?'

'An Indian boy, Hari Kumar.'

'I don't clearly recall, sir.'

'Coomer was the Anglicization, I believe. Harry Coomer.'

Merrick again leant forward.

'Does your driver remember the block? We're almost there. We ought to be slowing down.'

'I believe he does but I shall make sure.'

Bronowsky unhooked a speaking-tube and gave an order. The car which had already been slowing down just before he spoke now dropped to a crawl and came to a stop opposite the entrance to the flats.

'Didn't you know Coomer?' Bronowsky continued.

'We had an Indian boy or two but I don't recall the name, sir. They were rather junior to me.'

'Yes, I see.'

The footman or second chauffeur opened the nearside door and helped Count Bronowsky on to the pavement. Perron and Kasim stayed put on the bench until Merrick had followed and helped Miss Layton out.

'I should have liked you to meet my father, Count Bronowsky,' Miss Layton was saying, 'but Aunt Fenny and Uncle Arthur managed to persuade him to go out with them and they won't be back yet. Won't you and Mr Kasim come in for a drink, though?'

'My dear, how kind,' he said, taking her hand, 'but I couldn't claim your hospitality, having failed so badly in my own. And Mr Merrick is right. You have the journey tomorrow and your father to look after. I hope he'll be fit again very soon. My kindest regards to your mother and of course to your sister.' He raised her hand and kissed it. 'You accompany Miss Layton and her father as far as Delhi, Major Merrick?'

'Yes, I do that.'

'Then it is au revoir to you both. If you have time when you're in Delhi do call on Mohsin.'

'Mohsin?'

'Nawab Sahib's elder son. He is at the Kasim Mahal most of the year. He's rather a dull fellow but his wife is very hospitable. Mirat bores her. She likes to be in the swim, but *her* parties are beyond reproach. I shall write to them and mention you, so do send in your card.'

'Thank you,' Merrick said. 'And goodnight.' He shook the Count's hand and turned to wait for Miss Layton who was talking to Mr Kasim.

'I often think of it,' she was saying. 'And our ride that morning. Do you still go out regularly?'

Perron did not hear young Kasim's reply because Bronowsky had turned to him to say goodnight.

'If you are ever in Mirat, Mr Perron, a note to the Izzat Bagh Palace would always reach me even if we're up in Nanoora.' He gave Perron his card. 'The Izzat Bagh Palace was built in the eighteenth century. The interior has been much modernized but there's a lot there that would still interest you.'

Perron thanked him, shook hands with him and with Mr Kasim and as the two men returned to the limousine followed Merrick and Miss Layton into the block of flats. The lift was still out of order. At the foot of the stairs Merrick muttered something to Miss Layton. She nodded and began to climb.

'I think the form is, sergeant, for you to change into your other uniform and call in on your way down. There is, of course, no document for Major Beamish. Incidentally, *are* you going to need transport?'

'No, sir.'

'Where actually are you going?'

'Kalyan?'

'Tonight?'

'Yes, sir.'

They went up the stairs. The servant whom Purvis had

nearly knocked over was just opening the door to Miss Layton who went in without looking at either of them.

'We'll see you presently, then.'

Perron went up to the next floor and rang the bell of Purvis's flat. This time he noticed the nameplate. Hapgood. Hapgood the Banker. Mrs Hapgood the Banker's wife and Miss Hapgood the Banker's daughter. One of the happy families currently relaxing in Ooty. He rang the bell again. From inside he heard men's voices. The door was opened by the servant who had originally met him on the stairs. He looked wildly at Perron and began to talk rapidly in what sounded to Perron like Tamil – of which he understood only a few words. At the first opportunity he interrupted, speaking in English.

'What's the matter? I don't understand what you're saying.'

There were two other servants at the dark end of the corridor, the cook and his boy, probably. The boy was grinning. Perron shut the door. The bearer had resumed his incomprehensible complaint but was clearly inviting Perron to follow him into the living-room.

Arrived there his first impression was that there had been a visit by thieves who had torn the place apart to find what they had come for. The drinks table lay on its side surrounded by broken glasses and bottles. Cushions from the settees were scattered at random. The glass protecting two of the priceless Moghul paintings was smashed and the paintings themselves damaged. Inspecting them Perron realized that a bottle of rum had been shied at them. He could smell it. Stains ran down the wall. On the settee beneath he found bottle-fragments.

The bearer was now referring repeatedly to 'Purvis Sahib'. The cook came into the dining-room. His responsibilities did not extend beyond the kitchen. What was a disaster for the bearer was for him an interesting break in routine. The scene fascinated him because he was not going to be blamed for it.

'What happened?' Perron asked him in English.

'Purvis Sahib,' the cook said. He waved his arms about then mimed a man drinking, staggering, throwing things. He tapped his forehead. Purvis Sahib had gone mad.

'Where is Purvis Sahib now?'

'Room.' He shut his eyes, put his head on one side, let his tongue loll, imaging a man in a drunken stupor.

Perron went back to the corridor. The cook came with him. 'Locked,' the cook said. 'Sahib ish-shleeping.'

Perron tried the handle. He knocked. He called, 'Captain Purvis? It's Sergeant Perron.'

The bearer joined them.

'How long has he been here?'

'Half-hour, Sahib.'

The cook said, 'Drunk. Ish-shleeping.'

'What happened?'

The bearer started to explain. Perron interrupted him, asked him to tell him in English.

A telegram had come. When? Soon after Sergeant Sahib had left with the bottle of whisky. A telegram from where?

The bearer went back to the dining-room. Perron followed. The telegram – actually an official military signal – was under the telephone on a side-table.

When Purvis Sahib read the telegram he was very angry. He used the telephone. He rang people. Nobody he wanted to talk to could be found. He tried to ring Delhi. While he waited for the call he drank. He kept ringing the operator. Because he could not get through he was shouting all the time and drinking, and swearing.

Perron asked the bearer to be quiet while he read the signal. It was prefixed Secret and Urgent. It informed Captain Purvis of his secondment to the department of Civil Affairs and ordered him to report to Headquarters, South-East Asia Command, by August 9. Copies had been sent to an impressive list of authorities. No explanation was given but that was hardly necessary. In Ceylon, Purvis would find himself attached to a group of Civil Affairs officers bound for Malaya either with or in the wake of Zipper.

'Did Captain Purvis Sahib eventually speak to Delhi?'

Yes. The call had come through. During the conversation Purvis Sahib had become like a wild man, shouting and screaming. Then the line had been disconnected. Purvis Sahib began to throw the cushions, and then the bottles. Finally he kicked the table over. No one had dared go near. They had watched from the corridor. When Purvis Sahib staggered to his room they ran into the kitchen. They heard the door slam. Then they heard him shouting and throwing things again.

79

After a bit they heard him crying. Cook had tried to open the door but it was locked. Now he was unconscious with drink. What to do? What would happen when Hapgood Sahib returned from Ooty? What would Hapgood Sahib say when he saw the damage? Was the telegram not from the army sending Purvis Sahib to another station? Did not this mean that when Hapgood Sahib returned Purvis Sahib would not be here? Would the Sergeant Sahib write a chit to Purvis Sahib asking Purvis Sahib to write a chit to Hapgood Sahib offering to pay for the damage and making it clear that the servants were not to blame?

Perron, already on his way back to the locked door did not answer. He knocked loudly and called Purvis again. He grasped the handle and rattled. There semed to be only one bolt.

'I'm afraid I shall have to break in. I'll write a chit for the door.'

Perron launched himself left shoulder forward. The impact was as bad as the jarring shock of walking into a tree or a lamp-post. The door remained shut. The bearer started shouting again. A broken door, apparently, would be the last straw.

'Is there another way in?'

The bearer did not understand but the cook did. He sent the boy for some keys and then opened the door into the adjoining room and switched on the light. The room must be Miss Hapgood's. It smelt of stale powder and self-satisfaction. There was a great deal of chintz and several numdah rugs on the stone floor. The french-doors on to the balcony were open to keep the room aired but the way out on to the balcony was blocked by a thick wire-mesh screen. This was padlocked. While they waited for the boy to bring the key the cook explained that between this balcony and the one outside Purvis's room there was a gap of only a foot or two. The Sergeant Sahib would find it easy to step from one parapet to the other. Perron hoped this would be so and that Purvis's wire screen was not closed and padlocked too. The bearer assured him it would not be; but this remained to be seen.

The boy came with the key and in a moment Perron was outside. The balcony overlooked a broad passage between the block of flats and its neighbour and also had a view of the backs of other blocks. It was a world of hot night air and lighted windows. From some of them music came. The gap between the balconies was as narrow as the cook had promised. The cook allowed his shoulder to be used as a support while Perron got up on the parapet, steadied himself and stepped across. Without pausing to lose momentum or balance he jumped on to the floor of Purvis's balcony, barely managing to avoid twisting his ankle. One foot had landed within an inch of a potted plant which looked both virile and belligerent. The curtains in Purvis's room were closed but the wire-mesh screen gave at a touch. He entered.

The room was unoccupied. He tapped at the bathroom door and called. There was no sound from inside. He tried the handle. This door was locked too. He unbolted and opened the one into the corridor. The three servants were waiting outside.

'Did Purvis Sahib have his bath before the telegram came?'

No. All Purvis Sahib had done after Sergeant Sahib left was to sit drinking.

'In the flat below,' Perron said, slowly and carefully, 'there is a Major Rajendra Singh of the IMS. A Doctor Sahib. Please go downstairs, ring his bell and ask him to come quickly if he is there. If not come back at once.'

The cook volunteered to take the message but Perron said, 'No, you help me.' The cook looked tougher than the bearer. 'Purvis Sahib may be very ill. We have to break into the bathroom.'

Perron did not wait to watch the bearer go. He rattled the bathroom door, kicked the bottom and punched the top. The bolt was at waist level. Again he launched himself, right shoulder this time. After three attempts he stood back.

'Together. Okay?'

The cook lined himself up. On Perron's count of three they attacked the door together. There wasn't really enough working surface. Two shoulders needed a wider door. But Perron thought he felt something give. He fingered one of the panels. The door was a good solid piece of carpentry; which was a pity because breaking in looked like a chopper or axe job.

'Once more.'

This time the sound and feel of cracking wood was unmistakable. The bolt-hole was being forced out of the door-frame. Some of the frame would come with it.

'I think I can manage now.'

He stood the cook aside, made an anchorage for his left arm on the cook's shoulder and kicked hard at the door just above the handle with the flat of his shoe. He did this four times. At the fifth kick the door gave, swung open and revealed their own reflections in the mirror above the hand-basin: an unlooked-for and disturbing confrontation.

Perron went in. The water in the bath-tub had a pink tinge. In it Purvis lay, fully clothed except for his shoes which were placed neatly on the cork mat. His body had slumped and the head, turned into one shoulder, was half submerged. The source of the pink tinge was a series of cuts on the inner side of the left arm which was bare to the elbow. From these cuts slicks of blood rose. In his right hand, which lay under the water, the fingers touching but not grasping it, was the broken-off bottle neck that he had used to inflict the wounds. Other fragments of the bottle were visible. The label – from the second of the two bottles of Old Sporran – floated on the surface.

There was space enough between the wash-basin and the head end of the bath. From there Perron reached down, grasped the collar of Purvis's bush-shirt and heaved him up far enough to get the head out of water and a hand under one arm. He had to struggle to get a grip under the other. He glanced round. The cook was standing in the doorway looking as if he had come to announce that the dinner was ruined through no fault of his own.

'Help me with his feet,' Perron said.

'Sahib dead?'

'I don't know. Help with his feet.'

Reluctantly the man came in. After one glance at Purvis's face he looked away, studied the feet and presently leant over and grasped them, none too firmly.

'Up.'

Shoulders and feet came clear but Purvis was a dead weight. He sagged in the middle. The feet fell back in. The cook was drenched. Perron's eyes began to sting with sweat. The bathroom was like a hothouse. By contrast Purvis's body felt alarmingly tepid through the sodden khaki material. Changing tactics, Perron heaved the shoulders further up and then began to turn Purvis over on to the rim of the bath. As the face disappeared from the cook's view his attention to the mechanics of the problem improved. He grabbed Purvis's knees and heaved. Purvis was now face down and half out of the bath at the top end. Perron readjusted his grip and began to pull. The cook got hold of the thigh and knee of the left leg. At one moment Purvis was balanced entirely on the rim and in danger of falling off it. Perron walked backwards to the door, dragging Purvis with him. The water sloshed out of Purvis's pockets. The cook now got a secure grip on both ankles. They carried Purvis through into the bedroom.

'Bed, Sahib?'

'No, here.' Perron lowered his end to the floor. The cook followed suit.

'Towel.'

While the cook went back for this Perron turned Purvis's face sideways and adjusted the arms, straddled the body and began the exhausting drill for first-aid to the drowned. While he did so he looked at the left arm. There didn't seem to be much blood on the floor. Perhaps the slashes on the arm were superficial. A towel dangled in his face. 'Sahib,' the cook said. Perron broke off, took the towel and wound it tightly round the slashed arm. Then he resumed. A thin trickle of water and what looked like vomit came from Purvis's mouth.

'Doctor Sahib not answering,' came the bearer's voice. The cook repeated the message. 'No answer, doctor sahib.'

Perron continued exerting and relaxing pressure. A large trickle of water came.

'Go downstairs,' Perron said, between pressures. 'Ring Colonel Grace Sahib's bell. Ask for Major Merrick. Anyone. Say: Doctor, ambulance, Purvis Sahib. Quick. Okay?'

The cook repeated the instructions to the bearer.

'Go with him,' Perron said. 'Doctor. Ambulance, Sergeant Perron's request.'

Alone, Perron paused to wipe sweat. He looked at his watch. Twenty minutes altogether was what was recommended. Say another fifteen yet to go. After that Purvis could be presumed dead. He was probably dead now. Perron was tempted to pause again and listen for heart and pulse beat but he supposed the most important thing now was to keep up the rhythm. He resumed. He had studied the drill but this was the first time he had had to put it into practice. The action he was performing suddenly struck him as distasteful. Not only was the body very likely dead, it was Purvis's. It would have been preferable if the inert figure, prone between his thighs, had been that of a complete stranger. The fact that he had sat and talked to Purvis strengthened the unpleasantness of their present positions. He wondered whether Purvis would thank him if he succeeded in reviving him. The suspicion that he would not made the task that much more objectionable. There was another ejaculation of water and vomit. Perron turned his head, closed his eyes. He began breathing in and out through his mouth, slowly, to the rhythm of his own body's movement. He breathed audibly, thinking that perhaps by some quirk of nature Purvis's moribund brain and water-logged lungs might be stimulated into action by an association of ideas.

From breathing just audibly he progressed to doing so hoarsely through a half-closed throat, and continued so after his throat had begun to ache; the point being that he wanted Purvis to *hear* what he himself now began to despair of hearing from Purvis. His back hurt. His arms and shoulders hurt. Sweat poured unchecked over and around his closed eyes. His knees were numb from contact with the tiled floor. Pain stabbed through them down the shins and up the thighs with each forward and backward movement. Only his hands, pressing into Purvis's thin bony back and rib-cage, still seemed capable of doing their work indefinitely. He went on, exerting and relaxing pressure and breathing hoarsely until suddenly his throat dried up. He closed his mouth, swallowed and tried to make saliva. The effort put him off his stroke. He stopped for a moment and then, alerted, opened his eyes and stared down at Purvis. From Purvis's open mouth was coming a sound and under Perron's hands the rib-cage was moving. Purvis was breathing, or anyway fighting for breath.

'I think you can stop now, Sergeant,' someone said. He looked up and round. Merrick stood just behind him. 'I'll get another towel. We've rung for a doctor. He's just up the road so he'll be here in a tick.'

Perron nodded and looked down at Purvis. The struggle for breath seemed immense. Surprisingly it was not without a certain dignity. When Merrick returned with the towel Perron took it from him and spread it over the vomit and then, folding a clean section, tucked it under Purvis's cheek and stroked a lank bit of the mousy hair away from the closed eyes. As he did so Purvis's mouth shut and then opened again.

Merrick said, 'I think a blanket would be a good idea if there is such a thing.' He found one in the almirah and brought it over. Perron helped him cover Purvis with it.

'We'd better have a look at this.' He leant down and lifted Purvis's left arm. Perron unwound the towel. The inside was fairly bloody now but only one of the cuts was seeping seriously.

'I think just wrap the towel round again, Sergeant, until the doctor gets here,' Merrick said. 'It wasn't a very effective job, was it?'

'He was pretty drunk.'

'What on? More of the whisky the Maharanee didn't like?'

'To judge by the broken bottle.'

'And the smell in this room.'

'Is there a smell?'

'Very much so. Haven't you noticed?'

Perron sniffed. He noticed it now.

'Not the most prepossessing chap by the look of him, is he?' Merrick said. 'Do you know what was wrong?'

'I think he'd just had enough.'

'You look as if you have. Where did you leave the bottle you brought back from the Maharanee's?'

Perron told him he thought it must be in the living-room.

'I think you should have some. I'll bring it.'

Merrick went. Purvis's breathing was shallow but fairly regular. Perron got up stiffly. A man's voice in the corridor called 'Hello?' There was an exchange between Merrick and the new arrival. Merrick came back into the room with an English IMS officer. The officer knelt, lifted Purvis's eyelid and felt his temple.

'You're the chap who found him, are you, Sergeant?'

'Yes, sir.'

The doctor unwrapped the towel from the arm.

'Bath, I gather. Face completely submerged?'

'Right side, sir.'

'D'you know how long for, roughly?'

'No, sir.'

'How long were you resuscitating?'

'About ten minutes, sir.'

The doctor had his stethoscope out. When he had finished and slung the earpieces round his neck he glanced up.

'Well done. You'd better go next door and have a bloody strong drink and get out of that wet uniform. Major Merrick – perhaps a couple of the fellows outside will help me get him on to the bed while you ring for the blood-wagon?' He gave Merrick the number as Perron left the room.

*

After Purvis had been taken away Merrick came back from downstairs and into the wrecked living-room where Perron sat drinking some of the Maharanee's whisky and admiring the vivid and lively effect of the Guler-Basohli technique. The paintings were the only things he felt able to concentrate on. They were about one hundred and fifty years old. Even the two damaged ones maintained that air of detachment and self-sufficiency that went with a talent for survival.

Before Merrick could speak Perron said, 'Until I told Purvis what those pictures were he'd no idea. If I'd kept quiet he'd probably have left them alone.'

Merrick inspected them.

'It's what's called Kangra painting, isn't it?'

Perron nodded. Kangra was close enough.

Merrick said, 'Actually I find all oriental art unattractive.' He turned from the paintings. 'I don't think you need worry further about Captain Purvis unless he does the unexpected and dies, which would mean an inquest. But Simpson says he'll be all right. When he's recovered they'll hand him over to the psychiatric people. Are you going to be fit to drive back to Kalyan?'

'I should think so, sir.'

86

'Then get your other things and come downstairs and clean up. We'll give you something to eat. How much of that whisky have you had?'

'This is my third glass.'

'Rather a strong one, isn't it? When you're downstairs you'll remember which subjects are taboo, won't you?'

'The subjects of Havildar Karim Muzzafir Khan and Harry Coomer.'

'Good. Incidentally I liked the way you handled Count Bronowsky, but I was surprised he thought fit to raise the subject.'

Perron sipped whisky. He had not liked lying. He felt he was owed an explanation. 'Perhaps you'll tell me what Coomer did, sir?'

'He and five of his friends raped an English girl called Daphne Manners, the niece of the Lady Manners whose name also came up. It was a squalid and extremely nasty business and I find it inconceivable that a man should refer to it in front of a woman.'

Perron sipped more whisky. How old-fashioned. His inclination was to laugh. He wondered whether it was Merrick's intention to make him.

'Was a charge of rape the one you said he wriggled out of, sir?'

'Yes. But as I told you we got him and the others on political grounds.'

Perron drained the glass and stood up. 'It all sounds so melodramatic. I find it difficult to imagine Coomer raping anybody.'

'But then you didn't really know him, except with a bat and ball. Are you one of those people who think that if you teach an Indian the rules of cricket he'll become a perfect English gentleman?'

'Hardly, sir. Since I know quite a few Englishmen who play brilliantly and are absolute shits.'

'Do you?' Merrick said. He stared at Perron. 'What are you going to do about the Maharanee's whisky?'

'Keep it, I should think.'

'In view of what Miss Layton said about her father's fondness for that particular brand I was wondering whether it would be a nice gesture for you to leave it with her as a sort of thank you.'

'Thank you?'

'She's putting herself out to see that you have something to eat.'

'I didn't ask for anything to eat, sir.'

'I did that for you. I don't want you driving on a stomach full of nothing but liquor. And then there's the danger of delayed shock impairing your judgment and leading to an accident.'

'It's nice of you to have my welfare at heart, sir.'

'My concern is quite unaltruistic. I have a vested interest in your continuing capacity to perform efficiently. Now, let's go down and get you cleaned up and fed.'

'May I ask what vested interest, sir?'

'I'm arranging to have you attached to my department. The signal ordering you to report for an interview is probably waiting for you in Kalyan but the interview will be no more than a formality. You can assume you'll be working for me. You'll find it pretty interesting.'

'It's very kind of you, sir, but I imagine my department will think its present commitments much too important to allow me to go elsewhere.'

'You'll find they're overruled without much fuss.'

'The point is, sir, I shouldn't want them overruled.'

'Well that does you credit. One becomes attached to one's own unit. But I imagine you'll bow to the inevitable with more equanimity than our friend Purvis. Let's not keep Miss Layton waiting any longer.'

Perron picked up the bottle and went to Purvis's room to collect his pack. Back in the corridor he found Merrick instructing the bearer to leave everything as it was until morning. Perron preceded him through the open door, waited for him and then followed him downstairs. Just short of the door of the flat, which was ajar, Merrick said, 'I'll relieve you of that, shall I?' and took the bottle.

Going in, Merrick called, 'Sarah? I've got Sergeant Perron here.'

Perron followed. In layout the flat was a mirror-duplicate of the one upstairs. She was coming through the dining-room area towards them.

'Hello. Are you all right?'

'I think he's still a bit groggy,' Merrick said before Perron could answer.

'If you are I don't wonder. I'll show you where you can relax and freshen up. Ronald, you go and sit down.'

Her manner was brisk but sympathetic. The bedroom she took him to corresponded with the one Purvis had occupied upstairs but was properly furnished. The light and the ceiling fan were already on. There were two beds; between them a writing-table and a chair with an officer's bush-shirt draped over its back. The bush-shirt looked brand new. The woven shoulder-tabs were those of a Lieutenant-Colonel of the Pankot Rifles.

The door to the bathroom was open and the light switched on. She said, 'Do bathe or shower if you want to. You'll find a large green towel on the rail that hasn't been used.' She had made simple but efficient preparations. She looked at his damp uniform. 'I know father wouldn't mind your borrowing his dressing-gown if you want to have anything dried out and pressed quickly.'

'It's very kind of you, Miss Layton, but I've got a change of clothes in here.' He indicated the pack. 'My correct uniform. The one you saw me in this afternoon.'

'Yes, of course. I'll leave you to it, then. How hungry are you?'

'I'm not at all hungry but I suppose I ought to eat something.'

'I think you ought to if you possibly can. Not that there's much to offer you. Aunt Fenny assumed we'd all be out so she gave cook the night off and Nazimuddin isn't very inventive.'

'Whatever's going will be fine.'

'I'm afraid it's only soup, cold chicken and salad, and what Aunt Fenny calls a shape. In other words, blancmange.'

'I'm rather partial to shape.'

'Good.'

They smiled at one another rather gravely.

'Well,' she said, 'come along whenever you're ready. I'll send Nazimuddin in with a drink. What would you like?'

'Major Merrick thinks I'd just better eat. I've had some of the Maharanee's whisky. Incidentally, he thought your father might like what's left of it. Will he be insulted, being offered left-overs?'

She hesitated. 'Not of that particular whisky. How very nice of you. Are you sure you wouldn't like a glass while you're changing?'

'Quite sure.'

'Did Major Merrick tell you I tipped him off that there was a Field Security man in disguise at the party?'

'Yes, he did.'

'I wasn't sure whether to tell him or not so it was a relief when he said you'd already met and were coming to work with him.'

'You were quite right to tell him. You weren't to know which uniform was the masquerade.'

'Actually that never crossed my mind.'

There was a knock on the open door. The curtains parted and Merrick looked in.

'What is it, Ronald?'

'You've been such a long time I thought our sergeant friend was suffering a reaction from his exertions and that you were having to minister.'

'Actually, sir,' Perron said, 'we've been discussing the attractions and nutritive value of that homely pudding, the blancmange.'

'Oh,' Merrick said, not looking at Perron, speaking to Miss Layton. 'You're having shape again, then. Well, if it's one of the sergeant's favourite afters we'd better let him get changed.' He pushed the curtain further aside: a gesture of command rather than a mark of good manners. Miss Layton hesitated and then went through, murmuring 'Thank you, Ronald' as she did so. Still without looking at Perron Merrick followed her.

Perron put his pack on the nearest of the two beds. Taking out his carefully folded jungle-green issue uniform, spreading it, considering it, he said aloud suddenly, 'I'll be buggered if I will.'

The Zipper-bound boats out there in the roads riding the gentle swell of the Arabian Sea, patient in the night and the persistent rain, seemed infinitely welcoming; his working clothes (in comparison with the jacket that hung on the chairback) purposeful, appropriate. Going into the bathroom he felt his chin. It could have done with a shave but he didn't go back for his razor and brush. A day's growth of bristle was appropriate too. He stripped off the damp harlequinade and stepped into the tub, on to Purvis who lay there invisibly entombed in the smooth white porcelain. Perron's feet went right through him; but when he turned the shower faucet and gasped under the impact of a needle-sharp cold spray he felt the sodden flesh of Purvis's left arm take shape against his shins and the hand take hold of his ankle. Be not afeared, Perron began to declaim, the Isle is full of noises, sounds and sweet airs that give delight and hurt not.

When Purvis had been half-drowned for the second time that evening and Perron had dried himself on the green towel (put out on the rail by Miss Layton's own charming hands?) he returned to the bedroom and put on a clean set of cellular cotton under-shorts and clean socks – the second of two changes carefully packed that morning. Soldiers, he thought, acquired old-maidish habits – especially in the tropics. He got into the green trousers and bush-shirt, unrolled the sleeves and buttoned them at the wrists. Then he sat on the bed and put his boots on, folded the trouser-bottoms and secured them with the webbing anklets. All that remained in the pack now was his shaving kit, small towel, clean handkerchief, webbing belt, holster, pistol and lanyard. If Purvis had known about the pistol would he have gone to the trouble of getting it out of the pack? He put these things on the bed and went round the room and bathroom collecting the stuff he had discarded and cramming it into the pack, so that the damp clothes were at the bottom. This done he replaced the stuff from the bed and secured the pack straps. He checked his breast pocket for the piece of paper on which before leaving for the Maharanee's he had got Purvis to write down the address of the place where they had left his jeep, and which he'd fortunately not put in the pocket of the khaki uniform. It might have been illegible now, from bath water. He looked at it, rememorized it.

Finished, he glanced round the room until his attention was again taken by the brand-new khaki bush-shirt that belonged to Sarah Layton's father. It was, Perron supposed, one of the first things Colonel Layton would do on his return from prison-camp in Europe: get himself fitted out afresh, no doubt from necessity but also to look trim for the arrival in Pankot with the regiment. How would they march in? With bags of swank to make up for the silence in the hills?

But there was nothing particularly swanky about the bush-shirt. It hung on the chair back without distinction, like a jacket on a coat-hanger too narrow for it. There were eyelets sewn on the left breast which showed where two broad bars of medal ribbons would be pinned, but these were not there, nor on the table, and their absence struck Perron as eloquent, as a clue to some special attribute the jacket had which he hadn't identified.

He identified it now. The jacket was new but the slip-on shoulder tabs, although pressed and starched, were old, much laundered. The cream and brown cottons of the embroidered pip and crown, and the black cotton of the regimental name, were faded.

The attribute was twofold, a combination of economical habit and modest impulse. The way the bush-shirt hung on the chair back, shoulders drooped, ostensibly in possession of chair, room, suggested a claim to occupation, but – Perron thought – a claim made in awareness of the insecurity of any tenure. He tried to give the jacket a perkier look by twitching the shoulders back up. They slipped off again. This was because the chair was too narrow, not because Layton was a man of impressive build. Perhaps he had been, before years in prison camp wore him down.

The bush-shirt began to depress him; it was threatening to undermine his confidence in much the same way that the whole experience of being in India had so often seemed on the point of undermining it. Staring at the bush-shirt, on a perch it clung to which did not properly support it, he was struck by its mute indication of the grand irrelevance of history to the things that people wanted for themselves. As in Beamish's office, earlier, he again tuned in the inner ear, the one that could catch the whisper of the perpetually moving stream; but now caught nothing. It began to ache from the pressure of a marble silence so smooth and dense that the plop of a drop of water – the built-in residue in the nozzle of the bathroom shower hitting the porcelain – came as a relief, an excuse to tune back in to the world in which the most significant sound was that made by a hall full of men, ignorant of and indifferent to their history, and giving it the bird.

He got out his notebook and recorded Purvis's remark: 'Six years waste of the world's natural resources and human skills. I don't think I shall ever be able to forgive it.' That was at once a moral judgment and a revelation of thwarted ambition.

'Sahib?'

Perron looked up. The servant Nazimuddin stood in the doorway holding the curtain aside. He indicated a direction – that of the dining-room. Perron nodded – a little surprised to be invited to eat there. He let Nazimuddin go, put his notebook away, waited for a moment or two and then followed, carrying his pack, fighting an urge to open the front door when he got to it and leave without another word.

As though to forestall him Merrick was stationed near it. Through the dining-area, beyond the archway, Perron could see Miss Layton, in profile, seated, talking to someone in the living-room who was hidden from view.

'Leave your pack here, Sergeant.'

Perron put it down near the door. When he had straightened up Merrick continued. 'I told the servant to hurry you up because Miss Layton's father has come back unexpectedly. He's had dinner out and wants an early night but I've been telling him about you and he'll have a few words, so come along.'

Hearing them coming, she broke off what she was saying. Her father sat at one end of a large cretonne-covered sofa. Perron stopped and, briefly, held himself in an attitude akin to parade-ground attention.

'Father, this is Sergeant Perron. My father, Colonel Layton.'

'Good-evening, sir,' Perron said. He stayed where he was. The colonel got up but they were too far from each other to shake hands. He was tall, very thin, slightly stooped. He wore a replica of the bush-shirt in the bedroom. At the head of the row of medal ribbons was the MC.

'Hello,' he said. 'Hear you've been in the wars a bit tonight.' His voice was mild and pleasant. His upper lip was covered by the regulation bristly, cropped, moustache. His head was balding, his complexion pale; a washed-out, rather worn sort of face, but with the same bony structure as his daughter's and so perhaps once more resolute and attractive than it now appeared.

'The evening has been on the hectic side, sir.'

'Mine was too. Thought I'd give the rest of it a miss. Perron. Perron, is it?'

'Yes, sir.'

'Perron. Well, let's sit down again shall we, unless I'm holding the kitchen up.'

'It's only a question of heating the soup, the rest's cold so there's no hurry.'

'Splendid.' He turned to look behind him, as if the act of getting up had disoriented him, left him uncertain about the location or even the continuing existence of the sofa; then, remembering the other two, he indicated vacant places and waited until Merrick and Perron had chosen seats and settled in. There were two floral cretonne-covered sofas at right angles to each other, a small tapestry-covered wing chair in which Miss Layton was sitting, and a larger matching chair which Merrick took. Perron sat on the second sofa; in this way he faced the company. The furniture was arranged round an Indian carpet. There were Benares brass coffee-tables in front of each sofa. The room was not elegant like the banking Hapgoods' living-room, but comfortable, attractive in a homely English way. On the wall behind Colonel Layton hung a couple of faded portraits – conversation-pieces in the Zoffany style – with eighteenth century ladies and gentlemen under trees, with attendant servants: in one case transfixed in expository attitudes and in the other restraining cheetahs on leashes.

'There are cigarettes in the box, Mr Perron,' Miss Layton said. 'And the lighter works. So do help yourself whenever you want.'

'Perron,' Colonel Layton repeated, as if trying to place the name.

Before Perron could speak Merrick said, 'There was a man called Pierre-Cuiller who was known as Perron. He became Governor of what was called Hindustan and commanded the armies under Daulat Rao Sindia. Originally he was a sergeant.'

'In the French Army?' Layton asked. The question was open to both of them but Merrick took it up. 'I can't recall the early origins exactly. But I seem to remember he began life as a pedlar as a result of his family losing all its money. It must be in Compton, but it's some time since I read him. Perron was certainly in the French navy and I think he was in the French Army before that. He came out on a French ship but I can't remember whether it was on the Coromandel or Malabar coast he deserted. Anyway he disappeared up country to seek his fortune with the mercenary Europeans who helped the Indian princes run their armies. What I do remember is that he was among the remnants of Lestineau's brigade when they were taken over by another mercenary, de Boigne, Mahdaji Sindia's chap. Perron was still a sergeant then but rose pretty rapidly and when de Boigne retired after Mahdaji's death and Daulat Rao's succession Perron took over. But of course the two Wellesleys were in control of British interests by then and the French were practically finished. The Mahratta power was fading out and Perron never acquired a reputation as high as de Boigne's. Would you agree, sergeant?'

After a moment Perron smiled, to convey his appreciation of the point Merrick had made: that he was to be reckoned with.

'Yes, I'd agree, sir. But compared with de Boigne Perron was second-rate. Of course he was handicapped –'

Perron stopped – silenced by the impact of one of those unexpected shock-waves, scarcely more than a ripple, of delayed response to a forgotten factor. He had meant that Perron was handicapped by political and military circumstances more complex and threatening than de Boigne had ever had to contend with, but in the split-second before he used the word handicapped he recalled another impediment, one that he was always forgetting because it had seemed to play so insignificant a part in Perron's career. He looked at Merrick's left hand. The gloved artifact was at rest, just off the chair-arm.

Merrick said, 'I suppose you could call it a handicap but I

don't remember it ever being said to worry him. Which hand was it by the way?'

Monsieur Perron had lost a hand while throwing a grenade that exploded prematurely. Perron said, 'The right, I imagine, unless he was left-handed or being particularly hard-pressed.'

Merrick said, 'I don't think it was important.' He turned to Colonel Layton. 'The real answer is that he didn't have de Boigne's luck and of course it's difficult stepping into the shoes of an outstandingly successful man. It's an interesting coincidence to come across a modern Sergeant Perron, especially one who's making a study of British-Indian history.'

'Are you connected?' Layton asked amiably. 'I mean descended?' Perron said he was not.

'But the mercenaries are what you'd call your subject?'

'No, sir.'

'What is?'

'At the moment, sir, Field Security in the Bombay Presidency.'

Layton waited a few seconds then put his head back against the sofa. 'Ha!' And then added, 'Jolly good answer.' He crossed his legs, glanced at Merrick, then returned his attention to Perron. 'All the same, war over and all that, what'll be your subject then?'

'Eighteen-Thirty to the Mutiny, I think, sir.'

Layton narrowed his eyes. 'Good period. Bad too, I suppose. That your point?'

'I haven't got a point yet, sir. Choosing a period's rather like sticking a pin in a map of likely runners. Eighteen-thirty or eighteen-thirty-three to eighteen-fifty-eight is simply the period between the East India Company's loss of its trading charter and its metamorphosis into the Indian Civil Service. So it represents about thirty years' dress rehearsal for full imperial rule. Some of the clues to what eventually went wrong are probably there. That's an over-simplification but it's the neatest way I can put it.'

Colonel Layton was still observing him through those narrowed eyes, apparently paying close attention, but his next remark showed that his attention was on Perron himself and not on what he was saying.

'Perron. I've remembered now. There was a Perron at the school I was at. Younger than me, but a big boy. Remarkably fine athlete. Before the First World War. Place called Chillingborough.'

'That would have been my father, sir.'

'Would it now?' Did Layton's eyes stray to the stripes on his sleeve? Had the reference to Chillingborough been carefully prepared? Or had Merrick said nothing to Layton? On the whole Perron preferred to give him the benefit of the doubt.

'So you're Perron's son, then. Don't suppose I've thought of him since I left. Is he still going strong?'

'He was killed in 1918, sir.'

'Oh. I'm sorry.'

'Ironically enough, on November the tenth.'

'What awful luck. And your mother?'

'She died in 1919, of Spanish 'flu.'

'You poor fellow. Still, you'd be too young to know anything about it, I imagine.'

'Yes, sir. Actually I had a very pleasant childhood. I was brought up by some rather eccentric aunts and uncles.'

'Eccentric enough to send you to Chillingborough too?'

'Yes, sir.'

'Which house?'

'Bank's.'

'The same as your father.'

'No, sir. He was Coote's.'

'Ah. Yes. So he was.'

Layton turned his body rather awkwardly and put his left hand into the nearest of the two large side-pockets of his bushjacket. Coote's was a nickname. Perron had used it quite unconsciously but it was the sort of thing only someone familiar with Chillingborough lore would be likely to know.

'Did you know someone called Clark?' Miss Layton asked.

'I knew two. One with an e and the other without.'

She sat back and folded her arms, cupping the elbows. She said, 'I've always thought of him as Clark without an e. But now you mention it I'm not sure. My aunt and uncle would know. I only met him once. His first name was James.'

'They were both James. So we called them Clarke-With and

Clark-Without. Clark-Without otherwise lacked very little. I thought of him as someone who would go far in life.'

'Then the one I knew must have been Clark-Without. I met him on the sixth of June last year.' She had turned to speak to her father. 'I know it was the sixth of June because that's the day I visited Ronald in hospital in Calcutta and the day we heard about the second front.' She looked back at Perron. 'He was flying to Ceylon the next day to take up some glamorous-sounding job at South-East Asia Command Headquarters. I've not heard of him again, though.'

'Then it could only have been Clark-Without. Clarke-With wasn't what I'd call Command Headquarters material.'

He wondered about Miss Layton's brief acquaintance with Clark-Without. Clark-Without had not been officially expelled but, in Chillingborough's peculiar language, with-drawn by mutual consent. A Rolls had turned up and Clark-Without had driven away in style, not up-front with the chauffeur but at the back, smoking a cigarette. A mature boy for his age. Perhaps he had been excessively self-publicized in regard to his affairs with girls. Miss Layton did not look in the least embarrassed. In any case she had raised the subject herself. But why? To test for further proof that he himself had been at Chillingborough or to hear him speak the name of a man she had fancied?

'I think your father is tired, Sarah,' Merrick said.

'Ronald thinks you're tired, Father. Are you?'

'Not in the least. Tell you what I'd like, though. A peg of that whisky of Ronald's. Why don't we all do that?'

'It wasn't Ronald's whisky, Father. It was Sergeant Perron's. Before that it was the Maharanee's and before that Captain Purvis's. Nazimuddin !'

Colonel Layton looked from one to the other as if bemused by such a complicated history, and finally concentrated on Perron. 'Extraordinary thing,' he said, 'in the last conver-sation I had with a very civilized Oberleutnant at the camp I was at, the name of this particular brand came up. We were saying goodbye and he told me he'd be thinking of me in a week or two's time sitting in a comfortable chair in a cosy room, reading *Pride and Prejudice*, sipping a glass of special malt whisky and fondling the ears of my faithful black

Labrador, Panther. Apparently one day months before he'd said, "What would you most like to be doing at this very moment?" and it seems that's what I told him. I hadn't the faintest recollection of it. Memory's a bit haywire. But it was pretty well in line with the sort of thing I'd often thought, so obviously I had done. Well, he got the names right. I didn't have the heart to tell him I never knew the dog except as a puppy and that I'd since heard the poor beast was dead anyway, that there wasn't a hope of getting a bottle of that particular whisky in India, so that the only accurate part of his picture could be the comfortable chair and Jane Austen. He'd remembered the detail so accurately. I must say I found that rather touching. Um? Something one says quite casually capturing another chap's imagination and staying in his mind. A nice fellow. Very formal. Very correct. But fair. Yes. Fair. Very fair.'

Nazimuddin who had come in while Colonel Layton was talking and had collected glasses and the bottle at Sarah's low-voiced instructions now brought them to her. She told him to put the tray on the coffee-table nearest her father.

'Will you join us for supper, Father?'

'What?'

'Supper.'

'No, no. Had my supper. Any case, got the unexpired portion of the day's rations if I get peckish.'

She told Nazimuddin they would eat in ten minutes. The man went. Her father leant forward and picked the bottle up. He stared at the label.

'Extraordinary,' he said. 'I've not held a bottle of this for years.'

He put his free hand above his eyes like a shield, as though there was too much light, then folded it until it was across his eyes; and seemed to become fixed in that position, still gripping the bottle.

Miss Layton got up and went to him, bent down, took the bottle, put it on the table and then took his hand in hers. 'Come on, daddy, you've had a long day.'

Perron got up and moved away, making for the folding glass doors that gave on to the balcony but which were closed to keep out the rain. Through the windows he could see little except the reflection of the lighted room, the dark bulk of the back of the wing chair in which Merrick was obviously still sitting, Sarah Layton's bent head, strongly lit by the lamp at the side of the sofa. He could still hear her voice but she was speaking too quietly for any words to reach him. He was glad; he did not want to hear; he did not want to see, either, but wherever he looked the room and its occupants were there in the window. He saw her help Colonel Layton to his feet and lead him out. The colonel still had one hand over his face. The other rested on his daughter's shoulder.

After they had gone Perron did not move. He stared at the reflection of Merrick's chair. He could see the top of Merrick's head and the elbow of the shattered arm. There was the click of a cigarette lighter. In a moment he saw the smoke spiralling gently through the diffused ray cast by the lamp and, after it had vanished, a thinner wisp, rising from about the level of the shattered elbow, which meant that Merrick must have stuck the cigarette between two fingers of the black-gloved artifact.

Perron re-entered the sitting area and did not look at Merrick until he had taken a cigarette from the box Miss Layton had invited him to use, lighted it and sat down. Merrick was supporting his chin in his good hand and holding the cigarette in the artificial one. The unblemished side of his face was comparatively in shade.

'How did you come by that arm, sir?' Perron asked.

'Pulling a certain Captain Bingham out of a burning jeep, under fire, near Imphal, in 1944.'

Such precision. 'Is that what you got the decoration for? Rescuing Captain Bingham?'

'There was an Indian driver to get out as well. He survived. Captain Bingham didn't. He was Miss Layton's brother-in-law.'

'Since when you've been a sort of friend of the family, sir?'

Merrick released his chin, reached across and retrieved the cigarette.

'I knew them before. I was Captain Bingham's best man when he married Susan Layton in nineteen-forty-three.'

'Susan. Yes, that was it. Susan-mem and Sarah-mem. And the wild dogs in the hills.'

'You have a memory for detail. Good.'

'Difficult to forget the wild dog bit, sir.'

'Why?'

'Well, you nearly had him there, sir, didn't you?'

'Had him?'

'"Your wife will not hold her head up and even the wild dogs in the hills will be silent." The chap nearly cried.'

Merrick drew on his cigarette, then rested his chin again on the free fingers of the good hand; arm supported at the elbow by the chair-arm; the smoke floating up.

'He cried later.'

'Yes, sir?'

'When we examined him a week or so ago in Delhi.' Merrick stroked the outer corner of his right eye with his little finger, as if to remove something that irritated it. 'The evidence of his possible complicity in the death of the sepoy in Königsberg is quite strong.' Merrick flicked ash and then put the cigarette back between the black-gloved fingers.

'Is that why the subject's taboo down here? Because it upsets Colonel Layton?'

'It's taboo because it would particularly upset him to know about Königsberg. Actually neither he nor Miss Layton yet know I've seen the man and questioned him. I've tried to give them the impression the man's case isn't a priority. You realize that these men's old officers aren't allowed to go anywhere near them, don't you?'

'No, I didn't, sir. Why aren't they?'

'Because we'd be inundated with requests for interviews. Colonel Layton is a good example. He's convinced he could straighten Havildar Muzzafir Khan out in ten minutes. The attitude is quite admirable, of course, but given half a chance a lot of these men's old officers would try to deal with their own cases at regimental level, and the only sensible course is to keep them firmly out of the picture, otherwise it will get hopelessly confused. And of course it increases the prisoners' sense of isolation, and readiness to talk.'

From behind, in the dining-room area, came the sounds of plates being set out on the table.

'So not a word about the Havildar. I shall break the news to Colonel Layton in my own good time.'

101

They heard her voice, calling Nazimuddin.

She came into the dining-room. 'Come on, Mr Perron. You must be starved now. Are you ready too, Ronald?'

She waited for them to join her. The table was laid with places at either end and a third in the middle, facing the living-room. She asked Perron to sit in the middle and took the place on his left. Merrick sat at the other end. While they waited for the soup she asked him how long he'd been in India, how much of the country he'd seen and whether it was all as he'd pictured it. After Nazimuddin had brought in the soup and served it he expected her to give Merrick some of her attention, but she did not. For a few moments they drank soup and did not talk at all. He broke the silence by asking her how long she'd been in India herself.

'I was born here. Up in Pankot. So was my sister. We came back out in the summer of 'thirty-nine.'

Perron asked how long the journey to Pankot would take. She said the train left Bombay at two o'clock the following afternoon and that they would be home early on Wednesday morning – unless they decided to break the journey at Delhi. She looked across at Merrick. 'He mentioned it again just now. I've done all I can. It's up to you, Ronald, I'm afraid.'

'It's quite pointless,' Merrick said. 'A complete waste of time.'

'I know. But it's for you to explain why.'

'I thought I had.'

'I mean again.'

'When?'

'Tonight, preferably. Tomorrow morning at the very latest. I want it cut and dried before we get on the train because if we're going to stop off at Delhi I must try to get through to mother and tell her. It's only fair.'

'Personally, I think it would be better to let things lie. Once he's on the train the idea of getting off it will have less appeal.'

'But we get off at Delhi anyway, to change. There's a wait of at least two hours for the Ranpur connection. I don't want to stand around there not knowing whether we're going on or staying. And I certainly don't want to find myself trying to get through to mother from there and telling her we won't be home next day after all.'

'Very well. I'll have a word with him tonight. Incidentally, sergeant, where and what is this transport of yours?'

Perron told him.

'Well that's just round the corner if we take a short cut. We can walk easily, then you could drop me off.'

'That's kind of you, sir, but I'm sure I can find it on my own if you give me directions.'

'Major Merrick isn't staying here, Mr Perron. He's at the Taj.'

'Oh, I see.'

Nazimuddin had cleared away the first course and now brought in the second. Miss Layton made her selection from the tray. Merrick was provided with a plate of pre-prepared chicken and salad that he could deal with single-handed. The servant now reached Perron's side.

'I'm sorry,' Miss Layton said. 'We were talking just now about something you probably don't know about. The point of getting off at Delhi is for father to try to see one of his NCOs who's in trouble. The only man in the regiment who joined the Frei Hind force in Germany. But Major Merrick says it's a waste of time because of an order prohibiting contact between INA prisoners and their old officers.'

'Yes. It seems rather hard.'

'Understandable in one way, but father's rather upset because he's known the man in question since he was a boy of six or seven. Father was present when the boy and his mother were given the posthumous VC the boy's father won in the last war and he says he showed up awfully well in the fighting in North Africa, so he simply can't understand what got into his head.'

'Presumably Subhas Chandra Bose got into it,' Merrick said.

'But why?'

'It's the sort of thing we'll have to find out.'

'Father thinks he could find out better and quicker than anyone.' For Perron's benefit she added, 'According to the other men in the regiment, Bose and some Indian officers from another regiment who'd already turned coat came to the camp they were in and told them it was their duty to fight with the Germans for India's freedom. Then over the next few days the vcos and senior ncos were taken off separately for interviews. Some didn't come back for quite a while but the only one who never came back was this man my father's concerned about. The others thought he'd been tortured and killed because some of the ncos who were interviewed had a rough time if they told Bose's officers what they thought of them, and Havildar Muzzafir Khan had a reputation for being pretty outspoken. When another lot of Indian officers visited them a few months later and said Muzzafir Khan had joined the Frei Hind army and that they should all follow his example, one of them stood up and asked why Havildar Muzzafir Khan wasn't there to tell them himself. The poor man was carted off, didn't come back for a month and had a ghastly time. Now it seems that the officers were right, but most of the men in the regiment think as daddy does, that something awful must have been done to him to make him join Bose and that even then he'd only have joined to muck things up or escape to the allies at the first opportunity.'

'But he didn't escape,' Merrick said. 'He was among a group of Indians captured by the Free French when the Germans were on the run. The French were all for shooting them out of hand but an American army sergeant whistled up a helicopter and took them back to his unit as prisoners. The sergeant was a Negro, if that's relevant.'

'You've never mentioned that.'

'No. It's what drew my attention to his case, the discovery that one of the men listed in the report of the helicopter incident was a havildar from your father's regiment.'

'That will count against him, won't it? That he was actually fighting?'

'It's not clear whether he was fighting. The report didn't say. And he's just one man out of several hundred in the European and several thousand in the Eastern theatre.'

'Ought I to mention the helicopter incident to Father?'

'It's up to you. I'd prefer not. There's absolutely nothing he can do and the less he knows just now the easier it'll be for him to accept that.'

'Yes,' she said. 'I suppose so.'

'It's not as though your father's opinion of Havildar Karim Muzzafir Khan won't be asked for. When we reach the stage of dealing with the case someone will come up to Pankot to take statements from people who want to make them.'

'Will the person coming up be you, Ronald?'

'Possibly.'

They concentrated on their food.

Presently Perron said to her, 'I suppose it'll be quite a homecoming on Wednesday? Is there a special train laid on for the regiment?'

'There was hardly a train-load left. But they went back about three weeks ago. My father stayed on in Bombay because when the boat docked there were some men who had to go straight to hospital and he didn't want to leave them behind at this stage of the game.'

'That was very nice of him.'

'Yes, I thought so. The men appreciated it. A bit tough on my mother of course. She couldn't come to Bombay because my sister hasn't been well. But she's talked to the sick men's families and passed on messages and of course father's visited the hospital every day and been able to cheer them up.'

'How many sick men were there?'

'Only six. Five sepoys and a havildar.' She spoke across the table. 'If Father's obstinate about getting off at Delhi to get permission to see Havildar Muzzafir Khan we'll probably find the sick men obstinate about not going on alone to Pankot, especially the havildar because he and Karim Muzzafir Khan were friends. In fact they're related.' She turned again to Perron. 'The first battalion is very close knit. Hill regiments often are. My father can look at the nominal roll and draw a family tree of nearly every man on it. I mean if Naik X is married to a daughter of ex-Havildar Y, he'd know. Does that strike you as silly?'

'No,' Perron said. 'As admirable.'

'Yes. Admirable. And sad. Wouldn't you say sad? Particularly if you'd watched most of them die and seen the rest carted off as prisoners, and felt responsible.'

Merrick put his fork down. Nazimuddin offered him the tray but he declined another helping. Throughout the meal the gloved hand and artificial arm had been disposed on the surface of the table. He leant back, hooked the good arm over the back of his chair and stared at his empty plate, waited for the others to finish. When they had done so Nazimuddin came in with the shape: shapes, rather – three of them, turned out into glass bowls from individual fluted moulds. The shapes were white and looked tasteless but there was a bowl of jam to liven them up. Having served Miss Layton Nazimuddin went across to Merrick.

'Since your Aunt Fenny isn't here to feel hurt, do you mind if I say no?' Without waiting for her answer he said to the servant, 'Give mine to the sergeant. It will build him up. Not that you look starved exactly, but then sergeants seldom do. You manage to do yourselves pretty well, I suppose.'

'Usually, sir.'

'Even in India?'

'I think rather better in India, sir. One doesn't depend so much on diverting rations meant for the officers as one does at home.'

Merrick looked at the mat that marked his place at table, and at the spoon and fork he was not going to use. Miss Layton said, 'I'm afraid there's no savoury, Ronald. Perhaps you'd like to go and talk to Father, then we could all have coffee and Mr Perron could be on his way.'

'Perhaps that will be as well.' He began to get up, rather awkwardly, tucking the artificial arm close to his body. When he had gone Miss Layton said, 'You must have known someone called Rowan, too.'

'Nigel Rowan?'

She nodded.

'Only as one of the minor figures on Olympus would know Zeus. He came out here to the army, didn't he? I remember, because he was always walking away with prizes for classics and I thought he'd carry on in that field or at least go into the ICS if he really wanted an Indian career.'

'Yes, he is in the army, but he was transferred to the political department in 'thirty-eight or 'thirty-nine. He had to go back to his regiment when the war started. He was in the first Burma campaign and got fever badly. At the moment he's ADC to the Governor in Ranpur. He told me he was trying to get back into the Political.'

'Does he still have what I recall as a very detached and patrician manner?'

She smiled. 'I think it is only a manner. Will you have the other shape?'

'No, thank you.'

'They weren't very good, were they? Shall we go in then?'

Nazimuddin had carried the coffee tray through into the livingroom. Following her, he stood for a moment and studied the Zoffany-style pictures and then watched while she poured coffee from a silver-plated pot. He took the cup from her, sat down.

'What does your uncle do?'

'He runs a course about civil and military administration in India in peace time. To attract young officers into the ICS or the police when the war's over.'

'English officers?'

'Indians too. But mostly English.'

'Does he have much success?'

'More in Bombay than in Calcutta. He expects even more in view of the result of the election in England.'

'Yes, I suppose some people must think the prospects at home are now pretty bleak. But aren't the prospects for an Indian career even bleaker?'

She was stirring *ghur* into her coffee, occasionally stopping, tapping the spoon on the rim of the cup and then resuming. 'It's some years since anyone in their right mind thought of India as a career, if you mean India as a place where you could expect to spend the whole of your working life.'

'Is your father coming up to retiring age?'

'He hasn't long to go now. He'll be one of the lucky ones, I should think. The hardest hit will be men like Nigel Rowan, I mean men of his age. It depends on how power's eventually transferred. If there's a prolonged handing-over period, and if Uncle Arthur's right when he says the Indians will be glad to have experienced Englishmen working with them, then men like Nigel might have quite a few more years useful working life out here. But I don't think Uncle Arthur's right, do you? I don't think there'll be a prolonged handing-over period.'

'Why?'

'Because that would be the logical thing and I think the whole situation's become too emotional for logic to come into it.'

He waited for her to continue but she seemed to have come to a stop. He said, 'How will you feel about it, when it happens?'

'I shouldn't want to stay on.'

'Why, especially?'

'I don't think it's a country one can be happy in.'

'You'd be happy in England?'

'I didn't care for it much when I first went home as a child. But it's where I really grew up and started to think for myself. It's where I feel I belong. I know India much better, but ever since my sister and I came out again after going home to school I've only felt like a visitor.'

'Does your sister feel the same?'

'I think a bit the same. She tried not to. But it's difficult to say what she feels nowadays. She's had rather a bad time.'

'Major Merrick told me what happened to her husband. I'm sorry.'

'Did he mention his part in it?'

'Yes.'

She drank her coffee. She said, 'I'm sorry you don't remember Hari Kumar. Nigel does.'

He thought she intended to say more but just then they heard Merrick's footsteps.

'I think that's settled,' he said. She glanced at him as if to judge from his expression how gently he had dealt with her father. Perron glanced at him too but could tell nothing. As in the dockyard-hut the night of Karim Muzzafir Khan's interrogation, Merrick lifted his right hand and looked at the watch which he wore with the face on the inner-side of the wrist.

'I'll skip coffee if you don't mind. I've got some work to finish back at the hotel. And before that, of course, I must help the sergeant to find his jeep.' He nodded at Perron. 'If you're ready.'

'There's surely time for a cup? Mr Perron, perhaps you'd like another? Or the drink you never got?'

'The sergeant has to drive.'

'Does he really have to? Weren't you on duty of some sort at the Maharanee's party, Mr Perron?'

'Yes, I was.'

'Well who's to say when it might have ended? If you don't really have to report back to Kalyan tonight we could always give you a shake-down here. Frankly I don't think you should go all that way after the sort of evening you've had. We can send Nazimuddin out scouting for a taxi if your work is all that urgent, Ronald. Or you could wait until Uncle Arthur's back. He's using the staff-car.'

'I think you're asking the sergeant to risk getting into trouble.'

'There'd be no risk of that, sir. I'm allowed to use my discretion to a great extent and there are a number of perfectly adequate reasons why I might stay in Bombay overnight if that's what I decided.'

'Good. Then you'll stay, Mr Perron?'

Momentarily he was tempted to accept, help her get rid of Merrick which is what it seemed she wanted, and be alone with her for a while. But very soon the flat would be invaded by its owners, her aunt and uncle, and there would be explanations to make, chat about Purvis, chat about the course, chat about staying on in India. *Raj* chat. And she would fade back into that dreary predictable background. He was sorry for her. He felt she deserved better of life. But so many of them did. There was nothing he could do. Their lives were not his affair. He had his own to live. Their dissatisfaction, their boredom, the strain they always seemed to be under, were largely their own fault. The real world was outside. Impatient, he stood up. If you allowed yourself to sympathize too much they would destroy you. You would lose what you valued most. Your objectivity.

He said, 'It's very kind of you, Miss Layton, but what I have to do in Kalyan tomorrow is more important than what I might do in Bombay, so the quicker I get back the better. In any case, I've already offered Major Merrick a lift to the Taj.'

'Then I won't press you. Incidentally, my father asked me to make sure you know how grateful he is for the whisky and how sorry he was to be so much under the weather.'

They were all on their feet now. Merrick began to go into details of the arrangements for getting to the station the

109

following day. Perron moved away since none of this concerned him. He retrieved his pack and occupied himself pretending to check the straps. That done he stood up and humped the pack on his left shoulder and waited. Merrick was still talking as he and Miss Layton came through to the archway between dining-room area and passage, where Perron stood. Her arms were folded in the manner Perron assumed was characteristic – hands gripping elbows; one grip loose, the other tight. Too tight? An attitude more of self-control than of self-possession?

Merrick said, 'Tomorrow, then,' and with his right hand reached for and held her left shoulder and bent his head. Instinctively she bent hers away so that the kiss was placed somewhere near her right ear. Her eyes were closed. She smiled, as if to herself, and said, 'Tomorrow.' Merrick let her go. He nodded at the closed door, mutely commanding its opening. Miss Layton called Nazimuddin and then put out her hand.

'Goodbye, Mr Perron.'

The hand was cool and dry. The delicate aroma of the scent she used added to his pleasure in holding it. He thanked her for her hospitality and said goodbye. 'Perhaps we'll meet again,' she said. From behind him Nazimuddin asked if a taxi were wanted. Told that it wasn't he opened the door and salaamed to Perron as he went out. Merrick said goodnight to Miss Layton. Just before the door shut on them Perron caught her slight gestures: a nod, a movement of one hand. They were meant for him.

*

The rain had stopped some time ago but there were no stars, no breaks in the cloud-cover. Neither had the last downpour cooled the air, although there was a hint of freshness in the warm intermittent breeze that played around the palm-fringed *maidan*. He walked a pace or two behind Merrick until they reached an intersection where Merrick stopped. A taxi had drawn up to let its passengers out. 'We'll take this, sergeant, since it's here. It might save us getting wet. I'll drop you and go on to the hotel.' He got in after giving the driver instructions and Perron followed, glad to be saved the walk and the prolonging of the effort of being civil to Merrick which the walk and a jeep drive would have involved. Escape was imminent.

'A very nice girl, Miss Layton, sir.'

Merrick took his time replying.

'She has many admirable qualities. Her father certainly has cause to be grateful to her.'

'Oh?'

'When a man leaves a family of women behind one of them has to assume responsibility for keeping things going. I think she assumed most of it. But of course it tends to develop a girl's domineering instinct. As perhaps you noticed.'

'No, I didn't notice that, sir.' He added, 'This looks familiar. It was somewhere about here.'

'The next road on the left, in fact. Did she refer at all to Kumar when you were alone?'

'Only to say she was sorry I didn't appear to remember him.'

'What did you say?'

'Nothing.'

As the taxi pulled up Merrick said, 'I'll wait until you've made sure of your jeep.'

The gates of the house at which the taxi stopped were shut, perhaps padlocked, and the house apparently in darkness. Perron was almost grateful for Merrick's suggestion. Arrangements made by Purvis were probably not very reliable.

But in this case they were, in all respects except that of security. Directly Perron reached the closed iron gates a lamp was shone on him and a cockney voice said, 'Come for your gharry, Sarge?' Perron said he had and went back to the taxi.

'Everything's in order, sir.'

Merrick was looking out of the other window. He did not move.

He said, 'One case you should find interesting when you join me is that of the brother of the young Indian you met tonight.'

'Ahmed Kasim?'

Merrick turned his head, put a finger to his lips, and nodded in the driver's direction. 'He went over to Bose in Malaya. We got him in Manipur last year. It is interesting when you think

111

who the father is. Right. I'll see you in Delhi. In a couple of days or so, I expect.'

Perron shut the door and threw up a smart one which so far as he could make out Merrick acknowledged in the languid manner officers cultivated. The taxi drew away. Perron watched it go down the poorly-lit tree-lined street.

'Oh no you won't. You bloody well won't,' he said aloud.

*

Half an hour later, soaked to the skin by the renewed downpour, he gave up trying to trace the fault in the brand new jeep's electrical system and accepted the guard-commander's offer of a bed-down for the night. The guard-commander, a British corporal – seemed to welcome company. In the guardroom, keeping his voice low so as not to disturb the three huddled shapes disposed on charpoys in corners away from the dim light of a lamp that hung centrally above a trestle-table littered with mugs, playing-cards and worn copies of *Picture Post* and *Reader's Digest*, he offered Perron a shot of buckshee rum.

'Found its own way here, Sarge,' the corporal said, and winked. Outside, in the dark, he had called Perron sir at least twice but had got over any embarrassment this might have caused him. While they sat smoking and drinking rum the corporal explained that he and his bunch had been in India for a whole month and were still wondering what had hit them. They were part of a formation that had been under orders for France just before – as the corporal put it – old Hitler packed it in. For a while they'd been looking forward to becoming part of the army of occupation. There were chaps making fortunes there right now and from what he'd heard the frauleins would do it for a packet of cigarettes or even a Naafi sandwich. The corporal had been in the army for a year and some of the men in his unit less than that. They had reckoned Germany would be a cushy billet in which to see their time out and from the way 'old Slim's lot' had given the Japs 'the bum's rush out of Burma' the last thing any of them had expected was to be sent out East. When you looked at the map (the corporal said) you could see that the Japanese had had it. You could hardly see where places like Malaya were. But here *they* were. Had the Sarge ever known such a bleeding awful place. How long had the Sarge been out here?

'Two years,' Perron said.

'Christ.'

The corporal studied him, respectfully, but looking for signs of deterioration. 'I reckon I'd be round the twist if they kept me out here that long.' His tone became even lower, confidential. 'What's it like, Sarge. With these Indian bints?'

'The colour doesn't come off.'

The corporal shook his head. 'I couldn't fancy it somehow. Some of the half'n'halfs look okay but the one's who're white enough not to put you off are only interested in officers, aren't they? We been warned to watch it too. They say there's always a coal-black mum waiting in the parlour to get the banns read if you so much as touch the daughter. That true, d'you reckon, Sarge?'

'I've heard of cases.'

The corporal shook his head again. Perron glanced at the sleeping men. Only one of them had his face turned towards the light. He looked about nineteen; so, come to that, did the corporal. The faces were those of urban Londoners and belonged to streets of terraced houses that ended in one-man shops: newsagent-tobacconist, fish and chip shop, family grocer, and a pub at the corner where the high road was. What could such a face know of India? And yet India was there, in the skull, and the bones of the body. Its possession had helped nourish the flesh, warm the blood of every man in the room, sleeping and waking.

'Where do I turn in?' Perron asked.

'I'll show you.' The corporal looked at his watch. 'Then I got to change the guard.' He led the way out into a passage. 'There's a coupla wog clerks that sleep down that end, and there's a duty officer upstairs with the phone put through. He's a wog too. I think the officers that work here take it in turns to sleep in, not that anything ever happens, but there's a safe in the room the duty-officer sleeps in, so I reckon there's a lot of secret papers. There's a spare charpoy here, though—' he opened a door and switched on a light – 'and a bog through that door. You got a blanket, Sarge?'

'No.'

'I'll bring you one in.' He switched on the fan and went out. The room was an office, so sparsely furnished it looked like a monk's cell. Along one wall, under a shuttered window, stood a bare charpoy. Aslant one corner, there was a trestle-table covered by an army blanket, with one folding canvas chair behind it and a folding wooden chair in front of it for visitors. A neatly positioned telephone and blotting pad, a pen and pencil tray, an empty in-basket and an empty out-basket told a story of meticulous attention to work or of a complete absence of work to give attention to. Facing the visitor, parallel to the top edge of the blotter and the pen and pencil tray, was a triangular wedge of wood on which the name of the desk's occupant was painted in white.

Capt. L. Purvis.

Here behind the desk Purvis had sat, waiting for a call from Delhi that never came, and presumably here he had lain, on the charpoy, gazing at the alien geography of the ceiling, nursing his invaded gut and his invincible Englishness. And, on the wall behind the desk, he had marked off with a blue crayon the days of his martyrdom. Perron looked at his watch. Not yet midnight. Even if Purvis had learned to cheat by crossing a day off immediately before he left the office in the evening Perron did not feel he could cancel out August 5 for him until his watch showed 0001.

'Here's your blanket, Sarge, and something for a pillow. Anything else?'

'No thank you, Corporal.'

'We brew up at 0600. Okay for you?'

'Fine.'

'Pleasant dreams then, Sarge.'

After he had taken off his damp uniform, hung it over the chair back under the fan and mopped himself reasonably dry with the green handtowel from his pack, Perron sat in his underwear on the edge of the charpoy and slowly performed the nightly task of trying to obliterate from his mind all the disturbing residue of the day's malfunctioning and so leave it free to crystallize, to reveal the point reached in a continuum he was sure existed but, in India, found so difficult to trace.

He lit a cigarette and stared at his stockinged feet, then

reached over to his jacket and got out the notebook and pencil. After a while he wrote: 'Two continua, perhaps, in this case? Ours, and the Indians'? An illusion that they ever coincided, coincide? A powerful illusion but still an illusion? If so, then the *raj* was, is, itself an illusion so far as the English are concerned. Is that what she meant when she said she did not think India was a country one could be happy in?'

Dissatisfied with this he drew a pencil line lightly across the entry and tried again.

'For at least a hundred years India has formed part of England's idea about herself and for the same period India has been forced into a position of being a reflection of that idea. Up to say 1900 the part India played in our idea about ourselves was the part played by anything we possessed which we believed it was right to possess (like a special relationship with God). Since 1900, certainly since 1918, the reverse has obtained. The part played since then by India in the English idea of Englishness has been that of something we feel it does us no credit to have. Our idea about ourselves will now not accommodate any idea about India except the idea of returning it to the Indians in order to prove that we are English and have demonstrably English ideas. All this is quite simply proven and amply demonstrated. But on either side of that arbitrary date (1900) India itself, as itself, that is to say India as not part of our idea of ourselves, has played no part whatsoever in the lives of Englishmen in general (no part that we are conscious of) and those who came out (those for whom India had to play a real part) became detached both from English life and from the English idea of life. Getting rid of India will cause us at home no qualm of conscience because it will be like getting rid of what is no longer reflected in our mirror of ourselves. The sad thing is that whereas in the English mirror there is now no Indian reflection (think of Purvis, those men I lectured to, and the corporal here in the guardroom), in the Indian mirror the English reflection may be very hard to get rid of, because in the Indian mind English possession has not been an idea but a reality; often a harsh one. The other sad thing is that people like the Laytons may now see nothing at all when looking in their mirror. Not even themselves? Not even a mirror? I know that getting rid of

India, dismantling all this old imperial machinery (which Purvis sees as hopelessly antiquated, a brake on economic viability – his word) has become an article of faith with the intellectual minority of the party we have just voted into power. But we haven't voted them into power to get rid of the machinery, we've voted them into power to set up new machinery of our own for our own benefit, and for the majority who voted India does not even begin to exist. Odd that history may record as pre-eminent among the Labour Party's post-war governmental achievements the demission of power in countries like this? Could it be that, in power now, and with a mandate to demit power, the party will forget or omit to demit it? It could be. But we shall see. The machinery for demission is wound up and there are, as Purvis knows, overriding economic arguments for setting it in motion as soon as the war's over. In England the war *is* over. It ended on May 6. In England the war's a dead letter except for people with sons, brothers and fathers and husbands out here. And the fact that they're still out here simply adds to an English sense of grievance that England ever got involved with anything or anywhere south or east of spitting distance of the white cliffs of Dover. Terrific insularity. Paradox! The most insular people in the world managed to establish the largest empire the world has ever seen. No, not paradox. Insularity, like empire-building, requires superb self-confidence, a conviction of one's moral superiority. And I suppose that when the war is really over the recollection that there was a time when we "stood alone" against Hitler will confirm us in our national sense of moral superiority. Will it be in those abstract terms and on those shifting grounds that we'll attempt to build a new empire whose cornerstone will be the act of relinquishing for "moral" reasons the empire we actually had?'

He hesitated, then added, 'Tonight I am a bit drunk.'

Then, looking at his watch he saw it was tonight no longer. He put pencil and notebook back in the jacket pocket. The evening at the Maharanee's was over. Standing, staring at that name, Purvis, he realized that curious and complex as it had been the evening had had shape. Beginning with Purvis, it had ended in Purvis's office. He appreciated the symmetry of that.

He visited the bathroom. Returning, he went over to the light switch, changed his mind and crossed to the desk, found the blue crayon and went to the wall calendar. He drew an X through the 5, stared at the 6 and said aloud, 'That, anyway, is the crystallization, the point reached in the *time* continuum.'

He turned the fan down to its slowest rate of revolutions, switched off the light, opened the shutters on the unglazed barred window and breathed in. Bombay. Bom-Bahia. Part of an inheritance. His monarch's. His own. The corporal's, Purvis's, the Maharanee's. The street beggar's. He lay, adjusted the cushion the corporal had brought as a pillow, and the blanket so that it just covered his abdomen, the most vulnerable part of the body when there was a fan going. For a while pictures of the day just ended flickered across the screen lowered by his eyelids, but all at once there was the disturbing invasion of shots of Coomer, from all angles, long, medium and close; Coomer opening his shoulders, hitting out at a sequence of balls whose pitch and pace were subtly varied by the invisible bowler; or team of bowlers; the deliveries were in too mercilessly rapid a succession for one man alone to send down.

The cameras of Perron's imagination began to tire. Presently only one remained, and this zoomed in close to recreate a memory of the boy's face. There was a face, an idea of a face, a man's rather than a boy's, and formed from a notion of an expression rather than from one of features: an expression of concentration, of hard-held determination, of awareness that to misjudge, to mistime, would lead to destruction. There was no sound. And suddenly the face vanished. A flurry of birds, crows, rooks, rose from the surrounding elms, startled by a sudden noise, although there had been no noise. And they were not elms, but palms; and the birds were kitehawks. They circled patiently above Perron's head, waiting for him to fall asleep.

Journeys into Uneasy Distances

In view of what once happened there the countryside through which the mail train passes on the first stage of the journey from Mirat to Ranpur is surprisingly undramatic. The passenger who has what initially seems the good luck to be alone in a compartment soon grows restless as mile follows mile with nothing to catch the attention or work on the imagination other than what in India is common-place: the huddles of mud villages; buffalo wallowing in celebration of their survival from the primeval slime; men, women and children engaged in the fatal ritual of pre-ordained work.

Only the slow train stops at the wayside stations. On their single platforms people wait with bundles and a patience that has something exalted about it, although this impression could be the result of the express passing through too quickly for individual faces to be clearly noted. There are three such stations all of which are reached within thirty minutes of leaving Mirat cantonment. Thereafter, the villages become distant, but there is one, abandoned and ruinous, which appears suddenly and unexpectedly, close to the line.

Those ruins don't look old. For an instant the traveller conjures images of flames, of silhouetted human shapes running distractedly, stooped under burdens. But the moment of imaginative recreation is a brief one. The crippled dwellings and crumbled walls slide quickly out of sight and the panorama of wasteland, scarred by dried-out nullahs and rocky outcrops, appears again and expands to the limit of the blurred horizon where the colourlessness of sky and earth merge and are distinguished only by a band of a different intensity of colourlessness which, gazed at long enough, gives an idea of blue and purple refraction. Everything is immense, but – lacking harmony or contrast – is diminished by its association with infinity.

The ruined village is explained. The land is eroded. The exodus must have been slow, quite unremarkable. One by one the men would have gone, taking their women and children and driving their thin cattle, while inch by inch the soil was swept away and the implacable rock exposed until there was nothing but the empty waste; and the wind blowing hot in the telegraph wires that border the railway.

The land now seems to be at peace. It requires some effort to see such a place as a background to any sudden or violent event. Perhaps there was no bloodshed, no murder on this stretch of line. But, as if remembering violence the train slows and then draws to a stop. There is a clank under the carriage; cessation, immobility. The compartment – not air-conditioned, one fan not working – grows warmer. Presently there comes the hollow sound of unevenly clunking goatbells and in a moment or two the straggling herd comes into view, driven by a lean man and a naked urchin, in search of patches of impoverished grazing. They go by without a glance, drugged by the heat and the singleness of their purpose. When they have gone there is silence but their passing has disturbed the atmosphere. The body of the victim could have fallen just here.

A few moments before, he is said to have gestured at the shuttered window of the compartment door on which strangers outside were banging and said 'It seems to be me they want', and then smiled at his shocked fellow-passengers, as if he had recognized a brilliant and totally unexpected opportunity. In a flash he had unlocked the door and gone. Briefly, a turbanned head appeared, begged pardon for the inconvenience and then removed itself. The door banged to. One of the passengers stumbled across luggage and relocked it. After a moment he lowered the shutter and looked out. Those nearest to him might have seen his horrified expression.

Just then the engine driver up ahead obeyed an instruction and the train glided forward. It was the smooth gliding motion away from a violent situation which one witness never forgot. 'Suddenly you had the feeling that the train, the wheels, the lines, weren't made of metal but of something greasy and evasive.'

Without warning it glides forward now, from the place where the herd of goats has been, seeming to identify a spot marked with the x of an old killing by its mechanical anxiety to get away before blame is apportioned and responsibility felt. Increasing speed, the train puts distance between itself and the falling body and between one time and another so that in the mind of the traveller the body never quite achieves its final crumpled position on the ground at the feet of the attackers.

'It seems to be me they want,' the victim said. Perhaps he said no such thing but gave the impression of thinking it because of that look on his face of recognizing some kind of personal advantage. This look may have been due to nothing more than a desire to reassure the other occupants of the carriage that they had nothing to worry about themselves and that he would be quite safe so long as he went of his own free will. But all the evidence suggests that the witness was right about the words and the expression. The victim chose neither the time nor the place of his death but in going to it as he did he must have seen that he contributed something of his own to its manner; and this was probably his compensation; so that when the body falls it will seem to do so without protest and without asking for any explanation of the thing that has happened to it, as if all that has gone before is explanation enough, so that it will not fall to the ground so much as out of a history which began with a girl stumbling on steps at the end of a long journey through the dark.

The train is cautious in its approach to Premanagar. Tracks converge from the east, coming from Mayapore. To the left, some miles distant, is the fort, no longer a prison, infrequently visited by tourists; peripheral to the tale but a brooding point of reference and orientation. To the south, now, lies Mirat with its mosques and minarets. North, a few hours journey, is Ranpur, where a grave was undug, and farther north still, amid hills, Pankot, where it was dug in too great a hurry for someone's peace of mind. Beyond the fort, the west lies open, admitting a chill draught. The erosive

123

wind, perhaps. After a short halt the train moves on to its final destination.

*

It is dark by the time it clatters across the bridge and worms its way into the city of Ranpur, as it was dark on Tuesday August 7, 1945, when Sarah Layton and her father, and the handful of soldiers released from hospital, arrived from Delhi and disembarked to pick up the midnight connection to Pankot; and since the railway station has changed little it is easy to picture them, to pick them out of a crowd which behaves as crowds on platforms do (with a mixture of hysteria, impatience, gaiety and – in isolated cases – resignation). The platform is one of several protected by the vaulted, glassed and girdered roof that rests on steel ornamental pillars. At the base of these pillars people congregate, waiting for trains or inspiration. The lighting is yellow, intermittent. There are areas of light and half-light and areas of shadow. Through these areas passengers walk or run, and coolies trot bare foot, erect under head-loads, shouting warnings of approach. The grey paving is spattered with new and old spittings of betel-juice which a stranger to the country may confuse with bloodstains. There is a smell of coalsmoke, ripe fruit and of cotton cloth which human sweat has drenched and dried on and drenched again. It is a smell by no means peculiar to this station but for those to whom Ranpur represents a home-coming it has a subtle distinction, a pungency of special intensity, a benign and odorous warmth which even Sarah who had not been away for long was conscious of as she got down from the coupé and joined her father. Patiently he was choosing three coolies from the gang that had run alongside for fifty yards or more.

There had been no problem at Delhi. Ronald Merrick had waited to see them off on the Ranpur train, to be on hand if at the last moment Colonel Layton again had to be dissuaded from breaking the journey. But he had been docile, good-humoured, quietly intent on the morning papers with their latest reports of the significance of the bomb of 'devastating

124

power' which the Americans had dropped on the Japanese city of Hiroshima on Monday morning.

News of the attack had reached them on the platform of the Victoria terminus in Bombay, half-an-hour before the train was due out. Some English people said they had just heard it on the lunch-time radio. Aunt Fenny sent Uncle Arthur off to see what more he could find out. He had put on weight and did not walk quickly, was away some time, nearly missed them, had to accompany the moving train shouting 'Seems to be true but I can't make head or tail of it. Have a good trip.' In the evening when they stopped to take on dinnertrays there was confirmation in the evening papers. It had been an atomic bomb. The ultimate weapon. The question was whether Hirohito would now surrender to save other cities, Tokyo itself, from devastation. Sarah thought: It might be over, then. And knew relief. Excitement even.

'The moral reservations' (she has said) 'came later. At the time you could only feel glad. Awestruck, I suppose, by the sheer size of the thing. And by the miracle. I never met anyone who felt otherwise until long after. If we had doubts about the wisdom of letting off bombs like that they were very long-term. Too long-term to bother us. The short-term was the important thing.'

In the short-term, above all, it might mean safety for her father. He'd said nothing about further active service. The prospects were shadowy but they existed. No one expected the liberation of Malaya and the conquest of the Japanase mainland to be accomplished quickly or cheaply. If the war continued he would probably manoeuvre for a command before he was fully fit. But now the chances were that it would not continue and, walking with him along the platform, with one coolie ahead and two behind, to rendezvous with the havildar and the five sepoys who had travelled in a compartment a long way separated from their own, she was able to entertain an illusion of serenity, of entering a period of life which by contrast with the one just ended might be described as free, uncluttered, open at last to endless possibilities.

II

For a few seconds she awaited confirmation that the child had whimpered, but there was no sound of Minnie stirring in the spare room to pick him up and comfort him. Wondering whether Susan was still asleep or up to something odd, she felt for the switch on the bed-side lamp. The shock of no contact brought her fully conscious. She sat up in unfamiliar surroundings, a wall on one side, nothing on the other. She recalled, then, where she was; and because there was utter stillness, assumed that probably what had woken her was the jerk of the train coming to a halt. From her upper-berth she glanced down into the well of the coupé and saw her father – his shape, rather – standing at the carriage door. The window was lowered. She could smell the pine-trees – the scent of the hills. The air was chill. The light of Wednesday was just beginning to come.

'All right, Father?'

She spoke quietly but he drew his head in and glanced up at once, as if caught doing something forbidden.

'Did I wake you? I'm sorry.'

'No. It wasn't you. It must have been the train stopping.'

'Afraid that was ten minutes ago. I made a duff hand of opening the window. How about some tea? There's plenty in the flask.'

'I'll come down and get it for us.'

'No, no. You stay there.'

She felt for her dressing-gown. 'I'll come down anyway.'

'Do you want some light?'

'No,' she said. 'That would spoil it.'

He said nothing. She felt that he understood her mood. She climbed down and removed the steps from their hooks. He had his back turned, pouring tea from the thermos into the cups Aunt Fenny had packed in the hamper. The tea in the thermos had been bought the night before from the station restaurant at Ranpur. He handed her a cup. She stood near the lowered window, warming her hands on it.

'In the old days,' he said, 'we used to stop round about here to get up a proper head of steam. Then we got the new locomotive and were able to get up the gradient in a brace of shakes. I suppose the new engine's getting old. Listen.'

There was a faint noise, an abrupt exhalation, followed by a clank. It came again, then again. It sounded far off. The coupé was in a carriage at the rear of the train which was halted on a curved stretch of line. The window her father had opened looked east towards the plains they had left, across a deep valley, at the moment full of mist – below eye-level so that it looked like the surface of a lake. On the other side of the carriage was the rock face. The road, which took steeper gradients, was above them. She turned her wrist until she was able to make out the position of the hands of her watch. He saw what she was doing and said, 'Just over two hours to go, or should be if we keep to the time-table.'

She moved away from the window so that he could resume his vigil if he wished to, and sat on the lower bunk. He went back to the window. She wanted a cigarette but resisted temptation. In Bombay he had said to Aunt Fenny, 'Isn't Sarah smoking rather a lot?' and Fenny had tipped her off. She had tried to cut down, not for fear of his disapproval but as part of her campaign to guard him from as many sources of irritation as was in her power. She had warned her mother by letter how easily he could be upset, of the prison-camp habit of saving 'the unexpired portion'; pocketing bits of bread to eat later; the mark of a man who had known hunger. The habit was dying hard, as hard – no doubt – as recollections of conditions of which he never spoke. And he had been uninquisitive about affairs she had been prepared for him to question her on.

He had never mentioned the death of Teddie Bingham, the son-in-law he had never seen, nor delved into the nature of Susan's illness. Neither had he referred directly to the death of his stepmother, Mabel, from whom Rose Cottage had been inherited. Sarah had once begun to warn him that her mother had made a few changes in the place, but he had interrupted, saying Fenny had mentioned 'something about a tennis-court'. He'd added: 'Pity about the roses, but I suppose they needed a lot of attention and the court's a good idea for you girls.'

What else had Fenny said 'something' about? She was the kind of woman who let things slip without necessarily meaning to or even knowing that she'd done so. But in the case of the destruction of the greater part of the rose garden to make room for the tennis-court, Sarah was grateful to be

127

relieved of the job of telling him herself. She had feared doing so; unnecessarily, it seemed, judging by the casual way he had taken it.

But had he taken it *in*? From Germany after he got their letter telling him Mabel had died, he'd written: 'It's sad news but not a shock because she was getting on. I'm glad my last memory of her is in the garden the time I went up from Ranpur to say goodbye to her and to arrange your accommodation in Pankot once the regiment left for overseas. I'm sorry I wasn't able to fix up anything better than those cramped quarters in the lines, but Mabel was quite right. Even if she'd given marching orders to that PG of hers the three of you with Mabel would have been just as cramped at Rose Cottage, and however poky a place is there's nothing like having your own, is there Millie? Anyway I have this picture of you now, moving in to the cottage, all amid the roses and the pine trees. I long to be with you all again and not just have to picture it.'

It was possible that as he stood at the open window of the coupé any picture he had of his homecoming was of the house and garden as he remembered it and that the tennis-court had not penetrated visually, as an idea. Even after all these months Sarah could get a shock when she went through to the verandah and instead of the rose-beds saw the high netting, the lime-marked grass, the centre net or the bare posts if the net had been taken down by the *mali*. The court was seldom used. Sarah didn't play well and watching bored her. And the days were gone when her younger sister used a tennis-court and a tennis outfit as two more ways of ensuring that she was the centre of attention. That role had been discarded and the new one precluded violent exercise. Only Mildred, their mother, seemed to get any pleasure out of the court, not by playing, but by having it there as one might have anything that made an invitation attractive. 'Come up to the house at the weekend,' she might say to someone new on station, of whom she approved, 'and if you're keen bring a racquet and things. We've a sort of court you can get a game on.' And there was usually someone there to protest: 'Don't be deceived. Sort of court! Binky swears it's better than the number one here at the club.' And then her mother would raise her eyebrows and smile, that characteristic downward-curving smile that Sarah was afraid she might acquire, having once or twice got a glimpse of herself in a mirror smiling in that way. There was a way of sitting too and she had caught herself at that on more than one occasion, on the verandah of Rose Cottage, glancing from the tennis to her mother and recognizing her mother's attitude as the origin of her own: well settled in a cane chair, legs out-stretched and crossed at the ankles, elbows supported by the chair-arms; and the hands, drooping at the wrists, bearing the burden of a glass of gin-sling. She had sat up, put her glass down, leant forward and folded her arms, but that was becoming a habitual attitude too, and just as defensive.

Up ahead the whistle sounded and presently the train moved, taking the curve. The mist-filled valley flowed away and they entered a cut where the rock-face loomed on both sides. Her father stayed by the open window for a while, breathing in the scent of damp stone, wild ferns and mosses. When the scent became pungent with captive drifting smoke he ducked back in and raised the window. There remained in the carriage an opacity as if some of the eastern light had stayed inside.

He sat down. Unexpectedly he said, 'I haven't thanked you for coming to Bombay and for what you've done while I've been away. Your Aunt Fenny told me what a brick you've been, what a help to your mother and Susan. I just wanted you to know before we get in how grateful I am.'

As soon as he began she looked down at the cup in her hands. They had never been a demonstrative family. When he finished he put an arm round her shoulders, very briefly, just long enough for her to acknowledge the embrace by leaning into it for a moment.

'Shall I pour you another cup?'

'No thank you, daddy. Later perhaps. What about you?'

'I'll wait a while. Keep some in reserve in case we're held up again and get thirsty.'

'I'll rinse the cups then.'

'No, I'll do that. Unless you want to go in there.'

'Not yet.'

He took the cups into the w.c. cubicle, leaving the door ajar. The train was making slow time. She heard him humming. In

129

the past three weeks she had learnt to interpret this as a sign of restlessness, of anxiety to be occupied. She wondered whether it was light enough for a game of chess. She looked for and found the travelling set which he had brought back from Germany and on which he had taught her to play in Bombay. She had a beginner's enthusiasm and in one case what had seemed like beginner's luck. No doubt he'd deliberately contrived that, to encourage her; but she felt she had learned enough at least to give him a bit of a game.

Unable to see it clearly she put the set away. She wondered how long it would be before they played again, or whether they ever would. Once home, the pattern of relationship established in Bombay would change. He came back with the cups. She took them from him and put them in the hamper, protecting them with a napkin from contact with the neck of Sergeant Perron's bottle of whisky; of which he had said, 'Let's save some for your mother.' She doubted that her mother would want any. Not whisky.

He said, 'If you're sure you don't want to go first I think I'll shave and get done.'

She nodded, watched him potter around – potter was the only word for it – collecting sponge bag, shaving kit, towel, clothes, and finally his uniform from the hook on the wall. His movements were slow, thought out. Perhaps this had always been his habit. She did not remember it but not remembering was probably further evidence of how little she knew him, as little now as she had known him – and her mother – on her return to India in 1939 after the years of unavoidable separation. He switched the light on in the cubicle and this time closed the door but there was no sound of the bolt being shot. Had the Germans ever put him in solitary confinement? If so, for what crime? Attempting to escape? Eventually her mother would question him and get answers or he would regain confidence in his freedom and volunteer information, and then they would be able to put the story of the past few years of his life together piece by piece; as he would be able to put theirs together. But in neither case the whole stories. Probably never that.

She lit a cigarette now and settled closer to the window. In her imagination she had often rehearsed the circumstances of

130

her father's return but had not pictured them like this, with the two of them travelling alone from Bombay to Pankot. He confessed he had rehearsed them too but said there had always been a moment when his imagination failed, the moment following the actual reunion, and that this was probably because the scene of reunion was not determinable in advance: a railway station, a dockside, even an airport, the old house in Kabul road in Ranpur, the front verandah of Rose Cottage, the compound of the grace and favour bungalow in the lines of the Pankot Rifles depot. The reunion itself was the important thing, one did not think beyond it. He told her of a fellow prisoner-of-war, a Catholic, who had shocked a padre by confessing that he had always wondered what after spending six days creating the world and then resting on the seventh God had done on the eighth. The day of reunion was like the seventh day. Today, Wednesday, was the seventh. She could not visualize tomorrow except as a continuation, an emotional perpetuation, of today which of course it could not be. One thought about a day of reunion but the reunion itself was only a moment in a day. She and her father had had that moment in Bombay. He had another to come this morning but of this she would be no more than a spectator; perhaps not that because he had asked that no one in the family should be at the station. His request that the families of the sepoys and havildar should also be dissuaded from coming to the station, his warning that the only reception committee he wished to find would be at most the depot adjutant, Kevin Coley, plus an NCO and a truck to take the men back to the lines and some kind of transport for himself and Sarah, was an indication of his fear of any kind of scene that might affect him.

It would be nice, he had said, just to drive from the station with her in whatever transport could be arranged and to arrive at Rose Cottage much as though he had simply come home for breakfast after early morning parade. She had conveyed this wish to her mother and knew that it would be respected. She was prepared to let him go into the bungalow alone and busy herself outside in the garden or on the side verandah where probably little Edward would be, in Minnie's charge, playing with the new Labrador puppy.

131

Neither Sarah nor her mother had wanted the puppy. It was Susan's idea that they should have one, as like as possible to Panther who had been little more than a puppy himself when her father went abroad on active service. Susan said it would be a nice surprise for him and persisted until their mother said they'd see, but that black Labradors weren't to be had just like that. Susan then played her trump card. Maisie Trehearne knew some people down in Nansera who had some puppies ready.

The job of trying just once more to talk her out of it had fallen to Sarah, but when she tried she drew nothing except the look of hostility with which she was now familiar but had never got used to, so in the end she went down to Nansera with old Maisie Trehearne who loved dogs and had seen Panther die, and who made the morning's car journey down tense by continually referring to that episode, and the afternoon journey back exasperating by talking incessantly to the trembling little creature that was Panther's successor and had cost two hundred rupees and was guaranteed house-trained, a qualification which it showed evidence of being unaware it possessed by making a mess in its own basket, perhaps out of fright or a combination of fright and uncertainty about which of the two women abducting it was to be its new owner. Do pet it, Sarah, Maisie kept saying, in between bouts of petting it herself. But Sarah refused. 'It's Su's dog. I want Su to be the first to show it affection.' 'Of course, you're right. Isn't she, little fellow?'

And Susan had shown it affection. For a while the old Susan was there, on her knees, flushed and pretty, pushing a dark curl from her forehead with one finger and holding out her other hand, invitingly, caressingly, letting the puppy squirm up to her and sniff, bending down until her face was close, allowing it to lick her cheek, then hugging it and taking it to introduce it to Little Master who was sprawled on a rug on the verandah, dabbing at a toy dog, and who, after a moment's disbelief in this confrontation with a real one, screamed, so that the puppy – already named Panther the Second by Susan – backed away, puzzled, wholly at a loss until he found Sarah's by now familiar-smelling feet. He sat down against them and stared at the strangers. Susan stared back at him and then up at Sarah, so that on impulse Sarah pushed the puppy away with the side of her shoe and went to the verandah rail.

Ayah was comforting the child and Susan turned to help her. From the rail Sarah watched the puppy. Noting how it looked from the three on the rug to her and back again and then settled on its haunches on the spot where she had left it, ducked its head down and up again but made no sound, she realized that it had character and that she must harden her heart against it for both their sakes. She went indoors and called for Mahmoud to tell the *bhishti* to draw her bath. From the bedroom she heard Susan taking the little boy to task for being afraid of a puppy. The child had not yet learned to speak. Sometimes Sarah wondered whether he ever would, whether he knew whose child he was; his mother's, Ayah's or Sarah's. With the puppy it would be different. Dogs made their own decisions in such matters, as Panther 1 had done, choosing Susan as the owned and owning object of adoration despite her variable response to him and, finally, her absolute neglect.

She had always had that power, still had it, a power of immediate attraction for animals and people, and Sarah understood her sister's own attitude to that power, her inability to believe that she truly possessed it and something of the terror she felt knowing that she did. 'Come on, puppy,' she was calling. 'There. Nice puppy. Mummy's not afraid of puppy, see? Puppy loves mummy already. Come on now, stroke puppy. Show mummy what a brave boy you are.'

Gradually the boy had lost his terror and for a day or two the puppy was petted, played with, fed on the verandah by Susan and overseen by Minnie or Mahmoud during his periodic visits to urinate and defaecate, which he announced his intention of doing by going to the head of the steps into the garden and trying to get down them. The veterinary officer, Lieutenant Khan, came up from the Remount depot, examined his mouth and teeth and ears and gave him injections and powders which made him look miserable but did not dampen his playful spirit. Returning at lunch times and in the late afternoons from her work at Area Headquarters, Sarah noted the situation but knew that it would change.

On the fourth or fifth day (she could not remember which) she came back for lunch, was aware of the puppy's absence but said nothing until Susan went to their room for her afternoon nap and she and her mother were alone. 'I didn't see Panther Two,' she began. 'Is he all right?' Her mother supposed he was all right. Mahmoud had him in the servants' quarters. He had made a mess on the verandah. That's all her mother knew; that and that there had been a scene with Minnie crying and the child crying and Susan angry and then retreating into one of her moods. 'Do you *have* to go back to the daftar this afternoon?' her mother asked.

'I'm afraid I do. Why?'

Why didn't matter in that case, her mother said, and got up and left her alone. Sarah knew why and knew her mother knew she knew. But oppressed by the apparently unalterable rhythm of life at home she felt justified in pretending not to and it helped to get out for a few more hours. Nothing would happen during them. It took some time for a crisis to build up, if there was to be a crisis.

Her father came back into the compartment.

'There, all done.'

'How smart you look.'

'Dressed for the part.'

In the old days he would never have said that. He seemed to have acquired a sense of charade. He wore KD with Sam Browne, collar and tie. The rainbow ribbons above the left breast pocket added colour to his occasion. He had on one of the pairs of hand-made shoes which he had left behind in 1940 which throughout the war Mahmoud had kept dubbined and had recently polished to a deep conker-brown. She had taken two pairs to Bombay. This was the first time he had worn them.

'Are they comfortable?'

'I think,' he said, 'my feet have lost weight too. But they're good and soft.'

'I'll get dressed,' she said, 'then we'll have the other cup. Unless you'd like it now.'

'No, I'll tidy up here, then we'll have more room.'

Tidy up was one of the new expressions. He had become used to doing things for himself. In Bombay Nazimuddin had been scandalized by the sight of Colonel Sahib cleaning his own shoes, washing out pairs of socks, drawing his own bath, packing his own cases. Rather than tell him that in England many Sahibs were used to looking after themselves Sarah tried to explain that doing such chores helped her father get well again after being so long a prisoner in Germany.

He had left the w.c. cubicle immaculate. The hand-basin glistened, the speckled mirror gleamed. The stone floor looked newly swept. At Pankot the sweepers would have nothing to do but clear up after her. She wondered how her father had achieved such spotlessness. There was no brush or mop or cloth. Perhaps he had used handfuls of toilet paper.

In her valise which she set down against the door she had her civilian skirt and blouse and her WAC(I) uniform. While sitting on the closet smoking another cigarette she wondered which to wear. He had not seen her in uniform yet. She'd intended to wear it this morning, partly as a compliment to him and partly because she anticipated there being a moment when it might be better for her to leave her mother and father and Susan together and go down to the daftar to report back and arrange the day and time to resume duties. Which were not onerous. Never had been.

She decided on the uniform and emerging later and finding him with his head out of the farther window stood waiting for him to become aware of her, turn round and react. It was years since she had considered to what extent two girls had been a disappointment to him, years since she had been conscious as the first-born of being under some sort of obligation to make up to him for not being a boy; but standing there in uniform she realized that putting it on, today, was also partly an act of contrition, a way of saying: It's the best I could do. She was seeking approval as a boy might have done and this embarrassed her suddenly. She heaved the valise up on to the upper-bunk, heard him move, felt his appraisal. She glanced round.

'I say,' he said.

She faced him, smiling, awkward.

'How nice,' he said. 'How very nice. But you didn't tell me about the third stripe.'

'It's very recent.'

'All the same. Sergeant. Jolly good.'

'I'll get the tea. Would you like a cold bacon sandwich?'

'Cold bacon?'

135

'Cold fried bacon. I got some last night in Ranpur from the station restaurant.'

'Did you, now! Then you ought to have a crown as well.'

She laughed and opened the hamper which he had lifted on to the seat in readiness for breakfast. She loved train journeys. In England as a child she had been disappointed to find how quickly they were over. In an Indian train one could put down roots, stake out claims, enjoy transitory possession for a day or so of a few cubic feet of carriage which even a change of trains did not seem to interrupt.

The hamper belonged to Aunt Fenny and was zinc-lined, with compartments for flasks, cups, knives, spoons, forks and food. The cold fried rashers for sandwiches were in grease-proof paper.

'And a new loaf!' her father said.

'I got them to slice it. I hope it isn't dry.'

'When was all this?'

'After we'd had dinner and you were seeing to the men. It's a surprise breakfast. Have a hard-boiled egg first?'

'Hard-boiled eggs too. Well done. No, I'll have a sandwich first.'

When she was a child and before the years of exile at school in England they had trekked on ponies through the Pankot hills, making camp at tea-time, striking camp at dawn; rather, the servants had made camp ahead of them and done all the striking. What's for breakfast? her father used to say. Hard boiled eggs and cold bacon sandwiches. With mugs of hot sweet tea. Eaten and drunk before the sun had risen and scorched the mist away. Night found her so tired that she slept before she had time to fix in her mind the position of the jackal packs in relation to the camp. That was the year of the map-reading lessons when she had been initiated into the mysteries of orientation, six point references and compass bearings; lessons begun on the verandah of Rose Cottage which had a view of the hills and distant peaks which he taught her to relate to the hatchings and contours of a map pinned to a board, under talc upon which the coloured chinagraph pencils left marks you could rub out with your finger and obliterate entirely with a rolled-up handkerchief. He taught her the tewt – the tactical exercise without troops –

and she had seldom looked at a landscape since without being alerted to its topographical influence on what was or was not militarily feasible to perform in it. But she had never grasped as a man could do the points of weakness, the conditions that were favourable for the daring stroke that spelt success. Everything, hill, valley, hedge, tree, lake, river, bank, forest, seemed – militarily – overwhelmingly dangerous. So her military accomplishments really began and ended in the commissariat – providing hard boiled eggs and cold fried bacon sandwiches. These she could understand, appreciate, hunger after, and happily leave to him and to men like him the things that sharpened different appetites. Preparing a bacon sandwich now she thought of how he had virtually lost a regiment. She handed the sandwich to him, as it were in compensation.

He waited until she had made one for herself and then, looking at each other like old conspirators, they bit in, holding their hands up to catch crumbs.

'They taste better on a train,' he said, after swallowing. 'Something to do with the smoke and soot.' She poured tea into the mugs. Because they both liked it sweet she'd had the milk and sugar added in the flask: a thick strong picnic brew. The regular puffing sound of the engine came and went as it negotiated the bends and gradients on the hillside. She looked at her watch. One hour to go. He was at the window again, mug in hand.

'There they are!'

He waved and made room for her. Several carriages along the sepoys had their heads stuck out of the window of the special compartment Movement Control had reserved for them. They were grinning and waving. She waved back. One of them pointed. Perhaps his village was visible from here, or in this vicinity. But most of them came from the higher hills beyond Pankot. What a lot they had seen. What tales they could tell. In their villages they would be important men. They had seen the world and would be accounted wise in its ways. Their advice would be listened to. They would swagger a bit. The hands of the unmarried ones would be sought by parents with dowries and daughters. And a special distinction attached to them because Colonel Sahib had waited in

Bombay until they were all fit enough to travel. That tale would be told far into the future. It was something he had done for them. They would always remember.

She waved again and turned back in. He was on the bench looking up at her, smiling, as if proud of them, of her; as if happy. But she knew he was not; not deeply happy. She offered him an egg and a twist of pepper and salt to dip it in after he'd cracked and shelled it. He began this operation and she sat beside him similarly occupied. In India, yes, one could travel great distances. But the greatest distance was between people who were closely related. That distance was never easy to cover. Is Sarah heartfree still? he had asked Aunt Fenny in private, but Fenny had told her and added, Are you pet? So that for a moment it seemed that she would refer to what had never been referred to since it happened. And what had happened constituted the greatest distance there could be between her and her father. Or did it? She would have liked to tell him. She believed he would understand. But the train rattled on and she said nothing. They cracked eggs.

I particularly remember the eggs (Sarah has said), the moment when, simultaneously, he became conscious of the mess we were making and I became conscious that it irritated him.

*

There followed the moment of revelation, that in his valise her father had an old clothes brush. He used this to sweep the crumbs and sharp little fragments of shell into *The Times of India* – after they had brushed down their clothes and the seat with their hands. He carried the folded paper into the w.c. and poured the contents down the pan.

When he came back he made no comment. Gradually her embarrassment spent itself. She looked at him encouragingly, alert to the possibility that he had something special to say for which the clearing up of the mess may have been a delaying tactic as much as anything else; and looking at him, came up against the barrier of his inarticulate affection, his restraint, his inner reservations – as solid an edifice as the rock-face that marks the end of the line from Ranpur to Pankot where the

138

traveller gets down from the train several hundred feet below the hill-pass that leads into the Pankot valley.

Here there is a sound, neither far nor distant, but because the arrival of a train is always noisy the traveller may not notice it except perhaps as a faint singing in the ears or a gentle pressure on the back of the neck, a sound that does not vary in intensity. Full awareness may be delayed but when it comes identification is immediate. It is the sound of the streams and waterfalls that emerge from fissures and secret places in the rock: invisible from any part of the station or the concourse, above and around which the rock looms, softened by vegetation and (most mornings) mists which may gradually reveal themselves as drizzle, or burn away as the sun gets at them.

Somewhere along the road that winds up from the station the sound of rushing water is lost, but to know precisely where you would have to travel on foot, or order the taxi or the tonga to halt at every likely turn and twist, and listen, and in the one place where the driver would be prepared to obey such an order (the brow of the hill, at the pass where in the turning between rocks the whole panorama of the Pankot valley is suddenly disclosed) the sound has already gone and the ear is blessed by the holy silence that only the biblical clunk of goat-bells interrupts.

'*Thairo,*' her father said, at the same time leaning forward and touching the shoulder of the lance-naik driver whom Captain Coley had sent with the staff car to meet the train. Ahead of them the truck-load of ex-invalids careered on down the long straight road that led into the valley, making for the depot where some of their families waited for them. Her father's wishes had been scrupulously carried out. The arrival had been unremarkable; departure from the concourse delayed until only the truck and the staff-car remained. He had waited for a while in the carriage and, later, on the platform, until – within twenty minutes – the entire train-load of passengers had found or chosen their transport and gone. The sounds of the streams and the water were louder, then. Now on the brow of the hill, with the engine switched off and the windows open, he sat for a moment and then got out. She did not follow him.

139

After a while he got back in. He said 'Everything seems so much closer together,' as if in his absence Pankot had shrunk, the three hills which enclosed the valley been edged towards one another and squeezed up against the bazaar whose upper storeys of wooden balconies under steep-pitched wooden roofs rose above the mist into the clear morning air (which, Sarah saw, made them look nearer than they were).

Ten minutes later the car entered the V-shaped bazaar, at the low point of that letter: the square, with its war memorial, the meeting place of the road up into West Hill and the steeper road that thrusts assertively into the other hill upon which the British had chosen to build when they discovered in Pankot an ideal retreat from the hot weather in Ranpur. The main street, flanked arcaded shops, probably looked narrower to him. Passing the general store he said, 'Jalal-ud-Din', and smiled, shook his head, as if the store-sign was evidence of the indestructibility of Pankot's principal contractor. Jalal-ud-Din's shutters were still up. The first servant with a chit would not appear until nine o'clock. It would be ten o'clock before the first memsahib arrived to give an order and inspect the new stock. At this present hour there were few people and the car was not obstructed by tongas, cylists or cows. It continued, making for the junction of Church and Club Roads where the driver changed gear for the long uphill climb and where Sarah (as nowadays she always did) saw what her father couldn't: Barbie Batchelor's overturned tonga, the horse struggling, its leg broken, and the tin trunk, the cause of the trouble, upended in the ditch where it had burst open on impact and scattered its contents of missionary relics. From this scene of disaster Barbie had walked away, up Church Road to the rectory bungalow, mud-stained, clothes torn, still dazed and, according to the chaplain's wife, Clarissa Peplow, demanding a spade, still apparently harping on that old question: whether Mildred had buried Mabel in the wrong place, in the churchyard of St John's in Pankot instead of by the side of her second husband, Colonel Layton's father, in the churchyard of St Luke's in Ranpur.

'What was that?'

Had she spoken? He seemed to think so. She had been thinking: Poor Barbie. She might have said it aloud. She

140

smiled, shook her head, looked out across the golf-course which had played a part in a dream Barbie had had and had liked describing, a dream that had ended in St John's and which Barbie interpreted as heavenly reassurance that her old friend Edwina Crane had been forgiven for taking her own life. But that was three years ago, after the riots of 1942. Now Barbie's dreams were waking ones, lived behind barred windows in Ranpur. I have nothing to give you in exchange, she had written, not even a rose: written on a pad because she no longer spoke – which made it more difficult than ever to tell what she remembered, if anything. But 'not even a rose' had shown some grasp of the past, some stubbornly held recollection of the time when she had been happy, with Mabel, in Rose Cottage.

The car was getting near to the cottage now and she found herself suddenly short of breath, as though her heart had begun to beat for both of them, and this seemed extraordinary to her because at the same time she was conscious of having, just now, as they passed the entrance to the club, also passed the point of any further personal involvement in his home-coming. When she thought of the things to be done and said during the next quarter of an hour her skin prickled with irritation. The familiar names at the entrances to the bunga-lows in the last stretch of the road to Rose Cottage increased her uneasiness. Her body pressed back hard against the seat, ostensibly to give him a better view, but he was not leaning forward to look, in fact he was pressed back too, or so it seemed to her from the sense she had of his body's alignment with her own. So far as she could tell they both sat thus, wedged into their corners, staring straight ahead or gazing obliquely away from one another through the nearest win-dow, passive and reluctant rather than active and eager, and it occurred to her that perhaps he was as aware as she that so much more could have been made of their time together and that now it was over and the opportunity to know each other better gone, perhaps for ever.

'I think,' he said suddenly, and then jerked forward, touched the driver's shoulder. 'Stop here.' And hesitated before saying to her, 'If you don't mind. I'll walk the rest.' She

141

nodded. He got out. Before he shut the door he asked her, 'Will you give me time to cope? Say five minutes?'

'Of course.'

She understood. In this way he could achieve a small measure of surprise. It did not offend her that he wanted to achieve it alone. He set off, striding easily, alert and upright, already – as he had said – dressed for the part but now performing it. The driver was puzzled, glanced over his shoulder, uncertain whether he was supposed to drive on, follow slowly or stay put. She said in Urdu: Wait here for five minutes. He switched off. He was too new to the regiment to remember her father personally. He had not been overawed by the occasion; proud, rather, of the part he was playing in it. She wondered whether he felt cheated of its climax. This was the time when she should jolly him along, like a good colonel's daughter, but she was disinclined to ask the formal questions, which her father had also omitted to do: What is your name? What village do you come from? What other family members have served in the regiment? Instead she lit a cigarette. As she clicked the lighter off her eyes met his in the driving-mirror. He looked down immediately, too quickly for her to judge his reaction but she supposed that smoking was one of the things that made Englishwomen sexless to boys like this; smoking, short skirts, uniforms; and the white skin that probably made the body appear composed of a substance that was not flesh but an unsatisfactory substitute whose erotic qualities only men similarly endowed could appreciate.

As she exhaled, this notion seemed to take form in the smoke and hang with it until it was sucked through the open window, leaving her with a profound sense of her mis-placement in these surroundings. But there was no compen-sating sense of release from them because she could not easily imagine alternatives: to Pankot, yes, but the alternative to Pankot was still an Indian alternative, a variation of Pankot, and Pankot was already crowding in on her, threatening that illusion of serenity, of future possibilities, which had excited her the evening before, getting off the train at Ranpur. She was still in India, still of India. You could exchange one surroun-ding for another but not the occupation, an occupation less and less easy to explain and to follow except by continuing to perform it and seize opportunities to demonstrate – like the artist who carved angels' faces in the darkest recesses of a church roof and countered the charge that people couldn't see them by saying that God could – that dim as the light had grown it was still enough by which to see an obligation.

Five minutes had gone but she sat motionless, watching the smoke from her cigarette, unwilling to give the order to start up, unwilling to stir sufficiently to lift the cigarette to her mouth. From somewhere in the forested slopes a coppersmith-bird began its insistent high-pitched calling, a monotonous tapping sound of which she was usually only subconsciously aware but whose single rhythmically repeated note, coming just now, seemed to be counting the seconds away for her; and then, as it continued, encouraging her not to move but to listen, to surrender to its nagging persuasion until she entered a state of torpor or stupefaction, of which it might take some predatory advantage, reveal itself as a bird of more ominous intention, a bird of the species Barbie watched beyond the barred window, planing the sky above the invisible towers.

Abruptly it fell silent. The driver looked round.

'*Panch minute, memsahib?*'

'*Han,*' she said, '*lekin –*'

But what? Carefully she stubbed the cigarette in the chromium tray on the panel of the door, reluctant to bring the journey to a conclusion. Her capacity to feel or show family affection had diminished and in one area all but vanished. She felt closest now to Aunt Fenny who had seen her through the thing that happened to her. They had seen it through together, if such a lonely and love-less experience could ever be thought of as anything but solitary. Where there might have been recriminations between them there had been only a wounded but finally healing silence; healing because it had been warmed once by physical contact – Aunt Fenny's plump arm round her shoulders, Aunt Fenny's head against hers. Between herself and her mother there had been neither word nor gesture. Nothing. For her mother it had never happened. It was her mother's assumption of ignorance that hurt her most. Sometimes, holding Susan's baby and chancing to find her mother watching her, she felt she would have welcomed any response, even disgust, that showed her mother appreciated that the act of ministering to her sister's child was one that could fill her with the anguish of her own physical deprivation; and then, seeing no glimmer of recognition in that steady dispassionate gaze, she felt deprived again, of part of herself, of everything really except her guilt.

Her guilt was unquestionable but there was only one aspect of it which she was truly ashamed of, and this she bitterly regretted. She knew that behind her longing to talk about it to her mother lay a need for consolation and that this was a weakness, a form of self-indulgence. Understanding this she could live with her mother's silence, endless though it was as a punishment. For her mother the silence was part of the code, the standard: the angel's face in the dark. Or was it a demon's? Whichever it was it helped her mother to preserve an attitude of composure and fortitude and Sarah was able to admire her for it and see the point. In this way Sarah carved angel faces of her own and only at moments of acute distress had destructive impulses to tear the fabric of the roof and expose the edifice to an empty sky.

I shall walk the rest of the way, too, she told herself. And opened the door, got out, shut it, before she could change her mind. She told the driver to go ahead to the bungalow and wait. She stood in the road until the car had started then, following slowly, watched it as it took the last section of the hill. Rose Cottage was behind the next bend.

The coppersmith had resumed but from farther off, having flown to try its luck elsewhere or to plot another point in the boundary of its territory. She knew nothing of its habits, little of the lives of wild creatures whose co-existence with her own species created a mysterious world within a world; or rather, worlds, a finite but to her uncountable number, self-sufficient, separated, but intent on survival. She walked faster, to the tune of the distant coppersmith, and recalled with clarity the night of Susan's wedding in Mirat, wandering amidst the fireflies in the grounds of the palace guest house and saying aloud to her absent father: I hope you are well, I hope you are happy, I hope you will come back soon: and then turning back towards the house where Uncle Arthur sat alone on the lit verandah, a long way away from her, in a pattern of light, a circle of safety. My family, she had thought then. My family, my family.

She had said the words aloud and said them aloud again as she approached the entrance to the front garden of Rose Cottage. My family. My family. Before repeating the words she had not expected anything of them but at once she felt the tug of an old habit of affection and then a yearning for the powerful and terrible enchantment of inherited identity, which she had spent most of her adult years fighting to dispel; fighting as hard as Susan had fought to feel herself touched by it; and drawn into it, to its very centre, where she would no longer feel, as she had once confessed to Sarah she felt, like a drawing that anyone who wanted to could come along and rub out; that there was nothing to her except this erasable image. The first psychiatrist, Captain Samuels, had shown no special interest when Sarah mentioned it. He had simply said, What do you think that means? But had turned away to arrange things on his desk as if uninterested in her amateur opinions. So she had not answered and the question of Susan's idea of herself as a drawing people could rub out had never come up again, either with Samuels or with his successor, Captain Richardson.

But it had stayed in Sarah's mind as an explanation of her sister's self-absorption and self-dramatization. She did not understand what it was that had made Susan feel so inadequate and the discovery that she did had been a shock. Until then, the self-absorption had seemed to her that of a girl who not doubting her attraction demanded that others should provide her with constant evidence of its existence, and paid obsessive attention to the smallest detail when setting the scenes for these necessary acts of recognition. But the sequence of scenes that had made up – still made up – Susan's life could no longer be thought of as Susan playing Susan. It was Susan drawing Susan, drawing and re-drawing, attempting that combination of shape and form which by fitting perfectly into its environment would not attract the hands of the erasers. What Sarah feared now was that the game had stopped being a game, had become a grim and conscious exercise in personal survival; that Susan now drew and redrew herself attempting no more than a likeness that she herself could live with, and that she might tire of the effort.

When she reached the open gateway which was flanked by two stone pillars, she paused, convinced that her father had done so too a few minutes ago. In Mabel's day the name of the bungalow was set out in metal letters fixed to an unpainted wooden board planted in the high bank that bordered the road. Over the years the colour of the metal had become hardly distinguishable from the wood. They had faded into the background, as Mabel had faded into hers, and left the board with a look of being indifferent to the arrival of strangers. The board was still there but was partially hidden by the wild growth on the bank. To see it at all you would have to know it existed. Its identifying function had been usurped by neat white boards, one on each of the stone pillars, announcing respectively in bold black lettering the name and number of the house and the name of its occupier: Colonel J. Layton. Yes, he would have stopped, confronted abruptly by this evidence of ownership, and then perhaps searched for the old board until he found it, probably in a place that didn't quite conform with the one he remembered.

She set off along the curved gravel drive between the rockeries which were vivid with the blue, white, yellow and purple stars of flowering plants. There had been rain in the night and the air was fresh, chill in the shadows of trees and bushes, but the sky was now cloudless and as she came to the end of the rockeries the sun heated her face.

The staff car was parked opposite the steps up to the square-pillared verandah. There was no sign of the driver. The thick-set white stuccoed bungalow looked deserted, but in the way a place could do that had only just been abandoned. Again she stopped. If she entered she would find the occupants gone, the signs of their presence still fresh and warm, and a strong odour of the danger from which they had fled. She had felt this once or twice before, but this morning the sensation was particularly strong.

And, looking at the bungalow, as it were through her father's eyes, she thought she saw for the first time what it was that sometimes gave this impression. By stripping it of anything that made it look 'cottagy' – pots of plants on the

146

balustrades, flowering creepers round the square pillars – her mother had restored to it not its elegance (it could never have had that) but its functional solidity, an architectural integrity which belonged to a time when the British built in a proper colonial fashion with their version of India aggressively in mind and with a view to permanence. Exposed by the cutting back of trees and plants, set off by the new gravel on the drive and the widening of the forecourt (the rockeries were also earmarked for destruction) its squat rectangular bulk was revealed, and with it its essential *soundness*. The secluded, tentative air which Sarah had often associated with it in Aunt Mabel's time had quite gone. The name, Rose Cottage, given to it by a previous owner, a tea-planter, was now all too clearly, absurdly, inappropriate, and only the difficulty there would be with the *dak* had stopped her mother scrapping the name entirely and identifying the bungalow as 12 Upper Club Road.

In restoring it to a likeness of its former self, Sarah knew her mother had intended to create a setting that would speak for itself and also for her and her family's claim on history through long connection. The name Layton, and her mother's maiden name, Muir, under portraits on the walls of Government House in Ranpur and Flagstaff House and the Summer Residence in Pankot, on the drunken headstones in the churchyards of St John's and St Luke's, performed the same function of austere advertisement. In their dumb immobility they avoided the vulgarity of the words whose meanings they conveyed; but conveyed with so remote, so mute a self-awareness that even when identified they seemed thinned by irony. Service, sacrifice, integrity. And she had succeeded, but at a cost. By cutting away inessentials, the accumulations of years, she had robbed the place of a quality that belonged to that accumulation, the quality of survival and the idea behind it – that survival meant change. Restored, the bungalow no longer reflected the qualities of the people living there, it no longer fitted them as they truly were, so that – even when they were in it – from outside the bungalow looked empty, like a place of historic interest, visited but not inhabited. And, more than usually oppressed this morning by the sensation that she had arrived at a moment when it was deserted, she

saw the bungalow in a sudden, shatteringly direct, light –
looking as it looked now but even starker, uncompromisingly
new amid the raw wounds left by space having been cleared
for it; and on its verandah a white man in Indian clothes at
ease in a cane lounging chair, or on a charpoy, attended by
servants or by one of his Indian mistresses, and contemplating
through the mists of claret fumes and cheroot smoke the
fortune he had made or hoped to make out of private trade.
The words whose meanings her mother had wanted to convey
belonged to a later age, an age when the bungalow was already
old. Unwittingly she had exposed the opposites of those
words: self-interest, even corruption.

She made her way quickly, avoiding the steps, taking the
path round the side, then stepping off it because the new
gravel crunched, on to the new turf that had been put down on
ground cleared of shrubs. The side verandah was empty but
there was a spread blanket, a coloured ball and some bricks
where the child had been playing. The doors to the room she
shared with Susan were open. She hesitated. There was no
sound of voices inside the house. Ahead she could see one side
and corner of the high netting surrounding the tennis-court,
and moving forward, widening the angle of vision, saw
Minnie, the little ayah, inside the netting at the far end of the
court, walking behind the child whose arms she held aloft by
the wrists as he took faltering bandy-legged steps towards his
mother. The centre net was not up and Susan sat on a blanket
in the middle of the court at the point where the lime-marked
centre lines met, with her back to the house, leaning on her
right hip, her left arm stretched back, grasping one ankle, the
other arm taut, hand palm down on the blanket, taking the
weight. Close to this hand Panther II sat watching the child,
scraping the blanket with his tail. Susan wore one of the full-
skirted flowered cotton dresses that made her look eighteen
still, too young to be a mother, touchingly too young to be a
widow; and, round the shoulders, tied by its sleeves, a
cardigan. The hairdresser had been – perhaps yesterday. The
dark hair sported a crisp new set, a thick fringe of tight curls at
the back that left her neck bare. When she spoke her voice
carried. 'Come along then.' More faintly Sarah heard Edwar-
d's gurgling response. But suddenly he squealed. Minnie had

picked him up and was running forward. She placed him on the blanket close to Susan and then retreated, ran to the opening at the side of the court and through it across the lawn towards the servants' quarters, as though this were part of a game of hide-and-seek.

But Sarah knew that it was not; guessed that the girl had seen Colonel Layton coming out into the garden and – partly out of shyness (for she was still very young and had never met the head of the household), partly out of unwillingness to intrude, or to receive yet the look or expression of gratitude which she had earned – put herself out of reach.

As if alerted by Minnie's sudden action, Susan had looked round, and now got to her knees, picked Edward up and stood facing the bungalow with her head down talking to the boy, holding his right hand out in the direction of his grandfather who now entered the court from the gate on the verandah side of the netting. At first Sarah thought he was alone, but presently she saw her mother following slowly, arms folded, one hand at her neck, pressing down her string of pearls. The hairdresser had attended her too. And Sarah did not recognize the jumper and skirt. Nor the shoes. They were new. Beside her mother and sister she felt travel-stained, dowdy in her uniform, excluded from the scene: from what she recognized *as* a scene – for all its appearance of evolving naturally from a sequence of haphazard events. It bore, for Sarah, the familiar mark of Susan's gift for pre-arrangement, or her continuing and frightening attempts to reduce reality to the manageable proportions of a series of tableaux which illustrated the particular crisis through which she was passing.

It would be better, she had said to her mother, *for you and daddy to be alone for a bit when he gets here, wouldn't it? So I'll be in the garden with ayah and Edward.*

In this way the true climax of his homecoming had been delayed, transferred from the scene with his wife to the scene with the daughter who had a grandson to present. And a dog. But no husband. Instead, the ghost of the soldier whom she had married. The ghost, and the living likeness of the man in the child. These were her gifts to her father and her current explanations to herself of what she was in the world's eyes and in his particularly: a promise for him of his continuity and in that promise perhaps she saw a dim reflection of promise for her own.

He stopped just short of mother and child, raised his arms, inviting a triple embrace. *It's grandpa*, Susan seemed to be saying. She held Edward up and after a moment's hesitation her father took him and holding him firmly under the arms raised him high. Edward gazed down at the stranger with an expression that from a distance struck Sarah as oddly dispassionate for a child so young. It was an expression she had seen before on Edward's face when confronted by men. He seemed to have a reserve, amounting to a vague antipathy, for grown members of his own sex. Almost alone among them, Ronald Merrick had inspired an early positive response, in spite of the burn-scars, the artificial hand. These had not frightened the child.

The one thing Edward seldom did when men touched him was cry; but his grandfather did not know this and perhaps interpreting Edward's failure to show pleasure or interest in being raised aloft as a warning that tears could quickly follow, put him carefully down on the nearest corner of the blanket and, straightening up, gazed at Susan.

Hello, daddy, she seemed to say. Then she covered her face with both hands and, standing so, was embraced. When she uncovered her face and raised her head to kiss and be kissed her eyes were closed and she was crying. Sarah could hear her. He began saying things to comfort and jolly her out of it. And although he must have noticed the puppy before he chose this moment to exclaim about it. They both looked down at Panther, broke apart and knelt together on the blanket. Introductions were made. Panther wagged his tail and skittered a bit, happy but cautious under the flurry of attention. Colonel Layton scratched the puppy's head, ruffled Edward's red curls, placed an arm round Susan's shoulders. She wiped her left cheek dry with the palm of her hand. The scene was over.

I can enter now, Sarah told herself.

III

By the time the car had negotiated the narrow lanes from the

Samaritan Hospital of the Sisters of Our Lady of Mercy in the old city of Ranpur, through the Koti bazaar to the Elphinstone fountain, the street lighting was coming on.

Only one police squad remained of the force that had been out in the afternoon. The men were relaxed, awaiting the order to return to barracks. Traffic was flowing freely around the circus and access to the Mall and the Kandipat road was no longer restricted – signs that His Excellency the Governor had made the journey from the airfield out at Ranagunj back to Government House without incident and that news of Mr Mohammed Ali Kasim's brief stop in Ranpur, *en route* from Mirat to Pankot with the body of his secretary, Mr Mahsood, had not led to a popular demonstration in the latter case nor to an anti-government demonstration in the former – or certainly not one of the kind that got out of hand and at nightfall left the air charged with anxiety and irresolution.

As the driver turned into the Mall an Indian Sub-Inspector broke off conversation with a head constable, came to attention and saluted: the car rather than its occupant.

Rowan touched the peak of his cap then leant back and looked ahead to the still distant bulk of Government House, dark against the deep mauve northern sky and the grey pink-tipped storm clouds. The avenue of approach was bordered on each side by double rows of shade trees and the compounds of Ranpur's oldest European houses and bungalows. The sidewalks were as wide as the road. It was a processional route but seldom used for such an occasion because the way from the airfield where people usually arrived now lay to the east of Government House, beyond the cantonment.

The Mall, running for a measured mile and a half from the Elphinstone fountain to the Governor's residence, was bisected midway by Old Fort Road. In the middle of this intersection rose the bronze canopied statue of Queen Victoria. In 1890 that statue had been the cause of serious deliberations by the committee of the Ranpur Gymkhana Club. Unwilling quite to believe the story, since it seemed so perfectly apocryphal, Rowan had tackled the club secretary and eventually been shown the faded but still legible page of the committee's minute recording a bare majority vote against a proposal to paint the statue white to meet the criticism of members that, in bronze, Victoria – particularly in profile – bore an unhappy resemblance to a Rajput warrior lady of the kind who defied the British in the early decades of the century. The motion had been lost on the grounds of impracticability. A further motion that representations should be made to the appropriate department to try to ensure that any future replica of the Monarch should be executed in the best white marble was carried unanimously.

Although the Civil Lines officially began at the Elphinstone fountain, the Victoria statue was now regarded as the threshold. She stood on permanent sentry duty, accoutred with orb and sceptre, gazing with an air of abstraction towards the city. Behind her back the Mall continued, but on this second stretch there were no houses. The double lines of shade trees now bordered areas of flat open ground on which the military and police authorities could quickly establish command posts and hold reserve forces at time of civil disturbance. The line (or front) formed by Old Fort Road was considered the furthest that a civil demonstration should be allowed to march on Government House unless its intentions were clearly peaceful. Coming up the Mall from the fountain, riotous marchers invariably found the way blocked by squads of police, or soldiers, deployed across the road in front of the statue. The old houses and bungalows on the Mall between the statue and the fountain had long since been abandoned by the British and taken over by rich Indians. According to the British it was the inconvenience of places built in the late eighteenth and early nineteenth centuries which had caused their removal to the newer and better accommodation provided by subsequent building along Old Fort Road and on the cantonment side of Government House, although it was occasionally admitted that it would have been tedious to live on a route so frequently used by crowds of people making nuisances of themselves. The joke still current among the Indians, though, was that the British had lost their nerve and decamped, leaving their Queen behind.

To reach the Gymkhana Club Rowan would have to tell the driver to turn right at the statue and go along the eastern arm of Old Fort Road. He was tempted to do so. Since 1800 hours it had been his twenty-four hours off-duty. The prospect of beginning it with a dip in the club's pool, a drink or two on the terrace and a quiet supper alone in the annexe to the main dining-room, attracted him. He could send the driver back to Government House with a note for the duty-officer to say where he was. Or he could ring the duty-officer from the club to ask whether HE had asked for him, although that was unlikely. The twenty-four hours off-duty once a week was treated by Malcolm with rigorous respect.

But he gave the driver no instruction.

*

Having passed the sentries and the checkpoint inside the west gate they came out on to the forecourt of the west wing and pulled up at a certain point below the flight of steps leading to the great colonnaded terrace. Rowan signed the man's log-book, got out, went up and pushed through half-glazed double doors into the hall, full as usual with white-uniformed servants. He signed the duty book, marking himself OD, added his name to the mess list, went to check his pigeon-hole for letters and was handed two by the hall steward. Both felt like formal invitations. He went through the open half-glazed doors out on to an inner terrace, one of the four that flanked the inner courtyard: an immense rectangle laid out with intricate geometric precision and formality with lawns, paved walks, ponds and fountains. On ceremonial nights the fountains were floodlit but in the wet season were usually not even turned on. This evening the courtyard was lit only as far as the light from ornamental lanterns that hung from the apex of each section of the vaulted ceilings of the terrace could reach. Between the square pillars there were set great whitewashed tubs of hydrangea, geranium and bougainvillaea, and the ubiquitous crimson canna lilies. To reach the entrance to the staircase to his quarters Rowan had to walk past these almost to the end of the terrace and past the offices which coped with the routine work of the household. Most of these were shut and the benches provided for messengers empty, except outside the telephone exchange and the signals office which were manned round the clock, as was the cypher office, in the east wing, where Rowan spent most of his working day. He glanced across the courtyard. The first-floor windows of Malcolm's private rooms were lit.

Reaching the narrow door and the narrow staircase Rowan began to climb. His quarters were high up, on the second floor where the corridors were narrow, the rooms small, the ceilings low and the windows perpetually grimy. He had a sitting-room, a bedroom and a bathroom which suffered the drawback of having no running hot water. This had to be brought up from the basement in kerosene tins.

Without his bell, his telephone, and without the servants who manned the corridor, he might have felt himself marooned in a little oasis of inconvenience and for the first few weeks of his temporary appointment as an *aide* he had in fact suffered mild attacks of claustrophobia. But he had grown to see only the advantages of the place, even to be fond of it, and when offered something better on being transferred from temporary to official duty he had elected to stay. The quarters were supposed to provide short-term accommodation only and he was now the corridor's oldest inhabitant. One of the advantages was that the servants allotted to the corridor looked upon themselves now as virtually in his personal employ. He knew their histories, their weaknesses, their aspirations; helped them with their private problems and settled their disputes. He had never felt himself cut out to be a good regimental officer; but he was sufficient of a soldier to miss contact with men for whose welfare he was responsible. The servants were a surrogate.

Two of them greeted him now. One took a key from its hook on the board and another a sealed envelope from the pigeon-hole used for internal messages. Jaiprakash opened the door of his sitting-room and switched the lights and fan on. Rowan handed him the key to his drink cupboard and asked him to pour a whisky-soda. Jagram meanwhile went into the bedroom and bathroom, turning on lights and fans, then came back and went out to the corridor to call the bhishti. So it was, night after night.

To drink his whisky Rowan sat in his one comfortable chair. He opened the invitations, neither of interest to him, and then the envelope containing the internal mail. Two of the smaller envelopes inside contained bills. In addition there were various memoranda, the daily communiqué from the press office, a copy of a bread-and-butter letter from a senior officer of Eastern Command who had spent a few days at Government House and mentioned Rowan among those he thanked for making his stay comfortable. The largest envelope contained several cyclostyled pages: the general programme for the next few days, giving dates, times, functions, and the names of those members of the Governor's staff who were required to attend. Wherever his own name appeared the clerk had inked in an asterisk. Since Rowan had drafted most of the itinerary himself he glanced through it now mainly to refresh his memory and to check whether the Governor's private secretary, Hunter-Evans, had had to make any last minute changes.

Tomorrow night at 1930, when his day off was finished, he was to be at the reception in the state rooms for members of the Department of Education, the Municipal Board and the Ranpur Chamber of Commerce and at 2100 at the dinner for Mr Kiran Shankar Chakravarti who in the past few years had made several crores of rupees out of army contracts and had donated a sufficient number of them to found a department of electrical engineering at Government College.

At 10 a.m. the day after, he and Priscilla Begge (representing Sir George and Lady Malcolm respectively) were to welcome and escort to Government House Lady Burke from Delhi, whose interests were the Red Cross, the wvs and the work of women's committees, and in the afternoon he had another reception committee at Ranagunj airport to collect a popular English entertainer who had been touring Burma and Bengal and who was to stay at Government House and give a concert at the Garrison Theatre in the cantonment. On the evening of the same day he was to accompany the indefatigable Lady Burke and Mrs Saparawala, the vice-chairman of the Ranpur Women's War Committee, back to the station to catch the night train for Calcutta where they were to attend a conference. The day after that there was a morning meeting of the Executive Council followed by a lunch party for HH the Maharajah of Puttipur, and an afternoon visit to the quarries out at Rangighat. That was new to him. He hesitated, then remembering that the Maharajah was greatly addicted to the sight and sound of dynamiting, he took up a pencil and marked Rangighat with a stroke, to remind himself to check that someone had thought not only to warn the Ranpur Quarry and Construction Company of the Maharajah's visit but to tell them to be sure to have a few decent bangs laid on, even if they weren't scheduled, and whatever the weather.

In the evening the job of helping to entertain His Highness fell to a fellow *aide*, Hugh Thackeray, who was to accompany HH and General Crawford to the mess of the Ranpur Regiment. HH's son and heir, the Maharajkumar, was an officer in the fourth battalion. He had served in Burma and was presently in Rangoon. Thackeray, a Ranpur Regiment man himself, was also to accompany HH the following morning to pick up his private aeroplane at the airfield. In the afternoon of that day Rowan was to go with the Governor, the Member for Finance and the Member for Education, to the foundation-stone laying ceremony at the site of the new Chakravarti extension in the Government College grounds.

He put the itinerary away and thought how narrow his life sounded when set out like this. Jagram came back and went through to the bathroom. The familiar click of bolts on the corridor door meant that the bhishti was on his way up with the hot water. He took his whisky over to the desk, emptied his pockets and then his briefcase of all the papers connected with the day's assignments: at General Crawford's office, at the CID, at old Chakravarti's house. And – a private visit – at the Samaritan Hospital of the Sisters of Our Lady of Mercy. Among these last was the letter from Sarah Layton which had been written two days ago, on Saturday the 11th of August. She would not expect to hear from him so soon, nor perhaps when she did, by telephone. But it was to ring her, really, that he had come back and not gone to the club.

He unfolded the letter. The telephone number was there in the printed heading. He sat at the desk, spread the letter out and sipped whisky. This morning, because of its length and careful exposition, the letter had given him the impression of there being more urgency about the inquiry she asked him to make than she thought it fair to convey. He had already done what she asked. It would be nice to ring her to say so. But, exposed again to the letter's apparently casual tone he wasn't sure that he should.

Dear Nigel (she had written)

When we last met that time I was on my way to Bombay to meet my father you were generous enough to tell me never to hesitate to let you know if there were anything you could do for me in Ranpur. I hope you'll forgive me for taking you up on that so soon.

I think you'll remember my mentioning that whenever I came down to Ranpur I took the opportunity to visit a Miss Batchelor who used to live here at Rose Cottage as a PG of my father's step-mother, Mabel Layton. I'd just come away from seeing her that day you turned up at the Spendloves where I was staying a couple of nights before going on to Bombay. I was more grateful to you than you may have realized for persuading me to go along with you to those friends of Hugh Thackeray's, because seeing her in the state she'd reached was always discouraging. Her memory had gone, and so had her voice – she wrote everything down – but they said that was psychological. They assured me she was perfectly happy but it was such a depressing place I found that hard to believe.

Yesterday I heard in a roundabout way that she was dead and I confirmed this by ringing the Mother Superior at the Samaritan Hospital, where she was. I'd intended to ring ever since getting back from Bombay (just three days ago, on Wednesday) to find out how she was but kept putting it off. According to the Rev. Mother she died on Monday morning and was buried the following afternoon at St Luke's in Ranpur. She wasn't a Catholic, and was at the Samaritan because as you know theirs is the only place in the city that caters for Europeans who are ill in that way. All the arrangements both for her being there and for the funeral were made by the Bishop Barnard Protestant Mission Schools, which Barbie used to work for.

The line between Ranpur and Pankot is sometimes very bad and was yesterday. On top of that the Rev. Mother has a habit of not talking straight into the phone so she always sounds far away and if you keep asking her to repeat things she gets nervous. I mention this because I can't be sure whether

157

the things I gathered remain to be dealt with are things the Bishop Barnard people have neglected or said they weren't interested in. She said she'd been going to write to me, so I asked her to do that, but she said she'd told me now and perhaps I'd call in (just like that, from Pankot!). I've never found her anything but competent and efficient but she has that curious nun's vagueness about anything she's not dealing with on the spot, face to face.

The trouble is that in all the time Barbie was a patient there I was the only person who knew her before she became ill who visited her, and the staff got into the habit of thinking of me as a sort of go-between if there was anything to settle between the Samaritan and the Bishop Barnard who – I must say, did rather keep their distance and seemed to think it was sufficient that the bills were paid regularly although that was all done by their lawyers who were also Barbie's. I didn't mind going to and fro, whenever I was down there, settling odd things the Samaritan had just let pile up until my next visit. I did rather want them to feel that I had an interest in Miss Batchelor and that poor Miss Batchelor had someone taking an interest in her. I'd always assumed I'd be told if she suddenly became dangerously ill or was dying. They had my Pankot address. The fact that I was in Bombay when it happened doesn't alter the fact that neither the hospital nor the Bishop Barnard seem to have tried to contact me. I suppose the Reverend Mother would have written to me eventually – all of which suggests mainly that whatever it is that seems to be a loose end can't be very important.

I rang the Bishop Barnard too but the Superintendent is on tour. Her deputy didn't know of anything still to be dealt with. She said everything of Miss Batchelor's had been removed from the Samaritan and signed for and was now in the Superintendent's room awaiting disposal. Since then she may have been in touch with the Samaritan and sorted out whatever it is that seems to be a loose end. 'Things you should deal with,' is all I could really understand when I spoke to the Rev. Mother.

Unfortunately the only person I know in Ranpur well enough to ask to look into it is on holiday in Kashmir. (Mrs Fosdick, Mrs Spendlove's sister.) And perhaps it's not a place

I'd want to put Mrs Fosdick to the trouble of getting in touch with. Here, the Peplows, the rector and his wife, who took Barbie in for a while after she had to leave Rose Cottage, are in Darjeeling. Clarissa Peplow is one of the very few people who know that I kept tabs on how poor Barbie Batchelor was making out, and I know if she'd been here she'd have rung the Vicar at St Luke's and asked him to clarify things with the Rev. Mother. So I turn to you. If you have a moment, could you ring the Rev. Mother (The Samaritan Hospital of the Sisters of Our Lady of Mercy, Latafat Hossain Lane, Tank Road, Lower Koti Bazaar, Tel. 3124) and try to find out what 'has to be dealt with' and then let me know – by letter? I'd be awfully grateful. The line between GH and the hospital will probably be clearer and you always sound so calm and collected and in control of things she may be encouraged out of her vagueness.

Since there's been a Governor's conference in Delhi I realize you may still be up there with HE, in any case I know you'll be busy. Anyway, there's absolutely no rush about this, so really don't worry if for some reason or another there's nothing you can do. I've dropped Rev. Mother a line mostly about Barbie but adding that I didn't quite get the hang of the query she raised and have asked a friend in Ranpur to get in touch with her, since I can't get away myself just now. I expect if it's anything important she might write to me, but she never has before.

I was longer in Bombay than I expected. I expect you know why because I gather Sir George Malcolm had a reception committee waiting to welcome back the main body of the regiment when it got back three or four weeks ago. Father wasn't in awfully good shape and as a few of the men had to go into hospital in Bombay we stayed on until they were fit enough to travel. Incidentally, on my last day in Bombay I met Count Bronowsky and Ahmed Kasim and so was vividly reminded of first meeting you on Ranpur station and the game pie and champagne. We went on to an interesting but rather odd party at a flat supposedly belonging to a Maharanee but had to come away before the hostess had all the drinks locked up and turned us all out. Ronald Merrick was with us – my reluctant escort. He'd turned up in Bombay. He didn't want to go to the party but I insisted on going so he insisted on coming. He warned me not to say anything to the Count or to Ahmed about the job he's doing. Perhaps he didn't trust me not to. Anyway it was quite an evening, I'll tell you all about it when next we meet.

It looks as if everything's more or less over now that the Americans have bombed Nagasaki too and Russia has come in (some caustic comments here, about that). It will seem odd not to be at war with anyone. Father is looking much better now. I go riding with him every morning and don't turn up at the daftar until eleven or so, so I'm having an easy time of it.

Love, Sarah.

*

He lay the letter aside, glanced at the package and envelope the Reverend Mother had given him and then at his watch. At 7.45 on a Monday evening there was a good chance of finding her at home. But in the second reading he had been struck by that phrase 'and let me know – by letter'. It occurred to him that the members of her family might not be among those few people who knew she had kept tabs on Miss Batchelor and that her concern for the old missionary's health was one they did not share and would not approve of. He thought it would be very like her to respect their lack of concern by keeping her own concern to herself; just as a year or so ago she had respected their reasons for not calling on Lady Manners when they found themselves on neighbouring house-boats in Sringar, but had herself ignored the barrier the conventional world put up, by crossing the few yards of water on a day when she was alone and could do so without causing fuss or offence, and visited that old and enigmatic woman. She had attributed her action to curiosity. Initially she had used the word morbid, but then said, 'No, that's not right. But I was curious to see her, and the child.' Later she had said something odd, which interested him. 'In a way I think I envied her. But I'm not sure why.'

From the bathroom came the sound of water being poured into the tub. Deciding it would be better to relax in a tepid bath before making up his mind whether to ring her or write

160

to her, he went into the bedroom and began to undress. While
he did so he thought of their last meeting and of the time they
had spent together; and of their first meeting, just over a year
ago.

IV

Her quiet self-reliance had been the first of her qualities to
impress and attract him. Her unexpected entrance ahead of
Dmitri Bronowsky into the gilt and red plush railway carriage
had caught him unprepared, caused him some difficulty –
sitting as he was with briefcase on knee and a finger keeping
the page of the file of documents he had been studying during
Bronowsky's absence.

It was an intrusion he would have welcomed if she had
brought into that baroque interior a classic air of feminine
elegance. But she was in uniform, and this was crumpled. She
looked travel-worn, hastily pulled together, like someone
Bronowsky had just rescued from a crush on the platform,
although the side platform where the Nawab's private train
was drawn up was almost empty. It was not until she had
taken her cap off and was sitting next to him on one of the
ornate Louis xv-style salon chairs, in the light of the crimson
shaded lamps, drinking champagne and smoking one of
Count Bronowsky's pink-papered and gold-tipped cigarettes,
smiling at the old man's gay reminiscence of his earlier
émigré life in the south of France, that the first impression
was overtaken by another: that in her unusual, perhaps plain,
way she was beautiful. The bone structure of her face was
prominent but lacked the arresting emphasis which would
have made it striking. Her face had to be studied before it
revealed its natural and incontrovertible logic, and then one
felt instinctively that it would endure, that in old age it would
be marked by the serenity of understood experience and the
vitality of undiminished appetite.

'What a sad story,' she said when Bronowsky finished the
tale of the eighteen-year-old English boy who had loved and
lost a Spanish girl; lost because he could talk to her only in
English or in the schoolboy French Bronowsky had been hired

to correct and improve. The story was subtly turned. Many girls would have laughed blankly – or, had they been aware of Bronowsky's reputation and hence of the fact that he was probably recounting the tale of a lost love of his own (the boy), not even smiled. But, 'What a sad story' was what she said and then glanced at Rowan. It was no more than a glance but to him extraordinarily eloquent, and continuing to watch her it struck him that she was in love herself, that she was sustained by that, protected from all malice and unkindness and shallowness by the intensity of her commitment to the man she had chosen and the depth of her conviction that her own life was now set on a course that would bring more happiness than sorrow. The expression on her face was like that on Laura's when Laura broke it to him that she had changed her mind and was going to marry a man called Ratcliff.

He believed that what Laura must have felt for Ratcliff this girl – whose first name he did not know – felt for an unnamed man. This was so clear to Rowan that his mind played the trick of confusing her with Laura and the unknown man with Ratcliff, and he recalled quite vividly the feeling of helplessness which had underlain the stronger emotions of jealousy and anger and which had come full circle when he heard that Laura and her planter husband had become prisoners of the Japanese in Malaya.

Bronowsky called for another bottle of champagne. It was his seventieth birthday, he explained. Spending it on duty, he had equipped himself with special comforts. The salon, got up to look like that of a travelling nineteenth century European monarch with cosmopolitan tastes, was an appropriate setting for such a celebration.

'What news of your father?' Bronowsky asked, turning the conversation from himself to Miss Layton. All Rowan knew from Bronowsky's introduction was that Miss Layton was the sister of a girl who had been married in Mirat and that she had stayed with her family at the palace guest house before and after the wedding. Her father seemed to be away – at some distance – she had not heard from him recently. There was a mother. The sister was mentioned again. Miss Layton said they were both well. She herself had just been to Calcutta. She had an aunt and uncle there whose surname was Grace.

'And the officer who was best man at your sister's wedding,' Bronowsky went on. 'Captain Merrick. Have you had news of him? He interested me considerably. I thought him an unusual man.'

Spoken casually like that in these strange but civilized surroundings the familiar name, Merrick, had the same disconcerting effect as a sudden change in the intensity of light. He found himself concentrating on certain essentials. The girl was a stranger, not Laura. The Merrick she and Bronowsky knew need not be his Merrick. But her manner had altered. The prominence of bone seemed more accentuated. This, perhaps, was imaginary. She said that it was to visit this Merrick in hospital that she had gone to Calcutta. This Merrick, her Merrick, had been wounded and a Captain Bingham killed. Her Merrick had tried to help someone called Teddie and had lost an arm. He had pulled Teddie out of a blazing truck while they were under fire. He was in for a decoration. Captain Bingham and Teddie must be one and the same man. She had gone to see her Merrick in hospital because her sister was anxious to find out if there were anything they could do.

This Merrick had been best man at her sister's wedding. Whose best man? Teddie's? It sounded like that. If so the sister was already widowed; still prostrate, perhaps; well in health but not fit to travel; which might explain why she had sent her sister all the way to Calcutta to talk to the man who had lost an arm trying to save her husband. 'Physical courage,' Bronowsky was saying, 'you could see he had that.' Meaning *her* Merrick. On asking which arm Merrick had lost and being told the left the old man was quiet for a moment. 'That's something,' he said. 'I observed him picking up bits of confetti, also stubbing a cigarette. He was right-handed.'

How painstakingly observant. Rowan glanced up and found Bronowsky watching him through that one appraising eye.

'You may remember the man we're speaking of? Merrick?'

'No, I don't think so.'

'I don't mean you would remember him personally. He went into the army from the Indian Police. He figured rather

163

prominently in the case involving an English girl, in Mayapore in 1942. The Bibighar.'

Her Merrick. His Merrick. The same man.

'Oh yes. That case.'

'He was District Superintendent. In Mirat I had a long and interesting talk to him and found him utterly convinced that the men he arrested were truly guilty. I myself and I suppose most people since have come to the conclusion that they couldn't have been.'

Bronowsky was wrong. At the top of the administrative hierarchy, yes, one could say that, but even there the suspicion that Merrick had blundered was tempered by a determination not to allow it to be officially admitted. Uncorroborated and inadmissible evidence that in the case of Hari Kumar the blunder was one of a peculiarly unpleasant kind looked like having to remain a haunting burden on the consciences of a few. The irony of Merrick's act of bravery and the recommendation for a decoration was not lost on Rowan. It would justify the opinion originally held by the rank and file of the administration, and never truly altered, that in the Manners rape case Merrick had acted with that forthright avenging speed which had once made the *raj* feared and respected, and India a place where men did not merely operate a machine of law and order, but ruled and damned the consequences of ruling.

'It would have been understandable,' Bronowsky went on 'if Merrick had begun to waver in his opinion – unless you accept that he left the police temporarily under a cloud and harboured a grudge. But he had tried for years to get into the army. He was a very ordinary man on the surface but underneath, I suspect, a man of unusual talents. Are those boys still in prison?'

'Which boys are those?' Rowan asked.

'The ones arrested, not tried, but detained, as politicals.'

'I'm afraid I don't know, Count.'

The old man smiled, possibly to convey that his inquiries were made only out of general curiosity.

'I hope they are not forgotten and just being left to rot. The provincial authorities have an obligation in this matter, surely?'

'I'm sure they are not just forgotten.'

'The Indians remember. Unfortunately not only Indians of the right sort. There is a venerable gentleman of Mayapore who last year visited Mirat and engaged in some tortuous processes of intimidation.'

Another name clicked into place in Rowan's mind, but again, as in the case of Merrick whom he had never met, a name without a face. The name was Pandit Baba but the face was Harry Coomer's – Kumar's rather, quite unrecognizable, unidentifiable with the boy Rowan had known as Coomer: hollow-cheeked, prison-pale under the brown skin: the voice was Kumar's too, describing Pandit Baba of Mayapore in that halting staccato way: *I knew him as a man my aunt hired to try to teach me an Indian language – He smelt strongly of garlic – He was very unpunctual – the lessons weren't a success.*

Between each short sentence there had been a pause, as Kumar focused on an image, probably long forgotten. The manner in which he answered the question was what first suggested to Rowan that the documents he had studied and which were damning, damning to Kumar, were not going to stand up. It was the manner of a man talking to himself as well as to the two men on the other side of a table; searching his memory for certain details to convince himself of the reality of things he knew had happened to him but had preferred not to think about for a long time. For Rowan, this careful answer to his unimportant question about Pandit Baba had been the first of a series of answers, brief spoken meditations, which drove a persistent unwavering line through recurring doubt and uncertainty, until they culminated in that shatteringly casual remark which he believed he would never forget and which had finally convinced him Kumar must be telling the truth: *It's difficult to breathe in that position. It's all you think about in the end.*

Was Pandit Baba the man Bronowsky meant, the venerable gentleman from Mayapore who had been in Mirat? What he had gathered from Kumar of the Pandit's talent for avoiding trouble and leaving his young followers to carry the can made 'tortuous process of intimidation' sound right. But whom had he intimidated?

Bronowsky had turned to Miss Layton. 'The stone,' he said, 'you recall the stone – was certainly thrown at the instigation of this slippery customer. He is one of those on whom we keep a watchful eye. I am told he has recently left Mayapore, but I am not told where he has gone or why. Forgive me, it is an uncheerful subject.' Again he looked at Rowan and then began to rise. 'And Miss Layton must eat. We shan't wait for Ahmed. In any case he's probably only going to be interested in the champagne.'

Rowan looked at his watch. Young Kasim and his mother were already half-an-hour late. He hoped they wouldn't cut it too fine. After half-past midnight the line to Premanagar would be closed to them by the regular service. It would be 2 a.m. before it could be opened again for the Nawab's private train.

Bronowsky leant over him, lightly touched his arm. 'We shall be able to leave on the scheduled time. Ahmed will see to it. Come.'

As he followed Miss Layton in to the dining-salon he smelt the delicate scent of cologne and pictured her dabbing her wrists and neck and forehead with it to relieve the tensions and staleness of the journey from Calcutta. She turned round and spoke, saying something complimentary about the *fin-de-siècle* splendours of the Nawab's train, but he did not quite catch it. He bent his head inquiringly. He was very close to her. He was disturbed again, but in a way that did not become clear to him until later when they were eating game pie and drinking more champagne and she was telling them about her uncle's new job in Calcutta, which was to run courses of lectures to attract wartime officers to the post-war civil administration.

She discussed the logic of this. She spoke well and clearly, in control of a line of argument that was undogmatically developed. He suspected that she was not strong on small talk, that in company she found uncongenial she might even appear shy or withdrawn. The champagne helped perhaps, and Bronowsky was a skilful and encouraging listener, capable of charming anyone out of shyness, particularly good-natured and well brought up girls for whom he presumably felt the gallant, undemanding and guarded affection of the aging homosexual.

As she spoke Rowan saw how, indirectly, she was making a point: that the situation of these men who attended her uncle's courses – those who would succumb to the obvious temptations and those who would take a calculated risk – was in exaggerated form the same situation in which she, every English person of her generation in India, Rowan himself, found themselves. The outlook was shadowy but one could not (she implied) make this an excuse for working at half-pressure, nor for standing back from a job that was there to be done. In the course of her argument she used the word Indianisation, which suggested that the one criticism of her uncle's efforts she would accept as valid was that they were not officially directed as thoughtfully as they could have been to that end. In a girl of her type such a view was unusual. It was one he shared. It had lain immature and unformed behind his youthful decision to seek a military and not a civil career in India, a decision he had regretted and sought to remedy before the war by undergoing a probationary period in the Political Department, in the hope of transferring to it permanently and applying what talent he had to the problems of the constitutionally backward Princely states. It was in these that he still saw the most satisfactory opportunities, the chance, when he was fit again, to do some useful work.

The oval table was covered in white damask, it glittered with silver. From the centre-piece – a gilded wicker basket of white and scarlet carnations set amid ferns which trembled in the currents of air from the electric fans – came the dry delicate scent of the flowers. Watching her, still thinking yes she is in love, he put his finger on what it was that disturbed him. Had Kumar after all been lying? It didn't seem possible to place the image of Kumar's Merrick alongside Miss Layton and then see them in a relationship at all, let alone one of intimacy. She had not contradicted Bronowsky when he said that most people now assumed Merrick had made a mistake but she had not agreed either. She had said nothing. But Calcutta was a long way to go even on a mission of the kind he'd gathered it was – one involving the gratitude – in other words the honour – of the family. Her aunt and uncle could have undertaken it far more easily and just as effectively.

He sat patiently, talking little, awaiting an opportunity to find out more about her. Bronowsky was now telling stories of pre-revolutionary St Petersburg, of his émigré life in Berlin and Paris and Monte Carlo, but omitting (as he was reputed always to omit) the most interesting tale of all, which was perhaps apocryphal; the story of his successful negotiation between the Nawab, then a young man, and the European woman whom the Nawab had followed from India in a towering Oriental passion at being deceived: a negotiation for the return of jewelry the young prince had given her as any ordinary young man might give a girl a diamond engagement ring on the assumption that she would return it if she backed out. What pressure Bronowsky had brought to bear on the woman was a matter for conjecture (Rowan had heard several versions) but when the Prince returned to Mirat without the woman, according to the story, he had the jewelry, and he also had Bronowsky for whose tact and skill he was supposed ever since to have had the deepest admiration; an admiration that was not shared by the Political Department until they could deny no longer that under Bronowsky's guidance the wild and potentially dissolute young prince had become a model of rectitude and political wisdom.

The return to the salon for coffee brought no change of subject. The old man talked on and presently Rowan noticed that Miss Layton had become anxious about the time, about what was happening on the platform. Obviously she had a connection to make. It was twenty minutes to midnight. The only train he knew of due to leave Ranpur at that hour was the nightly train up to Pankot.

'I must go, I'm afraid,' she said, putting down her cup. Bronowsky pleaded for another five minutes but she said, 'If I stay another five minutes I shall never want to go, and I've got my compartment to get unlocked.'

They stood up. Bronowsky kissed her hand, thanked her for her company, asked her to visit Mirat again one day. She said she would like that, then turned to Rowan.

'Goodbye, Captain Rowan.'

He said, 'I'll see you to your compartment.'

But Bronowsky claimed that as his own privilege and there was nothing for it but to stand aside and let her go.

*

Just before midnight while Bronowsky was still absent young Kasim arrived with his mother, who was in purdah. He did not introduce her to Rowan but took her straight to the adjoining carriage where there were sleeping berths. At five past midnight Bronowsky came back. There were consultations with railway officials. Rowan settled in a corner, smoked, read documents, trying to reconcentrate on the matter in hand. The train left on time. He declined to join Bronowsky and young Kasim in the dining-saloon. From behind the closed curtains he heard Bronowsky's voice. He considered going to bed but the steward had brought him brandy and he sat on, drinking this, and doubting that he would sleep in the few hours it would take to reach Premanagar where he and Ahmed were to leave the train for the rendezvous at the Circuit House with Mohammed Ali Kasim, who was probably sleepless too, keeping watch through the small hours of his last night as a prisoner in the Fort.

Rowan did not envy young Kasim the task he had undertaken, that of breaking the news to his father that Sayed had been captured fighting in the INA and that the release from the Fort was only a partial release, that he was to live now under restriction, in the protection of his kinsman the Nawab. Rowan's own part in the affair was of minor importance. Officially he was merely representing the Governor, but it was the second time Malcolm had given him a job that fell outside the ordinary limits of the duties of an *aide*. The first had been the examination *in camera* of Hari Kumar at the Kandipat jail, little more than three weeks before. It interested him that tonight he should have found himself face to face with two people who knew Merrick.

But how well did they know him? He sipped his brandy, closed his eyes and put his head back. The kind of knowledge he had in mind was the sort one could describe as elusive; to her, perhaps, inaccessible; as obscure as the dark side of the moon. It irked him that he could do nothing to warn her of its

169

existence. Its possible existence. Merrick was protected by shadows of doubt that could never be dispersed, and by the iron system of the *raj* itself. If there had been a weakness, a fissure through which rumour and conjecture could flow and adversely affect Merrick's future, it had now been sealed up by the heroic act.

Rowan smiled, but at the irony of it, and – opening his eyes – found Bronowsky sitting opposite him, smiling too. The carriage, well-carpeted and sprung, ran smoothly and quietly. Bronowsky must have come in at a moment when the train was crossing points.

'Have I woken you?' he asked, raising his voice just sufficiently above the muffled rhythmic clatter for Rowan to hear him clearly across the width of the carriage. 'If so I owe an apology. Your dreams were obviously pleasant ones.'

'Satisfying recollections. I hadn't expected such a splendid supper.'

'Nor such charming company? I met her but the once, in Mirat, when they were staying there for the wedding, and tonight out there on the platform I didn't recognize her in uniform. Many girls would have been piqued, at the same time thankful not to have to stop and exchange banalities with an elderly foreigner. But Miss Layton made herself known. In Mirat I underestimated her. I marked her down as shy, even as a trifle colourless in the way – forgive me – that only well-bred English girls can be colourless. But I now see what it was. In Mirat she was taking a back-seat because it was her sister's wedding and the sister is extremely pretty and vivacious. Or was. Now she is expecting a baby, and already a widow. She and Captain Bingham had such a brief time together. He was killed in Imphal in April. I saw the notice and wrote to them but I knew nothing of the dramatic circumstances until tonight.'

Rowan nodded. A pregnancy could explain why Miss Layton rather than her sister had travelled to Calcutta.

'I've not been in Ranpur long enough to know everybody,' he said. 'Are they a Ranpur family?'

'Yes, but they've been in Pankot since the father went abroad on active service. He commanded the 1st Pankots in North Africa. He's a prisoner of the Germans. Then there was

170

her grandfather, who was a distinguished civilian, Finance Member of Council here in Ranpur during the previous war. And her maternal grandfather, General Muir, was General Officer commanding, also in Ranpur, early in the Twenties.'

Rowan nodded.

'And you, Captain Rowan? I see you were in Burma, presumably during the retreat. But nevertheless effectively. Or do you affect the traditional indifference to the Military Cross and pretend that it came with the rations?'

'It sometimes seems the only satisfactory explanation.'

'Were you wounded?'

'Only exhausted. It was a long march.'

'You have been ill?'

'I think, rather, debilitated.'

'The malignant and endemic fevers that used to cut life short but have learnt subtler methods of invasion. Quite. Our court physician, who doubles that far from onerous rôle with the slightly more exacting one of Minister of Health in our little Council of State and runs a hospital in his spare time, has a theory that it is only the lethargy induced in Englishmen by low but persistent tropical fevers, the lethargy and its corollary, the concentration of mental and physical resources on a particular task, that has kept the *raj* stubbornly intact. He says that the moment medical science finds a way of rendering the English bloodstream and the English bowel system immune to the attacks of Indian microbes and amoeba, then the English will all perk up, look around and wonder what on earth they are doing out here, and as a consequence roar with laughter and resign. He cites as an example of depressive and obsessive behaviour the case of General Dyer, who shot all those unarmed Indians in Amritsar in nineteen-nineteen, believing that by doing so he was saving the Empire. Habbibullah is convinced that the poor old fellow's brain was inflamed by the accumulation in the blood stream of the poisons of chronic amoebic infection. Of course he tells me all this because he is convinced that as a European I am similarly infected, in spite of my protests that for my age I am in vigorous good health and have never shot anyone, armed or unarmed.'

'Actually I believe General Dyer had arterial sclerosis and

171

died of it quite a few years later, but it's one of the slow diseases, isn't it? Someone did once suggest to me that it could have affected his judgment at Jallianwallah.'

'I didn't know that. I must tell Habbibullah. How nice to meet a young Englishman who knows a bit about the country's history. Dyer was another man who made a mistake, or acted controversially, and remained convinced to the end that he had been absolutely right.'

Rowan did not reply immediately. He wondered whether the allusion to Merrick was intentional.

'It surprises me a little, sir. That you should feel that. Most Englishmen who work out here have to be pretty well informed, surely. Not that knowing about Dyer is much of a test.'

Bronowsky smiled at him and leant forward, with his hands one on top of the other, supported by the ebony cane that was probably not as necessary an aid to balance as he made it appear.

'I exaggerated, yes. But one meets so many young officers who turn out to be here only because of the war and who know nothing. Mention General Dyer to them and they say, Oh, which division is he? It's different with the hard core of the professionals, which I take it you belong to. Do you have family connections with India?'

'Only on my mother's side. My father was out here at one time, but in the British Army.'

'Ah. I have been uselessly sifting my old memory for a Rowan. What was your mother's maiden name?'

'Crawley.'

The old man lowered his head, raised one finger and placed it on his chin.

'Crawley,' he repeated. 'There was a Thomas Crawley who was Resident at Kotala. He ran things very successfully during the ruler's minority. Were he and your mother related?'

'He was her brother, but considerably older. Did you know him?'

'Only by reputation. In latter days he experienced some difficulties. It was a pity. Have you had anything to do with the Political Department yourself?'

'I worked a probationary year just before the war.'

'Indeed. Your ambitions lie in that direction? But the army reclaimed you for the war no doubt. Where were you? Presumably not in Kotala?'

'No, but I did meet the Maharajah in Delhi.'

'How did that go?'

'Not at all, at first. When I told him Crawley had been my uncle he sheered off.'

'You told him voluntarily?'

'It would have been unfair not to. He was in one of his expansive moods, inviting people at random.'

'Inviting them to what?'

'One of his famous parties at the palace in Kotala.'

'That must have been a temptation. To see the place where your uncle spent the best part of his working life.'

'Yes, it was. My mother lived with him at the Residency for two or three years before she went home to get married. I'd seen all the photographs and heard all the tales about how it was in those days, and quite a bit about what happened after the ruler came of age. But I felt I'd only get the best out of a visit if I went openly as Tommy Crawley's nephew.'

'You said the meeting with the Maharajah didn't go well at first, that he sheered off. Did he change his mind?'

'Yes but I don't know how quickly. He must have kept tabs on me through his grapevine, though, because a couple of months later when I was touring with the agent for a small group of states north of Kotala I got a letter from him inviting me to call. It was a bit of a poser because it meant getting clearance from the department as well as from the Resident in Ranikot.'

'Why Ranikot?'

'When Uncle Tommy left Kotala the agency was transferred to the group that came under Ranikot. The Resident there put an assistant in at Kotala but everything had to go through him.'

'That can't have pleased the Maharajah.'

'It wasn't meant to. By regrouping his state and severing his direct link with the Crown Representative, the department thought he'd be upset enough to withdraw the accusations he'd made, that my uncle was interfering in private and state matters to an intolerable degree, not only withdraw but beg to have him sent back. I think they were looking forward to telling him it was too late and were rather surprised when he made no complaint.'

'Why too late?'

'Well my uncle was getting on and the strain of their constant bickering had ruined his health. My mother came out to see him in Simla while he was on sick leave and tried to persuade him to retire at once and not wait the two or three years he still had to go. She wasn't at all surprised when we met her off the boat and told her Uncle Tommy had died while she was on the passage home. The Maharajah wrote to her offering his sympathies. She'd known him well when he was a boy but didn't feel up to sending him more than a formal acknowledgment. When I was coming out, though, she said that if ever I bumped into young Kotala I should give him her salaams.'

'And did you?'

'Yes. He was very touched.'

'You accepted his invitation, then, in spite of the red tape. Good.'

'I'm afraid I couldn't. The officer I was touring with was dead against it, and actually a private trip on the side would have been a bit much for him to agree to because I was dogsbodying for him in a fairly hectic programme and supposed to be learning the ropes. So I wrote begging off. But I gave him my mother's message and said I hoped there'd be another opportunity of meeting. A week later he turned up at our next stopping place. He'd driven more than a hundred miles.'

'Was he so anxious to apologize for his treatment of your uncle?'

'He apologized for sheering off. I was afraid of the other thing too. I'd worked it out years before, from all the things my mother told me or let slip that the fault had really been my uncle's. I think she'd reached the same conclusion. As you said, he virtually ran the state while the prince was a minor and apart from that they'd formed an extremely close and affectionate father-and-son relationship. When the prince came of age all that should have stopped. My uncle should have stood back and been content to let the young man assume full responsibility, but he made the error of continuing to treat him as a minor, of forgetting that he was a ruling Hindu prince. And, of course, that must have led to a situation in which the prince's relatives and his state officials made it clear that they despised him for letting the Resident browbeat him and that if he had an ounce of real spirit he'd start showing my uncle where to get off. Unfortunately he did that in a young man's over-exuberant way, spending money wildly on personal extravagances, drinking too much and womanizing, all the things that gave my uncle the opportunity to press his criticisms. In fact after a year or so you only needed evidence of cruelty and corruption and complete disregard for the welfare of his poorer subjects to have had a case to depose him.'

'And there was no such evidence.'

'I imagine the only harm the Maharajah ever did to anyone was to himself. And I think he felt that. I'd say it still rankled. I got the impression he would really have liked to be abstemious and upright, all the things my uncle no doubt represented to him as virtues when he was growing up, hated being unable to resist other temptations and blamed my uncle for that as well. Well as I say he apologized for sheering off when we first met but when it got to the point where it was obvious one of us ought to mention Uncle Tommy he became very edgy. He'd driven all that way so I felt the ball was in my court, but I was reluctant to play it. I'm ashamed to admit I thought there might be a price-tag on the whole thing, that the idea was to soften me up by a display of magnanimity or remorse so that I'd agree to put a word in for him over some scheme he might have going.'

'Well, you'd been in the country just long enough to suspect he might think you new enough to try it on. How did you play the ball?'

'I didn't. I shirked it. So just before he got into the car to go back he confronted me. It's the only word. Have you ever met him?'

'No. Not the maharajah. We've never been to Kotala and he's not in the Chamber. Insufficient guns.'

'Quite tall. Very plump. He uses scent and wears rings.

Diamonds mostly. There was even a small jewelled cockade in the centre of his turban. I think you could call Kotala the walking effete-looking Indian potentate of popular English imagination. It isn't an image that conveys what *we* mean by dignity whatever it may convey to Indians, but ever since that day I've tried not to prejudge from appearances. I don't think anything could have been more dignified than his parting speech. He said he was glad to have met Tommy Crawley's nephew, trusted we'd meet again and have the opportunity to build a relationship on the friendly basis he hoped we'd established, but that this wouldn't be possible from his point of view unless I knew and accepted that although he had loved my uncle as a boy and had happy memories of those times, he had had a terrible time with him later, which he would never forget and could never forgive. He said, "When I was young your uncle was always saying, when you know you are in the right, fight for it, never give in, never retreat and never retract. My opinion is that in that matter I was right and he was wrong. If I regret anything it is the nature of the weapons he forced me to use and the nature of the balm he forced me to resort to to heal the wounds he inflicted." I was so impressed that when he'd gone I went straight to my room and wrote it down.'

'A prepared speech,' Bronowsky said, 'but effective. I should think sincere. Yes. Very English in its sentiment, but of course very Indian too. He was testing your mettle and temper as well as getting something off his chest. What did you say?'

'The first thing that came into my head. Afterwards I realized I was lucky he hadn't made a speech like that when I first met him. In the interval I'd been around and cottoned on to the system, the one that calls for the ruler to stand his ground and you yours but for you both to open up the ground between without committing yourself to occupy it. I said I personally knew very little of the quarrel between them except that my uncle had been deeply affected by it, had presumably felt as strongly about the correctness of his own behaviour, that I'd always regretted my uncle's career should have ended on such a note but would regret it far more had it seemed now that their differences after all hadn't been so serious that they couldn't somehow have been overcome, and was most grateful to His Highness for speaking so frankly and relieving my mind of any such supposition.'

'Were you alone with him?'

'Yes, why?'

'A pity. If your superior officer had heard that, I imagine you'd have received a most favourable report.'

'Actually I'm not at all sure it didn't raise a doubt about my fitness for political work. I was questioned pretty closely about what we'd said to each other and was made to feel I might do better if I applied myself more conscientiously to routine matters.'

'Young men with an aptitude usually excite caution rather than enthusiasm. It has ever been so. But you will probably survive. I trust so. If you have ambitions there still. Do you?'

Rowan smiled. He said, quoting, '"The body's fever, dying like a fire, Sheds little light upon the heart's concerns." '

'Ah,' Bronowsky said after a moment. 'Gaffur. But a somewhat more elegant translation than the one in the existing English version. The fading fever in the blood is like a dying fire, de dum de dum etcetera. But how apt. Gaffur, recovering from a bout of malaria or dysentery. Is that other version your own? Yes? Then we have one vice in common, although my own translations from the Urdu come more under the heading of extra-curricular activities for Nawab Sahib. Of course you know the Gaffur connection?'

'He was court poet in Mirat, in the eighteenth century.'

'And connected to the ruling family. A Kasim. Nawab Sahib had never read Gaffur in English. But he has many exquisite volumes in the original. Whenever people feel they should give him a gift that shows forethought but not extravagance they usually hit upon the poems of his distinguished ancestor. For instance, the Laytons presented him with a copy when he offered them the hospitality of the guest house at the time of the wedding. But the habit is rarer in English people than in Indians. He was very pleased and expressed the wish to learn some of his favourite verses in English. He was horrified when he read Colonel Harvey-Fortescue's Victorian effusions and since then I have had to try my own hand. I shan't assume the false modesty of the complacent amateur and pretend I'm not highly satisfied with some of the results. In fact I've become quite addicted to the exercise of this latent skill and sometimes fancy myself quite a little Pushkin. But it is hard on the eye. Having only one it is sensible to take care of it, but difficult to remember to do so. One adjusts so easily to such a slight impediment and seldom thinks of oneself as handicapped, unless one sees or hears of someone in the same or worse condition.'

The stories of Bronowsky's blind left eye and lame left leg ranged from the possible to the scurrilously unlikely. It was Rowan's chance to hear one of them and his chance to approach the subject of disability, the subject of lost limbs, the subject of Merrick. A chance again deliberately contrived? It was worth taking up. He realized how much he was enjoying talking to the old *wazir* and it pleased him to think that the conversation was no more than a ritual, a courtly circumnavigation of a subject they were both interested in but both too skilled to raise directly. Each had stood his ground. The space between was wide open. One could step on to it now without giving much away.

'I notice,' Rowan said, 'that the blind eye and the lame leg are both on the left side. Does that mean there was a common cause or is it a coincidence?'

'Oh, common. And common enough in those days. St Petersburg. A makeshift bomb. An explosive little incident at dusk on the drive from the Winter Palace.' Bronowsky leant back in his chair. 'An explosion like a scarlet flower in black foliage, thrusting out of the snow. A little summer miracle in winter. That and the pressure. One did not recall a noise. Perhaps the snow muffled it. Such are one's recollections. Later the discomfort. And the strange remote satisfaction of knowing it was no worse. No limb lost. A mere eye. A bad leg. Growing pleasure. The distinction of a limp and an eye-patch. The poor young fellow who threw the bomb was the only fatal casualty. He mistook me for Another. I made a callous joke. That now I had only one eye to weep with and mourn his useless little death. But that was to disguise less insensitive feelings. I thought, How strange. He did not know me, nor I him, but all through his life, from birth, for twenty years, without realizing it he had been moving towards me, step by inevitable step, and I had been waiting for him, preparing to set out on that drive through the snow, to keep an appointment, wrapped in my furs, well muffled, well disguised, so that he would not recognize me at the very last moment as the agent of his death. I saw his photograph. They had it, of course. And one from the morgue of his remains. They showed me this too, as if it would please me. Extraordinarily his face was unmarked. Very pale against the blackness of his hair and the wispy adolescent growth of beard on cheeks and chin. A dark young man, I thought, of random destiny and private passions. It was a revelation. As I looked at the photograph I realized that *he* could have been *my* death, that perhaps fate had decreed this, but had wound the machinery up wrong and was now aghast at the error. It struck me that, well, I must watch out, that perhaps even now a birth was taking place in some remote village, to rectify things. It seemed to me that fate would work this way, that the destiny so apparently random must be shaped even so from the beginning, that I had at least twenty years grace before I must keep the next appointment, this time with a young man who would complete the task. I pictured his life. How it would be. Not privileged like mine but harsh and sombre, so that his heart would grow into a habit of sadness which it pleased me to think of as also a sadness for me, because of what he must do that he did not know. I fell a little in love with him. And there were times when things were not good with me that I wished to hasten the consummation. This was in nineteen hundred. When I left Russia nearly twenty years later it was with the feelings almost of a deserter. By then, you see, he would have been in the prime of youth with only a few years to wait. In Berlin and in Paris I watched out for him, at first only among the young men of our emigration but then among young Germans too and young Frenchmen, because I realized that the appointed agent need not after all be of Russian nationality and that one of fate's little jokes might be that I should think myself secure merely because I had crossed a frontier. Even in India I used to watch.'

'But not any longer?'

'Oh, sometimes. India particularly is rich in possibilities. It is easy here to be a marked man. I spoke of this to our friend

Merrick during the interesting conversation I had with him in Mirat.'

'Merrick? Oh, you mean the Mayapore case. Miss Layton's friend.'

'When I say spoke of it I mean spoke in general to him of being a marked man, of the part played by these young men of random destiny and private passions. I did not mention my own case. Mine after all is illusory. His was real. He had been a marked man ever since Mayapore. Persecuted even, but in subtle ways to remind him that he was not forgotten, that his transfer into the army had not shaken off whoever it was, whoever it is, who wishes him to be under no delusion, but know that his actions in Mayapore will have to be answered for one day. To give him that uncomfortable impression, anyway. My own feeling was that these people were less interested in retribution than in the use that could be made of a controversial figure, such as Merrick's, to stir young men up to create trouble, to achieve some particular political or religious objective.'

'People like the venerable gentleman from Mayapore? The one you said was in Mirat last year engaged in some tortuous process of intimidation?'

The train passed over a network of points, rocking gently. The lights dimmed, then brightened, flickered out, came on again. In the very brief spasm of darkness it seemed to Rowan that Bronowsky had altered position. But there would not have been time for him to do so unobserved: a second or two. But he looked different. Rowan could not say in what way. It was strange.

'The venerable gentleman, yes.' Even his voice had altered, it seemed, but the whole thing must be a trick of the mind, or something to do with a change in the pressure in the carriage. Perhaps the country through which they were passing had altered. Or someone had opened a door or a window further down the coach.

'You mentioned a stone being thrown. Thrown at this man Merrick, did you mean?'

'Quite so.'

'At the instigation of this slippery customer?'

180

'How accurately you recall my words. Let us simplify things for each other. His name was Pandit Baba.'

'And he went all the way from Mayapore to Mirat to incite someone to throw a stone at poor Mr Merrick?'

Bronowsky laughed. He said, 'Precisely. Such a gesture would also strike me as excessive. The pandit, I think, would not expend energy on such an inconsiderable thing. Which was why I took note. It is too long a story, the story of the stone and Mr Merrick. In itself irrelevant and in its wider context of concern only to me, in so far as it concerns me as well as our chief of police to protect Mirat from these tiresome infiltrations.'

'I'm not quite with you.'

'When you people in British India clamp down, when you have a sweep and clap subversives and firebrands into jails, proscribe political parties or in any way make things unhealthy for Indians who stand up to you, then those who escape your nets go to ground. And where better than in the self-governing princely states where your formal writ does not so easily run? When you had that grand round-up in nineteen-forty-two, at the time of the Quit India campaign, I do not know how many activists, terrorists, anarchists, militant communalists or simple Congress extremists hitched up their dhotis and hot-footed it to places like Mirat. I know which of them turned up *in* Mirat, because I saw to it that they quickly hitched their dhotis up again and hot-footed it back across our borders.'

'Your chief of police must be very efficient.'

Bronowsky glanced away, smiling to himself. 'I suppose one or two escaped our combined vigilance. But we were very vigilant. It is wise to be. The states offer a wide variety of opportunities for political intrigue and some states I think deserve what they get in that way. But I will not have political or communal disturbances stirred up in Mirat by people who do not belong to Mirat. Both the major Indian political parties have been guilty of attempting it in the past twenty years. I need not elaborate. Quite apart from the fact that Nawab Sahib is by definition an autocrat he is also a Muslim. The majority of his subjects are Hindu. My life in Mirat has been spent trying to ensure that the two communities have equal

181

opportunities, which was not always so, that they live in amity and have reason to be perfectly content to live as subjects of the Nawab, and do not hanker after the democratic millennium promised by Gandhiji on the one hand or the theistic paradise-state on earth envisaged by Mr Jinnah on the other.'

For a while he was silent, looking now at the shoe on his left foot, which was thrust out, the heel on the thick carpet that helped to muffle the drumming of the wheels. He said, 'Eventually, of course, there can be no separate future for us, and latterly I have been directing my thoughts to the problem of how best to ensure a smooth and advantageous transition.'

'No separate future?'

'When the British finally go. No freedom separate from India's freedom. No separate future for Mirat nor for any of the states, with the possible exception of the largest and most powerful such as Hyderabad or those whose territories merge into each other and who might combine administratively. The alternative is Balkanization, which of course even if permitted would be disastrous.'

'There is an obligation to the princes on our part. I should say that it's been made clear often enough that we recognize it.'

'Well. Come. Come. You are all going, aren't you? One day. When? In five years? Ten years? Even five is not long. Perhaps I shan't live to see it. On the whole I hope not, because when you go the princes will be abandoned. In spite of all your protestations to the contrary. They will be abandoned. I have told Nawab Sahib so. He pretends not to believe it. I show him the map. I point to the tiny isolated yellow speck that is Mirat and to the pink areas that surround it which are the provinces directly ruled by the British. Since India passed under the Crown, I say to him, you have relied on the pink bits to honour the treaty that allows the yellow speck to exist. But you cannot have a treaty with people who have disappeared and taken the crown with them. The treaty will not be torn up but it will have no validity. It will be a piece of paper. A new treaty will have to be made with the people who have taken the pink parts over from the British. You will have to negotiate a new treaty with Mr Gandhi and Mr Nehru. You can forget Mr Jinnah because even if he gets Pakistan it will be so far away from you that it will be meaningless. So you will have to bargain for the continuing existence of the yellow speck which is Mirat with Mr Nehru and the Congress High Command. Nawab Sahib smiles. He can see it as clearly as I can see it – the form such bargaining might take. But he smiles also at what he likes to persuade himself is my simplicity. No, Dmitri, he says, we have supplied the British with money and men in two world wars. And there are over five hundred little yellow specks, and some not so little. The British are pledged to protect our rights and our privileges and our authority. I nod my head. I say, this is true, Nawab Sahib. But they are pledged as well one day to hand over *their* rights and privileges and authority to Mr Gandhi and Mr Nehru. They are pledged in two directions but can only go in one. Nawab Sahib smiles again. That, Dmitri, is where they are so cunning. He does not say what cunning he sees. He knows that if he puts it into words his illusion of it will collapse. So the words will not come. But in his mind he tells himself that the pledge to Mr Gandhi and to Mr Nehru cannot be fulfilled because of the pledge to the princes, or that it can only be fulfilled if the princes agree that it should be and that the princes will only agree if their territories are first secured to them in perpetuity. Therefore, my dear Captain Rowan, with Nawab Sahib adopting this reverent attitude to his piece of paper, you will appreciate that I am very much alone in this business of working and planning for the most advantageous position for my prince. And because I need peace and quiet to work and plan I do not welcome venerable gentlemen from Mayapore, or any of their like from wheresoever, who seek to cause the sort of unrest which our future masters will point to as proof that Nawab Sahib's subjects groan under the yoke of an iron, archaic dictatorship. A Muslim dictatorship at that. I do not welcome venerable gentlemen from Mayapore, because in their wake, in their footsteps, springing up like sharp little teeth, are these dark young men of random destiny and private passions – destinies and passions that can be shaped and directed to violent ends.'

Rowan nodded, leaving Bronowsky to guess what opinion he himself held about the future of the states. Since he had

accepted Malcolm's invitation to officiate at the transfer of
Mohammed Ali Kasim to the protection of the Nawab, he had
been checking on Mirat's status. There was no political agent
actually resident in the state. Mirat's relationship with the
crown was conducted through the Resident in Gopalakand
and this was old Robert Conway, whom Rowan knew only by
reputation. It had surprised him a bit when Lady Manners
mentioned him as an old friend of hers. Holding a high
opinion of Lady Manners he decided there was probably more
warmth in Conway than people usually admitted, but even
she had described him as an unemotional man with rigid
views. Bronowsky would not find it easy to communicate
with him, nor – Rowan imagined – was Conway a man who
would encourage Bronowsky in what he called his search for
the most advantageous position for his prince. From what
Rowan heard of Conway he suspected the Nawab would be
encouraged to believe that he would be abandoned only over
Conway's dead body and the dead bodies of every member of
the Political Department.

'Well,' he said, 'let's hope the venerable gentleman stays
clear. Some other time you must tell me about the stone. It
does seem a bit far-fetched to go to all that trouble. I suppose
he's safe now.'

'Who?'

'Miss Layton's friend – Merrick.'

'Frankly I doubt he was ever in much danger. Harming a
white man in this country is a hazardous occupation. But I
agree he's probably safe from further persecution, if only
because he's probably long since served his most useful
purpose from Pandit Baba's point of view. His own purpose –
well – that is another matter. And who can say what is the
purpose of a man like that?'

Rowan stretched. 'Perhaps just to do his job.'

'Few men have aims as simple as that.'

'Are he and Miss Layton old friends?'

'As I remember they met only at the wedding. He wasn't
even a close friend of the bridegroom. What you might call a
last-minute substitute for a best man who was ill. No one
knew he was the Merrick in the Bibighar Gardens case until
the wedding-day. He'd kept it dark, but it came out then

because of the stone and because I identified him at once directly I heard this Captain Merrick had been in the Indian Police. The stone, by the way, hit the poor bridegroom. Why do you ask?'

'Only that she seemed such a nice girl and that it would be tough on her if they're committed to one another.'

'Committed to one another?'

'Engaged, for instance.'

'Tough on her because of his lost left arm?'

'She didn't strike me as the sort of girl who would back out, and it would be hard on her, wouldn't it?'

'Oh, I agree. I doubt that Miss Layton would back out. But such a thing hadn't occurred to me.' With the ebony cane clasped in both hands he raised it to his chin and put his head back, gazed at the ornate ceiling. 'Committed. Such a thing hadn't occurred to me. There would hardly have been time for such a relationship to develop when they were in Mirat and no opportunity for it to have done so since, except by correspondence. No. I doubt there could have been time for a relationship of that nature even to begin, even if everything else had been normal.'

Tapping his chin with the silver knob of the cane Bronowsky continued to contemplate the view above his head. Rowan waited.

'But I see why it might occur to you,' Bronowsky went on. 'That she was just back from a long journey undertaken for the reasons she gave but also for her own private emotional satisfaction.'

The ceiling ceased to interest him. He looked at Rowan but still tapped his chin.

'Let us hope you are wrong. It would be a somewhat one-sided affair, I should say. Unless, in Mirat, I was mistaken, which is always possible.'

'Mistaken in what?'

'In my assumption that he didn't really like women.'

Rowan said nothing.

'It is what makes the Mayapore case interesting. It was interesting from the beginning but in a rather cliché-ridden way. Well, there was this girl, this poor Miss Manners, recently out from England, untutored in and unsympathetic

185

to the rigid English social system here. Good-natured and intelligent – a little like Miss Layton but in comparison with her an innocent abroad, so far as India was concerned. For a time she lives with her aunt Lady Manners in Rawalpindi, a liberal-minded old lady whose husband once governed Ranpur and incurred the hostility of the die-hards with his pro-Indian policies. Nowadays the old lady has almost more Indian friends than she has British, they say. Her niece, this Miss Manners, is invited by one of them, a Lady Chatterjee, to stay with her in Mayapore where the social structure is even tighter and more provincial than in Rawalpindi. And in Mayapore she becomes friendly with an Indian boy. Not one who moves in the small official circle of socially acceptable Indians but one out of the black town. Cliché number one. The princess and the pauper, but with a racial variation on the theme. And then there is cliché number two: the boy although now a pauper is really a gentleman, brought up in England entirely and educated at an English public school. A family misfortune alone accounts for his presence on the wrong side of the river, from which from time to time he ventures into the cantonment in the capacity of a humble reporter for the local English language newspaper. The friendship with Miss Manners ripens but almost clandestinely because there are so few places where she can go that he can go. But she is impatient of these artificial barriers, so they are noticed together. She is warned against the association. She ignores the warning but the friendship is now under a strain. In other words, cliché number four. And then, what really is the boy after? Cliché number five. The warning proves more than merited, or so it would seem. One night she is attacked and assaulted. She swears she did not see her attackers. Later she swears that although she did not see them she knows who they were not – not in other words the kind of boys who have been arrested who of course include her young Indian friend. Who in Mayapore doubts though, or doesn't guess who led them? Certainly the head of the police does not doubt. Within an hour of her return home after the assault her boyfriend and his companions were in custody. But now comes cliché number six. The head of the police himself has a regard for Miss Manners of an even tenderer kind than he would feel for any girl of his own race who gets into trouble. How tender a regard? No one is sure but it is whispered that he loves her or loved her once and was spurned. He does not actually deny it. In confidence he will tell you that his erstwhile regard for Miss Manners made it that much more difficult for him to keep a properly detached view and ensure that all his actions are performed dispassionately in the service of justice. Such manly frankness is appealing. If in the past there were people who had marked him down as not quite pukka, as not really out of what you English call the top drawer, they admit that in this business his behaviour has been impeccable as well as energetic. So the story seems to go, proving yet again that if fact is no stranger than fiction it is just as predictable. But did the story go like that? I think not quite. When I met him I talked to him at length and as we talked I got this other impression that Miss Manners had never really interested him at all, that he had scarcely noticed her until her association with the Indian boy had begun, and that he could not avoid noticing her then because he had had his eye on the young man for a long time. The young man was an obsession, an absolute fixation. Perhaps even Mr Merrick does not fully appreciate all the possible reasons why.' Bronowsky paused. 'Perhaps that is cliché number seven. At least in life if not in tales. Cliché number eight is that with a job to do in a few hours from now you should get some rest. I will ask the steward to wake you at 4.15, shall I?'

'Thank you.' Rowan reached for his briefcase.

'I hope it isn't only good manners that have kept you up. For me sleep is a waste of time, it being my seventieth birthday, although strictly speaking that was yesterday. I've enjoyed our talk. I shall cheat for a few hours more, drink some more champagne and read Pushkin.'

As Rowan got up Bronowsky said, 'You'd better disregard what I said, unless the question of those boys ever crops up at Government House. I hate to think of them lying forgotten in some inhospitable jail, if they were innocent. I do hope you are wrong, by the way.'

'Wrong?'

'About Miss Layton's reasons for going so many miles to see the wounded hero. I believe he has a number of admirable

187

qualities but none of them strikes me as likely to promote the cause of anyone else's happiness. Not even his own. He is one of your hollow men. The outer casing is almost perfect and he carries it off almost to perfection. But, of course, it is a casing he has designed. This loss he has sustained – the left arm – even this fits. If he regrets the loss, presently he will see that he has lost nothing or anyway gained more in compensation. What an interesting thought. I am tempted to say that had he not suffered the loss he might one day have been forced to invent it.'

Rowan smiled. 'To the extent of removing part of a limb?'

Bronowsky laughed.

'But absolutely!'

For a while he gazed at Rowan and then said sedately: 'I speak metaphorically, naturally.'

V

Bathed and dressed Rowan went back to his sitting-room. Jaiprakash poured him the second routine whisky-soda, the one he used to wash down the evening dose of pills. He picked up the telephone and asked for the Pankot number. The operator said he would ring him back when a priority call on the Pankot line had been cleared: probably in ten minutes. He asked to be put through to the mess steward. He ordered a tray and a tankard of beer. He did not feel like going into the dining-room. He then rang the signals office and checked how long he had to get a package down to go in the night bag to Area Headquarters in Pankot. The answer was an hour and a half to be on the safe side.

The telephone rang almost as soon as he'd put down the receiver. He picked it up again. Through atmospherics he heard the male operator in the exchange downstairs saying that the Pankot number was on the line and distantly a woman's voice saying 'Hello? Hello?' The crackling ceased abruptly. The connection sounded a good one. He asked to speak to Miss Sarah Layton.

'Speaking.'

'Sarah, this is Nigel. Nigel Rowan.'

'Oh, hello.'

'I got your letter.'

'That was quick.'

'I've done what you asked.'

'Already? How good of you.'

'I'm sorry to ring. Is it inconvenient?'

'No, of course not.'

But she sounded a little guarded.

'I thought I should let you know what I intend to do. If it's all right just say yes. It was only a matter of collecting some envelopes and a package. I'll get them done up and sent in the bag tonight to Area Headquarters. I don't think there's anything important. The Reverend Mother said you may decide to throw the lot away. I've rung just to make sure you knew to be on the look-out for them. If I mark the package private and personal will it reach you without any problems?'

'Yes, that would be fine. I'm awfully grateful.'

'She's nice, isn't she? The Reverend Mother.'

'Yes. Just vague on the phone.'

'How are things?'

'Pretty good.'

'I'm longing to hear about the party. The one in Bombay where the drinks got locked up.'

'Oh, the Maharanee's.' She laughed, sounding relieved to get off the subject of Miss Batchelor. 'If there's such a person. She didn't put in an appearance.'

'Which Maharanee was she supposed to be?'

'I'm not sure Count Bronowsky ever told us. He referred to her as Aimee.'

'Aimee? Was this at a place called Sea Breezes on the Marine Drive?'

'Yes. Do you know her?'

'She's the ex-Maharanee of Kotala. Has Bronowsky known her long?'

'I got that impression.'

'The old Machiavelli.'

'Why?'

'We talked about the Maharajah in June last year, the night you and I first met. He never mentioned knowing the ex-wife.

189

Kotala was the Maharajah I was telling you about a few weeks ago. The one my uncle had the trouble with.'

'Really? I wish I'd met her.'

'She's someone I try to avoid.'

'But you've been to the flat in Bombay?'

'No, only to her place in Delhi. I remember the name Sea Breezes because she was always sending notes from there when I was in Bombay with HE last Christmas. I thought Sea Breezes rather funny because she has a reputation for being hermetically sealed-in whereever she goes.'

'The flat was breezy enough.'

'Perhaps the room she was hiding in wasn't. She told me in Delhi she hated fresh air, light, the sound of doorbells and talking on the telephone and that her idea of true repose would be to have a magic wand to conjure up a party and make it disappear when she was fed up with it. You were lucky only having the drinks locked up. When she was Kotala's wife they say she kept a tame leopard and made it snarl to order. It could empty the palace of unwanted guests in one minute flat. When it bit one of his favourite girlfriends he sued for divorce. He wanted to cite the leopard as co-respondent but decided not to because it was a female leopard and people said he'd only be able to accuse it of alienation of affections.'

'Oh, Nigel.'

He smiled. 'It's true.'

'You're making me think your uncle was right after all. Actually she did have a sort of leopard, but he was on our side and warned us about the drinks being locked up. So we beat a dignified retreat before it happened. He was rather nice. His name was Perron.'

'Perron? Don't tell me he was a sergeant in the French Army.'

'He had two different uniforms, but he was a sergeant in both of them, yes.'

'Whatever is she up to? Raising an army? Anyway she's got her history mixed up. She's a Rajput not a Mahratta. The Rajputs weren't a bit keen on Sergeant Perron.'

'You know all about him too?'

'The Perron who succeeded De Boigne.'

'His real name was Pierre-Cuiller.'

'Was it? I don't think I knew that. Oddly enough we had a Perron at school. I was told to chastise him once for persistent slackness at games. The consensus of House opinion was that his incompetence on the playing field was a deliberate exhibition of eccentricity and the unpleasant task of persuading him to conform fell to me.'

'You mean you had to cane him?'

'I'm afraid so.'

'He was in Bank's, then?'

'That's right.' Rowan hesitated. 'I don't remember telling you which house I was in. What are you laughing at?'

'The picture of you caning Perron.'

'He thought it was rather funny too.'

'Did it improve his games?'

'No. He warned me it wouldn't. Actually I'm exaggerating. Violence wasn't necessary. I was supposed to apply corrective methods but he and I decided the best thing would be to talk it over. He told me he found team sports awfully depressing, all that waiting around at cricket on the one hand and what he called the incomprehensible hurly-burly of football on the other. Fortunately I'd discovered through another source that he rowed quite a bit during the holidays. We weren't a rowing school but there was a local canoeing and sculling club in the town so I got permission for him to join and that suited him down to the ground because it got him out of the school and off by himself on the river. When I last saw him he would have been about seventeen, but nearly six feet tall and with shoulders like an ox.'

'When was that, Nigel?'

'The same occasion I was telling you about at the party Hugh Thackeray took us to – when I visited the school between finishing at Sandhurst and coming out here.'

'And watched Hari Kumar playing cricket?'

'Yes.'

'He said he didn't remember Kumar.'

'Who said he didn't remember Kumar?'

'Sergeant Perron.'

'Sergeant Perron?'

'The Sergeant Perron who was at the Maharanee's party. The one who tipped us off about the drinks being locked up. I was only joking when I called him the Maharanee's leopard. He's a sergeant in Field Security. He came back with us and met my father and they talked about Bank's and Coote's. He remembered you but pretended not to remember Kumar.'

'A sergeant in Field Security?'

'At the Maharanee's he was a sergeant in Education. But when I first met him he was in Field Security.'

'You've met him twice?'

'Twice on the same day.'

'In one day he switched from Field Security to Education?'

'Education was only a disguise. I suppose I oughtn't to talk about it on the phone.' She sounded amused.

'Sarah, what *are* you talking about?'

'About your old friend Perron.'

'It can't be the same one.'

'Well he was over six foot. He looked like an oarsman. He remembered you. He remembered your first name. In fact he remembered you quite clearly. And still being only a sergeant is rather eccentric so obviously he hasn't changed. Does that convince you?'

'But he didn't remember Coomer.'

'Pretended not to.'

'Why should he do that?'

'I think probably Ronald could tell you.'

'Ronald? Ronald Merrick?' After a moment he said, 'Where does he fit in?'

'Sergeant Perron is going to work for him.' She added, 'I got the impression he wasn't very keen.'

'What made you think so?'

'The look on his face whenever Ronald ordered him to do anything. In fact I think he'll try to get out of it. I'm sorry. He was nice. He would have been an asset in that particular sphere. I'd better let you get on. I may get down to Ranpur again in a few weeks because daddy says he may be going. I'll let you know shall I? Unless you've gone by then. Have you had any news?'

'No. None.'

'It was awfully good of you to see the nuns. You must have been pretty busy if the *daftar* here is anything to go by.

They've been at sixes and sevens ever since they heard Mr Kasim's coming up to attend his old secretary's funeral.'

'Oh, why, particularly?'

'In case he takes the opportunity to make some sort of political announcement. There are quite a lot of people crowding in. Some are already camping out near the station.'

'Old Mahsood was a Pankot man.'

'But the police think it's MAK they're coming to see.'

'A popular demonstration or just taking *darshan*?'

'Taking *darshan*, we hope. Has there been any trouble in Ranpur?'

'Just a few crowds, directly it leaked that he was on his way from Mirat with old Mahsood's coffin.'

'Is Ahmed with him?'

'Not to my knowledge. Isn't he still in Bombay?'

'That was a week ago. The police here think it's going to be more like a political meeting than a Muslim funeral. They've drafted in men from Nansera.'

'I don't think they need worry. He was very devoted to old Mahsood. Bringing the body home is a mark of respect, I should say. If not he wouldn't have been at such pains to tell us what he was doing and ask for what amounts to official protection from excessive curiosity. That's probably the real reason why there are extra police.'

'Oh well. So much for that rumour. But people here are so used to nothing happening they'll probably be disappointed when it doesn't. I shan't be. It suits father as it is.'

'I'm glad he's better. Is there anything else I can do for you? Anything for your father, for instance?'

'Nothing I can think of, but thank you.'

'Let me know if there is. I'm afraid I've been keeping you. Look after yourself.'

'And you. Oh, and remember me to Hugh Thackeray.'

'I will.'

When they had rung off he collected together the envelope and package the Reverend Mother had given him. It seemed absurd to think of her actually having them in her hands tomorrow morning. The package, which contained something hard like a book and something soft, some sort of material, was inscribed: *In the event of my death: Dear Sarah.*

The envelope, inscribed by a different hand, probably the Reverend Mother's, was marked 'Oddments' and seemed to contain papers and other envelopes.

He put both the package and the envelope into a large manila envelope, sealed it and addressed it to Sarah at Area Headquarters, Pankot. The telephone rang. He picked it up immediately, thinking she might have remembered something important and rung back.

'Nigel?' It was Hugh Thackeray on the internal line.

'Oh, hello. Well. How was Delhi?'

'Like Delhi. More to the point, how is Pankot? I've been trying to get you but they said you were talking to Pankot. The fair Miss Layton, would it be?'

Hugh was still very young.

'It would. She asked to be remembered to you.'

'Very nice of her but quite unnecessary. I was thinking about her anyway. On your behalf, I hasten to add. What are you doing?'

'Nothing right now. I'm off-duty.'

'I know. But you're not under the weather, are you?'

'Not in the least. Why?'

'They tell me you've ordered a tray.'

'And a tankard of beer.'

'They kept that dark. I was a bit worried. I imagined something more on invalid lines. HE would like a word.'

'Right.'

'I mean over here in the study. Shall I tell him five minutes?'

'Yes, I'll come right over.' He hesitated. 'Any news?'

'What news did you have in mind?

'From Tokyo, say?'

'We think they're still agonizing about how to surrender unconditionally on condition that the Emperor remains sacrosanct. I can't think why he doesn't commit *hara-kiri*.'

'I don't think sons of heaven can. Any suggestions about which subject I could usefully mull over on the way down?'

A moment's silence. Then: 'MAK perhaps?'

'Right.'

He replaced the phone. He had hoped for something else, something more personal. He called Jaiprakash, told him where he was going. He took the envelope down to the signals office and then crossed over to the east wing. Here there were several people in the main hall: General Crawford and his *aide* – a slim and handsome Sikh in a pale blue turban – the Deputy Inspector-General of Police; old MacRoberts, the senior Member of Council, with Henderson of the Finance Department and his pale and angular wife who caught his eye and smiled; Mrs Saparawala and Doctor Bannerji, the Member for Education, and another fellow *aide* of Rowan's, Bunny Mehta. Some of them had been at Ranagunj airfield to meet the Governor. All except Bunny were on their way home, awaiting cars, calm among the servants who were coming and going intermittently. Rowan made for the narrow corridor to the private staircase: a spiral enclosed by wrought-iron that took him up to the small landing on the first floor and a green baize door through which he passed into the lobby of the air-conditioned private quarters. Here the public grandeur of pillars and black and white tiled floors, of busts on plinths and of immense potted palms in brass bowls, gave way to homelier oak-panelling and thick Turkey carpeting. With its magazine-cluttered central table, leather chairs and sofas set around the walls, it always reminded him of a doctor's waiting-room.

Priscilla Begge, looking both competent and harassed (he had never quite worked out how she managed to convey at one and the same time such apparently mutually exclusive qualities) was standing with her hockey-player's legs astride next to the little corner desk, talking on the telephone, watched by the two duty-bearers whose job was to ensure that the lobby was never unmanned. She gave Rowan a smile of welcome and a frown of pained exasperation, put her hand over the mouthpiece and stage-whispered, 'You can cross off –' then uncovered the mouthpiece and went on with her conversation but made a pleading (also commanding) gesture with her free hand, which he supposed meant she wanted him to wait. The door to the room of private audience opened and Hugh Thackeray looked in. He grinned at Rowan and then mouthed something at Priscilla who turned her back irritably and said, 'Will you repeat that please?' as if Hugh had distracted her.

195

'Poor old Bully-Off,' Hugh said when he and Rowan were alone in the empty audience room. 'Lady M's not well again and HE wants her to go down to Ooty to decide what's best to be done. Hang on here a moment. I'll just make sure he's ready.'

Thackeray went back into the study and shut the door. Rowan stood by the uncurtained window, looked down into the darkened grounds. He felt sorry for Priscilla. Much as she adored Lady Malcolm whose cousin she was, as well as secretary, and much as she loved the crisp healthy air of Ootacamund, her sense of duty, and the obligation she felt she was under to hold the fort during Lady Malcolm's frequent illnesses and absences, always made an order such as Malcolm had just given her seem to her like an instruction to abandon her post. Not that she saw herself as indispensable. Priscilla only lost her harassed look when Lady Malcolm was in residence and then it was replaced by one of thankfulness and hearty devotion. Rowan liked her because she had virtually no notion of her own capabilities. It was as if she could never quite credit it that she got anything right. The senior women in Ranpur who found themselves co-opted to act as hostess at Government House when poor Louise Malcolm struggled asthmatically for breath or retired to the one place in India that turned out to suit her affected to be amused by but never impatient of old Bully-Off's indefatigable efforts to help them to endure a rôle that actually gave them pleasure to assume. Malcolm had once said to him, 'If Priscilla could only stop thinking of herself as a prefect and start seeing herself as Head Girl what a good Governor's wife she would make.' But that Priscilla could never do. It was against her nature. On the night she was told that her name was on the next Honours List for an MBE all the colour left her face and for a day or two she had seemed pre-occupied, as by intimations of some kind of lost innocence.

He turned from the window at the moment Thackeray opened the Library door. He nodded. As Rowan passed through Thackeray whispered, 'See you later, maybe. I'm going to hold Priscilla's hand and assure her that everything will be all right so long as we remember we're a team. Aren't I a tease?'

The Governor was at the far end of the room where the desk – already cluttered – was angled to take light from one of the tall windows. The desk-lamp was on but Malcolm was standing gazing out of the window, as Rowan had been a few moments before, hands behind back, holding his horn-rimmed spectacles. He was in dressing-gown, slacks and slippers.

Rowan said good-evening. Malcolm turned round and smiled and went to the desk, putting on his spectacles.

'How was New Delhi, sir?'

'New Delhi?' He sat and rummaged. 'New Delhi. Here we are.' But whatever he had looked for and found he then seemed to lose interest in. He sat back, removed the glasses and rubbed the bridge of his nose. 'New Delhi. Very bad for one's sense of proportion, New Delhi.' He put the glasses back on and started making notes on a memorandum pad. 'Have a drink, Nigel. I'll have one too if you'd be so kind.'

Rowan crossed over to the area in front of the fireplace. Three sofas were arranged round it. The live-coal effect was on below the unused elements of an ornate electric fire. The drinks tray was set out on the main sofa-table. The light from the fire was caught in the facets of the cut-glass decanters. An illusion of cosiness. The air-conditioning hummed gently. The private rooms could strike uncomfortably chilly. The imaginary live fire was Priscilla Begge's idea. She said it cheered one up. He poured whisky for himself and Malcolm his usual brandy. No ice for either of them. Not too much soda. He took the drinks to the desk and set the Governor's on a cork mat next to a square cut ashtray. Malcolm nodded his thanks but continued writing his memorandum.

'Be with you in a tick,' he said presently. 'Do sit down. I'm sorry about this by the way, you're supposed to be off, aren't you? Off. Making hay. That's it, then.' He threw down the pencil, looked at what he had written, pushed the pad aside, reached for his glass and said, 'Cheers.'

'Cheers.'

'Well now. New Delhi.'

'Interesting developments, sir?'

'Confirmation of assumptions.'

'Elections?'

'Yes. War virtually over, so – elections. To the central legislature first, then in the provinces.'

'When sir?'

'When do we do anything in this country if there's a choice?'

'In the cold weather?'

Malcolm was playing with the horn-rimmed spectacles. 'The cold weather. How comforting it always sounds. Never do today what you can put off until the weather cools down.'

'I suppose it's soon enough in this case. And elections are what everybody seems to want.'

'Quite. Jinnah wants them. Nehru wants them. Even we poor overworked provincial Governors want them. Some of course more than others. Most important of all the fount of all wisdom in Whitehall wants them. I suppose we ought to be worried. Such universal agreement.'

'And the Viceroy, sir?'

'Oh, yes. Wavell wants them. What man could fail to seize the opportunity of at last doing something which everyone approves of? He'll announce the decision to hold elections in a week or two, and then pop off back to London to make sure everyone is talking about the same thing, and that the British Government understands that an election in India is rather different from one at home at any time of year.'

'Will there be an extended franchise?'

Malcolm smiled and put the spectacles back on. 'Heaven forbid. That would take two cold weathers. Central legislature first, then the provinces that have responsible ministries, after that our kind, in Section 93. How does that strike you?'

After a moment Rowan replied, 'It strikes me as rather problematical in regard to Section 93 provinces.'

'Elucidate.'

'Constitutionally, you'll have to dissolve the existing legislature before calling for new elections. It wasn't the elected legislature that resigned in 1939. Only Mr Kasim and his colleagues resigned. From the ministry.'

'Quite. What's your point?'

'Only that constitutionally there's no difference between provinces where ministries still exist as a result of the 1937

198

elections – most of them Muslim majority and Muslim League provinces – and provinces where ministries don't exist because they were Congress ministries and resigned when Congress told them to resign. In the provinces where ministries as well as legislatures still exist the assemblies will be dissolved by due process, prior to new elections. In Section 93 provinces the Governors will have to order dissolution.'

'Well, that's because Section 93 provinces are under Governor's rule. Are you suggesting that I can't dissolve the existing assembly which exists virtually only on paper, without inviting Mr Mohammed Ali Kasim kindly to reform his ministry first?'

'I'm not saying you can't, sir, obviously. I'm wondering whether it's wise.'

'I'm under no constitutional obligation to recall Mr Kasim.'

'The Viceroy was under no obligation to release certain political leaders from jail last June. But he could hardly have held the Simla conference without doing so.'

'A thoroughly bad analogy. But of course, I thoroughly agree with you.'

'Oh.' Used as he had become to Malcolm's habit of arguing aloud for the opposition he was often uncertain what the Governor actually believed himself. 'May I ask why you agree, sir?'

'I'd prefer to hear your own reasons first.'

Rowan smiled. 'Well, I suppose the idea of elections at this stage is to inspire confidence and create an atmosphere of letting bygones be bygones.'

'One can do that without reverting to a bygone status quo.'

'But if you don't revert to it the Congress will be at a disadvantage.

'They may think so ...'

'Isn't it what they may think that will count? It's not our fault their ministries resigned in the provinces and not our fault that the ministries that stayed were predominantly Muslim, nor our fault that nowadays that virtually means Muslim League. But the fact is that the League will go into the elections with all the advantages usually enjoyed by a party already in ministerial power while the Congress will have to fight from scratch with all the disadvantages of a party that has been proscribed, its members imprisoned and its funds largely sequestrated. They might interpret the failure to invite them to reform provincial ministries as a first step to new elections as proof that we secretly sympathize with the Muslims and the idea of Pakistan and are still set on punishing Congress for non-co-operation in the war.'

Malcolm pushed the spectacles down his nose and looked at Rowan over the rims. 'I advanced the same arguments myself but with more tactful allowance for the hostility they were bound to arouse. Unfortunately I couldn't answer the logical and inevitable question.'

'What question, sir?'

'The question what I thought Mr Kasim's response to such an invitation would be in the unlikely event of it being agreed I should extend one.' He pushed the glasses back on. 'How would you have answered that?'

'I suppose by saying I'd find out the moment it was agreed I should try.'

'That wouldn't have been an answer. The question was, what do you *think* he would say? And the answer is that one simply doesn't know. One has so little idea that one suspects he might decline as easily as accept and that he would decline because an invitation like that would force him to show his hand, and that he isn't ready to do that yet. And if one is the least anxious, as I am, to see Mohammed Ali Kasim again heading a Congress ministry in Ranpur one is disinclined to do anything that will force him into a false position. So I am perfectly content to fall in with consensus opinion and let provinces under Governor's rule remain so until after the elections. One doesn't even know whether MAK will stand again, or for which party, or if he stands for his old constituency he now has a chance of holding it against the League. One knows absolutely nothing of his present intentions, let alone of his future prospects. One knows nothing about his attitude to his elder son, either.'

Malcolm took the glasses off, picked up his brandy and held it at eye-level as if examining the colour and clarity of the liquid. Then he drank it down.

'And not knowing has become onerous. By the way, I'm losing you.'

'What, sir?'

'They're taking you back into the Political Department. One of the Crown Rep's people mentioned it and said I could tell you. I won't say I'm sorry because I know you'll be pleased. I'll miss you though. You'll get instructions in about a week's time.'

'Did he say anything about where?'

'No. You've done your probation so I should think they'll put you in as assistant at one of the Residencies, wouldn't you?'

'So long as it isn't Frontier Tribes.'

'He asked how fit you honestly were now. So I said you were blooming. Are you? Young Thackeray seems to think you ought to have a spot of leave before you go. He was under the very odd impression that a few days in Pankot would have a therapeutic effect on your liver.'

'Oh?'

'But I suppose he only said that because he was afraid of being sent himself.'

'Sent himself? To Pankot?'

'Pankot's where I'm told Mr Kasim is to be found in the next day or so. I want you to go up tonight, see him as soon as you can and give him the letter I've written. After that I want you to do whatever is necessary to persuade him to arrange the earliest possible private meeting with me, preferably here, but I shan't absolutely insist. I'm sending V. R. Gopal with you. They're rooting him out now. Don't worry about the bandobast, it's being coped with. All you have to do is pack and be ready by eleven-thirty. Is that all right?'

'Of course, sir.'

'Sorry it's such short notice but I don't want him slipping the net and turning up in Bombay or 'Pindi or Lahore or even back in Mirat before I've had a chance to talk to him.'

'I take it you rule out exerting official pressure?'

'To cause him to appear? Yes, I do.'

'Is he expecting the letter?'

'Possibly. I got Hunter-Evans to ring his house. His new secretary said he was resting because he was going up by car tonight.'

'The car's a new idea. Presumably the coffin still goes by train.'

'Yes, I think Hunter-Evans said it did.'

'And Mr Kasim wouldn't come to the phone himself.'

'He was resting.'

'Perhaps he'll ring back once he's rested.'

'Aren't you keen to go?'

'Perfectly keen, sir. I was just thinking of short-cuts. Obviously there aren't any. How do I and Gopal travel?'

'By train. They're putting on the special coach so you should have every comfort. A car from Area Headquarters will meet you in Pankot and take you up to the Summer Residence guest house. All that's laid on.'

'What's Gopal's rôle exactly?'

'Go-between. He and Kasim have always had a great respect for one another as you know. You'd better wear mufti incidentally.'

'I take it I don't hand the letter to anyone but MAK?'

'Preferably not. I leave it to your discretion. If Kasim can't or won't see you then Gopal will have to give it to him. He'll be involved with the funeral most of tomorrow, but get Gopal off to try and contact him directly you arrive. Gopal was an old friend of Mahsood's too. He can melt into the background without arousing anyone's curiosity. I shan't provide you with a copy of the letter but you'll have a separate sheet of notes for guidance which might help if MAK asks questions you feel you have to answer to get him to agree to a meeting.'

'Will Gopal be as fully informed?'

'No. My approach to Kasim is personal and in one way I may be sticking my neck out. It's nothing to do with inviting him to form a ministry before the elections, though.'

Rowan looked at his watch.

Malcolm said, 'You'd better go and get packed. I'll send the letter and notes up. Ring down if there's anything you want clarifying. And ring me from Pankot tomorrow night to say how things look.'

'You'll be rather busy tomorrow night, sir. You've got the reception and dinner for Chakravarti.'

'So I have. And the foundation stone ceremony later in the week. You'd better take a copy of the days' arrangements in case MAK asks you to suggest a time. I'll try to fit in but I'd prefer not to cancel the Chakravarti ceremony.'

'The stone-laying? Perhaps Mr Kasim would like to attend, sir.'

'Which day is it?'

'Friday, in the afternoon.'

'Would Chakravarti be offended?'

'Not so long as MAK doesn't steal the scene. Chak's been contributing heavily to secret party funds.'

'And hedging his bets by contributing to the Hindu Mahasabha too, so they say. Perhaps the odd lakh finds its way to the Muslim League as well. After all he's a business man with interests all over India. It's a possibility. By all means suggest it. And ring me tomorrow night however late. If Kasim drives down from Pankot on Thursday, say, I could meet him here on the Friday morning.'

'You have HH of Puttipur until mid-morning.'

'But not for lunch?'

'No, Hugh takes him to the airfield just before midday.'

'Then Kasim and I could lunch here and go on to the ceremony at the college. Separately, naturally.'

'Should I come back with him by car?'

'No.' Malcolm smiled. 'Your job's finished the moment he agrees to a time and place. He'll keep his word. The special coach can be held up there until you ask for it to be coupled on. But let Gopal come back directly neither of you sees any further point in his staying. He can use the coach if you like. You can stay on and relax for a few days. I think you should, don't you? Get some hill air into your lungs. Let's say I shan't expect to see you until a week today. By then instructions ought to be through from Simla or Delhi.'

'That's very good of you, sir.'

'You'd better get a move on, then.'

Rowan stood up. Malcolm had never welcomed references to his wife's frailty but he felt he couldn't leave without saying something.

'Thackeray tells me Lady Malcolm isn't well, I'm very sorry.'

'Yes. Thank you.' He took off his spectacles again and put them down. 'I'm sending Priscilla down.' He stood up and, unexpectedly, came round the desk and put out his hand. Surprised, Rowan clasped it briefly.

'I won't actually say goodbye but I suppose there's always a chance of our not coinciding again. One gets punted around like a bloody football in this job. Thank you for everything you've done, Nigel.'

'Thank you, sir. It's been a very happy and very useful experience.'

'Good. I hope things pan out. Today's rather one of those days when I can't quite see how anything pans out for anybody. It was a real horror, I'm told.'

'What?'

'Hiroshima. Absolutely and inconceivably bloody awful.'

'Unexpectedly so?'

'We shan't have the answer for quite a while. Someone said twenty years. That's food for thought, isn't it? And so is the idea that if a high-ranking Japanese delegation had been persuaded over to the States under a flag of truce to watch them test the thing, they'd have gone back and forced the Emperor to surrender then and there.'

'As impressive as that?'

'According to observers God knows how many miles away from the test area in the middle of the New Mexican desert. It leaves one with a rather humiliating sense of the essential parochialism of one's own concerns.'

'Yes. I suppose. I'd better go and get on with mine. Goodnight, sir.'

'One thing before you go.'

Malcolm thrust his hands into his dressing-gown pockets.

'I've always intended to say this when the time came. In my opinion you're admirably suited for the job you've done and even more for the one you're going to do. We have the same sort of views and much the same sort of way of expressing them to each other. We can gauge each other's thoughts and feelings pretty accurately. But the Indians can't, so easily. Sometimes not at all. I know it's a wretchedly difficult thing and nothing's worse than going to the opposite extreme, relaxing and unbending so much that you don't even convince yourself, let alone them.'

'But you think I need to unbend more than I do, sir?'

204

'It might help. The English manner is a formidable obstacle to mutual understanding between the races. As a young man of your age I used to believe precisely the opposite. But I was confusing mutual understanding with mutual respect and lack of understanding with lack of respect. Take young Thackeray.'

'In what way?'

'He's an awfully kind-hearted boy. Full of fun. Splendid with visiting brass from Eastern Command or GHQ and with young Indian officers like Bunny Mehta. But put him with a handful of senior Indian civilians, any distinguished Indian who's not in uniform, and he's a different fellow. Actually he's terrified of upsetting them or putting a foot wrong. But they don't know that. They look at what to me and you is his rather touching but sometimes exasperating expression of boyish concentration and they interpret it as one of a fully mature sense of racial and class superiority. I don't honestly think he feels that. But the English manner has never been much of a medium for communicating feeling. Sometimes I think that's at the bottom of half our troubles. Wavell's a good example. One of the sincerest and best disposed men who's ever held that wretched post. But also one of the most silent and unbending and outwardly austere. It's the English manner come to perfection. It won't do. And the irony is, Nigel, that at home it's been going out of fashion for years. Rather like one of those strains of indigenous plants that turns out to flower more profusely abroad and withers away in its home soil. Anyway. It's worth bearing in mind.'

He began moving away from the desk to the centre of the room. Level with the sofa table he came to a halt.

'One other thing. This girl in Pankot young Thackeray assured me would make a few days up there quite an attractive proposition for you. Miss Layton.'

'Miss Layton. Yes.'

'The same Miss Layton?'

Rowan nodded.

'Have you heard from her recently?'

'Actually we were on the phone this evening.'

'Anything to do with a havildar of her father's regiment who went over to Bose in Germany?'

205

'No, sir?'

'He's now with a batch of prisoners that came over from Bordeaux, in a camp near Delhi. General Crawford has a letter from Colonel Layton asking to be allowed to see him. Apparently he's the son of a Pankot Rifles Subedar who won the vc in the last war.'

'No, she said nothing about that.'

'Did she refer at all to our friend Merrick?'

'Only in passing. He was in Bombay when she was. I don't know why or for how long.'

'Has Colonel Layton met him?'

'She didn't say so. I imagine he must have done.'

'Is Merrick still in the department that's working up these INA cases?'

'Yes. He hadn't been in it long when she told me about it. That's only six weeks ago. And she and Merrick were at a party in Bombay last week. Ahmed Kasim was there. Merrick told her not to let Ahmed know he was connected in any way with the brother's case.'

'Ah. Well that's one thing. The other thing is Merrick's bound to know about the Pankot Rifles havildar too, presumably. Is he sufficiently in with the family to want to help Colonel Layton have an interview with the man?'

'Probably. In with the family, yes. I don't know about the other thing.'

'No. Perhaps Layton's letter to Crawford indicates he's tried that string and Merrick wouldn't play. Perhaps you'd try to find out. Crawford was going to write back and say there was nothing doing but I've asked him to sit on it for a few days. If Merrick's playing along and pulling strings, let me know. We could pull a few from here. If he's not there isn't a hope. But in that case tell her how sorry I am her father can't see his havildar. He may appreciate knowing that I've been consulted personally by Crawford.'

'Right, sir.'

Malcolm hesitated.

'Is young Thackeray barking up the wrong tree? Perhaps I shouldn't ask. But I can't help wondering. The only times you've mentioned her to me have been to pass on what she's told you about Merrick. Very helpful on that first occasion.

206

Interesting on the second. But I've assumed your interest in her was, what, limited to that subject? The way Thackeray spoke made me feel I've been insensitive.'

'I can't think why you should feel that.'

'No. Well. How much have you told her – about our view of Merrick?'

'Nothing, sir. Nothing specific.'

'Well, that would be difficult. Even if one disregards the element of doubt. But what impression do you have of her attitude?'

'I know she believes he made a mistake in the Kumar case.'

'How did the subject come up?'

'I asked her how the chap she'd visited in hospital was. And she told me he was all right and had gone to Delhi to deal with the INA cases –'

'Yes, I remember that. We were both struck by the idea of Merrick conducting a whole series of interrogations. How did she happen to mention the Kumar case?'

'She said she hoped he wouldn't start every examination of INA men with a preconceived conviction of the man's guilt. We went on from there.'

'Did you tell her you knew Kumar?'

'I only mentioned the school part of it. It interested her because her father went to the same one. She knew Kumar had been brought up and educated in England but hadn't heard definitely where.'

'Why is she so interested in Kumar?'

Rowan had asked himself the same question. He did not know the answer. He could only base an answer on Gopal's: that Kumar was really an English boy with a brown skin and that the combination was hopeless.

'I think she sees him as a man who couldn't have existed without our help and deliberate encouragement. I should say that in quite an impersonal way she thinks of him as a charge to our account – guilty or not guilty. But believing him not guilty makes the charge heavier.'

'She sounds an unusually thoughtful person.'

'Yes, I think she is.'

'Did you tell her he's free?'

'No.'

'So she doesn't know you keep an eye.'

'No.'

'I imagine she'd approve? Well –,' Malcolm smiled, '– I expect you have more than one reason for hiding that particular light. I take it Kumar remains in ignorance too?'

'I hope so.'

'Does he still suspect Gopal's man of being CID?'

'That, or one of Pandit Baba's creatures.'

'The CID still keeps tabs, presumably?'

'Very much so. On Gopal's man, too.'

'Does he mind?'

'Gopal says not.'

'What will you do when you've left Ranpur? Leave everything to Gopal?'

'I shall have to. There's not much to leave.'

'Yes, well, it's a minor matter. How are things with him though?'

'He lives much as you'd expect. Coaching a few students at a few rupees a time.'

'How is the aunt?'

'She still looks after him.'

'Is he as devoted as she deserves?'

'According to Gopal's man, yes.'

'Good.' Malcolm paused. 'I hope we did the right thing, that's all.'

VI

The car, which had been sent first to pick up Vallabhai Ramaswamy Gopal at his home, reached Government House a few minutes after eleven-thirty. Rowan had retrieved the envelope from the Signals Office and had it packed in his case. As he got into the car the old man said, 'Keep away, Nigel. I have a cold you see.' There was a smell of eucalyptus. Having spoken, Gopal clamped a square-folded handkerchief to his nose. He was wearing a grey flannel suit and had a woollen scarf round his neck.

'How did you manage that, VR?'

'I am catching cold easily nowadays. My wife tells me to keep an onion in my pocket. She has these outdated ideas.'

'How is Mrs Gopal?'

Gopal jerked his head. 'Okay. Very angry because I am not taking her to Pankot. She says what is the use of being married to a man who is always rushing off.'

'Are you always rushing off?'

'It is what I ask. When was I rushing off last? To Puri, isn't it, two years ago and who was that with me? But it is useless to talk fact and logic to Lila when she is angry. Please excuse me for bringing so many things.'

Mr Gopal's feet were hidden behind an assortment of luggage and oddments, among them an aluminium tiffin set. Outside on the roof rack he had already noticed a bed-roll and a wooden chest. His own suitcase was being put on.

'While she quarrels with me also she gets the servant to pack this and that. It is best not to argue.'

Rowan had visited the house once. The Gopals' quarrelling was not to be taken seriously. Jaiprakash announced through the open window that the suitcase was safely stowed. As the driver got in Mr Gopal spoke to someone on the other side of the car: a youth. He got in too and sat next to the driver.

'It is my nephew Ashok coming to see me off. Making sure for Lila I am not rushing somewhere I shouldn't be. Ashok, say how do you do to Captain Rowan.'

The boy turned round, ducked his head shyly but formally.

'Ashok is doing his BA here, isn't it, Ashok? But now he is talking of going to Calcutta for BSC.'

'Why Calcutta?'

'It is what we are asking. From Government College he can get BSC also, but no, he is insisting Calcutta. Ashok, tell Captain Rowan what you told Auntie Lila.'

Judging that the boy was too embarrassed to speak Rowan said, 'Perhaps the real question is why not Calcutta?'

'No, no, the question was definitely why Calcutta.' Mr Gopal sometimes took a very literal line. 'And the answer is for physics. Isn't it, Ashok? In Ranpur he tells his Auntie there is no decent teacher in physics. For the past few days it has been physics, physics. You know what the trouble is with him, Nigel? He wishes to be the first Indian to make an atomic bomb. He says only for power and energy but I know what is in his mind. He will blow us all up. And only last week it was Wordsworth and daffodils.'

They were through the west gate heading for the Mall and the western arm of Old Fort Road which would take them the longer but less congested way to the station. The car was now accompanied by two motor-cycle outriders – military police who had been waiting one hundred yards beyond the gate.

'Look Ashok, what a story you will tell your mother and father. Driving from Government House with a motor-cycle escort.' He turned to Rowan. 'Lila said I should not bring him but I said you would not mind.'

'Of course not. But what about getting back?'

'He lives near the station. He is Lila's sister's youngest boy. He was only visiting us. It is a lift home for him very nearly, otherwise I would not have brought him.'

'It's very late.'

'I'm often out as late as this, sir,' the boy said, turning round. 'I shall be perfectly all right.'

Rowan glanced at Gopal, but Gopal had the squared handkerchief covering the lower part of his face.

'You speak English very well, Ashok.'

'Thank you, sir.' He faced front. Again Rowan glanced at Gopal who jerked his head slightly, an affirmative answer to Rowan's unspoken question. 'He has found a very good coach and visits him two three times a week after classes. Other evenings he is attending YMCA and doing Ju-Jitsu. *Mens sana in corpore sano*. Ashok? You know the meaning of this?'

'Yes, uncle.'

'What a bright boy. Now physics. What will be the use of mind or body if you blow us all up? Will your physics cure my cold? What a state we are in. In one pocket the formula for splitting the atom and in the other an onion.'

'Do you know the English cure for cramp, VR?'

'No?'

'A raw potato in the bed.'

Gopal laughed. Ashok looked round, smiling. Rowan thought: I unbend easily enough with Gopal.

He looked out of the window. He remembered the time when neither of them had quite trusted the other. Now they were friends. Before that Rowan had known of him only as a shrewd and conscientious civil servant who was said to owe his position in the Department for Home and Law to Mohammed Ali Kasim. A member of the uncovenanted provincial civil service his advancement might otherwise have been blocked by the preference given to British and Indian members of the august ICS. Rowan didn't know in just what way he had caught MAK's eye when MAK was chief minister but he had been a good choice for the senior position he now held in the secretariat.

They had turned off Old Fort Road and were headed south down the ill-lit Upper Tank Road with the barrack-like PWD buildings in darkness on their left and on their right the grounds of Government College – the principal's bungalow, the playing field, the building-site for the Chakravarti extension, and finally, at the intersection with the brightly lit thoroughfare of Elphinstone Road, the old Victorian Gothic building of the College itself.

The car turned right into Elphinstone Road and was filled with sliding slanting bars of light and shadow. The motor-cycle escort shortened the distance between themselves and the car to mother it through the crowds that walked freely on the road. At the Lux Cinema they were still showing *Jawab*.

'Did you know old Mahsood well, VR?'

'He was not so old. He came to see us when MAK was released from Premanagar and sent to Nanoora in Mirat. He was very upset because he wanted to go too, and Mrs Kasim would not take him because she was afraid he would tell Kasim how ill she had been. When he went Lila said "He says Mrs Kasim is ill, but he is ill also." Then of course Kasim sent for him, so he closed the house up and joined them.'

'He lived in the Kasim household didn't he?'

'Since many years. He was never married. "What do I need with wife and children?" he used to say to Lila. "MAK and Mrs MAK are like brother and sister to me and Sayed and Ahmed are like sons or nephews." It was from Mahsood that Lila and I first heard about Sayed and INA. He said he suspected MAK would not forgive the boy and that this would be terrible for Mrs Kasim.'

'How much do you think is generally known now about Sayed?'

'How much? Or by how many people? Everyone is knowing something. No one is officially knowing anything. This is why the press keeps quiet. It is afraid of libel. Ask Ashok here what the students are saying. Tell Captain Rowan, Ashok, what the students are saying about Lieutenant Sayed Kasim. No? He does not want to say in front of you. The students are calling Sayed a hero because he fought with Netaji's army against the British. They know he has been kept in prison-camp awaiting court-martial ever since he was recaptured in Manipur, but they say he will never be tried because the British are afraid that MAK will conduct the defence himself and bring proof that Indian King's commissioned officers were left in the lurch by their English colleagues when the Japanese invaded Burma. And all things of that sort, isn't it, Ashok?'

'Not all students say this, uncle. Some concentrate on their studies. They aren't interested in Bose. He is only a Bengali.'

'Only a Bengali? You say this, Ashok? Are the physics teachers in Calcutta all non-Bengalis, then?'

'It's not what I say, uncle.'

'Who is saying, then? Your friend Vidyar Awal for one, isn't it? Ashok's friend Vidyar is very anti-Bengali, very anti-Bose. His father is a major in the Engineers and comes from UP. You see how these distinctions arise.'

'Yes, I do.'

Gopal sat forward suddenly.

'What are they doing? They should have gone down Chowpatti. This is the old way to the special shed.'

'That's where we're heading.'

'To avoid crowds? There will be no crowds. Everyone knows MAK has gone up by road now.'

'But you and I are going in the special coach, VR. Didn't they tell you?'

'The special coach? Oh, dear God.'

'HE wanted us to be comfortable.'

'Then we should go third class or in the wagon with poor old Mahsood's coffin. Ashok, you must say nothing to your

212

mother and father about this. Say nothing to anyone. Above all say nothing to your Auntie Lila.'

The boy was grinning. 'Why, uncle?'

'Oh, dear God.'

Rowan smiled, judging that Gopal was not really displeased. The little convoy turned left into the road that would bring them out at the coal and goods-yard area. They were already going past go-downs and repair sheds. Cyclists and car-driver had dipped head-lamps on. The road was not lit except where light fell from the high arc-lamps in the yards of the warehouses. There was a warm smell of drains, the acrid odour of coal and oil. They bumped over an uneven level-crossing. 'Oh dear God,' Gopal said again as if every spasm of discomfort were an indication of sustained discomfort to come. They approached a white post-barrier guarded by railway police. This was raised and the convoy entered an arc-lit cinder-yard and drew up at the entrance to a covered stairway to a covered footbridge. An English officer and an Indian station official were waiting for them. There was a batch of coolies to carry the baggage. The Englishman wore the armband of Movement Control. The Indian wore a sola topee. Rowan got out first. The MCO, not Captain Carter, but a man Rowan didn't know, addressed him as sir and announced that everything was laid on. Gopal was still in the car directing the removal of his hand-luggage. The MCO spoke to his Indian colleague. 'See to that lot, old son.' Then he turned to the staircase as if he expected Rowan to go on ahead.

'Okay, sir?'

'Yes, fine.' Rowan remained where he was. 'Incidentally I'm not a civilian and I don't outrank you. Has it been a problem getting the coach ready at such short notice?'

The MCO looked wary. 'All we had to do was see the thing shunted out of the shed to the side platform. I didn't know what the message meant at first because I didn't know there was a special Government House coach. I've only been here three weeks.'

'There used to be several.'

'Just for the Governor?'

'Governor, staff, secretaries, clerks, files. Government used to go up *en masse* to Pankot every hot weather.'

213

'What happened to the other coaches, then?'

'You've got them in general service. You'd probably have this one too if the interior would adapt.'

'Yes. I looked inside. If you don't mind me saying so I thought it was bloody ridiculous nowadays.'

'It was built for an earlier age.'

'And there's really just the two of you tonight?'

'That's right.'

'The message said two but about four or five servants turned up.'

'That would be about the normal complement.'

'They've been making beds and putting flowers in vases. I thought probably some ladies were coming along.'

'I think the flowers are the usual drill.'

'There's a drill is there?'

'It simplifies things.'

Gopal had emerged now. He carried an umbrella. Ashok held the tiffin-set. The coolies were dividing the luggage up among themselves. Gopal called out to one of them to be very careful with the box because the clasps were unreliable and the box was heavier than it looked. To anyone not knowing Hindi it probably sounded like a complaint. The MCO looked at his watch. On his face was that familiar English expression of utter detachment from an Indian activity. As Gopal and Ashok approached he said to no one in particular, 'Right then.'

He led the way up the staircase to the covered bridge. Their footsteps sounded hollow on the worn and grimy boards. Rowan had never travelled on the special coach himself but he had accompanied Pankot-bound guests from Government House to catch the train on several occasions. The previous MCO, Carter, had appreciated the fact that there *was* a special coach. Most of those who travelled on it had priority passages. Without the coach Movement Control would have found itself turfing passengers out of the ordinary first-class compartments to make room for them.

The covered bridge always reminded him of his schooldays. There had been one at Chadford where he changed trains on the journey between London and Chillingborough. This one smelt much the same, impregnated with decades of engine smoke. Briefly, above the undoubted Indianness of the station at Ranpur, he could imagine himself back at Chadford.

As they came down the stairs the station that was not Chadford presented itself, raw and uncompromising. They were at the front of the train. The special coach stood directly opposite the exit from the covered bridge. It was flanked by two guard's vans, one separating it from the engine, the other from the first of the first-class carriages. Beyond this the train stretched back a couple of hundred yards or more. The platform was crowded but a rope barrier guarded by police kept the area in front of the Governor's coach clear of everyone except people who had business there. Of these there did seem rather a large number.

Gopal was talking to the MCO's Indian colleague, apparently putting Ashok into his care. Two Government House servants stood at the foot of the steps that led to the coach's observation platform, which was also the point of entrance. They saluted Rowan when they caught his eye. The MCO was talking to a British sergeant who had a clipboard of papers. The luggage was going up into the coach. Beyond the barrier charwallahs were collecting money and taking back mugs from hands at windows. Further beyond where the crowds were greatest Rowan could still make out bouncing headloads – the luggage of late arrivals. He wondered where the coffin was and eyed the guardsvan-like coaches which flanked the one he and Gopal were to travel in. And had his suspicions.

'You could help me out, maybe,' the MCO said, arriving with his clipboard at Rowan's elbow. 'I know it's supposed to be sacred territory but I've got six officers in three of the four-persons only compartments and three officers in most of the coupés. Now I've got a GHQ priority who's just come in on the Delhi train.'

'The one due in at 2130?'

'It was ninety minutes late.'

'And you want to put him in the special coach?'

'According to my calculations after you and the Indian gentleman are settled in the two single-berths there's a couple of coupés going spare. Unless of course the servants are travelling in style.'

'What rank is your GHQ priority?'

'Lieutenant-Colonel.'

'That's not senior enough to qualify as a possible exception. But I'll ask Mr Gopal if he has any objection and then see how we're placed. Has Captain Carter been transferred?'

'Carter?'

'The MCO here.'

'I'm the MCO here. The previous chap's name was Carter.'

'Did he hand over to you?'

'He'd gone when I got here. Why?'

'He would have explained the uses and abuses of the special coach.'

'I don't know where abuses comes in.'

'Abuses come in if the coach kept to save Movement Control inconvenience from sudden Government House priorities is treated as a convenient way of solving routine problems of overcrowding. If Mr Gopal and I weren't going up to Pankot tonight the coach wouldn't be on the train.'

'It is on the train.'

'Because we're going up.' Rowan looked at the top paper on the clipboard. 'Is that a copy of the GHQ priority?'

The MCO pulled it from the clip and handed it to Rowan. 'See for yourself.'

Rowan took the paper, the usual carbon copy of a movement order, with an illegible signature – someone signing for an officer of the Advocate-General's branch. Rowan read the text. Then read it again and handed the paper back.

'It says Colonel Merrick is accompanied by a sergeant and a servant. Where are they all at the moment?'

The MCO referred to his own sergeant, who said there was no problem about the servant and that the colonel's sergeant had been 'fixed up'. But the colonel himself was waiting, hoping for something better than a third place in a coupé. He had a disability. The MCO said, 'What sort of disability?'

Rowan broke in. 'I know the officer in question. Just a moment.' He went to Gopal who was lecturing Ashok. 'May I have a word, VR? Let's go in.'

From the observation platform one entered directly into the sitting compartment. The coach had been equipped to look as much like a houseboat on the Dal lake as was possible. The sofa and over-stuffed chairs were covered in chintz. Numdah rugs added to the thickness of an Indian carpet. There were chintz curtains at the windows. A faint smell of sandalwood.

'Oh dear God,' Gopal said yet again. He had brought the tiffin set with him and the umbrella.

Rowan put his briefcase on one of the chairs. 'An interesting situation has arisen,' he began.

'We are to travel in an ordinary compartment?'

'No, they're all full up. The MCO wants us to take some of the overflow.'

'To me this sounds like a confusion. Why do you call it interesting?'

'The overflow happens to be Merrick.'

Slowly the smile and frown of pretended exasperation left Gopal's face. He seemed to take a firmer grip on the umbrella and the tiffin-set, making them look like defensive weapons. Offensive, even.

'Merrick? Ex-Superintendent of Police? Now Major?'

'Major no longer apparently. Lieutenant-Colonel.'

'You have seen him?'

'Not yet. I wouldn't know him by sight anyway. But there's no doubt it's Merrick. Would you object?'

'Object to him travelling with us? Is that open to me? You are His Excellency's chief emissary. It is for you to say.'

'It could be useful.'

'Useful? What could be useful about being with this man?'

'Aren't you in the least curious to see him?'

'Not in the least curious, Nigel. I will have nothing to do with it, but please don't bother about me. They can make up my bunk and I can nurse my cold.'

'The beds are already made up in the two main single berths.'

'No, no. I must have my own bedding. I have it with me. They can put it in one of the old *aide's* coupés. Your Mr Merrick can sleep in His or Her Excellency's berth.'

'We'll have to talk about what we do tomorrow before you go to bed. I'd better tell the MCO it's no go. Obviously you feel strongly.' It surprised Rowan a bit that he did.

'And obviously you want him. You say useful. You are the better judge of this. So let him in. But first let me sort out my

217

sleeping quarters and disappear. If we must talk let us do so in there. And please send Ashok in to say goodbye.'

Gopal went through into the dining-compartment. Rowan returned to the platform and gave Ashok his uncle's message. The MCO was standing with arms folded, his weight on one leg, advertising his patent amusement.

'We'll take Colonel Merrick and his party. The servant will have to muck in with our own but I don't suppose he'll be any less comfortable.'

'You mean you're offering two berths?'

'For Colonel Merrick and his sergeant, yes.'

The MCO's assistant said, 'There's that Major Hemming sir, the one who kicked up a fuss.'

The MCO nodded. 'If it's two berths going spare the answer is two officers, surely. Colonel Merrick and this Major Hemming.'

'The berth's aren't going spare. There's one for Colonel Merrick and one for Sergeant Perron.'

'Is that his name?'

'So it says on the Movement Order.'

'The sergeant's settled in.'

'Then you'll have to unsettle him or squeeze his officer into a coupé.'

'We're due out now.'

'That's up to you. But there'd be no point in bringing Colonel Merrick without the party specified in the movement order. The officer, the sergeant and the servant.'

'You're saying all or nothing?'

'Yes.'

'It beats me.'

As the MCO and his sergeant set off Ashok came down from the coach. Rowan spoke to the Indian official to confirm that he would see the boy safely out of the station. He bade Ashok goodbye, wished him luck in his exams and returned to the sitting-room compartment. The head bearer was putting out bottles and glasses on the marble top of a waist-high mahogany corner cabinet. A miniature brass rail held them secure. He ordered a brandy and soda and presently carried the glass out to the observation platform and placed himself where he could see fairly far down the train. The rope barrier was still in position but a section of it had been opened up. There was a sound of warning whistles. The platform was still crowded. The only Englishwomen he could see were in a group: girls in uniform, QAS, seeing someone off, probably on short leave or on posting up to the General Hospital in Pankot. They had some RAF and American officers in tow and looked merry.

Then they moved in closer to the carriage making room for people to pass: the MCO and an officer whose left arm hung stiffly by his side. Behind them Rowan just made out the tall jungle-green clad figure of a man wearing a green slouch hat and, next to him, someone in a pugree. Luggage bobbed on the heads of the coolies in the rear.

Rowan went back into the coach and drank his brandy down and returned to the observation platform. He went down the steps as the party passed through the opening in the rope barrier.

'Colonel Merrick?'

The man tucked a swagger cane under his left arm. Momentarily Rowan was appalled by the scar-tissue that disfigured the left side of Merrick's face. Sarah had never mentioned that. He took Merrick's right hand, briefly.

'My name is Rowan.' He had been steeling himself to say 'sir'. The word did not come. But he managed the rest of what he'd rehearsed. 'I think we have a mutual friend in Sarah Layton. I already know your sergeant.' Before Merrick could react he turned to Perron. Yes. No mistake. He offered his hand. 'How are you, Guy?'

A little muscle ridged itself on Perron's cheek.

'Fine, thank you, Nigel.'

They shook hands. Rowan readdressed himself to Merrick.

'We'd better sort things out so that the luggage can go in. There's a spare coupé which has its own bath cubicle, and then there's a single berther that's probably more comfortable but it shares washing arrangements with another. There's no one using the coupé.'

'I should be more than content with either,' Merrick said. 'But I do have a certain handicap. The coupé would suit me very well if it's really not wanted. Then I could have my servant in with me. In any case, it's very civil of you.'

'I'll have the luggage put in then. Is this your servant?'

Rowan glanced at the man who stood to one side of Guy Perron. Extraordinary. A cap of gold thread swathed with stiff white muslin, an embroidered waistcoat over a white tunic gathered at the waist by a belt, and baggy white trousers. Into the belt was tucked a miniature axe on a long shaft decorated with silver filigree. The face was clean-shaven but pockmarked. The eyes looked as though they were rimmed with kohl. A bazaar Pathan: handsome, predatory; the kind of man Rowan instinctively distrusted.

'Yes, that's Suleiman,' Merrick said. 'There isn't much luggage. We came in a hurry and fairly light.'

Rowan called over one of the servants from the coach. He gave orders for Merrick's luggage to be placed in whichever coupé wasn't occupied by Mr Gopal.

'What have you got, Guy?'

Perron indicated a kit-bag by his side and a briefcase in his hand. 'Just these.'

'Well we can sort you out later.' He told another bearer to put Perron's kit-bag in the sitting-room. 'I expect you could both do with a drink. Let's go up.' He led the way to the observation platform and stood aside to let Merrick up. Perron waited. Rowan waved him on. When they had both gone up he watched the Pathan follow the porters into the coach at the other end. Then he smiled at Ashok, nodded to the MCO and went into the sitting-room.

Merrick had removed his cap and placed it with the swagger cane on the small table between the two armchairs. He looked younger than Rowan had expected and, by Perron's side, curiously unimpressive. Perron, in this confined area, appeared large and heavily built. The jungle-green uniform added a special note of aggressiveness. His hair was fairer than Rowan remembered and the face, in maturity, less mobile in expression. As a youth Perron had smiled constantly.

'Thank you for taking us in,' Merrick said. 'I imagine it's meant bending the rules a bit.'

'Imperceptibly. What will you have, Colonel Merrick?'

'A whisky would do very nicely, thank you. And perhaps Perron may have one too. Then I think he'd like to get his head down. He's spent most of the past week travelling.'

'There'll be a light supper next door in ten minutes or so,' Rowan said. Warning whistles were being blown. 'What about it, Guy? The MCO said the Delhi train was very late in. Haven't you missed dinner?'

'I haven't had it but I haven't missed it.' Perron's tone was edgy and abrasive. 'Incidentally, no whisky for me. Unless it's Scotch.'

'It is.'

'Really? Well, that fits.'

'Fits what?'

Perron didn't answer. He stiffened his trunk and limbs as if coming to attention. 'With your permission, sir,' he said to Merrick, 'I should like to do as you suggest and get my head down.'

'Shall I continue in custody of the bag, sir?'

'No, leave that here.'

Rowan signalled to a servant in the dining-room and pointed at Perron's kit-bag.

'If you want to tuck down I'll show you where you can settle in.'

The bearer was handing Perron a glass of whisky and soda as Rowan went past him. In the dining-room he paused, heard Perron say, 'Goodnight, sir', and Merrick's reply, 'Goodnight, Sergeant.' The train began to glide forward. When Perron came in, holding his glass, Rowan went to the far door at the right-hand side of the dining compartment and passed through it into the corridor. Merrick's Pathan, on guard outside the farthest coupé, watched him. Rowan slid open the door of No. 1 compartment. The lights were on. His case was on the luggage rack. Perron followed him in.

'Which would you like, Guy? This one with the bed arranged so that your head faces away from the engine?' He opened the door into the shower and B.C. cubicles and then another door into a duplicate berth. 'Or this one where the head faces towards?'

Perron looked round the rosily-lit compartment.

'Have you nothing in between?'

'I'm afraid not.'

'Then I'll make do with this.'

'I'm told the last Governor's lady preferred it.'

'What about the present Governor's lady?'

'She never comes up to Pankot. If HE has to he goes by road.'

'The coach is something of an anachronism?'

'You could say that.'

'That fits too.'

'Like Scotch. Why? Fits what?'

'The generally hallucinatory atmosphere I currently exist in. Your health.'

The servant came in with the kit-bag, stowed it on the rack and left by the sliding door that gave on to the corridor. When he had gone Perron shot the bolt.

'Guard your property and your life,' he said, as though it were a quotation. In one corner of the compartment there was a diminutive armchair, chintz-covered. He squeezed himself into it. 'The Red Shadow is at large. Did you ever see anything quite as camp?'

'Camp?'

'Suleiman.' Perron hesitated. 'Never mind.' Then, 'Sandhurst, wasn't it? Chillingborough and Sandhurst. Now this. ADC to HE. The Governor in Ranpur. Unless I've been imagining it all and still am, which seems likely. I believe something may have happened to me a week ago tonight. It *is* Sunday?'

'No. Monday. The thirteenth. What happened to you a week ago on Sunday?'

'There was a Maharanee mixed up in it somewhere. And then there was poor Purvis. Are you sure it's the thirteenth? I could swear it was still Sunday.'

Rowan looked at his watch. 'Actually we're both wrong. It's now Tuesday the fourteenth.'

'Good,' Perron said. 'Two days nearer.'

'Nearer what?'

'The successful conclusion of Operation Bunbury. She'll have had my telegram by now. She will have given the first little tug to the first little string. What should we allow? A month, conservatively? Can I hold out even for a month? Or shall I commit murder? What do they do to sergeants who murder their officers?'

'Hang them, I think.'

'Very degrading. A firing squad would be different. Aunt Charlotte would approve of a firing squad.'

The train clacked over a series of points. Rowan steadied himself. Perron produced a hip flask from a sidepocket of his jacket and topped up his whisky and soda. 'Scotch,' he said. 'A parting gift from my previous officer. A pleasant enough but finally very ineffectual man. The only alternative he had to propose was that I apply at once for a commission. He thought it likely it could have been immediate but I said immediate or delayed made no difference because accepting a commission at this stage of the game would simply be a policy of despair.'

'There's no need to drink your own whisky, Guy. Just press the bell.'

'I don't suppose you have the slightest idea what I'm drivelling on about, have you, Nigel?'

'Some of the details are a bit obscure but oddly enough I get the general drift.'

'Do you? I wish I did. I find the general drift elusive. So here's to Aunt Charlotte and Operation Bunbury. I hope you're not going to ask me to explain Bunbury as well as camp.'

'No. But how will an imaginary sick friend solve your problem?'

'He died. At least he did according to the telegram I sent Aunt Charlotte. You remember Aunt Charlotte?'

'The sister of your balloonist uncle?'

'That's the one. The one who got on awfully well with that stunning girl you were with at School versus Old Boys. I can't remember her name. Did you marry her, by the way?'

'No.'

'Are you married?'

'No, go on about Bunbury.'

'Bunbury was Aunt Charlotte's idea. When I told her I couldn't delay my call-up any longer she said I obviously wasn't trying and that it was most unpatriotic of me because it wasn't going to be fair on the men for whose lives and welfare I so thoughtlessly intended to accept responsibility. She only became resigned to it when I got it through to her that I intended to serve anonymously in the ranks and when I agreed to tip her off the moment I wanted her to pull strings to

223

get me out. Throughout my relatively short but not uneventful military career, from Salisbury Plain to Kalyan, I've kept her informed of my state of mind by reporting on our friend Bunbury's state of health. His death last week will have galvanized her into action.'

'What sort of action?'

'She has several friends in what are called high places. Permanent establishment, not politicians. And fortunately I have a pleasant little niche awaiting me in what poor Purvis's benefactor called the groves of Academe. Perhaps more fortunately, our new government is both anti-imperialist and pro-education. In every graduate they will discern a future pillar of an expanded state school system. Not that I intend to be one. But I have the utmost confidence in Aunt Charlotte's ability to arrange a priority demobilization especially if she works in unison with a certain professor of modern history.'

'Who is this Purvis you keep mentioning?'

'Was. Not is. He's dead too.' Perron drank deeply, not quite finishing what was in his glass. 'I don't think I want to talk about Leonard Purvis. I'd rather talk about Bunbury. I had to follow up the telegram to Aunt Charlotte with a letter just in case the cable went astray. Would you like to know what I told her about how Bunbury died?'

'How did Bunbury die?'

'He committed suicide. Twice.'

'Twice.'

'The first time he did it in the bath-tub but I managed to revive him but when he did it again I wasn't there. They'd put him in an upstairs ward and when they weren't looking he threw himself out of the window and broke his neck.'

'A very determined Bunbury.'

'I'm glad you appreciate that. It's what I feel. In determination of that calibre there is something heroic. The thought first struck me at the hurried little inquest which they dragged me up from Kalyan to attend. They made out it was suicide while of unsound mind but you could tell they knew he was as sane as they were. On the other hand what *I* knew was that there wasn't a man in the room with anything like so profound a sense of what he was in the world to do, nor anything like so profound a sense of the criminal waste of human energy that we've seen in the last six years. I'm glad he didn't survive to hear about the new bomb.'

'Are you sure about not eating, Guy?'

'Could I have something in here?'

'Of course.'

'Then I'd better.' He poured more neat Scotch into the over-rich mixture. 'Normally, you know, I'm quite abstemious, but I've spent the past few days discreetly stoned to the eyeballs, a condition which the Red Shadow observes with envy and malicious longing to get his corrupt and filthy thieving hands into my kit-bag to see how many bottles I have left. I for my part long to catch him at it, so that I can boot him in the arse. And believe me, Nigel, before I leave, boot him I shall, with or without provocation. It's a point of honour. The arses of the Suleimans of India exist to be booted by British sergeants. It's traditional. One for the sergeant, two for the regiment and three for the *raj*. And then the women of the Suleimans of India will laugh like drains, the wild dogs of the hills will yelp their satisfaction and there will be peace again on the Khyber. I think you'd better go, because Suleiman will be making a note of the time you and I have been alone in a locked compartment and will make his report accordingly to Major Merrick. I beg his pardon. Colonel. But it's difficult to keep up. He was a major when I saw him in Bombay on Bunbury Sunday. A colonel when I reported at his office in Delhi on Thursday. I entertain this illusion now that it's dangerous to be parted from him for more than a day or two. Every night I go to sleep terrified that in the morning he'll be a full colonel or even a brigadier.'

'I take it you're not enamoured. Why, particularly?'

Perron sipped.

" 'I do not love thee, Dr Fell, the reason why I cannot tell" .' He sipped again. 'On the other hand I've been working out why. He's the man who comes too late and invents himself to make up for it. Even that arm, you know, is an invention. You needn't think it happened in a flash, with a bang, or even on an operating table. It appeared quite gradually, like the stigmata on a saint's hands and feet and side. So that the world would notice, and pause. The pause is very important. I think you'd

225

better join him. He doesn't like being neglected or kept waiting.'

'What takes him to Pankot?'

'The case of one Havildar Karim Muzzafir Khan, late of the Pankot Rifles.'

'I think I may know a bit about that.'

'You were always insufferably well-informed. About rowing for example. What bit do you know?'

'If it's the one who joined Bose's people in Germany' – Perron nodded – 'then Miss Layton's father has put in a request for permission to see him. Is Merrick arranging it?'

Perron drank more whisky.

'No. We're going up to take statements from the havildar's former fellow NCOs.'

'No chance of an exception being made.'

'An exception?'

'No chance of Colonel Layton being allowed to see him?'

'None at all. What's so special about Colonel Layton?'

'Nothing. But what's so special about Havildar Karim Muzzafir Khan that Delhi sends a half-colonel all the way to Pankot to take statements?'

'Oh, that's easily answered. The havildar was special because Merrick chose him.'

'You mean as an example?'

'I mean he was a chosen one. It's part of the technique of the self-invented man. Merrick looks round, his eye lights on someone and he says, Right, I want *him*. Why else do you think I'm here. I'm a chosen one. I expect Coomer was.'

'Coomer?'

'Coomer. Kumar. Harry. Hari. Don't tell me you don't remember him. Miss Layton said you did. It puzzled her when I said I didn't. It aroused her suspicions. Very embarrassing. It made her wonder whether I was only pretending to have gone to Chillingborough. So she dropped a name or two. Yours was one. And then there was Clark-Without.'

'Clark-Without? How did she come to know him?'

'I think she said they met in Calcutta. You remember his reputation, I expect. Hasn't she ever mentioned him?'

'There's no reason why she should.'

'But of course she's told you about meeting me. Obviously.'

'Not all about it. Why did you say you didn't remember Coomer, by the way?'

'The subject was taboo. Not fit for mixed company. Merrick ordered me not to discuss it. The easiest way to avoid being drawn into a discussion was to pretend I didn't know him. Did you know our friend Coomer put cricket behind him and went in for rape and that our friend Merrick caught him at it?'

'Is that what he told you?'

'Has he got it wrong?'

'There are two schools of thought. How did you come across Merrick? Just by being posted to his department?'

'Attached. Not posted yet, thank God. But no. I met him one warm night. On the docks. At Bombay. It sounds romantic, doesn't it? Then I didn't meet him again until the evening at the Maharanee's. But, already I was chosen. Fate. It has driven me to drink, to Bunbury and Aunt Charlotte, and to a refutation of Emerson.'

'Emerson?'

' "Society is a wave. The wave moves onward, but the water of which it is composed does not. The same particle does not rise from the valley to the ridge. Its unity is only phenomenal. The persons who make up a nation today, next year die, and their experience with them." Emerson failed to see that there were exceptions. People like you and me.'

Rowan smiled. He made neither head nor tail of it and on the whole saw no reason to try. But a penny had just dropped.

'Did you meet a Count Bronowsky at the Maharanee's? Sarah told me he was there.'

'He was certainly there. Why do you ask?'

'He put that idea into your head, didn't he? About Merrick inventing himself and the arm?'

'He certainly didn't. It's my copyright.'

'Coincidence then. He has much the same idea. I'd better leave you to it, Guy, and get them to bring you in some supper. By the way, when I was still out on the platform just now did Merrick take the opportunity to ask you how you and I knew one another?'

'He did.'

'What did you say?'

'I said we knew one another quite well before the war. I don't think it satisfied him. He probably thinks we've been in touch recently because neither of us showed any surprise at meeting.'

'You didn't mention Chillingborough?'

'I had a feeling it wasn't necessary.'

'It doesn't matter either way but one likes to be prepared.'

'Because of Coomer? What interests you and Sarah Layton about Coomer? The fact that he's an old Chillingburian who has been in what used to be called a Spot of Bother?'

'I suppose that provides a very rough basis for an interest.'

'As for everything else? This, for instance?' He gestured round the compartment. 'I imagine Colonel Merrick's coupé isn't half as comfortable. This cosy little compartment is symbolic, don't you find?'

'I hadn't thought of it. What is it symbolic of?'

'Of our isolation and insulation, our inner conviction of class rights and class privileges, of our permanence and of our capacity to trim, to insure against any major kind of upheaval affecting our interests, and of course of our fundamental indifference to the problems towards which we adopt attitudes of responsibility. Not moral responsibility, ownership responsibility. A moral responsibility would be too trying. Even poor underprivileged Purvis was clearheaded enough to admit that. Property on the other hand can always be got rid of and new property acquired. New property, new responsibility, but the same manner, the same deep inner conviction and the same snug cosy sense of insulation. I know where I shall find mine when I'm back home. Where will you find yours, Nigel, I mean when India is got rid of?'

'I've really not thought about that, Guy. It's just a shade too far ahead.'

'You haven't thought about it. But of course you don't need to. Neither of us does. Nothing can erode our ingrained sense of class security. Your face has taken on that remote patrician look that tells me you would find what I say offensive if you thought for one moment I meant it. Well I do. Every bloody word. Emerson was obviously too much of a peasant to appreciate the significance of you and me. Society is a wave. The wave moves onward. You and I move along with it.

Emerson was writing for the Merricks and Purvises of the world. The ones who get drowned. Merrick hopes not to be. But he will be. Can't the fool see that nobody of the class he aspires to belong to has ever cared a damn' about the empire and that all that God-the-Father-God-the-*raj* was a lot of insular middle- and lower-class shit?'

'An uncle of mine took God-the-father God-the-*raj* quite seriously, I should say.'

'You mean he had principles?'

'Yes, I think so.'

'I bet that if you cut right through the principles you'd find all he took seriously was his unassailable right to deploy things and people to his uttermost personal advantage and private satisfaction.'

'Is Merrick a principled man?'

'Principled as a rock. He thinks people like you and me are scum. He believes we've abandoned the principles we used to live by, what he would call the English upper- and ruling-class principle of knowing oneself superior to all other races especially black and having a duty to guide and correct them. He's been sucked in by all that Kiplingesque double-talk that transformed India from a place where plain ordinary greedy Englishmen carved something out for themselves to balance out the more tedious consequences of the law of primogeniture, into one where they appeared to go voluntarily into exile for the good of their souls and the uplift of the native. The transformation was illusory of course. A middle-class misconception of upper-class *mores*. But a man like Merrick can't be expected to see that. He's spent too long inventing himself in the image to have energy left to realize that as an image it is and always was hollow. He only notices it has become rarer. Poor Coomer obviously never stood a chance. An English public school education and manner, but black as your hat.'

'Not so black.'

'Black enough for Merrick. But most of us are as bad as black to him. There aren't many real white men left. And the odd thing is that when he comes across any he despises them. Colonel Layton for instance.'

'He despises Colonel Layton? Why?'

'White man gone soft. Guide *and* correct, remember? The two pillars of wisdom. Despises because Layton has and is everything Merrick covets. But Layton hasn't the nerve or guts to live up to it. He'd clasp the Bose-tainted havildar to his bosom, for instance. Tears of sorrow rather than the lash of anger. Too many bloody tears altogether. Even over a half-empty bottle of Old Sporran. So God help us tomorrow. Have you got any by the way?'

'Got any what?'

'Old Sporran. Doesn't Government House run to it?'

'Not nowadays. Why God help you tomorrow?'

'Not nowadays. No. Nowadays Old Sporran is reserved for the Purvises. Damned proletariat getting in everywhere. He hanged himself.'

'Who hanged himself? Purvis?'

'No, Purvis fell. The havildar hanged himself. Havildar Karim Muzzafir Khan, son of subdar Muzzafir Khan vc.'

'Oh. When?'

'Tuesday you said? So, a few minutes ago it was Monday. Sunday morning, then. Some time on Sunday morning. Before daylight. Which is why there's no chance of Colonel Layton being allowed to talk to him. There's no poor weary shagged-out shamed and insulted havildar to talk to.'

'Shamed and insulted by whom?'

'Merrick of course.'

'You witnessed it?'

'Only the beginning and the end. Bombay in June and Delhi on Friday. I expect I missed the best bits in the middle.'

'What happened in the middle?'

'I don't know. The real working-over I expect.'

'Physical working-over?'

'No sign of that on the body. I don't think that's Merrick's style.'

Perron emptied the flask into his glass. The liquor was now neat.

'You saw the body, then.'

'Oh yes. "Come over to D block, will you, sergeant? There has been an interesting development." At four o'clock in the morning.'

'Interesting?'

'That's what he said. It was quite deliberate. So that I should be unprepared. He presented the scene like a *tableau vivant*, well not so vivant, but one he'd set up which he wanted me to react to. I'm surprised he let them cut him down before I got there.' Perron swigged whisky. 'The whole thing was unspeakably ugly and sordid.'

'What did he use?'

'The havildar? You mean for rope? Torn strips of shirt and vest knotted together. He'd tried to cut his throat first with a broken bit of mess-tin. I'd prefer not to talk about it. I'll just tell you what Merrick said. "Not a very prepossessing looking chap, was he, sergeant?" '

'Yes, I see. So the real reason for the journey is to report the death to Colonel Layton?'

'No. The real reason is to sustain the connection. The role of friend of the family. Nothing brash of course. Nothing pushing. Just a persistent air of quiet competence and capacity and authority. Occasional sudden concentration of effort and flurry of activity that show the range and depth of feeling and concern. Like this visit. The human touch. And all these statements to be taken from the havildar's ex-comrades. As if anything that can be recorded now in the havildar's favour is not only welcome but a white man's duty to discover and put on the file.' Perron closed one eye and stared at Rowan as if he suddenly found it difficult to focus. Then he nodded and said:

'He's chosen the Laytons, too.'

Perron opened the closed eye and added: 'But don't worry. I mean if you do worry, don't.'

'Worry about what?'

'His choosing the Laytons. I said Laytons; not any one Layton in particular. At least I shouldn't think so. So don't worry. What *was* her name?'

'Whose?'

'The stunning girl Aunt Charlotte took a shine to.'

'Laura Elliott.'

'Laura Elliott.' Perron put his head back as if tired. 'What a sad name. What happened?'

'She married someone else.'

'Anyone I know?'

'I shouldn't think so. She met him in Rangoon. His name was Ratcliff. He planted rubber in Malaya.'

'What was she doing in Rangoon?'

'Visiting me.'

'When was this?'

'Nineteen-forty-one.'

'How did she get to Rangoon in nineteen-forty-one?'

'Her parents were in Mandalay. Civil service.'

'I always thought of her as army.'

'Her brother was.'

'Sandhurst together?'

'Yes.'

'Same regiment?'

'Yes. The three of us came out on the same boat.'

'Were you and Laura Elliott ever engaged?'

'Eventually.'

'When you went to Burma.'

'No, we became unengaged in Burma.'

'Were you in the Burma show in 'forty-two?'

'I never think of it as a show. Just as a retreat. I was in that.'

'Well, show or retreat, you survived. Did Laura Elliott's brother?'

'No.'

'Did Laura and her rubber-planter get out of Malaya?'

'The parents got out of Burma but only Mrs Elliott's still alive. She lives in Darjeeling and writes to me occasionally. She heard from Laura once early on, after she'd been interned by the Japanese. There was no news of Tony and Laura's never written again. At least nothing's been received.'

'Poor Laura. I said it was a sad name.' Perron brought his head back level. 'Does it upset you still?'

'Not any more.'

'What about Sarah Layton?'

'What about her?'

'She referred to you with what I'd call respect and admiration. Mutual?'

'Yes.'

'Pity. I mean for me. Given half an opportunity making a bit of a pass at Sarah Layton was the one thing that made the prospect of several days in Pankot bearable. But I expect I'd better behave, hadn't I? Yes. Well. Incidentally, do you mind very much if in future I call you sir in front of other people? You can go on calling me Guy if you like but it offends my sense of military decorum to call you Nigel in public.'

Smiling, otherwise ignoring this, Rowan said, 'Do you know where you're putting up?'

'You mean quartered. No, but I have every confidence in my officer. He's the kind of man who knows it's good form to look to the needs of horse, groom and self in that order, although his own comfort is assured, naturally, so it can always be safely left until last. Why? Were you thinking of keeping in touch?'

'We ought to arrange an evening if we can. You can reach me by ringing Two Hundred.'

'The Governor's hill palace?'

'It's the guest house attached to what used to be the summer residence.'

'Used to be? Has the weather deteriorated?'

'I mean it's shut up.'

'With accommodation so short?'

'People complain, but like this coach it doesn't convert very easily. And the next Governor may revive the old seasonal system of six months in the hills and six on the plain. Anyway ring me there. We'll fix something.'

Perron nodded.

Rowan said, 'I'll send a bearer in with the menu. He'll bring you a drink too if you want another. I'll leave that to your discretion. And feel free to ring the bell at any time.'

Again Perron nodded.

'Sleep well,' Rowan said, and began to go.

'Thanks for the bed, Nigel. I'm very grateful.'

*

The corridor was empty. No Red Shadow. In the dining-room two tables were laid and were being set out with chafing dishes. He smelt, fleetingly, carnations. And the scent of cologne. But there were only marigolds. He told one of the bearers to attend to the guest in compartment number two and then went through into the saloon.

Suleiman was kneeling, easing one of Merrick's feet into crimson leather slippers. Between the stiff first and second fingers of Merrick's black-gloved left hand was a lighted cigarette. Merrick and Suleiman both turned their heads. Suleiman grinned, showing handsome teeth. Merrick smiled, an odd lopsided smile – or so the scar tissue made it appear; and Rowan, in spite of everything, felt touched and under an odd kind of compulsion to forget what he knew, what he thought he knew; what it was unfair, after all, to allow himself to be affected by when he had scarcely said more than a few words to the man. As he took his seat on the sofa and nodded to the bearer indicating that he wanted another drink before eating, and listened to what Merrick was saying about Suleiman's theory that it was bad for the circulation to wear walking shoes when one wasn't walking, he also felt himself being supported, braced up almost, by an unexpected sensation of being once more – away from Guy Perron – in control of things, of himself, and in surroundings that matched his mood. And presently when Suleiman had gone, taking Merrick's shoes with him, and he and Merrick were alone, eyeing one another with what Rowan supposed an observer would interpret as cautious interest, it struck him as being odd that the one man he might have expected to be a disruptive or abrasive presence was not, but seemed to fit in and to share with him this feeling of repose, or anyway of momentary relief from the pressures which had been piling up, undermining his confidence: a feeling accentuated, perhaps, by the way the coach absorbed and muffled the vibration and clatter of the wheels without diminishing the flattering sensation of a speed and movement forward that were absolutely effortless.

The Moghul Room

I

My Aunt Charlotte's knowledge of India and Indian affairs
was very limited but her enthusiasm for any subject that
interested another member of the family was quickly stirred
and once it had been stirred it was difficult to moderate. For
example, the technique and mystique of ballooning continued to exert a fascination for her long after her brother, my
Uncle Charles, had abandoned it as a sport (having come
down near Cobh in Ireland after setting out from Kent for
Essex). For years, subsequently, she maintained a scrap-book
into which she pasted cuttings of anything she could find that
was connected with the subject of unpowered aerial naviga-
tion.

Flattering as her sharing of one's interests was it could be a
little tiresome even if one's own enthusiasm remained
unflagging. The clippings of newspaper articles and reports
about India which she sent or saved for me until her first and
fatal illness were, in a sense, an unnecessary duplication.
However it is to her I owe a comparison between Operation
Bunbury and the last Viceroyalty.

'Your viceroys are all Bunburyists,' she declared. (From the
moment of my return home in 1945 all Indian personalities,
policies and problems, were referred to as mine: your Mr
Gandhi, your Mr Nehru, your Kashmir problem, your non-
alignment policy, your confrontation with the Chinese, your
application for foreign aid, your green revolution, your family
planning.) 'Your viceroys' in 'Your viceroys are all Bunburyists' was just one of many examples of this habit of placing
everything Indian as it were in my gift. Asked to justify this
statement, though, she pointed out the regularity with which
at certain climactic moments in talks and negotiations my

viceroys withdrew, packed their bags and came home for consultation.

This, she said, was 'pure Bunburyism', clear evidence of pre-arrangements between my viceroys and my Secretary of State for India in Whitehall to ensure the continuation of whatever policy the British Government was currently pursuing in regard to the sub-continent. 'Take your present policy' she said once, when Wavell was still Viceroy (I always kept notes of our conversations), 'this is clearly a policy of conducting serious talks about a future constitutional change within a general framework of an assumption on our part that the existing status quo will be maintained. Which means that when your Lord Wavell detects that the serious talks are about to break down – or look like continuing so successfully that the status quo is actually at risk – he has himself called from the conference room as if to the telephone and returns a few minutes later to announce that there has been a development in London that requires his immediate presence there. It is merely another way of saying as Mr Worthing would have done, "I'm afraid my poor friend Bunbury has taken a turn for the worse and that I must catch the 3.15." '

I thought this a bit unfair to Wavell but on reflection saw that there was something in it in regard to viceroys in general, and said so. Thereafter whenever the Viceroy – Wavell, and then his successor, Mountbatten – arrived back in London, Aunt Charlotte sent me a postcard (usually of aerial views of the countryside) with a brief message: 'Bunbury unwell again.' 'Poor Bunbury giving cause for anxiety,' etc. The Mountbatten viceroyalty, though, produced this (an extract from one of the many letters of hers which I have preserved):

'If Attlee *means* that power is to be transferred as early as 1948, then Bunbury's ill-health has undergone a change. I don't mean he's better or worse, merely unwell in a different way. If our policy now *is* to get out, then you will begin to see that Bunbury's delicate constitution will respond admirably to every turn of events which advances our policy of demission of power by 1948 but suffer serious setbacks on any occasion when impediments to it are put in our way.'

In reply I pointed out that for the first time a viceroy of mine (Mountbatten) appeared to have plenipotentiary powers and

238

that although this was advantageous administratively it meant that the Bunbury gambit might well have had its day. Aunt Charlotte declared at once that a viceroy with plenipotentiary powers would be the greatest Bunburyist of the lot, because it meant he would have taken Bunbury to India with him. This was not clear to me. I asked her to elucidate. She wrote:

'I mean that Bunbury has at last emerged in his true colours as The British Presence in India – traditionally seated (I mean bedridden) in Whitehall, but at last visiting with Dickie (how well that boy has done) the scene of his hitherto only vicarious triumphs and failures. Attlee has said (it is so plain to me I wish it were to you) that a holiday in India until 1948 might be beneficial to him. A valedictory tour, so to speak, like the personal appearance of a famous film-star known to millions but only as a shadow on the silver screen. After the valedictory tour he will return home, retire and be content to fade away to look at his press-cuttings. So henceforth any deterioration in Bunbury's health will occur only when it looks to the Viceroy as if your Indians aren't going to let Bunbury leave as planned.'

The force of her argument was driven home early in June 1947 when the Viceroy – having had what the papers revealed day after day as the greatest difficulty in finding someone among the contenders both able and willing to relieve us of Indian responsibility and letting Bunbury go (I recalled Purvis's warning) announced that power would be transferred not in 1948 but in ten weeks' time.

Telegrams between Aunt Charlotte and myself crossed. Mine read: Bunbury stop looks like experience of personal appearance proved too much. Hers: Doctors here have re-examined Bunbury X-rays stop condition worse than thought stop vital expedite his return otherwise fear worst in that climate stop Dickie coping but suggest you fly out observe and supervise stop will arrange passage and underwrite reasonable expenses.

Reading this I realized that Aunt Charlotte had become a convinced Purvisite. 'Condition worse than thought' argued that a British Presence in India was as Purvis might have said no longer viable economically or administratively. 'Vital to expedite his return' was a hint that the members of the Labour Government after nearly two years in office were getting desperate at the prospect of having to continue to support this presence. Considering the complexity of the moral, political and historical issues which surrounded the attempted transfer of power in India and considering that these were the only issues ever publicly discussed I think Aunt Charlotte showed remarkable perspicacity. She thought so herself and as the years passed took undisguised pleasure in heavily underlining confirmatory passages in the articles and books she sent me – the writings of soldiers, statesmen and civil servants, journalists and historians – to draw my attention to admissions of the kind that supported what, misunderstanding me slightly, she claimed with my authority as her own entirely original opinion: that as a result of the war, the policy of Indianization, the running down of the machinery of British recruitment to the civil service and police, and as a result of the infiltration of political, communal and nationalistic modes of thought into the Indian armed services (the Naval Mutiny in Bombay in 1946 was always cited as an example) it would have been difficult, even impossible, to maintain in India any form of stable government with a responsibility to Parliament at home and for law and order and national defence in India, except at a cost which even if the will and the means were available would have been excessive and just not on from the British taxpayer's point of view.

In the delirium of pneumonia (at an advanced age she unwisely took an interest – an active interest – in her grand-nephew's passion for duck-shooting at dawn on the marshes) she spoke of many things which made sense to a member of the family. 'What, there, the penny black. Who would have thought it had so much blood in it?' Such a statement, sinister from the point of view of the medical staff, was perfectly rational if you remembered Aunt Hester's craze for philately and Uncle William's frustrated theatrical ambitions which dated from his appearance in a school production of Macbeth. Other remarks, obscure to the nurses, clear to me, showed that she was thinking turn and turn about of the things that had interested or obsessed her brothers and sisters. I should explain that my father was the only Perron of his generation who got married. The other brothers and sisters paired off: George (who was the eldest and who inherited) and Harriet, William and Hester, Charles and Charlotte. Cousins Henry and Sophie were my grandfather Perron's only brother's children. They paired off too. My father, Aunt Charlotte used to say, only got married because he was the odd boy out. Insisting on being sent to Chillingborough with a view to an Indian career, joining the army at the outbreak of the great war and getting married (not even to a relation) were, I suppose, the forms which Perron eccentricity took in his case. I was sent to Chillingborough really as an act of devotion to my father's memory. It was felt that he had never had a chance to show what – as a Perron – he could do – but that being killed on November 10, 1918, suggested he had been on the right lines. His brothers – who all had brilliant minds but unadaptable personalities – were in the main privately tutored between expulsions from a number of establishments of varying reputations and competence.

I am trying to convey as clearly and economically as I can something of the background of the last surviving member of that generation of Perrons who as she lay dying revealed herself to me as a woman whose life, so apparently full, had been in so far as original enthusiasms and direct experience were concerned (with that single and fatal exception) empty. A croaked reference to speed bonny boat could have been related either to my rowing or to the punt in which she had set out with her great-nephew to see for herself what so enthralled him about shooting duck. Drugs succeeded in reducing her temperature and there was a lucid interval before she relapsed into sleep, unconsciousness and coma. Opening her eyes and finding me there she said – indicating what she obviously recognized as a private room – 'Well I see that I am dying beyond my means' – closed her eyes and never opened them again, nor communicated, except by smiling intermittently at thoughts she did not share with me. That explicit reference to Bunbury's creator was the nearest she came to touching on a subject that had been a bond between us ever since I first set sail for India; but in making it she was just as likely to have been thinking of her Thespian brother as

241

of her 'Indian' nephew, or even of neither but of her late brother George who, inheriting the bulk of the Perron estate, had made a number of foolish investments.

She was such an unegotistical person, such a champion of other people's causes, that it seems grossly unfair to connect her in any way with responsibility for a death roll that was never accurately counted but which has become widely accepted as reaching the one-quarter million mark.

'Your Punjabis,' she said when I got back from the euphoric and bloodstained country after taking the trip to 'observe and supervise' which she had subsidized in 1947, 'Your Punjabis would appear to have taken leave of their senses.'

She was referring to the massacres that accompanied the migrations of communities after the decision to partition. I told her that the murders of Hindus and Sikhs by Muslims and of Muslims by Hindus and Sikhs had by no stretch of the imagination been confined to the land of the five rivers, but Punjab was a word which had always had a strong appeal for people like Aunt Charlotte and she probably felt that once you had pronounced it (particularly as she pronounced it, with a rotundity of mouth and emphasis of jaw – Poonjawb) then you had said all that needed to be said about the golden land below Afghanistan. She therefore continued to demarcate the zone of violence on this provincial basis and I think succeeded too in mentally reducing the slaughter to the manageable proportions of an isolated act of insurrection which was the result of allowing things to get a bit out of hand.

It would never have occurred to her to examine her conscience in regard to those one-quarter million deaths, although she had, in fact, as I had done – voted for them. It would not have occurred to her because she held single-mindedly to the Purvis principle, the view that a British presence in India was an economic and administrative burden whose quick offloading was an essential feature of post-war policy in the welfare state. I'll give her this, though: in adhering to this principle she never once introduced the ethical argument that colonialism was immoral – an argument that supported so many of us. I don't think the ethical

argument ever entered her head. She was esentially a pragmatist. The only moral argument I ever remember her advancing
was the one she used to try to convince me that my joining up
would be unfair to the men she assumed I would accept
responsibility for.

Needless to say, I never told Aunt Charlotte that she, as
well as I, was responsible for the one-quarter million deaths in
the Punjab and elsewhere. But I did once ask her who, in her
opinion, *was* responsible. She said, 'But that is obvious. The
people who attacked and killed each other.' There was no
arguing with this, but it confirmed my impression of her
historical significance (and mine), of the overwhelming
importance of the part that had been played in British-Indian
affairs by the indifference and the ignorance of the English at
home – whom Aunt Charlotte, in an especially poignant way
had in my mind come to represent; and upsetting though I
found it, nothing was more appropriate than that in that
delirium, when images of all the acquired and borrowed
interests of her life flowed swiftly through her heated
imagination, images of India were totally forgotten.

*

In investing someone with historical significance one should
proceed cautiously but I think the conclusion I came to about
her share of responsibility for disorder and bloodshed can be
traced back to that grey humid morning in Kalyan when I
stood up and spoke for half an hour to a hall full of restless and
inattentive men about the territorial ambitions of Mahdaji
and Daulat Rao Sindia, and realized how little any of us knew
or cared about a country whose history had been that of our
own for more than three hundred years and which had
contributed more than any other to our wealth, our well-
being.

Less than a month later I was passing through Deolali to
embark at Bombay on a homeward-bound ship in a mood
alternating between the exhilaration of a man released to
follow his own bent and the depression of one who retires
from a situation gratefully but with some doubts about the

means he's adopted to extricate himself. There were as well some unexpected regrets.

If I had been with Ronald Merrick right up to the time when the signal came ordering me to report to Deolali, I doubt that I should have felt anything except relief and grateful astonishment at the speed with which Aunt Charlotte had apparently worked. But I wasn't with him; rather, he wasn't with me and the signal happened to arrive at a moment when I was aware of being comfortably situated and pleasantly occupied.

*

In the morning, after that night journey from Ranpur in the Governor's special coach, when Rowan and I bumped into each other in the narrow passage between Their Excellencies' compartments (w.c. on one side, shower on the other) he was polite but (I thought) a little cool. I think he assumed I was lying when I told him I had no hangover, or assumed that I had already started on one of the bottles in my kit-bag so that I could face up to another day with Merrick and the Red Shadow.

He may have been right about the hangover because my recollections of the arrival in Pankot aren't very clear. But there could be another reason for that. To have travelled on the same train as a coffin without knowing it is one thing. To be greeted by a large crowd banging on drums another. I don't recall how soon it was before I connected the crowds and the drums with a funeral, or the funeral with a coffin that had come in on the train, or the coffin with the body of Mr Kasim's secretary, and I'm not sure whether it was Merrick's information alone, or Merrick's and the Red Shadow's plus other people's that helped me to fit the pieces together. What I do remember is that it was nothing Nigel Rowan said because he said very little. An impression I had that morning was of not inspiring his confidence; another was that as a result of whatever conversation he'd had with Merrick the night before there was an amiability between them now which seemed, on Rowan's part, advertised to show me that he discounted everything I had told him about that officer's behaviour. Without caring much what the answer was I

244

wondered whether Nigel had said anything to Merrick about my attitude to him, and whether Merrick's silence in the 15 cwt that Area HQ had sent to the station for us was especially ominous.

Nigel's detachment, Merrick's silence, the distracting crowds at the station, the drums and the shouting, the revolting stink of the Red Shadow's stale breath and unwashed body in the confined luggage-loaded space at the tarpaulin-covered back of the truck: these have stayed with me as parts of the jig-saw. Another part of it is waiting, in several places, keeping upwind of the Pathan if on the same verandah with him and moving if he came too near. The waiting was done in the complex of old Victorian barracks and huts of more recent origin that was Area Headquarters. A dry sunny morning? Something cool but hard – metallic – in the air, the smell of a century or more of Pankot's experience of military occupation. A late breakfast in a British NCOS' mess. Eating it alone at a long table as yet uncleared of used plates and cups and saucers. The depredations of white ants in wooden window frames set in crumbling plaster. Views from these windows of the hills. The sound of a coppersmith. Shafts of sunlight? A padlocked glass-fronted cupboard that displayed a few silver cups, sporting-trophies. A dartboard and last night's chalked scores. A little bit of Salisbury Plain in the Indian hills. I had never hated the army so much as I did in this hour or two in this drearily familiar and horribly anonymous area of roads and pathways, directional signs, inhospitable huts and characterless rooms – the makeshift impermanent jerry-built structures that seem to rest for sole support on the implacable and rigid authority of military hierarchy. The fire of hatred (so intense, so unexpected, so out of character) was stoked and fanned by a sudden and utter lack of confidence in the machine I thought I had set in motion with the telegram and letter to Aunt Charlotte. The illusion of imminent escape withered away in this uncompromising and heartless reality.

Another piece of the jig-saw: as I sat beneath the dartboard, stupefied by this misery, there was a distant crackling fusillade of shots whose echoes bounced from one hill to another. When the echoes were finally spent I heard the uninterrupted song of the coppersmith. No barking. The birds and dogs of Pankot – wild or tame – were used to the sound of range practice.

And I remember relief when the truck came back from wherever it had been with Merrick and the Red Shadow and I was taken by the driver (a surly, solitary man) from the NCOs' mess; relief that was short-lived because it ended in another anonymous room, an annexe in the grounds of the General Hospital (military wing) which I later discovered lay approximately half-way between Area Headquarters and the lines of the Pankot Rifles depot.

From the window of this room there was no view at all. The hospital was well provided with shade trees and the annexe was half-hidden in bushes. I didn't bother to ask the driver why I was to be quartered there, nor did I ask where Merrick and the Red Shadow were. One of the pleasures of being a sergeant is of feeling under no obligation to satisfy your curiosity about the background to events. You don't originate *anything* if you can help it. Delivered by the driver, admitted by a servant (who must have had an instruction from somewhere) I entered the room in the annexe and because it had a bed had no difficulty in assuming that this was where I was to sleep while in Pankot. I dumped pack and kit-bag and lay down.

Out of this phase (morning of August 14 to morning of August 16) one important minor figure emerges: that of an RAMC corporal, a young man from Bermondsey. I shall call him Corporal Dixon. The British NCOs on the hospital staff messed together and formed a little clique. It was a very unmilitary set-up: sergeants, corporals, but not lance-corporals. Driven by hunger to leave the room in the annexe and find the mess-hut I found I was expected, but I think only as a man with a name and the barest identification. I was received in a friendly easy-going fashion and given a beer. The mess conveyed an idea of intellectual superiority. There was a Van Gogh reproduction on one wall and the sound of Mozart from the portable gramophone. A few of the NCOs had seen service in the field. For them, Pankot was a relief station. Among these front-line veterans was Corporal Dixon, known affectionately as Sophie, or Miss Dixon, or Mum.

I was told that he kept the patients in the wards in stitches and that he had tamed the QA nursing sisters and the medical officers. I was also told that a wounded officer who had watched him at work at a casualty clearing station in the Arakan and listened to the stream of morale-boosting queenly chat – a mocking commentary on the sounds of battle near by – had said: 'You deserve the MM, Corporal.' Sophie had said, 'Oh that would never do, sir, I wouldn't presume, and where would they pin it, the cheeky things?'

But these tales came later when I set about trying to find out how I had offended, what had caused the temperature to drop. Between the friendly reception and the freezing up no more than a few hours passed. Dixon's first appearance was at lunch. 'A copper!' he said, fingering my green armband. 'Has someone been at the drugs? It's no good looking here, sergeant, we're all clean-living boys. It's that Matron over at Private. She's never been the same since she visited Cox's Bazaar looking for a bargain and found it closed for stock-taking.'

I laughed and was introduced. Dixon was rather welcome comic relief. Perhaps if I hadn't laughed he would have been tipped the wink to quieten down. Lunch was at a long table. White cloth. A vase or two of marigolds. I was at one end, as I remember, and Dixon at the other. The atmosphere was amiable. Once it was established that I wasn't at the hospital on duty but only quartered temporarily in the annexe I don't think any further questions were asked. I remember that towards the end of the meal all conversation died away because Dixon had taken the stage and was recounting a series of scurrilous but very funny stories, most of them delivered in a tone of prim outrage, of astonishment at the trickery and under-handedness of the world. It took me some time to sort out the code. After failing to see the point several times I realized that 'she' almost invariably meant 'he'. A sentence such as 'Well you should have seen her, got up to the nines in her new frock, preening she was, poor old thing, well she doesn't often have one does she?' didn't, I discovered, refer to a matron at a hospital dance but to a senior officer of the RAMC or the IMS who was wearing a new uniform, hadn't been looking where he was going and had bumped into and knocked Corporal Dixon over at a moment when he happened to be carrying a bed-pan full of urine. 'So there she was, drenched with Private Thingummy's piss, new dress ruined, and there was me flat on me bum and covered in piss too, thinking I'd really ask for me cards this time. But you can't beat breeding, can you? "Is that Corporal Dixon?" she says to Matron looking down her nose, oh very ladylike. "I'm afraid it is," Matron says. "I see," she says. "I suppose it was not entirely his fault so we won't hold it against him." Well as to *that*, I thinks to meself, chance would be a fine thing.'

How much of Dixon's tale was true one could only guess. (Did RAMC corporals carry bedpans in India?) What was clear was his rôle. He was the safety-valve. How well-timed and sustained his performances were over a period I could not judge except from the behaviour of his companions in the mess. Presumably he knew when to play up and when to give it a rest. I detected no signs either of boredom or aggression. Before the meal was quite over the steward brought in a note. It was for me; from Merrick. The truck-driver had brought it. I got up to leave.

'Are you with us for long, Sergeant?' Sophie Dixon called out. I told him probably for a day or two; added that I'd see them tonight anyway.

'Coppers,' he said for my benefit before I reached the door. 'The competition's been something cruel since they started sending them to college.'

A row of men, smiling, interested to see how I took it. Still smiling when I left. The next time I saw them they were not even civil; as though in the interval the gloom that began to settle on me during the long irritating afternoon had conveyed itself to them. I was deprived of the comic relief, of an antidote to Merrick who had surpassed himself to the extent when for two pins I would have set about undermining the whole subtly balanced structure of mystification and intimidation which was what he erected to get what he wanted.

From the medical NCOs' mess I was translated to a world of old barracks and hutments, parade grounds, flagpoles in beds of white-washed stones, the smell of creosoted wood warmed by the sun; a hot breeze blowing in from hills which were rigid in the torpor of an Indian afternoon. The distant coppersmith.

I was delivered to the adjutant's office in the lines of the Pankot Rifles and conducted from there to a low block – square stuccoed whitewashed pillars of brick supporting the overhang of a steep-pitched roof to form a verandah – into a room that was being emptied of benches by a squad of sepoys. A school- or lecture-room. The walls were hung with posters, aids to recognition of enemy planes, tanks and personnel. At a table on the daïs sat Merrick. Three officers stood round him: a pale middle-aged Englishman (who was the adjutant, Coley), a youngish Indian captain and a very young English subaltern, smart as paint, stiff as starch with a lot of fine blond hair showing on his arms between immaculately turned up and laundered sleeves and on his legs between the hem of knife-edged khaki shorts and the tops of stockings worn with puttees and brown boots. Of the four only Merrick failed to respond to my energetic entrance and salute. But he was facing the door and although he didn't look up from the file he was reading he knew who it was. There were a couple of jemadars, a havildar who looked like a clerk and a naik in charge of the sepoy work-squad.

When the last bench had been taken out Merrick said, 'We shan't need the daïs either.' The three officers got down from it. Merrick remained. 'And if it's not too much trouble, Coley, I'd like this table placed where the light falls as fully as possible on whoever's sitting behind it.'

'Of course.'

No one asked why he wanted this light. He had the trick of directing people's minds from strategy to tactics. The table was tried several ways while Merrick stayed enthroned on the daïs. The subaltern was used as a stand-in to test for the light. When the right place was found Merrick got up to allow the chair to be taken over and placed behind the table. Then he went across and sat down again. The sepoys took the daïs out. 'We shall want another table and several more chairs,' he said, 'including another one with arms to go in front of *this* table.' All this was attended to. Then a medium scale map of the Pankot District was sent for. A box of pins with different coloured heads. A pair of compasses. The maps were brought. The jemadars pinned them to the wall in sequence. Mugs of tea arrived, followed by the compasses and pins which turned out to be my cue.

'This is where you can make yourself useful, sergeant,' he said. He gave me a copy of the list of VCOS, NCOS and men who had been prisoners-of war in Germany. Against each man's name was the name of his village. With the compasses a circle was described on the map with its centre at the depot and with a radius equal to five miles on the ground. Then, as I read out the men's names and villages the jemadar stuck a pin in the map, a different coloured pin for each different rank. Whenever a pin was stuck inside the pencilled circle I had to mark the name on the list with an asterisk.

We must have been occupied thus for well over an hour. Merrick came and went, sometimes with Coley, sometimes with the Indian officer. The subaltern remained with me and the jemadar, absolutely enthralled because he had no idea what we were up to. By the time we had finished the map showed at a glance how many of the ex-prisoners-of-war, now on leave, could be fairly easily got hold of; how many of them, in other words, lived within five miles of the depot. When I explained this to the subaltern he seemed quite bowled over at such an efficient – and humane – bit of staff-work. No one liked to interrupt such well-earned leave, so the first set of interviews would be with men who could be collected from and returned to their villages in the course of a single day.

He also saw why the table had been placed so that the light fell on the faces of the officers asking for statements and not on the faces of men who were to be encouraged to make them. The table tops had already been covered by blankets, and there was a vase of flowers on one of them. From Delhi Merrick had brought with him poster-size blow-ups of smiling victorious generals: Monty, Alex and Wavell (chosen for their connections with the Middle East where the 1st Pankots had fought). There were also posters of Bill Slim and Dickie Mountbatten as Supremo. These were all pinned in strategic places on the walls. The master-stroke was the inclusion of a much enlarged photograph of a group of Indian officers leaning out of tanks and shaking hands with Americans, and of VCOS, NCOS and sepoys being matey with

European other ranks in what looked like a street in devastated Berlin or Cologne. Everything in the room now conspired to make the ex-prisoners-of-war who had been true to the salt and not gone over to Bose – proud and helpfully talkative. The subaltern, so obviously newly commissioned, and perhaps secretly relieved that he would now never have to lead his men into battle, was almost visibly moved. He interpreted the whole *mise en scène* as a compliment to men of a fine regiment and as a stroke of genius on the part of the one-armed Lieutenant-Colonel who, although coming from Delhi, obviously knew a thing or two and respected what he knew.

What the subaltern didn't know (how could he?) was that the whole business of the interviews and statements was utterly pointless. The Indian lieutenant suspected of being implicated in the death of a sepoy in Königsberg was himself dead – so I had discovered from the files in Delhi. Karim Muzzafir Khan's name, far from 'cropping up several times' in depositions taken in Germany about the dead sepoy had cropped up once. Moreover, the death of the sepoy might well have been due to natural causes. Suspicions had arisen solely from accusations and counter-accusations among Frei Hind sepoys who had been questioned after the Germans collapsed and who had no connections with the Pankot Rifles and one of whom may well have chosen to cast doubts on Havildar Karim Muzzafir Khan's conduct simply because he was an infantryman from a stuck-up regiment. There was no statement to be taken from any of the returned Pankot Rifles prisoners that could have any bearing on the dead sepoy, the dead lieutenant or on the dead Karim Muzzafir Khan's behaviour. The only things the ex-POWs would be able to tell us were the things they had already told Colonel Layton and their other officers directly they were reunited: their experiences of being talked to or intimidated by Bose's officers. Brief statements were already on the file. Eventually these might have to be elaborated but the cases against the Frei Hind officers were a long way down on the list of priorities.

I said the arrangements being made for these interviews were utterly pointless. That's not quite accurate. They

weren't pointless in terms of Merrick's passionate exploration outwards from the hollow centre of his self-invented
personality, and in these terms they were in every detail an
exposition of his determining will and of his profound
contempt for anything, for anybody, that crumbled without
resisting. Some hindsight here; but whenever I think of him
nowadays this little *mise en scène* comes back to me as a vivid
illustration of the extraordinary care he took to manipulate
things, people and objects, into some kind of significant
objective/subjective order with himself at the dominating
and controlling centre.

What arguments he used to convince senior officers in his
department in Delhi that he should leave at once on a
statement-taking mission, accompanied by his newly
acquired sergeant, I don't know. If there was opposition I
wasn't aware of it; the operation was mounted smoothly,
swiftly – as if Merrick had anticipated the havildar's suicide
and planned in advance so that the only impediment to the
scheme had been the havildar's tiresome stubbornness in
staying alive. I certainly had no doubt that one of the chief
reasons for the sudden journey was his desire to tell Colonel
Layton to his face that the havildar was dead.

He had this effect on me. I attributed to him the grossest
motives and the darkest intentions without a scrap of real
evidence. The interesting thing is that I was convinced that
he knew this, that my instinct to hold him in such intense
dislike and suspicion was clear to him from the beginning and
was one of the reasons why he had chosen me. I believe he
found it necessary to be close to someone whose antagonism
he knew he could depend on and that without this antagonism he had nothing really satisfactory by which to measure
the effect of his behaviour. My antagonism was like an acid,
acting on a blank photographic plate which had been exposed
to his powerful and inventive imagination. It made the
picture emerge for him. This excited him, the more so
because my antagonism could not be expressed openly
without risk to myself of being guilty of insubordination.
There were moments in our association when I felt that my
animosity inspired in him a gratitude and a contempt both so
overwhelming that he felt for me the same tender compassion

252

that is often said to overcome the inveterate slaughterer of game in the split second before he squeezes the trigger.

*

Pankot, then: the evening of August 14, 1945. On this same evening things were taking place of much greater consequence; for instance, in Tokyo, where the Japanese War Cabinet, persuaded by the Emperor, had finally decided to 'bear the unbearable'. In the past week since the incident in Hiroshima and its follow-up in Nagasaki it had become obvious to them that when the bomb-owning governments said Unconditional Surrender this was precisely what was meant. No trimming; no understanding even as between gentlemen that there would be no allied occupation of the Japanese mainland (that had been tried). No promise that the Emperor's person would be respected (that had been sought). So, on this evening the decision to surrender unconditionally was made, and perhaps as Merrick and I were driven away from the Pankot Rifles depot, having left the *mise en scène* in a state of readiness for the commencement of the charade the next day – the Emperor of Japan was at his desk recording the edict which was to be broadcast to his weeping subjects at midday tomorrow August 15, well before which time the decision would have been conveyed to us through the Swiss.

And at the very moment Merrick and I drove out into Rifle Range Road heading for Cantonment Approach Road and the Pankot General Hospital, it is probable that the handful of dissenting Japanese officers who tried to break into the Emperor's palace later that night to destroy the recorded edict before it could be broadcast were already gathering and working out ways and means and the odds against the success of this last ditch Samurai act of patriotic defiance.

In Pankot the height of the surrounding hills made for a longer evening than one was accustomed to down on the plains and instead of encroaching from the east night seemed to lap slowly down the inner slope of west hill (where rich Indians had built their hillstation houses) and glide across the valley and then inch its way up east hill where the English lived and on whose peak, amid conifers, one could make out

253

the roofs and upper-windows (last reflectors of the light of day) of the Summer Residence. Once the light had gone from the roof of this dominant but unoccupied building night fell – you might say – with the Government's permission. Sarah smiled when I suggested this to her. She knew the view well from the lines of the Pankot Rifles but its symbolism had not struck her before.

My recollection is of seeing it first when waiting on the verandah outside the room that had been got ready for the interviews with the ex-POWs, because I'm sure I retained a visual impression of it on the journey back and that when Merrick turned round and said, 'You know where to reach me?' I pictured him standing at the window of one of those blazing upper rooms of the Summer Residence, getting burnt on the other side of his face but feeling nothing. The real answer to the question where he could be reached was only slightly less impressive. He was staying at Flagstaff House with the Area Commander.

One question I longed to ask him was how Colonel Layton had taken the news of Karim Muzzafir Khan's death. I assumed the news had been passed on and that by the afternoon it was generally known by the other Pankot Rifles officers and the senior NCOs and VCOs, and that this had accounted for the heavy pause – the brief but significant silence that followed my intentionally clear announcement of his name and village when I got to it on the list and the jemadar fumbled with the coloured pins as if looking for a black one.

But I restrained my curiosity and said nothing; even when the truck drove inexplicably *past* the hospital entrance and made for the bazaar. The crowds who must have attended the funeral seemed to have gone but left hostages, groups of people still *en fête* and bunches of idle police. We stopped outside a general store. The driver got out and walked down the crowded road towards War Memorial Square – by prearrangement, obviously, since Merrick didn't question him. In fact he lit a cigarette. Without turning – addressing the windscreen – he said, 'Do you expect to see your friend Captain Rowan again while he's in Pankot?'

I told him we had no actual arrangement.

254

'It might be useful,' he said, 'for us to know just what he's up to.'

It was typical of Merrick that he should describe Rowan as being 'up to' something – and 'up to' something that had or might have a bearing on what Merrick himself was up to. It so happened that Nigel was in fact up to something, on the Governor's behalf, but I wasn't aware of this until later when Rowan – stung by certain developments – dropped his guard and disclosed that his distrust and dislike of Merrick were almost as great as my own. Discounting what he called an element of doubt, he had cogent reasons but wouldn't at first say what they were.

But it irritated me that because I now worked with Merrick he thought I could be used to pump an old friend for information which he hinted I not only could but ought to get for him. My polite but thick sergeant act (the NCO equivalent of what is known as dumb-insolence in private soldiers) saved me from actually promising something I had no intention of performing. And it may have sufficiently served Merrick's purpose to observe the effect his suggestion had on me. There was no reason why he shouldn't ask Rowan himself what brought him to Pankot. He had more opportunity, officially and socially. I discovered later that he and Nigel had both accepted an invitation to dine that night at the Laytons' and that each knew that the other would be there.

The driver came back; not alone. He had the Red Shadow in tow. The Red Shadow climbed into the back, disposed some parcels (presumably bought for Merrick) and gave me one of his malevolent grins. I never worked out the significance of these grins. More often than not he stared at me unsmiling. But since it was clear that he wished me no good in either case I never gave much thought to the matter, and on this occasion responded as usual with a gaze as blank as I could make it.

The truck was now reversed and we drove back to the hospital. The manoeuvre that had taken me past the hospital, to the bazaar, and now back again, seemed quite pointless, but it was all part of Merrick's mystification technique and I was becoming used to it. We drove through the gates of the hospital and for a sickening moment I thought that the Red Shadow was to be quartered where he could keep an eye on

255

me. This suspicion hardened when we stopped outside the medical NCOs' mess and the Red Shadow vaulted over the tailboard and arrived on the asphalt, legs apart, like an acrobat fetching up in a standing position at the end of a sequence of spectacular leaps and somersaults. He was, thank God, only making room for me to make a less agile descent. He climbed back in again directly I was out. But now Merrick also got out. He came round to where I stood dusting my hands.

'I can't guarantee transport in the morning, sergeant.'

'No, of course not, sir.'

'The Pankot's adjutant says he can produce two of the men we want to interview by 1030 tomorrow morning. I shall get to the office by ten so if nothing's come to pick you up by 0930 you'd better get a tonga down to the depot or scrounge some transport from one of the NCOs here. Are you quite comfortably situated, by the way?'

I told him very.

'I ran into one of the medical officers who helps me from time to time with this arm. He said his NCOs had a spare billet or two. I thought you'd find it more congenial than any of the alternatives.'

'It was very thoughtful of you, sir.'

He stared at me for rather longer than seemed necessary. Then he said, 'Tomorrow will be rather interesting. Goodnight, sergeant.'

I stamped on the asphalt and threw one up. I thought he blinked but couldn't be sure. A really good salute requires one's eyes to be fixed fair and square on the bridge of the officer's nose. He touched the peak of his cap with the tip of his swagger cane. Before the truck had started up I was off down the path past the mess to my quarters feeling in my pocket for the key to the padlocked steel ring that secured my kit-bag. In the bag there was the last of two bottles of Scotch and one of rum: sweeteners from my previous officer – a man whose experience of Poona had in my opinion had a dampening effect on his initiative. Otherwise he would have fought for me.

*

256

So far I have said nothing about my private life in India and the time has come when it ought perhaps to be dealt with. I should describe it as moderately satisfactory, as achieving its peak (perhaps appropriately) in Agra with the wife of an officer who was having an affair with the wife of another and its nadir in a massage parlour in Bombay which had been recommended and which I had first visited after a rough journey through warm rain on a 500 c.c. Norton, had vowed never to visit again but dropped in on during the afternoon following the inquest on Leonard Purvis, which was the same afternoon Beamish told me I was to go to Delhi to join Merrick. Otherwise the graph of satisfaction, while giving me no cause for smug self-congratulation at the time, does not in retrospect go quite so far as to suggest positive deprivation.

I mention it because, while sitting in my tin tub, drinking whisky, the cool invigorating air of the Pankot hills suddenly hit me and twenty minutes later I was setting off for the mess, turning over in my mind the interesting possibility that the friendly senior NCO (whom I shall call Sergeant Potter) might turn out accommodating in regard to whatever arrangements there were to maintain a good relationship with the Eurasian nurses (or even with the less snobbish of the QAs). Not caring much for rum I took the bottle with me, to present it to the mess, and arrived there, matily, full of good intentions. These very quickly withered.

To begin with the rum was declined on the grounds that the drinking of anything but beer in the mess was strictly regulated and that mess rules did not allow members, let alone guests, to bring bottles in. Then there turned out to be a non-treating rule which, broken on my first appearance at lunch-time, was now rigidly re-applied and meant that I couldn't sign a chit to repay earlier hospitality but only for whatever beer I wanted myself. All this was explained by Potter as the others drifted away from the bar to the sitting area. He stayed with me, but less out of friendliness than a determination to protect his colleagues from me, or so it began to seem.

But it wasn't until Sophie Dixon arrived that I really came to the conclusion that for all practical purposes I was in Coventry. He swept in, came to the bar, ordered a beer, signed a chit, acknowledged Potter, ignored me and then went over to the others. Then he started.

There was a smell in the room, he said. Had anyone let wind? If not, was it the drains? Or something in the cookhouse? It really was a very peculiar smell. But vaguely familiar. Given time he'd identify it. Meanwhile it quite turned him up. It made him feel very queer. He didn't think he'd last out. Especially after the day he'd had. Guess whom he'd seen? Her very self. Miss Khyber Pass of 1935. Prancing around like a two year old. Positively cavorting. She'd do herself an injury if she didn't look out. In fact he wondered how she had the energy considering she had two of them in tow this time. Count Dracula again, but also a new one, Golden Boy. Very superior, Golden Boy. Very posh. In fact you might say regal. But smart. Oh yes, very smart. Full of bull. When he came to attention it fair went through you. In fact you thought yours would drop off and you wondered why his hadn't. Well you did if you thought he had any in the first place, which you couldn't take for granted nowadays when they were letting anybody in and not even bothering to say cough.

At dinner, Potter who sat at the head of the table indicated I should sit on his right again but this time the place on my own right and the place opposite were left empty. The others crowded together and talked shop. Potter looked unhappy. Our conversation petered out. The others left the table as and when they'd finished. Eventually I was alone with Potter at our end. Dixon and another corporal remained at the other.

Potter said, 'Breakfast's a bit of a moveable feast. You could have yours in your room if you like.'

I said, 'I will if it's more convenient and what you'd prefer.'

Dixon muttered something. It sounded like, "ark at 'er.'

Potter, playing with the spoon and fork on his pudding plate, said, 'Just tell the boy.' Then he said, 'There's not a bad Chinese restaurant in the bazaar. We sometimes go there of an evening.'

'Actually,' I said, 'I'm not awfully keen on Chinese cooking.'

'Oh, Christ,' Dixon said, almost loudly.

'But I suppose they do egg and chips?' I added. For the first time Potter met my glance, pitifully grateful. He hated being rude. He said there was a good film on at the Electric Cinema. They'd all seen it themselves and enjoyed it. If I wanted to go tonight I could catch the second house.

*

I didn't go that night. I went the following night – after eating at the Chinese restaurant. August 15. Sergeant Perron's lonely vj day celebration. But it *was* a celebration. I began the day by having breakfast in my room, and so heard nothing about Japan's formal surrender until I arrived at the Pankot Rifles depot by tonga and went to the hut we'd set up the day before. Merrick wasn't there. I was told about the Japanese by the adjutant, Coley. He assumed that the interviews would be postponed. The depot commandant, Colonel Trehearne, had declared a holiday from all parades. The truck that was to have collected the two men chosen for interview hadn't yet set off.

The depot lines had a look of a Sunday morning make and mend. The air was bright. Things sparkled. The hills were in clear definition. There had been no rain for a day or two. Depot sweepers were sprinkling water to lay the dust on the road outside the hut and on the earthen floor of the verandah. The young subaltern arrived and was chatty. We walked up and down in the sunshine and he confided in me his intention to stay in India as long as he could. By eleven o'clock the truck still hadn't left and Merrick still hadn't appeared. Maintaining my policy of initiating nothing I hung round, talking to whoever turned up.

Merrick arrived at mid-day. He saw the adjutant first and then came out to talk to me. As a result of Japan's surrender Merrick had been recalled. He was to fly that evening from Ranpur to Delhi and thence to Ceylon – from where, providing the Japanese forces in Malaya laid down their arms, he would fly on to Singapore where he would be busy with the initial sifting of blacks, greys and whites among the INA men who had co-operated with the enemy. I never discovered how hard he had tried on the phone that morning to persuade Delhi to order me to accompany him. I'm sure he did try

259

because his attitude was unmistakably begrudging. He didn't want to leave me behind in Pankot. Delhi must have told him to. Another officer would be sent to replace him. Meanwhile I was to stay and get the interviews started with an interviewing board of a couple of Pankot Rifles officers and myself with a watching brief.

You will understand my euphoria. It became difficult to sustain my dumb-insolence act. This did not escape Merrick's notice. The unblemished side of his face acquired, just under the skin, a tremor.

'I may send for you in Singapore,' he said. He was about to take his leave. We were strolling up and down the road outside the hut where the truck was parked. He was giving me instructions about the conduct of the interviews and the importance of keeping them strictly within the terms of reference and not letting the Pankot officers get lost in irrelevancies. Then he stopped, and said, 'I suppose that is all.' We were by the truck. The Red Shadow was in the back, grinning. I affected not to notice him.

'Incidentally,' Merrick said. 'I saw Captain Rowan last night. We dined at Colonel Layton's house. Has he contacted you at all?'

I said he had not.

'I'm sure he will. So be careful what you say if he raises the subject of Mr Kasim's INA son. He was pumping me rather. I'd have liked to be more forthcoming because it was rather a special evening, but the department isn't so sure now that it would be at all helpful, whatever Government says, so I didn't want to raise his hopes. It would be better if you pretended to know nothing.'

He was back on form. I told him it wouldn't be difficult to pretend I knew nothing because I didn't.

'But you've read the file on Sayed Kasim.'

'No, sir.'

'I thought you would have done. I told you in Bombay it was one of our most interesting cases.'

I didn't answer.

He said, 'Perhaps it's just as well you didn't, though. Otherwise your old school-friend might have cross-examined you more successfully than he did me. He's been well trained to find out a lot and give little away. But so have I. Although in a different school.'

The time had come to say goodbye. Had he been about to offer his good hand? Was he aware of the possibility that we would not meet again? I gave myself no chance to find out. Smart step back. Stamp. One two three, up. The combination of muscular tension and emotional relief caused me to grunt. He smiled, tipped his cap peak with the cane and got in.

As he did so – and as I took in this *mise en scène* – the skin on the back of my neck and above my ears seemed to contract. Perhaps the hair stood up. Whatever the effect the cause was that I had apprehended not only the significance of Sophie Dixon's monologue of the evening before but the significance of the back-to-the-hospital-via-the-bazaar routine. In a different setting we had just re-enacted the end of that seemingly pointless journey. But it had been far from pointless. We had gone first to the bazaar because he wanted the Red Shadow in on the act. We had then driven to the hospital and into the grounds and stopped in view of the NCOs' mess because Merrick wished us – if possible – all to be seen together by the members of that mess. And obviously we had been. The three of us. Count Dracula, Miss Khyber Pass of 1935 and Golden Boy. Dracula and Miss Khyber Pass were known figures. Golden Boy was new. Accepted for myself on my first appearance – once identified as belonging to Merrick and the Red Shadow and transformed by some sinister magic flowing from them into Golden Boy, I was at once rejected. I did not know why. All I knew was that this rejection had been deliberately engineered by Merrick. He had sent me, unidentified and unaccompanied, into a nest of his enemies. And having established me there he had with meticulous attention to detail arranged to have me exposed as an enemy too. Nothing has ever convinced me otherwise.

He beckoned me to come closer.

'By the way, sergeant. I'm leaving Suleiman in your care. At least for a day or two. He'll continue to be quartered with the servants at Flagstaff House but I've told him to report to you here every morning. He has his month's wages and his return travel warrant. The officer who comes up to replace me may want to borrow him. If not I'll send word and then I rely on you

261

to get him on to a train and send him back to Delhi. Meanwhile, make whatever use of him you think fit. He knows his way round Pankot pretty well now.'

It was Merrick's parting gift to me, the only one he had available that he calculated would cast a blight on my day of liberation. But in this case he had miscalculated. The Red Shadow was still grinning at me. I grinned back at the Red Shadow, making calculations of my own. If the grin surprised the Red Shadow he gave no sign of it, but I think it surprised Merrick. Puzzled him? Interested him? Suggested to him a new line of attack for future dealings with me? It was difficult to say. When I turned from the Red Shadow to Merrick and snapped out, 'Right, sir,' there was a look on the looking side of his face that I can only describe as one of triumph and no-triumph, of contempt and no-contempt. And the scarred side was immobile and expressionless as if it had long since grown tired of living with its enigmatic counterpart.

*

Merrick left Pankot on the morning of vj day. I had my midday meal with vcos at the depot, and spent the evening at the Chinese restaurant and the cinema. Apart from breakfasts in my room, an evening bath and a night's sleep, I kept clear of the hospital set-up and could have done so more or less indefinitely. But Rowan came to the rescue. I'm fairly sure that he did so on Thursday, August 16.

He turned up at the Pankot Rifles depot, inquiring for me. He knew that Merrick had gone. He had finished his own job in Pankot but was staying on for a while. The Indian civilian who had come up with him, Gopal, had gone back to Ranpur. Nigel was alone at the guest house. He suggested I should join him. I said I'd be glad to. So it was arranged that I should transfer my stuff up there in the evening. He offered to send a car but I told him not to bother. He said he'd inform the billeting officer at area headquarters.

One reason for choosing Thursday as the day I moved in with Rowan is my recollection of the timing of certain events concerning the Red Shadow. Merrick left on the Wednesday, having told me that the Pathan would report to me every morning at the depot. I was prepared to find these instructions disobeyed so I was surprised when he turned up on – as it must have been – the first morning of Merrick's absence. He was waiting at the stick-guard post that controlled entry to the administrative block when I got there at 10 a.m. The first thing he asked for was a pass so that he could come and go freely on any errands I sent him on. I said I would think about it but not today because I had no errands for him to run. It would be enough for me if he reported again the following morning.

Seeing that I was about to pass through the gate he plucked my sleeve and held on and began to murmur at me confidentially. Presently it became apparent to me that he was offering to perform a particular service, that of procuring, and was anxious to hear what my special preferences were.

I put on a puzzled look and said, 'What do you mean?' and at the same time pulled my arm free of the grip. His kohl-rimmed eyes glittered and a sort of redness emanated from them – a rush of blood, but not I think of anger at my brushing him off so much as of irrepressible delight at the prospect now before us. He began to rehearse the range of Pankot's sex-life. The astonishing range. The impact on my imaginative sense and the smell of garlic which came in waves from behind his gleaming tombstone teeth combined to translate me momentarily from the prosaicness of white pole, sentry-box and wire fence (the charm and orderliness of the military lines of an old-established British hill station: monument to imperial rectitude and proper conduct) to a vantage point from which I had a sneaky glimpse in to the world within a world, hermetically sealed and composed entirely of a nest of boxes (Kama Sutra rather than Chinese), each offering successively its revelation of the inventive means by which one might secure release from the pressure of the biological urge. Could all that be available here? In Pankot? By comparison the Bombay massage parlour positively glinted as with a clinical aseptic light.

When the Red Shadow had exhausted either the list or his own imagination and fell expectantly silent, I said, 'Anything else?' Logic indicated that there could not *be* anything else but he took the question as seriously as I had seemed to ask it

263

and looked put out, even alarmed at the thought that there might be avenues of delectable exploration which he had never heard or dreamt of.

'Whatever Sahib desires,' he said at last and then smiled, popeyed, as if stunned by the elegance and ingenuity of his reply.

In the many barrack-rooms and sergeants' messes I'd lived in since getting into uniform – I might say in all of them – the one thing I'd be willing to admit had always distinguished me from my companions was my failure to acquire a *habit* of bad language. I don't mean that the soldier's words weren't in my vocabulary, they were; but they were reserved for special occasions. Like this one.

'What the Sahib desires,' I said, smiling generously, 'is that you should **** ***.' [I use asterisks because it always seems to me that written and printed the dignity of such phrases is lost and the pure metal of offensive *speech* debased.]

I did not wait to study the final effect of my remark. The immediate effect was sufficient – that is to say I was satisfied that his knowledge of the English language hadn't been put under any kind of strain and that what I said might even have had, for him, a ring of familiarity. Showing my own pass to the stick-guard (a very young but intelligent looking lad) I indicated the Red Shadow (now some ten yards away, staring, wagging his head at me) and explained that he was a notorious thief, currently on parole, but not to be trusted and under no circumstances allowed into the lines unless accompanied by myself. Any credentials he offered could be assumed to be forged or stolen and in any case better not touched by hand because he was suffering from a venereal disease now in an advanced, irreversible and highly infectious stage, a situation which made him reckless of his own life and the lives of others, especially the lives of young people (of either sex) under the age of twenty. I said twenty because the stick-guard looked like a raw recruit aged eighteen. A lot of what I said probably passed over his head, his military Urdu not yet being up to scratch and my knowledge of the local dialect being nil. But I think he got the general drift.

Thus, I had got rid of the Red Shadow for another twenty-four hours; but not, I admit, got rid of some of the impressions he had left me with of the arcane aspects of life in Pankot. Images tended to obtrude. Sometimes an odalisque appeared, scattering rose-petals for one to walk over in one's ammunition boots. Coley, languidly using a fly-swatter, appeared to me occasionally to be a eunuch dispensing attar from a silver shaker. A female sweeper, bent over her gently swishing broom, might have been performing a more delicate task; excitation of the dust the last thing in her mind, or in mine. The tea tasted odd. Goat's milk or bromide? And which, I wondered, of these men behind the blanket-covered tables, were sitting there satiated, just about getting through the day after a night's sampling of one or several of Pankot's erotic specialities? Coley? Yes, Coley perhaps. Not a eunuch after all. He had that remote washed-out look of a man whose secret life absorbed nine-tenths of his energy.

Having lunched with the vcos the day before, today I lunched with the havildars, and in the afternoon Nigel Rowan turned up and invited me to move into the Summer Residence guest house. As a consequence I spent the rest of the afternoon with a clearer and more practical focus for my wandering thoughts. The odalisque took on more and more the outward appearance of Sarah Layton whose part of Pankot I was about to enter, disguised in my fleece, shepherded by Rowan. By 4.30 or so when the second interview of the day petered out in cosy military reminiscences of the questioned man's experiences in North Africa, the transformation of the odalisque into colonel's daughter was virtually complete; the room, the hut, the whole precise military complex had reasserted itself and when I walked out past the stick-guard post the perfumed midnight garden of secret Pankot seemed as far away as the memory of the Red Shadow importuning that morning. I climbed into a tonga and felt the blessing of the ramshackle motion, the pine scent of the hills and the ancient smell of dung and wood smoke that hung in the invigorating air and mellow light. It had been my intention to keep the tonga waiting while I crammed into the kit-bag the few things I'd taken out, but as we got near the hospital I remembered I owed some money in the mess and would have to find someone competent to accept it. Realizing that this might take a bit of time my inclination became to bathe and change, postpone my arrival at the guest house and extract from the hospital the last ounce of the pleasure I would have in leaving it.

So I paid the man off at the gates and walked through the leafy grounds to the mess and to the hut where I had my quarters. It would have been about 5 p.m. The only men around were the servants. The room allotted to me was one of four or five under a single roof and sharing the same verandah, with its own bath-house and w.c. cubicle at the back, overlooking a courtyard or compound. At this time, apart from one sergeant (of whom I'd only seen the back view as he left in the morning for duty: it wasn't Potter) I was the only occupant of this particular block but there seemed to be plenty of bearers and bhishtis about. I never had any trouble getting what I wanted. The servants probably also looked after other huts and I was fortunate to be close to where they lived.

I had a key to padlock the front door from outside and the back door from inside. The drill was, once you were inside, to unlock the back door in the bath-house and then shout for the bearer or the bhishti. Actually to shout was seldom necessary. Directly you opened the back door bodies tended to converge and enter, the sweeper to sweep out (even if he had swept out in the morning), the bearer either to make your bed or to get it ready for the night, and the bhishti with the kerosene tins of hot water for bathing. If you waited for anyone it was usually the bhishti.

I told the bearer I was leaving, hustled the sweeper-boy out (giving him his bhaksheesh) and ordered a bath. Having unpadlocked my kit-bag I settled down to enjoy a Scotch and wait for the hot water to arrive. I decided to wear civvies and set them out on the bed with a change of underwear. The hot water came while I was undressing. I took the bottle of Scotch, my glass and another bottle of soda into the bath-house and settled in the tub for a leisurely soak.

The dénouement, after such careful scene-setting, is I suppose as obvious to you as it became to me before it actually occurred. Do you believe in a sixth sense? I don't think I heard a sound other than the noise the servants were making in the compound, shouting at one another, and the sound I was making myself, gently splashing water and humming a popular tune called 'Do I Worry?' But at one moment I was listening to the servants shouting and my own humming and at the next continuing to listen but, as it were, against a background of a soundless presence, a vibrating sense of intrusion.

Someone was in my bedroom and it needed no special gift of intuition to conclude that it was the Red Shadow. I went on humming and splashing, and kept my eyes well away from the door which, although closed, probably gave a man with an eye close to one of the hair-line gaps between door and frame, a view. I had little doubt – so strong was the sensation of being observed – that the Red Shadow was at the moment applying one kohl-rimmed eye to this gap, reassuring himself that I was doing what it sounded as if I was doing. I waited for the sensation of being watched to go away. When after yet another verse of 'Do I Worry?' it still hadn't I felt a powerful urge to grab the towel and hold it up like a purdah screen. I hadn't so far associated the Red Shadow with voyeurism, at least not when the observed object was a grown man long since past the peach-bloom of youth. Just, though, as embarrassment was giving way to simple outrage the eye stopped looking through the crack and its owner tiptoed towards the real objectives: my discarded uniform (wallet) and my kit-bag (bottles). This, you understand, was what my sixth sense told me. At the same time this sixth sense took control of my physical actions. It brought me, still humming, still scooping water, very slowly from the squatting to the crouching position. It kept me in the latter to minimize the change of level from which the hum was coming. Then it picked one of my feet slowly out of the tin tub on to the duck-board and then the other. It kept the water-scooping hand and arm going.

It then ceased to be inventive. There I was, stark naked, crouched and scooping and humming. The door was within leaping distance. But could one, should one, emerge, however furious, however vengeful, in a state of such wretched nakedness? Particularly after that voyeuristic interlude? The towel near by was not the kind one could wrap round with much confidence in its staying put during the energetic demonstration I had in mind. It was now that I noticed my discarded underpants. Still scooping, still humming, I hooked them with a toe and gathered them in and pulled them on. I leapt for the door, grabbed the handle and opened it.

The wallet was going back into the breast-pocket of my jacket. A ten rupee note from it had stuck to his fingers and (how dextrous he was) was disappearing into his belt at the same time that the wallet was disappearing back where it had come from. But both movements were now frozen at the point of completion and his head (looking stuck on his neck at a not quite convincing angle) was twisted round and presenting to me an O-shaped mouth.

I roared for the bearer – instinctively calling a witness – and this galvanized the Red Shadow.

'Sahib,' he said, opening his innocent arms, showing his empty hands and backing away, making for the door. As he backed I advanced and pronounced anathema.

'Rejected seed of a diseased pig-eater,' I began. 'Despised dropping from a dead vulture's crutch. Eater of sweeper's turds and feeder on after-birth. Fart in the holy silence of the universe and limp pudenda on the body of the false prophet.'

With each phrase I pushed him in the chest, out of the room, on to the verandah and then along its length. At each phrase he shook his head, wagged it rather in the Indian way, from side to side, an ambiguous movement suggesting both agreement and disagreement but striking a balance which seemed to mean: What the Sahib says, the Sahib says. And the Sahib continued saying, astonishing himself with a richness of imagery and fluency of Urdu he had never achieved before and has never matched since. Why didn't I write it down immediately afterwards? I've often wished that when finished the Red Shadow and I could have sat together and gone through it. But it has gone – like the Red Shadow but less precipitately and without my prompting. The verandah, elevated two feet from the ground but without a balustrade and giving on to a gravel path, made a perfect launching pad. And the Red Shadow when it came to it did not lack a certain grace and elegance of line. I've always felt that recognizing the inevitable the artist in him rejected resistance and settled for

268

co-operation. Our combined movements were balletic, slightly rough and ready and under-rehearsed but cumulatively not without poetry.

As we approached the edge of the verandah my flat-palmed pushes became closed fist prods – not punches; but they brought his arms and hands from the appealing to the protective position. We established a rhythm of prod and jerk and presently I grabbed his shoulders (this was the moment when he seemed to decide to go along with me) steadied him, removed the ten rupee note from his belt, and swung him round to face the way he was about to go, which he did, borrowing rather than receiving thrust from the sole of my bare foot, and adding some thrust of his own in an attempt to jump that wasn't made quite soon enough but contributed to the angle of flight and the arc of descent. He fell, rather heavily, spreadeagled, his lower body on the gravel and his upper on the grass on the other side of the path. And lay there; winded or pretending to be.

The sequence at an end and my week-old ambition fulfilled, I turned and found that there had indeed been witnesses. Apart from the bearer, the sweeper, the bhishti, and an unidentified person (no doubt of the kind who always turn up when there is an accident or act of God to contemplate with serene detachment – a freelance extra, as it were) there was Sergeant Potter.

What odd things one says to people, post-crisis. Seeing Potter I called out, 'Just the man I wanted. Will this cover everything? I'm leaving.'

'So I gathered,' Potter said, ignoring the ten rupees and looking down at the Red Shadow. 'But presumably not together?'

*

What Merrick had done was unforgivable. I had the story from Potter whose curiosity about my relationship with Merrick had been aroused by watching me deal violently with Merrick's servant. Ten minutes later he came to my room with my bar chits and the change from the ten rupees. By this time I was dressed and packed and I'd sent the bearer down to

269

the gates to get a tonga. The Red Shadow had gone; where, I neither knew nor cared. Potter asked what it had all been about so I told him. I bore Potter no ill-will because I was convinced that the NCOs' sudden change in attitude to me was entirely due to having seen me with a man they'd met before and had cause to dislike. But what cause? I wanted to know. Finding I was still friendly, Potter began to open up.

He said, 'Will that fellow make trouble for you with Colonel Merrick?'

I said it wouldn't bother me, but that as Merrick had gone to Ceylon and as I expected to be repatriated almost any day I'd probably be back in England before Merrick knew what had hit him or rather what had hit Suleiman. But I didn't refer to them as Merrick or Suleiman. I called them Count Dracula and Miss Khyber Pass. Potter blushed. He said, 'Look, I'm sorry. We thought he'd had the nerve to plant you on us.'

Potter didn't take much more persuasion to spill the beans.

*

It concerned a medical NCO. Potter didn't give me his name, but let's call him Lance-Corporal Pinker, Pinky for short, and let us imagine him as a reserved, studious and hard-working young man who had lived an institutional life with other men in uniform without ever seriously arousing the suspicion that he was what is called abnormal. Even Sophie Dixon wasn't absolutely clear on this score, or particularly interested. He liked Pinky because Pinky was harmless and friendly, quite intelligent and very conscientious. He had never served in the field, always at base hospitals. He had been in India for a few months and in Pankot for most of them. He was already in Pankot when Corporal Dixon and Sergeant Potter returned from Burma and were posted to the hospital's military wing.

At that time Pinky was working on the wards. His transfer to the office of Captain Richardson, the psychiatrist, came later. Pinky and Sophie were on the same officers' ward when Colonel Merrick (then Major) used to turn up for treatment and adjustment of his artificial hand and arm. He did this whenever he visited Pankot and on one occasion was admitted for two or three days because the chafing of the harness had set up inflammation and there was some question of infection.

It was now that Potter filled me in on Sophie Dixon's record in the field. His compassion for sick or wounded men sprang from the feminine side of his nature and he never left anyone in doubt about his physical preferences, but these were made entirely acceptable to the men he tended because it was his compassion and care – his dignified ministration to a sick man's needs that they were made to feel, never the other thing. They knew the other thing was there, they had only to listen to him camping it up in the casualty station tent or basha – but (as Potter put it) 'when he touched a man you could see that nothing was being conveyed except clinical reassurance'. In Potter's mind there was even an idea that Sophie's overt posture was a form of sublimation and that in fact he lived like a monk, on and off duty.

According to Sophie, the officer with the burnt face and artificial arm 'must have been quite a dish'. This was the irony; originally Sophie had liked Merrick, so had Pinky. Whenever he came for treatment, Sophie mothered him. He thought the wounded hero brave, patient and well-disposed. Merrick never seemed at all put out when Sophie put on his act. 'Sometimes I wonder about the Major,' Potter remembered Sophie saying. 'When I give him the bedpan this morning he looked at me ever so thoughtful. I nearly come out in one of me hot flushes. Watch it, Dixon, I says to meself. Hands off the tiller and leave it to the Navy.'

It would have repaid him to have listened to his own advice or rather to have watched not 'it' but Pinky. If he had watched Pinky closer he might have seen when the time came that Pinky was in trouble or heading for it. But by then Pinky was off the wards and in the psychiatrist's office. When Merrick next turned up for treatment he said to Sophie, 'I see your old colleague's working for Captain Richardson. Isn't that a waste of nursing skill?'

It didn't surprise Dixon that Merrick had visited the psychiatrist. Considering the nature of his wounds a chat with the psychiatrist would not have been in the least remarkable. Six weeks later Merrick was again in Pankot. He visited the hospital. This time he was accompanied by the

Red Shadow. Sophie saw them together and at once nick-
named Suleiman Miss Khyber Pass of 1935. A few days after
Merrick had gone back to Delhi, taking the Red Shadow with
him, Sophie found Pinky crying and packing his kit. It took
Sophie some time to find out why.

*

Working in Richardson's office Pinky (so it would seem) had
had his eyes opened for the first time in his young life to the
fact that his inclinations were not nearly as uncommon as he
had supposed. His was a typical case. Over-protected as a boy
he had preferred the company of girls until he reached the age
of puberty. After that he found himself attracted, mys-
teriously, to his own sex. He felt unique. Later he learned that
to be like this was wrong, and later that it was not so unique as
to have escaped being a criminal offence. As he grew older
still he also discovered that it made ordinary men laugh. He
knew he couldn't help being what he was and he didn't hate
himself, but he couldn't have borne to be found out. He told
Sophie that when he came to Pankot at the age of twenty he
had had no sexual experience with anyone except himself.

His job in Richardson's office was clerical and highly
confidential. It wasn't a hard job because the number of cases
in the hospital needing serious psychiatric treatment was
never high. There were a few disturbed men in one ward and,
now and again, in another, an officer or two whose
'equilibrium' had been upset. Psychiatry was still a bit of a
joke in Pankot but it had become vaguely fashionable in the
army. Just as potential officer-cadets in England had a routine
chat with a psychiatrist at the war-office selection boards so,
now, in Pankot's military wing, convalescent men had chats
with Richardson. It was almost a branch of welfare.

Richardson had a lot of time on his hands and Pinky
discovered that he made use of it by keeping separate sets of
private and confidential files for personal reference in his
future civilian career. As Richardson's confidence in Pinky
grew so did Pinky's opportunity to satisfy his curiosity about
the contents of these private files. Richardson told him that
psychiatry was a very inexact science and that there were

272

judgments it was wiser not to record officially because the army simply didn't understand the complexity of a man's emotional life and it was grossly unfair to penalize someone by recording an informed professional but far from conclusive opinion that might be interpreted subsequently in the naïvest manner and block a man's promotion. When Richardson found that Pinky was genuinely interested in psychiatric method he sometimes lent him 'closed files' of men who had been discharged and, during slack times, even discussed them with him. He never showed him files on men which were still 'open' and all the files, both the official and the separate private files, were kept under lock and key. If Pinky was lent a file he had to return it to Richardson before Richardson left the office.

What fascinated Pinky was the revelation that in Richardson's view (and who was Pinky to argue?) 'repressed homosexual tendencies' were not infrequently the cause or one of several causes of what – up there in the wards – might look simply like depression or apathy or a temporary inability to cope. He became intensely curious about the notes Richardson had made or was making about the men currently undergoing treatment – in particular one man around whom Pinky had been spinning private fantasies: a tough, good-looking corporal who had been in Burma with Wingate's expedition.

A timid boy, his obsession gave him courage. He stole Richardson's key – easy enough because the key was kept in a drawer of the desk which Richardson did not always remember to lock. What took nerve was getting a copy of it made in the bazaar and putting the original key back. Thereafter, night after night, he sat at his desk with one of the current confidential files, risking discovery but taking the risk because what he read absorbed him. The files changed his whole attitude to himself. The man in the ward, for instance, the one whom Pinky fancied, had admitted to Richardson that he had 'mucked about' with a fellow Chindit, still preferred women but wasn't ashamed of the mucking about because he thought of it as something that had 'just happened quite natural', just 'part of the business of being stuck in the jungle and being shot at' and if he were back there he'd probably do it again. What amazed Pinky was Richardson's diagnosis that this man was 'intelligent and well-balanced' with a 'healthy attitude towards sex', and that his depression was almost certainly due to a combination of the physical after-effects of the dysentery for which he had already been treated and an understandable but by him unacknowledged conviction that he'd had enough of combat. The note on the official file, which mentioned nothing about 'mucking about' closed with the comment, 'Fit for active duty from the point of view of this department but recommend further analysis of faeces'.

Intelligent and well-balanced. A healthy attitude towards sex. Pinky seized on the phrases as if they were lifebuoys. He acquired nerve. When he went down to the canteen or into the bazaar he looked about him, eyes open, newly confident. When he sat in the downstairs room of the Chinese restaurant (the floor reserved for other ranks) he glanced more boldly at men he liked the look of. Any one of them, judging by the files, might be willing to 'muck about'.

It was during this first extrovert phase that Merrick came back into his life, arriving at the office one evening after Richardson had gone and just at the moment when Pinky was at the filing cabinet selecting his evening's reading. He hadn't heard Merrick knock or come in but, looking up, saw him in the open doorway between Richardson's office and his own. Pinky's alarm was short-lived. Merrick was not to know that the cabinet was private. When Merrick spoke to him in a friendly manner, remarking on his transfer from the wards, Pinky stopped feeling guilty and asked Merrick what he could do for him. Merrick said he was in Pankot for a day or two and hoped he would be able to have a word with Captain Richardson. Pinky looked at the diary and made an appointment for the following afternoon. 'Merrick?' Richardson said next day, 'Isn't that the officer with the burnt face and amputated arm?'

When Merrick arrived Pinky sent him straight in. Presently he was called in himself. Richardson handed him the key and asked for a particular file. Without thinking – because he was now so used to handling them – Pinky brought him the official buff file and the private green one. Richardson handed back the latter and Pinky put it away. Merrick was in Richardson's office for about twenty minutes. When he had gone Pinky went in with some incoming mail and found Richardson studying the private green file. He gave both files back to Pinky. Pinky asked whether he should open a file for Major Merrick. He was told that Merrick wasn't a client. The files that had been got out in connection with Merrick's visit were known to Pinky. They weren't among those that interested him. They concerned a woman. He wondered what Merrick had been asking that caused the files to be got out, but did not inquire. The only other point of interest about this episode was that Pinky learnt for the first time that Merrick's peacetime job was in the Indian Police. The subject came up because Pinky said he supposed when the war was over the amputated arm would mean an end of Merrick's military career. Richardson said he'd no doubt go back into the police with a desk job and added, 'CID I shouldn't wonder. He's dealing with these INA cases already.' Pinky thought perhaps the woman's file was also connected with the INA business. He wasn't interested in the INA either.

*

Thus, lulled, Pinky rode for his fall. Several nights a week he went to the Chinese restaurant. Twice he thought he would have made it if he'd had the final ounce of courage it seemed to need to convey to a table companion that more than chat was on offer. After eating he often lingered in the bazaar, venturing beyond the area of light into the shadows and walking home, anticipating that longed-for voice calling out, Hey, soldier. And in the bazaar, during these patrols of his from shop to shop, he no longer shooed away the small urchins who pimped for their so-called sisters offering jig-a-jig, but grinned at them, shaking his head, listening for the miraculous change of tune from You want Girl, to You want Boy? Once, he heard it, but coward-like ignored it. It wasn't a boy he wanted, anyway, but someone of his own age.

*

Between Merrick's interview with Richardson and Pinky's next sight of him, several weeks passed, weeks which Pinky spent in the way I've described but which now culminated in what, had the consequences not been so terrible, he would probably have remembered ever afterwards as his unforgettable night. For a day or two before this memorable occasion, wandering in the bazaar he had been aware of the possibility that a young Indian lad was as interested in him as he – because this possibility was there – had become interested in the lad. He had never seen him in Pankot before but now they seemed to keep passing each other. The Indian was dressed western-style. He looked clean. He also looked vigorous: a dark-skinned version of the athletic kind of young Englishman Pinky was attracted to. On one occasion Pinky and the Indian were both looking at the window display in Gulab Singh's, the chemist, which was opposite the Chinese restaurant. The display was of clocks and watches. The next night Pinky stood outside the shop again. Again, as if from nowhere, the Indian turned up. They did not speak. Pinky wanted to but his mouth was too dry. When the Indian left Pinky stayed a moment longer and then left too. As he stepped into the road between a couple of parked tongas a man touched his arm and said, 'Sahib, you want woman?' Pinky shook his head. The man bent closer. 'Sahib, you want boy? That boy looking at watches? That boy very good boy. Like English soldier very much. He like you. He is telling me. Sahib wait here. Boy come.'

The man went – a turbanned whiteclothed figure, wearing an embroidered waistcoat and baggy trousers, walking quickly up the road openly and jauntily, stopping only once to make sure Pinky was waiting. Pinky began to tremble with excitement. To Pinky, this man looked manly and virile. East of Suez no shame attached to wanting boys. The man understood and casually accepted Pinky's need.

Pinky moved away from the tongas and went back to the arcaded pavement and strolled slowly along looking at the shop windows. When he came to an alley he stopped and looked back. The boy was coming, walking briskly. As he went past Pinky he smiled and walked up the alley. The alley was dark. For a few seconds Pinky was afraid. Sometimes alleys like this were patrolled by the military police and the west side of the bazaar, to which the alley led, was out of bounds to other ranks. Well, if the MPs stopped him and asked why he was following a boy he would say the boy had offered to introduce him to a college girl. Then he'd get off with a warning and an approving laugh. The blood began to pound in his chest. Pinky marched on.

*

'What was it like, love?' Sophie quite naturally had thought to ask Pinky, when he got to this part of his story. No go, apparently. He'd been over-excited. One gathers there was an encounter of some kind, prolonged but obstinately unsatisfactory. The Indian had explained his own failure by saying it made him unhappy to see Pinky so nervous. Then he had said it would be all right next time. He said, 'Come back tomorrow. Meet me outside Gulab Singh's at half-past nine and we will come to my room again.' When they were dressed the Indian became miserable and said he didn't think Pinky would come back. Pinky said nothing would stop him. 'Leave me a token then,' the Indian said. 'Lend me your wristwatch. Then I'll know that you like and trust me.' Pinky gave him the watch and told him to keep it. The Indian had already refused money. He refused to accept the watch except as a token of Pinky's intention to return the next evening. He took Pinky back down the rickety stairs into the alley and went with him until the light from the bazaar lit Pinky's way.

*

When I left for the summer residence guest house we got the tonga-wallah to drive through the hospital grounds along a path that led past Richardson's office. By we, I mean myself and Potter. He pointed the office out and then got off and walked back. After studying the place I gave the driver orders to move on.

The office was in a low building isolated from other blocks. It had the usual steep-pitched roof, the overhang supported by pillars to form a verandah. A small signboard outside announ-ced Richardson's name. One entered by a door at one end. This led to a passage. A window to one side of the door lit what had been Pinky's office. A window beyond lit Richardson's. The hut was presumably isolated to encourage patients to feel that anything they said to the psychiatrist went no further than here. Both Pinky and Richardson had had keys to the main door. The last to leave locked up. Outside the door, on the verandah, was a bench, a fire bucket and a cycle rack.

At about 6 p.m. on the evening of the day following Pinky's meeting with the Indian lad, he was alone in the office reading Richardson's private notes on the case of an ordnance officer who had collapsed under the strain of 'feeding the guns'. He kept looking at his watch and, because thrillingly it wasn't there, having to judge by the fall of the light outside how much longer he could afford to spend on this fascinating stuff before locking up, going to his billet to shower and shave and set out on his journey to bliss. He had just decided to call it a day and was closing the file when the door opened and Merrick walked in.

Pinky gave him a cheerful good-evening. Merrick asked if Captain Richardson was in. Pinky told him he had gone for the day but would be in the office tomorrow as usual and that if Major Merrick wanted an appointment he would be glad to look at the diary and write one in.

Merrick said that would be good of him. Pinky went into Richardson's office and came back with the diary. Merrick was now sitting. An hour was agreed and written in. Pinky took the diary back and put it on Richardson's desk. When he returned Merrick had the green folder and was examining the cover. For an instant Pinky was alert but Merrick didn't open the file and when Pinky was back at his desk he put the folder down. Then, smiling in a friendly way, he adjusted his artificial arm, as if it needed easing. The black-gloved artefact was held out, closed. He prised the fingers open. In the palm of the glove lay Pinky's watch.

He said, 'I think this is yours.'

Pinky did not remember with any clarity what happened next. On the whole he thought he just stared at the watch while Merrick sat waiting for him to react. The next thing

Pinky was fully conscious of was Merrick standing with the watch in the artificial hand and the green file in the other saying: 'My understanding from Captain Richardson was that these files were always kept under lock and key and were available to no one when he was not in the office himself.'

And then:

'I take it you have managed to obtain a key. You were at the filing cabinet the last time I came at this time of evening. If you have such a key you would be well advised to hand it over now.'

Pinky did so.

'Is this the only file you have removed tonight?'

Pinky nodded.

'Does this telephone go through to the hospital or the civil exchange?'

Pinky mumbled through dehydrated lips that it went through to the hospital exchange but that the hospital exchange could get any number.

'Right,' Merrick said. 'Wait outside. You will be wise to wait and do nothing foolish.'

Pinky stumbled into the passage. Merrick closed the door behind him. He found himself out on the verandah without knowing how he got there. Shock had affected his ability to co-ordinate what he did and saw with any sort of understanding of it. For instance he was aware of a figure leaning against a pillar, gazing at him, but the figure to him was simply a deformation of the pillar. When he realized it *was* a figure he assumed he must be hallucinating because it was a copy of the figure of the man who had procured the Indian for him the night before.

After a period of time, borrowed from and never repaid to him, he heard Merrick closing the door of the office. He got unsteadily to his feet, knowing the real shame began *now*, waiting somewhere for the military police, whom Merrick had obviously been phoning, to come and escort him to a guard-room.

But what happened was quite different. Without even a glance in Pinky's direction Merrick walked away up the path, followed by the procurer – or, let's give him his proper name, the Red Shadow. When they were out of sight Pinky began running. Then, wondering where he was running he ran back where it was safe. But it wasn't safe. So he was sick. After he had been sick he ran off again. Again he ran back and covered the vomit with sand. After he had done that he felt like a visitor, a stranger to the scene. Lights were coming on in windows of other huts that he could see through the trees. The evening was real. *He* wasn't real, but the evening was, and this unreal self had to lock Captain Richardson's office up. Before that he had to close Captain Richardson's office windows.

The green file was still on the desk. Automatically he went with it into Richardson's office. The cabinet wouldn't open. He felt for his key. Merrick had it. Or had he? Pinky turned on lights and started hunting for the key. There was no key; only the locked cabinet and the rogue file that couldn't be put back into it. If he could only get the file back into the cabinet and lock it he might be able to say he hadn't done it and that Merrick was lying. He knew this was impossible but that's the way his mind was working. Then he remembered that the key and the file were quite unimportant in comparison with the wrist-watch. Perhaps he could find the watch. If Merrick had left the file lying round perhaps he had left the watch. There wasn't a watch, though. Merrick had the key and the watch and he, Pinky, had the file. He hid the file in a drawer in his own desk. He shut all the windows and turned off the lights, locked the doors and ran back to his quarters. He went to the latrine. What he evacuated was liquid. He sat in the latrine in the dark with the liquid streaming from him. Then he did a very odd thing. He manipulated himself into a state of excitement and then out of it and leaned back exhausted. Subsequently this puzzled him. He asked Sophie if Sophie could explain why he did a thing like that. Sophie couldn't but remembered later and told Potter that he'd read somewhere that when a man was being executed by the rope he sometimes suffered an involuntary emission as though that part of him too was saying good-bye.

*

In the morning, unable to face what had to be faced, Pinky

reported sick. The duty MO couldn't find anything wrong with him but he looked so terrible that to be on the safe side the MO sent him to the staff sick-bay for observation. There was no one in sick bay except an Indian orderly. Pinky lay on a bed fully clothed. He was given a nimbopani and drank it gratefully but immediately afterwards brought it up. A QA sister arrived to chart his temperature and pulse. The temperature was slightly above normal and the pulse was rapid. An hour later he brought up another nimbopani. The duty MO came over. Specimens of urine and blood were taken. Pinky was put into hospital pyjamas and bedded down. He lay curled in the embryonic position. He hadn't slept at all the previous night. Mercifully he slept now, shutting the world out. He slept right through the most traumatic part of the day – the hour of Merrick's appointment with Richardson. When he woke in the late afternoon Richardson was sitting on his bed.

'My green file on the ordnance officer, Captain Moberley,' Richardson said, quite gently. 'Can you tell me where I might find it? I have an interview with him this evening.'

'Yes, sir,' Pinky said. He felt calm now. 'It's in the bottom left-hand drawer of my desk.'

'Thank you, Pinker.' Richardson stayed on the bed. Pinky could see that he was considering a number of alternative statements. Richardson was not a great talker. He was so used to listening. 'All things considered, Pinker,' he said eventually, 'I think you'd better remain here for a day or two, even though there is nothing physically wrong with you. I don't mean that you're malingering. I mean that your illness is psychosomatic. I take it you yourself are in no doubt of that?'

Pinky nodded. There was nothing Richardson could do for him but Pinky felt at least he understood. Richardson's was the last friendly face he was likely to see until he came out of prison. But he did not think he would ever come out. He would die of terror and humiliation. He hoped so. How could he ever face his parents again if he survived to be sent home? Two years. In an Indian prison. For a crime he hadn't committed and had never intended to commit. He had only wanted a bit of love.

The next morning he felt not better but somehow purged. The QA sister said she was pleased with him. He had expected that by now everyone would have heard about him and he had steeled himself to bear their contempt. So he guessed that whatever Richardson was doing he was doing as discreetly as he could.

Allowed up, he sat on the sun-verandah of the sick-bay and opened his mind slowly to his 'case' – the strange and puzzling aspects of it. The business of the files was of minor importance, surely. What Merrick was after was the nailing of men like him: queers. Probably Merrick had taken one look at him months ago and thought 'Ah.' His discovery that Pinky was sneaking looks at confidential files – gloating over them – would simply have reinforced a poor opinion of his character. And yet. And how long had Merrick had him watched and followed? When Pinky thought back to those weeks patrolling the bazaar he went cold.

Pinky had never seen the Indian procurer before but he must have seen Pinky. Was he in Merrick's pay or a fellow-victim of Merrick's cleaning-up operation? And what had happened to Tommy, the Indian lad? Had he been working with the procurer or had he been pounced on afterwards and made to hand the watch over? And then what happened? Had Merrick pounced on the procurer? Pinky became dizzy trying to work out the permutations. So he closed his mind to his case and lay on the sun-verandah all day trying hard to think of other things like home and times when he had been happy.

But throughout the day one question kept nagging at him. *Why me?*

*

After two days in sick-bay he reported for duty at Richardson's office. He had already packed a military criminal's kit – his small pack. When he arrived he found another NCO at his desk. The new lance-corporal said it would be helpful if Pinky could show him the ropes. He asked Pinky where he was going. All Richardson had told him was that he was to take over Pinky's job. Pinky said he didn't know yet but thought he'd better not interfere unless Richardson gave him official permission to hand over. He waited outside. Richardson arrived. Pinky saluted smartly. Richardson told him that since he was up and about he might as well show the new NCO some of the routine. A spark of hope was kindled. Logic said he should have been in a guard-room long ago. It was very odd. He spent the morning and afternoon helping his successor. Richardson came and went. He was neither friendly nor unfriendly. About five o'clock he came back and as he went into his office he told Pinky to come in.

When Pinky was inside with the door shut Richardson handed him a piece of paper. Pinky read it. He read it twice. It was a posting order to a Field Ambulance in a division that was preparing for something called Operation Zipper. When Pinky finally understood what this meant he sat down without asking permission and cried.

He cried from relief and out of gratitude. The only explanation he could find for his escape was that somehow Richardson had managed to suppress the terrible charge. How, he could not begin to imagine. For a moment he did not care.

Richardson let him cry the cry out. It didn't last long and wasn't noisy. The lance-corporal in the other room could not have heard it. Richardson poured him a glass of water and then went and stood in a characteristic position, with his back to the room, looking out of the window, his hands in his trouser pockets.

When Pinky had quietened down he stood up, ready to leave. He said that before he went he wanted to apologize for having abused Captain Richardson's confidence in the matter of the files. He knew it had been very wrong and he was very sorry. He didn't know what else to say because he couldn't bring himself to mention the thing that Richardson had only referred to obliquely – so obliquely that it was almost as if he hadn't referred to it at all.

Richardson said, 'Yes, I suppose it was an abuse. Between us we might have overlooked it, but in all the circumstances I decided you would have to go. If it's any comfort to you, Pinker, although I suppose I ought not to say this, I think you were extremely unfortunate to have come up against that particular officer. However, there it is. You did. And no experience, however disagreeable, is ever wasted.'

Richardson left the window, smiling, as if nothing much

had happened. 'Also, if it's any comfort to you, from observation I'd say that you'll actually be much happier in the field than in a place like this. Your conduct sheet is clean, there's no reason why it shouldn't stay like that, is there?'

Richardson offered his hand. Dumbly, Pinky took it.

'Tell me,' Richardson added, putting his hand back in his trouser pocket. 'How long was Major Merrick trying to get me on the telephone the other evening?'

'Get you on the telephone, sir?'

'He said he tried to ring me so that I could come over and deal with – this problem. He said he tried there and then, from this office.'

'He sent me outside, sir.'

'Yes. I see. How long were you outside?'

'I honestly don't know, sir.'

'Quite. Well, never mind, but actually I was in my quarters the whole evening. You didn't by any chance palm him off with a dud number?'

'He didn't ask for a number, sir. Just whether the phone was on hospital or civil exchange.'

'Well I only wondered, because my phone never rang. But it's of no importance. The operators probably ballsed the call up. That wouldn't be new, would it, Pinker? But perhaps it was as well they did. These things are much better discussed in the cold light of the day after. Wouldn't you say? Goodbye, Pinker. Good luck.'

Pinker said goodbye and thanked him. He tried to say more but couldn't. He had the impression that Richardson was really asking him to say more. But he shirked it. Just before he reached the door Richardson said:

'Oh, Pinker, I nearly forgot. This is yours, isn't it?'

He was holding out Pinky's watch.

'I think it must need a new strap otherwise you'll lose it again.'

Slowly, disbelievingly, Pinky took the watch. His face was burning. He mumbled something like thank you sir and goodbye sir, and then, remembering, came to attention. He was still at attention when Richardson said:

'If it's any interest to you, I found it among the Ms. I suppose it slipped off your wrist when you helped yourself to Captain Moberley's file.'

That evening, in the midst of his packing, Pinky stopped, sat down and looked at the watch: the gift of his parents when he joined up. Then he threw it on the floor and stamped on it with the heel of his boot until it was in pieces. This was what he had done with his life so far. He resumed packing, pausing every so often to wipe his eyes and cheeks. He kept telling himself to be a man. But that didn't help. Thus, Sophie found him.

*

There were only two explanations for the returned wrist-watch. The first was that Merrick had given it to Richardson and told him how it had come into his possession and that Richardson had persuaded him not to take the matter further but leave him to deal with it. This was the explanation Pinky believed was the correct one – the only one that made sense to him and which bore out his opinion of Richardson's stout character. It didn't make sense to anyone who knew Merrick as I knew him. It didn't make sense to Sophie and Potter but neither had an alternative explanation.

From their point of view here was an officer who had gone to a great deal of trouble to nail Pinky on a charge of gross immorality. Without compunction he had used another man (obviously, according to Pinky's description, his own servant) to act as agent provocateur and perhaps even a third man, the Indian lad, in order to get incontrovertible evidence. Sophie said he was familiar enough with British police methods in dealing with homosexuals not to find anything in the least remarkable about an officer of the Indian police using similar methods to shop a soldier. If Pinky had ever been charged and tried, Sophie said, we'd have been amazed at the transformation from fact to fiction in the statement made about how the evidence was obtained.

But then, after all this trouble, Merrick had done nothing more. Why? Had Richardson given Merrick a bad time? Had he seen through whatever story Merrick told him and warned Merrick that he would kick up a stink about the deliberate provocation he could see had been used? Had Merrick been scared off, been persuaded to hand over the prime bit of evidence – the wrist-watch – even been glad to get rid of it and slink off none the richer but wiser?

Pinky accepted this as the explanation because he wanted to. Sophie and Potter didn't accept it but couldn't conscientiously refute it. At one time after Pinky had gone Sophie was prepared to see Richardson and ask, but Potter dissuaded him. So, failing a revelation, they had both settled for the fact that Merrick had set Pinky up, sadistically using powers which were his but which finally he hadn't exercised to the full extent open to him – just possibly because after talking to Richardson (but why had he waited to do that and not called the MPs then and there?) he dared not take that risk.

Not dare take the risk? They didn't know Merrick. He certainly set Pinky up and having set him up used him. If there had been any further advantage to be had out of persecuting Pinky he would have taken it. He was the kind of man who worked for preference within a very narrow margin of safety where his own reputation was concerned. He courted disaster. Deep down, I think, he had a death wish. It came out in this way, pushing his credibility to the limit, sometimes beyond it.

But once he had got what he wanted – in the Pinky affair as in any other – he was no longer interested except to the extent that it pleased him to see his victim suffer. What he wanted in this case was not, I think in one sense, very important to him, but he had made up his mind to have it and had seen how he might get it. He had a talent, one that amounted to genius, for seeing the key or combination of keys that would open a situation up so that he could twist it to suit his purpose.

Originally Merrick went to see Richardson to discuss someone who had been one of Richardson's patients. This may have taken Richardson by surprise and like any psychiatrist he would have been reluctant to discuss the case in any detail. He would not have told Merrick much, only as much as an ordinary man would have realized he had to be satisfied with. But during that interview Merrick realized that there were files – a green one in particular – which would tell him far more, tell him as much as Richardson knew himself and which he was absolutely determined to have a look at. Sheer luck, coming upon Pinky at the filing cabinet the night before, acute observation and shrewd deductive powers, had already shown him the way in which to get that look.

So what Merrick wanted, *all* that Merrick wanted, was a look at the green file, the private file about the patient he went to discuss. It was as simple, as absurd as this. Even while Potter was telling me the sordid little story I was – because I knew Merrick – casting about for the unconsidered trifle, but the significance of the file did not really emerge until later when I talked to Rowan.

While Pinky was outside on the verandah counting the grains of sand in the fire bucket or whatever he subconsciously did when in the grip of that sense of unreality, Merrick telephoned nobody. He opened the cabinet with the key he had guessed Pinky had and which he had terrified him into handing over and at his leisure looked through the file. The Red Shadow was there to continue terrorizing Pinky but also on sentry-go to warn Merrick if someone not in the little *mise en scène* approached. When Merrick finished, he placed Pinky's watch in the cabinet – not in the Bs where the file he had been reading belonged but with the Ms which was the section to which he knew the file on Pinky's desk belonged, because he had looked at and memorized the name on the cover. He had then locked the cabinet and come away leaving Pinky sitting outside. He must have enjoyed that, leaving his victim in that sort of sickening suspense. He kept his appointment the following day, gave Richardson the key and shopped Pinky – not for sodomy but for abusing Richardson's trust. Precisely what Merrick said nobody knew, except Richardson.

In telling the story of Pinky, in trying to give an impression of my idea of what happened, I have filled the story out with some imaginative detail and also placed events in the order in which they occurred – not in the order in which they emerged during my talk with Potter. For instance, when Potter referred early on to Merrick's first visit to Richardson I said at once, 'What did he go to see Richardson about?' Potter said Pinky assumed he went to see him about the patient whose file

287

Richardson asked for. I said, 'What patient?' Potter said, 'Pinky said it was a woman, he'd had the file out at one time but put it back when he found out it was not about a man.' I said, 'Do you know what woman?' Potter said the answer was a woman called Bingham, but neither Pinky, Potter nor Sophie had ever heard of her.

I then asked him to continue with the story, but from there on I was on the alert because there was unlikely to be more than one Bingham in Pankot and surely Bingham was the name of the officer Merrick had tried to rescue from the blazing jeep, the officer Sarah Layton's sister married, who hadn't been well enough to go to Bombay to meet her father and whom Sarah had described as having had a bad time: obviously, in view of Richardson's file on her, not just a bad time physically but psychologically. And there was Merrick visiting Richardson to talk about her and becoming determined to have a look at her private file. Why?

It was rather late when I got to the Summer Residence guest house. This was a two-storeyed brick and timber building, appearing from the outside a cross between a shooting-lodge and the kind of villa you see half-hidden by fir trees and rhododendrons in the hills around Caterham. Inside, it was straightforward Anglo-Indian hill station stuff and smelt of damp and of aromatic wood. Rowan sat me down on a verandah whose floorboards sounded hollow underfoot so that it was rather like moving around in a sports pavilion or boat-house, except that the view was across an acre or so of rising ground to the Summer Residence (a dark hulk which in daylight proved to have been the inspiration for the guest house, architecturally speaking). On this verandah there were a lot of palms in brass pots and a set of white lacquered cane lounging chairs well upholstered by heavy cushions covered in durable royal blue cloth; and there was a smell of incense which presently I tracked down to a couple of joss-sticks smouldering away on a carved side-table. It struck me that if he went on like this and didn't get married soon Rowan might end up wearing Indian pyjamas indoors and eating pan prepared by himself from ingredients kept in little silver boxes, and discussing the Bhagavad Gita with a gentle down-at-heel professor from some nearby Hindu college; but only

288

during his leisure hours. And even then, in pyjamas, preparing pan and discussing the significance, say, of Krishna's remark to Arjuna that 'Learned men do not grieve for the living' no one would ever mistake him for anything other than an Englishman – one, moreover, of the kind it took a long time to get to know sufficiently well to be sure whether the amiable expression on his face was there for the benefit of the present company or for his own in dealing, as he constantly had to, with so many pressing and troublesome affairs.

For instance, having invited me there, having brushed aside my apology for lateness and sat me down, told the highly distinguished looking bearer to bring a whisky-soda for me and a gin-fizz for himself, he looked at me as if he wondered where I'd sprung from and what advantage I might expect to wrest out of this sudden and unexpected intimacy. He couldn't help it. It was an effect India had on a man whose manner was already naturally remote and uncommitted.

I said, 'Well, Nigel, tell me all about Merrick and Hari Kumar.'

His expression didn't alter. He said. 'Why?'

'I thought it would be a good way to bring the subject up. The subject of Merrick.'

'Why do you want to do that?'

'I thought you did. If we start right away wouldn't it make it easier for you to ask about Merrick and Mr Mohammed Ali Kasim's INA son?'

The bearer came with the drinks. Mine had far too much soda and ice in it. The coldness burnt my lips.

When the bearer had gone he said, 'I don't follow you.'

'Then I'd better start again. By the way, if anyone comes to put me under arrest would you be prepared to say that we spent the whole day together?'

Fractionally his eyebrows went up. 'I think that would depend on what they came to arrest you for.'

'Common assault?'

'On whom?'

'The Red Shadow.'

'Merrick's servant? Didn't he go back with him?'

'No. I just caught him pinching ten chips from my jacket.'

'If assault followed attempted theft I imagine you're safe enough.'

'In ordinary circumstances.'

'Were these not?'

'Are they ever where Merrick or one of his creatures is concerned? Who is Mrs Bingham?'

He picked up his gin fizz. 'Sarah Layton's widowed sister. Why?' He sipped.

'Tell me about Merrick and Hari Kumar first.'

'I'd rather you told me what you meant about Merrick and Mohammed Ali Kasim's INA son. Unless that would take you longer than we've got. We're dining out, if that's all right.'

'Should I change?'

'What you're in will do very well. If you could add a jacket. What gave you the idea I'd be interested in talking about Sayed Kasim?'

'Merrick told me to pretend not to know anything if you asked. But, as I said to him, that won't be difficult because I don't.'

'When was this?'

'Yesterday, just before we parted.'

'I saw him the night before. We discussed the case of Sayed Kasim – or rather a situation arising out of it – as fully as was necessary I'd have thought. So I really don't know what he means.'

'Weren't you pumping him?'

'Not at all. I asked a question and he answered it. Quite satisfactorily. It's all quite simple, Guy, but rather confidential. The thing is that since he was let out of prison MAK has consistently refused to see the son who fought with the INA and was taken prisoner last year. Government was prepared to let him but he said no. At least, he never took the offer up. All I wanted to know from Merrick, now that there's this department dealing with these cases, was whether he thought they'd co-operate about arranging a meeting if MAK suddenly changes his mind.'

'Has he?'

'Perhaps. But I didn't see Kasim until last night. When I spoke to Merrick the night before, the question was still rather hypothetical.'

'What did Merrick say?'

'That he didn't think his department would be keen now and might put up objections, but he was quite clear that Government might override them and could persuade the C.-in-C. it would be a good thing. He accepted that because his department doesn't initiate policy.'

'Well that's it, then. That settles it. Merrick's as mad as a hatter.'

Rowan watched me a while. He said, 'I hope not,' and drank more gin-fizz.

'What advantage does Government see in arranging a meeting between father and son? I take it it *is* a question of advantage. I met the other son, incidentally, at the Maharanee's.'

'So Sarah told me. I'm not sure there is much advantage now. But then I'm not personally in a position to judge. You know Kasim headed the pre-war Congress ministry in this province?'

'Yes.'

'He's in rather an unenviable position just now. Confidentially, Malcolm would like to see him back one day as chief minister, possibly because the alternatives to MAK are rather bleak. So anything one can do to help him solve his problems and clarify his position is done with that end in view. Does that surprise you? That a provincial Governor should have a soft spot for an Indian politician?'

'Why should it?'

'I thought perhaps it might. The *raj* is obviously not your favourite animal.' He looked at his watch and at my almost empty glass then glanced over his shoulder and summoned the bearer. 'Have the other half before we go.'

'May I have less soda and no ice this time?'

Rowan passed the instruction on but I sensed his disapproval.

'Is Mrs Bingham fully recovered?' I asked.

'Recovered?'

'Miss Layton told me her sister had had a bad time. What was wrong?'

'I think some kind of breakdown. She was pregnant when her husband was killed. Then she had the unpleasant experience of being alone in the house when Colonel Layton's stepmother died there. The baby was born prematurely. But it's quite some time ago. She seems all right now.' He added after a moment, 'You'll see for yourself. That's where we're dining.'

'At Mrs Bingham's?'

'At the Laytons. They all live together. Mrs Layton rang earlier and asked me to go round. I said you were now staying with me and she said she'd be delighted if you'd come along too. I didn't think you'd mind so I said yes for both of us.'

The other half arrived. Nigel had ordered nothing for himself. He still had some gin-fizz left. There was no ice in my whisky but the soda was over generous. I thought perhaps this was just as well after all, if we were dining at the Laytons'. Rowan said, 'Merrick told you then?'

'Told me what?'

'About Mrs Bingham.'

'He told me he was best man when she married the officer he tried to save.'

'Nothing else.'

'No.'

'Then what made you ask about her?'

'It's too long a story.'

'Oh.' He sipped gin-fizz. 'If she asks you tonight how you like working with Colonel Merrick you'd better tell her a lie and say you find it extraordinarily interesting.'

'Must I? My inclination would be to say I couldn't stop working for him soon enough.'

'I know. But she's going to marry him. It was announced at dinner the other evening.'

He studied me, as if for a particular reaction, then looked at his watch and got up. 'I've got a call to make. I'll be about five minutes, then we ought to go.'

I remained on the verandah, drinking my soda and whisky and considering the significance – the now clear and peculiarly distasteful significance of Merrick and Mrs Bingham's file. I thought: Well. It's none of my business. A few minutes later Nigel came back. 'I'm ready when you are,' he said.

I told him I was begging off because I didn't feel up to it.

'Aren't you well?'

'I don't think I would be if I had to spend the rest of the evening dissembling.'

He said, 'You wouldn't be the only one.'

'No. Miss Layton doesn't like him either, does she? But I suppose she'll have to learn to now. I won't. I'd rather not pretend otherwise to her poor sister.'

Rowan had propped himself against the balustrade, arms folded, ankles crossed. He said, 'When I said you wouldn't be the only one dissembling I really meant myself.'

'I thought you'd only just met him.'

'I've known about him, quite a while. But you guessed that, surely. Otherwise why ask me to tell you about him and Hari Kumar?'

'Is it what you've known about him or what you've just seen of him that puts you off?'

'Known was wrong. I'm sorry. *Heard*. One must be fair.'

'My Uncle George once said that the only reward in life for being fair is an obscure death.'

'He might well be right. Is he the balloonist?'

'No, that was Uncle Charles. Uncle George spends his life reading balance sheets and share prospectuses. We rely on him absolutely because he's the only member of the family who can count.'

'I never know when to take you seriously. I never did. How much time did you actually spend rowing on those Saturdays you got off?'

'Very little. The thing was to go about a mile up river to a place where a fellow-member of the club had found what he called a lot of spare local talent. We called it Knocker's Reach.'

'You mean that unwittingly I put you in the way of what Bagshaw called the temptations of the town?'

'Yes.'

Unexpectedly, Rowan smiled. 'Colonel Layton mentioned Bagshaw the other evening. He remembers him as a very junior maths master. I think it does him good to talk about things like that. Won't you change your mind?'

'An old boys' after-dinner session?'

'Would that bore you?'

'It would add no charm to the evening.'

'It would from his point of view, I think.'

'Does he find much charm in the prospect of having Colonel Merrick for a son-in-law?'

'Presumably he's not tried to stop it. The announcement was made in a friendly enough atmosphere.'

'What about Mrs Layton?'

'I expect her main concern is with Susan's welfare.' Rowan hesitated. 'The thing is, Merrick's extraordinarily good with the child.'

'How old a child?'

'Just over a year.'

'Boy or girl?'

'Boy.'

'In what way is he extraordinarily good with him?'

'He inspires the boy's confidence. I've seen it for myself. Watched them playing together with a box of bricks. They were both totally absorbed. Creatively absorbed. He has the knack of making a game seem important. Incidentally the child's not the least afraid of the artificial hand, or of the burn scars. I'm not much good with children so that the fact that I got no change at all out of young Edward is no guide, but Sarah says Merrick's the only man, more or less the only person of either sex who does. If Susan's main reason for marrying him is to give the child a father she'd have to look a long way before she found anyone more capable.'

'Do you think that is her main reason?'

'Wouldn't you agree it's a perfectly sound one?'

'So far as it goes. But I should say the important thing for a child is a sense of security. What's the point of having Merrick as an effective father-figure if the mother is unhappy?'

'Unhappy? One can't prejudge that.'

'You accept the possibility?'

'Susan's not a happy person by nature. But I feel quite incompetent even to hazard a guess about how a marriage like this will work out emotionally.'

'Or physically?'

He ignored this. He said, 'My worry really is about what might happen to affect Merrick's career adversely and make life difficult for her. When he was involved in the Mayapore rape case in nineteen-forty-two he went on the Indians' list of officials who were thought to have exceeded their authority in putting down the Quit India riots. If there's still such a list and I'm sure there is it would be remarkable if he's not still on it.'

'Were repressive measures taken?'

'The mood of the country was highly volatile.'

'In other words some officials acted beyond the limit allowed by law.'

'Well, yes. I think one has to admit it.'

'I can't think why you're bothered. They'll be well protected. They always have been.'

'But things have changed a bit, haven't they? The people now in Westminster know as little as their predecessors did about India, but I imagine they'll be more disposed to believe the very worst about the way India's been governed. I shouldn't think it will need more than a couple of ministers, men like Cripps, to come out here and hobnob with the Mahatma and the disciples of Annie Besant for the new Secretary of State to be rushed into setting up a commission of inquiry. The signs are that the Congress High Command may press for it.'

'Anything wrong in appointing a commission?'

'I think a very great deal. It might look like a genuine British attempt to see justice done impartially but the motive would be entirely political, a bit of window dressing in Westminster and damn the consequences in Delhi. And from the point of view of the morale of a frankly already overstretched Indian administration an inquiry of that sort would be pretty well disastrous. If there were cases of unduly repressive measures there were an infinitely greater number of cases of intense and by no means invariably nonviolent provocation. You have to put both the provocation and the methods used to meet it in the context of the atmosphere prevailing at the time, and that was a pretty tricky one. The Japanese were on the Chindwin, Singapore had gone and Burma had gone. Most of Europe had gone and North Africa was a mess. The plain fact is that strategically and I'm sure morally, India had to be hung on to. And I honestly don't see that any Indian leader who incited people to rebel against the *raj* and obstruct or sabotage its war effort has any right whatsoever to complain if quite a few of them got harshly treated. What else I see is that both sides would be wise to forget both the provocation and the reaction. Settling old scores is a fairly useless exercise at any time. When there's something else at stake as serious as trying to reach a sane and sensible agreement about the country's future government and constitution then it's worse than useless. It's damned stupid.'

'I owe you an apology.'

'Oh?'

'For thinking of you the other night as indifferent – how did I put it? – indifferent to affairs over which we adopt attitudes of concern and responsibility? So. My apology.'

'I don't actually feel owed an apology. But if you want to make one, the car's waiting at the front. We'd be no more than a minute or two late even if you want to wash your hands and comb your hair. But in any case, I must go.'

*

When Rowan told the driver to take us to Rose Cottage, Colonel Layton Sahib's place, I had a picture of what I must be in for, one so vivid that it depressed me. As a name, Rose Cottage wasn't quite as bad as say Mon Repos or Dunromin but I could not imagine anything much worse than dining there, among the cosy souvenirs of a lifetime of exile on the King's business. I pictured the Laytons surrounded by Benares brass and sweet briar, floral cretonnes and bronze gods; a Buddha smiling back at a yawning tiger-skin, and – above the mantelpiece – a watercolour of the Western Ghats and – on it – photographs of Sarah and Susan as little girls on ponies in Gulmarg. There might even be an imitation Chinese vase filled with dry bulrushes in a corner or on a grand piano; a standard lamp with a tasselled shade and dinner mats painted with hunting scenes from the English shires: Taking a Fence; The Water Jump; The Whipper-in; In Full Cry.

But directly we drove between two rather gaunt pillars my spirits rose. Had I heard right? Rose Cottage? One illuminated board simply announced '12' and the other 'Colonel J. Layton'. A moment of hiatus followed, a dark transit past dim ugly shapes which I feared might be rockeries, but then – lit from arc-lamps in the forecourt – I saw the beautiful proportions of an early nineteenth-century Anglo-Indian bungalow: squat, functional and aggressive, as well anchored to the ground as a Hindu temple.

'Good Heavens.'

'What's wrong?' Nigel asked.

'I hadn't expected anything so fine.'

'It's one of the oldest buildings in Pankot, I'm told. Is it your period?' He was smiling, taking something of a rise out of me but pleased that I was pleased. The verandah showed signs of vandalism: a wooden balustrade, obviously a later addition, but not recent; but apart from this the whole area was free of ornament, with one exception: a hanging lantern of iron and glass, plain, ugly and perfectly in keeping. In a niche near the door there was a handbell but the bearer, simply dressed in white linen tunic and trousers, was already receiving us. Nigel called him Mahmoud and told him I was Perron Sahib. The square hall was beautifully proportioned but ruined by oak panelling. I noted, though, that there were no wall hangings – no pictures, or trays. It looked as if something had persuaded the owner to leave the panelling to make its own vulgar statement. On the tiled floor there was a large Persian rug of a lovely silky texture. Heavy mahogany doors marked the positions of the rooms surrounding the hall. The one facing us was open. Mahmoud led us in.

*

I have tried to recapture events in some kind of sequence to give a lucid picture of my evening with the Laytons but it is as though after the shocks and surprises of that day I suffered a reaction of such intensity that I might have been hard put to it to write a coherent account the following morning let alone twenty-five years later.

Moreover, it was an evening during which nothing happened which contributed to what *you* would call a narrative line and which left me with nothing more useful from your point of view than impressions of members of the family – first impressions of the two I'd not met before and changed ones of the two whom I had. The most vivid impression of all was made by Mrs Layton, a woman whose personal distinction was heightened by an icy stoicism and by what was overlain but not disguised by that coldness: an unmistakable human sexual warmth, which I judged would be strong when aroused. Her air of detachment, the economy of movement and expression, the hard outer casing of the memsahib – so often tiresome in other members of that monstrous regiment – were, in her, peculiar graces. You felt that through them she was protected against the shock of life in general, and with them ready to meet the shock of her own head-on.

Rowan, in introducing us, told her how impressed I was with the house. She said something uncompromisingly direct like, 'Oh. Why?' My reply, whatever it was, helped to establish a tenuous bond between us. I understood that she had been making alterations both to the outside and inside and that there was still a lot to do which she was quite determined on in spite (was it?) of opposition from people who preferred it as it had been in Colonel Layton's stepmother's day. It must have been much later, probably when Nigel and I were leaving, that the question of the oak-panels in the entrance hall was raised. She described them as 'a pity', the more so because the damage done by removing the panelling might be considerable and the expense, in consequence, perhaps incalculable.

I describe the bond between us as tenuous because although I often felt a mutual empathy whenever we spoke to one another or when our glances happened to coincide, there were as many if not more occasions when a remark I made which she might easily have taken up was utterly ignored. She fascinated me. I observed with solicitude the portents of physical decline, the areas of flesh between eyebrow, cheek and ear, from which the resilience had gone, leaving the skin to find its own salvation, which it could only do with the help (presumably) of astringents which might, but didn't, never do, shrink it sufficiently to arrest the development of a network of minute folds and fissures which show up as lines and wrinkles and lend to the eyes a sad and perplexing beauty and luminosity, for the eyes do not age in the way that the flesh does, or do not when they are the eyes of a woman who is still handsome and armed with a proper measure of self-respect.

When she lifted her head – she had a habit of doing so and at the same time touching the necklace she was wearing – the pad of flesh under the chin was tautened and, for an instant, this and a consequent firmness of throat and neck created an illusion of youth, until you saw one, then two, obtrusive tendons and a faint blotchy discoloration in the region of the thyroid. On one occasion when my conscious critical self observed these marks of ageing, the other self, the self that weighed rather than noted evidence, was moved by a tender curiosity and a bold impulse to touch the skin as if to verify that what the eye saw was real, and as if, too, to communicate an opinion that it was virtuous in her to own such marks and that they inspired admiration, not pity. Perhaps it was her sensitivity to this reaction that caused her every so often to switch herself off from me, as a precaution against an unnecessary complication.

Possibly my reaction was an effect of the invigorating Pankot air acting in conjunction with the effect of that empathy, my recognition of Mildred Layton as an attractive older woman, one who, while conscious of the fact that one was borne along on the ever-flowing tide whose sound I sometimes listened for, did not allow the angle of her vision to be restricted to the view of here and now. She had, I believed, a vigorous sense of history, vigorous because it pruned ruthlessly that other weakening sense so often found with the first, the sense of nostalgia, the desire to *live* in the past. Throughout that evening she impressed me more and more as a woman who instinctively rejected the claims of years gone by if – unlike 12 Upper Club Road as I discovered she preferred to call it and to which she was in the process of restoring only what it could properly claim – these claims conflicted with her own claims, her determination both to survive and to defeat any force that currently threatened her.

Such strength of mind and character I attributed to her, and I judged it had probably not been sustained without effort and some assistance. She drank fairly heavily, like one accustomed (one might say disciplined) to it. One thing I noticed, the switching off became more frequent towards the end of the evening and was signalled by a lowering of the lids, a partial hooding of the eyes; but this was the only sign I could detect of the working of the alcohol.

*

Susan was the first of the two daughters to put in an appearance. If I had met her somewhere else and spoken to her for any length of time without knowing who she was, no familiar note would have been struck. Between this conventionally pretty girl and her sister there seemed to me to be no resemblance. Dark, carefully dressed hair and a high complexion, eyes that slid away from contact with your own and seemed emotionally disconnected from the smile of the neatly lipsticked mouth. The mouth alone performed the function of doing its social duty. Or was I *looking* for signs of disorientation? Her breasts were full, freckled above the deep cleft between them. She would be buxom in middle-age in spite of that narrow little waist (accentuated, I think, by a belt and a flared skirt). She was encumbered, distracted rather, by a Labrador puppy which had hectic manners which suddenly deserted it as if it had seen a ghost or had recollected some standing order about behaviour indoors. It retreated into a corner and sat awaiting a command or inspiration. It had the Labrador trait of looking at you in a way that revealed the white of its eyes – or so I think, having seen a similar animal recently that evoked these memories. Between Susan and this puppy there was a curious tension – a febrile acknowledgment both of the importance and unreliability of the other's presence. It did not take me long to recognize that for each the other was a symbol of a security desired but not felt. It took me a little longer to see that Susan Bingham felt no security in anything and longer still to work out one of the reasons why this insecurity made itself felt so strongly. The room was wrong for her, the room, the whole house. If the house had been as I'd expected, she would have fitted it. As it was it deprived her of the safety of a proper background. I noted how her mother kept watch, alert for any sign Susan might give of not intending to go through with something she had promised to perform. This is not hindsight. I was not at ease. Susan was difficult to talk to. I felt that the only way to break through to her would be to say: Tell me all about *yourself.* Her self-

300

centredness was like an extra thickness of skin. Without it, I believe, she would have died of panic or exposure. What she needed – the sense of human correspondence – was precisely what she protected herself from experiencing. I was appalled at the idea of the proposed marriage. As a victim, she was ready-made.

But it was – I reminded myself again – none of my business. None of this was. I was merely a spectator; as much but no more involved than someone in the audience of a theatre. The play had Chekovian undertones. For all the general air of easiness, the uneven co-operative effort to perform, *en famille*, each member of the cast was enclosed, one felt, by his own private little drama. Rowan, surprisingly talkative, did well – I thought rather too well – in his part of cheerful friend of the family. He wasn't cut out for it.

When Sarah came in at last it was as if someone had strayed on to the stage through error. She looked nondescript and her behaviour was colourless. She was quite unlike the girl I met in Bombay. My disappointment was profound. I assumed that in Bombay I must have been in a very uncritical mood where women were concerned. She was wearing the same dress, the one she had worn at the Maharanee's, but this time it did nothing for her. Her hair was dressed in the same way but lacked lustre. She did not even walk well. She had little to say to any of us. The one pleasant effect of her arrival was that Susan became a little more communicative and Rowan much less so. He had acquired the tentative air of a man who hadn't quite decided whether he was as fond of someone as he had imagined. Sarah gave him little encouragement. To me she gave none.

It was at dinner that it occurred to me that the evening had a motif; neither planned for nor consciously acknowledged. It was suddenly in the air. The motif was the forthcoming marriage and the part which I might or might not play in frustrating it. Only Susan and Colonel Layton, I thought, were completely unaware of this.

The motif first became apparent to me in the table arrangement. Mrs Layton put Rowan on her right and me on her left. Colonel Layton, at the other end, had his married daughter on his right and Sarah on his left, which meant that

Susan was next to me and Sarah next to Nigel. This strict adherence to an order of precedence that gave the married daughter seniority over her elder unmarried sister was, I thought, nevertheless open to more subtle interpretation, for there would have to come a point when I deliberately engaged Mrs Bingham in one of those table conversations which – even at so small and intimate a gathering – assume a semi-private character; and it would undoubtedly be my duty to mention her engagement to the officer I worked for and to offer my good wishes.

The subject of Susan's engagement hadn't arisen yet. After dealing with soup and responding to Mrs Layton's questions about the places I had visited in India, about the origins of the name Perron, about my balloonist uncle and my other eccentric relatives (Nigel must have briefed her well) I became very conscious that Susan was not communicating with her father nor (I felt) listening either to Nigel and Sarah or to her mother and me; that she was, in fact, waiting, self-contained, embattled; waiting for me to turn round and say: Well, tell me all about yourself.

This is the one moment in the evening I clearly remember. The soup plates were being cleared. Mrs Layton transferred her hostess's attention to Nigel, giving me the cue to transfer my own to Mrs Bingham. Protected, as I thought, by the conversation between Nigel and Mrs Layton I turned to Mrs Bingham and said Nigel had told me about her engagement to Colonel Merrick and that I should like to offer her my best wishes for their future happiness.

In the sudden silence in which I found myself ending it, my quiet little speech splashed as loudly as a stone thrown into a placid pond on a summer night.

After the ripples had died away Mrs Bingham looked round and smiled. 'Thank you,' she said. 'That is most kind of you. I'm sure we shall be. Very happy.'

Then she turned away, resuming contemplation of her place at table. I noticed Colonel Layton's left hand was occupied moving bits of bread from the middle of his side-plate to the outer rim and back again, as if he were counting cherry-stones that told his future. I imagine I tried several times to engage Susan Bingham in something approximating to conversation. I have no recollection of succeeding; instead I recall, chiefly, a sense of other people's resignation – particularly Mrs Layton's. Neither she nor Nigel (nor Sarah) could possibly have expected me to say anything except what I did say. Perhaps it was only when I said nothing more that they recognized their own subconscious expectations; resigned themselves to the inevitability of the marriage. Only Colonel Layton seemed unaware, unaffected. He smiled; ate sparingly. His demeanour suggested thoughts passing through his mind: How extraordinary – how nice – how lucky I am – whatever will happen to me next? The emotional instability of Bombay had gone. Rather, it lay hidden under the carapace, the hardening shell of reaffirmation.

*

When the women withdrew the servant brought a couple of decanters. One of them contained the remains of that much-travelled bottle of Old Sporran. I declined the whisky and had brandy; an act of self-denial which I followed up by mentioning Bagshaw and inviting what I would least welcome: a claustrophobic conversation about the hermetic world of school, that alchemy in reverse which transmutes the gold of life into the lead of tiresome recollections of immaturity. But Colonel Layton showed no enthusiasm for Bagshaw. He smiled benignly, uncommitted. He was suffering, I thought, from delayed reaction to the shock of homecoming. Here for him, briefly, was a likeness of the world he had just escaped from, a room occupied entirely by men. I don't think he liked it, suddenly. He raised his glass of malt whisky in a rather shaky hand and said, 'Strange thing. There was a young Oberleutnant at the last camp I was at –' and retold the story for – I assumed – Rowan's benefit, but when he had finished and I glanced at Rowan I fancied Rowan too had heard it before but assumed I hadn't.

'Extraordinarily kind of you, Perron,' Layton said, nodding at his glass. 'I feel it would be civil to write to the Oberleutnant and tell him it came true. Haven't actually sat down to Jane Austen yet, though. So mustn't deceive him. Not that one would know where to write. By the way, my future son-in-law told me that officer you rescued from the bath

303

succeeded on his second attempt. Sorry about that. It was his whisky originally, wasn't it?'

I agreed that originally it was.

'Odd thing,' he said, 'the compulsion to suicide.' Layton was studying the pale liquid in his glass, perhaps seeing in the whisky of one dead man the face of another. 'What do you say, Rowan? Odd? To be quite so at the end of the tether?'

Rowan said he was inclined to think there was a certain dignity in taking one's own life. Layton said he supposed the Japanese would agree but that it was wretched for the family and that that was what a man should think about. In the case he'd just had, the case of Havildar Karim Muzzafir Khan, it was the plight of the widow and her children that most concerned him. The regiment would have to make sure she didn't suffer unduly. But she had left her dead husband's village and gone back to her own. He feared that her neighbours had made life impossible for her when they heard what he'd done, in Germany. He turned to me. 'Perron, is anything that's worth knowing coming out of these interviews?'

The briskness of the military manner flared up in that one question and then went out again. I decided that he would prefer the truth so replied that so far as I was qualified to judge I should say nothing worth knowing whatsoever. He nodded.

'That's rather the conclusion I've been coming to,' he said. And nodded again. The images of the evening at Rose Cottage end there.

*

In my bedroom at the guest house I found on the bedside table a copy of Emerson's essays – heavily underlined and marked in the margins. Its owner, or one of its owners (it had obviously been handled a great deal) had written her name on the fly-leaf. Barbara Batchelor. The underlining began with the first familiar and sonorous paragraph of the essay on History: *There is one mind common to all individual men*: and continued intermittently. I flicked the pages to find the other familiar passage in the essay on self-reliance and found that marked too: *Society is a wave. ...*

'You've found the book, then,' Rowan said when I took it out on to the verandah to join him over what he called a night-cap. 'I'm sorry, I ought to have mentioned it, but forgot. It was among some things I brought up from Ranpur for Sarah. We thought you'd like it.'

Barbara Batchelor was an old missionary who'd once lived at Rose Cottage as companion to Mabel Layton, Layton's stepmother, now dead. Miss Batchelor was dead too. The book was among some things she'd left for Sarah.

When I was settled Rowan said, 'Incidentally, it needn't make any difference to you, but I've decided to go back to Ranpur tomorrow.'

I felt bewildered. 'Whenever did you decide that?'

'I suppose in the last half-hour or so.'

Recalling the tentative arrangement I'd overheard him making with Mrs Layton to play some tennis over the week-end I realized he was telling the truth. I didn't press for an explanation.

'I can't very well stay here once you've gone,' I said. 'I'd better see the accommodation people tomorrow.'

'That'll only confuse them. They know you're here. If I were you I'd hang on at least until an officer comes up to take Merrick's place, or you get ordered back to Delhi. I've signed you in as my guest. I'll mark it *sine die*, so all you'll have to do is sign any chit the servant asks for and sign the steward's register before you leave.'

'Who pays? Government or you?'

'Government. So long as you don't dine the station or do anything the auditors might think odd, like drinking three bottles of whisky before breakfast. They'd apply to me in that case.'

'You pay for the drinks anyway, don't you?'

'Don't let it inhibit you. You can drink to my future if you like. I'm going back into the Political. HE warned me about it before I came up. That's why I've been having these few days off. I rang him tonight before we left though and he told me the signal had come in. I fly to Delhi on Tuesday and then get told where I'm going.'

'It's only Thursday.'

305

'Oh, well. Clearing things up, packing. Better to get on with it.'

'Does Miss Layton know you're going?'

'She knows I'm expecting the posting.'

'Didn't you tell her it had come?'

'No.' He hesitated. 'Somehow the atmosphere tonight didn't seem right. I'm sorry it wasn't all that successful an evening.'

I asked him what time he intended leaving. He said the private coach was still in Pankot. It was just a question of getting it coupled on to the mid-day train. Gopal had gone back by car, with Mohammed Ali Kasim. He said, 'Perhaps there'll be a signal for you tomorrow too, from your Aunt Charlotte. Then we could go back together.'

'It's a shade early for my signal.'

'You were serious, though, about Bunbury?'

'Deadly serious.'

'What happens if it doesn't work?'

'A court-martial, I should think. Are you positive it's hanging and not shooting?'

But this irritated him. He stopped looking at me. He seemed to find the dark beyond the verandah the most rewarding of anything within his range of vision. I waited. Presently he glanced back at me. He said, 'Was it a surprise to see me the other night at Ranpur station?'

'Totally unexpected.'

'But you recognized me.'

'Easily.'

'Would you, if you hadn't met Sarah in Bombay and she hadn't mentioned I was in Ranpur, working as an aide to HE?'

'Perhaps not so instantaneously.'

'Even if we'd been contemporaries at school, same house, same year, and close friends. It wouldn't necessarily follow would it that we'd recognize each other if we met years later in a public place?'

'It could follow. Why do you ask?'

'Do you remember a boy called Colin Lindsey?'

'It rings a vague bell. Who was Colin Lindsey?'

'Harry Coomer's closest friend.'

'Then I may. I once asked Coomer to tell me the difference

between karma and dharma but he said he didn't know. I suggested he might ask his father during the summer holiday but he said he probably wouldn't see him because he was spending the holiday with – well – "Lindsay, here"?'

That was the picture: Coomer and 'Lindsey, here', standing together, the brown boy and the white boy, resisting an inquisitive prefect's invasion of their solidarity and privacy.

Rowan said, 'He saw more of the Lindseys than of anyone. His father encouraged it and kept himself in the background. He wanted Harry to grow up as much like an English boy as he could.'

I was about to say: How much like was that? But checked myself. Rowan was too delicately poised between confession and characteristic silence for me to take the risk of upsetting him with that kind of facile question. For a while neither of us said anything but he began to lose interest in the dark beyond the verandah, as if Kumar were no longer out there but had come in to shelter in our recollections of him. A third, empty, white cane chair might have been his. Well, not his, not Coomer's; but Kumar's, whatever Kumar was or had become; whatever he would look like now, sitting there, no longer interested in cricket, but rape. White women. It meant nothing to me. But I wondered how deep Rowan's prejudice lay. Of the depth of Merrick's I had no doubt.

He said, 'I suppose we ought to take into consideration the distinct possibility of our not meeting again for at least as long as it's been since we last did. What, ten years ago?'

'Next time it won't seem so long. I'm told the older you get the quicker time goes.'

Such cliché simplicity also seemed to irritate him. He asked me what it was that amused me. I told him that what amused me was the awful seriousness that seemed to overcome people who worked in India. He said he thought I'd only just stopped accusing him of not being serious enough. I said that wasn't quite what I meant. There was a difference between taking a situation seriously and taking oneself seriously.

He became interested again in the dark beyond the verandah. I thought I had done it this time and that soon he would drink up and say goodnight. Instead he said, 'Yes, but out here there are penalties for appearing not to. At least, that's one's earliest understanding. One is wrapped up in the cocoon of a corporate integrity. It's a bit like being issued with a strait-jacket as well as a topee. It makes it difficult to act spontaneously and you become so used to wearing it that you find it difficult to do without it.'

'They used to issue spinepads too.'

'I know.'

'But they went out. Like topees are doing.'

'I don't think the strait-jacket ever will.' But he was smiling again. He said, 'Sarah puts it well. She says that in India English people feel they are always on show. I think that's true and on the whole that nothing worries us more.'

'Why do you say that?'

'Perhaps because we feel that fundamentally there's so little to see?'

'The *raj* with a superior manner hiding an inferiority complex? I can't say I've come across much evidence of that.'

'You could begin with me. I've very little real confidence. But it would be dangerous to give that impression. I expect I overcompensate. Most of us do. It's probably what happened to Colin Lindsey.'

It was my cue but I didn't take it up. I wanted him to tell me about Kumar and Merrick but I suspected that any further prompting would result in my getting a watered-down account and that I would only get a reasonably full one if I left the initiative to him. He hesitated again. But whatever it was that made him want to tell me finally won the struggle with whatever it was that made him reluctant to do so.

*

In May of the previous year (1944) on the day Rowan resumed his duties as ADC after one of several spells in hospital, the Governor called him into his study, said, 'You're an old Chillingburian, aren't you?' and asked him if he remembered a boy called Hari Kumar or Harry Coomer. Rowan said he did. The Governor handed him the confidential file on a man currently detained under the Defence of India Rules. This was Kumar. Rowan found it surprising that the boy he had known should have developed into a political activist. The real shock came when he read further and realized that Kumar had not been arrested on political grounds but on suspicion of leading a criminal assault by several Indians on an English girl called Daphne Manners in Mayapore in August 1942.

Rowan remembered the Bibighar Gardens case quite well. He had been in hospital in Shillong still recovering from illness contracted during the long march out of Burma with what remained of his regiment. The Bibighar Gardens affair was something out of the common rut among the reported incidents of rioting, arson and sabotage that followed the arrest of political leaders, because it involved what in spite of that cautious phrase 'criminal assault' had clearly been the rape of a white woman. Rowan also recollected the sense of anti-climax when nothing further happened. A report that the men arrested had not after all been charged but sent to prison as political detenus was taken up by the Calcutta *Statesman*. It seemed odd, the *Statesman* suggested, that all six men originally reported arrested with such promptness, while presumably turning out to be the wrong men (since no charges had been made) should also all turn out to be politically active in a way that caused the authorities such concern that detention orders had had to be issued.

The *Statesman*'s interest in the case provoked no official comment; and when the riots were over, the Bibighar Gardens affair like so many others that had marked that period of violent confrontation between the *raj* and the population, simply passed into history together with the rumours that had added colour to it, the chief of which was that the girl herself had scotched the charges by denying that the arrested men were those who had attacked her and threatening to say such extraordinary things about colonial justice and colonial prejudices, if a trial were held, that it was decided there would be no point in attempting to hold one.

Rowan had heard these rumours, the accompanying explanation that one of the men arrested had been her lover and that she was so besotted or terrified that she had willingly perjured herself to save him, in fact had only admitted to being attacked because she couldn't disguise the awful state she came home in. She'd cooked up a story about the men being of the *badmash* or criminal type, not young educated boys like the ones in custody. He also heard the story that later she returned pregnant to her aunt in Rawalpindi and in the March of 1943 he had seen the notice in the *Times of India* of her death in Kashmir and of the birth of a child on the same day. The child, a girl, had been given an Indian name, and the notice had been inserted by her aunt, Lady Manners, the widow of Sir Henry Manners, one-time Governor of the province of Ranpur. At this time Rowan was again in hospital, in Calcutta. From there he went back to his regimental depot. Later he was in Delhi for a while. Early in 1944 he was appointed to Malcolm's staff at Government House, where Sir Henry and Lady Manners had lived during the late 'twenties and early 'thirties. But when Malcolm gave him the file on Hari Kumar he had not thought of the Manners case for months.

The next point of interest to emerge from the file was that Kumar was the man Daphne Manners was supposed to have been infatuated with. The longer Rowan studied the file the stronger the evidence seemed to him to be that Kumar, having formed an association with Miss Manners, had then plotted with several Indian friends of his to attack and rape her. In custody after the rape he had virtually given the game away according to the police report by mentioning Miss Manners's name before her name had been mentioned by the police. Moreover when arrested at the house where he lived with his aunt he had been bathing scratches and bruises on his face such as might have been given by a girl fighting her attackers in the dark; and the clothes out of which he had just changed were mud-stained. Throughout his interrogation he stated repeatedly, mechanically, that he had not seen Miss Manners since a night some weeks before when they visited a temple. (Miss Manners had used virtually the same words.) But he refused to account for his movements on the night of the rape or for the state of his clothes and the marks on his face. His almost invariable answer to questions was: I have nothing to say.

The one document in the file that caused Rowan uneasiness was one relating to the alleged discovery by a junior police officer of Miss Manners's bicycle in a ditch outside Kumar's house, and an accompanying document, attested by the District Superintendent of Police, stating that this curious piece of evidence (with its ridiculous implication that Kumar had cockily ridden Miss Manners's bicycle home from the Bibighar and then left it outside his own home) had been the result of a misunderstanding. The bicycle had actually been found by the superintendent in the Bibighar Gardens when the site was searched after the assault had been reported. It had been put into a police truck. The truck had then been driven to Kumar's house – to Kumar's house because of the known association between Kumar and Miss Manners and because the District Superintendent had called there earlier in the evening after Miss Manners had been reported missing by a Lady Chatterjee, at whose house Miss Manners was staying, and found Kumar not at home, and his aunt unable to say where he was. On the way to Kumar's house this second time (with the cycle in the back of the truck) the police's attention had been attracted by a lighted hut in some waste ground not far from the Bibighar. Inside the hut they had found five young men, all of them 'known to the police' for 'political affiliations' and several of them 'known to the police as friends of Kumar'. These men were 'fairly intoxicated' and were drinking home-made liquor, itself an offence that warranted arrest, but also in the District Superintendent's opinion certainly deserving investigation on a night when the authorities were on the alert for demonstrations against the government for its imprisonment of Congress leaders and when a European woman had been assaulted by five or six Indians. In arresting these young men, in putting them into one truck, in the continuation of the journey to Kumar's house, in the 'change of police personnel' from one truck to the other and the despatch of the five arrested men back to the police headquarters, 'a misunderstanding' had 'assumed that this was where the bicycle inspector finding the bicycle on the road outside Kumar's house' where 'it must have been temporarily placed, again as a result of a misunderstanding' had 'assumed that this was where the bicycle was found' and had accordingly put in a report which, even if that was not his intention, might certainly have led to 'this erroneous conclusion'.

The District Superintendent was Merrick. This was the first time Rowan came across his name. Someone, either in the Inspector-General's department or the Secretariat had minuted in the margin of this disclaimer about the bicycle, 'Pity about this'; an ambiguous phrase which did little to subdue Rowan's uneasiness; but initially the disclaimer gave him a favourable impression, not of the Mayapore police, but of the superintendent as a man who had not hesitated to sort out a muddle which would have been helpful in bringing Kumar to trial if left as it was. Subsequently, he was uneasy for a different reason. He could not help wondering whether the evidence of the bicycle had been planted by Merrick or with Merrick's blind-eye approval and then refuted by Merrick when he saw that it was too dangerous a piece of falsification.

Two other points of interest arose in the account of the actual arrest. In Kumar's room there were found (a) a photograph of Miss Manners and (b) a letter from England signed 'Colin' which referred to a letter Kumar had written to *him* but which he'd been unable to read because his father had opened and then destroyed it as one unsuitable for his officer son to receive – a letter, so it seemed, of a political and anti-British nature. The letter from Colin dated back to the post-Dunkirk era.

*

But, Rowan said, apart from this hearsay evidence of anti-Britishness, and unless the assault on Miss Manners could be interpreted as political, the evidence on the file of Kumar's political commitment was thin to the point of non-existence. He had – just once – been taken in for questioning because his attitude to a police officer had been unsatisfactory and arrogant.

The officer was Merrick. This incident occurred some six months prior to the rape. Searching an area of the native town for an escaped political prisoner called Moti Lal, Merrick had visited a place known as The Sanctuary, a clinic and feeding centre for the homeless and destitute run by a Mrs Ludmila Smith. Mrs Smith (also known as Sister Ludmila) went out every night with stretcher-bearers, searching for men and women who had come into Mayapore to beg, or to die. On the night before Merrick arrived looking for the escaped Moti Lal, she had picked up a young man found lying unconscious near the banks of the river.

This was Kumar, and all that was wrong with him was that he was dead drunk. When Merrick arrived in the morning he asked Kumar who he was, where he lived, what he had been doing. Kumar had a hangover. The interview went badly. Merrick decided to continue it at the nearest police station.

At this point in the file, Rowan said, there was a brief summary of Kumar's background. Kumar (according to Merrick) had not been frank about his identity but had 'finally admitted' that his name was Kumar, that he knew Moti Lal because Moti Lal had once been employed by Romesh Chand Gupta Sen, a contractor. Kumar had himself been employed by Romesh Chand who was in fact Kumar's aunt's brother-in-law. Romesh Chand had sacked Moti Lal because he didn't like his clerks to concern themselves with anything except the business, and that included not concerning themselves with politics. Kumar had left Romesh Chand later, when offered a job as a sub-editor and occasional reporter on the Indian-owned English language newspaper, *The Mayapore Gazette*.

There was then a statement that 'the man Kumar claimed to have been brought up in England by his father, Duleep Kumar, since deceased, and to have been educated at a public school which he named as Chillingborough College'.

Subsequent notes suggested that Merrick had investigated Kumar's claim and had got further information; that Kumar was born in the UP, that his mother died while he was still an infant and that aged two he had been taken to England by his father, who had sold his land to his brothers and now set up in business, anglicizing the name to Coomer. But in 1938 Duleep Kumar's businesses failed. He committed suicide. Hari was penniless. At the age of eighteen, through arrangements made between lawyers in London and his Aunt Shalini, widowed sister-in-law of Romesh Chand, and his own father's sister, Hari came out to India.

From the date Kumar was first questioned by Merrick he

was under surveillance. Kumar never explained why he was drunk but the names of his drinking companions were obtained and there were cross-references to other files kept on these young men. The surveillance seemed to have been fairly casual, but Merrick had been thorough in recording what was known locally about this English public-school educated Indian reporter. He'd discovered that Kumar had once applied to an English firm, British-Indian Electric, for a post as a trainee but been turned down on the recommendation of the technical training manager who thought him not intelligent enough.

A young man whose place Kumar had taken on *The Mayapore Gazette*, one Vidyasagar, was also under surveillance. Vidyasagar was now working on a nationalist local, *Mayapore Hindu*. There were notes of several occasions when Kumar and Vidyasagar had been 'seen together', but these couldn't strike a reader as very significant because the occasions were invariably those when they had simply been in the same place at the same time, as reporters (at District and Sessions Court, for example, and local functions on the *maidan*).

The most important items in Merrick's notes were those concerning Kumar's friendship with the English girl, Daphne Manners, who had come to Mayapore to stay with a Lady Chatterjee – a friend of Lady Manners in Rawalpindi. Miss Manners's parents were dead. She had lost her brother in the war and had come out to India quite recently to stay with her surviving relative, her aunt, Lady Manners. Since coming to Mayapore she had been doing voluntary work at the Mayapore General Hospital.

The notes about her association with Kumar began with one dated in April 1942. 'At the War Week exhibition on the *maidan* Miss M left her party to speak to K who was hovering in the vicinity.' The next note suggested that Merrick had taken the trouble to find out how Miss M and K had previously met. 'It seems K was invited to Lady Chatterjees's place, The MacGregor House, where Miss M was staying, shortly after K was questioned in the matter of Moti Lal, probably through the suggestion of the lawyer Srinivasan who was sent to police headquarters to inquire why I'd had K taken

314

to the kotwali for questioning. Srinivasan is Romesh C's lawyer.'

There were several further notes giving dates when K and Miss M were seen in one another's company, one of which – 'Miss M dined with K and his aunt at their house in the Chillianwallah Bagh extension' – Rowan found particularly distasteful since it indicated that Kumar could not even have someone to dinner without the fact being reported.

Finally, among the documents, there were two statements and a report from the Divisional Commissioner. The first statement, by Merrick, described how Kumar had first come to his notice and the opinion he had formed of him as a result of this, what was known locally about the characters of the young men in whose company he had been on the night he got drunk, how Merrick eventually thought it his duty to warn Miss Manners 'that the young Indian with whom she had struck up a friendship, which few Europeans on station had failed to notice, was not the kind of man one could recommend her to take into her confidence'.

Merrick's statements ended with an account of his own actions on the night when he had called on Lady Chatterjee and found her 'alarmed' at Miss Manners's failure to arrive home, and of his second visit when he found Miss M arrived at last but 'in a distressed condition as a result of having been attacked and criminally used by five or six men in the Bibighar Gardens'. He continued with a description of his discovery of the young men in the hut near by, of the state in which he found Kumar when calling again at the house in Chillianwallah Bagh and of the obstinate but suspicious behaviour of Kumar when taken into custody.

The second statement was a report made by three officers of the civil administration after a private interview with Miss Manners. According to this report, Miss Manners had not confirmed her earlier verbal statement that the men had come at her in the dark, covered her with her own raincape, dragged her off her bicycle and into the Bibighar, and that she had therefore not been able to identify them. She now stated that she had been *in* the Bibighar, alone, and that although it was dark, and the men came at her suddenly, and did cover her head with the raincape, she had had just sufficient glimpse and smell of them to swear on oath that they were all of the badmash or criminal type, not educated or westernized boys of the kind who had been arrested; that it would be ridiculous to bring such boys into court, that she could not fail to deny that they were the men involved, and that it would be just as reasonable to bring in a group of young British soldiers and accuse them of having blacked their faces in order to attack her.

The report from the Divisional Commissioner was simply to the effect that he had studied the files on the arrested men and all the statements and while agreeing that in view of Miss Manners's attitude the evidence against them in the matter of criminal assault was insufficient on which to charge them and bring them to trial, he agreed with the opinion that quite apart from suspicion of criminal assault the evidence obtained over several months of their conduct and political affiliations warranted their detention under Rule 26 of the Defence of India Rules.

When Rowan had studied all this material he returned the file to Malcolm who asked him whether he thought Kumar wrongfully imprisoned. Rowan said he thought so, technically, but that suspicion of complicity in rape was strong enough to take the view that he may have got off extremely lightly. The Governor then asked him whether there was any doubt about this Kumar being the Kumar Rowan had known at school – and handed him a police photograph; full face and profile. He hadn't seen Kumar since Kumar was about fifteen, but he thought the features were like those of the boy he remembered; apart from which everything on the file about Kumar's history fitted what he had known of Kumar's background. The Kumar he knew *had* spent all his life in England, was known as Harry Coomer. His accent had been as English as Colin Lindsey's and Rowan's own. You would only have to hear him speak to know whether they were one and the same man.

The Governor said Rowan would have an opportunity to confirm this. He was to arrange and lead a private examination of the prisoner at the Kandipat jail, in a room known as Room O. He would have a shorthand writer and an official from the Department of Home and Law to assist him.

There would also be a fourth person, a woman, who would watch and listen to the interview from a specially equipped adjoining room. The Governor had had many pleas from Kumar's aunt, Shalini Gupta Sen, to review the case against her nephew, and the poor woman had in fact come to Ranpur to be near by in case some steps were taken. But the request for this examination and the request to be present were from Lady Manners. Her visit was to be kept secret. Of the members of the examining board only Rowan was to know of her presence. The examination would not be made under oath and the entire affair was to be conducted in as discreet and confidential manner as possible.

*

With this Rowan had to be content. For the moment Malcolm would discuss it no further. Rowan made the arrangements at the Kandipat and on the day he met Lady Manners at Government House he was already hating the whole business. Kumar had been in jail for more than eighteen months and Rowan had decided that the only explanation for Lady Manners's sudden emergence from the obscurity in which she had lived since the tragedy of the assault and the tragedy of her niece's death in childbirth was that she had been biding her time, perhaps obtaining further evidence against Kumar and now wanted vengeance.

The impression did not survive his first short meeting with her the day before the examination; and on the day itself driving with her to the Kandipat, observing her physical frailty, noting her gentleness of manner, it struck him rather forcibly that here was a woman who felt that her life was coming to an end and that there were dispositions to make. He knew from Malcolm that she was staying under an assumed name at an hotel in Ranpur and that the child and its ayah were with her. To minimize the risk of being recognized by old servants at Government House she wore a deep veil over an old-fashioned sola topee, which she only raised in the car to look at the photograph of Kumar, whom she had never in her life seen.

But – Rowan wondered – if the object of the examination

was to secure the release of a man she felt, or knew, to be wrongfully imprisoned, why had she waited so long? Or was it so long? More than eighteen months since the assault, but only half that time since her niece died. As they drew near Kandipat, Rowan began to pull down the blinds of the car. They entered the jail precincts in semi-darkness.

*

The deeply subjective feelings, like joy, fear, love, are the most difficult to convey. One has to make do, more often than not, with the crutch of the words themselves. Very occasionally if an experience has been vivid enough, the quality of it comes through without there being much conscious attempt to communicate it. This was the way Rowan conveyed to me what the examination in the Kandipat jail had been like, for him. It had been a claustrophobic experience. I have thought of Rowan's experience of the Kandipat often, tried to shed light on it, as a scene, but the light coming out from the scene always seems stronger. One ends up a bit dazzled by it. The eyes hurt. You glance away, to rest them, and then momentarily there's the illusion of blindness, blankness. You feel shut in. I hit on the word claustrophobic while Rowan was describing it to me. Directly I hit on it I knew I had also hit on a description of the effect Merrick had on me.

That light I mentioned, the one coming out from the scene, was actually a real light: a light bright enough to interrogate by, but nothing crude; subtly balanced, tilted, as if haphazardly, but in fact shining on the examinee at an angle that would only worry him if he chanced to look up above the level of Rowan's head and wonder about the grille in the wall behind. But had he done so he would have assumed that it was part of the air-conditioning plant.

Another thing Rowan managed to communicate to me without putting it into so many words was the shock of this initiation into one of the *raj*'s obscurer rites, the kind conducted in a windowless room with artificial light and air, an early form of bugging system and spy-system, and making an uncompromising statement about itself as the ominously still centre of the world of moral and political power which hitherto he had known as one revolving openly in the alternating light of good intentions and the dark of doubts and errors. The room in the Kandipat emitted nothing but its own steady glare. It illuminated nothing except the consequences of an action already performed and a decision taken long ago. These could never be undone or retracted. In the world outside new action could be taken and new decisions made. But the light of what had been performed would glow on unblinkingly, like radium in a closed and undiscovered mine.

*

When the prisoner entered Rowan thought: No, that's not the man, the whole thing is a ludicrous mistake. The man is an impostor. It was not even the man in the police photographs. He had expected some change but not such a devastating one. This man looked middle-aged. He seemed not to understand English. Rowan asked him to sit down but it wasn't until the assistant examiner from the Home and Law Department, an Indian, said '*Baitho*' that he did so; and then the contours of the chair seemed to puzzle him, as if he lacked physical co-ordination. Rowan asked him whether he wished to have the examination conducted in English or in Hindi. He asked him this question in Hindi. The prisoner answered in Hindi, using the single word *Angrezi*, meaning 'in English'. As he answered he looked directly at Rowan for the first time and the conviction that the man was the wrong man weakened.

The eyes, Rowan said, were those 'of one man looking out of the eye-sockets of another' and the man looking out could have been Kumar; his answers to the routine opening questions whose object was identification all added up to an admission that he was, but still the answers came in Hindi – the abbreviated word *hān*, repeated tonelessly. Hān. Hān.

At this point Rowan reminded the prisoner that he had elected to have the examination conducted in English. Questions had been put in English. So far he had answered in Hindi. Did this mean that he had changed his mind and would prefer the questions to be put in Hindi too? He hoped that the answer would come again, hān; then the onus of putting questions would fall on his colleague, and for him the whole thing would become a semantic exercise. For Lady Manners in the adjoining room it would become an exercise in patience. He doubted that her Hindi was even as good as his. But that didn't matter. He would prefer to take a back seat. He didn't want this gaunt shambling creature to be Hari Kumar; certainly not Coomer, whom he remembered Laura Elliott describing as 'that good-looking boy who caught you before you even scored'. Old Boys versus School. Rowan had approached him after stumps, congratulated him; asked him what he intended doing. The boy had said, 'Try for the ICS, I suppose, sir.' And gone out of Rowan's life.

To emerge here? It wasn't possible. The physical evidence was against such a transmigration. The eyes could have been Coomer's; they showed no recognition of Rowan but Rowan wouldn't have expected it. But he had expected something far more telling. A manner.

Rowan waited for the prisoner to respond. He seemed not to have understood the question and Rowan wondered whether he should repeat it in Hindi. He was about to do so when the man spoke. He said he was sorry, answering the questions in Hindi had been a slip; he seldom had the chance of speaking English, except to himself.

Rowan described the effect of this casual statement in straightforward English as electrifying. It was as though there were two men in the chair, the one you could see and the one you could hear. The one you could hear was undoubtedly Coomer and once you were aware that he was Coomer the unfavourable impression made by the shambling body and hollow-cheeked face began to fade. The English voice, released from its inner prison, seemed to have taken control of the face and limbs, to be infusing them with something of its own firmness and authority.

'I felt,' Rowan said, 'that quite unexpectedly our rôles were reversed or at least levelled up and that it wasn't Coomer who was being examined so much as a system that had ostensibly given us equal opportunities but had ended like this with me on the comfortable side of a green baize-covered table and him on the unpleasant one. And one of the interesting questions was, where precisely did this leave my Indian colleague and co-examiner?'

The Indian colleague was the same Mr Gopal who had accompanied Rowan up to Pankot and just gone back to Ranpur with Mr Kasim. Before Kumar's examination Rowan and Gopal were no more than casual acquaintances and one of the ironies of that examination, Rowan had always felt, was that whereas he himself had a common bond of sympathy with Kumar but could not absolve him from suspicion of some kind of connection with the attack on Daphne Manners, Gopal – as became obvious – believed him innocent on every count, believed that he had been victimized by the Mayapore authorities because he was an Indian, but at the same time disliked him for being the kind of Indian he actually was. Quite early in the questioning Gopal elicited from Kumar the fact that Kumar's father had admired the British and the British form of administration in India and that he had deliberately brought Kumar up in a way that should have enabled him to enter the administration with the same qualities and advantages an English boy had. At the same time, Gopal's form of questioning made it clear he believed this could only have been done at the cost of Kumar senior turning his back on his own people – which in fact had been the case and a major cause of the ensuing tragedy.

Kumar senior had been exposed as a man with an obsession that had cost his son dearly. One of Gopal's objectives in this line of questioning about Kumar's background was of course to establish that with an upbringing such as he'd had the very idea of his ever becoming a danger to the British was nonsensical. To Gopal, Kumar/Coomer *was* British. During the recess when Kumar had been taken outside for a while, Rowan admitted that he and Kumar had been at the same school but that Kumar didn't realize this, didn't recognize him. Gopal then described Kumar as 'an English boy with a brown skin' and said, 'the combination is hopeless'.

Rowan called the recess because he'd felt the examination was getting out of hand. He had tried unsuccessfully to keep it strictly to the question of Kumar's political affiliations. These, he believed, had been virtually non-existent and had now been shown to be non-existent. The only occasion when

321

Kumar had consorted with any of the young Indians who were found drinking in the derelict hut on the night of the rape was that other night, six months before, when he got drunk himself and was picked up by Sister Ludmila's stretcher-bearers. Until then and after then he had kept fairly clear of them. He felt no animosity towards them but they weren't young men whose interests he could share, whose experiences he had shared, or whose aspirations he could regard with anything except a detached kind of understanding. They were all young nationalists but, he said, why shouldn't they be? In examination he made no bones about that, but no bones either about his view of the limited form their nationalism ordinarily took. They were young, therefore inconsistent, laughing at the British, talking against them, but fond of wearing western-style clothes and with a tendency to copy British manners. They were friendly, at times deeply depressed, at times euphoric. They were educated to a standard a peg or so above the level on which society determined they could live.

The truth which Coomer had had to face was that this was a level on which he now had to live too: that of one young Indian among countless others who could never expect to achieve any kind of position of authority; young men doomed, it seemed, to spend their lives as members of a literate but obscure and powerless middle-class, thankful for jobs as ill-paid clerks in shops and offices and banks – a life infinitely poorer than the one he would have led if he had grown up in his father's ancestral village, or if Kumar senior's obsession about the value of an English upbringing had not been so deeply felt and so uncompromisingly followed that he had sacrificed his own security and – with that single exception of his young widowed sister – the regard of his family.

Hari never knew much about his father's business affairs in England but for many years these must have prospered. Hari's childhood was spent in security and considerable comfort. There had been housekeepers, governesses, tutors, a private school and then Chillingborough. In the Spring of 1938 he had been looking forward to his last term, the prospect of university and of preparation for the ICS examinations. Qualified, he would eventually have come out to India on terms of parity with young Englishmen entering the covenanted civil service and so fulfilled his father's ambitions. Duleep Kumar's death would not in itself have altered these prospects but pennilessness did. Probably it was the elder Kumar's realization of what his complete financial failure would mean to his son that led him to take his own life. As a boy himself Duleep Kumar had had to wear down his own father's opposition before getting himself a college education in India and wear it down again as a young man before going to England to study law. When he returned, unqualified, an academic failure, he had had no alternative but to settle down with the child-wife to whom he'd agreed to be betrothed before leaving England. The Kumars were well-to-do landowners, orthodox, rigidly opposed to any change in *status quo*. Their power and authority flowed from their wealth and possessions. With this they were content. The men were semi-literate, the women quite illiterate. The sole exception was Shalini, Duleep Kumar's youngest sister, whom he taught to read and write in both Hindi and English. India could hold more for an Indian than this, he knew. If he could not get it for himself then he would do so for the son his wife presently bore. She made it easier for him by dying. But still he wasn't free. His father, having divided the inheritance among the sons, left his family to earn merit by relinquishing his earthly ties and become *sannyasi*. Commending their mother to the sons' care he departed, with staff and begging-bowl. They never saw him again. The mother, living the life of a widow in the family house, survived two years. Shalini had gone to Mayapore as the child bride of one Prakash Gupta Sen. After his mother's death there was nothing to keep Duleep Kumar in India. He sold his interest to his brothers and departed, presumably quite well-off, and took Hari to England. Probably he still had friends and acquaintances in England from his law-student days, and such connections would have been helpful, but he must also have been enterprising and skilful. Just what eventually went wrong, Hari Kumar did not know.

What he knew was that his father was dead from an overdose of sleeping pills and that the lawyers said there was no money because the creditors would take everything. The only Indian relative he knew of, the only one his father had ever written to, was his Aunt Shalini. The lawyers wrote to her. The assumption was that money to keep him at school, at least, might be forthcoming. It was not. Shalini, widowed and childless, was a dependant of her Mayapore brother-in-law, Romesh Chand. She borrowed money from him to pay for Hari's passage. He would live with her. And still the assumption was that Hari would continue his studies and become an ICS candidate in India. His ignorance of India was as great as the lawyers' ignorance. When he sailed he had not the smallest conception of the devastating change made to his life by his father's failure and suicide.

*

Rowan told me that these facts emerged in the first five or ten minutes of the examination but that he had been able to build for himself a far more complex and disturbing picture, indeed had been unable to get it out of his mind since. He said that Hari's old life must have ended and the new one begun the moment he stepped off the ship in Bombay. His link with England would have snapped, then, with shocking abruptness.

Rowan said, 'Well. You know. Whatever kind of shock India is, pleasant or horrid, if you're a young Englishman coming out to the civil or military or to any kind of job, you're cushioned from the shock the moment you step off the gangplank because metaphorically you step off into a covered-way that extends from the dock – however many hundreds of miles – to your first station. When Elliott and I and Laura stepped off we were met by friends of Elliott's parents. I've forgotten who, people I never saw again, but I remember that within an hour or two we were at the Gymkhana Club having a drink and everything was very English and reassuring. Everything was done for us. We didn't have to lift a finger. I remember thinking, How good this is. But even if we'd not been met there would have been people to see us through, an agent to take charge of us, or people going up to the same station. And in any case we had our white faces and our official standing.'

Think, Rowan said, of Harry Coomer's arrival. The bewilderment he must have felt was scarcely imaginable. It was to be hoped that if no one met him he had at least fallen in with some people on the boat who were helpful. Perhaps the bewilderment had started on the boat. Rowan doubted that he would have had a first-class passage. And when it came to the train to Mayapore, he suspected he would have had to travel third but sincerely hoped not. The boy spoke nothing but English and the kind of people who spoke his kind of English would have been, suddenly, on the other side of the fence. He would have been one more face in the multitude. And the graver revelation was still to come.

A few months ago Rowan had accompanied Malcolm on a tour that included a three-hour visit to Mayapore. He had not been in Mayapore before and thought the cantonment charming. But the cantonment had not been where Kumar was bound seven years earlier, in 1938. Rowan would have liked to slip away from the Governor's entourage but this had been impossible. At one moment, though, the entourage was in the vicinity of the Mandir Gate Bridge, scene of one of the worst of the Mayapore civil riots in 1942, and there, across the river, he had a view and needed no further evidence.

Somewhere in that noisome mass Kumar had lived with his Aunt Shalini, had found himself put to work in his uncle's warehouse in the Chillianwallah bazaar, had been regarded as a man who had lost caste, who ought to undergo ritual purification to rid himself of the stain of having lived abroad. There was to be no more education, no degree, no ICS, no entry even into the lower levels of the provincial administration. This was the orthodox urban middle-class Hindu India which hoarded its profits and kept itself to itself, and served no interests but its own and existed, quite unmoved, side by side with the India of unspeakable poverty and squalor. And this was the India in which Hari was expected to settle, grateful for the charity bestowed.

*

Rowan said, 'I think if it had happened to me, once I'd realized that it was real and that there seemed no way out, I'd have cried myself to sleep every night. Perhaps he did, old as he was.'

His Aunt Shalini had adored her brother, Hari's father. They had kept up a correspondence through all the years of separation. She was proud of her 'English' nephew as she called Hari and there's no doubt that she loved him and did her best for him, her best to help him to adjust; but as a childless widow of Romesh Chand's brother she herself was little more than one of Romesh's chattels and the means she had to help were limited. How long Kumar worked in his uncle's warehouse Rowan didn't know, but in the examination he had found out more about Hari's attempt to get a job with British-Indian Electric. The technical training manager who had turned him down as 'not intelligent enough' was obviously the sort of man – self-conscious about his own education and background – who disliked his own English bosses and despised all Indians on principle. Hari Kumar, with his brown skin and public school voice and manner, was a sitting duck. Ignoring Hari's statement that he had no technical knowledge but was willing to learn he asked him a series of technical questions and when he'd finished and Hari had been unable to answer, he said, 'Where are you from, laddie? Straight down off the tree?'

Hari walked out. A mistake, perhaps, but Rowan thought it showed how deep his instinct still was, how automatic his response to any threat to what he still possessed and still prized; prized because it was all he did possess: his sense of what he owed himself and had to keep on paying to himself, even at the expense of a lost job; the debt incurred by his English upbringing.

*

He got his job on the *Mayapore Gazette* because of his knowledge of the language in which the paper was supposed to be printed. He had no ambition to be a journalist. By this time he must have picked up some Hindi, but he had abandoned attempts to learn it systematically. For a while his aunt had paid for him to have lessons from a local pandit, one Pandit Baba Sahib – apparently an unfortunate choice since

Baba Sahib was known by the police to recruit young men to the cause of Hindu extremism under cover of having scholarly discussions with them about Hindu mythology. From Hari's point of view the lessons weren't a success. Baba Sahib was always late and always smelt strongly of garlic. After a while Hari told him not to bother to come again. His association with this tiresome old man was brief but it probably counted against him eventually. Rowan imagined that Hari gave up learning Hindi because he did not want to pick it up sufficiently to start thinking in it, or to acquire an Indian tone of voice.

His knowledge of English was the one asset he had that could be put to practical use. When he joined the *Mayapore Gazette* as a sub-editor his uncle reduced his Aunt Shalini's allowance. Rowan imagined he'd been paid little or nothing for working in his uncle's warehouse. There couldn't have been any overall financial gain from the change of jobs but the offices of the *Gazette* were far more congenial. They were in the cantonment.

Hari crossed the river from the native to the English quarter. The new job brought him into closer physical contact with the kind of people he thought he knew because he had once been one of them. He realized he no longer was and that he had become invisible to them. But there was always Colin to write to and Colin to get letters from although Colin's letters changed in tone as he responded to the political crisis in Europe. To Hari, Europe seemed so far away that he could not share Colin's concern. He was aware of growing areas of estrangement. Colin might have been aware of them too had Hari ever described the kind of life he was living now. This he never did. He allowed Colin to go on thinking of India as a glamorous sort of place. He didn't want to appeal to Colin for pity and he wanted to keep in touch.

Colin joined the Territorial Army and thereafter wrote of nothing else. When war broke out he at once became a full-time soldier. It was between the outbreak of war and the defeat of the BEF and its evacuation from Dunkirk that Hari wrote the letter Colin's father destroyed because it was full of what he later described to his wounded son as 'a lot of hot-headed political stuff'. According to Hari, this letter had just been an attempt to discuss the pros and cons of the Congress resignation from the provincial ministries in protest against India's automatic involvement in the war against Germany. If the British Government could not declare war on behalf of dominions like Canada and Australia, but had to leave them to come in voluntarily, why should war be declared on India's behalf through the Viceroy, without consultation even? That was the basis of the Congress argument. Legally, of course, this was the only way war could be declared; but a point which Hari must have made (after the liberal education which men like Bagshaw had ensured remained a Chilling-borough tradition) was that with Dominion status ranking as a declared principal aim of the British for India, the outbreak of war had been as good a moment as any to show that the spirit rather than the letter of the law was to be the guiding factor in the British–Indian relationship. But there hadn't been even a pretence of consultation between the Viceroy and his provincial ministers and central legislative assembly. Piqued, the Congress had resigned, declaring that a war against the European dictator could only be waged by free men.

Rowan said it must have been the kind of letter 'one old Chillingburian would have written to another', as strong in its arguments for the Viceroy as in those against him. It was unfortunate that it had reached Colin's home at a time when Colin was in hospital recovering from wounds and when – as Mr Lindsey probably put it – Britain was 'standing alone'. One could imagine all too easily the sort of man Lindsey was or had become; the sort who, if he had tenants or male servants would have liked to round them up and march them to the nearest recruiting office; the sort who stuck pins in maps and nursed a sense of personal injury if anyone, man or nation, cast any doubt whatsoever on the conduct of those whom God had raised to positions of power and responsibility. The attitude of Indian politicians since 1939 wouldn't have endeared any Indian to him. Deliberately opening Hari's letter he would have had his suspicions of that country's population confirmed.

'A lot of hot-headed political nonsense.' A thoughtless, empty phrase. But how damaging it had seemed two years later when the police found the letter from Colin in which it was repeated and apologized for. It was the only letter from Colin which Hari kept. That was unfortunate. It was like preserving the one real piece of evidence against oneself. Hari kept it because it was the only letter he had had from Colin which struck him as coming from the fair-minded boy he had known. Young Lindsey's baptism of fire had knocked some of the jingoism out of him. He had stopped flag-wagging. The war had become too real for that. Perhaps for the first time since Hari left for India Colin wondered what *Hari's* reality was like.

In 1941 he was to find out. His regiment came out to India. He wrote to Hari in Mayapore saying he hoped he would get down to see him or that somehow they could meet. He wrote again from another station, this time saying how difficult such a trip would be. Then he stopped writing. Hari told himself that the regiment had probably been sent down into Burma or Malaya; and at the turn of the year when the Japanese attacked, he felt sorry for him, in the thick again, having a bad war.

*

Rowan hesitated. I took the opportunity to interrupt, to ask a question that had been nagging for the past few minutes.

'He could have joined up himself, couldn't he? He'd have got in at once as an officer-cadet.'

'I know. It's a question I intended to ask him, but didn't, because I realized he'd have been quite justified in saying something like, "Why the hell should I have? Why should one pip on my shoulder have made me visible and acceptable to English people all of a sudden?" An answer like that, however justified, would have looked bad on the record.'

'Evidence of anti-Britishness?'

'On paper, yes. But I haven't told you the other thing that technical training manager said to him. "I don't like bolshie black laddies on my side of the business." If you have a thing like that said to you by a member of a firm like British-Indian Electric in Mayapore, I think it follows that you don't rush to join the colours when their country goes to war in Europe.

What I don't think followed in Hari's case was a rush to join the opposition. I don't believe he saw any *political* significance in what was happening to him.'

As a reporter on the *Gazette* he often attended English social functions such as flower-shows, gymkhanas, cricket matches. Occasionally an Englishman would compliment him on his English accent, ask him where he'd acquired it, and show such disbelief when told that Hari stopped saying 'Chillingborough'. A Chillingborough man didn't end up as a tuppenny-hapenny reporter on a fifth-rate local Indian newspaper. So he steered clear of these embarrassing confrontations.

And then early in 1942 he saw officers and men of Colin's regiment in the cantonment. The battalion had come into Mayapore. He wondered whether he would arrive home one night and find that Colin had visited him. He rather hoped not. It was unlikely anyway. The city on his side of the river was out-of-bounds to troops and although an officer could always get an official pass Hari thought it more likely that Colin would write, or perhaps turn up at the office of the *Gazette*. No letter came. He never saw Colin among the officers who shopped in the cantonment bazaar. It was possible, he realized, that Colin was no longer with the battalion, but in his heart he must have suspected that a few months in India had shown Colin the truth about the kind of life a young Indian with no official position would have to lead. A glance at the map of Mayapore would have shown him how close they were, how far they were separated socially.

But Colin was in Mayapore. On the *maidan* – to report a cricket match – Hari saw him. They were within a few feet of one another. They looked at one another. Neither spoke. The kindest construction Hari could put on Colin's failure to speak was that he didn't recognize one brown face among so many. This, at least, was the suggestion he made when Rowan was examining him. Kumar described the incident in the course of answering the board's question, why – on a date in February 1942 – he had been found on waste ground near the river, dead drunk, and taken to Sister Ludmila's Sanctuary.

He said he'd always avoided intimacy with young men like

330

Vidyasagar and his companions, always refused invitations to go with them to coffee-houses. After the meeting with Colin on the *maidan* he'd met Vidyasagar and on the spur of the moment accepted an invitation to go home with him. It was as if he knew that his one true link with the past had now been snapped, as if he could see no reason to go on deceiving himself that he was any different from these semi-westernized youths. That night he discovered that they distilled or had access to illicit liquor. They were used to it. He was not. He got very drunk. They took him home but after they had gone he wandered off again, across the derelict ground where destitutes and untouchables camped out and where Sister Ludmila and her stretcher-bearers found him.

*

You could begin with me, Rowan had said, *I have very little real confidence. But it would be dangerous to give that impression. I expect I over-compensate. Most of us do. It's probably what happened to Colin Lindsey.*

Assuming mutual recognition, over-compensation for lack of confidence seemed to me a curious way of describing Lindsey's behaviour. Could one assume mutual recognition? Could one even assume that the man Kumar thought he recognized as Lindsey had been Lindsey? Apparently he must have been. Subsequently Rowan checked, through the military secretary's department. A Captain Colin Lindsey had been in Mayapore, not actually with his battalion but on the staff of the formation with which the battalion had been brigaded for training, and had then been transferred at his own request away from Mayapore to divisional headquarters.

Still, mutual recognition remains an assumption. But, if there was mutual recognition, one has to assume that Lindsey saw nothing so clearly as the embarrassment that would follow any attempt to renew an old acquaintance in such very different circumstances. His transfer to Division suggests that he probably applied for it directly he heard that he was going to Brigade, in Mayapore. Little to do with over-compensation for lack of confidence, but a lot to do with straight-forward self-protection from the consequences of having a

friend who was no longer socially acceptable and who might
turn out to be a pest, the sort of Indian who as the *raj* so often
said would try to take advantage, make demands it would be
impossible to satisfy and which it would be wiser and more
comfortable not to lay oneself open to.

Where I agree with Rowan is in pinpointing the meeting
with Lindsey as the one meeting in Kumar's life which,
leading directly to the other from which all his true misfortunes flowed, must bear a special significance: no Lindsey on
the *maidan* that day, no drinking bout with young Vidyasagar
and friends; no wandering on to waste-ground, no stretcher-
bearers, no Sister Ludmila, no Sanctuary; no morning waking
there, hungover, resentful and unco-operative.

No Merrick.

*

And yet how logical that meeting was, between Kumar – one
of Macaulay's 'brown-skinned Englishmen' – and Merrick,
English-born and English-bred, but a man whose country's
social and economic structure had denied him advantages and
privileges which Kumar had initially enjoyed; a man,
moreover, who lacked entirely that liberal instinct which is
so dear to historians that they lay it out like a guideline
through the unmapped forests of prejudice and self-interest as
though this line, and not the forest, is our history.

Place Merrick at home, in England, and Harry Coomer
abroad, in England, and it is Coomer on whom the historian's
eye lovingly falls; he is a symbol of our virtue. In England it is
Merrick who is invisible. Place them there, in India, and the
historian cannot see either of them. They have wandered off
the guideline, into the jungle. But throw a spotlight on them
and it is Merrick on whom it falls. There he is, the unrecorded
man, one of the kind of men we really are (as Sarah would say).
Yes, their meeting was logical. And they had met before,
countless times. You can say they are still meeting, that their
meeting reveals the real animus, the one that historians
won't recognize, or which we relegate to our margins

Neither Rowan nor I saw it like this, then. I doubt that he
would see it like this now. Simply, he would remain appalled

and puzzled, a man with a conscience that worked in favour of both men; more in favour of Kumar than of Merrick; but Merrick was given sufficient benefit of the liberal doubt to leave Rowan inert. What Rowan was doing, in telling me all this, was trying to set off against his own inertia someone else's positive action: mine. He wanted me to do what he could not do: help Kumar. His ideas on the subject, it goes without saying, were woolly.

*

Kumar had been washing under a tap, trying to clear his head, when Merrick arrived at the Sanctuary looking for the escaped prisoner, Moti Lal. The first ball of the over. The merciless succession of deliveries after all came from the same hand. Merrick saw him, a young man of twenty-two, washing under a tap; and chose him. I wondered how 'prepossessing' Hari Kumar had been before prison had had its effect and made him look like one man peering out of the eyesockets of another. Self-punishment being out of the question, Merrick punished the men he chose. After Karim Muzzafir Khan's suicide I was never in any doubt about Merrick's repressed homosexuality. Rowan always evaded this issue, and the result was that for him I think it assumed a graver importance than it merited, except perhaps in regard to the proposed marriage to Susan Bingham. But he had found it quite impossible, obviously, to convey any suspicion of this kind to Colonel Layton, or to anyone whom it might concern. One can understand this. It was no business of his, just as it was no business of mine.

For not answering Merrick's questions smartly and respectfully, Kumar was taken forcibly from the Sanctuary, pushed, punched and thrown into a police truck; not by Merrick but by one of Merrick's sub-inspectors (the same one, perhaps, who made an 'erroneous' report about the bicycle?).

But Merrick saw him being punched. So did Sister Ludmila. After the truck had driven away she sent word to Hari's uncle Romesh Chand. Romesh sent the lawyer Srinivasan to inquire why young Kumar had been 'arrested', but by the time he got there Kumar had been released. The word got round, though, that a young Indian of good character and good education had been roughed-up by the police and taken in for questioning – got round in those circles of Indian society which formed a link between the rulers and the ruled; Indians with a foot in both camps.

Four years after his arrival in Mayapore this world became aware of him. He had to be hauled into a kotwali first. It must have intrigued Merrick that this world now took note of Kumar. Srinivasan, first; and then, no doubt through Srinivasan, no less a person than the District and Sessions Judge, an Indian, who apparently inquired gently why this young Indian had been taken to the kotwali with no obvious justification. For Srinivasan and the judge Merrick can only have had contempt.

The *doyenne* of this official Indian society in Mayapore was Lady Chatterjee, a woman of cultured and cosmopolitan tastes, one imagines, since she was a friend of Lady Manners. *Persona grata* with the Deputy Commissioner, with whom she played bridge, she was neither blind nor deaf to evidence of the *raj's* high-handedness even if (as one supposes) she often had to be to its frequent vulgarities. What Srinivasan, the lawyer, or Menen, the judge, told her about the young Kumar, interested her sufficiently to cause her to invite him to a party at her house.

He went, one imagines, out of curiosity; prickly curiosity, as resentful of the interest his 'case' had aroused as he was resentful of the fact that it had taken so long for this privileged section of Indian society to notice him. Rowan gathered it had been a mixed party – a further irony. Kumar would have been under observation by both sides. Admitting to Rowan that from his point of view the party wasn't a success (nor, he thought, from Lady Chatterjee's, whom he failed to thank), he said he had forgotten how to behave in this sort of company.

One questions that until remembering that he had never been in that sort of company before, and realizes that what he really meant was that he had no idea how to behave in a gathering of people, white and brown, who even when they mingled were observing certain rules which hinted at segregation. These were rules which only Miss Manners seemed unaware of. At first he thought she was merely trying over-hard to put him at his ease. It was a long time since an English person had talked to him without either condescension or self-consciousness, which was what Miss Manners *seemed* to be doing and what subsequent events suggested she *had* been doing. And that would make her the first Englishwoman to have talked to him on the simple human level of woman to man. When last in England he had still been a schoolboy. One wonders about the effect this would have on him. Rowan had never seen a photograph of her. The one the police found in Kumar's room was not in the file. But he had heard her described as not much to look at; but this was afterwards, when people had no time for her and assumed she had rigged the evidence to save a man she was infatuated with or terrified of.

One really knew nothing about Daphne Manners except that she was in some degree or other attracted to Kumar. One knew nothing about Kumar's feelings. The history of their relationship could be made to fit almost any theory one could have of Kumar's character and intentions. Here he was, for instance, doing as little as he could to encourage her because he found her embarrassing. Or here, doing that same little in order to excite her more. Or here, genuinely fond of her, perhaps falling in love with her, but seeing no future for either of them and doing his best to make her see that there was no future. The theory most people had was that he egged her on, made her chase after him, to humiliate her, but subtly, so that she did not realize that she was being humiliated.

'Which theory do you subscribe to?' I asked Rowan.

'I think he was fond of her. I don't believe he meant her any harm. I think she fell in love with him quite early on. And eventually I think they started making love. I think they were making love in the Bibighar Gardens. It's the only explanation that makes sense of all the rest. They were making love and were interrupted by the men who assaulted her.'

'His friends?'

'They weren't his friends. He'd only been out with them once, the night he got drunk. They weren't his enemies either. And they were really only kids. If Hari and Miss Manners were making love in the Bibighar that night then I think the men who attacked them and assaulted her really were the kind she described later when she had to admit she'd had a glimpse of them. Badmashes who'd come into Mayapore to pick up what they could in the riots everyone was expecting and which had already started down in districts like Dibrapur. The Bibighar Gardens sounds like a public place but it was a derelict site. The kind of place men like that would collect in, waiting for dark. And the kind of place Kumar and Miss Manners would go to, to be on their own.'

'Didn't you ask Kumar whether this is what happened?'

'It only occurred to me later. Quite recently, in fact. In any case Kumar wouldn't have admitted it. He refused to say anything about her. He went on insisting he'd not seen her for something like three weeks, after the night they visited the temple. Exactly the same as he insisted when Merrick arrested him. And then of course don't forget I was trying not to examine him about the rape. I was taking a very literal view of the terms of reference, which were for the examination of a political detenu. But the rape couldn't be avoided. Everything came back to it because everything came back to Merrick. Kumar seemed to want it to come back to Merrick. So did Gopal. So for that matter did Lady Manners. Gopal started asking him about his first interrogation – I don't mean the one in February – I mean after Merrick had carted him away from his home on the night of the rape. He told Gopal Merrick had had him stripped and that his genitals had been examined. Lady Manners was listening in and watching through the grille. The microphone was in a telephone on my desk but she and I could use the telephone to communicate. When she realized I was trying to stop things going along these lines she rang through and told me I mustn't bother about her hearing unpleasant things. The other thing she wanted to know was whether Kumar knew her niece had died in childbirth. I pretended it was an outside call, naturally, and took that opportunity to call a break and send Kumar out. I tried to explain to Gopal that if we started concentrating on the alleged rape the record of the examination might be thrown out as irrelevant. But he insisted. I thought it pretty dangerous. You have to realize, Guy, that at this time I was fairly convinced that Kumar was mixed up in the assault somehow or other and that Gopal was being very naïve, over-anxious to show that Kumar had been a victim of *raj* terrorism. And, well, to be quite frank, it went against the grain to hear Kumar beginning to accuse an English police officer, a man who wasn't there to defend himself.

'Kumar wasn't on oath, the examination was private. The police officer couldn't legally be affected by anything Kumar decided to say or make up. And I wondered why he was suddenly so co-operative about answering questions he'd previously refused to answer. In 1942 his reply to every question according to the file had been that he had nothing to say. The only thing he still had nothing to say about was what he'd been doing between leaving the *Gazette* office as usual about six in the evening and arriving home about 9.30 in mud-stained clothes and with scratches and abrasions on his face. On the other hand –'

I waited.

'On the other hand, if he'd spent his time in prison making up fantasies about Merrick's treatment of him I felt he could have made up a plausible story to cover that ominous gap. But he hadn't. And whatever he said *sounded* like the truth. I didn't know what to think. But I felt like a defending lawyer who knows he can get his client off so long as he sticks to the point – the minor legal issue – and avoids anything controversial. I think I could have stuck to that and overridden Gopal if Kumar had co-operated. But he kept on saying that the real situation couldn't be avoided. He didn't mean the rape, he said he meant the situation between Merrick and himself. So when he came back after the recess I let everyone pull out the stops. I felt I'd exchanged briefs and was now prosecuting. If I let him talk about what he called the situation I thought he'd inadvertently give something away. It wasn't what I wanted. It was what I felt I couldn't resist any more. Do you see that? Or do I sound like someone covering up a prejudice and pretending the prejudice was never there?'

It was a difficult question. I couldn't answer it. I didn't try. What worried Rowan was the thought that after all his suspicion of Hari's complicity in the rape was not based so much on the evidence in the file as on the fact that Hari was an Indian and the colour of his skin coloured one's attitude to

337

him, and that in fact it was a relief to exchange his brief, throw off the mask and let Hari condemn himself while he was trying to condemn Merrick.

And I think it was then, with Rowan sitting opposite me, showing not a trace of anxiety (carve him in stone and nothing would have emerged so clearly as his rigid pro-consular self-assurance, remoteness and dignity), that I understood the comic dilemma of the *raj* – the dilemma of men who hoped to inspire trust but couldn't even trust themselves. The air around us and in the grounds of the summer residence was soft, pungent with aromatic gums, but melancholy – charged with this self-mistrust and the odour of an unreality which only exile made seem real. I had an almost irrepressible urge to burst out laughing. I fought it because he would have misinterpreted it. But I would have been laughing *for* him. I suppose that to laugh for people, to see the comic side of their lives when they can't see it for themselves, is a way of expressing affection for them; and even admiration – of a kind – for the lives they try so seriously to lead.

*

It was Gopal's theory that the cuts and abrasions Kumar was said to have been bathing when the police turned up at his house hadn't been there until after the police turned up, or until he arrived at police headquarters, or even until later; that is, not there until they started getting rough with him and needed a report on the file that would explain the state of his face and at the same time harden the evidence against him. When the examination got under way again Rowan read out to him Merrick's statement about his arrival at Kumar's house and his discovery of Kumar, bathing his face, which was cut and bruised, and of the discarded muddy clothes.

Was that an accurate report? Rowan asked.

Yes, Kumar replied. It was.

*

Gopal was deflated but bided his time. There was another report on Kumar's file, quite a brief one, a copy of a statement

338

by a magistrate who'd been asked by the Deputy Commissioner to question Kumar on two rather unpleasant aspects of the handling of the case. Word had got round in Mayapore that to try to make them confess the arrested boys, all Hindus, had been forced to eat beef. Also that they'd been whipped. The magistrate's name was Iyenagar. Rowan hadn't seen the files on the five other boys, he'd only been shown Kumar's. According to this file Kumar told Iyenagar that he had no complaint to make about his treatment, a simple enough refutation of the rumours and one that seemed to be borne out by the report from the medical officer at the Kandipat jail who examined Kumar physically the day he was sent there as a detenu – more than two weeks later. The only mark of physical violence noted down by the prison doctor was a contusion on his cheek. But that had been there when Merrick found him bathing his face.

The bruise, however, gave Mr Gopal an argument which he tried to turn to Kumar's advantage. He said that the marks on Hari's face, which Hari himself refused to explain, had been interpreted by the police as marks got from Miss Manners in the struggle with her attackers. He said that in a court of law a lawyer might reasonably have asked whether a woman could hit a man hard enough for a bruise to stay on his cheek for as long as two weeks. He was still trying to get Hari to say that the police had beaten him up. But Hari wouldn't say this. He said it was a good point but that in a court a prosecuting counsel might well have turned it against him by suggesting that the men who attacked Miss Manners also fought with each other.

'I saw an opening there,' Rowan told me. 'I asked him casually if that was what had happened. I remember how he looked at me. He said he'd no idea what happened among the men who attacked her. But he realized I'd exchanged briefs. I tried again to get him to say what had happened to him that night, gave him the chance to go back over the ground, back to the question of Colin, back to his relationship with Miss Manners, but all I got out of him was the information that sometimes he and Miss Manners had helped Sister Ludmila at the Sanctuary, occasionally visited one another's homes, and sometimes on a Sunday morning met in the Bibighar Gardens, the kind of places where they could go without attracting what he called abusive attention, but that all this ended on the night they visited the temple, when they had some sort of tiff.

'I saw another opening. I said, "But you made the quarrel up later." He didn't fall for that. He pointed out that I was forgetting he and Miss Manners hadn't seen each other since that night – the night they visited the temple. So I let Gopal take over, which meant letting Gopal get Hari to say what happened after Merrick arrested him.'

Almost at once they were in what Rowan called very murky waters. While they'd concentrated on the political evidence it had been possible to show that the conflict was not a conflict of evidence so much as of interpretation. Directly Hari began to describe what happened after he'd passed through the room in which the five other boys were being held behind bars, euphoric with liquor, and down into the air-conditioned basement of Merrick's headquarters, it became a question of setting Merrick's official statements about the interrogation against Hari's recollections of it. Recollections, or fantasies?

For example, from the police file: this – 'At 2245 hours the prisoner Kumar having continually refused to answer questions relating to his activities that evening asked for what reason he had been taken into custody. Upon being told it was believed he could help the police with inquiries they were making into the criminal assault in the Bibighar Gardens earlier that evening he said: I have not seen Miss Manners since the night we visited the temple. On being asked why he named Miss Manners he refused to answer and showed signs of distress.'

When Hari was asked to say whether this was accurate he said it wasn't. He had refused to answer questions but the statement left out the fact that he'd said he would refuse to do so while he was left in ignorance of why he'd been arrested. It may have been 2245 hours before Merrick finally said he was making an inquiry, but he described it first as an inquiry about an Englishwoman who was missing, then added, 'You know which one,' and then made what Hari called an obscene

340

remark. He didn't know what was meant by a distressed condition unless this was a reference to the fact that he was shivering as a result of being kept standing for a long time, naked, in an air-conditioned room, after Merrick had inspected his genitals. After that inspection Merrick had said, 'So you've been clever enough to wash?' and later, 'But she wasn't a virgin, was she, and you were the first fellow to ram her'. After that, according to Hari, Merrick had sat on his desk, drinking whisky, and talked to him about the history of the British in India, every so often interjecting remarks about the boys in the cell upstairs, suggesting that they looked on him as a leader, that they'd do anything he said, and again making the comment that 'she hadn't been a virgin' and that Hari had 'been the first to ram her'. From this sequence of events, Hari claimed, he gathered that he and the others were suspected of rape. He claimed that he didn't mention Miss Manners until Merrick finally told him, at 2245 hours – a time he didn't dispute – that an Englishwoman had been criminally assaulted, and added, 'you know which one' and then made an obscene remark. He refused to say what the remark was but admitted that he now told Merrick he hadn't seen Miss Manners since the night of the visit to the temple.

Gopal pointed out to him that unless he repeated the obscene remark his explanation for naming her remained unsatisfactory. But he would not repeat it.

*

It annoyed Gopal that he wouldn't. He went on pressing. Hari went on refusing. Gopal became heated, as if he were suddenly on *Merrick's* side and intended to show that if Kumar wouldn't repeat the remark that was because he couldn't; it had never been made; everything he had said about Merrick's behaviour was a pack of lies.

Hari remained unmoved. Rowan joined in again. He went over Merrick's statement point by point, forcing Hari to agree that in a number of details it was correct. Hari *had* named Miss Manners. The time was not in dispute. And he *had* been showing signs of distress if only because he was shivering.

The rhythm of question and answer quickened. How long

had Hari been kept standing naked? He couldn't remember. Why? He lost track of things like time. One hour? Two hours? Perhaps. Was he alone with Merrick? Not all the time, other people came in. Who? Two constables. Anyone else? Yes, there may have been others. Couldn't he remember? Why couldn't he remember? Was he saying he was confused, giddy and cold from standing all that time? He wasn't standing all the time. He was allowed to sit then? No, he wasn't allowed to sit.

Gopal said he didn't understand. If Kumar wasn't standing and wasn't sitting, what was he doing, lying down?

Hari said, 'I was bent over a trestle, tied to it. For the persuasive phase of interrogation. A cane was used.'

*

Rowan said, 'I read out Iyenagar's report and asked him whether that was an accurate record of his interview with the magistrate. He said it was. In a way I was prepared for that answer because when I began reading Iyenagar's report *aloud* it struck me for the first time how very carefully the questions had been framed. They were the kind of questions a cautious authority would ask if it was suspected that a man would be too frightened to say he'd been ill-treated and if it was felt that a denial would be better for everybody's sake. "Have you any complaint to make about your treatment in custody?" was the first question. Hari said "No." Most of the questions were like that. And if Hari couldn't actually reply "no" he just said he had nothing to add to his first answer. Before I began reading it I thought I'd make it impossible for him to explain why he now accused the police of physical violence when he'd had the opportunity to do that at the time. He'd agreed that the Iyenagar report was accurate. I intended to show that he was being inconsistent. But he wasn't. I knew the answer to this before he gave it. He'd told Iyenagar the truth. He had no *complaint* to make. Just that. No complaint.

'The question wasn't so much why he didn't complain then as why he was complaining now. And was he telling the truth? I read out the prison doctor's report, the one that didn't note any visible marks of physical violence apart from the bruise on his face. But I couldn't shake him. He implied that the doctor had seen other marks but hadn't recorded them. We asked how many times he'd been hit. He said he couldn't remember. Whenever they stopped hitting him Merrick talked to him to encourage him to confess. He said Merrick told him Miss Manners had already named him but that he didn't believe her story. He believed she'd egged Hari and the others on and then got more than she bargained for and wanted them punished. Hari said that every time Merrick felt he was getting nowhere he told the constables to start again. I asked how long they had gone on. I still didn't really believe him. He said he didn't remember. Gopal asked if he was implying he lost consciousness. He said he never lost consciousness. He simply couldn't remember how long he was on the trestle.'

Rowan paused. 'Then he explained why he couldn't remember. He said it was difficult to breathe in that position and that breathing was all you thought about. I believed him then. It's not the sort of thing a man could easily make up, is it? And the trouble was that believing him made the next bit that much more difficult to write off as pure invention. He said Merrick sent the constables out of the room and spoke and acted even more obscenely. I asked him what he meant. I rather wish I hadn't. He said Merrick – fondled him.'

'Fondled him.'

'I told the shorthand writer to strike that out, leave his note-book on my desk and wait outside until I called him back. Then I really started on Hari. I put it to him that he was lying, taking advantage of the examination of his case as a political detenu to make baseless accusations in the mistaken belief that these would protect him if a charge of rape were made even as late in the day as this. I really pitched into him. I told him he had the chance to retract and advised him to think very carefully before passing the chance up.'

'Did he retract?'

'No. He apologized.'

'What for?'

'For what he called misunderstanding the reason why he was being examined.'

'What had he thought was the reason?'

343

'He thought Miss Manners had managed to persuade someone at last that he'd done nothing to deserve being locked up and that this had been his chance to prove it.'

'He wasn't far out, was he?'

'No, but I should have stuck to the political evidence. As soon as we went into the business of the rape I couldn't hide my suspicions and so he thought no one had really been persuaded of anything except that it was time to interrogate him again. Either that or that we were trying to salve bad consciences. He asked outright if something had happened to her. He'd had no news of her of any kind. I told him what had happened, that she'd died of peritonitis a year before, after a Caesarean operation. He asked whether she had married. She hadn't of course. He didn't ask if the child survived. At first I thought he was quite unmoved. Then I saw he wasn't. I asked if he wanted time to compose himself. He said he didn't but that we should have told him. It was very odd. His voice was quite unaffected. Physically he was composed. But he was crying. I asked him whether what he meant when he said we should have told him was that he would have answered the questions differently if he'd known she was dead. He said he only answered them because he thought she must have wanted us to ask them. If he'd known she was dead he wouldn't have answered them at all. I reminded him there was one important question he still hadn't answered. He knew I meant the question about where he was when she was being attacked. He said he'd never answer it. I was ready to bring things to an end but Gopal began again about the situation between Hari and Merrick. The clerk was no longer in the room. Officially the examination was over. He realized that. He seemed willing to talk – about that situation – even anxious. I didn't stop him. I believed he'd told the truth about the caning. I accepted that. I think you have to. I don't condone it. I'm not sure I can condemn it. It would be unfair to single Merrick out. Caning's a normal judicial punishment in this country. There were a lot of such sentences dished out in 1942 and I don't doubt a fair number of beatings-up in cells to get confessions. What I didn't accept, don't accept, without question, is – well the other thing. He could have imagined it.

By his own admission he wasn't in full possession of his senses. I see you don't agree.'

'The violence makes more sense if you do accept what you call the other thing. Was Merrick kind to him at any point?'

Rowan stared at me. 'Kind to him?'

'Afterwards.'

'He gave him water. But he made him thank him for it.'

'It's the sort of thing I mean. Tell me about it.'

'I can only tell you what Hari said. It doesn't mean it happened.'

'Well tell me what Hari said.'

'He said he was taken into another room and manacled to a charpoy. Merrick was alone with him. He gave him a drink of water and made him say thank you. He bathed the cuts. He told him there'd be no more questions until morning. He said the whole evening had been an enactment of the real situation between them and that now they both knew how matters stood and what that situation was.' Rowan paused. 'It was a master and man situation, a simplified way of putting it, but near enough. At one point Merrick said, What price Chillingborough now? At another point he told Hari that there were only two basic human emotions, contempt and envy, and that a man's personality existed at his point of equilibrium between the two. But when I met Merrick the other day I simply couldn't imagine him behaving and talking like that.'

'I'm sure he did.'

'Yes, I thought you'd believe it. It's one of the reasons I'm telling you.' Again he hesitated. 'Hari said that it was to punish himself for thanking Merrick for the water that he decided to answer no more questions. He said the situation between himself and Merrick wouldn't exist if he dissociated himself from it and refused to say anything more to Merrick or to anyone else. Does that make sense to you?'

'It makes very good sense. It's what I've been trying to do. Dissociate myself from the situation that arises out of being chosen.'

Rowan was silent for a while. Then he said, 'Has he chosen Sarah Layton's sister?'

'I don't know. I don't think so.'

'Just the Laytons as a family?'

That suddenly didn't fit entirely either. But I saw what did. I said: 'In the way I mean by choose I should say he's chosen the child.'

*

'The child,' Lady Manners had said (meaning that other child fathered by a person unknown). 'The child. But even now I can't be sure, only surer. She was so sure.' The other thing she said was, 'He spoke the truth', but qualified it later as they drove through Kandipat, blinds down. She said, 'One has to make do with approximations' and that this was what one meant when one said he spoke the truth. When Rowan left Room O he too was sure he had heard the truth. He told Lady Manners that Kumar would be released but regretted this later when various impediments to such a release had all contributed to a partial revival of disbelief, to a renewed conviction that Kumar *had* somehow been involved in the assault. Lady Manners had asked to be taken back to her hotel and not to Government House. As they parted she thanked him for having undertaken such a distasteful task and asked him to give Malcolm a message: a very short one. 'I know my niece did not lie, that he never harmed her and is very wrongfully imprisoned.'

When he gave the message to the Governor, Malcolm said they would discuss it when the record of the examination was typed up and he'd had the chance to read it. He was going to Calcutta for a few days and preoccupied with other matters. He told Rowan to give the confiscated shorthand book to Cynthia, Her Excellency's private secretary. He thought it unwise to have it transcribed by the shorthand writer at the Secretariat. 'Don't worry,' Malcolm said. 'Cynthia's pretty broad-minded.' All the same, Rowan tore out the page which the shorthand writer had drawn a line through before handing it to her.

She must have worked late. The following morning she sent him a sealed envelope containing the notebook and a top and two carbons of an impeccable typescript. When he rang through to thank her she merely said, 'Oh, well. Press on you know. Only way to get round the course.' When he read the typescript through he was astonished at her apparent equanimity. It sounded even worse in print. He kept notebook and typescripts in a locked drawer until Malcolm returned, and hourly expected Gopal to ring him and ask when the shorthand writer could complete his job by typing the record. But Gopal didn't ring.

When Malcolm had read the typescript he told Rowan it was a pity he hadn't been able to stick to the political evidence. The transcript showed that he had tried and also why he hadn't succeeded. But it was a pity. He explained that although senior police officers had always stood by Merrick, and that included the Inspector-General, the Inspector-General's private opinion was that Merrick had botched the evidence by being over-anxious and emotionally involved because he had been fond of the girl himself. If the IG saw this transcript he would be so shocked by Kumar's accusations that he would write them off as pure fantasy and point out that the only result of the examination had been to revive suspicion of Kumar's guilt, and that this would be sufficient reason to keep the fellow locked up until the end of the war. The IG would say that to release Kumar now would be as good as recording a reprimand on Merrick's personal file and that this could count against him, very unfairly, when he returned to the police after his army service.

'Then the best thing,' Rowan had said, 'will be to file the transcript away and forget all about it.'

But Malcolm said he didn't think he could allow that. In Kumar's case Rule 26 had fairly clearly been abused. The abuse was less obvious in the case of the other boys. If they had had a political leader at all it would have been Vidyasagar who wasn't among those arrested for rape but who was arrested a couple of days later for printing seditious literature on the press in the *Mayapore Hindu* office. In comparison with Vidyasagar even the others might be thought of as lambs led to the slaughter. Kumar, Malcolm was sure, hadn't even been a member of the flock. 'By the way,' he said, 'why did you confiscate the book and end the examination so abruptly?'

Rowan told him.

'It isn't in the transcript.'

347

'I removed the offending page.'

'And deprived Cynthia of the dénouement? What happened after you sent the shorthand writer out?'

Again Rowan told him.

'And Lady Manners heard *all* this?'

'Yes.'

'Did she make any other comment in the car coming home apart from giving you that message?'

'I gathered she was now surer Kumar was the father of the Manners child, but not as sure as her niece had been.'

'What did you infer from that?'

'That Miss Manners told her aunt she and Kumar had been lovers.'

'Her niece told her nothing. She left a written statement absolving Kumar completely. The old lady found it after her death, but she wouldn't show it even to me.'

* * *

Rowan felt like exploding with irritation.

'If we'd had Miss Manners's statement we might have had a more successful examination,' he told the Governor. But the Governor pointed out that the examination had been of a man detained for political reasons. Miss Manners's statement, presumably, dealt entirely with her emotional involvement with Kumar. The only value a statement like that would ever have would be in the event, now highly unlikely, of a charge being brought against Kumar for rape, when defending counsel might construct his case from it. In Malcolm's view, Lady Manners was perfectly justified in otherwise keeping it to herself. Neither she – nor her niece – had ever had any answer to the political charges, which lay outside their competence, however deep the conviction was that political detention had been imposed out of sheer frustration; the frustration felt by the civil authority which had wanted to nail Kumar much more effectively. And in *that* regard, in the matter of the charge of rape, Malcolm suggested, Miss Manners's silence, Kumar's refusal to answer questions, during the period when a charge of rape might so easily have been brought, had not only been effective then but was eloquent now. Just how eloquent, Malcolm wasn't sure. Except that he believed it suggested that they had loved one another and that, loving him, she had been afraid for him.

Just as eloquent, he thought, was the fact that Lady Manners had let a certain amount of time elapse before trying to hoist the civil authority with its own petard: Kumar's 'political' crimes. Clearly non-existent. He could order Kumar's immediate release simply on the basis of the transcript of the examination but was reluctant to do so without the approval of both the member for Home and Law and the Inspector-General. That approval, he thought, wouldn't automatically flow from the transcript of the examination.

'He left it to me,' Rowan said, 'to find a *modus operandi*.'

The first thing Rowan did was to edit a copy of the transcript to isolate the political content. When he'd done this he persuaded Cynthia to type copies of the revised version. 'Very neat', she said, when she handed the revised version to him. He thought so himself. It was now the kind of transcript that could be shown – for instance to the Inspector-General – without much fear of blood-pressures rising or of waking departmental sensitivities.

However, there was one man who might upset the applecart. Both Rowan and Gopal would have to initial the transcript before it went on file. Gopal could wreck everything by refusing to put his initials to a document that was obviously rigged. The question was, in what was Gopal most interested? In the release of an unjustly imprisoned Indian detenu or in the eventual exposure of a British police officer? Rowan rang Gopal at the Secretariat. He asked if they could meet somewhere, unofficially. Gopal didn't bite. Rowan had no option but to go to the Secretariat. He took with him a carbon of the full typescript and a carbon of the edited version. He asked Gopal to read both documents and then get in touch with him so that they could discuss the problem.

The following day Gopal rang. He asked Rowan to have dinner with him at his home that evening and gave instructions how to get there. It was the beginning of an association that ripened into friendship and affection. Gopal had seen the

349

point of the edited typescript at once. He was on Kumar's side. He said he would be prepared to initial the edited typescript at once, with one proviso, that the title of the document should include the word Abstract and that the general heading should make it clear that the examination was in regard to a warrant issued under the Defence of India Rules. He produced a draft of the kind of heading he had in mind. Rowan accepted it at once.

'Are we doing the right thing, though?' Gopal asked as they parted. 'In prison at least he has an identity.'

*

But even with the edited typescript in front of him, the Inspector-General threatened to prove stubborn. An unexpected nigger in the woodpile was Pandit Baba. Since 1942 this man had become much more actively involved in affairs which attracted the CID's attention. Kumar's disclosure that he had been taught Hindi by Baba interested the IG considerably. Kumar had refused to answer questions about the Pandit at the time of his arrest. His admission now surely showed how well-informed Merrick had been, how right to suspect a connection, how right to ask questions about a connection. Until now it hadn't been clear why he did. At the time the Pandit's activities had been too unimportant for one's attention to have been attracted to his name on the file. But he was nowadays believed to be a subtle and potentially dangerous leader of Hindu youth, anti-Congress, anti-Gandhi, anti-British, with affiliations with the Hindu Mahasabha and its activist group, the Rashtriya Swayam Sevak Sangh. And what was the connection between the pandit and the detenu's aunt – who had bombarded Government with pleas for her nephew's release and was now in Ranpur without visible means of support? The examination showed that the aunt had paid for the Hindi lessons, and that it was she who had chosen Baba as Kumar's teacher. Did her persistence, her constant pleas, suggest prompting by Baba Sahib? Was she being used by this man? He had always been much too clever to get into trouble himself. Currently he had disappeared from the scene. But if one released Kumar mightn't he be the

350

very type of young man the Pandit would find it useful to have as a disciple?

Rowan suggested to Malcolm that if the main obstacle to Kumar's release was the suspicion that he would fall at once into the Pandit's net of eager young disciples perhaps the thing to suggest to the IG was that if the CID wanted to nab the Pandit a free Kumar might be more helpful than an imprisoned Kumar.

But Malcolm said, 'Either we believe Kumar and his aunt have no political commitments or we don't. If we don't believe it we're not justified in releasing him. Frankly I do believe it. The Pandit's just a red herring the IG's suddenly noticed. So, let it lie. Have you ever understood Einstein?'

Rowan said he hadn't. Malcolm said he hadn't either, but that sometimes when faced with this apparently insoluble and intricate problem of reaching a solution through the thickets of departmental vanities he applied his own theory of relativity, which was that although people seldom argued a point but argued round it, they sometimes found the solution to the problem they were evading by going round in ever *increasing* circles and disappearing into the centre of *those*, which, relatively speaking, coincided with the centre of the circle from whose periphery they had evasively spiralled outwards.

So Rowan let it lie. His belief in Kumar's innocence or guilt was like a pendulum. He wished he could get that to lie too, wished he could stop it at the vertical point which represented non-commitment. It was a relief when a couple of weeks later Malcolm gave him another confidential assignment – one which called for him to officiate on the Governor's behalf at the transfer of another detenu – Mohammed Ali Kasim – from imprisonment in the fort at Premanager to the protection of his kinsman, the Nawab of Mirat; a form of parole, an ostensibly compassionate act but not without its element of political shrewdness.

And it was on this assignment that he'd met Sarah Layton – changing trains on her way back to Pankot from Calcutta where she had visited the wounded hero, the best man at Susan's wedding. There she was, a rather travel-stained *Deus ex machina*, bringing news about wounds and decorations

351

which might solve the problem of departmental concern for Merrick's reputation and Merrick's future; but for Rowan, I thought, rather more than that. Was he, by the time I met him on the same station, more than just rather fond of her?

I thought so. His decision to go back to Ranpur the next day suggested he had had hopes which he had suddenly given up. I should have liked to see them together, not as I had done that evening, but in Ranpur during two or three days of what I judged to have been a tentative exploration of airier regions that promised to be in common ownership. Mutual antipathy to Merrick was no more than a way in to those regions. Rowan, of course had not – and never would have – disclosed to her what he knew, and she had nothing to disclose except her instinctive woman's prejudice. These meetings between them had taken place during the brief time she spent in Ranpur before going down to Bombay to meet her father. Before then, they had met only that once when she had just come in from Calcutta and her visit to Merrick. He hadn't been sure what her relationship with Merrick was. It was a relief to him, he said, to discover that in one sense there was no relationship. Another discovery was that she had once met Lady Manners in Kashmir, had seen the child; believed Merrick had made a terrible mistake. It was now that he told her he'd known Kumar as a boy, at school. But that was all. He might have told her more this time, on this visit to Pankot, but naturally hadn't done so.

'Naturally?' I asked.

He said, 'Well, of course.'

It was silly to have questioned it. Merrick was to be Miss Layton's brother-in-law. That being so, from Rowan's point of view the subject of Merrick and Kumar was utterly closed as one he felt able to discuss with her. I wondered when she had first heard or suspected that Merrick planned to marry her sister. Almost certainly the answer must be that she'd suspected nothing until she and her father got back to Pankot. Most certain of all was that it had been a shock to Rowan. I began to see the fullness of Rowan's little tragi-comedy. He had, after all, had hopes of her. The brief holiday in Pankot had been intended as an opportunity to convey to her that his resumed career in the political was one he hoped she might share with him. Perhaps his hopes had only finally been dashed, or shelved for future exploration, during the few hours we'd spent that night at Rose Cottage. Perhaps, with Merrick gone, he had hoped to find her recovered from the shock, less weighed down, looking and acting like the girl he knew (the girl I remembered). Had he at any time said anything to her at all about his hopes? Had she rebuffed him?

His attention was again directed to the darkness beyond the verandah; and suddenly I saw this other, faintly ludicrous aspect of the affair; one that inclined me to believe that because Rowan was the kind of man he was he had said nothing to her at all. He would have taken his time anyway, and before an opportunity arose the wind had been knocked out of his sails by the announcement of Susan's engagement. Well, imagine it: imagine, for instance, Rowan shaving, brushing his hair, facing up to his reflection; thinking what he *must* have thought because every man would. Imagine him thinking this: Could I honestly spend the rest of my life knowing what I think I know about the man who would be my brother-in-law and say nothing?

And the answer would be, no. The other answer would be that knowing himself incapable of saying anything he knew that his own hopes had to be abandoned.

*

Malcolm was on the point of leaving for Delhi when Rowan got back from the Kasim assignment and told him the news about Merrick's gallantry in the field. 'I'll check it,' Malcolm said. 'Meanwhile we'll say nothing. It would be best if the Inspector-General got to know through his own sources.' It meant another delay, the possibility too of this development making the IG even more stubbornly opposed to any course of action that belittled Merrick's earlier performance as a guardian of the law. But the farce was coming to an end. Quite suddenly, without fuss, it was over. The IG withdrew his objections to Kumar's release. Kumar was informed and told the date on which he would be free and instructed to report to the police in Ranpur once a week for six months. He was allowed to write to his aunt to prepare her for his return.

The aunt was living in rooms above a shop in the Koti bazaar. So Gopal told Rowan. They met the night the order of release was signed – a form of gentle celebration by two conspirators. Rowan was thinking: Yes, but release to what? Gopal had already formed a plan. He said it would be possible to put Kumar in the way of beginning to earn a living as a private teacher of English. He knew a reliable young man who would help him and who had already made contact with the aunt. The poor woman was very nervous and suspicious. It had been difficult for Gopal's young man to gain her confidence. He had had to ask her to trust him when he said the authorities had at last taken an interest in her nephew's case, trust him when he said there was every reason to hope that Hari would be released, and trust him again when he said he would help him to find work and keep out of the way of people who might want to exploit him.

'I suppose I was sticking my neck out,' Gopal said, 'but that is what necks are for.'

*

It was ironic, Rowan said, and salutary, that of the two of them it was old Gopal, who had begun by not liking Hari, who had put his mind to the question of Hari's rehabilitation.

Kumar had been free for over a year now. Rowan hadn't seen him, neither had Gopal. He relied on Gopal for news and Gopal relied on his reliable young man. Kumar no longer had to report to the police but the CID still kept an eye on him. It had been weeks before Kumar trusted Gopal's young man enough to fall in with the scheme for teaching English. He made the excuse that he would himself have to learn Hindi properly, first. But eventually, probably when it occurred to him to wonder what they lived on and he realized that his aunt had come to the end of her small resources and had always been too proud to beg help from her brother's family and only too anxious to cut herself off completely from her dead husband's, and had now sold the last bit of her jewelry, he agreed to help cram a couple of candidates for entrance to the Government College. Their success brought him other boys, including a nephew of Gopal's. He seldom visited their homes. He seldom left the apartment. He was paid very badly but he refused anything that smelt of financial help. The reliable young man, when he could do so without Kumar knowing, gave the aunt small gifts, as if in return for the cups of tea and coffee he had when he visited them; gifts of a few vegetables, flour, ghi. The young man's own means were limited. Some of these gifts, Rowan suspected, came from Mrs Gopal.

Rowan had been able to do very little. He knew no Indians of the kind whose sons would go to an anonymous private teacher in the Koti bazaar. Rowan's Indian friends were rich. Gopal was the exception – the only middle-class Indian with whom he had ever become on intimate terms. At the same time perhaps the only Indian with whom he had ever been on such terms.

And now Rowan was leaving Ranpur. He had no idea where he would be sent. Even that little which it had been open to him to contribute, so vaguely, so anonymously, would come to an end, now. He would keep in touch with Gopal as far as that was possible. Gopal and he had always had an idea that as circumstances changed, politically, it would be in their power unobtrusively to guide Kumar back into life. What he was living now was hardly a life. The reliable young man reported that Kumar seemed to have no ambition and that it was distressing to listen to the aunt painting an optimistic picture of a happy future when you only had to look at Kumar's face to see that Kumar's window on to the world was still closed and darkened. And once, coming on her alone, the young man had found Aunt Shalini crying. 'Why should he hope?' she asked, 'when there is nothing for him to hope for? He understands only English people and they will never forgive him because of the girl. The doors will always be closed to him.'

She meant the doors Hari had been brought up to open – the doors into the Administration. And what she said was true. Rowan himself was in possession of no key that would enable Hari to enter. Neither was Gopal. Even the way in to a junior teaching post in a Government College was barred.

*

'I've often thought of writing to old Bagshaw,' Rowan said. 'I don't really know why. One couldn't put it all in a letter anyway. And perhaps the old boy's dead now.'

'Is that where you see a future for Kumar? Back home?'

'I don't see much of a future for him here. I'm just broadening the perspective. It occurred to me that back home, if that's really where you're going, you might chance on something that could help. Anyway, I'd appreciate it if you'd write to me sometimes. Would you like another drink?'

I said I would, but that I'd take it to my room. It was nearly one o'clock.

'I'll send it in.' I imagined him sitting up for a while yet.

He didn't send it in. He brought it himself, calling to me through the half-open bathroom door. With a glass of brandy he gave me a large manila envelope.

'It's a carbon of the full typescript. I thought you might like to keep it. Take it home with you. To the groves of Academe. Officially it doesn't exist. HE told me to lose the copies of the full record. I destroyed the top and the shorthand book. I kept the carbons. I still have one.'

'Do you always carry this around?'

'No. I thought of giving it to Mr Gopal as a parting gift but thought better of it. Sleep well.'

On the way out he stopped.

'You'd better destroy it if you find Operation Bunbury snarled up and you're still stuck with Merrick. I mean in view of his light-fingered servant. Incidentally, you've never told me why you asked who Mrs Bingham was.'

'It's still too long a story.'

'But connected in some way?'

'Where Merrick's concerned everything's connected.'

'Yes. I suppose it is.'

When Rowan left me I opened the envelope meaning just to glance through it while I drank the brandy, but it was two o'clock before I'd finished reading and except for a sip or two the brandy was untouched. Far more than when Rowan described the examination I was attracted, appalled, riveted, firmly convinced of Kumar's innocence but deeply puzzled by his stubborn refusal to answer that vital question. If Rowan's object had been to ensure that I would find it difficult to get Kumar out of my mind then he had probably succeeded.

I put the transcript in my kit-bag and padlocked it, drank the brandy and went to bed.

I'd read the transcript using Rowan's final interpretation like a sieve, to isolate scraps of gritty evidence – the interpretation he'd only recently arrived at, the only one he thought made sense. I agreed. Kumar and Miss Manners had become lovers. They had been making love in the Bibighar. The marks on his face were got in a scuffle with men who pulled them apart, beat him up, knocked him unconscious or sat on him while one by one they raped the girl.

That, I thought, made sense; but thereafter there was no sense – only a silence which however hard I listened to it seemed incomprehensible. Nothing emerged from it after I turned the light out except pictures of Kumar: the man I had never seen not the boy whose face I couldn't clearly remember; but sweeping and cutting and blocking that merciless succession of contemptuous deliveries. Elms and rooks; but then again, not these, but palms and crows: the view from the flat which Purvis contemplated, retreated from, saying, 'I'm an economist', then coming in and pushing me further and further back into that elegant room with its priceless paintings in the Ghuler-Basohli style. Standing there, drink in hand, I lurched into sleep and Purvis was Kumar, seated, looking up at me through the eyes of this other man who kept saying: I don't think I'll ever forgive it.

*

Rowan had left a note. The steward brought it with my breakfast and the morning papers at 8.30. Rowan wrote that he'd had to make an early start to Area Headquarters to arrange about the special coach. He would have to go down to the station too. A tonga could be got to take me to the Pankot Rifles depot and he'd try to call in there to say goodbye. In case he couldn't he gave me an address in Delhi (that of a bank) for future correspondence. Very thoughtfully he gave me the name of the officer at Area HQ who would know of any signal arriving for me.

357

I got to the Pankots' depot at ten o'clock. They had suspended the interviews. I waited an hour but Rowan didn't turn up. I went to Area Headquarters. He had been there but had gone (I imagined) to say goodbye to the Laytons. In the signals office I introduced myself to the signals sergeant and made sure he had my telephone number. I went back to the guest house and was told that Rowan had just rung to say goodbye. For the rest of the day and throughout the evening, Ulysses-like I lashed myself to the mast of my quarters, deaf to every seduction except that of the sirens of the telephone exchange and signals office; afraid to go out, just in case a miracle had speeded Operation Bunbury up and a movement order was already on its way to me, one that required immediate action to be considered valid.

Saturday is a blank. All I remember is a reduction in the guest house staff. An invisible garrison commander had issued orders to reduce the rations and send the cooks and bhishtis, every able-bodied man, to fill the gaps at firing-ports and listening posts, leaving me attended by one shabby fellow who scavenged somewhere for pallid meals of thin gravy soup, dried meat and miserly salad and got steadily drunker, deafer and more difficult to conjure either by electric bell, handclap or parade-ground order. His name was Salaam'a. One yelled this greeting at empty space unoptimistic of his filling it. It puzzled him that I wore a sergeant's uniform. He thought it was some kind of disguise.

*

Sunday: the first Sunday of the peace. When I woke I knew I couldn't spent another day cooped up. I persuaded myself that Aunt Charlotte couldn't have moved quickly enough to justify my absurd expectations unless she had pre-empted the situation some weeks ago and decided that since the war in Europe was thoroughly over there was no reason for me to carry eccentricity to the absurd length of staying out East and eating the rice needed by starving natives.

Among the notices in the guest house was one from St

358

John's (C. of E.). Communion at 8 a.m.; morning service at 11.
I had missed the first but felt I ought to attend the second. I got
out my best khaki. I polished a pair of brown shoes and rubbed
up the dazzle on the badge of my side-cap. I darned a small
hole in the heel of a clean pair of socks Then I shaved – twice –
until the lower half of my face looked properly baked and
glazed.

These were acts of contrition for the destructive and
mutinous mood of the morning of my arrival in Pankot;
gestures of voluntary submission to the military system. At
ten-thirty I set off and marched myself to church at heavy
infantry pace.

St John's was packed. It was like poppy day at Chillingborough; hymns and prayers in chapel. All that lacked was an
old boy to give an ambiguous address about the obscenity and
waste of war. I glanced round, looking as it were for Harry
Coomer; but met only the mass of pale and ruddy com-
plexions of an all white congregation. Were there no Indian
Christians in Pankot? No Eurasians at St John's on this
Sunday of all Sundays? Perhaps there were. My view, from
one of the back pews, and to the wall side of it, close to an exit,
was limited. I was among the soldiery, a lone volunteer
among the pressed men. Far ahead, towards the pulpit,
shoulders glittered with pips and crowns making angular
shapes between decorative hats.

But no dark face that I could see. I began to feel oppressed,
slightly agitated, and glanced at the nearby door. The chaplain
was reading a lesson. In a moment there would be another
hymn. I checked the advertised number in the borrowed
hymn book. From Greenland's Icy Mountains, From India's
coral strand, They call us to deliver, Their land from error's
chain. When the congregation got up to sing it I slid out of the
pew and in a moment was in the open, going down a gravel
path between ancient drunken gravestones. Outside on the
road under shade trees tongas waited, their drivers slumped in
their seats or disposed on the ground in twos and threes
smoking bidis. I flashed a two rupee note and commandeered
someone's equipage. It could be back at the church by the
time the service was over. I only wanted to go to Area

359

Headquarters. As I climbed in I thought I heard a voice from the church saying: That's right. Aunt Charlotte's voice.

The signals sergeant was leaving his office as I approached it. Seeing me, he stopped dead. He ignored my courteous greeting. He stared at me as if I were his worst enemy. I followed him into the office where without a word he handed me a signal.

Bunbury.

After I'd read it, twice, he said, 'How d'you manage it, then? That's all I ask. How?'

But there was no vice in him. He just envied my luck. Where had I been, he wanted to know. He'd rung Pankot 200 only ten minutes ago and got no answer. I told him I'd been to church. He said, as if this explained the signal, 'I must try it some time.' Then he became very helpful. He took me and my AB 64 and the precious piece of flimsy paper ordering Sergeant Perron to proceed immediately to Deolali for onward transmission to UK for demobilization (War Office instruction Number Such and Such and Stroke This Stroke That) to the Admin office where he enlisted the help of a havildar-clerk who, having no axe to grind about speeding an English soldier out of the country, set to work with detached efficiency.

Interpreting a string of references at the end of the signal he told me that I ought to arrive in Deolali in possession of certain important documents including a medical on my fitness to be allowed back into the UK at all. He checked my AB 64. So recently Zipper-bound my jabs were up to date. He told me other things I would need. He seemed quite happy telling me. I wasn't much interested. Nothing worried me. Somewhere just behind my eyes were rosy vistas, shimmering images of a world that had become benign. Area Headquarters was full of this benevolence. It was at low-pressure, staffed by nice people who seemed to have lent themselves voluntarily to the idea of simply keeping it going between Saturday and Monday. I felt the clerk was relieved to have something to do that he could put his mind to. I could rely on him utterly. I could rely on the Signals sergeant too. He kept close to me as if he thought some of my luck might rub off.

'Let's find the Duty Officer,' he said. We walked along

shady verandahs. The fire-buckets, I noted, were painted an enchanting shade of red. The sand in them sparkled. We went into a semi-darkened airy room where the desks and empty chairs were waiting for tomorrow and then through into a room whose windows were unshuttered. A girl in WAC(I) uniform was at a filing cabinet.

'Morning, Sarge,' my sergeant said.

She had three stripes. She turned round. It was Sarah Layton.

But the original Sarah, the friendly one. I said, 'Good Lord, you're a sergeant too.'

'Well I am when I'm playing soldiers.'

'Is that what you're doing?'

'Yes. I'm glad you looked in. I've just tried to get you on the phone.'

'You know each other,' the Signals sergeant accused us. We agreed that we did. He gave me an odd look but said that would make it easier. He told Sarah what I represented: a problem which Area Headquarters had to solve. He explained what the problem was, how much of it was already being tackled and what remained to be done.

While he spoke I watched her, on the look-out for any sign of disappointment that the chances of knowing each other better were limited to here and now. I thought there was such a sign but couldn't be sure. If she had been anticipating a quiet morning on duty with nothing much to do, the expression I marked (a slight darkening of the eyes) could just as well have been irritation at the interruption as of sorrow at my departure.

'The duty officer's gone off somewhere, but I'll cope,' she said. 'You can leave Sergeant Perron to me.'

The sergeant caught my eye, nodded in her direction. 'You're lucky. Most of the others slope off at the first smell of anything like work. O.K. Miss Layton. Buzz me if you get stuck.'

*

She spent a lot of time on the telephone. I sat watching her, wondering at the change in her. Probably it was only life at home that got her down. Eventually she said, 'Right, that's tied up so far. Let's go.' I followed her out of the office. She locked the door.

'Where to?'

'Just relax. The army's taking care of you.'

'What about your office? Can you just leave it?'

'I was only sorting things out for tomorrow. I'm not officially on duty. But everyone at home has gone to church.'

We went back to the havildar-clerk. She went through documents with him, collected a batch. We went to another block. She told me to wait outside. Ten minutes later she came out with more documents. Then to another office. She came out with another batch. I said, 'You're making me feel redundant, that I exist only on paper.'

'The next bit is more personal.'

She hailed a 15 cwt that was driving towards the exit. She told me to get in the back. Five minutes later I recognized the grounds of the hospital but when I got out I didn't recognize the building. She explained it was the private wing. The duty MO had promised to 'do me' if we came to the private wing at mid-day. It was five to. This time it was she who waited outside. The MO was a pleasant fellow. 'Feeling all right?' he asked. I said I was, really. 'Silly question,' he muttered, filling in spaces on the form. We worked out my height and weight without the aid of scales and measures. 'They'll do you in Deolali, too,' he warned, 'but if you arrive without a medical sheet you could be held up.' He signed the sheet and handed it to me. 'Lucky chap,' he said. 'Just try not to get clap between here and Deolali. It sometimes happens.'

He came out with me and chatted to Sarah. He said if she'd finished repatriating Sergeant Perron he'd take her up to the club. She said there was still some documentation to do but that she'd probably see him there later.

Back in the havildar-clerk's office she gave him all the documents we'd collected. They checked through them, detaching copies for different files. Finally he handed me all that I apparently required from this storm of paper: a few sheets which went into an envelope.

Outside she said, 'Well, that's it. All you have to do is to be at the station before mid-day tomorrow – unless –'

362

Without another word she led the way to the signals office. The sergeant was just coming out, going to lunch.

'Is there any transport going into Ranpur tonight?' she asked him. He said there probably was. She turned to me. 'If you could get down to Ranpur during the night you could get the train that leaves at 8 a.m. You'd gain over twelve hours, and that might make a lot of difference at the Deolali end.'

I said it was a good idea. She said to the sergeant, 'I'll ask at the club. Perhaps you'd have a look round too, Joe, and ring Sergeant Perron at 200 if there's anything going in.'

He said he'd have a word with a Sub-Conductor Pearson in the mess. I could go along with him now, if I wanted. I made an excuse about having food laid on and packing to do. We shook hands in case we didn't meet again.

Sarah and I shared a tonga back up the hill. I thanked her for everything she'd done and said the food at the guest house wasn't much cop since Nigel had gone but that it would be nice if she could have lunch with me. She said there was a lunch party at the club which she couldn't get out of. I asked her what she'd tried to ring me about earlier. She'd rung because she knew I was on my own and wondered if I was all right, since I hadn't rung her. I asked her whether she could manage tea. She wasn't sure. She'd be in touch some time, though.

As she got out of the tonga at the club entrance she looked at me and said: 'I envy you, Guy. But I'm glad for you. And I'm not at all sure you don't deserve a medal. Ronald Merrick's going to be furious.'

*

I told Salaam'a to bring beer to the verandah. I sat studying the precious documents. For the first time I noticed that the signal hadn't come via Delhi, via Merrick's department, but had originated in Poona. The first War Office instruction must have been signalled from Delhi to Poona and my old officer must have rung Delhi, been told where I was and then copy-signalled direct to Area Headquarters in Pankot. I went to my room and wrote him a note of thanks, added a PS, to the effect that my tin trunk which had been left in Poona could either be repatriated too or broken open and its contents (a greatcoat and winter uniform) disposed among the needy. Then I had a couple of gins, a pallid replica of yesterday's pallid lunch, and composed myself to sleep, having first told Salaam'a to attend to the telephone and in any case wake me with tea at four.

*

Zipper was coming to grief. Speeding towards the beaches in landing craft on the September tides near Port Swettenham we were opened fire on by rogue Japanese who had opted out of the Emperor's peace, chosen to die, but to take us with them. For a moment I listened, aghast, at the guns and the water rushing against the steel hulls of the boats, aghast because of the danger and of the miserable realization that Bunbury had been only an Indian ocean dream.

I raised my wrist to check the time of landing and, doing so, woke to the reality of Pankot time which said ten to five, a thunderstorm, but all well. But not wholly all well. From the bedroom I wouldn't have heard the telephone and it looked as if Salaam'a wouldn't have been hearing it either, being either asleep or dead drunk at last. I pressed the bell-button. Like those at Ishshee Brizhish one could never tell what effect pressing the button had unless someone turned up. No one did inside the half-minute I allowed before getting out of bed, tying a towel round my waist and going in search.

I went through the living-room shouting that ridiculous name and then out on to the verandah from whose roof water was cascading from an invisible pipe or leaking gutter on to the gravel path. Beyond, vertical rods of water obscured the view of the Summer Residence.

From contemplation of this same scene Sarah Layton turned her head, to glance up from the cane lounging chair where she rested, smoking. A tray of guest house tea was on the table by her side.

She said something that I couldn't hear and I was too conscious of my near-nakedness to go closer and cup an ear. She indicated an unused cup. In dumb show I told her I'd be

364

out again in a minute, and went back, splashed my face, combed my hair, and got into a shirt and slacks and sandals.

'I hope you don't mind,' she said when I joined her. 'The boy was just going to wake you when I got here. I told him to leave you for a bit.' She felt the pot. 'We'd better ring for some more.'

I did so. I asked her when she'd arrived. She thought it must have been nearly an hour ago. I wondered whether she had been waiting for me to wake or for the rain to stop, but didn't ask. She said, 'You'll be glad later, I mean to have slept on a bit because I'm afraid you won't have a very comfortable trip if you decide to go tonight. The best we could do is the back of a fifteen hundred-weight that's leading a convoy down. But it'll take you right to the station in Ranpur.'

She opened her bag and gave me a slip of paper with a name – Sub-Conductor Pearson – and a telephone number written on it. 'The convoy leaves at ten this evening. Call him just before seven. He'll tell you where to go to get it. I'm afraid I drew a blank at the club, so I liaised again with Joe Baker. He was going to ring you but I said I'd call and tell you.'

Our hands touched as the paper was transferred. The softness and gentleness of her fingers balanced out the impression of hardness, of military efficiency. It occurred to me that the time she'd devoted to me could perhaps best be repaid by giving her the chance to take up some of mine if she wanted to. I didn't *have* to leave Pankot tonight. And now that it came to it I wasn't sure that I wanted to.

'On the whole,' she said, as if reading my thoughts, 'I'd settle for the discomfort if I were you. Joe Baker's had another signal. There's a Major Foster arriving tomorrow morning on the night train. You're asked to meet him, so I suppose he's Ronald's replacement.'

I'd met Major Foster. He was a ditherer, the kind of well-meaning chap whom it could be fatal to get near. If I met him and told him I had to leave on the mid-day train, on repatriation, he might out of sheer good intention invent so many problems that we would still be solving them two hours after the train had gone.

I said, 'Yes, he is the replacement. I'll settle for a night's discomfort. I may as well ring Sub-Conductor Pearson now. Then we'll know how long I've got.'

'I shouldn't if I were you. Not for a while. Joe Baker said six-thirty or so.'

For some reason she reddened slightly and returned her attention to the rain, which was stopping.

Salaam'a appeared.

'Would you prefer a drink to more tea? Nigel said I could make free so long as I didn't dine the station. You're not quite the station.'

'No, I'm not, am I? I'd like a drink very much.'

I told Salaam'a to bring out the drinks trolley. When we were alone I said, 'Can you stay and have an early meal with me?'

She didn't answer. She must have heard. The rain had now stopped entirely. She continued to stare ahead of her. Her cigarette was nearly finished. I glanced over my shoulder to see what apparently held her attention. The sun was just coming out. The Summer Residence rose – base to roof – out of the fast-moving shadow of a retreating cloud. Sunshine had already flowed across the garden. It pressed hard against the line of the balustrade, warmed my back and made me conscious of the hastiness with which I'd put clothes on.

'You've seen the house, I suppose,' she said. 'I expect Nigel showed you over.'

'No. Isn't it shut up?'

'The servants will always let you in.'

'There seems to be only one servant left.'

'They live in the main quarters. They only come down if there are people at the guest house. The house itself was built in 1890. Most of it's plain Anglo-Indian but there's a Moghul suite where they used to put up pet princes. The throne room's very ordinary, just a couple of chairs on a daïs, and the ball-room's quite small. But they danced on the terrace too. There used to be coloured lights in the trees.'

'That must have been nice.'

'It was all rather stiff and starchy. At least on the surface. And that's about all you see when you're young and just back out from home. Not that I'm really competent to judge. People here sigh for what they used to call the full season

366

when the Governor and his wife moved up for the hot weather. But there hasn't been a full season since 'thirty-nine, and Susan and I missed that. I remember it best as part of childhood. We had ghastly parties here.' She smiled at a memory. 'When the new Governor took over in 'forty-one he was rather unpopular at first for not continuing the tradition of six months in the hills. Mother says the dances Susan and I have been to were very scratch affairs by comparison, but people get used to anything. At Flagstaff House we used to rate a major-general but since the beginning of the year we've only had a brigadier. People complain but they're getting used to that too. And now that the war's over I suppose it'll alter even more, with people whose retirement's been postponed upping sticks and going home, or settling here and growing old and tiresome and complaining that their pensions don't go far.'

'When does your father retire?'

'In about three years. But I've no idea what they'll do.'

'Rose Cottage belongs to them?'

'Yes, they're luckier than some. The army stopped people buying or building property in Pankot years ago – I don't mean on West Hill, only Indians build there. But father's step-mother got hold of Rose Cottage a few years before the embargo. She left it to him along with everything else she had. I expect you could see what a lot of money's been spent on it recently. I've always imagined father and mother spending the rest of their lives there, but now I don't know.'

Salaam'a wheeled the trolley out. We both chose gin. While he prepared the drinks I excused myself and went inside to wait for him. When he came in I told him I was leaving for Ranpur that evening, that he should arrange supper for two because the memsahib might be staying. I gave him his baksheesh and an extra few rupees to tip his invisible assistants. Then I told him the memsahib and I wanted to look at the house, that we would go over in about fifteen minutes. How did we get in? He said the head chaukidar would let us in. He would go now and make sure the head chaukidar was there.

She was waiting, glass poised to drink. I faced her, leaning against the balustrade. We toasted the space between us.

After drinking we remained silent. I gave her a full minute by my watch and the same full minute to myself to prove beyond reasonable doubt that my idea about the immediate future was not all that different from hers.

The minute gone the silence continued, but delivered us slowly from any sense of the strain that slightly marked its beginning. Eventually I said to her, 'I never thanked you for Emerson.' She put her head back against the cushion, studied me, as if she knew the passage which had come into my mind and which had caused me to mention the book:

The world rolls: the circumstances vary every hour. All the angels that inhabit this temple of the body appear at the windows, and all the gnomes and vices also. By all the virtues they are united. If there be virtue, all the vices are known as such; they confess and flee.

*

On the way there I looked for them but they must have scattered; but remembering the distant view of the upper storey from the lines of the Pankot Rifles depot I asked her whether she had ever noticed how the sun setting behind West Hill seemed to have to pause until the upper windows of the Summer Residence released its last reflection, and the *raj* allowed night to fall. Well, she said, she was familiar with the effect but had never identified its cause. She was smiling, her head up, one hand shielding her eyes, neck curving from the brave little angles of jaw and chin. Something dazzled her – the suddenly exposed sky, sunshine on wet surfaces, or the drops of rain strung in the trees to dry. We had left the path, chosen the director way across the lawns for which she was more suitably shod than I. My feet and trouser bottoms were wet, the chappals clung to my bare soles. A week later, unpacking and repacking my kit-bag in Deolali, the chappals, still slightly damp to the touch, smelt of grass, and the trouser bottoms were tide-marked. The chappals were in my possession for a number of years, and – even after a long time unused – discovered in a cupboard, dried, cracked, the buckles rusty, the smell of dampness and the smell of grass still seemed to be in them like a perfume of their own recollection of that occasion; their recollection of the persistence of damp when moving across dry flagged terraces and interior floors of stone and parquet and carpet, through chill shadow and hot streaks of filtered light when shutters were opened like doors on the tombs of flies and moths whose mummified bodies lay on dusty sills; taking the weight of the wearer's heels as he gazed upward at vast chandeliers enveloped in balloons of muslin; or substituting for weight the stickiness of suction when the ankles were crossed for the enthronement of the substitute Governor and his Lady on two shrouded chairs; the weight redistributed again, concentrated on the toes as the sightless painted eyes of Muirs and Laytons and fellow members of a pro-consular dynasty were met by live eyes in a head thrust forward – the body canted to achieve a position where the light on dark varnish less obscured the detail and colour of pigment underneath.

Stairs, corridors; doors opened by keys obtained earlier for a consideration from the ancient chaukidar who was lost below in a dream of opium and the vanished splendour of which he was the guardian and we no more than observers. Sensibly and more drily shod she moved through the Summer Residence like a visitor who had been before and had little to gain except the satisfaction of her companion's curiosity, which was minimal, overriden by preoccupation with the way she walked through this maze of imperial history, or stood revealed by the chance falling of light and shade, responding to changes in the pressures that different rooms imposed on her recollections which seemed to be of a time she no longer recognized as real.

And yet, turning from some object pointed out in one particular room, an object that had failed like so many in so many rooms to recommend itself to me as having continuing substance or sustained meaning, she seemed to me to have only this unreality in her possession and to belong to it like a prisoner would belong, after a time, to a cell his imagination had escaped but whose door he was not permitted to open.

We chose this particular room, I think, because at first glance it represented in itself a form of release: release from the stupefying weight of nearly a century of disconnection from the source. But the Moghul suite was no less burdened

369

by that weight; it was the inner box of a nest of boxes. Through one unshuttered window, westering sun filtered through the intricate fretwork of a screen on to the tiled floor where the chappals lay, temporarily set aside. A smell of old incense permeated the fabrics of the covers and cushions of an immense divan such as might have been used by court-musicians. One fancied that dust rose from it, gently enveloping us in a dry benevolent mist in which hung minute particles of the leaves and petals of garlands of flowers: jasmine, roses, frangipani and marigold, and all the names of Allah. One observer: a mouse. Are you afraid? I asked. No, she said, I'm not afraid. Eyes closed, at rest, I realized that we had been both observed and accompanied. The distant coppers-mith still continued, beating out his thin, endless, strip of metal into the alternating shapes of the sounds and silence of the Pankot hills.

*

Returning the keys to the chaukidar, I make my own way out and look for her; and, mistaking the place, think for a moment she has taken the opportunity I gave her (out of delicacy, thinking she might prefer not to have to bid the chaukidar goodnight) to abandon me too; but she is waiting, out there on the lawn, gazing up at the highest windows where the day awaits permission to end. Joining her, I glance up and find that it is already ended. There are no faces, either, unless they are our own, watching us go – not only as we do, across the lawn back to the guest house – but further, much further, on separate roads that may never cross again.

Having poured her another drink I go inside to telephone Sub-Conductor Pearson. A woman answers. Her voice has a Eurasian lilt. She leaves the phone. I hear her calling for 'Leonard'. Pearson, not Purvis. Calling him from his Sunday afternoon in married quarters? Waiting, I wonder what Sergeant Baker said to make Sarah blush when she recom-mended not disturbing the Sub-Conductor until 6.30 or 7 (until an appetite for beer and curry and Sunday love had been appeased and been slept off?). His voice is full of nuts and bolts, of oil and graphite; and sober irritation at being

reminded of a promise given earlier when all the Sunday
pleasures were ahead. But he is a man of his word. He tells me
where to go and when to be there and whom to ask for. I have
about two hours.

*

She said she would not stay to supper. She would have liked to
but she had left it too late to ring and say she had made other
arrangements. She ought to get back soon.

'Then let me take you.'

'No. You've too much to do. I'll wait while you pack and
change. Then I must go and you must eat.'

My packing was a hit and miss business. First I had to
change back into uniform. In doing so I seemed to change my
flesh. I was a sergeant again. She, in her uniform, remained a
colonel's daughter. Theoretically a rule had been broken. I
began searching in the kit-bag for some tissue-paper packages
– scarves and stoles for the Perron women (and a few for non-
Perron women). My hand kept touching the transcript of the
examination.

'Guy?'

She was standing just inside the bedroom door.

'I just wanted to say I'll make sure that someone meets
Major Foster tomorrow. Is that servant of Ronald's still
around? Nigel told me you caught him thieving.'

'I've not seen him.'

'Major Foster will probably ask. Where was he quartered?'

'At Flagstaff House, I think, with the other servants.'

'I'll make sure. I'm going now.'

'Going *now*?'

'Yes, I must. Write to me some time. Let me know how you
get on.'

There are situations in which it is very difficult to know
what to say. One of the tissue-packages was in my hand.

'I bought a few things for people back home. I've nothing
else.'

She took the package because I really gave her no alternative. 'It's only a scarf. At least I think it is. Perhaps we'd

371

better open it in case it's something like a tie for one of my uncles.'

'Whatever it is I shall like it.'

We went back to the verandah.

'One more drink.'

Her back and shoulders felt so much thinner than they really were.

She shook her head and said there wasn't time. She must go. She didn't need a tonga. It was only a short walk up the hill. I went with her to the front of the guest house. The light had almost gone. I said I couldn't let her go home alone.

'I shall be perfectly all right. It's what I'd prefer. Honestly. Goodbye, Guy.'

She turned and set off down the narrow drive. I called after her. She glanced round, waved the package. I began to follow her, but stopped, understanding that her wish to go now and go alone was genuine. In a moment the curve of the drive had taken her away. I went back to finish packing my kit-bag. As I shoved the typescript well in to make room for the slacks and shirt and chappals I remembered that particular line: *We haven't seen each other since the night we visited the temple*. I rolled down my sergeant's sleeves, the drill for night-time. While buttoning the cuffs a trick of light made my hands seem brown.

*

They had emerged, erupted violently, from the shadows of the Moghul Room, attacked me, pulled me away, hit me in the face. Later when they had gone and we held each other again I said: Let me take you home. She said, No. No. We haven't seen each other. We haven't seen each other since the night we visited the temple. She saw the danger I would be in if I dared to go with her, dared to mutter to someone, a white man, an official, any of the men who would ask questions, 'We were making love. These men attacked us.' She had seen the danger of implicating me in any way, but she hadn't seen the marks on my face, because it was too dark. And I hadn't thought of them until I got home.

*

I don't remember eating. I remember sitting on the verandah drinking the last of the ADC's brandy and staring out into the dangerous Indian night until it was time to send Salaam'a to fetch a tonga to take me to the rendezvous with Sub-Conductor Pearson's convoy and the first leg of the journey back to the source, where all these things, becoming distant again, would count for little and seem to belong to another world entirely.

The Dak Bungalow

I

The scene was over. I can enter now, Sarah told herself.

*

But I did not enter. None of us did. I thought I saw the reason.
What had held us together as a family was father's absence;
his return showed how deeply we were divided. You could feel
him making the attempt to come to terms with each of us
separately. There was a time for mother, a time for Susan and
Edward, and a time for me; and a different kind of time for the
servants, for Pankot, for the regiment.

My time was before breakfast. Between seven and eight-
thirty every morning father and I rode. He associated me with
these early hours of the day and during them treated me with
a special solicitude, as if the pattern of intimacy which had
been established on the journey from Ranpur when we shared
tea and bacon sandwiches and were careful with crumbs,
might develop through repetition into something complex,
mysterious and satisfying. At times he had the look of a man
with a secret he was patiently waiting to share; at others that
of a man empty of knowledge and recollection.

After a couple of days I noticed on these morning rides that
we were taking the same route – down the northern slope of
East Hill into the valley – and stopping at the same place. The
view wasn't spectacular. About a mile ahead you could see a
village. That was all. But he reined in and sat motionless,
gazed at the distant huddle of huts and the terraced fields that
traced the contours of the hill. The earth was tawny. There
was always a mist. You could smell the smoke of wood and
dung fires. After five minutes or so he would look at his wrist-

watch and say, 'Well, better get back.' Apart from this single comment he kept silent during the halt.

An obvious explanation of the choice of turning point was that it was fixed according to a formula involving time available, distance to be covered, expected time of return. But we did not always take the same route home and got back to Rose Cottage anywhere between say 8.15 and 8.45. The only part of the ride I could be absolutely sure of – the part that I began to feel was plotted by an obsession – was the route out and the halt and the five minutes' silent contemplation of a village whose name I wasn't certain of but checked on one of the large-scale maps at Area Headquarters. It was called Muddarabad.

We had never kept horses at Rose Cottage. Such stabling as there had been had – long before Aunt Mabel's time even – become merged with the servants' quarters and store-rooms. A syce brought horses up from the depot. In the past year or two I had ridden seldom, mother less and Susan not at all. In Bombay father had said that one of the things he was looking forward to was getting accustomed again to the saddle. He hadn't ridden for nearly five years. I assumed that it might be a week or two before he felt fit enough to go out and that in any case it would be mother who went with him, but on his first evening at home he said, 'What about riding tomorrow?' and he said it to me. He rang Kevin Coley and I looked out my things but didn't discover until I put them on in the morning that my jodhpurs were uncomfortably tight round the waist. Mounting, I was as nervous as I had been as a small girl. He wore slacks and chukka boots. He led off as though he had been going out every morning of his life.

This would have been Thursday, August 9. He rode a few paces ahead of me. We spoke very little. I felt some reserve – embarrassment – in regard to his physical presence – imagining mother still lying in their bed considering through half-shut eyes the pillow beside her which bore an impression of the head of the man who kept looking back at me, smiling, as if in delight in rediscovery. Do children, when grown up, even nowadays, quite believe in the reality of their parents' sexual life?

Logic told me that in the past few years there must have

been moments when my father lay in his bed in prison-camp and thought, God, God, I must have a woman. Suspicion rather than logic told me that in my father's absence my mother had had an affair. Logic in fact didn't come into it. Kevin Coley looked incapable of physical passion; a dry desiccated creature whom nothing would arouse except a threat to the professional obscurity in which he'd been content to live since his wife's death in the Quetta earthquake. But, nursing my suspicion – and my growing understanding of the complexity of physical needs and physical responses – I had to throw out the idea of non-capability, non-culpability, and – in consequence – try to suppress every emotion except that of ironic acceptance, which wasn't easy – so difficult in fact that I couldn't sustain it for long and had to try to counteract suspicion by telling myself that it was based on nothing more reliable than poor Barbie Batchelor's delirious imagination, coupled with the workings of my own which, alerted by Barbie's at first incomprehensible ramblings in the Pankot hospital, had since stretched the evidence (things seen, overheard, intuited) to make a case which the strictly rational side of my nature rejected, because even if adultery were the kind of game I could imagine my mother playing, adultery with Kevin Coley struck me as ludicrously out of character. So, I was back at the beginning of the circle of conjecture, and beginning to go round again, all the time conscious, naturally, that what chiefly nourished the retaliatory instinct to suspect her was her treatment of me, her utter disregard, her pretence of knowing nothing while knowing everything about the sordid abortion in Calcutta – everything except the name of the man who would have been the child's father, which she could have found out easily enough not from me but from Aunt Fenny who couldn't have been in much doubt but respected my silence and was fondly and foolishly guilt-ridden at the thought that she had been initially responsible for putting me in his way, or putting him in mine (it came to the same thing).

It was on the Friday – after our second ride to Muddarabad – that I heard poor Barbie was dead. Major Smalley mentioned it to me at the daftar, having heard it from his wife, and she was invariably well-informed. When I rang the Reverend Mother of the Samaritan Hospital in Ranpur and she talked vaguely of papers meant for me or my family I feared some kind of revelation, a written statement, a letter to my father whom Barbie had hardly known but on whom I knew she relied to settle once and for all the question whether mother had buried Aunt Mabel in the wrong place – a letter perhaps referring to mother's association with Coley. I didn't believe Barbie capable of malice. What I feared was an unintentional accusation by a woman whose wits were scattered – as scattered as the contents of the trunk she'd left at Rose Cottage where she'd been Aunt Mabel's companion, and which she removed on the morning of the accident – the trunk that was the cause of the accident because it was too heavy for the tonga.

The trunk was full of things connected with Barbie's work as a mission teacher, old textbooks, exercise books she'd kept to remember special pupils, gifts from the children and their parents, and a copy of the picture her old mission friend Edwina Crane had been given as a reward for heroism in the North West Frontier Province during the Great War. Barbie told me that the trunk wasn't particularly important but it was 'her history and without it according to Emerson she wasn't explained'. When Mabel died she had to move into a small room at the rectory bungalow. She'd taken things down there bit by bit during the week or so mother gave her to give us vacant possession of Rose Cottage. The rectory wasn't a permanent arrangement and Clarissa Peplow was worried about the amount of stuff she seemed to have. Barbie asked me if she could leave the trunk with the *mali*. I offered to take care of it myself. Susan and I would be sharing the room that had been Barbie's and I saw no reason why I shouldn't look after the trunk until she found a permanent home. But she knew mother would object. She said that if the *mali* put the trunk in his shed then providing I knew it was there that would be good enough. So that's what was done.

*

Muddarabad was the village Havildar Karim Muzzafir Khan came from. We stopped there because father couldn't bring

380

himself to ride on and enter it and confront the havildar's wife and family. Each morning, I think, he set off with that intention and then, reaching the halting-place, found the intention collapsing under the weight of his notion of its futility. *Man-Bap*. I am your father and your mother. This traditional idea of his position, this idea of himself in relationship to his regiment, to the men and the men's families, had not survived his imprisonment; or, if it had survived, the effort of living up to it had become too much for him. Was it lack of energy or lack of conviction, I wondered, that caused him to rein in and sit straight-backed as if posing for his portrait as a military officer watching the course of a battle for whose outcome he would be held responsible, or studying the ground over which, tomorrow, conclusions would be tried?

And, watching *him*, it struck me how very rare after all were men whose genius lay in active warfare. For one genius there would be almost countless plodders who were commanders in name only, men to whom the structure of a landscape would present almost as great a problem in military understanding as it had always done to me, but who had been taught to apply a set of ready-made formulas so that it was upon these and not the terrifyingly wide margins of error that their minds were concentrated. As a child he had seemed godlike to me, revealing some of the secrets of his profession. I had the feeling now that he believed himself dishonoured – not by anything he had done but by his talent, which turning out limited had narrowed the whole area of his self-regard.

Waiting at the halting-place on the third morning, the Saturday, I recalled my mother's words overheard the night before, when I came home late, having stayed on at the daftar to telephone the Reverend Mother at the Samaritan. 'It's a question of your presence more than anything. It was the same for me when you all went into the bag.' And in retrospect it seemed scarcely any time at all since she had ridden out with Kevin Coley from one village to another to talk to the women whose husbands, sons and grandsons and brothers were either dead or captured in North Africa.

For her to visit every village would have been impossible but on other occasions she talked to women who came in from outlying districts for confirmation of the news, receiving them outside the adjutant's office and even in the compound of the grace and favour bungalow where we lived in those days. Colonel Sahib, Colonel Memsahib. Two aspects of the one godhead. My mother was not built to look like a woman another woman could be comforted by – but at these meetings her very stiffness seemed right. The important thing was that she was there, in the shell of her flesh which if hard seemed trustworthy. She told these women the truth always, for instance that as prisoners of war the men would be separated from their officers and that it would be virtually impossible for father himself to ensure their welfare. But, subsequently, in many unobtrusive ways, she had kept an eye on the widows, and the wives who like herself could only wait patiently for their men's return. She did this entirely out of her sense of duty. It was an act, but she played the part with a perfect sense of what would be extraneous to it. She did not make the mistake of identifying herself too closely with it. When she came back into the bungalow she shed it, or seemed to shed it. And called for gin.

So, 'Why don't you?' she had said the night before, meaning why didn't he ride on into Muddarabad. But it was different for father. *Man-Bap.* That act had been an inseparable part of his life as a commander of Indian troops. *He* had to identify himself closely with it. It was supposed to go deep into him, right down to the source of his inspiration. Every morning, when we stopped after riding down the northern slope of East Hill, it was as though he waited there for the inspiration to return and lead him down into the village. But, 'Well', he would say, and said it again that Saturday, 'Better get back'. On the way home we usually rode abreast and talked about the things that had happened yesterday and the plans there were for today.

*

After riding we had breakfast and then I went down to the daftar. Officially he was on station leave but sometimes he went down to the Pankot Rifles lines. The immediate future was very uncertain. There was a question of long leave, the possibility of taking it at home, but the more important questions for him were of his fitness and of his next appointment. Long though I did for home leave the prospect wasn't one I considered likely even if the war ended as people expected. He was too close to retirement to waste time in England. He had too much time to make up. He and mother were now well enough off, having inherited Mabel's money, not to go after promotion simply to earn a higher pension, but he would go after it, I believed, to redress the balance. And it would be something to put his mind to. The obvious job for him was that of commandant of the depot which Colonel Trehearne had held throughout the war, postponing his own retirement. But now I got the impression that mother had set her sights higher and that she wanted to get out of the station. I couldn't blame her. The expense she had gone to in altering Rose Cottage couldn't in her case be seen as evidence of an intention to make it a permanent home. Even the prospect of final retirement there now seemed questionable.

*

Feeling I must do something about whatever it was Barbie had left which the Bishop Barnard Mission hadn't collected or didn't want and about which the Reverend Mother was so vague and yet so insistent, I wrote to Nigel Rowan to ask him whether he'd ring her and get the facts clearer. That was on the Saturday. On that evening we dined with the Trehearnes.

Maisie Trehearne was tall, pale and stately, and so upright that it was rumoured she was supported by a steel corset. Lately she had taken to wearing flowing dinner gowns of grey or blue georgette which gave her the appearance of a metallic ghost. When she moved she created the illusion of cooling breezes which weren't necessary because the Commandant's house was the draughtiest in Pankot and wretched to dine at on a winter evening. The Trehearnes were the last people to order fires lit and the first to order the hearths to be cleared and guarded by brass trays. And never, in the rainy season, when the evening could be chilly – which fortunately it wasn't on this occasion – was an electric fire brought in and switched on. Her husband, Patrick, now sixty, had the same frail, febrile but inflexible look: highly tempered steel worn to the thickness of a wafer. There was scarcely a line on their faces. They were the faces of people who had never had a sleepless night or a moment's worry, or, if they had, had somehow acquired an almost oriental sense of spiritual detachment from the cares of life.

The other obstacle to comfort at the Trehearnes was the pack of dogs, a strange hybrid collection ranging from puppies to full-grown brutes, seldom less than three altogether; raw, savage, the terror of servants, cause of concern to timid guests; obstinate, disobedient; objects of Maisie's devotion and her husband's sufferance. The dogs seemed natural victims of the disasters that were always befalling them. Ruling the roost at Commandant House they seemed disinclined to learn that the world outside was a hostile place. One, attacking a tonga horse, was kicked to death; another was bitten by a krait; yet another run over by a staff-car from Area Headquarters which it had thought had no business on the same road as itself. One, straying, was shot on the rifle-range. Others simply succumbed to one of the diseases domestic animals in India were always dying of. You would have thought that a woman so genuinely fond of animals, particularly of dogs, would have lost heart, but Maisie never did, she was always acquiring replacements for those that had fallen, and you always felt that her attachment was deep, her sense of duty to them strong, her horrified reaction to any tale of cruelty to animals of any kind absolutely real. You could still feel this about Maisie even when sitting in their dining-room under the glazed eyes of the creditable number of mounted shikar trophies for whose deaths she and Patrick were just about equally responsible. The trophies were seldom referred to. Perhaps they were there merely as relics of youthful exuberance which had long since been grown out of. I once heard Lucy Smalley say she wondered that Maisie didn't mount the heads of the dogs too: a typical Smalley remark but not (which was also typical) wholly unjustified.

*

'Watch out for the dogs, John,' mother had warned father when we set out in the car Colonel Trehearne had sent up. The warning was unnecessary. Perhaps for once Patrick Trehearne had put his foot down, or Maisie and Patrick had both had the foresight to see that the usual kind of welcome you got at Commandant House didn't sort well with greeting a man who had been locked up for several years. Instead, the dogs had been locked up and we entered unmolested.

It was father's first dinner out and Maisie had promised mother to keep the party small. It turned out even smaller than planned because Kevin Coley's servant rang just before we arrived to say that the Adjutant Sahib had gone to bed with a temperature. 'Actually,' Maisie said, 'we're rather worried about Kevin. He suddenly seems restless. After all these years resisting any attempt to move and promote him he's acting as though he thought it was time something was done about him.'

The Trehearnes' bedroom where we left our stoles, exposing necks, shoulders and arms, like Spartan women, to the chilly rigours of the interior, was immense. In it the twin beds looked diminutive, mere sparrows' nests. High above them, suspended from the raftered ceiling, were circular frames for the mosquito nets which were hardly ever necessary but which Maisie had a fondness for. It was the kind of room, sparsely furnished, which always looked camped-out in rather than occupied, and where you wouldn't have been surprised to find bird-droppings on the floor.

It was while we were in the bedroom that the subject of Barbie came up and I discovered that mother also knew she was dead. Susan was momentarily out of the room, powdering her nose in the adjoining bathroom (people in Pankot had learned not to refer to death and disaster in front of her, if they could help it). Maisie said, 'Mrs Stewart at the Library tells me that according to Lucy Smalley, Miss Batchelor died the other day. Did you know?'

She addressed the question to both of us. I was standing at the foot of one of the beds. Mother was peering into the glass of the dressing-table, making a minor repair with her lipstick. Perhaps this provided her with an excuse not to speak. But she didn't react at all, her expression remained constant, concentrated. I was forced to answer. I said that Major Smalley had mentioned it to me at the daftar.

'There was nothing in the *Ranpur Gazette*,' Maisie said. 'And the death columns are the first thing I read. It used to be the births and marriages but you seem to reach a time of life when you know only the people who die. How did Lucy hear?'

'I don't know,' I said, truthfully.

'Do you, Mildred?'

'Do I what?'

'Know how Lucy Smalley heard Miss Batchelor was dead.'

'All I know is what Mrs Smalley told me when she rang, but I suppose in this case one can take it as more or less true.'

'What did she say?'

'Only that the Bishop Barnard people had written to Arthur Peplow and that the chaplain who's filling in for him opened the letter and asked her who Miss Batchelor was. Mrs Smalley, it goes without saying, had only dropped into the rectory bungalow to see if she could help with any little problem.'

'Had the Peplows kept in touch with the Mission, then?'

'I don't know about keeping in touch. But the rectory was the woman's last address. I expect the Mission wanted to be sure she's left nothing here that they ought to have and I'm sure their solicitors will be already on to ours making a fuss about the annuity Mabel willed her. I suppose the estate will have to cough up what she'd have received if we'd ever got round to buying it. Thank God I had the presence of mind at the time to tell our own solicitors in London to drag their feet, and thank God she went off her head as soon as she did because that gave them a good excuse to drag their feet even harder. Mabel must have been off *her* head, making that sort of provision for an elderly spinster.'

'I've never really understood about annuities,' Maisie said.

'You buy the damned things to provide an income for life which is all right if the person the annuity's bought for lives a long time. The catch is, once it's bought, the capital sum has gone forever. Even if you die the next day. I must say it would amuse me if the Bishop Barnard people think they've got several thousand rupees coming to them. They have complete control of her estate, apparently, for what it's worth.'

'Poor Miss Batchelor,' Maisie said. 'I sometimes think she had a sad life.'

Mother put away her lipstick. As she did so she glanced up, regarding me through the mirror. Then she snapped her handbag and turned round.

'I don't think you'd feel so sympathetic, Maisie, if you'd had to watch her encouraging Mabel's eccentricities and anti-social instincts and at the same time be pretty sure she was feathering her own nest pretty neatly, and then making all that macabre fuss about where Mabel should have been buried. I had Mabel's funeral to cope with and Susan's premature labour to cope with and I had to cope with them virtually alone because Sarah was down in Calcutta visiting that man Merrick in hospital. And on top of it all I had this damned silly woman running all over Pankot saying I was shoving Mabel into the ground at St John's when she'd wanted to be buried at St Luke's in Ranpur, next to John's father. Even that elderly admirer of hers, Mr Maybrick, thought it was a bit much. And of course John tells me he never heard Mabel say a single thing about where she wanted to be put. I took him to see the grave this morning. He thought it very suitable.'

Susan came out of the bathroom and the subject was dropped.

'How pretty you look,' Maisie said, which was no less than the truth, the kind of thing Susan still needed to hear but which was nowadays inspired more by the obligation people felt under to encourage her back to life and happiness than by spontaneous admiration. I imagined that Susan herself was aware of this not very subtle undercurrent of intention, and that she responded to praise in the same way that someone who is enjoying remission from the pain of a disease they know they're not yet cured of must respond to being told how well they're looking. And, because it had happened before, I was now prepared to wake up that night and hear the sound of her crying. Her crying was terrible, because when she cried and I tried to comfort her we seemed very close, closer than we had ever been as children; but within a day or two we were farther apart than ever. Every measure of love and affection had to be paid for by a larger measure of antagonism.

'How pretty you look,' Maisie had said, and then as if by an association of ideas, and leading us out, she said, 'We have invited young Mr Drew.'

Edgar Drew. Eager Edgar. I tried to catch Susan's eye but she had assumed her party rôle. Eager Edgar had been to Rose Cottage once or twice. In a rare conspiratorial moment between us Susan and I had christened him thus.

'We thought,' Maisie was saying to mother, 'it would be nice for him to meet John.' By which she really meant he would be suitable young company for Susan and me.

He had obviously arrived before us because Maisie didn't greet him when we went into the sitting-room where he stood with Colonel Trehearne and father, one hand behind his back, the other clutching his sherry glass, his head adjusted to a slant of attentiveness and inquiry, the wary look of a young man whose heart wasn't quite in what he had been taught he had to do to get on; of a man who having no inner resources of strength and energy – at least none he dared trust – saw no alternative to the perplexing business of flattering his elders. His father was an insurance broker in Byfleet and he had been to a public school of which I think he'd just reached the stage of feeling slightly ashamed because he realized it ranked as 'minor'. Physically he was attractive but he nullified this attraction every time he opened his mouth. His conversation was excruciatingly dull and he seemed to have no opinions of his own. He worked hard to sound self-confident, so hard that one became aware of the effort it cost him.

The Trehearnes had taken to him because they thought him a cut or two above most of the last year or so's intake of newly-commissioned English subalterns from Belgaum and Bangalore who had arrived at the depot, stayed a few weeks and then departed to join the 4/5th and the 2nd battalions in Burma. Moreover, Second-Lieutenant Drew had expressed interest in the idea of applying for a regular commission and this ambition counted in his favour when it came to comparing him with some of the rougher-spoken and rougher-mannered men who had got into the regiment with (I suspected) higher qualifications from OTS as potential leaders of infantry.

He was what was never actually called but certainly thought of as regimental depot material which meant it was thought he would eventually prove to be perfectly adequate for active regimental duty but was meanwhile presentable enough in the mess and at dinner parties such as this to be put temporarily by and employed more pacifically.

I could tell that he had had little or no experience of women; his attentiveness betrayed anxiety. Someone, his mother probably, may have told him that a gentleman never looked lower than a girl's nose. The result was that when he talked to you he kept his chin up and head back and made you feel disembodied below the neck. He had beautiful hands; not fine and elegant but firm and shapely. But you seldom had a chance to admire them. They were usually clasped behind his back or bunched into fists. Even at table they tended to disappear between mouthfuls, presumably to clutch one another or be wiped surreptitiously on his napkin. When you had the opportunity to touch or be touched by them – that is, when he danced with you – they were uncomfortably moist, but at least they were a connection; although a distant connection because he danced you at arm's length – which made it seem like dancing with a draught. I admit I had occasional fantasies about Mr Drew's hands, and after seeing him in the club swimming pool I also had occasional fantasies about the rest of him. Perhaps I should have told him, not for my own good, but for his. He can't have been unaware of his physical appearance, but I think he probably needed confirmation from outside before he could relate his own awareness to other people's. I had a distinct impression that he might be the only child of elderly parents. He seemed to belong to a generation earlier than his own – that of the Edwardians, say – which would explain his enthusiasm for the outward forms of Anglo-Indian life.

He was, of course, more directed towards Susan than to me (interested or attracted would be the wrong words). She aroused his masculine instinct to protect. Confronted by me he was always on the defensive. It was I who reminded him that fundamentally he was a bit afraid of all of us. Sometimes when talking to him I heard in my own voice tones like those Clark-Without had used when talking to me, tones calculated to provoke; and then I stopped, a bit appalled at the ease with which one followed disreputable examples, and at the ease with which bitterness, once felt, lodged itself, dug itself in and hardened all the edges of your personality.

When we went into dinner Maisie put him between mother and Susan. I had been intended to sit between Colonel Trehearne and Kevin Coley, which would have been rather like sitting between a couple of posts. As it was, I sat between Colonel Trehearne and my father, which while not greatly different was more comfortable. And from here I was able to watch Mr Drew more or less undistracted and, while mother talked to Colonel Trehearne, attend to what Susan and Mr Drew were jointly building that might rank as a conversation; and occasionally contribute to it myself, talking across the table when Mr Drew found himself at a loss. One advantage Mr Drew had in making a go of sitting next to Susan was that he took the shy man's way out; he kept the ball rolling by asking her questions about herself; about what she had been doing, about whether she had enjoyed that, about what she thought she might do next week and about the chances she saw of enjoying that too or enjoying it more. I suppose it was really due to her that the conversation was a success, because once he had got on to the subject of what she had done or had thought, she was able to take an interest of a kind that encouraged him to go on feeding her with questions, scraping the bottom of the barrel of his imagination, but managing. When a change of course signalled a change in talking duties and mother turned to him he became at once less articulate. A faint flush of anxiety spread across his face and stayed there. You could see the gleam of perspiration on his forehead.

I don't remember what she talked to him about nor, now that Colonel Trehearne was free, what subject or subjects he and I chose in order to avoid talking about others. What I do remember clearly is the way in which I suddenly became conscious of the yelping and whining of the dogs. While Maisie talked to Susan and mother talked to Mr Drew and Colonel Trehearne and I exchanged trivial bits of information, the imprisoned dogs moaned and barked and snarled somewhere at the back of the compound. If Maisie heard this distant accompaniment of protest she gave no sign of it. The talk continued. The noise never stopped except to change key.

Father was the only person at the table not talking, and at the moment I became conscious of the dogs I became conscious of this too; aware of the nervous intensity of the silence in which he listened to the cries of those chained animals. He stopped eating. Maisie glanced at him and then very quickly turned back to Susan; which made it plain that mother had warned her to take no notice of anything he did which she thought odd, like putting his fork down, covering a piece of bread with a napkin; staring at the plate.

But this was different. It was the effect of the barking of the dogs that left him unable to eat another mouthful, unable to speak (I felt) or even to move, because of what the dogs reminded him; what, locked up, they represented. I was afraid of what he might do. I took an opportunity to say something to him. He looked at me. His smile was benign. Beneath the table his right hand was trembling. Perhaps my speaking broke the spell. He resumed eating. But sometimes when the sound of the dogs reached a crescendo his knife and fork shook.

*

'If I were you, Maisie,' my mother said, when we were out of earshot of the men, having left them to drink their whisky in the draughty dining-room, 'I'd let those hounds loose. It's worrying John, hearing them yelp.'

Intermittently she had this capacity to astonish me with unexpected proof of having noticed things she'd seemed protected from or unconcerned about; but on this occasion my reaction to the revelation was very strong. Waiting my turn for the lavatory and my turn at the looking-glass, it struck me that there was now absolutely nothing to keep me living where I was living, doing what I was doing. It had all come suddenly to an end. I sat on Maisie's bed and opened my mind to the prospects, the joyful prospects of being free because there was no further family duty for me to perform, no one it was necessary to keep an eye on, or stand by, see through a crisis, make excuses for as I'd had to do in the early days at the grace and favour bungalow before there was Mabel's money to be extravagant with and bills ran up, card debts were being forgotten, and too much gin was being drunk (so elegantly, so discreetly); no one now for whose return I had to wait. Even Susan no longer needed me. She only needed everyone.

So I could go home, stay with Aunt Lydia in Bayswater, find myself a job, a place of my own, and a man I could look at and not feel that he was tortured by an affection for the country I'd not been happy in and to which he would always be longing to return, as if to prove something to himself. I could finish with India before it had quite finished with me, rusted me up, corroded me, corrupted me utterly with a false sense of duty and a false sense of superiority.

I emerged (a little over-painted I think – I noticed mother look at me) and determined to be nice to Mr Drew. I tried to get him to talk about Surrey (where great grand-father had lived and where, walking with Aunt Mabel to show her the stream where Susan and I played together I had been stung by a wasp at the moment of one of what I called my funny turns, which might have been growing pains and made me feel immense in a diminutive landscape); but when Mr Drew did talk about Surrey it sounded to me like a different country – a foreign place – so I made him dance with me to Maisie's portable, out on the verandah where it was no draughtier than indoors, while Susan sat inside, not watching us, but with an expression on her face that I recognized but tonight refused to do anything about. Then the dogs came in and there was pandemonium. Susan's coffee cup somehow got knocked over (or was deliberately spilled to distract attention from the dogs). Her new dress was stained down the front and before you could turn round the pieces on the board had been rearranged and Susan was there in the middle of the scene, with people sponging her, inviting her to have another cup, while she tried to embrace the hound that had caused the trouble; and Mr Drew got down on his knees to collect bits of broken china, and then realized he'd made a gaffe because what else were all these servants for? Still outside, I re-wound the gramophone and played another record of which no one took any notice except towards the end when father came out and said, 'Years since I did this,' and shuffled round with me for the last few bars. Then we went inside where two of the dogs had their devoted heads on Maisie's and Patrick's knees and the third was lolling, tongue out, enfolded by one of Susan's arms: the two of them leaning against one another, squatting in the centre-piece of the rug, in front of the empty hearth.

*

But those intimations of freedom continued. My limbs felt as though they were made out of a substance that wasn't always obedient to the law of gravity. I seemed buoyant, almost on the verge of levitation, to have become in relation to Pankot a dominant but disinterested force. I was no longer ashamed of the dreams I had and had considered shameful, dreams in which I also played a dominant rôle, loving a man who was an amalgam of Major Clark and the young American officer in Darjeeling who was Clark-Without's only successor so far, and who had so impressed Aunt Fenny with his courtly Boston manners that she never suspected him of having other than a brotherly interest in the girl she was supposed to be chaperoning, the girl who was supposed to be convalescing from a spell in a nursing-home in Calcutta, and whose problem was no longer emotional but physical, and who let him into her room three nights in a row, because unlike her Aunt Fenny she hadn't been deceived, had recognized in the American the same single-minded and powerful sexual drive that had distinguished Clark-Without and which she wanted – perhaps for a number of reasons – to appease and be appeased by.

For not least among those reasons was the need to satisfy again her own fully awoken physical desires. I oughtn't to say 'not least'. The need was pre-eminent. An almost unbearable ache. Perhaps I should leave it at that and perhaps it is only some lingering old-fashioned idea that desire without love needs excusing in a woman that makes me not want to refer to this episode without also groping for other explanations. The danger of doing so is that one could come up with another idea, equally false; the idea that I was deliberately debasing

393

myself, paying myself out, being consciously promiscuous because that was now all I was fit to be; a well brought up young woman who had betrayed her upbringing by lying on her back for the first man with the power to persuade her on to it, and who had then had to get rid of the result in the usual sordid way, going in for a d and c and coming out foetus-free but permanently stained, soiled.

Well, I was not debasing myself with John J. Bellenger III but I was not in love with him either. Nor was I hoping that he would fall in love with me so that I could laugh in his face and have my own back on Clark-Without, on men in general. Perhaps all these possibilities were there, in my mind, like echoes of explanations, other people's explanations, but fundamentally there was only the desire, and if it was enclosed by a kind of anguish that anguish was for the loss of a scarcely begun life, the destruction of a child I had conceived, should have carried, loved and looked after. Appeasing the ache of physical desire, I was – yes, I think so – also comforting that anguish, trying to numb it.

But I do not know. The American told me with some understandable pride that I was the twenty-third girl he had had, not counting the ones he had had to pay for. I wasn't sure whether he wanted to amuse or shock me, hurt me or excite my admiration. It could have been that he was unsure himself because when I asked him which of these reactions he expected he looked confused, then laughed and said I had struck him as a girl who was naturally inquisitive and who would be interested in statistics, and that he'd never told a girl before which statistic she represented. I didn't believe him. Afterwards, when he had gone back to what he called States-side (he was in Darjeeling getting in some leave at the end of a tour of flying duties) and Fenny and I went back to Calcutta where mother and Susan were to join us, I worried rather about the possibility of having caught a disease, which would have been the last straw as far as mother was concerned (if I was unable to keep it as secret from her as she was determined the other business officially had to be).

*

The anguish had been part of the dreams, but now it had gone, or been sublimated in images of extraordinary sensuous tranquillity. One's moral sense sleeps while the subconscious mind works out its logic. Here we were, in perfect amity, revealing to one another the purity of a simple physical connection, myself active, they supine, eyes closed, mouths smiling faintly, free of that grim alignment which in real life reflected tensions. I now woke up from these dreams gradually enough to suffer no shock. For a few moments the tangible quality of pleasure lingered, so that the pleasure seemed to come with me into the actual world and colour all my responses, even my response to the knowledge that I'd only dreamt. Lying in the dark I luxuriated in my own ability to smile. And when up and about, getting on with the dull repetitious routine of coping with things and with other people, I had the idea of this smile in my head, in my whole body, as if a smile were a newly developed faculty.

*

Saturday, Sunday night, Monday. On the Monday night, because he had unexpectedly rung me, Nigel Rowan came into the dream too, not centrally, but on its misty periphery, as if he were waiting for me to finish and resume some kind of moral responsibility.

'Who was that?' my mother had asked when I'd put the phone down in the hall and joined her and father in the living-room. I told her. 'Is he in Pankot, then?' she asked.

No, I said, he was ringing from Ranpur. She expected to be told more than that and when she wasn't told she said, 'Was he ringing to say he's coming up?'

She'd heard more about Nigel Rowan from Clara Fosdick than she had ever heard from me. Clara Fosdick had probably given her a good report of him and exaggerated the amount of time Nigel and I spent together in Ranpur before I continued on to Bombay to await father's arrival.

'No,' I said. 'He's not coming up.'

'Did we ever know any Rowans, John?' she asked father.

'I don't remember. Why?'

'Sarah's met a Rowan who's one of Malcolm's *aides*.

According to Clara Fosdick he had a relative in the Political but the name Rowan doesn't ring a bell. Did you know a Rowan at school?'

'I don't remember one.'

'Clara said this Rowan was at Chillingborough. Perhaps his father was too.'

'Do you mean Perron?'

'No. Not your eccentric sergeant. A Captain Rowan.' She looked at me again. 'What did he ring about?'

'About something I asked him to do.' I turned to father. 'Nigel Rowan's uncle was Resident at Kotala. He's just told me.'

My father nodded. He wasn't taking it in. But mother said, 'Then he must be Tom Crawley's nephew. You remember, don't you, John? All the fuss there was! How interesting. Are you sure he's not coming up?'

'He didn't say he was.'

'Did you tell him about your eccentric sergeant?'

'I mentioned Mr Perron. Yes.'

'Did he remember him?'

'Yes. Very well.'

'Not an impostor, then.'

'No, mother. Not an impostor.'

'He won't go to sleep,' Susan said, coming in with Edward in her arms and the ayah just behind her. 'He won't go to sleep until he's said goodnight again to grandpa.'

The child was as good as asleep, but this scene was part of the day's programme. I had delayed it a bit by being so long on the telephone. The child turned his head into Susan's breast when his grandfather dutifully leant over him and said, 'Goodnight, old chap.' Satisfied, Susan transferred him to Minnie's arms.

'Is there time for me to have a drink, or have I held things up too long already?' Susan asked.

'We couldn't have gone in before because Sarah's been on the phone,' mother explained.

'Oh. I'll take it in shall I then?'

'There's no hurry,' father said. He went to the side table where Mahmoud as instructed had set out the bottles and glasses so that Colonel Sahib could mix the drinks himself.

396

'Do you know,' he said, 'I realized today that I've put up a fearful black? I'm not sure I shan't have to send in my papers.'

'What dreadful thing have you done, John?'

'I've been on station very nearly a week and I've neither sent up my card to Flagstaff House nor signed the book. Back in 'thirteen, in Ranpur, it took me the best part of two weeks, doing nothing else, just leaving my card, ticking off the names on the list that Mabel gave me. Had to dress right for it too, and it cost a fortune in tonga-fares and shoe-leather.'

My mother smiled. She said that in the circumstances she imagined his failure to call at Flagstaff House might be overlooked.

'Really?' he said. 'Things have changed.' He caught my eye. 'Not sure I approve.'

It was the first joke he had made. I laughed. I said we could ride past Flagstaff House the next morning.

'So we could.'

*

But we didn't. On that Tuesday morning he was late joining me on the front verandah where I waited, smoking, watched by the two syces who had brought the horses up. Usually only one syce came, riding one horse and leading the other. When I first came out it was drizzling slightly but now it was clearing rapidly in that way which foretold a hot sunny morning. Remembering the funeral I asked the syces whether the bazaar was very crowded. The syce I knew said no, but it was said there were many people at the station, and he had seen people making for there. The bazaar would be crowded later, with people who had nothing better to do than look at a Congresswallah. That was why he had brought a companion; in case when they went back the crowds were big enough to worry the horses.

I said that was wise, and smiled because almost invariably the people who served us spoke contemptuously of politicians. A form of flattery. It was nearly twenty-past seven before father came out. The syces stood to attention and salaamed him.

'Well done,' he said. 'Well done,' as if bringing the horses up

397

on time stretched their mental and physical resources. He said this every morning. And every morning he kissed me lightly on the cheek. This morning he did not kiss me. He put his arm round my shoulders and exerted faint pressure but did not look at me. He looked at his watch instead and apologized for being late. I asked him whether he had got his cards with him. I had to explain what I meant.

'Oh, lots of time for that. Lots of time.'

He led off as usual and once out on the road turned to the north, towards Muddarabad.

As I trailed behind him (the wisest thing to do on this narrow twisting section of road whose high-banked bends could mask the noise of trucks that sometimes used it) I felt vaguely disappointed. A change of route would have suited my buoyant mood. I had hoped that this morning would be different but obviously it was going to be like all the others unless I could force a variation, persuade him past the halt, into the village.

But it was he who forced the variation. About a quarter of a mile before we reached the halting place we came to a road that led in from our right. We had taken this road once or twice on the way home. Now, without more warning than a glance behind to check my position, he led into it, then reined in to let me come up and said, 'I thought we'd take a look at that.'

That was the old dak bungalow, wedged in the hillside, about a quarter of a mile away. A track would take us up to it. The bungalow hadn't been used for years, to my knowledge. It had always looked derelict to me. But this morning as we approached I saw the figure of a boy on the verandah. I said, 'There's someone there.'

'So there is. Good Lord.'

He was a poor actor. And getting closer I now recognized the *mali's* boy. He had on the blue mazri shirt that had originally been one of father's, which mother had handed on to the gardener who had since had it cut down to fit his son.

'Isn't that *mali's* boy?' father asked, forcing his tone. 'Well I never. What's the young scamp doing here?'

The boy had begun to unpack a haversack. I said, 'Playing truant I expect. It looks as if he's brought food for the day.

Wouldn't it be nice if he'd got sandwiches and coffee and offered us some?'

'Shouldn't think much hope. All the same. Jove. Yes, wouldn't it, just? Still, mustn't count our chickens.'

We came up the steep and partially overgrown track in file. Far off I could hear the coppersmith. The sun had got up well into a clear sky. The old bungalow looked as if it were resting on the vapour which clung to the green hillside. Beneath my horse's rather clumsily placed hooves small wet pebbles slithered and crunched.

What is all this? my father called to the grinning urchin, in Urdu. *What are you doing here? Making arrangements for breakfast, Sahib*, the boy called back. Father laughed. He shouted up, *Will there be breakfast for us also? For Sahib and Memsahib-miss*, the boy called back.

'I say, we're in luck. Free scoff.'

Another urchin appeared to hold the horses. A well-bred urchin. Ignoring the burra sahib he stood first by me while I dismounted. I thanked him and asked him whether he was Fariqua's friend. He said he was. I asked him his name. He said, 'Ashok.' Ashok and Fariqua. A Hindu boy and a Muslim boy. Ashok led the horses round to the back. We went up the rickety steps to the ruinous-looking but in fact still quite stout verandah. On the wooden table Fariqua had spread out the feast on a coloured cloth: thermos, cups, pot of sugar, pot of salt, spoons, plates, unnecessary knives and forks, stacks of sandwiches wrapped in paper already appetizingly stained with what looked like bacon-fat.

'Well done,' father said. '*Bus.*'

The boy saluted and ran off to join his friend. (Later they came and squatted on their hunkers at some distance, in silence, observing us gravely.)

We sat side by side on the old bench. I reached for the thermos. 'No, let me,' he said. Pouring tea his hand scarcely trembled. He said, 'Better than leaving one's card.'

'Much better.'

He'd woken early, he explained, and had the idea, had got the servants moving, but it had taken longer than he imagined. The boy hadn't been able to leave with the picnic breakfast until ten to seven, so he'd hung around, made a long

399

business of shaving and dressing, to guard against our catching the boy up. He'd wanted it to be a surprise.

'It's a lovely surprise.'

I'd never been to the old dak bungalow before. There had never been a reason to – even as a child. It was too close to home, wherever home had variously been in Pankot, a different home every summer, practically. The dak bungalow (open in those days, now declined, neglected) had been a point of reference in a familiar landscape. From it I now had a view of Pankot new enough to make the place look oddly unfamiliar.

He opened the first package of sandwiches.

'They won't be a patch on those we had on the train,' he said. 'Bacon sandwiches have to mature a bit, don't they? Crisp but not brittle. Not too moist, not too dry. I'm afraid this batch only got put down an hour ago. All the same, they don't smell too bad.'

And they tasted good. We munched for a while, content. It must have been now that the two boys came back to watch us.

'Did you know about our young supernumerary?'

'Fariqua's friend? Is he a supernumerary?'

'Well, I think he's attached himself to our strength. I caught sight of him the other day when I went round the servants' quarters. Thought he was just visiting because he dodged out of the way. But this morning I found him and Fariqua curled up in the goat-shed.'

'Hasn't he a home?'

'Probably several. None permanent. Orphan. Ambitious boy, though. Tells me he's going to Rajputana one day, to become a mahout, ride an elephant for a maharajah. Meanwhile he scrapes a living running errands in the bazaar and sleeping where he can, I suppose. I should have told *mali* to boot him out but hadn't the heart. Trouble is, once you've recognized the existence of a boy like that you're in a fair way to having to pay for services rendered but not wanted. *Mali* doesn't need two boys to help him, does he? Not with the little he has to do nowadays.'

What he meant was: now that the rose beds are gone. He missed the garden more than he would ever admit. From where we sat I could see the fold near the peak of East Hill behind which Rose Cottage lay. I tried to make out the fir tree that stood at the farthest point of the grounds. I said, 'Well, the tennis-court needs some keeping up.'

'I expect it does.'

I waited. I thought he was going to talk about Mabel. The roses. Or the grave. It hardly mattered which. They were all connected. But he went on, 'We must have a game presently. Bit strenuous for me at the moment though. But don't you and Susan give it up just because I'm back. I'd enjoy watching. You could get up a foursome. Young Drew maybe. And some other young fellow.'

He hesitated. 'I expect there *are* other young fellows? Been up before, waiting for a chance to come up again?'

'It shouldn't be difficult to make up a four.'

'With anyone in particular?'

I pretended not to understand, tilted my head at him, filling my mouth with bacon sandwich.

'Any young fellow who'd be particularly keen? This young ADC for example. Nigel Rowan?'

'Nigel Rowan's down in Ranpur.'

'What I mean is, well, forget tennis. Any young fellow in particular, special from your point of view, that I don't know about?'

I continued munching sandwich and considered the situation from what I imagined must be *his* point of view, looked at a woman, now twenty-five, who had been back in India for six years, and who must surely long since have worn out the excuse that of two sisters she was the less obviously attractive. Statistically, the odds against her remaining single or unattached must have been higher than in any comparable period. India had been jam-packed with eligible young men, and proportionately shorter than ever of eligible women. There were several possible explanations, none of them comforting to anyone who had her happiness at heart: she was frightened of men, she was one of the world's born old maids, she was consumed by a passion for a man who hadn't noticed her or who was married or for some other reason unattainable; or, she preferred women. Of these possibilities the consuming and unrequited passion was the one that most fathers would find the least disturbing and I wished badly that I could have

401

confessed such a thing to him. Being unable to, being unable to confess to any of these things, I felt unsatisfactory and inadequate. I said, 'There's no one in particular so far, daddy.'

We went on, munching bacon sandwiches and Ashok and Fariqua continued to observe us, as though we were exhibits which it was only part of their job to look after, the other part being to watch us closely for clues to the trick we were performing to sustain an illusion of our ordinariness, the illusion that the Sahib-log too liked to eat and take a rest and did not live like birds of paradise, perpetually in flight, feeding on celestial dew.

'Has there never been anyone in particular?'

'You mean someone I wanted to marry?'

'Yes. That sort of in particular.'

I shook my head, pushed the sandwiches closer to him. He took one – seemed to think about it – and then placed it on one side. 'Tell me,' he said, 'what are your feelings towards Ronald Merrick?'

I stopped chewing and stared at him. I remember that: just staring at him, and suddenly wondering whether there was a plot to try to pair me off with the only man I could easily think of who appalled me. To avoid answering I turned the question. I asked him what *his* feelings were.

He regarded me rather sombrely.

'He wasn't what I expected. Being a friend of Teddie's – the same rank – I'd expected a younger man.'

'He wasn't a friend of Teddie's. They only shared the same quarters in Mirat.'

'But he was best man.'

'A last-minute substitute.'

'Yes, I see. Not that it matters.'

'I think it mattered to Teddie.'

'What makes you say that?'

'Well, I was there. I think Teddie regretted it. If I'd been in Teddie's shoes I'd have regretted it too. Hasn't mother or Aunt Fenny told you what happened at the wedding?'

'I know about the stone some chap threw that hit Teddie and delayed the ceremony.'

'The stone was thrown at Ronald but nobody realized that at the time, or why a stone had been thrown at all. The only explanation seemed to be that it was intended for the Nawab. The Nawab had lent us cars and the cars had crests on them. So we imagined the stone was thrown in error by someone who didn't like the people at the palace. We ended up guarded by MPS. That was a mess too. When the Nawab and his party turned up at the Gymkhana Club for the reception, the MPS didn't know who he was and tried to stop him coming in because he was an Indian. Then when we were seeing Teddie and Susan off at the station we were bothered by a poor old woman who prostrated herself at Ronald's feet. The whole thing was a mess but by then we knew who Ronald was. We knew the name of the district where he'd been superintendent of police.'

'Yes, I know all that. Ronald's told me himself. But I shouldn't think Teddie held it against him for long. It was hardly Ronald's fault.'

My father picked up the sandwich now and bit into it. I poured us more tea.

'What was Teddie Bingham like?' he asked.

'A bit like young Mr Drew. But not so shy.'

'Your Aunt Fenny told me he was rather attentive to you, at one time, before his engagement to Susan.'

'Yes. Actually it got to the stage where I was afraid he might propose.'

'Why afraid?'

'I realized how easy it would be just to say yes. A girl can, you know. It's a kind of inertia. You think well, why not? It's what's expected. Getting married to a fairly presentable man. Decent background. Good regiment. Nothing known against. And it's very flattering to be wooed a bit. Even by someone as automatic and predictable as Teddie.'

I should have liked to tell him about the night things came to a head, with Teddie obviously thinking the wooing drill had gone on long enough and that it was time to clarify things between us; the night he shifted gear and became fastidiously amorous, kissing me for so long that it was like a breath-holding contest and we both longed to come up for air, and then knew beyond any doubt that we were both bored with one another. But I felt you couldn't tell your father a thing like that about the man who had gone on to marry your sister. So instead I said, 'Why did you ask about my feelings towards Ronald Merrick?'

'I asked because – well, I've been given to understand that you had some special – no, that's wrong – that you *might* have some special regard for him.'

'Who gave you to understand, daddy?'

'Your Aunt Fenny. She's very fond of you, you know. She has your happiness very much at heart.'

'And I'm fond of her. But I can't think why she should think that. I told her a long time ago what I felt about Ronald Merrick.'

'Yes, but she wondered whether there might have been a change of heart. No, I'm exaggerating again. She said a change of heart couldn't be ruled out.'

'Well it can. I can't imagine how Aunt Fenny could get such an idea. She saw us together often enough when he turned up in Bombay. So did you, daddy. I don't like him. It must show.'

'I wouldn't actually say that.'

'Well whether it shows or not, that's the situation. Furthermore he knows I don't like him.'

'Oh?' He hesitated. 'I don't think he does.' He leant back. 'Neither does your mother. She has much the same impression as Fenny. That you might have a special regard for him.'

'*Mother* told you I might have a special regard for Ronald Merrick?'

He studied me very seriously.

'Yes. Have you?'

'No, daddy.'

'I didn't really think so, but I wouldn't hold out as an expert, you know, not against Fenny and your mother. So I wanted to be sure. Can I be sure?'

'Absolutely sure.'

'Why don't you like him?'

'I can't easily explain why.'

'I know he's not, well – how stuffy it sounds – but not quite our class.'

'It doesn't sound stuffy at all. It's true. He's not quite our class. Class has always been important to us. Why should it suddenly stop being important?'

He had leant forward, arms on the table. He was smoothing

one side of the close-cropped moustache with his knuckles. He seemed puzzled. It wasn't the kind of reaction he expected. Not from the rebel of the family.

He said, 'It's only important over quite a narrow area of life, although I agree it's an important area. The private bit. It's easier to be intimate with someone who comes out of the same box. But there are other areas where it's not important at all. Areas where it's actually harmful, I'd say. Anyway, in Ronald Merrick's case, does it honestly arise? Unless we insist on looking only at the background?'

'You mean he's our class now? That he's made the effort to raise himself to our level and if he keeps quiet about his origins no one will know they weren't much cop. Is that what you mean?'

'He doesn't try to hide them. That's one thing in his favour.'

'One thing? All right. One thing.'

'Surely he has a lot of admirable qualities?'

'Like what, daddy?'

'Like physical courage, moral too, I dare say. No, I don't dare say, I do say. Don't you agree?'

'I prefer a bit of moral cowardice myself.'

'Oh?'

'Or whatever it is that makes you admit there can be two sides to a question, other points of view as good as your own.'

'That's not moral cowardice.'

'I said moral cowardice because you said moral courage. And moral courage is so often what you say people have who really only have their minds rigidly made up to suit themselves.'

'Yes,' he said. He smoothed the other side of the moustache. 'I suppose it can be. I'd not thought of it like that. And I grant you in Ronald's case a certain inflexibility. But you often find it in men who've had to fight their way up the ladder. They have to work so much harder. Did you know he lost both parents when he was only fifteen?'

'He mentioned it once.'

'You know what they were?'

'He said they were in a very small way. I didn't inquire how small or what way.'

'They had a small shop in North London. Newsagent,

405

tobacconist. That sort of thing. I got the impression that before the First World War they were both in service. The shop did pretty well and they took over a larger one. Ronald began at a local boardschool but got scholarships and ended at quite a good grammar. Then the parents were killed in a motor-accident. There was a country uncle somewhere but he wasn't interested in the boy. The assistant headmaster of the school was, though. He took him in to live as a ward and to stay on and matriculate. This fellow had some sort of Indian connections or interests. Socially it was a leg up. Ronald said he imagined if his parents hadn't died he'd have been shoved into something like insurance or accountancy. He knows he owes everything to the schoolmaster. Not just the chance to complete his education but the chance of a better background as well. A good enough one to scrape him into the Indian Police. Physically and academically he must have been more than good enough.'

'You've learnt a lot. More than any of us.'

'Only what he openly volunteered.'

'I realize that. What puzzles me is why he volunteered it.'

'Does it puzzle you? Really? You've no idea?'

'None.'

'Yes, I see. And I'm sorry. I mean sorry you don't much like him. But at least that's better than the other thing. He told me all this because he wants to marry Susan. He said Susan had given him reason to believe she wasn't averse to the idea but that no decision could be made until I got home. Fenny and your mother were surprised. Very surprised. They thought that if he had that kind of regard for either one of you it must be for you. I wanted to be sure how you felt. But it's taken me a bit of time to pluck up the nerve to mention it to you. I was afraid of it hurting you. ...'

'It doesn't hurt me.'

He took my hand. I said: 'It doesn't hurt me, it appals me. I don't honestly believe it. She's said absolutely nothing, but if he's right, if she's thinking on these lines, you've got to stop it. Really. She's not fit to marry anyone yet, let alone Ronald Merrick.'

'The psychiatrist apparently says she is.'

'Which psychiatrist?'

'The one here.'

'Who told you that?'

'Ronald. He saw the fellow a few weeks ago.'

'With Susan's approval?'

'No. He saw him before he spoke to Susan. He wanted to know what effect a proposal of marriage might have on her, whether it would set her back at all. Whether he should wait a bit before saying anything even to me.'

'What a bloody nerve.'

'I thought it rather sensible.'

'Well of course – you thought exactly what he planned you should think. I hope Captain Richardson gave him bloody short shrift.'

'Oh? Why? If you were Richardson and a man who's short of an arm and has half his face burnt off came to you and said, Look I want to marry one of your patients, what are the problems likely to be from her and your point of view?'

'I know, I know. It's all beautifully logical. Absolutely square and above-board. Admirable. On the surface. On the *surface*, daddy.'

'He's very good with young Edward.'

'Yes. He's very good with young Edward.'

'Better than I.'

'Better than you. Better than any of us. Better than anyone. Better than Susan. But he wouldn't be marrying Edward. He'd be marrying Susan. How good will he be with her?'

Directly I'd said that the blood came to my face. I guessed what he probably thought. For one wild moment I wondered whether it could be true, wondered whether if I went to Richardson and described the situation to him he would say, It's clear of course, Merrick appals you because he attracts you and your exaggerated concern for your sister is simply a reflection of your fury at being rejected in her favour.

But it wasn't true. What I believed *was* true was that my mother had deliberately tried to manipulate things. She couldn't possibly want Susan to marry Ronald Merrick, but rather than say so she had grasped the opportunity offered by Aunt Fenny's foolish but well-meaning hint to make father believe that it might break my heart. It could even have been in her mind that in time if the idea of having Ronald Merrick in the family persisted he could be paired off with me because neither of us deserved any better.

'What I don't understand,' father said, 'is your having no idea how the land lay. From Susan's point of view.'

'Did mother?'

'No. But sisters share confidences, surely. You've been very close to her. I know that. At least I know what your Aunt Fenny says.'

'What does Aunt Fenny say?'

'If it hadn't been for you Susan would have had a complete breakdown.'

'She had a complete breakdown, daddy.'

'I meant, might have had to be put somewhere.'

'She was put somewhere.'

'But only in the nursing home, here.'

'In a room with barred windows. They thought she might hurt herself. They were afraid of violence. She'd put the baby at risk. Hasn't mother told you that?'

After a while he said, 'I suppose I've been told just as much as it's thought I can take in. Fair enough. Anyway, that's all over, isn't it? She's quite better now, surely. And quite capable of weighing things up and making a decision she'd have no reason to expect to regret?'

'What does that mean? That she's decided?'

'Yes, I think she has.'

'You've actually discussed it with her?'

'Yes.'

'Did *Susan* say I might be upset?'

'She seemed to think you were expecting it. She was surprised her mother wasn't. She thought it must have been obvious to everyone for a long time that if she married again it would be to Ronald. She's given it a lot of thought, you know. She said she couldn't expect to fall in love more than once in her life, but she does respect him and she knows she's got to think of the boy's future. She assured me there wasn't any element of pity or gratitude in her decision – I mean gratitude to Ronald for what he tried to do to save Teddie. And she's also not blind to the fact that his disabilities make his future career a bit chancy. All in all, I was rather impressed by the way she's thought it all out.'

408

'Was mother impressed?'

'Your mother was chiefly concerned about the effect it might have on you.'

'She raised no objections on her own account? She hasn't gone so far as to say she doesn't want Ronald in the family?'

I could have phrased that better. Again he regarded me seriously, still not entirely convinced that I was being frank about my own interests in the matter. But I let it go at that. I had to become used to the idea that I no longer had responsibilities. It was no business of mine whom Susan married. He had much the same thought, apparently. He said, 'Well when you come down to it Susan's free to marry whoever she likes. It would be nice if we all liked him too. Your mother hasn't actually said she doesn't. Being the mother she's obviously not too happy about one of her daughters marrying a partially disabled man. Come to that neither am I. It *is* a liability. He's very conscious of it himself. If for any reason you think he and Susan have been over-secretive, do take the disability into account. A girl's got to think pretty hard before she commits herself in a case like this. Think it out on her own. So does the man.'

'He's ten years older than Su, at least.'

'It's not much.'

'Why hasn't he married before? Have you asked yourself that?'

'My dear, what's that supposed to mean?'

'It's not supposed to mean anything. It's just a question.'

Eventually father said, 'I don't see anything in particular to question. I'll admit he's probably been keen to make the sort of marriage that, well, he could congratulate himself on making, but I see nothing wrong in that. Good luck to him. Why not? Senior police appointment, the guts to pester his department for a wartime commission, a DSO. It's not a meagre record, not as though he's bringing nothing worth while. I suppose you can say India's made him what he is, but after all isn't it India that's given *us* whatever distinction we have? Without India, I wonder what we'd have been? Lawyers like my grandfather? Merchants like his father? And on the Muir side – Scottish crofters? A long way back, but not all that long way. It's only a difference in timing. India's always been an opportunity for quite ordinary English people – it's given us the chance to live and work like, well, a ruling class that few of us could really claim to belong to.'

'It's no longer an opportunity.'

'That's hardly Ronald's fault.'

'I didn't mean it that way. I meant it's no longer any use looking at Susan's future from that angle. It's all finished. She ought to go home. Ronald's the kind of man who'll never let her. He's worked too hard to get here. It would be different if they were in love. But they're not. They can't be. I don't believe he's capable of feeling that for anybody.'

My father leant back, folded his arms.

'It's not his first proposal, though, is it?'

'Isn't it?'

'Didn't you know?'

'Know what?'

'That he was very fond of the girl in that wretched case that caused him so much trouble.'

Again I stared at him. I could tell from his expression that he was still ready to believe that any reference to Ronald and another woman hurt me. 'Daphne Manners? Ronald told you he was very fond of Daphne Manners? Fond enough to propose to her?'

'Yes. He did.'

'It's not the impression he originally gave me. All he said was that he once thought he liked her but that he went off her pretty quickly when he realized she wasn't sound.'

'Sound?'

'He may not have said sound. It's what he meant. Not sound. Meaning bluntly too friendly with Indians.'

'He told me he proposed marriage to her. I don't see it as a thing a man would invent.'

'And I don't see it as a thing a man would talk about. Why did he?'

'I suppose I asked him. I don't mean directly. It just came up. We were discussing the case. Talking about his future. He said his Inspector-General had supported him but he wasn't sure what the long-term effects would be on his career as a whole. He was very frank.'

'He thinks he made a mistake?'

410

'No. I didn't get that impression. Rather the reverse. But I believe it's often worried him that his feelings for the girl might have influenced him, made him act too hastily, not wrongly, just too hastily. Well, I don't wonder. Wretched case altogether. Wretched to talk about.' He hesitated. 'I'd really prefer not to.'

'All right, daddy, we won't talk about it. That doesn't mean we may not have to live with it, Susan especially, if people start pressing for inquiries into some of the things that were done at the time. But I mustn't say that, must I? The mere prospect might make you feel sorry for him. You should never feel sorry for Ronald.'

'I'd feel sorry for any man who was victimized.'

'Victimized, yes. So would I.'

I'd started to fold the paper in which the sandwiches had been packed. Noticing some still ungathered crumbs I unfolded it again, swept them in, and refolded. I had repaid him badly for the care and trouble he'd taken, for the love and affection he'd shown, making arrangements like these before telling me something he thought might upset me. I'd neither set his mind at rest nor, in the last few minutes, even spoken kindly to him.

'It was such a lovely breakfast,' I said. 'I'm sorry if I've spoilt it. I honestly didn't mean to. Now I suppose we ought to be getting back.'

'You haven't spoilt it. What is the time?'

'Eight-thirty.'

'Are you on duty again?'

'Yes, I'm afraid so.' I remembered the Government House bag, with stuff in for me from Nigel. I'd meant to get to the daftar quite early to round up Sergeant Baker to make sure I got the packages.

'What will you say to Susan?' father asked.

'Nothing. She won't ask my opinion. The thing has been for me to be there when she's wanted me to be there. To be there and go along with whatever she's decided to do. Oddly enough, I've been quite good at that. If marrying Ronald is her new interest she'll be all right so long as she's making plans and seeing everything in terms of the next step ahead.'

'If she stops seeing things like that, would you know?'

'Yes.'

'Sooner than your mother?'

'Probably.'

'Would you tell me?'

'If I'm here, daddy.'

'Might you not be?'

'I can't live at home indefinitely.'

'I do understand that. But – well, for a while. At least until after the wedding.'

'That might depend on when the wedding is.'

'I'd not imagined anything impulsive.' He felt for my hand again. 'Don't *you* be impulsive. What had you in mind?'

'Going home, really. I'd like to get myself a job of some kind. Aunt Julia would take me in for a bit, I expect.'

'Going home? But that's a long-term plan, surely?'

'I thought of going to Aunt Fenny in Bombay for a while. Then on from there when I've really decided. I can pay my own passage. Aunt Mabel left us each five hundred pounds of our own. Susan and me, I mean. And I've got a bit more.'

'That's your nest-egg. There's no question of forking out your own fare, if going home's really what you want. But I hope not yet. Not yet, Sarah. Give me a bit of time to enjoy my whole family.'

I felt the net closing in again. I said, 'Well the war's not quite over yet.'

'No, but if it is, try not to be in too much of a hurry or think me too selfish. It'll be easier for us all to make plans when we know what's to happen to me. The Trehearnes will be going after Christmas. It looks as if I'll take over. But there's just a chance of my getting the Area. Your mother's a bit restless, she'd really like a change of scene, but if we got the Area that would rather please her. Flagstaff House. All that goes with it. And it would probably see out my time.'

'You'd like it too, wouldn't you?'

'Yes, I would. As a young man I assumed I'd end up a general. Small chance of that now. I'd settle for brigadier. Or just full colonel doing Trehearne's job.'

'Then I'll cross my fingers, daddy.'

'Would it make any difference to your plans?'

'Flagstaff House?'

'You were practically born there. And, well, if it happens I'd be sorry to think of your missing it altogether. You've had your share of stale gingerbread. Opportunity for a bit of gilt. But perhaps I shouldn't have mentioned it. Raising hopes.'

He would never understand how little the idea of moving into Flagstaff House raised my hopes. And just then they needed raising. Looking at that oddly unfamiliar view of East Hill it seemed to me that once long ago I'd been marooned there and that now the flood had receded, receded so far that you would have to walk miles to find water and even then have to wade on, endlesssly, without coming to a depth sufficient to swim in.

For one moment I believed, perhaps illogically, my only hope of getting away lay in confessing to my father what had happened to me. I could say: Look, I'm no longer a virgin. I was bedded by one of those officers Uncle Arthur's paid to make enthusiastic about having a career in India, only this chap turned out only to be enthusiastic about what Uncle Arthur would call the wrong things, and I was left in the club, also the wrong one, like any tiresome little skivvy, but unlike her we were able to arrange to have it brought off, and boringly unconventional though I've always been from most people's point of view, I simply didn't have the nerve to walk round pregnant and unmarried in Pankot. I know I'm not by a long chalk the first colonel's daughter to wander down the primrose path, but the catch is that I would never marry a man without first telling him what had happened, which mother knows. I made it clear to Aunt Fenny and if Aunt Fenny's run to form she's obviously told mother that I'd never marry under false pretences. Mother's probably guessed it anyway. And she doesn't really mind because it would go against her patrician scale of values to let me marry a man she really approved of and she thinks the ones she'd approve of are the ones who'd turn tail once they knew. So she's written me off. You'd better too.'

I glanced at him, and then, summoning the nerve, I began to tell him. I got as far as 'Look –' and then, after a second or two, departing from script, 'There's something I want you to know, something I must tell you,' but I got no further because

413

he suddenly grabbed my hand and, not looking at me, said, 'No,' quite sharply, and then repeated it more gently.

'No. Nothing to tell me. Better be off.'

Still without looking he let go of my hand; briefly but quite strongly put his arm round me and then let go altogether and stood up and shouted something to the boys who scrambled up and ran round to get the horses. Then he went to the head of the steps and down them. He was calling something to me, pointing, perhaps at the fir tree high up on East Hill which his better-trained eye had sighted; but half-keeping his back to me, giving me time to let the reason for his reaction sink in.

He knew about the pregnancy and the abortion. Fenny or my mother had told him. Fenny probably; perhaps only hinting at a cause of unhappiness which my mother had more coldly identified. I went to the head of the steps, pretended to look where he was pointing, shading my eyes.

The boys brought the horses. Ashok helped me to mount. When he'd done so I thanked him and led off without waiting for father, heading down the stony track. Half-way down my horse began to miss his footing. The effort of keeping control, slight as it was, seemed immense; the last shameful straw. By the time I reached the road I couldn't see clearly. I waited until he came up. We could go one of two ways. He chose the shorter, and I fell in behind him. But presently he moved over to his right, waited until I was level and, apart from having to drop back a couple of times when a vehicle went by, stayed silently abreast of me until we reached home.

*

Susan was in the bathroom which meant I didn't have to talk to her. I changed quickly into uniform and to avoid seeing anyone set off for the daftar without even washing the smell of horse off my hands. Momentarily I'd forgotten the reason for wanting to be early on duty, but recalled it when the tonga approached the spot where Barbie's accident had been, the spot Clarissa Peplow once pointed out to me, where after careering down Club Road out of control the tonga had overturned, spilling them all into the ditch. From this point Barbie had walked, mud- and blood-stained, presumably

414

refusing assistance from passers-by, making for the rectory bungalow into which she strode, calling for a spade and announcing that she had seen the Devil. The spade was for resurrecting Mabel. The devil was Ronald Merrick.

Rose Cottage had been shut. Mother, Susan, the baby and ayah had gone down to Calcutta to join Fenny and me after our holiday in Darjeeling, a reunion intended to maintain the illusion that everything was well with everybody. In the family's absence Mahmoud had discovered the trunk in the mali's shed and complained about it to the man mother had asked to keep an eye on things – Kevin Coley. And Kevin had gone down to the rectory to ask Barbie to remove it.

According to Clarissa, Barbie didn't mind. When she went up to the cottage to collect the trunk she found a stranger there. Ronald. He'd come up to the Pankot hospital to have the artificial hand fitted and had called at the cottage to see us. According to Ronald he and Barbie sat and talked, mainly about her missionary friend, Edwina Crane, whom he'd known in Mayapore. She insisted on giving him the copy of the picture which she associated with Edwina. Then she asked him to supervise the loading and securing of the trunk in the back of the tonga. He said he'd advised her against it; it was too cumbersome, too heavy. But she wouldn't listen. He said she struck him as over-excited, in fact, he said, 'Exalted might be the better word.'

It was quite a while before I talked to Ronald about his meeting with Barbie. He had left Pankot before we returned from Calcutta. At that time I'd only met him twice. I'd not liked him. But the real animosity came later when he began to turn up in Pankot on the excuse of visiting the hospital, but in fact it seemed to me to attach himself to us. I realized that he was a very lonely man in the ordinary sense of the word and without my realizing quite how it happened I found myself more often in his company than seemed explainable. At the pictures, for instance, or eating out at the Chinese restaurant when it was inconvenient to entertain him at home (when Susan wasn't well, or had taken too much of her sedative). Going out with him when he was in Pankot, so far as I was concerned, was no more than a duty, one more duty to add to the many I'd got lumbered with or stupidly volunteered for and I assumed that this was understood by the family as a whole. What he assumed about it had been beyond me to work out. He knew I disliked him. Knowing he knew made me feel that we were all safe from him.

When we went to the Chinese restaurant he always ordered a particular table, the one in the window on the first floor (officers only) which looked out on to the bazaar, and which at least provided him with the view to which my silences too often forced him to give attention. I never felt that my being poor company upset him. We were at the Chinese restaurant when I first asked him to describe in detail his meeting with Barbie. I didn't tell him I'd just seen her, in the Samaritan in Ranpur, but I think he guessed. When he said, 'She struck me as being over-excited when she set off, in fact exalted might be the better word,' he studied me closely as if checking for the effect of that word exalted. The exaltation began (he said) when she opened the trunk to give him the picture and found a lace-shawl which she said didn't belong to her but which she thought Mabel's old servant Aziz must have put in the trunk when he temporarily had the key to it.

I knew which lace he meant, lace which Mabel had been given by her first husband's mother – lace like a web of butterflies, worked by a blind old French woman, some of which had been used for Susan's baby's christening, and some, years before, for my own. I had recognized it only a couple of days before at the Samaritan hospital, draped round Barbie's head and shoulders, stained brown with dried blood.

Ronald said, 'She put it on when she got into the tonga, like a bridal veil.'

The lace shawl, with its rusty stains, was among the packages that Nigel had been given by the Reverend Mother to hand over to me.

*

But of course there was nothing waiting for me at the daftar, nothing – Sergeant Baker told me – addressed to me in the overnight bag from Government House. I thought of ringing Nigel up but delayed doing so, finding an excuse not to do that until after five, because he would be busy, but in fact shirking it because the main reason for ringing him would be to tell him about Ronald and Susan and to try to coerce him into helping me to stop it; which seemed a bit unfair.

I remember sitting at the typewriter in the daftar, cutting a stencil from a holograph order written out by Major Smalley, and using so much red-sealer to obliterate mistakes that the wax paper began to look like a piece of the lace shawl Barbie had worn, seated at her window. She had on that occasion seemed to have found peace, the peace of absorption in a wholly demanding God, a God of love and wrath who had no connection with the messianic principles of Christian forgiveness, and it was like that I preferred to remember her, not – as at other times when I had visited her – unanchored, unweighted, withershins, attempting to communicate with the doomed world of inquiry and compromise.

When I was midway through the stencil the phone rang. The operator told me a Captain Rowan was on the line. It was as though I'd conjured him. I said, 'Nigel? I'm afraid there was nothing in the bag. Is that why you're ringing?'

'Partly,' he said. 'Actually I brought the stuff up with me.'

He explained the situation but I wasn't being very bright and it took me some time to understand that he was in Pankot, that he'd travelled up on the overnight train, was staying at the Summer Residence guest house and in the last few minutes had spoken to my mother on the phone and been given my Area HQ number and extension.

'Has she rung you at all?' he asked.

'No, yours is the first call I've had. Why?'

He said, 'In which case you probably won't know Ronald Merrick's here too. By chance I travelled up with him. He had our mutual friend Guy Perron in tow. Merrick's with your parents now. He's come to break some rather sad news to your father. A havildar from your father's regiment who was in the Frei Hind force in Germany committed suicide the other day. Merrick thought your father might be very upset. He wanted to break the news to him himself.'

'Yes. I see. I think he will be. Upset.'

'Merrick's now a half-colonel.'

'What?'

417

'He's been promoted to Lieutenant-Colonel. Did you know?'

'No, I didn't, Nigel. The other thing I didn't know was that he might also become my brother-in-law. Father told me this morning. He wants to marry Susan. And Susan wants to marry him.'

I may have got that wrong: the order in which things were said; but I plainly recollect then a very long silence. We were both trying to assimilate wholly unexpected bits of information: on my part, the poor havildar's death, Ronald's sudden and to me ominous presence in Pankot.

'What do you think of him now that you've met him?' I asked.

'He wasn't quite what I imagined.'

'How long are you here for? I'd love to see you. Is today possible, or is HE in control?'

'The Governor's not here. There's only a Mr Gopal. Actually your mother's just asked me to have dinner at Rose Cottage tonight. I'd like that but I'm not sure whether I can make it. I've got a thing to do for HE. I'm free once I've done it but I'm not sure when that will be. Could you lunch here?'

'You mean today?'

'Yes. Come up as soon as you like.'

I could do that now, I said; and did – leaving the wounded stencil in the machine and looking in on Major Smalley to make the excuse that I was feeling off-colour but hoped to be back in the afternoon.

*

A man came down the steps as the tonga pulled up in front of the guest house. I hadn't seen Nigel in mufti before and for a moment scarcely recognized him. A suit disguised some of the thinness which his uniform accentuated; he looked fitter, more relaxed, like a man released from some kind of duty which he'd found more and more difficult to do. We had never embraced. Just here, just now, an embrace would have seemed right, but we did as we'd done when parting in Ranpur; shook hands rather solemnly. He held my elbow as a token of support while we climbed the steps but at the top he

418

let go. We went through to the rear verandah which had the view I knew best – across the lawns to the closed Summer Residence – although I couldn't recall just when I'd last seen it.

On a table between two white cane blue upholstered chairs were the several packages he'd brought up from the Samaritan. I thanked him but for the moment didn't want to deal with them or even look at them. He ordered drinks, offered me a cigarette. While I smoked he told me something about the special job he had to do in Pankot. For the moment, at least until he'd had some word from Mr Gopal, he was more or less a prisoner at the guest house, since he might have to make himself available at any moment. He doubted, though, that this would be earlier than the following day.

'So you might be able to come to dinner tonight?'

'Yes, it's very likely.'

'And you might be here for a day or two at least?'

'A day or two certainly.'

The drinks came. While he dealt with the steward I settled back in the cane chair considering how in two days Nigel and I might effectively collaborate to stop a marriage I was sure ought to be stopped. He could talk to my father. I would talk to Susan. The main problem was that Ronald was in Pankot too. So far I'd hardly taken in that fact and now that I did so and had time to consider the excuse Ronald had found to come up from Delhi, the havildar's death seemed like something he had invented to suit his own ends; so that then I began to wonder what it could be that Barbie's death had been invented for. My mind was racing, but I could feel my body settling into a posture of embattled indolence and could hear a voice warning me: Don't say too much. Go carefully.

I'm trying to reproduce for you an occasion of awful disorientation. Failing probably. God knows how one could succeed.

'Well when did all this happen?' he asked. 'Your sister and Ronald Merrick?'

'I wish I knew. She's never said anything to me. Not the slightest hint. But there it seems to be. According to father. I've not talked to Susan yet but father has. And apparently Ronald's talked to him.'

'Your sister is serious, then?'

'So father believes.'

'Does he approve?'

'Let's say he doesn't know Ronald well enough not to.'

'Nor well enough to give his consent immediately?'

'The drawback is, consent's not actually needed.'

'No. Of course. So you have the impression it may be more or less fixed?'

'If it is, I want to unfix it. I hoped you might help me.'

He said nothing. But his expression was kind. I went on: 'It's a lot to ask. But if there's anything you can do to help, I'd be very grateful.'

He didn't answer at once. Then he said it was difficult to see on what grounds he could. He didn't know Susan at all. He and I had talked about Ronald only in general terms. He added, 'Now that I've met him I can't say he's the kind of man I'd want to go out of my way to have much to do with. I suppose one has to assume some serious emotional involvement on your sister's part. One's instinct isn't much to go on, if it comes to thinking of interfering.'

'Is it only instinct, Nigel?'

He thought for several moments and then said, 'From the family's point of view I'd be concerned mainly about the possibility – I don't say probability – the possibility of his name cropping up in any future fuss the politicians make about officers suspected of exceeding their duty in nineteen forty-two. Of course, there's no need even to anticipate a fuss. But if there is a fuss, Merrick might be involved. Not that that would make the slightest difference to Susan, I imagine. Assuming a fondness. Nor to the family. But that's all I can offer – as a practical argument against. Perhaps your father should be warned. About the possibility.'

'I've already warned him. But it didn't have much effect because Ronald's already discussed that aspect of things with him. I was hoping you might dot a few i's and cross a few t's.'

He frowned, not at me but at his glass. He said, 'Well there's also the history of persecution, isn't there, but you know more about that than I do. If it's resumed, your sister could be hurt by it.'

'I've told father about the persecution, but I think it just makes him feel sorry for the man. And Ronald naturally has been very frank about the effect the Manners case could have on his career. It's part of his technique. What I meant was being able to tell father something I don't know. But which you might know. Something on a confidential file, for instance? I may be wrong, but whenever we've talked about Ronald you've always left me with the idea that you know far more than could be expected of a man who'd never met him. So. A file?'

After a while Nigel said, 'I should think all a file would tell you about Colonel Merrick is that he left the comparative safety of the police for active service in the army and was decorated with the Distinguished Service Order, since when there has been a history of regular promotion, no doubt well-deserved.'

'In which case there would be nothing much to fear from a political fuss later, would there, if the files show him as such a paragon?'

Hearing the sharp edge to my voice I suddenly pictured what perhaps I looked like – a hard-bitten little memsahib interfering in other people's lives to stop herself shrieking with the boredom and frustration of her own – or (and perhaps Nigel wondered about this too) trying to stop a marriage because she coveted the man for herself, in spite of all she had ever said to the contrary about her attitude to him.

'I'm sorry, Nigel, I shouldn't try to involve you. It's not your problem. I'd better ring home and tell them I won't be back for lunch. Then I'll go through this stuff of poor Barbie's.'

He accompanied me inside, showed me where a telephone was and a bedroom-bathroom suite that I could use, should I want to; in fact, he said, the phone could be switched through to the one in the bedroom if I preferred that. The steward could get the number. I said that might be best and went into the bedroom, sat on the bed, waiting. The phone rang. Mother was at the other end. She said, 'Where are you?' I told her.

'Good,' she said. Apparently she had rung the daftar and had been expecting me to arrive at any moment, "off-colour". She had rung to tell me Nigel Rowan was in Pankot and that if he got in touch I should do my best to persuade him to accept the invitation to dinner at Rose Cottage. She added, 'Presumably you know by now who else is here.'

'Yes. Nigel told me. I'm sorry about the havildar. Is daddy very upset?'

'Not too upset not to have invited Ronald Merrick to dinner this evening. I don't want just a family dinner. I want Captain Rowan here too.'

'He'll come if he can.'

'I want you to make sure he does. I must have another man at the table.'

'If you want to make sure you'd better invite someone else. Nigel's not definitely free. There's always Edgar Drew.'

'I said man, not boy. And a man of our own sort.'

'Then ask Ronald to bring Guy Perron. I gather he's brought him up to Pankot.'

'So we've all gathered. We've all been having to admire the invisible feather in Colonel Merrick's cap. Colonel! But you can hardly ask a colonel to bring his sergeant along even if there was a chance of his agreeing to. Which in this case there isn't. What a pity the ranks aren't the other way round. I want Captain Rowan.'

'I can't promise.'

'I'm asking you to do so. I'm saying that the least you can do for me is to guarantee he'll be here.'

'The least?'

'The least. He sounds to me the most presentable man you've ever bothered to get to know. In the circumstances, in *all* the circumstances, I should prefer it if you brought him into the open and remembered that this isn't Calcutta, but Pankot.'

I said, very quietly, 'Why do you want that, mother? So that Susan can take one look at him and decided he's for her? I suppose that would solve everything from your point of view.'

'Not quite everything,' mother said. She put the phone down. A meaningless retort; the kind someone is stung into making out of sheer exasperation. I went into the bathroom so that I could calm down and stop shaking. I heard the telephone ringing again in the bedroom but before I could reach it – thinking it was mother calling back to apologize – it stopped, presumably because the call had been taken elsewhere. Going through into the living-room I found Nigel taking the receiver from the steward. I indicated that I would go out to the terrace and did so. The steward followed and asked if I would have another drink. While waiting for it I stood by the balustrade and smoked and then, remembering the packages on the table, decided I might as well look at some of them. The first and bulkiest (containing something solid, like a book, and something soft) was marked: *In the Event of my Death: Dear Sarah*.

Inside I found the butterfly lace which I hastily put down. The solid object was a book of Emerson's essays. I remembered her fondness for them. A quick flip through the pages showed that many of the passages were underlined. I read several of these but found them tiresome and self-righteous. I put the lace back in the wrapping and left the book on the table. The other package, an envelope, contained several smaller envelopes, variously marked: To Sarah: Not to be Opened Before My Death. Private and Personal: To Colonel Layton's daughter. To the Girl who Visits me. To the Girl with the fair helmet of Hair. To Whom it Might Concern. To Gillian Waller from a Friend.

Every glance – I found it too painful to give much more just then – and subsequent study showed heart-breakingly little except her continuing concern over the question of Mabel's grave – evoked images of her distraction and how, as time went on, she seemed not to have recognized me. In the end she had even given me another name, Gillian Waller. It rang a bell, but I couldn't remember why.

I stuffed the envelopes into my shoulder-bag and managed to push the lace in too. I didn't want the lace for one particular reason. For the same reason I couldn't throw it away. There remained the book. I picked it up again and was glancing through it when Nigel came out.

He said, 'Good, that's settled.' He looked pleased. 'Tomorrow. Probably in the evening.'

'Which leaves you free for tonight?'

'Yes.'

'You know Ronald Merrick's invited too?'

'I wasn't sure.'

'I'll make your excuses if that's what you'd prefer.'

'Would you prefer to dine here?'

'I think that's ruled out, Nigel. I'm not inventive enough to think of an excuse that would cover both of us.'

'In which case I'll come to Rose Cottage. Have the other half before we go into lunch.'

'I'm having the other half.'

'Well, have the next.'

'No, this is fine. I've a stencil to finish this afternoon. But you're one drink behind. You'd better catch up.'

He gave an order to the steward, then noticing that the packages had gone from the table leaving an unidentified book in their place he said, 'Mystery cleared up?'

'I don't think there was much of a mystery after all but I haven't looked through everything yet. I really am grateful though. Are you keen on Emerson?'

'I don't know him I'm afraid. Guy Perron's the Emerson expert. He was quoting him last night.'

'Oh? Barbara Batchelor was an expert too I should think, judging by the homework she seems to have done on him. I thought you might like to keep the book as a reminder of a pretty odd sort of mission.'

'I shan't need reminding. If you don't want it why not give it to Guy? It might cheer him up.'

'Is he very down-in-the-mouth?'

'I shouldn't say that. Fighting mad might be nearer the mark. He told me he has a scheme to wangle his repatriation. But I never did know when Guy was being serious.'

'I should say he's serious when it's necessary. For instance in Bombay he saved a man from drowning himself in the bath.'

'But not – I gathered – from chucking himself out of a hospital window later and breaking his neck. So Guy said.'

'I didn't know that. Poor Captain Purvis.'

I felt suddenly like laughing. Such a useless, farcical death.

Nigel had been leafing through the book. 'Here it is. "Society is a wave." One of Miss Batchelor's favourite passages too if the markings are anything to go by.' He handed the book back to me. I read the passage. It meant nothing to me. I put the book on the table.

'I think Sergeant Perron should have it if you don't want it, although a sermon on self-reliance is hardly what he needs. Will you be seeing him?'

'I'm not sure. I've given him this number to ring. He didn't know where he'd be billeted. Poor Guy. Two suicides in one week and an order attaching him to Ronald Merrick's department. Incidentally, coming up last night he told me you'd met another old Chillingburian, Jimmy Clark, or Clark-Without as we called him.'

'Yes, that's right.'

'Where was this?'

'In Calcutta.'

'What was he doing there?'

'Oh, passing through on his way to Kandy, looking up old acquaintances, including Uncle Arthur and Aunt Fenny. He'd been on one of Uncle Arthur's courses and was quite the blue-eyed boy.'

'Was that the only time you met him?'

'Yes, he flew to Kandy next day to take up some glamorous sounding appointment. Or perhaps he was just swanning around.'

'Probably. What did you make of him?'

'I thought he talked a lot of sense. He had us all sized up pretty well.'

'Us?'

'People like us. English people in India. Except that he didn't think we were really English any more. He said we got left behind. Preserved in some kind of perpetual Edwardian sunlight.'

Nigel laughed. 'Let's eat,' he said.

*

'Game pie of a kind,' he pointed out. 'And champagne also of a kind. Compliments of Government House. It came up in the ice-box.'

'Who are they meant for, though? Not me. Could it be the elusive congressman, Mr Kasim?'·

'No, for me, I think, from HE. This is my last assignment for him. They're taking me back into the political.'

'When? When are you going?'

425

'I'm probably leaving Ranpur some time next week.'

'It's what you wanted.'

'Yes, it is.'

'Where will you go? Kotala?'

'I shouldn't think Kotala.'

'What's your ambition? The Residency at Hyderabad?'

'Too late for that. I'd need another ten or fifteen years.'

'Then why go on? Why not just get out?'

'I thought we talked about that when we first met over Count Bronowsky's champagne. I thought you said nothing was an excuse for working at half-pressure, or standing back from a job while it's still there to be done.'

'Did I say that?'

'Yes.'

'And you've remembered. It doesn't sound like me at all.'

'I thought it did. Anyway. It's what you said.'

'I can't have been thinking straight.'

'Have some more game pie.'

'I can't even get through this.'

Suddenly I felt nauseated. Irregularity was one of my problems these days, so I was usually prepared; and it was better than the punctual but protracted miseries I'd once endured. I murmured an excuse, got up and went back to the guest bathroom and scrabbled in my crammed shoulder-bag for what I needed; panicking when for a moment I couldn't find it among all the things from Barbie's room at the Samaritan. But once I'd uncovered it the sensation of sickness seemed to change its nature. I found myself shivering, as if from a slight fever. But it wasn't fever, it was delayed shock, a physical response to the emotional strain of the ride home from the Dak bungalow after the realization that either my mother or Aunt Fenny had told father about the abortion in Calcutta. It had been for me to tell him; no one else. I seemed to have his forgiveness. If I wanted anything it was understanding.

Plugging myself against the unseasonable but likely menstrual flow I found myself weeping as I'd never done before, not even at that time Aunt Fenny took me in her arms in the hospital room and warned me that mother would never refer to what had happened because for her it hadn't, and that anything I wanted to get over should be got over there and then.

To muffle the sound of my crying I ran the taps hard, and bathed my face. The cold water was like a series of slaps. I stared at my ruined self, hating every pore, every line, every bone. But, ruined or not, as a face it was indestructible. A Layton more than a Muir face. Built to last.

The thought was not new, and thinking it again I recalled the last time I'd thought it: in the garden of Rose Cottage, bending my head to take the scent of a red rose. That was all. The garden. The rose. Barbie and I. And this conviction of being built to survive. But I couldn't recall the context. It might have been before or after Mabel's death.

I began to repair my Layton face, doing it with care and deliberation as if the end-result had to represent my conscious projection of myself into a particular future. And then the context came back: the context of the rose and Barbie and of Gillian Waller. It had been before Mabel's death, when Susan was still pregnant. Who is Gillian Waller? Barbie had asked me. We were walking in the garden, the garden as it had been before the time of the tennis court. Who is Gillian Waller? I don't know, I'd said. Why? And unwittingly Barbie disclosed that at night sometimes she went into Mabel's room, took off her spectacles, put away the book she'd fallen asleep over, tucked her up and turned off the light, and then waited until she could be sure the sleep hadn't been interrupted. In this sleep, this half-sleep, Mabel had sometimes muttered to herself, as old people do. Gillian Waller, she had said. So it sounded. So: Who was Gillian Waller? 'I'm afraid to ask,' Barbie explained. 'I hate to seem to pry. She's such a self-contained person. There are people like that. She's one. Is Susan more cheerful?'

Not cheerful, I said. Holding on.

I could feel Barbie's hand on my arm as she said, 'To what? Would you say she's dangerously withdrawn?'

I leant over the basin, stared at the white porcelain, smelt the rose. 'We endure,' I said. 'We're built for it. In a strange way we're built for it.' But at this point the context changed, led me to another similar occasion when Barbie and I were in the garden and she grasped my arm again and said, 'They say the child should have a father. I'd encourage it if I were you. If she doesn't marry again you'll never get away. Some people are made to live and others are made to help them. If you stay you'll end up like that, like me.'

*

'Are you all right, Sarah?' Nigel called from the bedroom.

'Yes, thank you,' I called back.

I waited until I heard the click made by the bedroom door as he went back into the main living-room. Then I considered my reflection very seriously and understood, slowly, the full irony of the situation. I said to my reflection: 'There goes a man I might have been happy with and who up to the time he rang me at the daftar and I told him about Susan and Ronald probably thought he could be happy with me.'

I completed the mask, exaggerating the lipstick and, before opening the bathroom door, smiled, to prepare for the entrance.

But I did not have to enter. I had entered already, long ago.

The Circuit House

The only light entering the compartment came from one of the arc-lamps that lit the siding, but a dim light was on in the corridor and when the door slid open he saw that it was Ahmed, not Hosain, who had come to wake him.

'It's time, father.'

'Has Mr Mehboob arrived?'

'Yes, half-an-hour ago. But Hosain said you hadn't bothered to go to bed and were only dozing, so I left you until the last moment.'

'Even on stationary trains I don't sleep. Just for me we could all have come by car and not bothered with this.' He wound his scarf round his neck and put on his cap. 'How far is the Circuit House? I've forgotten.'

'About half-an-hour's drive.'

'So near?' On that previous occasion, coming from the Circuit House, the journey seemed endless. But that had been a journey with a joyful reunion, not a painful one, at the end, and they had driven all the way to the station at Mirat, not this station. He made a mental note: I am not fully awake – guard against these muddles.

Outside in the carpeted corridor Hosain was waiting and took the briefcase from him, to relieve him both of the weight and of the supposed indignity of having to carry anything himself. Unencumbered he went to the door. The last time he got off a railway coach at this particular siding it had been with difficulty, climbing down backwards because there was no platform, the distance between the level of the coach floor and the level of the cinder-yard great, the steps perpendicular. He had had to beg help with his luggage from one of the conducting officers. That was three years ago, almost to the day. 'Where is this?' he had asked. The receiving officer had said, 'Premanagar'. Which meant they were imprisoning him in the fort. After that he had had to climb unassisted into the back of a police truck. He had barked his shins. But this morning – for it was nearly five o'clock – there were special steps already in position and two railway employees to steady them and him against every eventuality.

Mr Mehboob came fussily across the dimly lit and deserted cinder-yard to greet him and conduct him to the waiting limousine, whose driver held the door open. *Everything has meaning for you, Gaffur*, he quoted silently to himself, *the petal's fall, the change of seasons*.

The railway coach and the limousine both belonged to the Nawab. But this was the last time he would find himself in his kinsman's and Count Bronowsky's debt; or very nearly the last. When what had to be done at the Circuit House had been done he would return to the coach, which was filled with all the accumulated stuff of his life under restriction at Nanoora, and travel on by rail to Ranpur to reoccupy his home permanently. The limousine would return to Mirat. Mehboob had been right. There would have been no point in coming from Nanoora to Premanagar by car when the coach had to come anyway, would leave Nanoora earlier, and offer him a chance to sleep during the hours it was parked in the siding.

The secretary followed him into the Daimler and settled ponderously beside him on the softly cushioned back seat. He had wanted Ahmed beside him. But Mehboob was jealous of his own prerogatives. As a secretary he wasn't a patch on poor old Mahsood and as a man Mr Kasim found him irritatingly like an English caricature of an Indian – possessive towards people with power, arrogant to those with none. Even his physical characteristics now fitted him for the part he played with such breathless intensity. His plumpness was only just short of obesity. His nickname was Booby or Booby-Sahib – a kindly enough invention of Mahsood's (who towards the end when he was losing his grip but refusing to let go was always saying, 'I will ask Booby. I will tell Booby') but which was now used behind Booby's back and sometimes even to his face with less charitable intention. As Mahsood's assistant Booby's liabilities had been less apparent than his assets, chief among which was what had seemed an unrivalled knowledge of party political machinery acquired at grass-root level on the local sub-committees and in the corridors of the provincial legislative assembly. He had first come to Kasim's notice in 1937 as the backroom man largely responsible for the election campaign that had sent to the assembly another Muslim Congressman, Fariqua Hamidullah Khan. Khan had defeated a Muslim Leaguist whom the League had thought would walk away with the seat – a lean hawk of a man whose expression in defeat had been a sight to see.

In those days Mehboob had been lean too. Kasim had met him in old Hamidullah Khan's house on the painful occasion when he had had to tell the old war-horse that his name wouldn't be going forward to the Governor as a candidate for a portfolio in the first Congress Ministry in Ranpur. He had expected to be given the department of education and there were times, subsequently, when Kasim regretted not having given the old man his chance. A Muslim minister for education might have been quicker (even a man as slowed up by age, vicissitudes and disappointments as Hamidullah Khan) to pounce on or defy the hard-line Hindus who had made it compulsory in the district schools to salute the Congress flag, sing songs which had a Hindu rather than an Indian national connotation, and to teach history in a religious rather than a political context. It had been this more than anything throughout the country that had alerted the Muslims to the dangers of a Hindu-*raj* succeeding a British-*raj* and which had provided Jinnah with the kind of political ammunition he'd been so short of. But Kasim hadn't given Hamidullah Khan his chance and in July 1942 the old man died while on a visit to his ancestral home near Rawalpindi. The next month Kasim was imprisoned in the fort at Premanagar. Released in 1944 to the protective custody of the Nawab, joined by his wife, and presently by old Mahsood, he had looked at his ageing secretary and seen the unmistakable signs of deterioration. 'You need a young assistant,' he had said. 'Perhaps so, Mac-Sahib.' And a day or two later Mahsood had come to him. 'There is a man, poor young Mehboob who

433

got Hamidullah Khan into the assembly. Doing nothing since Khan Sahib died. Like Othello. Occupation gone.' 'Get him,' Kasim had said, recalling the lean young man.

And here he was, Mehboob, Booby, Booby-Sahib, sitting beside him, weighing the Daimler down at the left-hand side.

'Were there any letters after I left?' Mr Kasim asked, turning his attention from the window.

'I have them here,' Mr Mehboob said. 'Three are marked personal so I have not opened them. One of them is from Bapu. Another from your daughter, Mrs Hydyatullah.'

'And the third?'

'From our indefatigable suppliant, Pandit Baba Sahib.'

'You could have looked at that. After all CID will already have done so.'

The door on Mehboob's side opened. Ahmed leaned in.

'Everything is ready,' he said.

'Then come along.'

'I'm going in the escort vehicle.'

'You would be more comfortable here.'

'It's all arranged. An alteration would create confusion.'

Kasim nodded. Ahmed shut the door. The driver got in. Presently the car moved. Kasim closed his eyes and didn't respond when Mehboob said, 'Premanagar very depressed area. Here too much erosion, too much poverty, no industry. Government has just abandoned it as hopeless. Here presently we shall have communists, isn't it? Everyone very bolshie. Why else are they giving us an armed escort?'

Kasim didn't answer. It was mainly Mehboob's fault that Ahmed had elected to go in the other vehicle. His younger son and his new secretary had never pulled on well together. Mehboob despised Ahmed for having no political sense; Ahmed was simply indifferent to Mehboob. He was indifferent to everybody. He lived his own life. He was dutiful when it was necessary to be dutiful. But there was no affection. He had seemed to love only his mother. When she died he had acted as if her death need not have happened, and as if he blamed his father for the fact that she died without having seen Sayed again.

'Give me my daughter's letter, then,' he told Mehboob.

'Light! Light!' Mehboob instructed the driver.

434

'No, no, no light. Just give me the letter. I'll read it later.'

Mehboob opened his own briefcase, got out some envelopes, leaned forward, putting his face close to them, and eventually handed one to him.

'Did you notice the post-mark?'

'Yes, it is from Lahore.'

'Good. Then she is back from Srinagar.'

'Also I noticed it had been opened. You can always tell.'

'And Bapu's?'

'This too.'

'Achchha.'

He held the letter at an angle to the window getting what light he could to confirm his daughter's handwriting. Politically it didn't bother him that the Lahore Government had intercepted, opened and read the letter and reported its contents to Delhi. Any letter from his daughter could only strengthen the impression Government had that he was being tempted over to the League. Her husband, Hydyatullah, was now an ardent Leaguist and separatist. She had become one too and a potentially staunch supporter of the INA, therefore of Sayed. But privately Kasim was outraged to think that strangers had read the letter. He had never got used to the idea that his personal life was also government property. He folded the letter carefully so that it would fit neatly into the breast pocket of his coat.

'Did anything else of interest happen after I left Nanoora?'

'Government House in Ranpur rang confirming your appointment tomorrow, but I think really to make sure that you had left for Premanagar. Also there was a call from *The Statesman's* man in Ranpur. He asked if it was true that you were now coming back to Ranpur. I told him that if he was exercising patience the truth or otherwise of this rumour would be revealed to him in due course.'

'You are beginning to talk like Bapu. Was he content with this evasive reply?'

'He wasn't pursuing it further at the moment. He said his paper was very much anxious to obtain an exclusive interview. I said exclusive interviews had never been the Minister's policy.'

'Did he comment on your using that title?'

'No. He called you Minister himself, and was seeking favours. He said, "Has the Minister said anything about the Viceroy's broadcast announcing elections?" I said obviously the Minister has said things about it, all India is saying things and also wondering why really the Viceroy has now flown back to London. So he switched subject. He said, "What is Minister's view of the reports of the death in an air crash of Subhas Chandra Bose?"'

'What did you say?'

'I said the Minister had read these reports and assumed that they were probably correct.'

'And his response?'

'His response was that not everybody assumed this. But he did not pursue it. He was anxious to maintain cordiality and the prospects of an exclusive interview when you get back to Ranpur.'

After a while Kasim said, 'He did not mention Sayed?'

'No, Minister. He did not mention him but of course was thinking and wondering. The newspapers are still saying nothing for the moment.'

When Booby called him Minister to his face he always felt himself being flattered in a way that amounted to a rebuke.

*

Light was just beginning to come when they reached the Circuit House. Deliberately he kept his eyes lowered so that he would not inadvertently catch a glimpse of the fort. The compound and the Circuit House itself seemed smaller than he remembered them. A year – nearly fifteen months ago – after imprisonment in the fort the whole landscape and everything in it had looked immense. When the car stopped he said, 'I wish to see no one for some time. Ask Ahmed to come and collect me when it is confirmed that there is a room for me to go to and be alone. Then I shall wish to bathe and have breakfast.'

'All that is arranged, Minister. No, no, no, no, no! Wait! Wait!'

Someone had opened the door on Mehboob's side. The door shut again. In the compound Mr Kasim could see figures of

436

men, waiting, one of them with a slung rifle. The sight of the man with the rifle unnerved him. The presence of such a man suggested that they had already brought Sayed from the fort.

'Something is wrong,' he began.

'Nothing is wrong, Minister. All arrangements have been checked, double-checked. It is simply that the British always like to put on a show. Here is Ahmed now.'

Mehboob lowered the window and said, 'Your father is waiting here. Tell them to show you the room and tell them that the Minister will see no one for some time, isn't it? Also that all these people should disperse. It is like a bloody circus.'

'Ahmed –' Kasim said, but Mehboob held up a hand.

'Your father is not wanting anybody. I am waiting here with him until you tell us everything is as he wishes. Private room and no damned reception committee or all that nonsense.'

Ahmed went. Mehboob rolled the window back up and began to complain about the English weakness for making a *tamasha* of everything. 'Take all this show away from them and what is left? Look at all these people milling around in the name of security.'

But, Kasim thought, *tamasha* was precisely what the British could most easily dispense with; and presently when the shadowy figures in the compound had mostly disappeared and the man with the rifle had made himself scarce, going down towards the culvert-entrance, when the compound was quiet, unpopulated, he felt more than ever the weight of the *raj's* authority; and, feeling it, allowed himself to focus clearly on the dawn-image of the fort – on the place, rather, where the silhouette should be, some miles distant but elevated commandingly above the plain on a hill.

He did not at first identify it. And then did, and stared, fascinated by the evidence of its relatively diminutive proportions. It had originally been a Rajput fort. The Muslims had conquered it. It was they who had built the mosque and the zenana house in the inner courtyard where Kasim had spent his imprisonment. The Mahrattas had invested it. The British had acquired it. So much history in so insignificant a monument? Insignificant, that was to say, in relation to the vast stretches of the Indian plain.

Everything has meaning for you, Gaffur: the petal's fall, the change of seasons. New clothes to celebrate the Îd.

The regard of princes.

Rocks. These are not impediments. All water flows towards uneasy distances. Life also –

He had bathed and shaved. He had prayed. He had had a light breakfast. Now he had read for the planned ten minutes from the works of Gaffur. He put the book away, retained his spectacles and took his daughter's letter from the table where he had placed it ready. It was dated August 20, six days ago.

'We reached home yesterday and found your letter which of course had been opened. Guzzy suggests that we should send all our letters unsealed to save them this bother but I said why should we save them bother? If they want to pry into our private affairs let them go to whatever trouble is necessary. Tomorrow we are having a party to listen to Wavell on the radio which I expect will be the usual guff, everyone knows he is going to announce elections. Guzzy says he has no alternative but that the results will surprise him and force him to recognize the reality of the problems that divide the country. We were glad to get away from Kashmir. On vj day people excelled themselves. The place was packed with British and Americans and the drunkenness and vulgarity had to be seen to be believed. I am sorry, daddy, that we could not break off to go down to Pankot. Poor old Mahsoodi. I cried all night after getting your telegram (I hope you got mine? Your letter does not say).

'Poor Sayed has at last been allowed to answer my last letter to him but of course it tells me nothing that is necessary to hear. He writes mostly of childhood recollections. Please, daddy, write to him. He says little but I know he is hurt never to have heard from you and blames Government since this is the only explanation he can find as a dutiful and loving son much devoted to his father. He asks me to tell you to thank Ahmed for his last note. Soon I hope you will write and tell me you are back home for good in Ranpur. Then perhaps Guzzy and I can visit you and bring the children. I never liked coming to Nanoora since I knew you didn't like being there but stuck it out. Also it was bad having to get permission, even when darling mummy was so ill. Guzzy and I were much amused by the picture in the newspaper of the Governor's stonelaying ceremony in Ranpur. You looked very bored and distinguished, as Guzzy said "Like a man keeping his own counsel." I was very proud. In pictures so many people just look like hangers on. Your loving daughter.'

He refolded the letter and returned it to its envelope, opened his briefcase and put the envelope inside, then the book of Gaffur's poems, then his Astrakhan cap. From the briefcase he took the white Congress cap. In the old days he had been criticized for wearing it. It had not been worn for months. It was necessary to wear it now. He placed it on his head. The crown of thorns. It was nearly eight o'clock. At eight, promptly, Mehboob knocked and came in and stood arrested. Mehboob had never seen him wearing the cap, except presumably years ago before they were closely associated.

'It is eight o'clock, Minister,' Booby said. 'They are here.'

'And Sayed?'

'I have not seen Sayed, but they assure me he is here. He is probably still in the compound.'

'Has he breakfasted?'

'I will go and ask, Minister.'

'Please! Do not call me that. And by all means go and ask. It should not be necessary but do it now. You should think of these things. You should anticipate my questions. They have probably pulled him from his bed and brought him here without even asking him if he wants a cup of tea.'

'I will find out –'

'Yes, yes! Find out! I will see nobody until I am assured he has breakfasted. It should all have been thought of.'

Mehboob went. Kasim, after a moment, covered his face with his hands and whispered: 'Glory be to You who made Your servant go by night from the Sacred Mosque to the Farther mosque. Praise be to Allah who has never begotten a son, who has no partner in His Kingdom, who needs none to defend Him from humiliation.'

439

When Mehboob came back his pale copper-coloured face was flushed. 'I am unable to find out whether Sayed has breakfasted,' he announced.

'What has made you so angry?'

'It is impossible dealing with such people. They cannot answer even civil questions. They treat everybody like dirt.'

'Who are they?'

'Two English subalterns wearing revolvers. They are in the court-room, feet on the table and smirking and hardly bothering to reply.'

'Only these two?'

'There are also the people who were here when we arrived, a police inspector and another young Englishman who is assistant to the Divisional Commissioner. But they are only local, in charge of the general arrangements. They have nothing to do with the party coming from the fort.'

There was a knock on the door. Mehboob opened it just sufficiently to see who it was.

An English voice said, 'The party is fully present now but the senior conducting officer would appreciate a preliminary word with Mr Kasim.'

'Who is that?' Kasim called out. Mehboob opened the door wider. A young English civilian stepped in.

'Good-morning, sir. My name's Everett. I'm assistant to Mr Harding, the Divisional Commissioner. He asked me to apologize for not being here himself. I hope the arrangements have been all right, so far?'

'Thank you, Mr Everett. Perfectly satisfactory. Is Lieutenant Kasim here now?'

'Yes, sir.'

'He was not a moment ago and my secretary had difficulty in getting an answer to the question whether he had breakfasted properly.'

'Yes, I know. That was unfortunate. But I've just asked the senior conducting officer myself and he assures me your son had a good breakfast.'

'And the senior conducting officer wants to have a word with me?'

440

'Yes, if that's all right –', Everett broke off because Ahmed tapped at the open door and now came in–, 'and if it might be in private.'

'I'll let you know. I'll send word.'

Everett went out, closing the door.

'Have you seen your brother, Ahmed?'

'No, but I've seen the conducting officer. I thought I'd better warn you. It's Merrick.'

'Merrick?'

'The ex-police officer in the Manners case, the one Pandit Baba's been pestering you about. I didn't know Merrick had anything to do with the INA, but he was in the army in intelligence when we met him in Mirat. Actually I saw him again in Bombay about three weeks ago. He said he was working in Delhi.'

'Ah, yes. That Merrick. The one Dmitri told me was badly wounded. You never told me you saw him again so recently.'

'I haven't seen much of you since getting back. And the case didn't seem to interest you.'

'No,' Kasim said. 'But perhaps it will. He knows you know him in connection with that old case?'

'Yes.'

'So he will assume that by now I know too. In fact he would probably assume that you would be here with me to meet your brother, which means that he does not in the least mind my knowing who he is. But he must know, mustn't he, Booby, that he is on the List?'

'It is clear, Minister. He hopes to ingratiate himself somehow. You could always say you will meet nobody except Sayed.'

'What is his rank, Ahmed?'

'Major, I think.'

'Since you know him it would be a good idea if you went now and brought him along personally. Go with Ahmed, Booby. I shan't want you again until all this is over. Meanwhile open and read the letter from Bapu so that we can discuss it later. Ahmed – give me one minute, please, before you bring Major Merrick.'

When they had gone Kasim went to the single window, which overlooked the inner courtyard. A policeman with a

441

rifle was posted nearby facing towards him. There were bars but no glass in the window frame. Kasim closed the inner shutters. The only light in the room now came from the single naked bulb in the centre and from the high fanlight on the wall that faced the front compound. The furniture was sparse: a string charpoy with a mattress, two wooden armchairs and two smaller chairs, a table. He made a move to sit at the chair behind the table but then decided to remain standing.

*

'Major Merrick? Please come in.'

Ahmed, who had opened the door and stood aside without entering, let Merrick through and then closed it. Kasim offered his hand and felt a twinge of pity for a man with such a badly disfigured face and such an obviously useless left arm, clamped to his body with the cap tucked under it at elbow level and a briefcase suspended from the gloved fingers of an artificial hand. The man said, 'Actually Lieutenant-Colonel, since I and your younger son last met, Mr Kasim.'

The grip of the right hand was strong, like the voice. Kasim indicated a seat and sat down himself. He now noted the pip and crown on each shoulder tab, the regimental name and the ribbon of the DSO. He watched while Merrick dealt with his cap by removing it from under the left arm, placing it on the table, and with his briefcase by removing it from the artificial hand and placing it on the table too, next to the hat. He glanced at the inner side of his right wrist, checking the time.

'I'm sorry about the few minutes delay, but when we arrived your elder son asked for a few minutes alone before he came in. So I sent the others along and waited near the car. But I assure you his reason was not because he felt unwell as a result of not having had an adequate breakfast –' Merrick smiled. The effect was strange, lopsided. He continued – 'Nor as a result of inadequate sleep. We reached the fort early enough yesterday evening to let him rest up after the journey from Delhi. The journey itself was not very taxing. We flew to Ranagunj and came on by road. In fact I believe you'll be much tireder than he because I gather you travelled down overnight and only got here an hour or so ago. Incidentally, Mr Everett

442

tells me your secretary may have been upset by the two young officers' apparently unhelpful attitude over the question of what kind of breakfast your son had. The explanation is that they had no idea what he had, since I breakfasted with him alone. They are only temporary escorts. They reported to me at Ranagunj in exchange for two other officers who came with me on the plane. They have no information about any of us. All they know is that the Indian officer is in custody.'

'The question of Sayed's breakfast has already been satisfactorily answered, Colonel Merrick. So far as I'm concerned it is a closed subject. Incidentally, my younger son Ahmed had no idea you were in any way connected with Sayed. Does Sayed know that you know his brother?'

'The one is a social acquaintance. The other is not. So the answer is, no.'

'Please tell me what is the purpose of this preliminary private word?'

'The purpose is to tell you as much as possible about the charges which Lieutenant Sayed Kasim will probably have to face.'

Kasim hoped that he betrayed no surprise. But he was surprised. He said: 'I have not asked for this. I'm not sure that I wish to be told anything about such matters. My son must himself have a good idea what charges there may be. What can you tell me that he cannot?'

Merrick said, 'Naturally, Mr Kasim, it's entirely up to you whether we have a preliminary word. It wasn't my own department's idea, but Government seemed to think it fair.'

'Fair?'

'The charges and evidence in these cases aren't fully prepared yet by any means. But Government feels that your son would be much more at ease if he doesn't have to tell you everything himself.' Merrick paused. 'It could after all be a bit painful for him.'

'Painful?'

Merrick kept him waiting for a reply. He seemed utterly composed and in command. 'He has never struck me as being among those who are unrepentantly proud of the situation they find themselves in.'

For the first time Kasim was unable to keep his eyes

unwaveringly on the man. He glanced down and carefully covered his right hand with his left to control the familiar tremor before it began.

'Very well,' he said. 'Tell me what you wish. But as briefly as possible.'

'A charge of waging war against the King-Emperor is of course going to be the almost unavoidable common charge to be faced in these cases and in your son's case the evidence is incontrovertible since he was captured fighting in one of the INA units that accompanied the Japanese when they tried to invade India in 1944 and got as far as Manipur and Kohima. The unit he commanded surrendered voluntarily and seemed to have been abandoned in an untenable position by the Japanese, without access to any supplies or lines of communication. I'm afraid one often found that. Voluntary surrender or no, however, he was in arms, waging war.'

'You were in that theatre of war yourself, Colonel?'

'I was on the staff of one of the divisions that were brought up to mount the counter-attack. As an intelligence officer the INA became my special concern.'

'Were you present when Sayed was brought in?'

'No, I was out of the line by then.'

'Wounded you mean, thus?' Kasim indicated the arm.

'Yes. Thus.'

'By INA action?'

'There were INA about. Japanese as well. Why do you ask?'

'The reason is obvious, surely? A man wounded as badly as you could be forgiven for accepting a job that gave him an opportunity to redress the balance.'

'One does the job one is given. But I take your point. The INA were involved in the incident but I was wounded entirely by my own fault.'

'How was it your own fault?'

'I was trying to stop a fellow officer acting thoughtlessly.' Merrick paused. 'You asked me to be brief –'

'I know, but I should like to hear about this other matter. It is all relevant to my rather sparse knowledge of the INA.'

'Very briefly, then. I'd gone forward to collect an INA prisoner. At that time they were rather a rare species. The sepoys of the Indian Army tended to shoot them out of hand.

444

This prisoner was originally from the Muzzafirabad Guides. The officer who was on the same divisional staff as myself was also Muzzafirabad Guides. He insisted on going with me and when the man said there were two other INA ex-Muzzy Guides soldiers hiding in the jungle near by waiting to give themselves up the officer suggested we went to collect them. I said we shouldn't, but the next thing I knew was he'd taken our jeep, and the prisoner, and gone forward to do just that. I borrowed another jeep and went after them. When I found them the jeep was under fire and on fire. The prisoner had decamped, presumably to rejoin the enemy, and the officer was burning to death. I pulled him and the driver out but it was too late to save the officer.'

'Was he a friend of yours?'

'We knew one another pretty well. At least since I acted as his best man. At his wedding in Mirat. I expect Ahmed will have told you about the wedding. Ahmed, or Count Bronowsky.'

'The wedding. Ah, yes.'

'But I think it fair to say I went after the officer only to secure the prisoner, who was my responsibility. The result was hardly the prisoner's fault, nor was it really the officer's. I needn't have followed. He was one of those men with the not uncommon idea that any sepoy who'd been in the regiment would only have to come face to face with one of the officers of that regiment to throw his gun down and return contrite to the fold. I took the less romantic view that guns only got thrown down when the alternative was hunger and no other escape-route.'

'As in Sayed's case?'

'I don't think you'll find he pretends otherwise. And being an officer he was responsible for the lives of the men in what remained of his unit.'

'You've interrogated Sayed often?'

'Since joining the department several months ago I have talked to him quite frequently, yes.'

'Forgive these questions. An old lawyer's habit. Please go on. He was captured originally by the Japanese in Kuala Lumpur in nineteen-forty-two when the Japanese defeated the British Army there.'

'The British Army and the Indian Army. Yes. Of course you know he asserts he didn't join the INA until after August nineteen forty-two when he heard of the arrests in India after the Congress Quit India resolution – arrests which included your own. He told you this in his first letter home, after we'd recaptured him. I'm afraid copies of all his letters in and out have had to be made.'

'Don't apologize, Colonel. I am used to that sort of thing. In the same letter to my late wife he apologized for having failed in the march on Delhi.'

'It was probably the same letter. I remember the phrase from my study of his file.'

'Tell me, Colonel Merrick. How does this apology for having failed in the march on Delhi balance with your view that he is not among those unrepentantly proud of the situation he finds himself in? Which situation do you mean? His situation as a Lieutenant of the Ranpur Regiment, now your prisoner awaiting trial for waging war against the King, or his situation as a Major in the INA who failed in his march on Delhi to free India from the British but lives to tell the tale?'

'It's more than a year since he wrote that letter.'

'You mean he has had second thoughts?'

'Frankly, Mr Kasim, I should say he had had a great number of thoughts. For the past year he hasn't had much to occupy his mind except the single subject of why he decided to switch his allegiance.'

'And wage war against the King. Yes.' Kasim waited, then said, 'What other charges?'

'Incitement? Abetment? Bringing aid and comfort to the enemy? As I said, charges aren't framed. But your son has admitted to helping to recruit other Indian POWs into the INA and also to helping devise propaganda about the INA and broadcasting on one occasion to India, incognito.'

'Is there any more serious factor that may have to be considered?'

'More serious factor, Mr Kasim?'

'One hears gossip, tales, possibly exaggerated, or so one hopes, that recruitment was not always voluntary; that in a few cases certain methods were used to persuade sepoy prisoners-of-war to join.'

'You mean brutal methods?'

'Yes, I mean that.'

'And what you want to know is whether this is a factor that may have to be considered in your son's case and might lead to a charge that he used such methods himself?'

'Yes.'

After some moments Merrick glanced at the table. The one good eyebrow contracted slightly. Kasim wondered whether the full ramifications of the question of brutality were lost on him. They could not be if his reputation from the time of the Bibighar was deserved. But perhaps that reputation was simply the result of rumour too.

'A factor that may have to be considered?' Merrick repeated to himself. He looked at Kasim again. 'The only answer I can give you, Mr Kasim, is that I don't know. I can assure you it hasn't arisen yet but it would be quite unrealistic of me to assure you that it can't arise.'

'You mean there are indications that such accusations may be made against Sayed?'

'On the contrary. A lot of evidence has been collected of cases of torture and brutal behaviour and several officers and NCOs have been named, but your son's name has never been among them. In fact the men who surrendered with him have invariably spoken of him with great respect, particularly in regard to his care for their welfare and for the way he stood up to Japanese officers when this was necessary. No, my point is that the men we have access to, those already recaptured, represent only a percentage of the eventual sources of evidence. There are all those still in Malaya for instance. I can't vouch for what some of them may or may not say about your son's conduct once we've got hold of them. It was a very large army.' He hesitated, then added, 'I'm exceeding my brief expressing a personal opinion, but I shall express it none the less since you seem concerned. I should be very surprised if at any time between now and the completion of the collection of all the evidence in all the cases your son is implicated in any charges other than those I've mentioned.'

'Yes. I see. Thank you. And this is all you have to tell me?'

'I think so. I hope it's helped you in a general way.'

'Yes.' He made a snap decision. 'Tell me, Colonel Merrick – are you still troubled as I understood from Ahmed you were – I mean troubled by incidents devised to remind you that your conduct as Superintendent of Police in Mayapore – I should say suspected conduct – had made you unpopular in certain quarters and wasn't going to be forgotten?'

Merrick smiled. A cheerful smile, Kasim thought.

'Not until recently.'

'Another stone?'

Merrick reached for his briefcase and began to manipulate the artificial hand back round the handle while he continued speaking. 'No, there's only been the one stone. Chucking stones at British officers *is* rather a hazardous operation. They've reverted to the subtle approach. The bicycle again.'

'Bicycle?'

'A bicycle. Left on my verandah. Rusty and useless, naturally.'

'A rusty bicycle left on your verandah, Colonel Merrick? What purpose does this serve?'

'It's obviously a symbol of the bicycle I'm supposed to have planted outside the house of one of the boys who assaulted Miss Manners. Miss Manners's bicycle.' He stood up. So, after a moment, did Kasim. 'The bicycle's rather a good touch. They began after I'd left Mayapore just by chalking inauspicious signs outside the door of my bungalow. Then one day there was this rusty old bicycle outside my quarters. That was in Mirat, just before someone chucked the stone. The incidents have a twofold purpose, of course – to let me know it's known where I'm currently living and working – which they do – and to undermine me psychologically – which they don't.'

'When and where was this new incident, this second bicycle?'

'According to my cook, about a week ago in Delhi. I've been down in Ceylon and Rangoon and got back only just in time to accompany your son here. My cook said he found it leaning against the verandah rail one morning. He got the sweeper to take it to the back of the compound because there was a bad smell which he traced to the saddle-bag. He wouldn't touch it himself after that because the smell was that of a putrid pork chop. Since he's a Muslim I've had some difficulty in persuading him to stay. He's a very good cook. He cooks fresh pork chops for me quite happily. Just seems to draw the line at putrid ones in the saddle-bags of rusty bikes.'

Kasim averted his face to disguise his own revulsion.

'You should report such things to the police.'

'I always do. It doesn't bother me personally but then whoever is responsible for this kind of childish persecution isn't really in the least concerned either about me or about what are no doubt still called the innocent victims of the Bibighar. The Bibighar affair was used as an excuse to stir up trouble generally and it rather looks to me as if it's going to be given another innings in conjunction with the INA cases because it's been discovered I'm connected with them.'

'Given another innings by whom, Colonel Merrick?'

'By whoever prefers anarchy to law and order. Has Count Bronowsky never talked to you while you've been living in Nanoora, about the power exercised in India by uncommitted and irresponsible forces? He was very eloquent about it on the first occasion I met him.'

'Count Bronowsky and I don't have an intimate relationship, in spite of my younger son's connection with him. He and I are politically opposed. He is dedicated to the continuing autocratic authority of the Nawab. I am dedicated to the diminution and final extinction of the autocratic authority of *all* the Indian princes. My respect for Count Bronowsky has become quite strong since I've lived under restriction at the Nawab's court, but we are still political opponents and seldom exchange views.'

'I suppose you and I are potentially opponents too, Mr Kasim.'

'You and I?'

'I and your party. Surely I'm on the list?'

'What list, Colonel Merrick?'

'The list of officials whose conduct in nineteen forty-two may be inquired into. I'm told it looks as if I'm likely to be on it.'

'Told by whom?'

'The CID officer I reported the new incident to. Not that it

449

surprised me. The fact that the subject has come up at a political level is sufficient warning. Anyway, if I'm not on it yet I imagine from what I'm told that my old friend Pandit Baba of Mayapore won't be happy until I am. Of course it's he who's responsible for the childish persecution, but there's never been any clear evidence to connect him with it. He's not a very connectable man. You can't pin him down with any certainty even as a member of the militant wing of the Hindu Mahasabah. But he has a genius for inspiring young men to sacrifice themselves in whatever cause he's currently taken up. I admired him rather. In Mayapore whenever we caught one of his disciples as they called themselves breaking the law they always swore the only thing they discussed with the Pandit was the Bhagavad Gita and went willingly to prison. What I admired was his power to inspire such loyalty. In those days his activities were more tiresome than dangerous but I should say he's capable of graduating to better things. Assassination, for instance. You know the man I mean, Mr Kasim?'

Kasim smiled.

'I have never met him. I think now I must see Sayed. You are due to take him back to the fort when?'

'When your meeting is finished.'

'And when do you take him back to Delhi?'

'This evening.'

'By road to Ranagunj and then by aeroplane?'

'Yes. I must be in Delhi tomorrow. I have to fly back to Kandy and from there probably to Singapore.'

'Then I will say good-bye to you now, Colonel Merrick.' Again he made a snap decision. 'I don't think we shall ever be opposed in the sense you mean. Not you and I personally. I am not interested in past quarrels, only in solving present and future problems. It is the only way any of us will ever make progress.'

'Quite. Quite.'

For the first time Merrick looked uncertain of himself, disappointed, if the unscarred side of his face was anything to go by. Kasim thought: He's proud to be on the list, in which case what people said about his conduct in Mayapore is probably true.

The man reached for his cap. Kasim did not watch him go through the awkward motions of tucking it under his left arm.

'I'll bring Sayed now,' Merrick said. He hesitated then went towards the door.

'No, please do not bring him. I wish our meeting to be completely in private and in any case it would offend me to see him physically in the custody of anyone. And there is another thing –'

He went over to the window. 'This room is very hot and dark. It is like a cell. I closed these shutters because there is a guard outside whose presence disturbs me. I know that guards are necessary – if only as a formality since Sayed could hardly effect a credible escape in the middle of this desert.' He opened the shutters and breathed deeply. The guard was still there, just out of earshot. 'So I apologize for any inconvenience but I think I should prefer to see Sayed in the court-room. At least it will be larger and airier and they can post as many men outside as they wish. That should take only a few minutes to arrange, shouldn't it? Just a question of clearing the other people out. Perhaps you'd be so kind as to send someone to let me know when everything is ready.'

'I'll come myself, Mr Kasim.'

'That is kind of you.'

III

He realized how little he could have seen of the Circuit House on that previous visit fifteen months ago. He did not recognize the corridor that Merrick now led him along. They stopped at a door. Merrick opened it on to a small room.

'This isn't the court-room,' Kasim said. 'It's the magistrate's room.'

'It's the best way in.'

'No! The worst! How can I enter the court-room through the judge's door? Where have you put Sayed? In the dock?'

'I can bring him here if that's what you'd prefer.'

'I wish no one to *bring* him anywhere.' He felt ill. He turned back into the corridor whose series of grimy windows gave on

451

to the verandah of the inner courtyard. The place stank of unresolved cases, of the acrid odour of legal millstones grinding fine and slow between sessions; and of his youth, pleading interminable cases in court-houses such as this. After all, interviewing Sayed in the court-room would be a mistake. It would be like putting him on trial. But then, for Kasim, what was about to follow *was* Sayed's trial.

'Mr Kasim, are you all right?'

'I am perfectly all right. It is just that −'

He broke off. There was a third man whom Merrick was urging forward from the open doorway; a tall man, taller than himself, broad-boned, well-fleshed, dressed like an active-service officer in dark green cotton uniform; pale brown skin, dark-browed, brown-eyed. Between the nostrils and the lip a moustache grew, close-cropped in the British style. The hair was cropped too, but not too close. A fine-looking man. Only the eyes betrayed a weakness: the weakness that accompanied an uncertainty about the warmth of his reception.

But Sayed did not wait to find out what kind of reception he would get. Silently, effortlessly, in one flowing movement he knelt at Kasim's feet, placed his hands on Kasim's shoes, lowered his head to his hands and then raised it, at the same time removing his hands. As he rose Kasim instinctively performed his own task, putting his arms round him. So, for a moment, they remained.

'Come, let us go through,' Kasim said, and released his son. Merrick was walking down the corridor, his back to them; but he had been a witness. Kasim led the way through the magistrate's room, out on to the daïs in the court-room and down into the well of the court. He stopped by one of the pleaders' tables; that table at which Sayed must have been sitting. There were an empty coffee cup and a used cigarette tray. The smell of tobacco smoke hung in the air. He still drank too, probably, like Ahmed, but with at least the excuse that it was a habit acquired in army messes, just to prove equal capacity with British officers. But the smoking was new and despite himself Kasim found the dirty ashtray repugnant. He said nothing, but Sayed, also without a word, removed it, took it across to the other table.

452

'Please, there is no need. If smoking has become necessary to you, smoke by all means. It doesn't bother me.'

But Sayed left the ashtray where he had put it and came back, stood; the weakness was still discernible, the uncertainty was still there, in the eyes. Kasim sat. From this angle his elder son looked even taller and broader. Both Ahmed and Sayed dwarfed him but Sayed would make even Ahmed look slenderly built. The periods of privation must have been of short duration, unless the British had been feeding him up.

'Come, sit.'

Sayed did so.

'Have you seen Ahmed yet?'

'Not yet, father. But Ronald told me he's here.'

'Ronald?'

'Ronald Merrick. The chap you've been talking to. He said he'd make sure Ahmed and I had a word afterwards. He's quite a good fellow really. Very decent to me.'

The voice was strong too, the accent clipped, more clipped than Kasim remembered from their last meeting, certainly more clipped than it had been after Sayed had passed out of the Indian military academy when Kasim had told him, 'You sound like a British officer.' They had both laughed. He could have stopped Sayed choosing the army as a career. He had been criticized for not stopping him. It hadn't always been easy for him to explain why he had a son who held the King-Emperor's Commission. It couldn't always have been easy for Sayed when young Englishmen, fellow members of the mess, learnt who his father was. But Sayed had never complained and when Kasim became Chief Minister in Ranpur any embarrassment Sayed might have felt vanished. He remembered Sayed saying, 'You are a Minister. I am an officer. We are both necessary.' He had meant necessary to India and Kasim had been moved.

'How are you treated then? You look well. Put on an inch or two. Like Ahmed. As you see, I have taken off. Who is commandant at the fort nowadays? Still Major Tippet?'

'I don't know, father. I was only there overnight. You were there too?'

'Oh yes. Better than the Kandipat although boring after a bit. They gave me a room in the old Zenana House. I wonder whether my bed of onions is still flourishing? It was in a courtyard a few feet from the steps to the Zenana. I watered them mostly with the water from my shaving mug. So this is how they tasted. Of soap. What one will do to keep oneself occupied. But onions are good for warding off colds. So your mother always said.'

The muscular geography of his son's face momentarily revealed itself: an intricate map. The eyes hardened. Kasim folded his hands on the table. He said, 'When I was released to go to Mirat they brought me here first of all to meet Ahmed. Now that I'm going back home it seemed a convenient place to tell them to bring you. If I had come to Delhi the world and his wife would have been watching. Anyway, it gives you an outing. What did they tell you. Anything?'

'First they just told me to get ready for a trip. But then Ronnie Merrick got back from Rangoon and put me in the picture. He said Government had given permission for us to meet and that he was coming with me.'

'The impression was that I had petitioned Government and that Government had decided to be magnanimous?'

'Yes.'

'It is not entirely accurate.'

'Oh, I didn't swallow it whole. I know how devious they can be.'

'In this case devious to what end?'

Kasim waited. Sayed said nothing.

'Come. Don't hold back. Just because I am your father.'

Sayed looked down at the table. 'They know you've never written to me. They think this shows you disapprove of what I've done.' He glanced up. 'It would be very useful to them to have someone like you on their side. A member of Congress, ex-Chief Minister. And a Muslim. Someone to denounce us all as traitors. They realize such people will be in short supply.'

'Quite so. Both major parties will stand behind the INA. The true nature and extent of INA came as a surprise to many of us. But people who are locked up a long time have a lot of surprises in store when they mingle freely again and find out what has been going on. So among us at Simla it was generally agreed that INA would be supported.'

'Generally, not unanimously?'

'Quite clearly all parties will combine to organize the defence if these cases ever come to trial. Whether they will do so is up to the Viceroy and the Commander-in-Chief. It will be interesting to see how they solve the problem of who should be tried and who should not. From a legal point of view the entire matter is without precedent. Administratively it is farcical. Some kind of legal strategy will have to be evolved to uphold the spirit if not the letter of the law. But I am sure the British will find a way. They have considerable experience of how to deal pragmatically with situations which pose profound questions. They cannot just say, You have sinned, go home and repent, without running the risk of their entire Indian Army resigning *en masse* by way of protest and going home also. On the other hand they cannot court-martial every INA soldier because it would take several years to do so. On top of that, it is not in them to find a solution such as the Germans might have found. Or the Japanese. It is not in them to line you all up in a concentration camp and shoot you out of hand. It is not in them politically and it is not in them emotionally. What can they do? The answer is fairly clear. They must establish a scale of priorities. In such a scale every King's Commissioned Officer who joined INA will be at the top. He cannot hope to escape being cashiered at the very least. Your military career is finished, Sayed. You must make up your mind to that. Even if the British left India tomorrow it would be finished. Because whatever we politicians say and however stoutly we defend you, the loyal Indian members of the Indian Army will not defend you. Why should they? It is against their interests. They are on the winning side. Whatever military plums there are to pick when we are independent they will claim properly as theirs. Why should they share them with Subhas Chandra Bose's defeated people? Of course it would be different if the British had lost the war. Then you'd be in clover. But they've won it. Your first error, a very pardonable one, was perhaps to have assumed in nineteen forty-two they'd already lost it. Isn't this so, Sayed? Isn't it this more than anything else that persuaded you to join INA? Isn't it this more than the fact that you heard I and most other

Congressmen had been imprisoned and that the whole country was in turmoil that decided you?'

'No, father. It was entirely because you were arrested along with everybody else and that the whole of India was rising and telling the British to quit.'

'Who told you I was arrested?'

'Shah Nawaz Khan. General Shah Nawaz Khan. Originally a captain in the Punjab Regiment. But so far as I'm concerned, *General*. He came up to Kuala Lumpur in nineteen forty-two as commander of all Indian prisoners-of-war parties. I knew him slightly. He was a very good officer. He stopped the Japanese doing all sorts of things to us.'

'But he was INA?'

'He had joined, yes, but only to stop the Japs exploiting Indian prisoners and to wreck the INA from inside if necessary. I am talking of first INA, under Mohan Singh. But you must know all this.'

'No, tell me.'

'Mohan Singh was also Punjab Regiment. Shah Nawaz said he thought him a very average officer. Mohan Singh was captured somewhere like Alor Star. People say he had a bad time with his British officers and that they left him to face the Japanese alone. He started organizing the prisoners. When the British surrendered at Singapore all the Indian officers were separated from the British and made to assemble with all the Indian troops at Farrer Park and handed over by the representative of the British Government, to an intelligence officer called Fujiwara and given orders to obey the Japanese. Then Fujiwara handed them over to Mohan Singh. Fujiwara said Mohan Singh was their GOC and had power of life and death over them. I was not in Singapore then. But this is what I was told.'

'Who are you saying gave the prisoners orders to obey the Japanese?'

'The British Government representative.'

'All prisoners of course must obey the lawful orders of their captors. There is nothing much to be made of that. More interesting is the order for the separation of British King's Commissioned Officers from Indian King's Commissioned Officers. By whose order was this separation?'

456

'The Japanese, presumably. But I never heard any protests from the British. They were too interested in saving their own skins. As at Kuala Lumpur. "Hold this position, Kasim old chap," Colonel Barker said. So I held it while the rest of the battalion and all the British officers disappeared. I held it for four days. Nothing happened for three of them. In three days Colonel Barker and the others got down to Johore. He got one of the last ships out of Singapore or Malacca, I don't know which. All I know is that on the fourth day the Japs came and that on the fifth we couldn't hold them off any longer. We had nothing. Nothing to eat. No ammunition. At the time I said, Well, it is war. Somebody has to carry the can. Since then I thought there was another explanation. Here in India, father, the army looks very sound, very pukka, very good form and very secure, very gentlemanly. In Burma and Malaya you realized a lot of it was eyewash. They never wanted us. They never trusted us.'

He took his father's hand, leaning forward, lowering his voice. 'But I have seen senior British officers in Singapore and in Rangoon bowing to Japanese sentries. And I have seen senior British officers slapped and kicked for not bowing, and *then* bowing.' He leant back. 'So much for the *raj*. They too can be made to act like peons. I shall never forget.'

Hand free, Kasim held it out, palm towards Sayed and shut his eyes. 'Please. Forget all this. I have heard all this sort of thing before. It is of no importance. It will not help you in any way whatsoever. It's your conduct that is in question not the conduct or misconduct of this British officer or that British officer. Let us speak no more of disparities between British officers and Indian officers. If you try to do this in court-martial prosecuting counsel will eat you alive and spit you out as a silly boy with a grudge.'

'I wanted you to know –'

'I know. I *do* know. But when you are court-martialled you will be well advised to give quite a different picture and pretend it has never entered your head that your commanding officer treated his white officers in one way and his Indian subaltern in another. If necessary praise him. Adopt a soldierly attitude to this matter. Do not antagonize the court. It will be a military court. Even if one of its members is an

Indian officer – which is almost bound to be so to preserve the idea of impartiality – do not be tempted to raise the question of this disparity. Secretly he might agree with you but it will embarrass him and put him further against you. He will be already against you because he will be thinking: Here is this young fellow who is only a lieutenant but calling himself major and also being called a hero by the politicians and the people and here am I, still a captain after twenty years of loyal service to the *raj*.'

He hesitated, then said, 'What is wrong, Sayed?'

Sayed's eyes had become tearful. He bent his head. He said, 'I'm sorry, father. I prepared myself to find that you weren't going to help me. I was wrong. I'm ashamed to have thought it. All this is very good. Very helpful.'

Kasim felt himself begin to tremble. He said, 'Clearly I must help you. I'm not only your father but a man who happens to know something about the law and the way the law works. You are to clear your mind of every consideration except that of your defence. Neither of us can wish to see you sent to rigorous imprisonment or transportation for life. That you will be cashiered and finished for ever with the army is sufficient punishment.'

'Finished for ever?'

'For ever. It is my opinion. I have told you why. So. As I say. Clear your mind. Shah Nawaz Khan told you in Kuala Lumpur that Congress Party leaders in India had been arrested and that I was among them and that the country was rising against the British. This led to your decision to join INA. What you call first INA. Why did it? Let me suggest why. Naturally you were angry that your father had been put in prison simply because he was a leading member of Congress. But then you calmed down. You sat back and considered the situation. The British had been defeated in France. They had been defeated in Burma and Malaya. The Japanese held the Chindwin. Beyond the Chindwin lay India. In India the population appeared to have been driven to desperation and had risen against the *raj*. Although your father was a politician you yourself were politically uneducated. Like Ahmed you have never bothered much about such matters. You did not fully understand why Congress passed a resolution calling on the British to quit but broadly you understood it was because in a war for freedom India should also be free. Also you understood that everyone felt that so long as the British remained in Delhi the Japanese were bound to attack your country. Now. The Japanese were pretending to be friendly towards the Indians as fellow-Asians, but you did not trust them. If they invaded India and as seemed likely again defeated the British the very clear danger was that far from gaining the independence which the British themselves had promised, India would again become subject to a foreign government, this time a Japanese government. A Japanese *raj*. And what could you do about that, sitting in Kuala Lumpur as their prisoners-of-war?'

'What indeed?'

'It was a terrible problem. On the one hand you felt you could not just sit in Kuala Lumpur waiting to be told that Hirohito was now the titular ruler of Hindustan. On the other hand not to sit around would mean appearing to kowtow to the Japanese and disregarding your oath to the King-Emperor. To escape from prison-camp was one thing – virtually impossible though that was in the Far East. To secure your release by throwing in your lot with an organization which the Japanese had helped to bring into being was another. Moreover, should the INA ever march with the Japanese into India, march with whatsoever patriotic intention, there would be the inevitable armed confrontation with those of your own countrymen who were still serving under the British flag.

'How could these problems be resolved? The answer was they could *not* be resolved. You had to choose. And you could not see into the future. You had no crystal ball. You had to weigh one possibility against another possibility and make a decision. And then one day you looked around and perhaps remembered some of the things the Japanese had done. And you remembered how this Shah Nawaz Khan had stopped them doing such things in this place or that place. And you thought of the Japanese doing or trying to do these things in India and how it was necessary to stop them doing them.

'Then for the first time you saw clearly what the problem was, that it was a question of choosing between your own integrity and your country's integrity. Only an officer who was a national of a country already under foreign rule could ever face this dilemma. But this is an explanation, Sayed, not an excuse. Legally it isn't even a mitigating circumstance, so put that out of your mind. Go back to Kuala Lumpur and your decision to join Shah Nawaz Khan. You asked to see him and told him you'd made your mind up to join INA?'

'Not quite like that. And he made a point of never persuading anybody against their own judgment. I didn't decide until the end of September. He'd gone back to Singapore then. While he was in KL things improved for us but after he'd gone there were several incidents.'

'What kind of incidents?'

'For example. Before Shah Nawaz came to KL the Japanese were forcing our jawans to learn Japanese foot drill, things like that. He stopped them. He told me it was what the English prisoners in Rangoon were having to do and that it showed the Japanese intended to make us all puppets if they could. When he had gone it started again. I protested, but it made no difference. One sepoy who refused became very ill. The Japanese must have beaten him up pretty badly.'

'The sepoy's name?'

'I don't remember. It was happening too often.'

'More than one sepoy, then.'

'Yes, more than one.'

'And you took a risk, protesting?'

'That didn't matter.'

'You were in some kind of position of authority in this camp?'

'Only a section of the camp. And as a prisoner oneself one's power was limited. I was responsible for this section, though.'

'But you were only a lieutenant.'

Sayed glanced up.

'Shah Nawaz and Mohan Singh were only captains. How many Indian majors, colonels and brigadiers do you know of, father? Do you personally know any Indian generals? The British have always been careful to see that no Indian officer rises high enough to be in a position of much authority.'

'Again I must warn you not to say such things at your court-martial. Please try to concentrate. What steps did you take at the end of September when you came to the decision to join INA?'

'I spoke to two INA officers who visited the camp.'

'Officers visiting for recruitment purposes?'

'Only partly. Mainly to make sure for Shah Nawaz Khan that we were not being exploited. I told them about the sepoy who had been hurt. They got permission to take him to their house. They gave him good food and medical attention.'

'But you don't remember his name?'

'Perhaps it was a name like Laksham. He was a non-combatant. A sweeper, I think. I'm not sure.'

'I ask because if this man has survived his testimony might be useful to you.'

'I understand that, father. I don't know whether he survived.'

'Well, go on. You told these two INA officers that you'd thought about it very hard and had decided to join the INA.'

'Yes.'

'They were pleased of course.'

'Yes, but they advised caution and to say nothing to the Japanese. They promised to speak to Shah Nawaz Khan and Mohan Singh in Singapore.'

'Why this caution?'

'Things were very difficult just then. The INA faced a crisis. Mohan Singh was not strong enough. Many officers were afraid he would let the Japanese use the INA for their own purposes. Also there were many different opinions among INA officers about legality and such-like. They told me that at one time an INA party had even been sent to infiltrate across the Chindwin and contact Congress in India.'

'Seeking Indian political approval of the INA?'

'Yes.'

'I did not know this. This is new to me. What happened to the infiltrating party?'

'It failed. But one of them deserted and got through to the British and presumably told them everything that was going on. Meanwhile you were all being locked up so there was no one left to contact even if another party had been sent.'

'Good. Good. So you were all still in the dark and had no crystal ball. It supports the argument I am outlining. And here there is an attempt to act constitutionally in some way. Democratically. Patriotically certainly. What INA were pondering then is the question what is the will of the people of India in this matter? Do they want an INA? And now getting no answer and realizing that it will not be possible now to get an answer. Go on.'

'The two officers said I would be a useful officer in a properly constituted free Indian Army. They said they'd have a word with Shah Nawaz Khan and Mohan Singh but that I should be patient meanwhile and say nothing. They said Shah Nawaz had had a very disagreeable experience down in Singapore opening a new officers' training school and then having to close it almost at once because the Japanese told Mohan Singh it couldn't be tolerated or something like that. The Japs wanted complete control. In their hearts some of their officers despised us and Mohan Singh was unable to resist them effectively.'

'So you continued a prisoner?'

'Yes.'

'Taking care of your men. Good. Did you ever discuss these matters with them?'

'Sometimes I talked to the NCOs so that they could tell the sepoys and give them some hope for the future, poor fellows.'

'Then what happened?'

'Then I became quite unwell for a time.'

'Why was this?'

'A Japanese officer humiliated me in front of the jawans.'

'Tell me about this humiliation.'

'He assembled all my men and stood me in front of them. He said Lieutenant Kasim would now have personal lessons in Japanese drill and words of command so that he in turn could teach these lessons himself.'

'So you had these lessons. In front of your own men?'

'No, I refused.'

'You said you were humiliated. If you refused what humiliation existed?'

'The humiliation existed because of what he said in front of everybody after I'd refused.'

'What did he say?'

'He said, "Here is a Lieutenant called Kasim. The British

have put his father in prison. What sort of man is this who so loves the British that he will not take up arms with us against them?" Then he spat between my feet. Then he slapped my face and then I was taken away and beaten up.'

'This man's name?'

'Hakinawa.'

'Of course you will say nothing of this at your court-martial. You understand this? Only with the greatest reluctance should you answer questions about it if counsel happens to press for information of this kind. Then only should you give a hint and then leave it to him whether to go on pressing. However much he presses and however much you are inclined to speak out, you will discover your answers are of no importance to your defence. You understand? Try to let prosecuting counsel alone stand convicted of raising this kind of emotional subject in evidence. Only if the prosecution can be seen and heard to squeeze it out of you must you mention such a thing.' Kasim paused. 'Of course a clever defence counsel, knowing of this, might manipulate the prosecution into the mistake of pressing such a point. Now, go on. You were beaten up. What afterwards was the attitude towards you of your men, who had seen what you call this humiliation?'

'I don't know. I was separated from them.'

'How separated?'

'First I was put in solitary confinement for a week or two. Then I was sent to another camp.'

'How were you treated there?'

'All right, I suppose.'

'All right, merely, or very well? Well, which? Come, keep alert, do not think of me as your father but as your prosecutor. How were you treated? All right or very well? Let me suggest you were treated very well. Let me put it to you that a Japanese officer apologized to you and spoke of Hakinawa with contempt, also that perhaps he hinted you might find yourself back with Hakinawa unless you showed yourself more co-operative. Which month was this, by the way. October? November?'

'November, I suppose.'

'November, nineteen forty-two?'

'Yes.'

'In November, nineteen forty-two, then, you began to be treated well. Thank you, Lieutenant Kasim.'

Sayed stared at him.

Kasim said, 'You see? You see the dangers of this line of evidence and argument? At this point prosecuting counsel sits down. He asks no more questions so you cannot answer them. The court looks at you and thinks perhaps it sees a man who wanted no more beating up. Every other consideration goes by the board, swept off by this one emotional consideration. The court looks at you and thinks, Well he is a coward –'

'Father –'

'Coward! Coward! This is what they are thinking. At this point defence counsel rises and tries to demolish this unfortunate impression by going back over all that old ground when you were supposed to be thinking seriously and objectively about this matter and that matter, about what is constitutional and what is not, and what is for India's good and what is not. But he does not find it easy. Prosecution has tricked you into raising this emotional question of to what extent Lieutenant Sayed Kasim was thinking of his country and to what extent thinking of his own skin. Defence Counsel's voice begins to carry less conviction. He knows that nothing can obliterate that impression, that Lieutenant Kasim is a man who joined the INA to avoid being beaten up again by a Japanese officer called Hakinawa. Nevertheless he has his brief and must go on to the bitter end.'

Kasim took out his squared handkerchief and dabbed his forehead. 'I remember the first case I pleaded in front of a British magistrate. A very minor case to do with a land dispute between two brothers. In private consultation my client made much of the emotional rift in family feeling. Presumably his brother, the claimant, had been doing likewise because when we got into court his counsel began to present the case as though it were a dispute between Cain and Abel, with my client cast as Cain. I had to listen to many of my excellent pleas and arguments being turned against me before even I had a chance to speak. I looked at the young magistrate. For a moment I could not interpret his expression.

Then it suddenly struck me that he was wanting to hear none of this. It embarrassed and disturbed him. He was keeping his eye on his papers and trying to get it all down in writing. So when my turn came to stand up I proceeded very haltingly – at first actually because I had no alternative. I had lost all inspiration. I fell back on legal precedents, almost automatically, and he kept interrupting me, getting his clerk to show him this reference and that reference from this book and that book. While he did this I stood silent. At first I thought his interruptions were his way of accusing me of incomplete preparation. And then we happened to glance at one another at the same time and instinctively I knew that he was grateful just to be referred to points of law and the land records. Instinctively I knew I had provided him with a way out of this emotional situation that claimant's counsel had tried to establish. So then I became deliberately even more dry and boring, boring to the court but not to this boy-magistrate. And to make sure of this I sometimes made an old legal joke, old to the court, but new to him in the sense that while he had probably already heard the jokes from his tutors this was probably the first time he had heard them repeated in a court-room. My client was in despair. The claimant and the claimant's counsel were looking very smug. So I stopped looking at them. I looked only at the boy-magistrate and his expression was sufficient to encourage me to continue along these lines. I could see him beginning to feel that it was exactly for this that he had been trained for so long and so expensively. I could see him recognizing that this training had some point after all. I began to refer to the very old cases I knew he must have studied for his initial examinations. He became very confident, almost peremptory. Sometimes he rebuked me for getting a reference wrong. Mostly he rebuked the claimant's pleader for interrupting. His table became piled with books and documents. Sometimes he said, "What is your point in regard to such and such a sub-section, Mr Kasim?" I would tell him and at the same time refer him to another sub-section which I guessed he had had to answer questions about more recently. The public benches began to empty. The claimant's pleader pretended to go to sleep. People were yawning. It was the most boring case of the year.

But it was the one the boy-magistrate will probably never forget and the one I must always remember, Sayed. From this case I removed every last speck of emotion. I made him see that Indians too are capable of detachment. There was practically nobody left in the court when he found in favour of the counter-claimant, my client.'

'Yes, I remember all that, father. You told us many years ago. Many times.'

'Oh, did I?' He dabbed his forehead again and suddenly felt very old. 'The reason I tell you again –' he began.

'I know the reason, father. You've always believed that the English are very emotional but unwilling to show it in public.'

'This is so, isn't it?'

'I can't take it into consideration. What the English feel or don't feel is no longer important. We've finished with them, whether you like it or not.'

'Why do you say whether I like it or not? What has my life been, then? What have I been doing? Asking them to stay?'

'No. Not asking. But perhaps making it possible because you believe so much in the power of the law. Their law.'

'In this case you'll be well advised to rely on it too. You will be finished if you persist in making emotional appeals. Now, go back to November, nineteen forty-two. How long were you in this new camp where you were treated all right, as you put it?'

'Until the following February. One of the two officers I'd already spoken to came to see me. He said Mohan Singh had been arrested by the Japanese in December for withholding full cooperation and trying to insist that only the INA should deal with India. But now they'd had word that Subhas Chandra Bose was coming from Germany to take charge. Shah Nawaz was raising a new INA and determined that the Japs wouldn't be allowed to interfere, but made to treat us as equals and not as a puppet army they could do what they liked with.'

'So you yourself now joined?'

'Yes. I went down to Singapore.'

'Taking some men with you, other recruits?'

'Yes, I visited my old camp. I told the men my decision. I left it to them to make up their own minds. A few NCOs volunteered immediately. I took them to Singapore with me.'

'Was Bose there already?'

'No, he didn't come for several months. We concentrated on training and on stopping the Japanese from interfering. Someone in the Japanese Government had told them to treat us with more respect and when Bose did come it was a revelation. You only had to see and listen to him once to know that at last we had a real leader. And then of course he put everything on a pukka footing.'

'By pukka footing you mean his establishment of a so-called Government of Free India in exile?'

'Why so-called, father? What was de Gaulle's Free French Government, then? You don't hear people referring to that as so-called.'

'You know the difference between de Gaulle's and Bose's governments. There is no need for me to tell you. That sort of statement would be very smartly thrown out to sneered at as a quibble by the president of the court.'

'It wasn't a quibble to us. It made us independent of the Japanese. The Azad Hind Fauji became a properly constituted army, the armed force of a properly constituted and independent government.'

'You joined the INA before Bose took over. You would be sensible to say nothing on these lines. Tell me, why did you do this broadcast? Colonel Merrick says you admit to helping with propaganda generally and to doing a broadcast. I knew about the broadcast quite a long time ago. Someone listening in Ranpur thought they recognized your voice. I of course was in prison so heard nothing, but I was told about it afterwards. This *was* your voice?'

'Probably. I did one broadcast. Early last year. January, I think. After that I moved up into Burma in command of a battalion for the advance into Manipur.'

'What sort of thing did you say in the broadcast?'

'I just spoke in general terms, about the fight for India's freedom and the choice that had to be made by someone like myself, an officer in the Indian Army. They have a copy of the broadcast on their files in Delhi. All these broadcasts were monitored.'

'What was the main purpose of these broadcasts?'

'To encourage people here at home who had opportunities to listen. It was important for them to know that if the Japanese invaded, Indians would be with them. One couldn't say anything about not trusting the Japanese, but people listening could read between the lines. They'd realize that we'd be doing our best to stop the Japs giving them trouble.'

'Very well. Then you moved into Burma, you said. And then across the Chindwin and into Manipur.'

'Eventually, yes.'

'And waged war against the King.'

'Yes, I suppose so.'

'Not "yes, I suppose", Sayed. Just yes. Yes. Yes. You waged war against the king. It was the unavoidable result of the decision you made. We have already dealt with that. What remains to be dealt with is your attitude at this time to the Japanese.'

'It was the same as Netaji's.'

'Netaji? You mean Bose. What was Bose's attitude?'

'For him it was a question of wait and see. Under Netaji the lives of thousands of Indians in Asia were made better and the Japanese said repeatedly that we were allies, they'd no quarrel with India. But Netaji said many times to us in private that we must be prepared to fight them too if necessary. We should never fully trust them. Also he said they were perhaps afraid of us. I think this was why they kept us short of supplies and equipment and why in Burma they stopped us operating as a fully independent and major force. Whatever the Japanese Government said, we knew there were many Japanese officers who had their own ideas and way of dealing which wasn't in line with the official policy. They were the ones who didn't agree that India should be Netaji's sphere of influence. They only wanted to see the Rising Sun hoisted in Delhi in place of the Union Jack.'

'Good. Remember that. That could be a helpful point. But what does this mean, sphere of influence?'

'Surely it is obvious, it was fundamental. Netaji said –'

'I want it in your own words, not Netaji's.'

Sayed again hesitated. He said, 'What have you against

Netaji? He spoke to me about you with much warmth and admiration.'

'What did you expect? For him to tell you he thought I was a bloody fool? No matter. Just that he and I never got on. Anyway he's dead –'

'Perhaps –'

'Perhaps, perhaps. Perhaps Hitler did not die in the bunker. Perhaps Bose did not die in a plane crash. The world must always have its myths. Let us get back to spheres of influence. You should avoid that phrase. It is one used by journalists when they are really talking about a political carve-up. You must try not to give this impression, that Bose sat down with Togo and said, right, you keep Burma and Malaya, and all the rest. We'll have India.'

'What is wrong with that? It's our own country.'

'The British still happen to think that legally it is theirs. Just do not use that phrase. Rely more on what you said about the Rising Sun and the Union Jack. Rely entirely on the question not of what appeared to be agreed between your Netaji and the Japanese within a framework of spurious legality, but on the underlying distrust, the fear that if and when the British were defeated, which seemed imminent, the Japanese would run riot in the country, looting and raping and enslaving, and that the best way to try to stop them doing this was unfortunately to march with them.'

Sayed said nothing.

'So now there comes the question, of whether there was any deepening of your distrust as a result of your experience of marching with them into India. Did the distrust increase?'

'Yes, because they dealt with us unfairly.'

'How?'

'Over things like rations, supplies, arms and ammunition. In not giving us proper operational information. They tried to palm us off with coolie work. The men were getting browned off. I was always having to dispute with Japanese officers mostly junior to me in rank to get the men a proper deal.'

'Morale in your battalion was not as high as you would have liked?'

'Morale was always high. We were fed up only with the

469

Japanese. Among ourselves things were okay. I tried to share their hardships with them.'

'Sometimes no doubt you had to punish some of them.'

'Never to appease the Japanese. If a Japanese officer complained of any of my men's behaviour I told him to shove off.'

'I did not mean this. You were what you call a properly constituted army. You had a disciplinary code, no doubt, an army act laying down rules and regulations and punishments for infringement.'

'Everybody accepts this necessity. Our regulations were based completely on the Indian Army Act.'

'You cannot use the words based and completely together. Either they were a duplicate or based merely. Based with variations for local conditions and circumstances.'

'Yes, I see. You've been listening to all these rumours of ill-treatment. But where do such rumours come from except from men who joined us and have been recaptured like me but are hoping to suck up to the British with tales of tortures. I know nothing of such things. The only barbarity I have ever witnessed was in my old regiment in Kuala Lumpur when the officers' mess cook was ordered by Colonel Barker to receive six strokes of the rattan for stealing rum and selling it in the bazaar. We were all made to assemble and watch.'

'Under the pukka Indian Army Act such punishments are prescribed for menials. I am questioning you about punishments of combatant soldiers.'

'And I've already answered. I know nothing of brutal punishments. In Rangoon I ordered such things as extra fatigues, confinement to barracks, forfeiture of pay. And in the field, extra guard duties or heavy pack drill. I am not a monster. I am not a barbarian.'

'And you know nothing of this kind and worse kinds of violence in forcing men to *join* the INA?'

'Nothing.'

'You never had a case of desertion in your battalion?'

'No.'

'If you had, what would have happened if the man had been caught? Come. Think of me still as your prosecutor. What punishment did your INA prescribe for desertion, for instance in the face of the enemy, meaning in the face of the British and the Indian armies? Death?'

'That would have been the maximum.'

'In the eyes of the British who are not interested in INA acts or regulations, to execute such a sentence on an Indian soldier, even a traitorous Indian soldier, would amount to murder under the Indian Penal Code. You realize this? I am sorry to press you on the subject. Were such a sentence ever passed and executed, everyone concerned would be guilty at least of abetment to murder. You see how difficult things become when there is no political let alone legal recognition of the losing side by the winning side? I want to be absolutely sure there is no problem of this kind attaching to your case.'

'I've told you, father. You can be sure.'

'Because if there is any doubt, all my advice to you so far is valueless. You would have to work your case up on lines that would seek to establish the legality of what I have called Subhas Chandra Bose's spurious constitutional framework. You would need the services of an expert on Constitutional and International Law. On full consideration, do you think after all you might require such services?'

'All I know is that I've only told you the truth. What I understand of it. I am merely a professional soldier. I don't follow all these technicalities.'

'They are not just technicalities, Sayed. Never mind. Go back now and concentrate your mind on the situation that ended in your surrender in Manipur. But let me lead you a little. In court your counsel would not be allowed too much licence in that respect.'

He smiled, attempting to make Sayed smile too.

'In Manipur,' he went on, 'you find yourself in a difficult, perhaps untenable military position. No supplies, no ammunition, no lines of communication. You are somewhere in the hills near Imphal. The Japanese are suddenly nowhere. The British and the Indian armies are uncomfortably close. Now – were there among your men any who said, Major Sahib, this is our chance. Now we can do what we really joined the INA to do – escape from prison-camp and return to duty at the earliest possible moment?'

471

Presently Sayed said, 'Yes, there were some men who pretended to think like that.'

'How did you deal with them?'

'I tried to make them see what folly it was.'

'Folly? Why folly?'

'Folly to expect the British to swallow a story like that.'

'Folly is not a good word. I suggest you do not use it. It would make it sound as if you were thinking what was wise and what was foolish and not of what your position really was – that you had all made a certain decision as prisoners-of-war, with a certain idea at its end, and here was the idea in ruins, with the Japanese being beaten back and not any longer looking likely to march on Delhi to hoist the Rising Sun in place of the Union Jack. Which meant that all of you were in ruins too, unless you abandoned whatever post the Japanese had left you to hold before leaving you in the lurch, abandoned it and retreated and ran back after the Japanese to share their defeat with them. Perhaps to fight another day. Perhaps not. It seems to me, Sayed, that the one thing your INA never took into account was what was to happen if the Japanese *were* defeated. Or were you so convinced of their superiority that the eventuality never occurred to you? Were you by any chance relying on the defection of the Indian Army, the moment they saw Indians marching shoulder to shoulder with the Japanese? Did you think the Indian Army would at once turn on its British officers and join with you and the Japanese to massacre the British Army?'

Sayed did not reply. But he got up and went towards the other pleader's table. 'Yes,' Kasim said, misunderstanding. 'Smoke if you want to. And then tell me how you tried to convince these men of yours of their folly. But I hope you were thinking not of folly but of dishonour.'

But Sayed had gone on past the table, hands behind back. For a moment he stood near the rail behind which when the court was in session the public sat. Then he came back and stood looking down at his father.

'No,' he said. 'I asked them, "What folly is this? What mercy do you expect from the British or even from our own fellows who are commanded by them and dare not disobey? You will all be shot like dogs just as so many of our people

472

have always been treated like dogs. Isn't it better to die here?"
Then one of them said, "Major Sahib, we do not care. To
surrender is our only chance now of seeing our families again,
so let the British and our own old comrades shoot us if they
want to, it no more matters. We do not care either about the
British or the Japanese. Staying here we shall all be killed
anyway, and our women and children will starve, no one will
see to them or bother about them and it will all be up with
them." Then another said, "Here we are only so many, but
most of us are thinking like this, that we must risk being shot,
because it is our only chance. You have only to ask the others.
We are all thinking the same. That it is all finished with us!" '
'Please sit. I cannot speak to you while you are standing up.'
'It's easier for me to stand, father. So let me tell you. I sent
these men away and assembled the others. There weren't
many of us left anyway. I said, Well what is the decision of the
majority? Who is for surrendering and chancing being shot?
One hand went up and then another until there were only a
few hands not up. Including mine. Then I went away to be
alone for a bit. Perhaps you would have preferred me to do
what it was in my mind to do. Shoot myself. A very
honourable solution. But what is the good to India of a dead
Indian just now? And perhaps also I wished to see my family
again, only it was not even that I was allowed to see my own
mother before she died.'
'Sayed –'
'No. Let me speak please. You are talking about a world that
exists only in a court of law and I am not. In the world as it is it
is necessary to act sometimes according to the heart –'
'I do not advise this, Sayed. It is pure emotional rhetoric. It
will not get you anywhere.'
'Will not get me anywhere? Where is this place I am
supposed to be going? Where is all this supposed to be leading,
this advice you are giving me? The truth is that after all you
don't intend to help me. You are giving me a lot of ideas about
how to placate the British. Why should they be placated?
What right have they to say what I shall do and what I shall
not do?'
'I am helping you in the only way I can. I must make it clear
to you that I don't intend to make political capital out of this. I

cannot advise you to present your own case in a political framework. I do not intend to take that road. I advise you not to. I do not approve of what you have done. I do not approve of INA. I shall not identify myself with any committee set up for the defence nor shall I defend you in court, although to do so would be a very popular thing in the country generally. On the other hand I shall not criticize you, nor the INA, to anyone, which is perhaps what Government has been hoping I would do. I do not intend to commit political suicide, although you will appreciate that the situation I find myself in does not augur well for my immediate political future.'

Kasim paused, went on before Sayed had a chance to speak: 'If you plead guilty I will continue to help you. I will help to choose and to instruct your defence counsel, but in a wholly private and confidential manner. Everything I have been trying to put into your mind this morning as the proper way to conduct your case has been to this end: that you should plead guilty to waging war against the King, and then submit a reasoned statement setting out the considerations that led you to do so. Pleading guilty is the only way you can come out of court with any kind of personal integrity left.'

Sayed, still standing, had looked away, but now turned on Kasim. 'Integrity? What else have you ever done, father, except wage war against the King? Hasn't this been your whole life, to get rid of the British? What is the difference between you and me except that you went to prison now and again and I carried a gun?'

'You have just explained the difference, Sayed. If you cannot see it, then it is pointless to discuss it any further. So yes, come, come. Let us finish. We are simply aggravating one another.'

He got up.

'You are throwing everything away,' Sayed said.

'Not everything.'

'No one will trust or respect you if you don't stand up for us along with other political leaders.'

'I hope it is not my fear of this that you have been relying on?' He made to go, but stopped, unable to part with his son on such terms. 'It is you who have thrown away everything, Sayed. The men who did not are the Indian soldiers and officers who are still in prison-camp, who resisted all these perhaps understandable and pardonable temptations and suffered infinitely greater hardship, and who will now be coming home. In a year or so, if you are not in prison, where will you be? For a time yes, you will all be heroes. But when there is no longer any reason to treat you as heroes, then you will be forgotten or if you are remembered at all it will be with mistrust, as men who broke their contracts, men who voluntarily took an oath of loyalty and then disregarded it, men who treated their commissions as mere scraps of paper to be used or thrown away as they thought fit. And if you *do* go to prison for this meanwhile, I beg of you do not try to console yourself with the thought that you and your father have both in your time suffered the same punishment for the same crime. It will not be so. The only contract I have ever made of this kind is with myself, to do what I could to obtain the independence and freedom and unity and strength of this country. Whenever in earlier days I defied the law it was in performance of that contract, and I defied it knowing full well the penalty and indeed inviting the penalty and proudly admitting that I had incurred it. The last time I went to prison was because I would not repudiate my membership of a party that Government lawfully suppressed. Unjustly but lawfully suppressed. It is true that at one time I was sworn in as a minister and it is true that I and all my colleagues resigned when we felt we could not any longer participate in an administration under the British. But a soldier cannot resign in wartime. When you became a soldier, Sayed, this fact should have been clearly in your mind as defining the difference between us. I did not interfere with your decision to become a soldier because I asked myself what kind of independent country will India be if we do not have a properly trained and experienced professional army to defend that independence. That the British allowed Indians to become officers I have always taken as a sign of their good faith in the matter of eventually bowing to our demands to rule ourselves. But that is by the way. What is not by the way is that now you can no longer be a soldier, you can no longer help your country. And this is what angers me. Your life so far has been wasted.'

475

Sayed stared at him.

'It is not a country. It is two countries. Perhaps it is many countries, but primarily it is two. If I'm not wanted in one perhaps I shall be wanted in the other.'

'Ah!' Kasim exclaimed. And sat down. 'So this also has happened to you. Then we are even more deeply divided.'

'We're only divided by your refusal to face facts, father, and by your reliance on this and that legal interpretation, also I begin to think by your reliance on the British to act as gentlemen. I no longer believe in such concepts. I have seen too much of life. It is no good relying on principles and no good relying on the British who themselves have no principles that can't be trimmed to suit *them*. In any case, they are finished. They are no longer of importance and will drag us down with them if we aren't careful. They are only interested in themselves and always have been. But now they are afraid of the Americans and the Russians and will try to get rid of India as quick as they can, both to curry favour with the USA and USSR and not to have any longer the responsibility. They will hand us over to Gandhi and Nehru and Patel – and then where will you be, father? How can you trust Congress as a whole? How can you imagine that just because you've been useful to them in the past you – a Muslim – will be allowed to remain useful when they have power? They will squeeze you out at the first convenient opportunity. Congress is a Hindu party whatever they pretend. They will exploit us as badly as the British have done, probably worse. There's only one answer and that is to seize what we can for ourselves and run things our own way from there.'

Sayed leaned over the table.

'When you say my military career is finished, I would agree with you. It would be finished if the British stay and finished if we merely substitute a Hindu for a British *raj*. It would be finished because I'm a Muslim and they hate us. Also they hate each other. A Hindu from UP hates a Hindu from Bengal and both hate a Hindu from the South. A Hindu *raj* would be a catastrophe. They have nothing to hold them together. They hate and envy us mostly because we have such a thing. We have Islam. It will be madness not to resist them. The only thing that matters in this world, father, is power. We must grasp our own. Surely it is true you have been thinking of this too? Please, do not be too proud? I do not want to see you become neglected and bitter in your old age.'

Kasim kept his attention on his son's hands: good, square capable hands. No sign of a tremor. Nor perhaps of sensitivity. He kept his own clasped.

'You are asking me to throw everything away and go over to the League?'

'It wouldn't be throwing anything away. Guzzy and Nita are very keen on this, I think. Their letters are full of hints. Jinnah would welcome you. Almost I imagine he is expecting it, because you have been so difficult for people to get hold of.'

'And Ahmed? Is he keen?'

'What does Ahmed know about anything? He is still a child.'

'No,' Kasim said. 'He is not a child.'

'Well, no, no, not in that way. A man with a reputation I gather.'

'A reputation?'

'For liking the things a man likes.'

'Women? Drinking? This is so.'

'He should be careful. It must worry you.'

Kasim did not reply. He noted the solicitous tone in his son's voice. Which verged on condescension. Sayed added, 'Perhaps he is like this because he feels himself to be without chance or opportunity.'

'You mean he does not agree with the things I stand for?'

'How can I say, father? He is a good boy at heart, I'm sure. I shall try to find out what he thinks, shall I?'

'He does not think about much. Except these things you mentioned. And hawking.'

'Hawking?'

'He was always very keen on riding. Now he has trained a falcon. It is very difficult, you know. It demands much attention and concentration. Sleepless nights. All that sort of thing. But he is much attached to her. He goes out whenever he can.'

'But that is good! A good manly sport. I am glad. I should not like him to become dissipated.'

Sayed placed one hand on his father's coupled ones. Kasim

477

did not look up. But he felt, as a physical pressure, the steady way his elder son watched him.

'Perhaps we should say goodbye now, father. Thank you for coming to see me.'

'It is you who have come the greater distance.'

'That is my duty.'

Kasim stood up. Dutifully too, he held his arms out. They embraced. Speaking into his son's shoulder he said, 'Do not rely too much on this Colonel Merrick. He has known Ahmed for some time. He has told neither of you that he knew the other.'

'He told me just before he brought you in, father. But don't worry. I rely on no Englishman. He is of no importance either.'

'They will be waiting for you outside, no doubt. No doubt you can see Ahmed alone in here also, but you had better go out now. It would offend me to see you in custody of any kind. By the time they bring you back in I shall be gone.'

'You will write to me?'

Kasim nodded. He murmured: Allah be with you. Then released him and moved away. He heard his son's firm, heavy footsteps; and in a while the opening and closing of a door. He looked round the empty court-room and, familiar though it was, as such rooms went, it seemed to him lacking in the quality that gave such rooms meaning or even the dimensions of reality. Then he walked out by way of the daïs and the magistrate's room, through the corridor and along it in search of the room that had been set aside for him.

*

By the time they drove into the siding at Premnagar it was nearly half-past ten. There was barely an hour before the night train from Mirat to Ranpur was due to stop and pick them up. The stationmaster was fussing because the coach had to be shunted to a more convenient place for coupling and he had expected them by ten o'clock.

A puncture had delayed them. For half-an-hour Kasim had waited on the roadside, listening to the wind in the telegraph wires. The night sky had no luminosity. The wind held the smell of approaching rain; a small rain; but better than a heavy rain in country like this which the wet monsoon either avoided or flooded, first drying the top-soil for a couple of years, then sweeping it away. He welcomed the rain and the darkness of the sky. The fort, unsilhouetted, had entirely disappeared. He welcomed the wind and the air. It was good to feel braced and chilled after the heat and humidity of the room in the Circuit House; but he knew he might catch cold. Instinctively he had felt in his pocket for the onion that was supposed to ward colds off. There was no onion. He had given that up when his wife died.

Now to the stationmaster's fussing, Booby was adding his own. Where were the steps by which to mount? 'We don't need steps,' Kasim said and reached for the handgrips, heaved himself up only to find himself steadied unexpectedly from inside by Ahmed who had been in the coach collecting the small suitcase he'd brought from Mirat and was now going to take back to Mirat in the Nawab's Daimler.

'Surely you're not going yet?'

'Not for a moment or two, father. I didn't want to forget it though.'

'Well give it to one of the people to take to the car then come and talk to me for a moment.' He was conscious of the peremptory tone in his voice and wasn't encouraged by it. He went down the corridor. Hosain was waiting. He slid the door open.

'Tell them to bring tea or something.'

He entered the compartment. Before he could sit Mr Mehboob followed him in and put the briefcase on a seat.

'Where is Ahmed? I want to see him alone for a moment. And please shut the door. I've been standing all that time in the open.'

'You shouldn't have got out on to the road, Minister, when we had the puncture.'

'How can they change a wheel with two people like us sitting at ease in the back? It is bad for the springs, Ahmed says, and it is the Nawab's car and must be returned in good condition.'

Hurt, Booby left the compartment and began to close the

479

door but opened it again for Ahmed. Sulkily he shut it when Ahmed was inside.

'Come, sit, they are bringing tea.'

Ahmed looked at his watch but sat down. 'I've not time for tea, father, it's a long drive and the chauffeur wants to go to a garage to get the punctured wheel repaired so that we have a spare.'

'There will be no garage open at this hour.'

'He knows of one.'

'It will take hours. You will get cold standing around.'

'What he advises is best, father. So I mustn't be long. Anyway they're going to move the carriage at any moment.'

'I don't like you travelling alone in a car at night all the way to Mirat. It is a bad area round here. And the escort van has gone.'

'I shan't be alone, father. There's the driver. Anyway, Booby came down at night. I can take care of myself just as well as he can.'

'Booby is paid to risk his life,' Kasim said. But smiled. Encouraged by Ahmed's answering smile he said, 'We have had no opportunity to talk today.' That was untrue. He had deliberately avoided being alone with Ahmed. 'What I want to suggest is that you come back now to Ranpur. Come back for a few days. There is a great deal to do and a great deal you can help me with. Poor Booby is such a muddler. Ring Dmitri in the morning and explain the necessity. If you like, send a note back with the driver too.'

'I promised Dmitri I'd be away only two nights. There's a meeting of Council tomorrow.'

'Council, council. He doesn't need you. The Council is Dmitri. Anyway, you do not attend these meetings personally.'

His heart sank. It was so badly said. He wished he could withdraw the imputation that Ahmed's official duties in Mirat were negligible; although he knew they were. He should never have agreed to Ahmed going to work in Mirat – but then he should never have let his elder son go into the army. Both had seemed acceptable enough solutions at the time. He had found adequate explanations: that India would need experienced officers; that it could be useful to have a son

480

experienced in the administration of feudal survivals like the
princely states. But for months now he had found these
explanations less convincing than the other explanation –
that in his heart he had felt at the time that neither son was
capable of contributing much more. Neither son had
inherited the spark. Neither son cared deeply about the things
he cared for himself. The only thing he could still convince
himself of was that he had believed, hoped, that in time they
would, that their occupations would help to nourish in them
the necessary passion, determination, and restraint.

'Well,' he said, 'if you must go back, you must.' He was not
going to beg. Nor was he going to admit that he could not bear
the thought of returning to the empty old house in the
Kandipat road alone; although he believed that Ahmed
understood this. When he had said to Sayed, *No, Ahmed is not
a child*, he had not meant what Sayed thought he meant. He
had been thinking of the occasion when Ahmed startled him
with a shrewd assessment of the situation in which he might
find himself – indeed now found himself; startled him into
realizing it at a moment when he had been incapable of
thinking clearly; the previous occasion at the Circuit House
when they had brought him unprepared, without breakfast,
from the fort, telling him nothing, so that he had feared the
worst, that his wife was ill or dead and that they were
releasing him on compassionate grounds as they had released
Bapu when Kasturba was dying. He had nearly disgraced
himself – finding Ahmed there – pathetically crying out 'Then
God is good!' when Ahmed reassured him. Relief had been
followed by bitter resignation when the truth came out, that
his release was only partial, that he must suffer the
humiliation of living under restriction at Mirat, and the
bitter-sweet humiliation of learning that his wife was to share
that restriction with him. And after the relief, the resignation
and the humiliation, had come the shock of hearing Ahmed
speak so calmly of Sayed's capture in Manipur. Outraged, he
had not only called his first-born son a traitor, but had
insulted Ahmed. It had been unforgiveable, yet Ahmed had
seemed to forgive it, had gone on, speaking calmly still,
intelligently, about the motives Government might have in
releasing him from the fort. It could have been the turning

point in their relationship. His own stubbornness, his peremp-
toriness, his coldness of manner – carefully nurtured defen-
ces against the Islamic sin of betraying emotion – had perhaps
been the chief impediments to closer understanding. And yet
after that one moment, that opportunity they had had to be
closer to one another, Ahmed had seemed to withdraw again.
It was as if the spark of involvement and commitment had
failed to ignite. Subsequently, Kasim had tried tentatively to
kindle it again and sometimes Ahmed had seemed to respond,
but when his mother became ill, fatally ill, the capacity to
respond had seemed to be deliberately smothered, and he had
become again merely dutiful in matters where dutifulness
seemed obligatory. As now, when he was dutifully sitting on
the opposite seat, but leaning forward, hands clasped,
indicating imminent departure.

'Well tell me, Ahmed, how *you* found things with Sayed?'

'He looked very fit and cheerful, I thought. He says he's
treated pretty well.'

'I know. I know. Did he say anything you feel you should
tell me?'

'We talked about hawking mostly. We weren't alone. One
of the subalterns sat in the room.'

'But why was this?'

'Major Merrick said his instructions were that only you
could be alone with him. But he made the subaltern sit where
he couldn't hear easily. It didn't matter really. It was amusing
if anything.'

'He is now Colonel Merrick. Didn't you notice? Also he is
either equally unobservant or deceitful. He told me Sayed was
not among those he'd classify as unrepentantly proud of what
he has done. It wasn't my impression. Was it yours?'

'I'd no impression either way. We didn't talk about that
kind of thing.'

'Just about hawking?'

'No, but mostly about me. I'm afraid I couldn't think what
to ask him about himself. One day must seem to him much
like another, after all.'

'What things about you, other than hawking?'

'Oh, personal things.' Ahmed grinned. 'He said Merrick

482

saw me drinking whisky in Bombay. He said I should stop that.'

And, Kasim thought, they had probably talked about their mother's illness and death, the temporary burial at Nanoora that would have to be gone through again so that she could rest finally in the Kasim tomb in Ranpur.

'He said nothing about Jinnah, then?'

'Oh, yes. He said he thought Nita was becoming very pro-Jinnah.'

'Only that?'

'Well he said Nita was probably pro-Jinnah because Guzzy was, and that wives usually follow their husbands in such things.'

The steward knocked, slid back the door and brought in tea. 'You'll change your mind, Ahmed?'

'No, I haven't time. I must go in a minute.'

'Then bring it later,' Kasim told the steward. The steward went. 'Sayed did not ask you your own view of Jinnah?'

'No.'

'He did not tell you he had strongly recommended me to go over? And that he had undertaken to find out your own feelings?'

'No. Nothing like that at all.'

'Obviously he had begun to when he mentioned Nita. Were you interrupted soon after?'

'Yes, they came and said time was up. We'd had our ten minutes or whatever it was.'

'That's all they allowed? It doesn't matter. What matters is that he attempted to do what he said he'd do. So let me settle the question – what your feelings would be if I went over to the League. The League is very strongly placed. In the last few years while most of the Congress was in prison they have paved the way to divide the country. In the elections they are likely to win most of the seats reserved for Muslims. Even my own is not safe. If I offered myself to the League Jinnah would welcome me. I might even get a portfolio in whatever central government he's able to set up in whatever kind of Pakistan he is able to wrest out of us. To make sure of a portfolio I could also do what perhaps a father should. Publicly defend my son against charges of treason. I put it to you in these crude terms

483

because for once, Ahmed, for once I am asking you to tell me what your honest opinion would be if I did these things. You said a moment ago that women always followed their husbands in such matters. Your mother always followed me. It was not easy for her eventually because her own family became very Pakistan conscious and very Jinnah conscious, just as Nita and Guzzy have become. What I am asking you is whether you and Sayed and Nita and your mother were thinking that I was wrong all the time, and that you were all conforming and saying nothing out of family loyalty. Whether it is your view that now I should in turn conform for everybody's sake, including my own.'

Beneath them the coach wheels clanked. The coach had been coupled to a shunting engine.

'I've got no view, father,' Ahmed said, getting up. 'You know I don't understand all these ins and outs. They don't seem to me to have anything to do with ordinary problems, though I suppose they must. But however many solutions are found people are still always dying of starvation. All that kind of thing. Or if they aren't dying of starvation they're killing one another senselessly. It all means nothing to me, parties and such-like.'

Kasim got up too.

'Then it means you don't care either way? That is one question out of the way at least. I shan't have to consider your feelings, or rather shan't have to feel conscience-stricken about you as well as Sayed. That is a relief. You see I made my mind up long ago what I would have to do. I have only been waiting for the moment when I was forced to take action. Let me just say this to you, Ahmed, that whatever your answer had been, my mind would not have been altered. But one likes to know where one stands with one's own family. To me Sayed is a man whose actions remain indefensible because he broke his word, he broke his contract. It follows that I cannot break mine. Never in my life shall I go over to Jinnah. I did not say so to Sayed because I felt he did not deserve an answer either way –'

The train shoved forward a yard or two and stopped abruptly. They avoided being thrown together by reaching for different handholds to steady themselves.

'So that is the position,' he said, righting himself. 'You, I think, deserve to know. You had better go now, if you're not coming to Ranpur.'

He slid the door open and led the way down the deserted corridor. The train, after the clanking and jerking was unnaturally still, as if it had died. The carpet muffled the sound of footsteps. When he turned round, near the exit, it was almost a shock to find Ahmed so close behind him.

Formally he embraced him.

'Do not hang around too long in that garage. Find yourself some coffee or something.'

'Yes, father, I'll do that.'

'And something stronger, no doubt, I expect you have your flask.' He could smell the whisky behind the scent of garlic on his son's breath. He let the boy go, then stopped him.

'What I have said about Sayed, please never repeat. It might make things worse for him. The other thing, about Jinnah, is in confidence. It will become public knowledge soon, though. Since you profess political detachment I can't expect you to approve or disapprove, but I'm sorry if I've spoken roughly. I haven't meant to upset you.'

Again the train jerked and this time began moving slowly forward. Ahmed grasped one handrail and began to get down. 'Why should I be upset?' he asked. 'I've won my bet with Dmitri. He bet me you'd go over to Jinnah. I bet him you wouldn't.' The shunting engine's whistle pierced. He raised his voice. 'He wouldn't offer stakes, though. We both expected me to win really.'

Ahmed jumped and ran for several paces to maintain momentum.

'Ahmed!' Kasim cried, wanting him back.

'Mind yourself! Shut the door!' Ahmed shouted, coming to a halt in the cinder-yard.

'Ahmed! What do you mean? Expected, or wanted? Ahmed!'

But the cinder-yard had got up speed, taking Ahmed with it, taking him out of earshot, revealing more of its detail in the shape of coal bunkers and go-downs, the sudden glare of an arc-lamp, and then a suffocating smoky darkness which drove him in, back almost into Booby Sahib's arms.

'Minister, what are you doing? Why is the door open? Why isn't someone here looking after things in a proper way? It is getting so that no one can be relied on to look after you at all.'

'No, Booby,' he said, placing a hand on the fat pudgy shoulder. 'I am well looked after.'

IV

They paused in the ante-room while the *aide* who had called for him and Booby with a car at the Kandipat road knocked at the door, opened it, and then with a slight bow indicated that Kasim should go in and that Booby Sahib should stay where he was.

When Kasim entered, the Governor was half-way across the long high-ceilinged room. He had on what looked like the same crumpled chalk-striped suit he'd worn on the day of the laying of the Chakravarti foundation-stone. He carried his spectacles in his left hand; the right was being offered.

'Mr Kasim. Prompt as usual. How are you?'

'Very well, thank you, Governor-ji. But this time the promptness is due chiefly to your Captain Thackeray who brought the car on time.'

'The car didn't embarrass you? I'm told your house has been pretty well besieged all day.'

'Chiefly by well-wishers, fortunately.'

'Good. I thought we'd sit here. The fire's not really on. Just the imaginary coal bit. Say if you're cold.'

Without Malcolm having done anything visible to command it, the Government House magic worked, in the shape of doors opening and servants bringing in tea. There were five of them. Malcolm ignored them. They simply operated.

'How is Lady Malcolm, Governor? I hope better?'

'Somewhat better, thank you.'

'Not as good as you hoped?'

'No. I'm trying to get her to go home to see a particular chap. It's just a question of finding a way of persuading her to leave Ootacamund. Then we'll see.'

They were now surrounded by an English-Indian tea. Kasim could smell the curry-puffs without even looking for them.

The servants vanished as smoothly as they had appeared. When the last one had gone, Kasim said:

'I shall not be contesting the elections.'

'Yes, I see.' Only the voice betrayed disappointment. The face remained calm.

'I shall recommend to my colleagues in the Congress Party that a man called Fazal Huq Rahman should stand in my old constituency. He is still very anti-Jinnah very competent, and in my opinion stands the best chance of holding this Muslim seat for Congress, although undoubtedly my old sparring partner Nawaz Shah will leap at the opportunity to pass his own seat on to someone else and contest mine on behalf of the League.'

They sipped the tea which the servants had poured.

'Nawaz Shah?'

'Abdul Nawaz Shah. Not to be confused with Shah Nawaz Khan.'

The Governor smiled. He said, 'I wasn't Governor at the time, but I seem to remember you wanted Abdul Nawaz Shah in your nineteen thirty-seven Ministry.'

'He is an able and dedicated man and in nineteen thirty-seven there were constitutional grounds for forming a coalition, as well as reasonable hopes of satisfying the League that our policies were not after all anti-Muslim. Now of course such hopes are very slender.'

'Yes. I'm afraid they are.' Malcolm put his cup down. 'All this means that you're also not going to align yourself with the defence of the INA?'

'Yes. It means that.'

'Does it help if I point out that elections in this province won't take place until some time in the New Year? By which time the subject of the INA might not be so delicate?'

'Not really, Governor. The election *campaigns* will begin almost at once. It is clear that the subject of the INA will be taken up strongly by both major parties and just as clear that unless I align myself with the defence of INA personnel I should lose an important Muslim seat for Congress. The electorate would say, Who is this man who won't defend even his own son?'

'But my dear Mr Kasim, no one would blame you for defending your son, for defending the INA. I least of all.'

'I have imagined you would not. It is what you were delicately hinting when we had lunch a couple of weeks ago. On earlier occasions I detected from Government rather less delicate hints that it was hoped I might lead an attack on these fellows.'

'Is it your intention to lead an attack?'

'No. I do not have a suicidal turn of mind.'

'Well that's one good piece of news at least. On the other hand, if you don't publicly defend the INA and your son, how can you survive, politically?'

'I do not know whether I can survive. But I am an old enough professional to know that when you do not know how, you bide your time. I will do nothing to help nourish this idea that the INA are heroes. Eventually other people may agree with me. A free and independent India may not want to employ such officers. But personally I should not like to feel that at one time I defended them, and then refused to employ them. So for me it is simply a question of refusing now. Many of them had perhaps understandable and excusable reasons. But how can you judge which man had what reason? Let into your army one man of the suspect kind I have in mind and you plant the seed of a military dictatorship, you nurture a man who will throw away his commission again and challenge and even overthrow a properly constituted civil authority. I do not want a government of generals. I do not want to see such an India. I do not believe there will be such an India. But too much adulation of INA seems to me the best way of getting such an India. So, for the moment, I must be what you call *hors de combat* because I am out of rhythm with my country's temporary emotional feelings, and the country's temporary emotional feelings are out of rhythm with my own. I should be, as you also say, rusticated, for everybody's sake. So, Kasim, I tell myself. Go and cultivate your garden for a while.' He smiled. 'At Premanagar I had plenty of practice.'

Malcolm smiled too. He said, 'Not everyone has the taste for martyrdom, Mr Kasim. It rather surprises me to sense it in you.'

'Martyrdom? Oh, no, you've got me all wrong! A martyr is

the last thing I'm cut out for. I am a very practical man, even a pragmatist. The equal of any Englishman in that respect. But I have trained myself to take the long view also and taking the long view has taught me that you have to live for ever with a single moment of short-sightedness.'

'Well let's not say martyrdom. Just let's say you're putting a very high price on your conscience, your moral sense. Does it follow you've put a low one on the ultimate good of this province?'

'Governor, you know that this is a Congress majority province. Whoever you invite to form a government will be a Congressman. The price I exact for my moral sense is one Muslim seat, one minority seat in the assembly. So. My temporary rustication is bought very cheaply. I could not possibly win it in all the circumstances.'

'Temporary rustication? What have you in mind?'

'At the moment only cultivating my garden. Doing everything I can to promote the claims of Fazal Huq Rahman and disputing the claims of Jinnah and his League for partition. Oh, they will soon see that I am not in his camp. And, if I am asked my views about INA, I shall take – forgive me – the line of the English gentleman. I shall say, "How can I comment on such matters when I, my son, my whole family are involved? It is for others to speak." Also I shall fall back on the time-honoured excuse that certain family misfortunes and personal health do not make me a suitable candidate for elections in the coming cold weather. Now, what do you give me for my moral sense? You see what a Machiavellian viper you have been harbouring in your bosom?'

Malcolm put his head back, closed his eyes and laughed.

'So, Governor. May we have just another word about Fazal Huq Rahman?'

Malcolm put his spectacles on and looked at Kasim. He said, 'What more of Fazal Huq Rahman?'

'Should he defeat Nawaz Shah in the elections, which is very unlikely, and a misfortune for India which we can attribute to the late Lord Minto. ...'

'Why Lord Minto?'

'It was during his viceroyalty that the decision to provide separate electorates for Muslims was taken –'

'Entirely as a result of Muslim pressure –'

'That is technically so, but Minto need not have agreed. He and the British wanted to agree, he was unconsciously dividing and ruling. Lady Minto was dividing and ruling quite consciously. You never should have allowed your memsahibs into the country. It was she who greeted the arrangement for separate electorates with cries of amazon joy, because what she called Indian national subversion had been effectively blocked. It is to people like the Mintos we owe Jinnah.'

Malcolm was smiling. 'Go back to Fazal Huq Rahman,' he said.

'I was about to. I was merely reminding you, Sir George, of the political background to these constitutional absurdities. It is as though, Sir George, at home you had separate electorates for Protestants, Catholics, non-conformists, evangelists and Christian-Scientists. Communalism has been written into our political structure by the *raj*. The cold weather elections will be fought on a religious not a political issue. However, should Fazal Huq Rahman persuade his Muslim majority constituency that unity and not separation is the answer, which is doubtful, let me first of all say that he is not yet of ministerial calibre, and then reassure you that he is neither relative nor friend nor the friend of a cousin to whom I owe some favour –'

Again Malcolm put his head back. He took off his spectacles and wiped his eyes. He said, 'What should I do about Fazal Huq Rahman?'

'When you discuss portfolios with your new chief-minister designate, he will suggest a man for Education and no doubt like all good Governors you will raise no objection. But having raised no objection it would be useful if you could introduce Fazal Huq Rahman's name into the conversation and indicate some interest in seeing him in that department with a brief of some kind.'

'I'll keep my eye open, Mr Kasim. Perhaps nearer the time you'll help to guide it finally in the right direction?'

'I don't think that would be very wise. I don't think, you know, that we ought to see each other again except in public, socially.'

The Governor gazed at him steadily. He said, 'I should be

sorry for that. But I must leave it to you. Are you going back to practise the law?'

'No, no. I am a fortunate man. I don't have to earn a living, as you know.'

'I really meant, interest yourself in legal matters?'

'One never loses one's interest.'

'No, quite. What I meant was identify yourself with what I might call quasi-legal committees set up to look into matters involving possible legal processes or inquiries?'

'You are referring to matters that might arise from the civil disturbances that followed Government's arrests of Congressmen like myself?'

'Yes.'

'And the way they were put down?'

'And the way they were put down.'

'No, I am not interested in anything like that. To me it is all water under the bridge. Turbulent water at the time but to me it is foolish to re-disturb it. Now I think I must go.' He got up. Malcolm got up too. Kasim said, 'Thank you for what you arranged, and hoped to arrange. Next year you can forget all these things. I hope Lady Malcolm will soon be fully recovered.'

'Thank you.'

They began to walk slowly towards the doors that led to the ante-room. Then Malcolm stopped. He said, 'Mr Kasim, do you remember the last thing I said to you in this room, just before you went off to the Premanagar Fort?'

'Yes, I remember it very well. You said you would leave a thought in my mind, that one day this room might be mine.'

'Is it what you'd like? If so, I think I might almost guarantee it. It's not the same as heading a Ministry, but it has its compensations. Ranpur hasn't had an Indian Governor before but you wouldn't be the first Indian Governor appointed in the country.'

'You mean sworn in, not appointed.'

'Well, yes.'

Kasim felt the tremor beginning again in his right arm and hand. Almost unconsciously he steadied it by clasping the right wrist. For a moment the temptations of the peak – that splendid heady upper air, that immensity of landscape – made his head sing.

He heard himself saying, 'Well you see how difficult that would be, unless the Viceroy had been succeeded by a Governor-General of a self-governing dominion, and unless his executive council had been superseded by an Indian cabinet responsible to a freely elected central Indian assembly. And in that context a provincial governorship, if such a thing survives which I suppose it will, will be a job for an old man. Please don't misunderstand me.'

'I don't misunderstand.'

'Furthermore, for me to be sworn in, when you retire, would necessitate severing my active party political connections.'

'I understand that too. I suppose I was looking for a way of ensuring that your rustication isn't too permanent.'

'Well that is my problem but it is kind of you to involve yourself in it.'

'Not kind, Mr Kasim. I am involved whether I like it or not. But I prefer to like it. How serious were you when you said we oughtn't to see each other again in private?'

'Oh, very serious. I try not to say things lightly.'

'In that case is there anything I can do apart from saying goodbye and wishing you good luck?'

'Oh yes, one small thing. I am almost ashamed to mention it.'

'But please –'

'I know that any letters Sayed writes to members of his family and any letters members of his family write to Sayed must be opened and censored. That is quite correct in all the circumstances. But it has become onerous to feel that one can neither write nor receive letters from whomsoever on whatsoever subject that have not been looked at by strangers – no doubt perfectly disinterested fellows just doing their jobs. But it tends to limit one's sense of one's right to proper self-expression, and is so ridiculous when by contrast I know I can come here and frankly and freely speak my mind.'

'I attended to that a couple of days ago when a particular point was brought to my notice and I realized it was still going

492

on. But give it a day or two –' Malcolm smiled – 'you know how slowly any administration works.'

'Oh yes. I know, only too well. Thank you. Good-night, Governor.'

'Good-night, Mr Kasim.'

*

The crowds were still there in the Kandipat road, in the dark, patient, waiting to welcome him back from whatever great occasion he had gone out on. At the entrance to the house the progress of the car was interrupted. Thackeray was not in the car and there was nothing to identify it as one from Government House, but tomorrow it would be all round Ranpur where he had been. By then it would not matter and tonight it did not matter, to the patient crowds, where he had been or what he had done. It was enough for them that he had been out and done something in this sort of style, challenging the *raj*. With such crowds Booby was a different man. He beamed, he smiled, he rolled the window down and said cheerfully, 'Okay, okay, what is all this, what are you waiting for, he is tired can't you see, please let us pass. Tomorrow is another day. He will have something to say then. *Hán, hán! Jai Hind. Jai Hind.* All people go home now. Everything is okay.'

And rolled the window up as the crowd divided like a Red Sea and the car swept in through the iron gates. 'You see, Minister,' Booby said enthusiastically, 'here we are finally at home.'

*

Booby had even arranged that the fountain should play in the shallow pool in the miniature inner courtyard. Kasim leant on the railing that protected the second floor balcony and watched the dimly lit aquarium-effect for a while. Then he went back to the room he had asked should be set aside for him – the room his father had studied and meditated in during his own widowerhood – a room without ornament, with cream-washed walls, fretted windows, a simple bed, a desk, a

493

chair, two lamps (oil-lit in his father's day, now electric). He sat at the desk and again opened Bapu's letter.

'Minister?'

'What is it, Booby?'

'Can I get you anything?'

'No, no, but come in, sit down.'

There was nowhere for Booby to sit so Kasim vacated the chair and sat on the bed. Still Booby did not sit.

'You must sleep,' he said, 'you did not sleep all night again.'

'I am not tired. I must draft a letter to Bapu.'

'Please, dictate it. I have my pad and pencil.'

'No. I shall draft it. Then we can discuss it. Then it can be typed.' Booby's shorthand left a lot to be desired. Old Mahsood had had no shorthand. Somehow this had not seemed to matter.

'Very well,' Booby said. 'Then there is for the moment only the question of the letter from Pandit Baba.'

Kasim shut his eyes and flicked his hand, negatively. 'Oh, throw it away, Booby. It is all water under the bridge. We have never answered him before. Why should we answer now? We do not even know, only guess, what he is bothering me personally for. He is a tiresome man and of no account.'

'Yes, Minister. I will throw it away then. Mr Chakravarti has rung. Inviting you to dinner next week.'

'I cannot go to dinner with Chakravarti next week.'

'I will tell him so.'

'No, do not tell him. Accept and then decline later. The day before. It is so much less complicated. What else?'

'Mrs Nawaz Shah also rang.'

'So she can ring.'

Kasim looked up. Booby nodded. Expressionless. But somehow approving. Perhaps Booby would do after all.

'And?'

'Ahmed rang from Mirat this afternoon while we were out.'

'Saying what?'

'I couldn't get hang of it. We need more intelligent staff, Minister.'

'Perhaps. Tomorrow we'll discuss this, but primarily I shall leave it to you. What did the message say?'

494

'It is completely without meaning.' Booby referred to a note. 'Three words only. "Expected and wanted." '

'That is all?'

'That is all, Minister.'

Kasim smiled. 'It is enough. Thank you, Booby. That is all for tonight.'

*

After a while he got up from the bed and sat at the desk and began drafting the letter to Bapu. He inscribed the heading: To Mr Mohandas Karamchand Gandhi.

Dear Bapu, (he wrote)

Thank you for your letter and your kind expression of sympathy in the loss of my old friend Mahsood. As you know he was with me for many years and now all that is over. One feels such a loss. I am grateful for your letter because it helps me knowing the loss is shared.

It has, however, been a particular blow, coming on top of others and frankly I am in low spirits and prey to all kinds of doubts and uncertainties. Please do not misunderstand. I have no doubts whatsoever about our commitment to the cause of freedom and unity and non-violence to which you have given not only your life's work but also inspiration to the rest of us. This cause I shall never abandon. The uncertainties I spoke of arise from many different sources. For instance –

Momentarily Kasim's inspiration failed. Then he continued: For instance, I find myself uncertain which of two recent events – the election of a socialist government in London and the destruction of Hiroshima by a single atomic bomb – will have the profounder effect on India's future. It is this pressure from the world outside India that perhaps creates these uncertainties in my mind, although I am sure these outside pressures are reflected in pressures from within. On the one hand, there is the element that one might call purely political, and on the other an element one cannot but see as rooted in or flowing from a power that goes beyond the norm of what we morally understand by power –

Kasim broke off. He stared at the paper for a while. The words meant so little. What was in his mind seemed to mean

495

so little too. It was the world outside his mind, the world he felt he couldn't encompass that meant much. Tonight, it couldn't be reached.

Coda for Operation Zipper

Early that September, coming into the harbour of Georgetown on the island of Penang, where the tide was presumably low, the first detachment of re-occupying British troops observed what looked like an uncomfortably large number of Japanese soldiers assembled along the harbour wall, so that for a moment it wasn't clear to them whether they faced a reception committee or something less welcoming, whether Zipper which had begun life as an offensive operation and then been rescaled as an expedition of liberation of the people of Malaya wouldn't now become an operation again.

The matter was cleared up satisfactorily when a young Marine officer, attempting to mount the perpendicular iron ladder on the harbour wall from the light assault vessel that rocked up and down in the low-lying water, got into difficulties and the Japanese soldier nearest above him got down on his knees, stretched out an arm, and said, 'I help you, Johnnie?' Subsequently, most of the men, mounting at other points, found themselves momentarily relieved of their rifles, which certainly made the climb easier for them, but rather nullified the impression they'd had that the Nips were among the least accommodating people you'd be likely to find East of Suez (which was saying something). And Penang looked much more promising than Kalyan. Behind the line of Japanese soldiers were groups of pretty Chinese girls, grinning and waving.

Further down the coast, on one of what Leonard Purvis once heard fellow guests of the Maharanee's call the beaches around Port Swettenham, there was no harbour wall to scale, instead, an idyllic scene, an immense stretch of golden sand backed by elegantly disposed palm-trees. The senior officer riding in on a swift shallow-draughted landing craft was sardonically amused by the sight of three diminutive Japanese officers waiting for him on the sand, holding their

496

swords in a manner that indicated submission. Beautifully uniformed and shod, the Englishman had himself carried ashore through a few inches of water by two stalwart marines who placed him gently on dry land in front of the Japanese commander. After an exchange of polite formalities, the English officer said, 'Perhaps you'd like to see how we would have come in in less peaceful circumstances?'

He gave an order. A junior officer in the landing craft blew a whistle and raised a flag. From half-a-mile out, where waited a formidable line of heavy landing-craft (and further behind still, the big ships that had formed part of the Zipper convoys) there at once came the growling sound of marine engines starting up. Almost, one could smell the oily fumes. They came in, making impressive waves and wakes with their blunt bows and sterns: ten, twenty, thirty of them; and then stopped, crashed down their single fronts or dramatically opened their double ones. Being so heavy they had not come in further because it was known (through intelligence) that for the last two hundred yards the water was barely wading depth, not more than eighteen inches, insufficient to get way astern for putting back to the ships for more loads. They had stopped about four hundred yards out where there were three feet beneath them, sufficient for their purpose, and no obstacle either for the green-clad infantry or for the water-proofed trucks, carriers and armoured vehicles which now spewed out of them and began to advance, remorselessly shortening the distance between themselves and the observers on the sands.

After going fifty yards, though, something odd happened. The leaders of the files of soldiers in the centre suddenly disappeared beneath the bland, scarcely rippling surface, and on one of the flanks the line of vehicles sank equally suddenly – not completely like the men but up to their superstructures. Whistles blew, men shouted and thrashed around. Only on the other flank was the operation of landing going smoothly, but in that sector there was no treacherous and unexpected sandbank, nor any of the quicksand which nearly cost a life or two and claimed more than one armoured vehicle.

The senior officer on the beach, having run instinctively forward, was standing now, bemused, with his beautiful boots in several inches of water. He was concerned for his troops and had no opportunity of observing the Japanese officers behind him; but his *aide* did, and later – whenever he recounted the tale – said he had never until that moment really understood what was meant by the inscrutability of the Orient.

He also said he hoped that if his commander felt he'd suffered any kind of humiliation from this incident he'd been more than compensated a few days later when he went down to Singapore, freshly laundered, to watch the simple, precise, efficient and impeccably organized formal surrender by the Japanese in Malaya to the brisk and handsome naval officer, the Supremo, who in less than eighteen months' time was to mount a far less simple but equally precise, efficient and impeccably organized operation – not for receiving power back but for handing it over.

BOOK TWO 1947
Pandora's Box

I

1947

It was June, and there was a full year to go before the date the British Government had proposed as one by which it could be assumed that a satisfactory constitutional settlement would have been reached and the *raj* could withdraw in honour of its undertakings, and the long struggle for independence could be considered over.

But the bustling new Viceroy was back in Delhi. He had returned from consultations in London on the last day of May. Scarcely pausing to get his feet back under the desk, on June 2 he held meetings with Indian leaders and told them in confidence of the new plan proposed by him and approved by the British cabinet. On June 3 he broadcast to the Indian nation and said it was now clear that the division of India into two self-governing dominions, India and Pakistan, was inevitable, and added that the British Parliament would pass the necessary legislation to demit power on this basis during the present parliamentary session.

On June 4 he held a press conference (a feature of his vice-royalty which some old hands thought unnecessarily showy) and in answer to a question confirmed that this hastening through of legislation in Whitehall meant that Government would transfer power not next year but this year. He said, 'I think the transfer could be about the fifteenth of August.'

The astonished questioner did a rapid calculation. Ten weeks to go. Ten weeks. Ten *weeks?* It may have been that on this occasion several members of the Bengal Club at least looked like dying of apoplexy, but there is no reliable evidence, and they must by now have become inured to such rude shocks, however terminally rude this one seemed. It is

501

far more likely that in other places where a more sophisticated response was to be expected, people simply said, 'I wonder what Halki will make of it?'

Halki was the new pseudonym of a young Brahmin, Shankar Lal, a shy retiring man who had left his orthodox family in the Punjab to earn his living as a cartoonist in Bombay. *Halki* meant 'light-weight or counterfeit' and replaced an earlier pseudonym, *Bhopa* (a priest possessed by the spirit of the god he worships). The new pseudonym wasn't intended to hide his identity; his style was unmistakable; even the CID recognized it when his cartoons began to reappear after the several months of unemployment that followed the publication of the still-famous Churchill two-finger cartoon. As to that unemployment, the one or two close friends in whom he confided explained to others that his silence was not due to editorial cowardice so much as to Shankar Lal's strength of character. Lal had refused several offers from editors only too willing to uphold the freedom of the press. He had gone into seclusion to think about the nature of his political commitment and to perfect his style; but he had made a verbal agreement with the editor of a popular Indian-controlled English-language newspaper to offer his work exclusively to him directly he felt ready to publish again.

During this interim period his editor-designate sometimes went out to Juhu, where Lal lived in great simplicity, to look at his work and try to persuade him to start publishing right away. Lal declined, with his usual courtesy, but often gave the editor whichever of the private cartoons he had most admired, and these the editor framed and arranged round the walls of his office (which was where Perron now saw them).

Halki's most devoted admirers used to – and still – say that a retrospective exhibition would show how Shankar Lal's youthful political adherence to Congress's aims of unity and freedom had shaded off into a generally humanist view of life. Among the unpublished work from the watershed period between the Churchill two-finger cartoon and an equally famous cartoon that marked his reappearance was one drawn in late August, 1945, after Wavell's announcement of cold-weather elections. This depicted the then-Viceroy, statue-naked on a plinth (inscribed 'Vote!') in the attitude of Rodin's Thinker, his bronze shoulders caked with snow. Actually, there were two versions of this unpublished work. The first included in the distant background a hot and sweaty affray between Muslims and Hindus and was captioned 'The Solution?'. The second version, still featuring Wavell as the snow-clad Thinker, omitted the affray but substituted the figure of an undernourished child asleep at the base of the plinth, with one hand grasping his begging bowl. The word 'Vote!' had disappeared from the plinth but reappeared on the side of the empty bowl. This was Perron's favourite of the two.

A successor to this unpublished cartoon (also unpublished) was dated 20 September 1945, the day after Wavell's report to the nation on his return from London, where he had attempted (unsuccessfully) to wrest from Attlee's government the kind of clear statement of policy that would have given the already-announced cold-weather elections the special significance which all political parties in India felt was lacking: a clear statement about independence. This cartoon was captioned 'Box-Wallah', and portrayed Wavell in the garb of an itinerant Indian merchant and purveyor of ladies' dress materials, squatting on his hunkers on the verandah of a European bungalow, recommending his wares to a gathering of memsahibs who bore remarkable resemblances to Bapu, Nehru, Patel, Tara Singh, Maulana Azad and Mohammed Ali Jinnah. Jinnah was sitting somewhat apart from 'her' colleagues, consulting a glossy magazine marked 'The Pakistan Ladies' Home Journal'; but none of them was responding to the pleas of the box-wallah or to the sight of the avalanche of silks and woollens he was flinging hopefully in all directions (lengths marked: 'New Executive Council – Indian patterns'; 'Central Assembly Dress Lengths (for Cold Weather Wear)'; 'Constituent Assembly Fashion Designs, For All Seasons'; 'Provincial Election Lengths: Graded Prices'; 'Dominion Status Fabrics (Slightly Soiled)'.

Why didn't Halki want to publish this one? Perron asked. Oh, the editor said, Halki wanted to. It was he, the editor, who had refused. One couldn't dress such eminent men up in women's clothes, like so many transvestites, especially when the women's clothes were European-style. Look at Gandhi's legs, (the editor said) and at those flapper's shoes.

The next significant cartoon was the one with which Halki had made his public reappearance, in December 1945, when (after an adjournment) the 'show-piece' trials of three INA officers began at the Red Fort in Delhi. Perron had already seen this one, because his old officer from Poona days had sent it to him. It was with this cartoon that Perron's interest in Halki had begun.

The trials were described as showpieces because they seemed to have less to do with the seriousness of the cases chosen to begin the long legal process of bringing to justice men who had waged war against the king than they had to do with proving GHQ's and the C.-in-C.'s determination not to show partiality (or, conversely, to attack the three main communities simultaneously). The officers chosen for the grand opening trial at the Red Fort had been Shah Nawaz Khan (a Muslim), Captain P. K. Sahgal (a Hindu) and Lieutenant G. Dhillon (a Sikh).

Halki's cartoon was very simple. It consisted merely in a beautifully sombre and perfectly proportioned drawing of the Red Fort, and carried the bleak caption, 'The King-Emperor's Tomb.' That was all. From that day, the editor told Perron, circulation began to rise. The cartoonist had caught the right new mood and Halki became famous overnight. But he had remained shy, enigmatic. Some of his cartoons occasionally seemed almost pro-British, or anti-party. For instance there was this one, in 1946, at the time of the short-lived but tricky mutiny at Bombay in the Royal Indian Navy, a mutiny which had surely convinced the British, if they weren't convinced already, that their time had expired. But the cartoon had taken editorial courage to publish because it showed an Indian frigate, controlled by mutinous ratings who had trained the ship's guns on the Royal Yacht Club and were about to open fire. Bursting through the roped-off gangway to stop them was Patel, in full Congress garb, waving his arms hysterically. The caption ran, 'What are you doing, for God's sake? One day we may want it ourselves.'*

* Royal Yacht Club – traditionally the most exclusive in India – was actually closed down after independence.

Perron did not remember this one. Neither Bob Chalmers, his old officer from Poona, nor Aunt Charlotte had sent it to him. Nor did he remember the next two or three the editor showed him. The first of these pre-dated the naval mutiny joke and made a pair with the Red Fort cartoon. It was a meticulous drawing of a famous building, the Central Assembly in Delhi, in which in the first phase of the cold-weather elections the Congress had captured all the general seats but the Muslim League had won every one of the seats reserved for Muslims. Both parties had claimed a landslide victory and Halki's cartoon was captioned *Jai Hind* ! Closer inspection revealed a fissure in the foundation of the building and a crack spreading right up through one side of the fabric. Reluctantly, the editor hadn't published this, but he published the two-part cartoon in which Halki satirized the climax and anti-climax of the INA trials at the Red Fort.

The first frame showed a senior British officer mounted on a dome in the attitude of the statue of justice above the Old Bailey in London. Although blindfolded, the officer was recognizable as the C.-in-C. His scales were unusual since instead of two suspended trays there were three, each occupied by a mannikin figure representing the religion of each of the three accused, a Hindu, a Sikh and a Muslim. The C.-in-C.'s sword was held firmly aloft. In the second frame, which celebrated the anti-climax after the verdicts of Guilty and the C.-in-C.'s reduction of the sentences of life transportation, cashiering and forfeiture of pay to cashiering and forfeiture only, the scales were empty and his sword lacking its blade (it looked as if it must have fallen off through faulty workmanship). Beneath the blindfold the C.-in-C.'s expression remained unchanged: austere, determined and disapproving.

Yet one more cartoon was devoted to the subject of the INA, but Perron had to get the editor to explain it. After the anti-climax to the Red Fort trials it had become clear that except in several serious cases involving murder or brutality the *raj* could do nothing except cashier the officers and discharge the approximately 7,000 sepoys and NCOs who, classified as

505

'black', had not already been discharged as 'greys', or, as 'whites', returned to their units in semi-disgrace. The bulk of these 'black' discharges (after which the subject of the INA could conveniently be considered closed) occurred at Holi, 1946, the Spring fertility festival, traditionally celebrated by crowds roaming the streets throwing coloured powders and squirting coloured inks at everyone in sight. Halki's cartoon, captioned 'Holi', depicted a crowd of the discharged men emerging from a detention centre, being greeted by their families and throwing immense quantities of powder into the air and at one another. It took some time to discern in the distant background the plight of a loyal Indian Army sepoy still on guard-duty at the camp who had been sprayed with coloured ink by the departing prisoners and who was obviously being put on a charge by an immaculately dressed and irate British officer for being unkempt on duty. The editor published this cartoon too and received several threatening letters as well as a formal protest from the committee of the All-India Congress.

The next cartoon was one that Perron had also seen. Rowan had sent it to him as an enclosure with the only letter he had ever written. It illustrated a meeting of the Cabinet Mission of 1946 which had come out to India in the hot weather after the elections to seek an agreement on the major constitutional issue arising out of the continuing difficulty the British Government seemed to be having in establishing to whom to hand over when the time eventually came. The cartoon showed the three sweating members of the Mission: Cripps (merely President of the Board of Trade, but difficult to detach from Indian affairs), the Secretary of State (Pethick-Lawrence) and the First Lord of the Admiralty (Alexander). They were sitting staring at a large map of India which showed the country's provincial boundaries. A legend at one side of the map provided the clue to the different hatchings: perpendicular lines for Hindu majority provinces and horizontal lines for Muslim majority provinces (with a few areas of cross-hatching in the Punjab and Bengal). But nearly one-third of the map remained unhatched. The main caption was: 'A Paramount Question' and this was followed by a sub-caption in the form of a dialogue between the three ministers:

Sec. of State: I say, Cripps, what do the blanks represent?
Cripps: God knows.
Alexander: Perhaps the fellow ran out of ink.

Rowan's comment when sending this cartoon to Perron had been: 'Confidentially, it's said to be quite true, that three senior cabinet ministers between them had no idea that the self-ruling princely states, who have individual treaties with the paramount power (the Crown) respecting their rights to their own independence, cover so much of India.'

Another cartoon, which Perron hadn't seen, dated June 29, 1946, showed the cabinet mission returning disconsolately to London, climbing aboard a plane labelled 'Imperial Shuttle Service'. The Secretary of State was carrying the Imperial Crown and Cripps was surreptitiously handing him back a large diamond and saying, 'You'd better stick it back in, already.'

Halki's inventiveness here lay chiefly in the way he made the three British ministers look like three shady Jews from Amsterdam, and Nehru, Jinnah and Tara Singh look like three equally shady Arab merchants who had come to wave them off but were eyeing each other suspiciously, wondering if the jewel from the crown had been secretly handed over to whichever one of them had offered the highest number of piastres. Perron hadn't seen the cartoon because the editor hadn't dared publish it.

After this light-hearted cartoon came a series of tragic ones, every one of which the editor had published. They belonged to the period following Congress's decision to accept Wavell's invitation to join a new executive council which became known as the interim government, and to do this without the League. With governments formed in all the British-ruled provinces after the elections, some with League ministries but the majority with Congress ministries, the vital gap in government lay at the disputed and potentially federal centre. One of Halki's cartoons portrayed this enigmatically. It was the one in which he first reintroduced a characteristic figure from his 'Bhopa' days – the struggling and emaciated figure of Indian freedom and unity, last seen clenched in Churchill's two-fingered fist. Here he was now, the emaciated figure,

507

stretched on a pavement asleep, but in two sections. Nothing connected the trunk to the lower limbs. You could see pavement between them. The majority of its Congress admirers interpreted it as a criticism of the Muslim principle of partition, of a separate Muslim state as a *sine qua non* of independence. The editor told Perron that it was really Halki's criticism of the men who had it in their power to join the two portions of the body together by at least attempting to work together at the centre.

'And these,' he said, leading Perron to another wall, 'are what I call Halki's Henry Moore cartoons, all inspired by those drawings your artist did of English people living like troglodytes in the underground railway stations during the Blitz. I published all these and became very unpopular with the proprietors. A cartoon should make people laugh, they said, even if it is only to laugh at themselves. But I said, What is there to laugh about now? Well – look at this!'

'This' was a sombre pen and ink drawing of Calcutta, captioned 'Direct Action Day', August 16, 1946 and celebrated the result of Jinnah's decision to resort to violence in the belief that the Viceroy had betrayed him by allowing Congress to enter the central interim government without him. In this picture, though, it was difficult to distinguish Muslim dead from Hindu dead. Halki had just drawn a pile of bodies, such as might be seen on the streets of Calcutta on any night of the week, except that these were obviously dead, not sleeping; but ordered in rows, like sleepers, in diminishing perspective from a lit to an unlit area.

There were several variations on this theme, but it was always night-time and the street was always the same street, the foreground lamp-post the same lamp-post. The most striking (Perron thought) was the one that showed the street all but empty. There were no bodies on the pavement, bloodstains adumbrated the shapes of bodies cleared away. In the background you could just see Bapu, with his staff, accompanied by Jinnah (hands behind back) walking down the road towards the lit area. This carried no caption and was the last of the pictorially sombre cartoons. Sombreness, though, continued in the jokey ones that followed.

A cartoon dated 3 September 1946 marked the occasion of

the swearing in of the interim central government headed by Nehru, ostracized by Jinnah and overshadowed by the assassination of one of the nominated non-League Muslims, Shafaat Ahmed Khan, which caused riots in Bombay and Ahmedabad. Another, in mid-October, celebrated Jinnah's about-face, his decision to co-operate and enter the interim government to protect Muslim interests. To accommodate him three non-League Muslims had to resign. A third cartoon, dated in November, represented Halki's satirical view of this armed collaborative truce, a drawing of Wavell presiding over a round-table conference of his brawling Indian ministers (whose briefcases, leaning against their chairs, were bulging with fused bombs). A window gave a view of a rioting mob. A doorway was marked as the way into the Constituent Assembly where the future constitution of free India would eventually have to be settled. The door was wide open but clearly no one was prepared to enter. In this cartoon Wavell was drawn in diminutive proportions, crouched in an overwhelming viceregal chair, and with two heads – or rather one head drawn twice, with connecting lines denoting its swift turning to and fro, as he listened first to one argument and then to another. The caption ran: 'I see' and only readers who knew that this brief sentence was said to be the Viceroy's most frequent contribution to every conversation really appreciated the joke.

One of the unpublished Halki cartoons of the last phase of Wavell's viceroyalty was drawn early in December when Wavell had persuaded the British Government to invite a delegation (headed by himself) of Hindu, Muslim and Sikh leaders, to a consultation in London, which he hoped would break the deadlock. Once again there was the waiting aeroplane ('Imperial Shuttle Service'). The pilot, looking out of his window, was Attlee and the co-pilot Cripps. Advancing across the tarmac were Nehru, Baldev Singh and Jinnah and Liaquat Ali Khan. At the head was Wavell, but whereas the four Indian leaders were depicted as free agents merely prodding each other forward with a peremptory finger digging into the back of the man in front, Wavell's hands were manacled behind his back and the finger pressing into *him* was Nehru's. It was captioned 'The Invitation'. The editor had not published it because he thought it a shade too sympathetic to the Viceroy and potentially troublesome. Later he regretted his decision.

He had missed the point of the leer Halki had drawn on Attlee's face and only fully appreciated Halki's interpretation when in the following February (1947) after a further couple of months' variations on the theme of incompatibility (with the constituent assembly assembling without the League, and then the Congress threatening to withdraw from the interim government if the League insisted on remaining in it), Attlee announced his government's intention of transferring power peacefully and responsibly by June 1948 and hinted that if the constitutional issue hadn't been solved by then an award would have to be made and power transferred to whatever authority Britain felt would govern in India's best interests. This (as the editor pointed out to Perron, who agreed) was exactly the kind of clear statement that Wavell had always tried to get. But it was accompanied by another, to the effect that Wavell's 'wartime appointment as Viceroy' (which was the first anyone had heard about such a limitation to a traditional five-year term of office) would end in March and that his successor would be Louis Mountbatten, the victorious Supremo of South-East Asia Command in the recent war, a relation of the King's, but patently a man of the new world.

Halki celebrated this news with a cartoon which the editor published against considerable internal opposition but with popular acclaim. Again, it was a two-frame cartoon, each frame showing a different aspect of one of those old-fashioned cottage style barometers: a little rustic house from which a male figure emerged in poor conditions and a female one in summery.

Halki's rustic house was a simplified version of the main entrance to Viceregal House. Frame one showed Wavell outside the first of the twin doors. The sky above was black. Bulging monsoon clouds were pierced by a fork of lightning coming from the mouth of a heraldic, rather ancient, winged lion, labelled 'Imperialism, circa 1857'. In the second frame the sky was bland, lit by a sparkling little sun held aloft by a frisky airborne lamb (with Attlee's face) labelled 'Imperialism, circa 1947'. Below this bland sky the gaunt figure of

Wavell had retired into the gloom of Viceregal House and out
of the other door had come the fine-weather figure of a smart
toy-soldier (Mountbatten), magnificently uniformed, taking
the salute, smiling excessively and exuding sweetness and
light.

Subsequently, Halki had found his cottage-barometer
theme a useful one to hark bark to during the first month or so
of Mountbatten's appointment, weeks spent in seemingly
inexhaustible rounds of conferences and counter-conferen-
ces. These later cartoons portrayed the various problems the
new Viceroy had had to contend with and (perhaps) his
growing exasperation at his inability to solve them to his own
satisfaction. Political intransigence (from whichsoever party)
was portrayed in the shape of the stormy figure (for example,
Jinnah, but not invariably; there was once even Gandhi)
emerging from the dark door while the toy-soldier retreated
into his, and the bland sky was threatened by clouds that
never quite covered the frisky lamb (although the smile on
the lamb's face tended to get more and more strained).

'But that first barometer cartoon,' the editor said, referring
back to the Wavell/Mountbatten version, 'is the prime
example of Halki's gift for foreseeing the inner nature of
events before they have actually taken place.'

'When will Mr Shankar Lal be back in Bombay?' Perron
asked. The editor shrugged. 'He went almost without notice.
He came to see me just two weeks ago and said he must go to
the Punjab to try to persuade his parents to come down here,
because otherwise they would find themselves living in
bloody Pakistan. He said he had been working two or three
days on a cartoon for publication on August 15, in case he isn't
back by then.'

'But there's still a fortnight to go.'

'I know. But he said his parents are very stubborn people.
Anyway, I have the cartoon. It is terrible. I may not dare
publish it. It is in the safe at home so I cannot show it to you.
But you saw his June 3 cartoon? People say it is his
masterpiece.'

'No, I haven't seen that.'

'Oh you must, Mr Perron. It is very funny. I have the
original at home because even my wife laughed. Everybody

laughed. They rang me from Delhi and told me Mountbatten had laughed.' The editor banged his desk bell. 'I will get a copy of the relevant issue.'

*

For the June 5 issue, commemorating Mountbatten's announcement that Pakistan was now inevitable, and that the British would withdraw 'probably by August 15' Halki had worked throughout June 4 and drawn a picture of an immense Gothic building, or rather a structure which the architect had planned as one only to be frustrated (one had to imagine) over certain details of land acquisition. The attempt to create an illusion of a single façade, although admirably conceived and executed, hadn't quite worked, although it took several moments of close study of Halki's exemplary drawing to discern this. The cartoon occupied a whole page.

The main building, one such as citizens of Bombay were especially familiar with, was a huge emporium bearing some basic resemblance to the local army and navy shop. Across the façade the name ran: *Imperial Stores*. Between the word *Imperial* and the word *Stores* were the royal coat of arms and the announcement: *By Self-Appointment*. The building was several storeys high and drawn so as to show the main street frontage and one side-street elevation. The main entrance, curiously, was on the side street. Above this side street entrance there was another sign: *Proprietor:* Albert George Windsor; *Manager:* Clem Attlee.

At ground level, front and side, there were display windows crammed with goods but across each banners had been pasted proclaiming: *Grand Closing Down Sale. Expiry of Lease. Starts June 3. Bargains in Every Department. All Stock must be Sold by August 15.* Above this building the lamb held the sparkling sun aloft.

Outside the main entrance on the side street stood a tall, splendidly uniformed commissionaire who was looking at his watch, awaiting the moment to open the doors. Halki had caught Mountbatten's expression of detachment and self-confidence perfectly. All round the building there were queues of eager bargain hunters, mostly civilians but also soldiers and police. Each queue was separated from the others

512

by its own 'Queue Here' sign – and these were variously inscribed, Congress, League, Sikhs, Hindu Mahasabah, Liberals, Europeans, Anglo-Indians, Tribes, Scheduled Castes, and at the head of each queue was a clearly identifiable leader who was consulting his shopping list.

The queues were orderly and well drilled – you felt that the commissionaire had disciplined them to be so and that he knew, they knew, he would stand no nonsense. One of these queues stretched right round the side-street and along the main frontage. This was the one headed by Mr Nehru and Mr Gandhi and was by far the longest. But exactly mid-way along the main frontage this queue was interrupted to allow passageway from the road into the building, and it was this visual break that confirmed (or originated) the impression that the building was not really an architectural whole.

Sandwiched between what could now be seen as two interrupted halves was an older building, obviously still in the ownership of a small shopkeeper who had been surrounded, propped up, pressed up against and down upon, by the giant concern, but never wholly absorbed. A great deal of ingenuity had been shown in creating the illusion that the smaller shop was part of the bigger one, that the older structure was a mere decorative flourish that did nothing to diminish the architectural integrity of the whole edifice. The older building announced itself as 'The Princes' Emporium' and was labelled, 'Imperial Stores (Paramountcy, 1857) Ltd.' The sticker across its one narrow window said, 'Business as Usual' and its narrow little Moghul door was guarded by a commissionaire whom the editor told Perron was recognizable as the head of the British Political Department.

Free access to this door from the road was secured by ropes that separated the orderly Congress queue, and Halki had depicted a very old-fashioned Rolls Royce drawn up at the pavement. Emerging from this limousine were a Maharajah and the first two or three of what looked like a car-full of wives arriving on a shopping expedition. Standing in the road just behind the car was a policeman – looking exactly like Patel, the chief enemy in the Congress camp of the Indian princely states. He was noting down the car's registration number in a book labelled 'Traffic Offences (Obstructions)'.

The fun did not end there. Facing the main frontage on the other side of the road there was work in progress on a giant multistoreyed building, only the ground-floor of which was completed and occupied. A placard announced: *Anglo-American Atomic and Commercial Enterprises Inc and Ltd (Successors to Box-Wallah and Co)*. Through the ground-floor windows you could see men at work in the offices. An American executive sat with his feet on a desk, smoking a cigar and using three telephones. A British executive sat with his feet under the desk, smoking a pipe and talking into only one. Queueing to enter the building was a hybrid collection of Indian businessmen consulting attendant lawyers who were in turn consulting draft contracts. Already in the building too, were figures representing the great Indian industrialists (Tata and Birla). A separate side-street entrance gave access to a queue of Muslim (Pakistan) businessmen, most of whom seemed destined to end up at the desk of the American executive.

And still the fun did not end. In distant perspective, on a continuation of the main frontage of Imperial Stores, was a Labour Exchange, and here there were four queues of Englishmen and Englishwomen whose children were being comforted by faithful bearers and ayahs: a queue each for ICS, IMS, army and police. The queuers were going into and coming out of doors marked 'Pension' and Compensation'. Some of those who had collected their dues were walking across the road, holding moneybags, to join the queue waiting to enter the offices of Anglo-American Enterprises Inc and Ltd. Some, obviously elderly, were trekking in another direction, to the office of a travel agent whose windows were bannered: Cheap One Way Retirement Tickets. Bilaiti and All Best Hill Stations.

There was no caption. A caption would have been excessive.

'Tomorrow I have a party,' the editor said. 'Come and see the original. At my house.'

'I'm afraid I can't. I'm leaving Bombay tomorrow morning,' Perron said.

'Then take this copy. I have never yet had in my office an Englishman all the way from London who comes to see me entirely to discuss Halki. He will be very flattered. No, no, that is wrong. I have never yet succeeded myself even in flattering him.'

'Thank you,' Perron said. He felt rather moved. It was the special gift Indians had, to move you unexpectedly; unexpectedly because you felt that historically you did not deserve any consideration or any kindness.

*

Leaving the newspaper office he walked for a while along the crowded Bombay pavement, then saw and hailed a taxi. He told the man to go in the direction of the Gateway and the Taj. When the taxi reached the spot where he had drawn up his jeep just two years ago he told the driver to stop but wait for him. He walked the few yards to the wall of the esplanade, with its view on to the Arabian Sea; and its smell. Disgusting. Peaceful. I shall never go back home, one Perron cried. The other said: Take me back, for God's sake. When he returned to the taxi he threw annas at the little crowd of children and told the driver to go to Queen's Road.

*

He paid the wallah off, tipping excessively as though this munificence had become obligatory since Mountbatten had removed the last doubt that the British intended to go and so made them the only people left in India who were universally popular. He studied the blocks of flats. He couldn't be certain which block he wanted, but then – believing he recognized the forecourt – he entered it, imagining Purvis ahead of him barging into the servant and the girl. He climbed the few steps to the dark entrance and went along an unfamiliar passage to the lift-shaft. This convincingly announced itself as out of order and on either side the name plates stirred other recollections. Desai? Tractorwallah? He climbed the steps to the first floor and stood, perplexed, facing the door whose name-plate should be Grace but wasn't. He went to the door opposite. Major Rajendra Singh, IMS. That, surely, was right? He climbed the next flight and arrived at the flat above Rajendra Singh's.

Hapgood. Mr Hapgood, the banker, Mrs Hapgood, the

banker's wife and Miss Hapgood, the banker's daughter. One of the few remaining happy families in Bombay? He pressed the bell. Would the servant be the same servant? Would they recognize one another? The door opened. He did not recognize the servant. The boy was (God help us all, Perron thought) Japanese.

'Is Mr Hapgood in?' he asked. He handed in his card. The boy studied it carefully, ridging eyebrows as beautifully shaped as Aneila's. Not quite Japanese; a mixed-blood oriental from Sumatra? Singapore? Jakarta? A handsome, poisonous-looking young man who sported a gold wrist-watch. One could smell the starch on his arrogantly spotless white steward's jacket and trousers. He wore black shoes with pointed toes. 'I will see if Master is in.'

Perron thought: Master, now, is it? The British will always be safe.

The boy let him in, then shut the door and went in the direction of the living-room. Perron glanced down the corridor towards Purvis's old room. The door was shut; so was the door of the adjoining room. And the flat looked as if it had not been redecorated since then.

'Master says come.'

Perron followed the boy through the dining-room area and into the living-room which had once struck him as elegant, which now looked just a little disorganized. A quick glance at the wall behind the long settee confirmed the continuing existence of the Guler-Basohli paintings. A man stood on the balcony, as Purvis had done, holding a glass, looking out at the Oval. It was a clear evening, the sun not yet down. The man was tall and thin. For some reason Perron had always imagined Hapgood as short, rotund and red-faced, like the tea-planter at the Maharanee's. Hearing footsteps, Hapgood turned round.

'Mr Perron?'

'Yes. Mr Hapgood?'

'What can I do for you?'

'I'm sorry to bother you. I called downstairs on the off-chance of seeing Colonel and Mrs Grace. I see they've gone, but I thought I'd take the opportunity to come up, because I feel I owe you an apology.'

'Oh?' Hapgood was a man with formidable eyebrows. His face was yellow and very creased. His jaw and chin suggested firmness of opinion. 'Have we met?' he asked.

'No. You and your family were away, in Ootacamund I think. But there was an officer called Leonard Purvis billeted here – a couple of years ago. I was here the day things rather got on top of him. I wasn't here when he smashed things up, but I saw the results, and I've always felt it was partly my fault that two of your Kangra paintings were damaged.'

Hapgood's eyebrows twitched. He glanced at the wall.

'Oh?' Then, 'Actually they're Guler-Basohli school. But Kangra covers it.'

The servant had come in with a glass on a tray. He put this down on the drinks table.

'Scotch? Gin?' Hapgood asked.

'Gin, thank you.'

'Master will have gin,' Hapgood told the boy without looking at him. 'Why do you feel it was partly your fault?'

'Purvis had no idea what they were, until I admired them and told him how valuable they were. So it was probably my fault that he singled them out when he was throwing bottles.'

'Oh,' Hapgood said. 'Was that why? We often wondered. He never seemed to notice them.' He strolled across the room towards the paintings. 'But as you see, the damage has been fairly well disguised. They are exquisite, aren't they? My wife was pretty upset at the time. But as I told her, it needs more than a bottle of rum to destroy a work of art.'

Perron had forgotten it was rum. Hapgood hadn't. He turned to Perron suddenly. 'Did you know the man my old bearer told me about? The man who had to climb the balcony and pull Purvis out of the bath?'

Perron admitted that he was the man.

Hapgood said, 'Good heavens.' Then, 'My dear chap. How nice of you to call – to have remembered the paintings. My wife will be sorry to have missed you. She was awfully touched that you bothered to leave the servant a chit about the bathroom door.'

Perron recalled that the servant had asked for a chit. He didn't actually remember writing one. Obviously he had done, probably while sitting in this room afterwards, drinking Old Sporran.

'Perron,' Hapgood was saying. 'Perron. Yes, I remember now. But ...'

'*Sergeant* Perron,' Perron said, to clear up any doubts. 'Field Security, Poona.'

'Field Security? I see. Somehow we'd always imagined the Sergeant Perron who pulled Purvis out of the bath was something to do with his so-called economic advisory staff.' Hapgood led the way back to the balcony. 'Field Security, Poona. Did you know a fellow who's now in pharmaceuticals here? What's his name –'

'Bob Chalmers?'

'That's it. Chalmers. His firm banks with us. I don't know him well. I remember he said he was Field Security in Poona and liked it so much he stayed on.'

'Chalmers was my officer. Actually I'm staying in his flat here in Bombay. We kept up, after the war.'

'Well bless my soul. Have you come out to join his firm?'

'No, I'm only on a visit. Quite a short one. And I've not seen Bob yet and probably won't now. He had to go to Calcutta just before I arrived, but left everything laid on so that I could stay at his place.'

'Yes, I see. And you knew the Graces?'

'No, I knew their niece, and their niece's father.'

'I'm afraid Mrs Grace has left. Poor old Arthur Grace died last year. Very suddenly. My wife and I were quite upset. He'd had dinner with us only the night before. Mrs Grace had gone up country to see her sister. The niece was getting married. Yes, I remember now. She was here to meet her father, wasn't she, when we were in Ooty?'

'The elder niece was here. There was a younger one.'

'I don't remember that. Anyway, one of them got married. Which was why Fenny Grace was away and poor old Arthur was on his own for a couple of weeks. We used to have him up. I thought he was perfectly all right but my wife said she wasn't happy about him. She said he looked as if he didn't know what anything was about any longer. Curious phrase. But women have these intuitions. He had a heart attack. Went, just like that.'

Hapgood snapped his fingers, but to call the servant's attention to his empty glass. Perron's was still half-full.

'This was last year?'

'Last year, yes. Middle of February. When the Indian ratings here mutinied. Things were a bit of a mess, but Fenny came back the moment we wired. Actually we thought it a bit thick that no one from her family came with her to help her get through it. But you're right. There must have been two nieces. I remember her saying her niece wanted to come with her. She couldn't have meant the niece who'd just got married. Must have been the other.'

'Sarah, I should think. The one who got married must have been Susan.'

'It rings a bell.'

'Susan must have married a man called Merrick.'

'I think that was it. Chap with something wrong with him?'

'He lost an arm in the war.'

'That's it. Yes. Fenny left us some snaps she took at the wedding. She had them printed here once she'd dealt with the funeral. Pity my wife's away. She'd have details like this much clearer in her mind. If you're anxious for news of the family I'm sure I could turn up the sister's address. Pankot, wasn't it? Fenny must have given it to my wife, and my wife's very efficient keeping her address book written up.'

'I have the Pankot address. It's just that I've not heard since the end of 'forty-five. My fault really. One somehow lets things slide.'

'True. True. One lets things slide. The last we saw of Fenny was when she left for Delhi after the funeral. She was going to fly home to another sister in London. I expect the London address is in my wife's book too, but I don't think they wrote to one another because Fenny said it would only be a short trip and that she'd be back again. Then our daughter married an awfully nice Canadian Air Force chap we met in Ooty. We were in Montreal last year for the wedding. Pretty killing expense. But once in a lifetime. Now my wife's back in Montreal waiting to become a grandmother. I'm expecting a telegram almost any day.'

Perron lifted his glass. 'Good luck.'

'Thank you.' After drinking Hapgood said, 'Are you committed this evening?'

Perron lied. 'I'm afraid so, yes.'

'Tomorrow, perhaps?'

'Unfortunately I've left this call very late. I'm off tomorrow.'

'Oh. Where are you off to? Not home?'

'No, a little state called Mirat.'

'A long journey. They had some trouble there recently. Is that why you're going?'

'I didn't know that. What sort of trouble?'

'Usual thing. Communal riots. I think it's died down. Anyway, it's in the Punjab things are getting tricky. Too many people on the move in the hope of ending up in the right place. But what can you expect when you draw an imaginary line through a province and say that from August fifteen one side is Pakistan and the other side's India? The same applies to Bengal.'

'It is rather drastic, isn't it?'

Hapgood gave Perron a penetrating glance. He said, 'It's what an important minority felt they had to have and in the long term it's probably for the best.'

Perron nodded. Hapgood was probably more in sympathy with the Muslims than with the Hindus.

'Do you have press connections, then, Mr Perron?'

'Only rather marginal ones. Sufficient to help me move about and get seats on planes.'

'I asked because nearly every stranger from home you come across nowadays is either a journalist or a member of parliament swanning around ostensibly to observe the democratic process of dismantling the empire but actually making soundings for his private business interests. Nothing wrong with that, of course. India's going to be an expanding dominion market once it settles down. The thing is, we'll have to meet more outside and inside competition. Do you have business interests as well as marginal press ones, Mr Perron?'

'My interests are primarily academic.'

Again Hapgood snapped his fingers and again while they continued talking his glass was taken and replenished and returned. This time Perron had his own glass topped up. The Oval was under the spell of pink and turquoise light, fading into indigo shadows.

'If you have press connections, though, I suppose you're here to be in at the kill, if I may put it that way. Forgive me, but Mirat seems such an unlikely little place to go. If you want to be in at the kill you should go up into the Punjab and try to accredit yourself to the wretched chaps who've been formed into the boundary force and have the job of protecting the refugees and stopping them tearing at one another's throats.'

'Well as I said. My interests are primarily academic. And at the moment primarily concerned with the relationship between the Crown and the Indian states.'

'Well you could go up to Bahawalpur. They've had some high jinks there. Or down to Hyderabad. That's the one princely state large and powerful enough to prolong its independence for a while. Have you seen Patel? He's in charge of what I call the coercing operation. Have you seen the head of the British Political Department? He'd give you the other side of the picture. They say his department has been burning private papers for weeks now, all the scandalous stuff we've collected over the years about the way some of the Princes behaved. Couldn't let Patel get his hands on those, could you?'

'Well I have a definite invitation to Mirat. I think it will suit me very well, especially if it's had its troubles.'

'What sort of invitation, Mr Perron? I ask because I might be able to help you.'

'That's very kind of you. Actually the invitation's from the Chief Minister, Count Bronowsky. I met him here in Bombay during the war. He was kind enough to say I'd be welcome in Mirat at any time.'

'Then there's nothing I could do to smooth your way better. It was Bronowsky I had in mind. I don't know him socially, but he's had an account with us for years, and we usually meet in my office when he comes to Bombay. I haven't seen him for some time. Probably because of the troubles they've had there. How is he?'

'I've no idea, but well, I imagine. I wrote to him just before

521

coming out from England and there was a telegram waiting for me at Bob Chalmers's flat, inviting me to turn up whenever I wanted.'

'Well. Give him my regards.'

Perron looked at his watch, and prepared to finish his drink.

'Are you absolutely committed this evening? I've got a few people coming in, couple of chaps from the bank and their wives. Friends. Not all that boring. Actually it's buffet. Nowadays in Bombay you never know who'll turn up or who they'll bring. Being alone just now I encourage it.'

Perron was tempted. He had a brief and flaming image of the Maharanee floating in on the arms of a couple of English bankers, in her scarlet saree, subsiding on to the long settee under the Guler-Basohli paintings, showing her nipples; and of Aneila offering chairs, cigarettes, and dewy tumblers which she had rinsed under the tap in Purvis's bathroom to help the sinister little servant cope. And an image, then, of all the lights going out, because the light had virtually gone now from the forgiving Bombay sky, leaving only a gleam in the fretted edges of the palm fronds. And the sweet, grave, unforgettable unforgotten smell, drifting across from Back Bay.

'I'm afraid I am committed, sir,' Perron said. 'Perhaps if I come back this way I could give you a ring.'

'Of course,' Hapgood said, pleased to be called sir. But it was *now* Hapgood wanted. A new face to ease the ache of boredom. Hapgood's own face went out, as the nearby street-lamp came on, below and behind him. A trick of illumination.

'You have a new servant, I see.'

'Young Gerard? Yes. Bit of a mongrel. We inherited him from a chap who retired last year. Our agent in Ipoh. Gerard kept things going for him while he was in prison-camp. Very efficient fellow. Not like poor old Nadar, the one you'd remember. Trouble with Nadar, he couldn't keep his hands off stuff that got left around. We had to let him go. Mistake, probably. My wife says it's better to employ a dishonest servant you know inside out than one you'll never get on any sort of terms with. Not that it's going to matter either way to us next year. Our time will be up then. Learn to do our own cooking and washing up, I shouldn't wonder. Neither of us fancies Montreal. So it looks like Ewell or Sutton. Know anything about mushrooms?'

Automatically Perron thought of cloud formations.

'Mushrooms?'

'A friend of our Canadian son-in-law, an ex-RAF type who lives in Surrey, has gone in for mushrooms. Grows them in his garage. Making a fortune, I'm told. Not that we'll be looking to do that. But you need to put your mind to something, so preferably something with a saleable end-product. I don't fancy chickens. Mushrooms are quieter.'

Hapgood smiled. His face, re-illuminated as he guided Perron back into the living-room where Gerard had switched on some of the table-lamps, looked composed. And resigned. 'Well,' he said, 'if you change your mind, just arrive. Meanwhile I'd better get myself ready for the invasion.' Perhaps Gerard had run his bath (with the same imperturbable expression he had shown when running baths for Japanese officers in his previous master's house in Ipoh?).

Perron was about to say, 'Do you still have the same cook?' but realized in time that this might sound like an inquiry into the quality of the food to be expected. So he left not knowing whether that happy, co-operative, and sturdy little man still presided over the hot stoves in the Hapgood kitchen. On the whole, Perron thought, it was unlikely that he did. The bearer, the cook, and the cook's boy, had been a happy family too, in spite of the rivalry and the demarcation of zones of responsibility. When the bearer went they had probably followed him.

As Gerard held the door open, Perron glanced once again down the corridor, to get his last glimpse of Purvis's still-closed door.

*

Back in Bob Chalmers's rather odd flat he made a few notes about his visit to Hapgood. The oddness of Bob's flat consisted not merely in the unexpected situation of the house (in one of the narrow rather squalid roads behind the Gateway; not far, surely, from where the massage parlour had been?) but in the admixture of traditional and emergent Anglo-Indianism in its appointments. The rooms where basic European needs were scrupulously met (bathroom, bedrooms, dining-room) were furnished in the old dependable style. But in the living-room there was nowhere to sit comfortably. There were imitation Persian rugs on the floor, sparkling cushions from Rajputana, mattresses covered by durries or printed cotton bedspreads, a pair of tablas, a harmonium, and in a conker-coloured leather case – a tamboura, probably from Bengal. On the walls there were modern paintings by modern Indian painters. Impressionism had arrived (and a pointilliste school, after Seurat, to judge by a disturbing view of the burning ghats at Benares). Scattered round the room on cushions, on floor, on mattresses and in a unit-style bookcase, were the things that showed Bob Chalmers to be perhaps a little uncertain where his tastes lay. There were trade magazines dealing with pharmaceuticals and other light and heavy industrial subjects. There were literary magazines published in Calcutta and pale blue stiff-boarded editions of works by Radakrishnan about *karma* and *dharma* and the Hindu way of life. The bookcase held several volumes from the Left Book Club, a row of old Readers' Digests and the latest novel by Nevil Shute. On a very low coffee-table, among pottery ashtrays, were a translation of the poems of Gaffur by a Major Tippet, and the March 1947 issue of *The New English Forum* which Perron had sent him. This was an issue containing one of Perron's articles, the article originally entitled *Daulat Rao Sindia and the British Other Rank*, but subsequently retitled (for publication) *An Evening at the Maharanee's*, which title Perron had tossed out from the top of his head at the end of a rather drunken lunch at Prunier's with the young Tory MP who published the magazine and whose personal assistant in the publishing firm he directed had recommended Perron as a likely contributor, after reading Perron's review (in the *New English University Monthly*) of a book called *My Memories of* INA *and its Netaji*, by Maj. General Shahnawaz Khan, Foreword by Pt Jawahar Lal Nehru [*sic*], which Bob Chalmers had sent him from Bombay after its publication in Delhi in 1946 with a letter of which the only passage Perron clearly remembered was: 'Remember Bombay and Bordeaux? Well, this is connected. And get that last paragraph of "Jawahar Lal's" foreword, I quote: "I must confess that I have not been able, through lack of time, to read through this record, but I have read parts of it and it seems to me that this account is far the best we have at present." Unquote. How's that for shrewd fence-sitting, now that the trials are over?'

But then, Perron thought, putting his notebook away, and nodding assent to Bob Chalmers's bearer who was standing in the doorway indicating that supper was ready (which he could already tell, smelling the delicious scent of turmeric) where else can one sit, and remain in balance?

II

Perron woke. The silence was solid, as if he had been spun off the world into space. There were no echoes, not a glimmer of light in the primeval dark. Then he heard the engine breathe in the distance and re-identified himself as the lucky lone occupant of a coupé on the night train from Ranpur to Mirat. He sat up, reached for his cigarettes. The lighter illuminated his watch. Five a.m. He twisted his body round and raised the blind and then the shutter and gazed out at the pale frozen landscape. So vast a country. Its beauty unnerved him. The engine breathed again, sounding nearer. He held his own breath and listened to another sound: the cries of dogs hunting the plain in packs.

When he woke again light was streaming through the unshuttered window and the train was moving slowly, clacking its wheels rhythmically, reluctantly. The landscape was eroded. Nothing could live here, he thought.

He was cold. He got up, slipped his feet into chappals and reached for his robe. Enfolded in silk he rasped one hand against his cheeks. His eyes were gummy. They felt raw from the specks of sand and soot that had entered the compartment. Pushing through the door into the lavatory he felt the chill coming up through the hole in the pan. He wanted hot coffee. Comfort. There was none. In an hour or two it would seem impossible that he had ever felt cold.

*

Shaved, washed, dressed, he went to the sunny side of the compartment to warm himself. It was 7 a.m. He should have been in Mirat by now and drinking coffee or tea in the station restaurant, getting some bacon and egg. He had lost the knack of travelling in India. He hadn't even brought a flask of water. All he had was yesterday's papers, bought in Ranpur: *The Times of India* and *The Ranpur Gazette*. He now read through the *Gazette*, scarcely taking it in, flicking the pages. The only pieces worth reading were a waspish editorial and a quiet essay by someone calling himself Philoctetes. He couldn't remember who Philoctetes was. In this case, probably, the editor, exercising a gentle taste for *belles-lettres*.

He went back to the window. The train was passing a village. Water buffalo wallowed in the local tank. Women walked with baskets of cow-dung on their heads. Men drove skeletal goats and horned cattle. There was a smell of smoke. It would be a hot dry day.

*

It was gone nine o'clock when the train drew into Mirat (Cantonment): two hours late according to the new schedule. He was glad that he hadn't announced his arrival in advance and put anyone to the trouble of meeting him.

The platform was crowded. Officers, wives, mounds of luggage. Departing British. A train seemed to be expected in the other direction, from Mirat to Ranpur. The restaurant was crowded too. There wasn't a vacant table and he didn't want to share. He decided to push on and told the coolie to take him to where tongas were to be had.

The concourse was also crowded, mostly by squads of British troops squatting on piles of kit-bags, smoking. Perron's suitcase and hold-all were put on to a tonga. He told the man to go to the club. The tonga set off through the cantonment bazaar. Perron breathed in the familiar smell: an oily, spicy scent mingling with that of burning charcoal. And then they were out on to the first of the wide geometrically laid out roads of a military station, metalled roads with khatcha edges, shade trees, and lime-washed stones marking the culvert crossings over monsoon ditches, which gave access to the compounds of the old bungalows. The tonga passed neat white-shirted Indian clerks on cycles and was passed in turn by military trucks. Once you had seen one cantonment, it was said, you had seen them all.

It took twenty minutes to reach the club. The way in was by a broad gravel drive that curved through a compound darkened and cooled by trees and shrubs. The colonnaded façade was dazzling white. Against the white the sprays of red and purple bougainvillaea stood out exuberantly. After the tonga wallah had taken the luggage into the vestibule Perron paid him off.

There was no one in the vestibule. The hall beyond led to a terrace set with wicker chairs and tables. The vestibule was dark, high ceilinged. There were palms in brass pots. He banged a bell on the desk (which was discreetly positioned behind a pillar). A servant appeared from behind another pillar. Perron asked for the secretary. While he waited he studied some of the framed photographs that hung on the white-washed walls. These were mostly of victorious teams from old tournaments in the 1920s. Tennis, polo, cricket, golf. There was a photograph of Edward VIII when he was Prince of Wales.

A young Indian in European clothes came into the vestibule, asked if he could help, explained that the secretary was still having breakfast. Perron gave him his card and said he would be in Mirat for a little while and wondered whether the club could offer temporary membership, and if so whether it might include accommodation, say for tonight, and some breakfast now. The card he offered was the one that gave his London club address. The man glanced at it and said he was sure this could be arranged but that he would speak to the secretary. The bearer came back. The clerk told him to show the sahib out on to the terrace and serve him breakfast.

The terrace was longer and wider than the view from the vestibule suggested. Apart from the wicker chairs and tables which were arranged close to the balustrade to give occupants a view directly on to a long sweep of lawn and flowerbeds (with, beyond, behind a white painted fence, rougher ground set out for jumping and riding displays), there was also a line of club dining-tables and chairs ranged along the length of the inner wall. The tables were free of napery, their mahogany surfaces highly polished. Each had a silk shaded lamp. There were probably a dozen of these tables and, between each pair, casement doors which led into the interior. Half-way along the terrace one of the tables was occupied by two Indian officers and an Indian civilian (or an officer in civilian clothes). The rest were empty. At the far end of the line of wicker chairs and tables sat a European woman. She wore sunglasses and was drinking coffee. The Indian officers and the civilian were finishing breakfast. The bearer guided Perron to the first of the empty dining-tables.

He was a grizzled old man, white-uniformed, sashed, barefoot, gloved and turbanned. Having seated Perron he went away, returned almost at once with a tray from which he took things to lay a single place on the gleaming surface. Having done this he produced the final item – a menu secured in a silver-plated stand. 'Sahib,' he said, and went, leaving Perron to consult the bill of fare. Perron, picking the card up by its stand, suddenly leant back, gazed out at the sweep of lawn, the canna-lilies, the immense earthen pots of delicately tinted and scented flowers that stood sentinel between each batch of wicker chairs and tables. India, he thought. India. I'm back. *Really* back. Why, he wondered, was the Mirat Gymkhana Club so familiar? And then saw why. Once, both wearing civilian clothes, Bob Chalmers had breakfasted him at the Turf Club in Poona. The Mirat Gymkhana might have been a duplicate. The bearer came out again with a wooden contraption which he opened up and set behind the side-plate. A newspaper rest. Upon this he placed a folded newspaper called the *Mirat Courier*.

'No *Times of India*?'

'Not until midday, Sahib. Yesterday's is available.'

'I think not yesterday's. What is Fish Soufflé Izzat Bagh?'

'Local fish, Sahib. Caught daily in Izzat Bagh lake. Cooked with spice and served with rice. Today not recommended.'

'Oh, why?'

'Today not fresh, Sahib. Fish too long on ice. Fishermen not going out two day now.'

Perron ordered eggs and bacon and, when the old man had gone turned to watch the belligerent shining blue-black crows making hungry sorties on to the wet lawn. The Indian officers suddenly laughed aloud and slapped their napkins down. The European woman wearing the sun-glasses was getting up, gathering her things. She went through one of the open casement windows at the far end of the terrace. The civilian with the officers went on talking. Perhaps he was telling them funny stories.

'Mr Perron?'

An elderly man, short, stout, bald, stood by Perron's table. Perron got up, took the offered hand.

'Macpherson,' the man said. 'I'm the secretary. Please –' But Perron remained standing until, accepting his invitation Macpherson sat too. 'I hope you're being looked after all right.' Perron assured him he was. 'Don't have the fish, incidentally.'

'Your chap's already warned me off it.'

'That must be old Ghulam. Thank God for him anyway. Staff's difficult nowadays. Night train from Ranpur?' Perron nodded. 'Should have been in at seven. It gets worse every year. I see from your card you're from home. Been out here long?'

'About ten days. Can you put me up for the night?'

'For as long as you like. Nowadays we have more departures than arrivals. All the same, even for a night I'm afraid you'll have to pay temporary membership and I'm afraid the fee's for a minimum of one calendar month. War-time rule, dating from when young officers were coming and going and being posted overnight.'

'And forgetting to pay their bills?'

'That's about it. Still, a lot of them are dead long since, I expect. You've been out here before haven't you?'

'Yes, but not for long. A couple of years during the war.'

The Indian officers and the civilian had got up and were approaching. Macpherson looked up. 'Everything all right, Bubli?'

'Everything's fine, Mac.'

'Are you dining tonight?'

'Who can tell, with one thing and the other?'

'If you don't tell you're likely to get Fish Soufflé Izzat Bagh.'

'Oh, God help us. I'll let you know. See you, Mac.'

'See you, Bubli.'

'Nice fellow,' Macpherson said when they were alone again. 'Gentleman. But then most of them are. Which I can't say for some of our fellows.'

'How long have you been secretary, Mr Macpherson?'

'About ten years. Mirat was my first station. Oh, years ago before the other war. Artillery. I got a chance to come back in nineteen thirty. Jumped at it. Retired in thirty-five. Took this on. Don't regret a single day. Look forward to many more. No ties at home anyway.'

Perron nodded. He understood that here was where Macpherson would prefer to die.

'I had a job, though, back in 'thirty-seven, opening membership to Indian officers. It split the committee right down the middle. But I said if a man's got the King's Commission what does it matter what his complexion is. During the war the old members agreed I was right. It damned well disgusted us. We were damned well ashamed, I mean of some of our own countrymen. Do you know what they did once? Emptied all the chamber pots from the men's room into the swimming pool, because they'd seen a couple of Indian subalterns swimming there. I marched them out pretty smartly. Chamber pots in the swimming pool were just about their Kingston Bypass style. Of course, that was wartime, 'fortytwo, when the Indian politicians were kicking up a fuss. But do you know what happened here a few weeks ago?'

'No?'

'Swimming pool again. Someone excreted into a Gandhi cap and floated it. I never found out who. But I had my suspicions. Had to drain the pool, have it scraped, and get a Brahmin priest along to do a purification ritual before it was refilled. No Indian's been in it since. It'll be all right though.'

'Whom did you suspect?'

'The leader of what I called Mirat's second-fifteen rugger club. The English officer who let wind when I took Mirat's Chief Minister into the men's bar one evening.'

'Did the chief minister comment?'

'Not directly. He's not an Indian. If he had been he wouldn't have commented at all. But he couldn't resist saying, Shall we get some fresh air?' Macpherson waved a hand, indicating the terrace. Perron's breakfast began to arrive. 'Sorry, Mr Perron. Unpleasant subject. Enjoy your breakfast.'

Perron stood to acknowledge the secretary's leave-taking. He said, 'I know the man you mean, Dmitri Bronowsky? Actually I'm in Mirat to see him. Perhaps I can telephone from here and leave a message that I've arrived?'

Macpherson hesitated. 'Is he expecting you?'

'In general, yes.' Perron explained about the telegram that had awaited his arrival in Bombay. 'But I didn't wire back. I thought I'd just turn up.'

'I know he was here a few days ago but he may have gone to Gopalakand. I can find out easily enough. He's got a full plate just now. Not just Patel and company. Things haven't been too good here the past week or so.'

'It all looked quiet enough this morning.'

'Oh, in the cantonment. But across the lake, in the city. Not so good. That's why we don't recommend the Fish Soufflé Izzat Bagh. The fishermen are Muslims. They've fished the Nawab's lake since the eighteenth century. Tradition. Special sect. But they haven't dared go out the last couple of days since a couple of them were found drowned. They call it murder and blame the Hindus. So it looks as if we may be back to how it was last year and earlier this. There's a curfew in the old city. But we can always make you comfortable here, Mr Perron. I'll send my clerk along with the temporary members' book.'

Macpherson went. Perron drank his orange juice. The clerk came with the book. Perron filled in the columns at the top of the clean page at which the book was open. He resisted the temptation to turn back and check how long it had been since the club had last received a temporary member.

The front page of the *Mirat Courier* for today, Monday August 4, featured a muddily reproduced photograph of the Viceroy in Delhi with some of India's leading princes, which Perron had already seen in *The Times of India*. There was no reference in the accompanying article to Mirat's own prince, the Nawab, but the tone of the article suggested that the editor was anxious to convey an impression that the relationship between the princes and the Viceroy was of the friendliest kind; which, however true, was largely irrelevant to the political issue. The front page was, in fact, all sweetness and light. There was no follow-up to the rumour Perron had heard that Jinnah was accusing the Sikh leader Tara Singh of planning to assassinate him and sabotage the partition of the Punjab.

The bearer brought his bacon and egg and, glancing up, Perron saw that the woman in the sunglasses had come out of the further casement doorway and was walking slowly along the central strip of coconut matting. From a distance he'd assumed that she was middle-aged, perhaps because her hair looked dull, colourless, and because the sunglasses accentuated the rather disagreeable set of the mouth. Nearer to, he saw that she was quite a young woman, thin but well-shaped, with a good bust, and a graceful walk of the kind that suggested she had always been proud of her carriage and had worked at perfecting it: an acquired good carriage, rather than the natural good carriage that he remembered as characteristic, for example, of Sarah Layton. As she came nearly level with his table Perron smiled and said, 'Good morning.' She smiled too and murmured good morning and went slowly on. She reminded him (he realized) of a younger *Mrs* Layton. She had that kind of composure: indolence almost. She left behind her a whiff of scent just heavy enough to suggest that it was expensive.

Before starting on his breakfast Perron turned the *Mirat Courier* over to its back page. Here was another muddy photograph, illustrating a report headed 'Happy Occasion in Ranpur', and by-lined 'From our Ranpur Correspondent'. He settled to eat and read.

'The grounds of Government College in Ranpur were the scene of a happy occasion on Saturday when His Excellency the Governor, Sir Leonard Perkin, opened the new college building in which a future generation of Indian engineers will receive their education. "Let us hope," Sir Leonard said, "that these young men, on whose shoulders India places great responsibility, as she moves forward into a new industrial age, will look back on the times they spent here, in this handsome building, with a gratitude at least as great as we here feel today to its inspirer and founder and principal benefactor, Mr Chakravarti."

'Sir Leonard went on to recall how, just two years ago, when the future seemed less certain, his distinguished predecessor, Sir George Malcolm, laid the first stone for the new wing. "Many of you," Sir Leonard said, "will remember that occasion and perhaps regret as I do that Sir George is not here to open the splendid college that has arisen from that single stone. Be assured that I shall send him an account and appropriate photographs of it."

'Sir Leonard went on to speak of the gratitude he himself had always felt to the evening technical institute he had attended as a youth after a hard day's work in the industrial north of England. He then referred to the "grave doubts" he had had when, in 1946, Prime Minister Attlee had proposed to put his name forward as Governor in Ranpur. "Well, Len, the PM said to me, we've already sent Fred Burrowes to Bengal and he's an old railwayman too and not doing too badly. Unfortunately," Sir Leonard continued, "Fred has stolen my best joke, which was that while I knew nothing about shootin' and huntin' I knew quite a bit about tootin' and shuntin', so perhaps after all I could be of some service in the brief period I hoped it might take, which indeed it has taken, for us to climb down from the footplate and make way for you chaps, of whose skill and devotion and confidence in the future this college is both proof and symbol."

'Amid popular acclaim, Sir Leonard then led the way from the platform to the main entrance of the new building. Receiving the key he made a characteristically generous gesture, placing the key in the door and then inviting Mr Chakravarti to turn it so that he would be the first to enter the college which Mr Chakravarti described later as "the fulfilment of an old dream."

'Present among the guests was Mr Mohammed Ali Kasim, obviously recovered from the recent chill that prevented his attendance at the Chamber of Commerce dinner two weeks ago. Until the announcement also two weeks ago that Mr Trivurdi would succeed Sir Leonard Perkin, Mr Kasim had been widely tipped as the new Governor-designate. Answering your reporter's questions, Mr Kasim said he had no particular plans for the immediate future but that Mr Trivurdi's appointment as Governor was one that would have his whole-hearted approval. He declined to answer our question whether the Governorship had been offered to him first, and whether such a refusal was an indication that presently Mr Kasim intends to return actively to politics in the province.'

The article about the Chakravarti building had seen Perron through his bacon and egg and part of his toast and marmalade. The bearer asked if the sahib desired a fresh pot of coffee. Perron said he did. He took another piece of toast and folded the *Mirat Courier* to pages two and three. A glance at page two showed that it was taken up entirely by box-advertising, so he placed the paper on the stand with page three towards him.

Another muddy photograph; but suddenly he paused, a piece of toast on its way to his mouth, but never getting there. He pushed back his chair and took the *Courier* over to the stronger light near the balustrade. The face in the photograph was virtually unrecognizable. The heading alone made identification possible:

Lieutenant-Colonel Merrick, DSO

A moving ceremony

'The funeral service for the late Lt.-Col. (Ronnie) Merrick, DSO, whose tragic death we reported last week, was held last Saturday here at St Mary's, in a simple but moving ceremony conducted by The Reverend Martin Gilmour who, in his short address to a large congregation, spoke of Colonel Merrick as "a man who came into our midst, a stranger, and inspired us all by his devotion to duty, and has now gone, leaving us not poorer but richer for the example he set."'

The same Merrick? The three-quarter profile photograph did not itself confirm so. Perron scanned quickly down to the smaller print where the names of the chief mourners might be found.

'Supporting the widow were members and close friends of the family, Colonel John Layton, Mrs F. Grace, Captain Nigel Rowan (AAGG) and Mrs Rowan. Among the representatives of the cantonment were the station commander and his wife, Colonel and Mrs Rossiter and the Misses Rossiter; Brigadier and Mrs Thorpe, Colonel and Mrs S. K. Srinivasan, Major

Thwaite and Miss Drusilla Thwaite, Major and Mrs Peabody, Captain and Mrs P. L. Mehta.'

So, then, yes. Merrick. But who was Mrs Rowan? Sarah? She wasn't otherwise named. And what were they all doing in Mirat? AAGG meant assistant to the agent to the Governor-General. Was Rowan political agent in Mirat? He went back to the larger print.

'Referring briefly to Colonel Merrick's skilful handling of the far from easy task entrusted to him some months ago, the chaplain pointed out that the man whom they had gathered together to mourn and honour was one who had a disability that would probably have persuaded many men to feel that the period of their useful active employment and service had ended. "Ronnie," he said, "never felt this. Some of you have seen, many of us have heard, how this gallant officer who had taught himself to ride again, led his detachment of States Police during times of trouble, patiently and humanely but firmly restoring order and securing the peace of the state in whose service he was for all too short a time."

' "Today," he continued, "our hearts and prayers should be offered to Colonel Merrick's widow, in thanksgiving for a life so well lived, so abruptly ended, so sadly lost."

'After the singing of the hymn "Abide with Me" there was a moment's silence and then from outside the church came the clear sombre notes of the Last Post, sounded off by a bugler of the Mirat Artillery. An equally moving last touch to the simple service was made when the Chief Minister of State in Mirat, the Count Bronowsky, stepped forward and assisted the widow from the church.

'A few days earlier a post-mortem confirmed that Colonel Merrick died as a result of injuries sustained in a riding accident. The funeral was delayed to enable the widow and other members of the family to attend. The remains were cremated.'

*

'Sahib?'

The bearer had brought the tray of fresh coffee. He was asking Perron whether he wanted it at the breakfast table or at the verandah table where Perron was leaning against the balustrade. Perron nodded at the verandah table and then read the report again. And now the muddy photograph began to take on a sinister likeness to the Merrick he had known. He sat down, poured more coffee, and continued to study both the photograph and the report.

'I didn't know,' a woman's voice said, 'that the local rag could be so absorbing.'

Startled, he looked up. The woman in the sunglasses had come back and was sitting two tables away. Her voice was low-keyed, a bit hoarse, but attractive. He smiled, put the paper away and said, 'I'm sorry, I didn't see you.'

'That's what I mean. You are Guy Perron, aren't you?'

'Yes –?'

'You've been expected. So I did wonder when I saw you arrive. I've been nosey and had a look at the book you signed. No, please don't move.' She got up herself and came to join him. She took the sunglasses off, revealing rather pale eyes, blue-grey with a tinge of violet. A tiny scar, about an inch long, white, showed clearly beneath the left one. In spite of this blemish she was in a sad, rather exhausted way, beautiful.

'You won't recognize me. But you might remember me as Laura Elliott. At least Nigel told me you did.'

After a few seconds Perron said, 'Yes. Laura Elliott.' He offered his hand. Hers was rather clammy. He said, 'The coffee's fresh. Let me ask the bearer for another cup.'

'Thank you.' She sat down. He rang the handbell. When the old man came out he saw at once what was wanted and went back in. Perron sat. She was gazing steadily at him.

'I *think* I remember you,' she said. 'I mean I know I remember you but think I recognize you.'

'And I you.'

'No. I shouldn't think so.'

She had a directness that wasn't unpleasant, but having made this denial there was a hint of confusion in the way she replaced the sunglasses. He thought it possible that Nigel might also have said to her: Guy called you that stunning girl. She was stunning no longer.

The bearer brought another cup and another pot of coffee.

She poured for them both. 'Why have you come to the club, Mr Perron? Nigel said they were expecting you at the Izzat Bagh.'

'I never got round to wiring the day and time I'd get here. After a night on the train I thought it would be a good idea at least to get some breakfast and even make sure of a bed for the night without putting people out.'

'Well, and it's nice to be on your own for a while. Before putting on one's visiting face. Is Nigel going to be disappointed?'

'Why disappointed?'

'He said you'd be surprised to find him in Mirat. But you don't seem surprised. You haven't even asked me who I mean by Nigel. Did Dmitri give the game away after all?'

'No. And I am surprised. But the edge has been knocked off by what I've just read in the *Mirat Courier*.'

'Oh, have they said something about him? I never read it.'

'His name's included in a list of people who went to a funeral on Saturday. Mr Nigel Rowan, AAGG. And then the other names clinched it. The only person I don't know about is Mrs Nigel Rowan.'

Laura Elliott smiled. Her mouth went down with the smile. 'That's me, I'm afraid. Was I mentioned too? Nigel will be pleased. It worries him a bit that printed guest lists seldom refer to us both. But then how can they if I'm always making excuses or just not turning up? It's Dmitri Bronowsky who's expecting you really, isn't it? Are you going to ring him up?'

'The secretary said he mightn't be in Mirat but that he could easily find out.'

'In which case he's probably looking for me. Dmitri was in Mirat yesterday. He must still be. But you needn't ring. Nigel will either be ringing me here or arriving here some time this morning. You could go back with him. In any case I'll let him know you're here.'

'It's well over a year since Nigel and I were in touch. How long have you been married?'

'Rather less than a year. But do you mind if we don't talk about it? I was always very fond of Nigel and still am, but I'm afraid his marriage hasn't been a success.'

Perron studied Laura Elliott's face – turned, for once, away

537

from him as she watched the swooping crows; and thought he saw a woman who had had a bad time and was trying to pick up the pieces. She had rejected Nigel originally for a planter in Malaya. He remembered Nigel referring to a surviving Elliott parent in Darjeeling, who had only heard from Laura once, after she had ended up in a Japanese prison-camp. Presumably, unless there had been a divorce, the planter-husband hadn't survived. He felt he couldn't ask. He felt she would welcome a discussion about her and her first husband's captivity as little as she welcomed discussion of her marriage to Nigel. He said:

'Are you staying here at the club?'

'Yes, temporarily.' The sunglasses were redirected at him. 'I've just remembered.' She took the glasses off. 'You had a delightful but rather dotty aunt. Is she still alive?'

'She's paying for most of the cost of this trip and she's pulled most of the strings that make things easy when I want them easy.'

'I'm glad she's still alive. People like that deserve a long life.'

'People like what?'

'People who take an interest in other people, especially in young people. I felt that. I felt her reacting to me as if I were a person, not just another good-looking girl.'

'I'll tell her what you say.'

'Oh, she won't remember me.'

'But she does.'

A moment of nakedness. Then the glasses went back on. There was the sound of a telephone ringing. Perron said, 'Perhaps that's Nigel now.'

'We shall soon know. You'd like some more coffee?'

'Thank you.'

She began to pour. Hearing footsteps, Perron looked round. It was Macpherson. He said:

'Ah, there you both are. Already introduced yourselves. Good. Your husband is on the line, Mrs Rowan.'

She thanked Macpherson, pushed the glasses hard against the bridge of her nose and got up and went without another word or a glance in Perron's direction.

Macpherson said, 'It looks as if you're in luck and I lose an overnight guest.'

She did not come back. The clerk came ten minutes later with a message from her. A car would call for Perron at midday to take him to the Izzat Bagh. He stayed on the terrace for another half-hour or so. But still she did not return.

*

The car slowed to pass through a sentry-guarded checkpoint marked by a notice: *End of Cantonment Limits* and then headed along a straight road slightly below the level of the railway. He put on his own dark glasses and took out Rowan's note and re-read it.

'My dear Guy, I'm sorry I can't come to collect you personally. It's one of those pressing official mornings. I've not had the chance yet to tell Dmitri you've arrived, but will. Meanwhile, the best thing is for you to come to my bungalow. It's next to the Dewani Bhavan, Dmitri's house, where you'll be staying, but a lot has happened since he wired you in Bombay and you may find dossing down with me at least a good temporary solution. You're very welcome. Laura tells me you and she met and that you've seen the *Courier*, so know something of the score. Colonel Layton went back to Pankot this morning but Susan and her aunt are still here. They're staying at the palace guest house. Sarah's here too, of course, and has promised to be at my bungalow to welcome you and to see you settled in. I may have to stay at the palace for lunch, but I've organized things for you to lunch at my place. I expect you'll want to relax anyway. The bungalow is tucked between the Dewani Bhavan and the bungalow that was Susan's and Ronald's.

'You'll get a good view of the Izzat Bagh Palace and the guest house directly you fork right from the railway and the road starts to lead you round our side of the lake. Once you've passed the walls of the palace grounds you're at the Dewani Bhavan (and our bungalow which overlooks the waste ground between the palace and the city). See you soon. Nigel.'

The fork was ahead. He moved to the left-hand side of the car. Presently he saw the palace at the other end of the dazzling stretch of water: a rose-coloured structure with little towers, and on the lake-shore a white domed mosque with one slim minaret reflected. To one side, amidst trees, a palladian-style mansion. The guest house presumably.

At this upper end of the lake there were huts and boats (beached). A detachment of armed police patrolled the area. The lake seemed to be separated almost into two by an isthmus and an area of reeds. Where the reeds began the road curved away from the bank as though everything beyond the reeds was private property. The car became cooler, shaded by banyan trees. And to the left there suddenly appeared a brick wall mercilessly topped by spears of broken bottle-glass. The palace grounds. The wall continued for half a mile. Perhaps more. But suddenly ended, at a right angle, and the road was now edged on that side by an immense stretch of open ground, broken by nullahs. The car slowed. Just ahead on the right there was a grey stucco wall, a glimpse of a substantial bungalow, the Dewani Bhavan. But his attention was taken by a more distant view, the view of what lay at the far end of the waste ground, about a mile away: the blur of the old walled and minareted city of Mirat.

The car turned, across a culvert, into the compound of a small bungalow, a very old, squat building with square pillars to its verandah. The compound was rough and untended.

Standing in the shadow of the deep verandah was a woman wearing a blouse and skirt. Sarah. She had her arms folded (hands, as he remembered, clasping the elbows). As the car drew up she came down the steps ahead of a servant.

The first thing he noticed as he pushed the door open and looked up at her was a little pad of flesh beneath her chin.

'Hello, Guy.' She offered her hand. He took it and could not tell whether a warmer embrace had been expected, or would be welcome. Free, she folded her arms again and led the way on to the verandah which at this central point was deep, set out with tables and lounging chairs. There was a dusty uncared-for look about it. Whether this was Laura's fault or one of the reasons why Laura wasn't living here were questions whose answers might become clearer.

The interior hall was dark, sombre. You could smell damp. Sarah moved through it unaffected, he felt, by the oppressive weight of masonry, the brooding pressure of the thick square pillars that rose from the tiled floor up, up, into a remote raftered roof. She opened a door and the scale diminished to one that was more accommodating to the human ego. But this room was long, too narrow for its length. Here, he sensed the presence of hidden fungus, a sweet heavy smell which, mixed with the light dry scent of some kind of antiseptic, immediately depressed him. A white mosquito-net shrouded a narrow little bed. The main source of light was from the open bathroom door. It was probably from the bathroom that the smell of antiseptic came.

'It's rather spartan,' she said. 'Nigel asked me to apologize. But I probably don't need to. I expect Laura warned you they've not been here long and won't be staying.'

Perron let that go. He said, 'What date do you think? 1830? 1850?'

'I don't know. Shut up too long anyway. Watch out for scorpions. And I don't want to alarm you but there was a snake not long ago, on the verandah at the back. They had a good hunt after it was killed so I don't think you need worry, in any case Nigel says snakes are very misunderstood creatures and that the thing to do if you meet one is bow politely and ask it to go its way in peace.'

'I shall probably just yell the place down.'

She laughed, standing there, in front of him, arms still folded. He moved forward, put one arm lightly round her. She didn't move but in a moment briefly leant her head so that her hair brushed his chin.

'It's nice to see you again, Guy. You always made me laugh.'

She moved away. The servants were bringing in his suitcase and holdall. She said, 'I don't think Nigel will be back for lunch, but it's all organized for you to have directly you want it. So let's have a drink. Then I'll leave you to settle in.'

'Do you have to leave?'

'Yes. But I've got time for a drink.'

They returned to the verandah. She called out to the driver that she'd be ready in fifteen minutes. He went away, round the side of the bungalow. A servant had already placed a tray and bottles and glasses on a side-table. She told him to go and then asked Perron what he'd have.

'Out here I still like the gin.'

She poured, added ice and fizz and brought the glasses over. She said, 'I'd ask you to lunch at the guest house in ordinary circumstances but today I think you'd be happier eating here alone.'

'If you think so.'

He offered her a cigarette. She hesitated then took one. 'I've been trying to cut down, which means I've joined that boring gang of cadging non-smokers who never have their own. Thank you.' Bending forward to give her a light he noticed that the hand holding the cigarette was a bit unsteady; and that her hair, once so smooth and gleaming, looked less well cared-for. He felt this suited her rather better. She seemed more marked by experience. He said, 'I've come at rather a bad moment, haven't I?'

'Up to a week ago we'd certainly thought of your arrival rather differently.'

'How differently?'

'Nigel and I and Ahmed were going to meet you at the station. It was Dmitri's idea. I expect he'd have come too, because he likes surprising people. That's why when he got your letter from home he didn't answer but waited until there was just time to send you a welcoming telegram in Bombay. He thought he couldn't very well write a letter without mentioning the fact that Nigel and I were here. And Ronald of course.'

'You were here when my letter arrived then? I thought you'd probably come down just now. From Pankot.'

'No, I've been here for quite a time. It was Susan who had to come down. With father and Aunt Fenny. Father went back this morning. Did you come in on the night train?'

'Yes.'

'Then you must have been on the station at roughly the same time as father.'

'There was quite a crowd. Were you there, seeing him off?'

'No, but Aunt Fenny was. He has to get back to Pankot to go on handing over his command at the depot. He wanted us to go with him but at the last moment Susan wouldn't. So Fenny felt she had to stay too.'

'What about your mother?'

542

'Oh, mother went home last month to start house-hunting.'

'So no retirement to Rose Cottage?'

'No. Actually we moved down to Commandant House quite a while ago and rented the cottage to people called Smalley. We can't sell it, except to the army, but that's what will happen now. I expect the Smalleys will stay there a while because they're staying on under contract with the Indian Government. At least for a year or two. He's a bit too young to retire. A bit too old to fancy his chances at home. Father of course would have retired next year anyway. Neither of them wants to stay out here, though.'

'So back home for you too?'

'I don't know about me. Aunt Fenny and I went back for a month or two last year, after Uncle Arthur died. You never met them, did you?'

'No, but I know about Colonel Grace dying. I called at Queen's Road the other day and saw Mr Hapgood.'

'Hapgood?'

'The people upstairs. Captain Purvis's billet.'

'Oh.' She leant back, shutting her eyes. 'How long ago all that seems.'

'You never got in touch with me.'

'What?'

'When you were in England last year, with your Aunt Fenny.'

'No.'

'Nor answered my second letter.'

'No, I'm sorry. But that was a long time ago too.'

'Was the visit home a disappointment?'

'I don't suppose I gave it a proper chance. It might have been different if Aunt Fenny had gone home for good. But she had her return passage booked. And when the time came I felt I had to come back too.'

'You told me once that India wasn't a place you felt you could be happy in.'

'Did I? Yes, I remember thinking that.' She looked at him. 'I've been very happy since.'

'Has Susan been happy?'

Sarah didn't answer at once. Then she said, 'At the moment

543

she's in rather a bad way, probably worse than the family realizes. I can't remember what you knew about her history, but she's never been what is called really stable.'

'Didn't Ronald Merrick give her stability?'

Again she didn't answer at once.

'He's provided it now. You'll see what I mean if she talks to you about him, which is fairly likely. He's all she talks about.'

'It was a successful marriage, then?'

'I expected it to be disastrous. Of course, he adored the boy, and the boy adored him. Edward doesn't know Ronnie's dead, by the way. I ought to warn you.'

'Is the boy here?'

'Yes.' Sarah stubbed her cigarette. 'Su wouldn't leave him in Pankot, which is partly why Fenny had to come. Anyway, it's no bad thing for her to have him with her, but it's had its awkward side. I looked after him while the others went to the funeral. It was difficult explaining to him why mummy kept crying and why they'd come all the way back to daddy's house and not seen daddy. He said daddy had promised he'd still be here when their holiday in the hills was over and he'd made everything safe again. So of course I said that things were quite safe now but that daddy had had to go away for a while to make them safe somewhere else.'

'Ronald sent them back to Pankot because of trouble here?'

'Partly that, but to get them into the hills for the hot weather as well. Su wanted just to go up to Nanoora, but Ronald said if there was any more trouble Nanoora would be just as bad.'

'Has there been much trouble?'

'Off and on, yes. Quite a lot. That's why he was sent here in the first place. They were up in Rajputana. He'd become temporarily attached to the States Police. You know? The reserve pool that sends officers and men to states where the rulers' own police forces need helping out? He packed Su and Edward back to Pankot and came down here alone. They say he did a marvellous job. The Nawab's own police are practically all Muslims, and that was part of the problem, because they took sides in communal disturbances, lashing out at Hindu crowds and mobs and turning a blind eye if the Muslims were having a go. Ronnie stopped all that. He pretended it was easy. He said all he'd had to do was make the Muslim Chief of Police see he had a duty to the whole community, but it can't have been as simple as that.'

'When was all this?'

'Last December. He didn't expect the job to last long. But Dmitri was so impressed by the way he handled it he persuaded the States Police to let him stay on and help overhaul the whole Mirat Police Department and devise a new training and recruiting programme. It suited Ronnie very well. At one time there was an idea he might retire officially from the service and make a contract with the Nawab. Su and he set up house early last March. Then in May when the hot weather was really cooking up he sent her and Edward back to Pankot. As I said, partly because of the heat and partly because there was another outbreak of communal riots.'

'That was their bungalow next door, wasn't it?'

'Yes. It's not nearly as dilapidated as this. In fact he made it very comfortable. I stayed with them for a while after I helped Su move down from Pankot. But since April I've been living either at Dmitri's or the palace. Now, of course, I'll have to go back with Su. Fenny can't cope with the journey alone. And I don't know how badly Su'll take it when the reaction sets in.'

'I see there was a post-mortem.'

'Yes.' She got up. 'I really must go.'

Perron, getting up too, said, 'How long has Nigel been in Mirat?'

'About six weeks. The Political Department sent him down to try and sort things out. Actually Dmitri asked for him. Mirat comes under the Resident at Gopalakand and things got rather difficult. Nigel will tell you all about it. I'll be in touch, Guy. Probably this evening.'

The driver had come back. But just as she began to go down the steps another car came into the compound. 'You're in luck,' she said. 'Here's Nigel now.'

She went down to meet him. Perron stayed on the verandah. The car stopped several yards away from the one already parked. The driver got out and opened the door. A man emerged. If it was Rowan then he had lost even more weight. This man's skin was pale yellow and looked almost translucent, stretched over the cheek-bones. The man raised a welcoming hand to Perron, then said something to Sarah. They came towards the steps. Only now was the man's face recognizable as Rowan's.

'Hello, Guy,' he said. 'I'm sorry but I'm afraid I'm only here to pack a case.' They clasped hands.

'I'll see to the case,' Sarah said. 'How many nights?'

'Two at the most. I ought to be back tomorrow evening. And don't bother. Tippoo can do it.'

'Does it include black tie?'

'I've got all that in Gopalakand. Just one other suit. Isn't Tippoo here?'

'Yes, but I'll see he gets it right.' She went inside calling for someone named Tippoo. From the far end of one of the narrow wings of the verandah a middle-aged Indian in European clothes came out of a casement doorway: a clerk, not a servant. Rowan said, 'Just a second, Guy,' and went to meet him. They talked for a while. Then Nigel came back.

'Have you got a drink?'

Perron indicated his glass.

'Let me freshen it for you. I really do apologize. We're in the middle of what I suppose you'd call a flap. I've got to go up to Gopalakand.' He handed Perron the refilled glass. 'You're looking very fit. I'll be back in a moment.'

He went inside. Perron heard him calling Tippoo and Sarah calling something back. The clerk came out again, with a couple of files, but seeing Perron alone he went back inside, presumably to look for Rowan indoors. A telephone rang and was quickly answered. The two drivers were gossiping. Perron sat down and composed himself, to let the tide of India flow over him; presently it would ebb and leave him revealed: a visitor who was excluded from the mystery, the vital secret. I have been happy since, Sarah had said; as a woman might say if she were in love. In love with whom? Nigel? But he had been in Mirat only six weeks and she had been here since March, obviously content. Merrick? No, that was impossible. And Merrick's death didn't seem to have disturbed her in the way she would have been disturbed by the death of a man she had loved. The only answer seemed to be: in love with the land itself, after all; yes, in love with that, and content to be here

546

whatever happened. A strange but perhaps logical reversal of her old attitude.

'I won't apologize again,' Rowan said, coming back and sitting opposite, glancing at his watch. 'But I have to be off in five or ten minutes, so let's work out what's best for you. There are three possibilities. You're more than welcome to stay here, and you could rely on Tippoo to look after you. Dmitri asked me to tell you you're equally welcome to move into the Dewani Bhavan, but he's unlikely to be around much if at all in the next day or two. We've got a couple of States Department people over at the palace –'

'Waving the standstill agreement and the instrument of accession to Congress India, and asking for the Nawab's signature before August fifteen?'

'Good, you know about that. That cuts out a lot of tedious explanation. The other alternative for you while I'm away is the Gymkhana Club if you'd prefer that sort of atmosphere. If you opt for the club I could take you there now, as my guest it goes without saying. I've got to collect Laura. Sarah would keep in touch with you of course and there'd always be a car available to take you anywhere you want to go. But don't feel I'm pushing you out. My clerk will be here too most of the time and he'd help you in any way he can. Otherwise you can just forget about him. He has his own domestic arrangements. So, Guy, I leave it to you and in spite of what I said about not apologizing again, I do.'

'It's entirely my fault. I ought to have sent a wire. Checked that it was convenient.'

'The flap would have occurred anyway. It's not inconvenient for us. We're just worried about you.'

'I'd like to stay here, if that's all right.'

'Good. Actually it'll make things easier for Sarah, not that she ever complains, but we do all tend to load her with extra jobs. She could help look after you better here than at the club.'

'Tell me one thing, is the Resident at Gopalakand in what I call the entrenched opposition camp that's encouraging the princes to stand firm on their own independence?'

'Fundamentally, that is the problem.'

'What does Dmitri want?'

'Honourable integration.'

'And the Nawab?'

'I don't think the poor old man knows. But after all these years he's suddenly resisting Dmitri's advice. The Resident's trying to persuade the Maharajah in Gopalakand to sign nothing and reserve his position until paramountcy automatically lapses on August fifteen and leaves him technically independent. As a result the Nawab's taking that line too. It's quite hopeless of course. He knows it, but he's being very stubborn and the Resident isn't being in the least helpful. He's never really been interested in Mirat. Mirat should have had its own agent long ago.'

'Are you on Dmitri's side, then?'

'Let's say I agree that the only sensible course for Mirat is to accede to the new Indian Union on the three main subjects, sign the standstill agreement and then get the best deal possible. Mirat's entirely surrounded by what's been British-Indian territory and overnight becomes Indian Union territory. The Nawab can't live in a vacuum.'

Perron nodded. He said, 'How have things been for you, Nigel, this past two years?'

'I've moved around a lot. Little else. Perhaps I ought to have stayed in the army. It turned out to be the wrong time to come back into the Political. Still, the end would have been the same in either case.'

'What do you hope to achieve in Gopalakand, or is that confidential?'

'If I can come back with a letter from Conway to the Nawab making it clear that Mirat's on its own and that Conway can't advise either way, then we should be able to persuade the old chap to sign. And sign he must. There's no sensible alternative. Except chaos, if that's sensible. From what I've seen going on in the past few weeks I sometimes wonder whether the Political Department cares, so long as it can close itself down convinced that it's upheld the principles of the whole past relationship between the States and the Crown.'

' "Nothing can bring you peace but yourself," ' Perron quoted. ' "Nothing can bring you peace but the triumph of principles." '

'What?'

'Emerson.'

'Oh.' Nigel smiled. 'Did he say that? How apt. That sums up my department's attitude admirably.'

'Not just your department's. I think it sums up the attitude of everybody who's concerned in what happens on August fifteen.' Perron took a sip of his gin. 'I'm sorry about Merrick,' he said. 'Not that I ever liked the man. Still, he seemed to have made good in Mirat.'

'Yes.' Rowan looked at his watch again.

'And Harry Coomer? Any news of him? I'm sorry I decided there was nothing to be done at my end.'

'I don't think I really expected it, but I appreciated your giving thought to it, and appreciated your letter. One becomes involved for a time, and then the involvement ends. In any case, I don't think there was anything Kumar wanted.'

'Why do you think that?'

'He implied as much. We exchanged letters after Gopal died, last year. Poor old Gopal. He was always getting colds. He took his wife down to Puri for a holiday and caught cold and got pneumonia. I asked Mrs Gopal to put me in touch with the man who'd been helping Kumar rehabilitate himself. Got Kumar's address out of him, so wrote. Difficult letter to write. I didn't hear for ages. He'd moved, so my letter followed him around. When he wrote he didn't give me his new address but the letter was postmarked Ranpur so he must still have been there, I imagine. Probably still is.'

'What did he say?'

'What it added up to was that he was quite content doing what he was doing, coaching students privately.'

'A defensive attitude?'

'I don't think so. He seemed very grateful for the one or two things I'd suggested.'

'What sort of things?'

'Just general ideas about how he could make best use of his talents.'

'Commerce for instance?'

'Yes, but that would be open to him at almost any time.'

'Would it, Nigel? The kind of commerce we think of as commerce? I seem to remember he failed to get into it once, with British-Indian Electric.'

'Once.'

'Has British-Indian Electric changed?'

Rowan said nothing.

'Will anything ever really change in India, for him? Isn't Harry Coomer the permanent loose end? Too English for the Indians, too Indian for the English?'

'That, rather, is Sarah's view. Frankly, I think he's more interested in being just his own kind of Indian.'

'Have you told her you tried to help him?'

'Yes, but only quite recently.'

'I don't suppose you ever showed her a transcript of the examination?'

'Good God, no. She knows nothing about that.' He lowered his voice. 'Few people do now, except you. Everything in connection with the examination was destroyed, except the orders for Kumar's release.'

'To protect Merrick's reputation?'

'The issues involved ranged far wider than that. I imagine quite a lot of files were vetted, and re-arranged.'

'To make it more difficult for an incoming Congress ministry to smell out witches?'

'A witch-hunt was what certain sections of Congress wanted. An inquiry could have aggravated racial tension to an intolerable degree, coming as it would have done on top of the INA trials. If it interests you as a student of history, there was no inquiry because between them Nehru and Wavell put a stop to it. They both saw what it could lead to.'

'And Merrick got off scot-free.'

'Actually, I think it annoyed him. I believe he felt slighted. There were only a few individual inquiries into serious cases involving rather senior officials. It was all done very quietly. One or two people got retired, prematurely.'

'What happened to Kasim's son, Sayed?'

'He was cashiered. That's all.'

'What's he doing now?'

'I'm not sure. Living in Lahore, I believe, with his Muslim League sister and brother-in-law. In some kind of business. Ahmed will tell you.'

'No splendid appointment for one of the INA heroes?'

'They were only heroes for a while. In a way they still are.

But folk-heroes. People in a story or legend. When it comes to finding places for them in the world of affairs it's a bit different.'

Sarah came out. Behind her were a couple of servants with bags and the clerk with a briefcase. They went down to the car while Sarah said: 'You're all set, Nigel. If Laura asks, her green taffeta's in the blue case, along with other things she might need.'

'That's good of you.'

'Give Sir Robert my kind regards.'

'I will. Guy's going to stay here, by the way.'

'Good. Do you ride?'

'Off and on. Fortunately more on than off. But it's pure luck.'

She laughed. 'Perhaps we could go out tomorrow morning. I'll ring you later today, anyway.'

The three of them went down into the compound but after he and Nigel had said goodbye Perron stayed near the bottom step while Nigel saw Sarah into her car and then got into his own. He waved them both off.

'Sahib,' Tippoo said, behind him. 'Gin'n'fizz?'

*

Rain. Geckos. Clack-clack-clack. On the walls. Heraldic lizard shapes, pale yellow on the grey-white wash. Chasing one another, intent on copulation. He had woken erect himself – and, half-asleep, smiled, reassured both by this and the realization that the faint discomfort in his bowels had gone, that he was acclimatized. He peered at his wrist-watch. It was only half-past four. He had slept for two hours, after a lunch of chicken pulao, mutton curry lightly spiced in the northern Indian style, and Murree beer. Somewhere a gutter was overflowing. On the basket-work bed-side teapoy there was a tray of tea and a plate of bananas and bread and butter. It must have been the slight clatter of the tray that had woken him. He began to open the mosquito-net and, swinging himself up and round was about to get out when he remembered scorpions and paused, his feet well away from the floor. He reached down, tapped his slippers, and then thrust his feet into them. He grabbed a towel from the bedside chair, wound it round his middle and went into the bathroom.

But, returning, he paused on the threshhold of the bedroom, alert. There was a smell he hadn't noticed before. A foul, sweet smell. He glanced around. In a moment or two the smell seemed to have gone. He sat down and poured tea. He glanced up at the sloping rafters; then lit a cigarette, smoked the recollection of the smell away. The shrouded bed looked like a catafalque. There was a sudden flash of lightning that lit the bathroom and momentarily distorted the shape of the bed. After that, the thunder. And then the humdrum sound of continuing but gradually diminishing rain.

As he finished his tea the bathroom was flooded in sunshine. He called for Tippoo.

*

By five-thirty he was bathed and dressed. He went out into the compound. The shadow of the bungalow thrust itself across the drive. He walked round the side, seeking the sunshine and warmth. At the back the compound stretched for perhaps one hundred yards. There must once have been a lawn and flower beds, but the latter were overgrown. The grass needed scything. An immense banyan tree, its main trunk on this side of the wall dividing Rowan's bungalow from Merrick's, connected the two gardens through its aerial roots. From the other side of the wall Perron heard the high-pitched voice of a young child, a boy, and lower-pitched woman's laughter.

'Catch, Minnie!' the boy shouted. But the throw was too high. A ball sailed over and came to rest some thirty or forty yards away from where Perron was standing; but the ground was too rough for it to bounce. It died, disappeared. He moved off the path and struck out across the grass, wetting his shoes, the bottoms of his slacks. He cast to and fro. Eventually he found it: a grey, soggy tennis-ball.

He picked it up, then turned and saw an Indian woman and the child standing near the banyan tree. Beyond the tree a gate between the two compounds which he hadn't noticed before stood open. The child made a commanding gesture to the woman, as if bidding her stay where she was and then advanced towards Perron: a Pathan child dressed in baggy white pantaloons and shirt, sash, embroidered waistcoat, and cocks-comb pugree. Stuck in the sash was a toy dagger. A miniature Red Shadow. As he got nearer Perron saw that he was of course an English boy, dressed up. His eyes were bright blue, his eyelashes very pale. From under the turban emerged a lick of sandy red hair. He stopped and stuck his little fist round the handle of the toy dagger.

'Who are you?' the boy asked.

'I'm just a visitor. Who are you?'

'I live next door. Is that my ball?'

Perron stooped and showed it to him.

'It looks like mine. Has it got MGC on it?'

Perron inspected it. 'Yes, you can just see MGC.'

'Then it must be mine. MGC means Mirat Gymkhana Club. Mr Macpherson always used to give me used tennis balls.'

Perron nodded, handed the ball over. The child spoke with the assurance of a boy far older.

'It was Minnie's fault. Women can't catch. Thank you for finding it. If you hadn't, Minnie would have had to look and she didn't want to because she's afraid of snakes.'

'Aren't you?'

'No. At least, not very afraid. There were snakes here when Uncle Nigel came. He's not my uncle really. I don't have an uncle because my father didn't have a brother and my mother only has a sister. My stepfather doesn't have a brother either. I've got a stepfather because my real father was killed in the war.'

'You're Edward, aren't you?'

'Yes. My full name is Edward Arthur David Bingham.'

'My name's Guy. My other name is Perron.'

'They're both rather funny names, but I like Perron best. So I'll call you Perron.'

'Then I shall probably have to call you Bingham.'

'Okay.' A minor matter had been satisfactorily settled. A more important one was coming up. 'Can you throw, Perron?'

'Yes.'

'Which arm do you use?'

'The right arm.'

'I throw with my left arm because I'm left-handed. My

stepfather has to throw with his right arm because his left arm was cut off. But he's a very good thrower.'

'What do you call your stepfather?'

'Ronald. At least, I do mostly. My mother likes me to call him daddy, so sometimes I do. But he likes me to call him Ronald.'

'Do you know what Ronald means?'

'It means it's his name.'

'Most names have meanings. My name means wide. On the other hand it might mean wood. So you'd better go on calling me Perron which is probably just the place where we lived once. And I shall call you Edward after all. Ronald means the same as Rex or Reginald. It means someone with power who rules. Edward means a rich guard.'

'But I'm not very rich. At the moment I've only got one rupee and four annas.'

'I don't think it's a question of money. Anyway you're guarding the fort while Ronald's away. You're looking after your mother, aren't you?'

'Yes. My mother's name is Susan. What does Susan mean?'

'It means a very beautiful flower called a lily. Not the red ones you see here. White ones.'

'She is quite beautiful. Except when she cries. She's crying now. That's why they sent me out to play in the garden. She may have stopped crying though, if you want to see her. Come on. If she's still crying we can play in our garden. It's a nicer garden than this one.'

Perron got up. The child led the way. As he drew near the ayah he held the ball up and said, 'Here's the ball, ayah. We may want to play with it again.' The girl took the ball in one hand and with the other half-covered her face with the free end of her saree, to protect herself from Perron's gaze.

The Merrick garden was certainly 'nicer'. The lawns were well-cut, and there were signs of work-in-progress, in the form of beds recently dug into ovals, circles and rectangles. Edward pointed them out.

'That's where Ronald's going to try to grow roses.'

Beyond the beds, at the far end of the Merrick compound, was a tennis-court. A thick hedge of shrubs and bushes hid the servants' quarters. The bungalow itself had been re-stuccoed and painted. The rear verandah formed an elegant whitewashed colonnaded semi-circle which embraced the central set of steps leading to the house. Between the columns hung green tattis, some lowered, others at half-mast. Tubs of canna lilies stood sentinel. The bungalow had the slightly raw look of having been stripped recently of ancient creepers to allow redecoration.

The little Pathan marched across the lawn towards the verandah and then at the bottom step kicked off his chappals and climbed barefoot. Perron decided that this was part of a private game, not obligatory, so he climbed shod. The boy waited for him at the top, legs apart, fist on the handle of the toy dagger.

'Would you like to see my room first, Perron?'

'Very much.'

The boy strode off to the right, along the verandah and round the corner. At the side of the bungalow he pulled open a wirescreen door, held it, and let Perron enter first.

A small room, austere, remarkably unboylike. That was Perron's impression until he remembered that Edward hadn't slept or played here for several months. The narrow little charpoy was unmade, its mattress rolled, the net folded. Across the exposed webbing were the clothes he had taken off – diminutive khaki shorts, a blue shirt and grey socks. A cane chair, an almirah and a chest of drawers were the only other furnishings. The door of the almirah was ajar, which suggested that the first thing Edward had done was seek out his Pathan outfit and hasten to get into it.

'Do you like my room?'

'Yes, I do. Where does ayah sleep?'

'There of course.' He pointed at the floor near the casement door. 'Except neither of us sleeps here just now. We're staying at the palace guest house. I'll show you the palace if you like, but not today. Do you like my picture?'

Perron looked at the wall where the child was pointing. Above the chest of drawers was a coloured print in a gilt frame. He went to inspect it.

'Daddy gave it to me. It's called "The Jewel in Her Crown" and it's about Queen Victoria.'

Perron saw that indeed it was. It was the kind of picture

whose awfulness gave it a kind of distinction. The old Queen was enthroned, beneath a canopy, receiving tribute from a motley gathering of her Indian subjects, chief among whom was a prince, bearing a crown on a cushion. Ranged on either side of the throne were representatives of the *raj* in statuesque pro-consular positions. Disraeli was there, indicating a parchment. In the background, plump angels peered from behind fat clouds, and looked ready to blow their long golden trumpets. The print was blemished by little speckles of brown damp.

'But it isn't the jewel in the crown the prince is holding. The jewel's India,' the boy explained.

'Yes, I see.'

'It's an alle-gory.'

'What's an alle-gory?'

'Don't you know? It means telling a story that's really two stories. The Queen's dead now of course. I should think they're all dead, except the angels. Angels never die.'

'No. So I'm told.'

'Have you ever seen an angel, Perron?'

'No.'

'Nor've I. Daddy says mummy saw an angel once, an angel in a circle of fire, but I mustn't talk about it because it upsets her. Come on. Let's see if she's still crying.'

Reluctantly, Perron followed him to a closed door. The boy opened it, put his head out and listened. The silence coming from the other side was peculiarly oppressive. But Edward obviously found it reassuring.

'I think she's stopped.'

He opened the door wide. Beyond was the main entrance-hall, as encumbered with square pillars as the hall in Rowan's bungalow; but the tiled floor shone – except in the area exposed by the taking up of a carpet which had been rolled and corded and now awaited disposal.

Edward pattered across the hall on his bare feet, entered a room whose door stood open. There was a pause, and then a woman's shriek; a pause, a repetition of the shriek, longer drawn out, and then continuing.

The boy emerged, levitated. Simultaneously a magenta-coloured shape flowed past Perron – the ayah. The ayah grasped the boy out of the air, and so revealed the source of the levitation; Sarah, who turned immediately back into the room from which the shrieks were still coming. As the ayah carried Edward away he began to wail. A white-clad, sashed and turbanned servant ran in from the front porch, across the hall and into the room.

Then the shrieking stopped. Slowly, Perron approached the wide-open doors, uncertain what to do. The doors were double and from the threshold he could see that the room was a bedroom, but a very large bedroom, dominated by a bed which was centrally placed, raised on a stone-stepped daïs. Sarah was sitting on the edge of this bed cradling and rocking Susan in her arms. The servant stood nearby. Perhaps he had spoken because Sarah seemed to be shaking her head at him. Presently the servant took a few steps back, then turned, saw Perron, and came out, went past without a word.

Below the daïs there was an open tin trunk and scattered all around it what must be Ronald Merrick's relics: KD uniforms, Sam Brownes, leather cases, hairbrushes, a sword in a black and silver scabbard, mess dress, leather gloves, swagger canes, a Field Service cap, riding boots, jodhpurs, Harris tweed jacket, checked flannel shirts, a Gurkha's kukri, grey slacks, brown shoes, chukka boots: the detritus of a man's life in India.

Three tall casement windows, facing west, had been unshuttered. The evening light filtered through. The shafts of this light were alive with mobile particles of dust. He turned to leave. He didn't think Sarah had seen him, but just then she said, 'Don't go away altogether, Guy.'

He said, 'I'll be outside.'

*

He sat on the front verandah. The trees and bushes in the front compound were in a similar state of decay as those in Rowan's, but thick enough to screen the bungalow from the road. The servant was talking to the chauffeur of one of the palace limousines, parked near the foot of the steps. The servant came up and asked if the sahib wished anything. Perron shook his head.

He smoked. He thought: Why should she scream? It was her own son. He sat on the balustrade. As he finished his cigarette the ayah and Edward came out. Edward was now wearing his ordinary clothes. His little chappals clattered. He looked what he was – a small boy scarcely out of infancy, three or four years old. But when he spoke he was still the little Pathan.

'Hello, Perron. Are you coming to the guest house?'

'Afraid not, old chap. Not today, anyway.'

'If you do I can show you the palace after all.'

'I'd like that. Tomorrow, perhaps.'

The boy offered his hand. Perron reached down and shook it.

'Goodbye, Perron.'

Edward clattered down the steps and ran to the car. The ayah hastened after him. He shouted at the driver, 'Jeldi, jeldi. Ham ek dam Guest House wapas-jane-wale hain. Chalo!'

The driver, approaching, wagged his head and called back, 'Thik hai, Sahib.' He helped Edward get up on the running-board and open the rear door. The ayah followed him in but must have been told to go to the farther seat because when the door was shut Edward put his head out of the open window and shouted:

'I can show you the white peacock too, Perron.'

Perron made an appreciative sideways nod of his head. The boy sat back. The car set off.

'You've made a hit.'

Sarah had come out and was standing behind him. She said, 'The white peacock's his special secret. But why does he call you Perron?'

'We agreed to be informal. He's a remarkable boy, isn't he? How old?'

'He was three last June. I remember wondering whether he'd ever learn to talk.'

'Is Susan all right now?'

'Yes, perfectly. She'd like it if you came in and had a word. She may ask you to dinner at the guest house this evening. That was originally my idea too but I'd prefer it if you made an excuse. These upsets sometimes have repercussions later. So I'd rather we left anything like that until tomorrow.'

'What upset her?'

Sarah, arms folded in the characteristic way, shrugged slightly. She didn't look at him. Her manner struck him as evasive. He realized that this was not the first time today that it had. She said, 'Oh, the whole afternoon mainly. She insisted on coming over and sorting out some of Ronald's things, so I had to come too because Aunt Fenny's not feeling very bright. Then Edward insisted on coming with us. The whole thing was a mistake from the start.'

'Could you have dinner with me, at Nigel's?'

'I'd like to but I'd better not. Let's go out tomorrow morning, though. I'll try and rope Ahmed in too.'

'What time?'

'Could you be ready by seven? That's the best time.'

'Rain or shine?'

'At this time of year it only rains in the afternoon, if it rains at all.'

'I've got nothing special to ride in.'

'That doesn't matter. Well, let's go in. The guest house is only a few minutes away so the car will be back soon and I want to get Susan away before the light goes.'

*

'We met didn't we, Mr Perron? That time in Pankot just after Ronnie and I became engaged and you were working with him.'

She had on a cotton print dress with a full skirt, which was disposed to envelop her legs while she knelt on the floor by the tin trunk, her weight centred on her left hip, supported by a stiffened left arm. After they'd shaken hands she placed her right hand back on her left shoulder. The light which twenty minutes before had streamed through the unshuttered windows had diminished, but what was left of it lit one side of her pretty flushed face and picked out the red-brown tones of hair which in full daylight would look dark, almost black. She seemed perfectly composed now.

She said, 'Of course, you know that I've lost him. My son doesn't know. It's really a question of working out a way of how and what to tell him.' She reached out and touched the Field Service cap.

559

Sarah said, 'Why don't you leave it all, Su? Khansamar will put it away. Then we could all have a drink outside while we wait for the car.'

'No, I don't want a drink. But you both have one. I've still got a lot to sort out and I don't want Khansamar touching anything.'

'Then I'll help you start putting things back,' Sarah knelt and began to fold the tweed jacket.

'How little there is,' Susan said. 'I mean when you think of the years a man spends out here. So little he would want to keep. Will daddy have as little as this?'

'I don't expect there'll be much more.'

Susan fingered the pommel of the sword. 'And even the things they do have look like toys, don't they? I suppose that's because the things they play with when they're young are just smaller versions of the things they'll have to use later. It's different for us. A doll's house isn't at all like a real house. And a doll not in the least like a real baby. You didn't know my husband well, did you, Mr Perron? You were hardly with him at all, were you?'

'No. A very short time.'

'Ask anyone here in Mirat and they'll tell you what a fine man he was. I don't yet think of him as dead.'

Sarah gently withdrew the sword from her sister's touch and placed it in the trunk.

'And then my not being here at the time makes it seem it hasn't happened, and when I tell Edward we'll be seeing daddy again soon, that's what it seems like. That we will be seeing him. Please stop putting things back, Sarah. It's all that's left of Ronald and it's not even all here.'

'Oh?' Sarah said, not looking at her sister. 'What's missing?'

'His arm for one thing.'

Sarah pushed hair away from her right cheek and didn't comment.

'I mean the artificial one, Mr Perron. His harness. But we always called it his arm. It was one of the ways we made light of it. Where's my arm? he used to say. He took it off every night. Nobody knows the discomfort he was in, from the chafing. The first time I saw his poor shoulder and his poor stump, I cried. They were so inflamed and raw. That's because he never spared himself. He learned to ride again, you know. Getting up on what he called the wrong side. He played tennis too. He called it patball because he had to serve underarm by dropping the ball and hitting it on the bounce but he played a strong game otherwise.'

Sarah had got up and was opening a chest of drawers. Susan said, 'It's no good. I've looked in all the drawers and cupboards. I've looked everywhere, but I can't find it.'

'What's this, then?' Sarah held up a contraption of webbing and metal.

Without even looking Susan said, 'That's the one he couldn't wear. The new one. The one they said was much better, a much more modern design. But if you look at it you'll see it can't have been worn more than a few times.'

Sarah thrust it back into the chest and closed the drawer.

'I hope this doesn't embarrass you, Mr Perron. Talking about his arm. But you see he never, never, wore it in bed. He took it off every night. He had to be very careful not to let the stump get too inflamed. I know what a relief it was to him to get out of the harness, and sometimes what torture it was to put it back on in the morning. He wouldn't have worn it while he was laid up after his riding accident.'

Perron said, 'Perhaps the accident explains why it's not here, Mrs Merrick. It could have been damaged and sent away for repair.'

'Oh.' She considered him gravely. 'I hadn't thought of that.' She smiled. 'Ronnie was quite right. He always was. He said women have instincts, they know when something is wrong or not properly explained. But men work things out logically much better. It struck me as odd when I couldn't find it, because to put it brutally I couldn't see them putting the arm on, just to take – just to take his body to the mortuary for the post-mortem. And there had to be a post-mortem because he was found dead in bed and people thought he was getting better. I blame Dr Habbibullah, but daddy says I shouldn't. He said no one can foresee a clot of blood. But why was there a clot of blood? Unless there was an internal injury from the riding accident that Dr Habbibullah hadn't diagnosed?'

'Well you know, you can seem in perfect health one minute, and then –'

'Drop dead the next. Oh, I know. But all these doctors protect themselves and each other don't you think, Mr Perron? I mean whether they're English or Indian. And I do blame Dr Habbibullah even though Ronnie himself once said he was one of the best doctors he'd ever come across.' She looked round at Sarah. 'Khansamar would know about Ronnie's harness, Sarah. Whether it was damaged.'

'I don't think we should worry Khansamar over a thing like that, Su.'

'Why?'

'Because he's a servant. When you ask servants what's happened to something it always sounds as if you're accusing them of stealing. I'll ask Dr Habbibullah if you really want me to.'

'Yes, I do. But what about the other things that are missing? Where are his Pathan clothes? He was very fond of his Pathan clothes.' She turned to Perron again. 'He had to choose Pathan clothes because of his blue eyes. He had two sets but only one pugree and only one embroidered waistcoat.' She looked at the scattered stuff. 'There's only one set here, these trousers and this shirt. The other set's missing, and so are the pugree and the waistcoat. And the sash. And the little axe.'

'He probably gave them away,' Sarah said. 'It must be years since he used them.'

'Oh no. He went out in them in Mirat too. With one of his spies. He had to have spies, Mr Perron. I'm sorry if it sounds melodramatic, but this is a very melodramatic and violent country. If you're a police officer and take your job seriously you can't just sit in an office like a deputy commissioner. You have to get out into the bazaars and listen to what people are saying. You have to do all sorts of things that so-called pukka members of the *raj* pretend don't have to be done. Of course if you like you can leave it entirely to subordinates, but Ronnie wasn't like that. He knew it was his duty to get out and see and hear for himself. I expect a lot of people who sing his praises now for what he did to settle Mirat when he first came here would pretend to be shocked if they knew he ever had to go out at night dressed as an Indian servant. But he was prepared to do that for the job's sake. It was very dangerous.

562

That goes without saying. That's why he never told me. But I found out. Shall I tell you how I found out, Mr Perron?'

'Only if you want to.'

'Yes. I think I do. I don't know whether you know, but I haven't been very well. For quite a long time. I can't sleep without taking something. He was so understanding about that. And sometimes when there was any kind of trouble brewing or crisis or flap on, anything that kept him working late or might mean his being called out, he'd sleep in another room, so as not to disturb me, once I'd taken my pills. But the pills don't always work. And then I go through phases of not wanting to take them at all because you can't spend the rest of your life taking pills just to get to sleep. And one night I didn't take any pills at all, and Ronnie was working late and sleeping in this other room, and I just lay here trying and trying to get to sleep naturally. And that's terrible. When you're so tired, but can't sleep and you toss and turn and the night just seems to be slipping away and you start imagining all kinds of silly ridiculous things and there's this awful temptation to take not just one or two of the pills but enough to make you sleep forever. So I went to Ronnie's room to see whether he was still awake, so that I could tell him I had this awful temptation, and when I got to the door I saw the light was on. And at four o'clock in the morning that was just as if he'd stayed awake in case I needed him and I felt terribly beholden to him. But when I opened the door it didn't seem to be Ronnie there at all, but this terrifying Indian just standing there staring at me. But of course it was Ronnie. That's why I lost my nerve though, a while ago, when Edward ran in dressed just the same way. I don't mean I didn't know Edward had the same little kind of outfit, I only mean it was like seeing Ronnie again, and just at the moment I was wondering where his own Pathan clothes were.' She turned to Sarah. 'Can't we ask Khansamar even about the clothes?'

'No, we can't. That would be worse than asking him about the harness. The car must be here. I'll go and see. Then we ought to be getting back. Khansamar can put all this away.'

Sarah went.

Susan said, 'My sister isn't very intuitive.'

'No?'

'No. You see, Mr Perron. Ronnie's missing arm and Ronnie's missing clothes are like the dog that didn't bark in the night.'

'Conan Doyle?'

She smiled brilliantly.

'My favourite as a child was *The Speckled Band*. I used to read it by torchlight under the bedclothes at the school Sarah and I went to at home. *The Speckled Band* reminded me of India. Because of the snake. When Aunt Fenny told me last week that Ronnie was dead I thought first of a snake. Or of a scorpion. I've always been terrified of scorpions.'

'I'm terrified of both.'

'Oh, men always say terrified. But they're only pretending. Ronnie was afraid of nothing.'

'I imagine not.'

'I depended on him, Mr Perron. You see, I've always been terrified of almost everything.'

To his alarm he saw that quite suddenly tears were falling down her cheeks. But they fell as if her eyes were at a different season from the rest of her. She still smiled. Her voice altered not at all. She remained physically still. She said, 'I'll never meet another man who understands – I mean who understood me so well. He seemed to guess things about me that no one else in the family ever guessed, not even my sister. It was like living with someone who'd lived with you always, even in your secret life and knew the nice things and the not so nice things. Even things you'd forgotten and even the things you'd dreamt. Until I met Ronald I'd no idea a man could be so patient and understanding. It was a long time before I could help him with his arm. I mean help him to put it on and take it off, and help him with the salves and powders. He understood that. When I'd learned how to help him we became very close. Very close. Closer than at any other time. I've never been so close to anyone before. He realized that. I think he realized that helping him with his arm was a way of helping me to become close to people. Which is what I'd never been. Never felt. His arm was very important to me, Mr Perron. I prefer to think of it being damaged, not just thrown away. Although if it was damaged in the accident I expect it has been thrown away because people don't understand the importance of

564

symbols. But wherever we went, he was admired and respected. Especially here in Mirat. You see, he never *pretended*. He always said what he thought, so people knew where they stood with him. Some of them didn't like where they found themselves standing, but they couldn't blame him, or accuse him of being two-faced. He wasn't always easy on people. At one time I used to get upset when he was angry or disapproving or cold. But he was only angry when he found people out cheating or lying or pretending. And it was good for me. I'm not nearly as afraid as I used to be. I don't know what will happen now, though, but at least he's left me with Edward. When you look at Edward now you wouldn't credit what a poor miserable little boy he used to be. With nothing to say to anyone. Terrified of animals.'

The tears had dried. 'At least, at first. He grew out of that. Perhaps that's my one contribution. We had a labrador puppy and Edward became quite fond of him. But we had to get rid of him in Rajputana. Ronnie didn't like animals in the house.'

'Your son's certainly a friendly little boy.'

'I'm glad you think that.' Briefly she made that gesture more familiar in her sister: one hand reaching out to clutch the elbow of the other arm. 'But it's time he went home. He's very precocious. It's what happens out here. And you shouldn't order other people about like that. I remember doing it myself as a child. But that was because I was afraid of them.'

'I don't think Edward's in the least afraid.'

'No. But you can't tell. Aggression can be a sign of insecurity. Ronnie was never able to help me over that sort of thing. He was the most secure person I've ever known and when Edward talks to servants the way he does I sometimes think he's just copying Ronnie. Ronnie was always very firm. But fair. Don't misunderstand. The servants always adored him. What is it, Sarah?'

'The car's here,' Sarah said from behind. Perron wondered how long she had been standing there. 'We ought to go.'

'Yes, I suppose so. If Khansamar bolts the shutters and locks the door we can leave all this just as it is until tomorrow. I know in my heart he's trustworthy really, because Ronnie always said how reliable he was and he was a good judge. I was just telling Mr Perron, Sarah, how good Ronnie was with the servants.'

She stirred. Perron got up. He helped her to rise. As she came level and stood near him he felt that she was as taut as a bent bow.

'When we first came here,' she said, accepting his arm, and allowing herself to be led out, 'that's to say when I and Edward came down from Pankot to join Ronnie, he'd already had the old bungalow cleared and decorated. He'd started furnishing it, with Dmitri's help of course. Everything except the hall-carpet belongs to Dmitri. The whole compound at the back had been cleared too. Of course at that time it looked as if we might be here for quite a while but in any case that was the way Ronnie worked, to make a home whereever it was, however impermanent. He was so much better at that sort of thing than I'll ever be. He said it was a terrible mess when he first got here. Nobody had lived here for ages and at that time he only had Khansamar. Well. There was a cook and a sweeper, and a bhishti and a mali, but only as temporary people. He said it was for me to decide how permanent they should be. But I couldn't fault his choice. He had that knack of looking at people and knowing whether they'd be any good or not. So really from the start we had a full complement. But unemployment in the state is a terrible problem and I remember how week after week these young men and boys used to turn up, begging for a job. Ronald had such a good reputation for paying a fair wage and treating servants properly that they came here first rather than anywhere else. You'd have thought that eventually they'd have given up. But they never did.'

She stopped abruptly, in the dim entrance hall.

'Where *are* all the servants, Sarah? I've only seen Khansamar.' But she did not seem to need a reply. She placed one hand just below her throat. A theatrical little gesture, Perron thought. But in Susan, all such gestures were probably mute cries for help. 'The whole place is so quiet. As though everyone has gone.' She turned, offered her hand. 'Thank you for your kindness, Mr Perron. For being so logical. For being here. For knowing Ronald.'

It was an exit line. She went quickly across the hall out on to the verandah and then down the steps to the car. For a moment Sarah stayed with Perron in the hall. Then she murmured, 'Thank you, Guy,' and went out too.

III

He was dressed by five to seven and on the verandah as the second-hand of his watch ticked up the hour. It was a clear sunny morning.

At ten past he heard the growl of a vehicle being changed down to enter the compound. A jeep swept in. A khaki-clad figure was riding shot-gun on the high rear seat. Sarah was driving. Her head was bound in a silk scarf. She wore khaki too. She braked but kept the engine running and smiled up at him. This was the old Sarah of Area Headquarters who knew a thing or two about getting a move-on.

'Where's the horse?' he asked. She patted the seat on her right as though it were a saddle. He climbed in over the low port. She wore a khaki skirt too. In fact she had on her old WAC(I) uniform. He could see where the stripes had been. The Indian with the rifle was a soldier. His shoulder tab said *Mirat Artillery*. His face was pitted by smallpox. He looked cheerful. Sarah re-engaged gear, gave a burst of power and drove the jeep down to the exit.

Coming out on to the road he saw that the *maidan* opposite – the rough ground that stretched from the walls of the palace grounds to the walls of the old city – was now populated by military vehicles and groups of soldiers and armed police. He expected her to turn right, imagining that the horses were waiting somewhere on the *maidan*. But she turned left, passing the Dewani Bhavan and then the palace wall, going in the direction of the lake, but suddenly turning left again into a rough unmetalled road. The wind flicked her scarf and the collar of her khaki shirt. She drove very well. A bumpy road, but a smooth ride. Clearly she was familiar with the route.

Coming in from the right, a little way ahead, and from the left, were the spurs of two low wooded hills. Otherwise the countryside was open, poor, unfertile. There was no visible habitation. The land was tawny, flecked with patches of

567

dusty olive green scrub. As the jeep entered the section of road enclosed by the two wooded spurs, Sarah slowed. The road was straight and there seemed no reason for her caution; until, a long way ahead, he saw an elephant plodding rhythmically towards them. As they drove nearer he saw the elephant was pushing or urging something ahead of it with swings of its trunk. Sarah slowed almost to a crawl. Behind the elephant were two men and ahead of it, its calf, an absurdly small creature. Seeing the jeep the mother elephant advanced protectively and the calf went under the shadow of its huge head. Now that they were close Perron saw that the animal's hide was almost black, but red from the dust of the tawny earth. Just before they came level the elephant swung into a side-track, followed by the men. And Sarah drove on.

She said, 'They're the Nawab's. They belong to his forestry department. No one can build here. A hundred years ago it was all forest.'

The road began to descend into an area of scrub-jungle. The horizon was already blurred and violet with the day's promise of heat. A twist in the road brought them to an area of rising land, almost devoid of trees. On the brow of the hill Perron saw two horsemen, as still as statues. Sarah drove a little further and then pulled in behind an army truck and a large closed-in van: a horse-box. A couple of soldiers, with rifles slung, were standing on the opposite side of the road.

'We can watch from here,' she said, getting out. From the dash-board she took a pair of binoculars and handed them to him. 'Here,' she said. 'Now you can see something of the old India.'

Even in close focus the horsemen seemed perfectly still. The lenses blurred the colours slightly, isolated purple refraction so that the profiles of the men's faces seemed to be outlined by a dim reddish-blue glow. They were brown faces. What was so extraordinary was the lack of movement, the intensity of concentration. One of the men was turbanned, the other bare-headed. The turbanned man was dressed in what looked like a studded leather jerkin and tight dark pantaloons. The younger man with the bare head (Ahmed surely?) wore an ordinary pale blue shirt, corduroy breeches and riding boots. Around his raised left forearm was a leather shield which ended in a glove. Upon the forearm sat a hawk. Perron fancied that he could see the feathered shift of its neck, the gleam of its fierce eye.

Then the vision in the binoculars suddenly blurred and Perron lowered them and just caught the end of the flighting movement of Ahmed Kasim's arm, citing the hawk at its prey – a movement that produced in the bird apparent momentary lack of co-ordination, quickly righted, and developing into a powerful and breath-taking ascent, a great arc, the beginning of a spiral of such formal beauty that Perron caught his breath and held it until he discerned in the empty heavens, through the planned geometry of the hawk's attack, the objective, the intended point of killing contact: a dark speck intent on escape.

He felt Sarah's hand groping for his. But she only wanted the binoculars. He let them go and then gave all his attention back to the aerial hunt, one that left no vapour trails but reminded him of a summer that had mapped them. The hawk plummeted. Its shape merged with the speck. Sarah cried out, with pleasure and pain. He looked at her. All he could see was her hand gripping the binoculars, her slightly open mouth, the brave little thrust of chin and the tautened throat.

She gave the glasses back to him and said without looking at him, 'You must watch this.'

He took the binoculars and readjusted the focus. The horsemen had put their mounts forward at a slow walk. He searched the lower sky in the direction they were heading and, almost too late, picked up the image of the hawk just descending. The prey was invisible. The hawk's wings were still at stretch, but folding back in slow motion, in satisfaction. And then they were at stretch again, beating against gravity, intent on ascent. He followed its course, saw Ahmed throw something. It swooped down, clawed at ground level, attacking something with its beak. The older horseman was riding in the direction of the kill. Ahmed, motionless, watched the hawk swallow its gift – presumably an appetising and bloody piece of raw meat. Presently there came the far-off sound of Ahmed's voice, a sound like Tek, Tek, Tek-Allahallahallah. The hawk was now beating at the air again, rising, circling once round Ahmed, flirting at the lure of his leathered forearm, and then gently turning and coming in to alight. It ducked its head, arched its wings, then allowed itself to be brought near to Ahmed's face: the likeness of a kiss.

Unexpectedly, Ahmed flighted the hawk again, but not at prey, unless he himself were the prey. He cantered to and fro, round and round, gradually descending the hill, spiralling at ground level as the hawk had spiralled the sky, while the bird flew to and fro as well, sometimes swooping in mock attack.

'I wish he wouldn't do this,' Sarah said. 'But he trusts her utterly.'

It was like a game of love. Sometimes Ahmed called out and when he did the hawk seemed to turn away, spurning him, only to meet him again at the end of another swerving course. About one hundred yards from the road, Ahmed reined in. The hawk planed above him for a while and then as if breathless too, ready to call it a day, came in and settled gently on his proffered arm. Perron saw that Ahmed was securing the jesses. Again he brought the bird close to his face, then he sat erect and came the rest of the way at a sedate walk. Some distance behind, the falconer was following slowly down. He had a canvas bag slung over his shoulder. The kill.

'Hello,' Ahmed called. He kicked his stirrups away, brought his right leg up and across the saddle and slid down. The bird stayed rock-still on his forearm. He tickled her stomach. She glared at him and then at the strangers. But what else, Perron wondered, could a hawk do but glare?

'Her name's Mumtaz,' Sarah said. 'Come and meet her. Incidentally, don't offer to shake hands with Ahmed. She's very jealous and protective. Aren't you, Mumtaz? I'm not allowed to touch her at all, because she senses I'm female. But if Ahmed tells her it's all right she'll allow you to tickle her throat.'

Ahmed said, in Urdu: *Here is Perron Sahib, from across the black water. He is a friend. Say hello.* He stroked her breast feathers, then said in English, 'You can touch her now, Mr Perron.'

Perron extended a finger. The head turned. A glaring eye observed the finger. Risking the loss, he placed the finger on her breast and smoothed downwards. When he withdrew the finger the hawk's wing stirred slightly.

'Ah,' Sarah said. 'She liked that. Ahmed, you'd better keep your eye on her. I think she's a bit of a rover.'

Ahmed laughed, then, noticing her skirt said, 'Aren't you going to ride?'

'No, I thought not today.'

'What about you, Mr Perron? You can have Begum here. She's still quite fresh.'

'I'm more than content to watch you hawk.'

'Oh, no more of that. I'm glad you were just in time. We can have a run after breakfast if you like. Come, Mumtaz. You can go to sleep now.' The falconer had come up and dismounted. Rather tetchily Mumtaz hopped from Ahmed's arm to the falconer's. The falconer took her down to the truck and Perron now noticed that there was an awning attached to the truck's side and, under the awning, a table laid for breakfast. Nearby, in the shade of a tree, a portable perch had been set up, with a silver chain attached to its cross-pole. The falconer transferred Mumtaz to this, secured her and clapped a little scarlet velvet hood on her head.

'Come,' Ahmed said. 'I hope everybody is hungry.'

They went down to the table under the awning. Ahmed absented himself for a while. As Perron and Sarah sat she said, 'Are you glad you came?'

'Not glad. Enchanted.'

'I meant back to India.'

'The answer's the same.'

She smiled.

* * *

The convoy home was headed by the army truck. The soldiers sat in the back of it, the falconer up front, with Mumtaz. Behind, Ahmed drove the jeep with Sarah next to him and Perron in the back seat. Bringing up the rear was the horse-box which gradually got left behind. Perron, shouting against the noise of the engine and the currents of air asked what the bird thought of mechanical transport. Sarah leaned back and said: 'Ahmed thinks it's her favourite part of the proceedings. But she's very blasé. She goes to sleep.'

'What do the soldiers make of it all?'

'I think they get a bit of a kick out of it. It's still quite new to them.'

No one had explained the presence of the soldiers. If the hawking was quite new to them then presumably a military escort was a recent innovation. But how recent? And why was it necessary? Sarah turned round again and shouted, 'We're going to the palace if that's all right. I've got to visit Shiraz, but Ahmed will take you round and show you the interesting bits.'

Ahmed said something to her which he didn't catch. She laughed.

'Who is Shiraz?' Perron shouted.

'The Nawab's daughter.'

Perron nodded. He did not know the Nawab had a daughter. But he thought that between Ahmed and Sarah there was a special kind of empathy, the kind that two people betray in small gestures and in the way they have of dealing with one another in public. Well, if that was how the land lay he could only wish her good luck, slightly deflating though it was to his own ego.

He looked at Ahmed's back. He remembered him as a pleasant but rather unsociable young man, given apparently to whisky and women, a combination which might by now have begun to show signs of taking toll. Instead, young Kasim looked (as Uncle George would say) well set-up. Mounted, and flying his hawk, Perron appreciated that to Sarah he would even cut a heroic figure. And she was the kind of girl who would defy the convention that a white woman didn't fall in love with an Indian.

When they came close to the end of the unmetalled road Sarah called out, 'Go in through the guest house entrance, Ahmed, and drop me there. I've got a few things to do. I'll join you at the palace later.'

Ahmed nodded and then hooted and drew ahead of the truck, paused at the T-junction and raised his arm to indicate that the truck should turn right. Turning left himself he came to a halt to make sure the driver had understood. Perron looked back. As the truck came into view he saw the falconer's arm which was resting by the elbow on the open

window frame, and upon the arm, Mumtaz, hooded, head
slightly inclined –

*

(Extract From Perron's diaries)
(Tuesday August 5) – asleep, dreaming of what? The palace
wall is backed by trees. You can see nothing from the road. We
turned in at an unexpected culvert. Twin iron gates. Closed. A
smart sepoy opened them at once and we went in, past two
more who were armed and came to attention. The gates were
closed again once we'd passed through. The path is bordered
by rhododendron. Just where it forked (giving on the left a
glimpse of the guest house) Sarah made Ahmed stop. She
insisted on walking from there. We continued along the right-
hand fork and came out after a hundred yards into a large
formal park, with the extrordinary pink palace on the left. To
the right, half-a-mile away, was the main entrance gate and
frontage, facing on to the *maidan*. The park was laid out with
avenues, terraces and fountains. As we got close to the palace
you could see that parts of the pink stucco needed replas-
tering. The palace bears some resemblance to the Wind Palace
in Jaipur. We drove to a side entrance. Sentries again. Steps up.
The smell of ancient damp masonry. A long terrace, a lot of
servants and officials coming and going. Obviously the
business side of the place. Then through a narrow Moghul
arch into a dark stone corridor – the kind in which you feel the
weight of India: a heavy darkness which is a protection from
glare and heat but reminiscent of tombs and dungeons.

But the inner courtyard was beautiful. At the far end, facing
the paths and fountains was the old Hall of Public Audience, a
deep terrace with a high roof supported by convoluted pink
columns; and, with a marble canopy and daïs centrally placed,
the stone seat on which in the old days the Nawab was
enthroned on cushions: the *gaddi*. Behind the Hall of Public
Audience (Ahmed said) was a smaller courtyard overlooked
by the present Nawab's private apartments. Avoiding this
other courtyard we crossed and went out through another
series of dark passages to the other side of the palace. Lawns
swept down to the lake and the little white mosque which

was enclosed in its own railed courtyard. We went down to the lake shore. The glare was intense. Ahmed said they were fishing again this morning. Beyond the distant reeds you could just see a couple of boats and men casting large shimmering nets. Ahmed took me back inside the palace to see what he called the modern rooms. These were at the front. The old Moghul passages gave way to corridors, Victorian in style (dark lincrusta, hundreds of pictures cluttering the walls, as thick as postage stamps in an album) and then – fascinating! – a kind of salon which reminded you of the public lounge of a Ritzy Edwardian hotel, all gilt and plush and potted palms in gilt wicker baskets, ornate draught screens and a circular padded bench around a central marble column. Dmitri Bronowsky's influence, one would imagine.

*

It was in this *fin-de-siècle* foyer that Ahmed left him, to change out of his riding gear. He promised to be back shortly. He said, 'Would you like a swim later? There's an outdoor pool. We can provide towels and costumes.'

'Yes, I'd like that very much.'

'It can't be for about an hour, though. Sarah usually gives Shiraz her swimming lesson between eleven and twelve. I'll tell them to send you coffee and the papers.'

The coffee and papers came. Today's *Times of India* and *The Statesman* (which obviously reached the palace earlier than they reached the club), the *Mirat Courier* and *The Ranpur Gazette*. This morning in the national newspapers some play was being made with the latest difficulties Jinnah was said to be raising: questions about the precise status Mountbatten would have in Karachi when he made his last appearance there as Viceroy on August 13. Two days later Jinnah would become Governor-General of the new dominion of Pakistan (moth-eaten Pakistan as he had called it, when he found he wasn't getting either the whole of the Punjab or the whole of Bengal – least of all Kashmir or a corridor connecting the west with the east).

It seemed that Jinnah had been gently reminded that the Viceroy would still be Viceroy on August 13 and he himself only Governor-General designate, just as Mountbatten was also Governor-General designate of the new Dominion of India. There was no question of Jinnah taking precedence before the date of independence, and Mountbatten couldn't be in both Karachi and Delhi on August Fifteen.

There were depressingly familiar reports from Lahore, Amritsar and Calcutta of troubles with the Sikhs and of murders and arson, and equally depressing commentaries on the harrowing experiences of some of the refugees already making their way from what would be Pakistan to what would be India, and vice versa. But the photographs in the papers were only of smiling statesmen's faces.

The *Mirat Courier*, predictably, published similar photographs and gave up its front page to preliminary details of the official programme for independence day celebrations. A Muslim firm in the cantonment called Mir Khan Military Tailors and Outfitters had taken half a page to announce a grand cut-price sale of all items of uniform and sporting equipment. At the rear pages were brief details of a number of farewell parties held the previous week.

He turned more expectantly to the waspish *Ranpur Gazette*, and was not unrewarded. The editorial – a long one – was headed: *Pandora's Box*. It read:

'The pocket-kingdom of Mirat was, until 1937, except for a brief period in the early 'twenties, in direct relationship with the Crown through the agency of the Governor in Ranpur, which suited all parties and conformed with the geographical and political facts of life. Geographically and politically, Mirat has always existed and can only exist in future as part of the geographical and political territory by which it is surrounded.

'That it exists at all as a separate political unit is due to the pure luck and chance of the fall of the dice of history. Long drawn-out though the battle for power was between the European merchants and the ruling Indian powers in the seventeenth, eighteenth and nineteenth centuries, there came a point when the dominant European power, the British, made a settlement with what was left of the scattered remnants of Moghul India. That point was reached in 1857.

'Dare one say that as a result of the Mutiny the Crown

575

feared it had gone far enough with its policies of expansion or that it simply decided that the status quo, then existing, would prove the most profitable, if maintained? Be that as it may, with two-thirds of the sub-continent now under the direct rule of Whitehall and the real power of the remnants of Princely India reduced virtually to impotence, a declaration was made of "no further territorial ambitions" (what a sinister ring that phrase has nowadays!) – and treaties were made with the rulers of the nearly 600 remaining states, widely scattered and varying in size from mere estates to provinces the size of Ireland, treaties which secured to the rulers and to their successors their princely rights, revenues, privileges and territories, assured them of autonomy in all but the major subjects of external affairs and national defence, treaties which undertook to protect the princes from each other, from attack both internal and external.

'Separate though these treaties were – a series of private formal individual contracts between rulers and crown, they have nevertheless always been part of a larger unwritten treaty – or doctrine: the doctrine of the paramountcy of the British Crown over all the rulers; the paramountcy of the King-Emperor or Queen-Empress who, through the Crown Representative, could depose an unruly prince, withhold recognition from a prince's heir, and generally take steps to ensure the peace, prosperity and wellbeing of a prince's subjects.

'But none of the doctrinal powers of "paramountcy" could abrogate the treaty made with a state. From time to time the Crown has taken over a state's administration, but only in trust. The declaration of "no further territorial ambitions" has been, one may feel, upheld.

'Unfortunately, the doctrine of paramountcy has run counter to the doctrine of eventual self-government for those provinces ruled directly by the British parliament, through the Government of India. Paramountcy has always been illogical in the long run, and this illogicality is best exemplified by the dual rôle assigned to the Viceroy. In his rôle as Governor-General it has been his duty to govern and guide and encourage the British-Indian provinces towards democratic parliamentary self-rule. As Crown Representative, it has been his duty to uphold, secure, oversee and defend the autocratic rule of several hundred princes.

'Many princes have therefore assumed, or pretended to assume, or felt entitled to assume, that the demission by the Governor-General of power into Indian hands in provinces directly ruled by the British, could not absolve the British from treaty obligations to uphold, secure and defend the integrity of the territories the princes have ruled, for better or worse, and which they believe they have every right to continue to rule, irrespective of who rules the rest of India.

'It is fair to say that until quite recently they have been encouraged in this assumption by statements from Whitehall and New Delhi, and by the behaviour and attitude of senior members of the Political Department. Their chief fear was that "paramountcy" would be transferred by the Crown to the Crown's successors in British India (in this case, the Congress Party, which for years has made it clear that the survival of autocratic states, some quite feudal in their administration, could not be tolerated). But they were reassured. Paramountcy was a doctrine. You could not transfer a doctrine.

'But if you can't transfer it what can you do with it? The answer is, nothing. It simply lapses when the paramount "power" disappears. But what about the treaties? Can treaties lapse unless both parties agree to the lapse? Indeed they can. They lapse when one party no longer has the power (or the presence) to perform its part of the bargain. By abdicating in British-India, the British Crown no longer has the power to protect and secure and uphold the territorial integrity of Princely India, without running the risk of going to war with the new Dominion. One prince is rumoured to be consulting his lawyers in Switzerland with a view to suing the British Government in London for non-performance of contract. Another is rumoured to have gone to Delhi armed with a revolver. Other princes, of course, see the lapsing of paramountcy and of treaty obligations as the opportunity to declare their complete independence.

'What the British Crown has really done for the past hundred years is advance the territories it ruled directly to full democratic and parliamentary self-government, and maintain the territories it did not rule directly, but was paramount over, in forms of autocratic government alien in nature to the form of government itself advocates and which the British people themselves enjoy at home and seem convinced is everyone's birthright. You can hardly wonder that this left-hand/right-hand policy was entrusted to one man, the Viceroy, in order to create the illusion that there was a unity of purpose.

'Our new Viceroy has been, as ever, quick to grasp the irreconcilable details and see the immense political vacuum that technically follows the removal of British power in British-India. The new States Department is his efficient answer to nature's abhorrence of such a vacuum. You could say that Whitehall foresaw the situation in 1935. You could say that the princes themselves are largely to blame for refusing at that time to co-operate in the Federal Scheme for a united and self-governing India (but they were not the only people who were suspicious of the scheme and refused to co-operate). You could blame the princes for many things, including their haughty distrust of one another, or of anybody. You cannot in principle blame them for standing by their treaties, for acting out the Ruritanian farce currently playing up and down India (and Pakistan); a farce all too frequently encouraged by senior members of the Political Deparment who have served in India for years and have been brought up to take the treaties as serious and sacrosanct documents.

'This is a farce in which Muslim rulers of predominantly Hindu states which are hedged about on all sides by territory which from August 15 will be ruled by the Congress from Delhi, elect to join one of the two distant arms of Pakistan; or in which Hindu rulers of predominantly Muslim states in or contiguous to Pakistan declare allegiance to Congress India, or in which rulers of immense landlocked states declare their independence of everything and everybody. You cannot blame them because not only is the farce implicit in the treaties and the doctrines but these declarations and intentions do not in any single case contravene either the spirit or the letter of the law. They are simply devoid of any means of

578

reasonable implementation. From the princes' point of view, the long years of British power and influence have left them in possession of preserved but unpossessable goods. Geographically and politically they cannot survive individually once the Crown abdicates and twentieth-century India (or Pakistan) takes over.

'All this, and the terrible reports of the breakdown of civil authority in many areas of the Punjab, must make it seem that to achieve the objective of a political transformation scene in the long pantomime of the British-Indian Empire, the Viceroy, obeying the wishes of a well-meaning but ignorant British electorate, has found himself in the unenviable position of opening Pandora's Box and letting out all the evils that have afflicted this country probably since time began but which have been imprisoned, under a lid shut and locked by the single rule of British Power and British Law; evils which have not died of asphyxiation, but multiplied.

'Which brings us back to the small but not unimportant state of Mirat, which is not only geographically part of this province but traditionally and politically part of it.

'Under the present ruler, His Highness Sir Ahmed Ali Guffur Kasim Bahadur, and his Chief Minister, Count Dmitri Bronowsky, Mirat has made notable strides forward. A predominantly Hindu state, the administration used to be the almost exclusive preserve of Muslims, a situation common enough where the ruling family is Muslim, but one that always causes dissatisfaction and unrest. For the past two or three decades, official posts, including senior official posts have been open to Hindus. There are Hindus on the Council of State and for many years now there has been a Hindu College of Higher Education.

'The existence in the state capital of a large military cantonment and training area for troops of the British and the Indian armies has contributed (for nearly a hundred years) to Mirat's prosperity and no doubt to its peace and security. For the past year or two, however, there has been a great deal of unrest. Both the main Indian political parties must be held partly responsible for this because neither has been slow to take political advantage of the problems posed for India as a whole by the continuing existence of states whose rule, however benevolent, can hardly be called truly democratic.

'The Nawab is now faced with the problem of what action to take now that his treaty with the Crown and the doctrine of the Crown's paramountcy are lapsing. One may think it a pity that since 1937 his relationship with the Crown has been conducted through the Resident at the distant court of a much larger state, Gopalakand. Whatever advice Sir Robert Conway is giving the Maharajah of Gopalakand ought not, one may suggest, to be the same advice he should give to the Nawab of Mirat. But that is by the way. At this juncture, advice from the Political Department is largely irrelevant. The consideration that should be uppermost in the Nawab's mind is the well-being of his subjects.

'It is important to remember the tradition of intense loyalty and reverence felt by the subjects of a princely state for their ruler, the tradition of dependence on him to make wise decisions. The main Indian political parties may scoff at these traditions as outmoded and feudal, but they exist. And already we have reports of the first effects on the people of Mirat of rumours of indecision at the palace.

'For instance, the rumour that the Nawab has not been co-operative with representatives of the States Department of the government of the new Indian dominion and may declare himself an independent Islamic state, affiliated to Pakistan, has led to the murder of Muslims in the city of Mirat and in the villages by extremist Hindus, and to burning and looting of Muslim shops. Retaliation, by Muslim extremists, has led to the murder of Hindus and the burning and looting of Hindu houses and shops. In all this, the position of such British troops as remain in the cantonment is, to say the least, delicate, and that of Indian troops equally delicate since they are in the main troops allocated to the new dominion of India and most of the Muslim elements of regiments that are to be divided have already left the area.

'Nevertheless it is to the cantonment, which might itself turn out to be the scene of awkward confrontations, that Muslim refugees from the villages and from the city have gone, seeking temporary refuge. Some of these refugees are no doubt bona fide travellers *en route* to Pakistan. Most, one suspects, are there temporarily, simply to protect their lives, having lost their property.

'We cannot afford to have in this province of British India which in ten days time will become a province of the new Indian dominion, a pocket of such potential communal and political danger.

'The Nawab could defuse the bomb in an instant, by taking the logical, the only practical step, which is to sign the instrument of accession to the new Dominion of India on the three subjects of external affairs, defence and communications and the standstill agreement which will allow him time to negotiate a settlement with India on all the complex and vitally important points arising from the lapse of paramountcy and the end of his treaty with the Crown.

'If he signs, his subjects will then know where they stand. Since the majority is Hindu, one might say that the majority would approve such a step. The Muslim minority who until recently have lived in comparative harmony with the Hindus of Mirat would also accept his decision, as that of their ruler and co-religionist, but those of them who see a better future for themselves in Jinnah's new Islamic state could then peacefully wind up their businesses and affairs and leave – just as peacefully.

'One can sympathize with the Nawab. One should sympathize with any man whose traditional assurances and traditional courses of action are suddenly removed or closed to him. But it is *his* sympathies, not our own, which are under test and examination. One is fairly confident that the outcome will show them firmly placed with the present and future welfare of all his people.

'So at least one must hope. Classical scholars will recall that Hope was the only thing that didn't fly out of Pandora's Box but remained obstinately at the bottom.'

*

'Guy?'

It was Sarah. She had changed into a cotton frock.

'Ahmed asks me to apologize. He's got something urgent to

581

attend to. But Dmitri would like to have a few words and present you to HH, if you're agreeable.'

'Of course. Have you had your swim yet?'

'I can't this morning. I've got to go back to the guest house soon. But I can take you back to Nigel's bungalow after you've met HH. I'm sorry if we seem to be messing you about again.'

'Hardly that.'

She led him by a new way into the inner courtyard and then along one of the paths between the lawns and fountains.

Strolling up and down the colonnaded terrace on their left were four men; one of them in full Congress garb, another in a lounge suit, the other two in long-skirted high-necked coats.

'States Department?' Perron murmured.

'The two on this side are. The others are members of the Nawab's council. Finance member and food member.'

One of them called out, 'Good-morning, Miss Layton.'

She called good-morning back.

'That's the food member. He's an expert on agrarian economy. Dmitri pinched him from Calcutta before the war. I wish you could have gone to Biranpur and seen the model farm and village he set up. Perhaps you'll be able to, if you're staying for a while and things settle down.'

'Perhaps you'll go with me?'

'I wish I could. I'd like to see it again. But I can't think when that'll be. Susan's decided to go back to Pankot right away and I'll have to go with her. I don't know what will happen after that.'

'What does right away mean?'

'The day after tomorrow, I think. Ahmed's looking into the arrangements now.'

She moved ahead of him, through the Hall of Public Audience, to a narrow archway that gave on to the courtyard Ahmed hadn't shown him, the one overlooked by the private apartments. Going through the archway she suddenly stopped and said, 'Oh. Wait. Do you mind?' She went down into the courtyard leaving him alone, in the shadow of the archway.

Seated on the rim of a fountain at the centre of the courtyard was a young Indian girl dressed – how odd – in slacks and blouse. As Sarah approached her Perron saw two older women, in sarees, getting up from squatting positions on the terrace and making *namaste*. The Indian girl's back was towards Sarah but the movements of the women alerted her and she looked round, then down again, head bowed. Sarah sat beside her and after a moment put her arm round her.

Perron turned away and considered the Nawab's eye-view of the main courtyard. From here there was nothing that oppressed him. The courtyard was brilliant with sunshine and colour and splashing water. Then he saw the white peacock – at least, *a* white peacock – strutting across one of the lawns, its breast carved like the prow of a Viking ship, its long trailing tail quills making stern and wake. The quills were in moult. Should it erect them now they would look like the spokes of a moth-eaten fan. But the proud statement of the bird's slow stalking was only marginally impaired.

He went back to the archway in time to see Sarah and the girl walking slowly arm in arm, climbing up to the terrace. The women followed some distance behind. Then the girl broke away and ran in through a doorway. Sarah returned to the courtyard. The two women hastened after their charge.

He went down and waited.

'Shiraz?' he asked.

'Yes. Shiraz.' Then she took him up to the private apartments.

*

'My dear Mr Perron,' Count Bronowsky said, limping across the darkened, almost completely shuttered, room. 'How can I sufficiently apologize for not having greeted you before? I don't mean that Sarah and Nigel haven't tried their best to cover up for me, but I'm very conscious of my personal failure in the matter of hospitality. Please forgive me.'

A single shaft of light from the louvres of a shutter exposed the half-blind face and the parchment texture of the skin. The offered hand seemed made of nothing but frail bone. There was a faint smell of eau-de-cologne. A stronger shaft of light fell on to a couch near a window. It was to this that Dmitri led him, skeletal hand lightly resting on his shoulder. 'When I had your letter from England, I thought – Ah! Mr Perron may be persuaded to lecture at our college on the subject of the European mercenaries and the history of the Mahrattas. But in the event the college is temporarily closed owing to what one calls circumstances beyond one's control. The students are on strike.' They sat on the couch. 'In any case this was just a thing I selfishly thought you might agree to do for us. The important question is what we can do for you. You mentioned the possibility of writing and publishing something on the subject of the transfer of power as it affects states like this. I've forgotten the name of the paper.'

'It's a new quarterly review called *The New English Forum*. It probably won't survive more than a few issues. I'm afraid my journalistic credentials are entirely spurious.'

'I see you have this morning's *Ranpur Gazette*.'

Perron realized he still carried the folded newspaper.

'I hope you won't think it very discourteous of me, Mr Perron, if I ask you to hide it away. His Highness hasn't read this morning's issue and there's a long editorial in it which from my point of view has come out a shade prematurely. You've read it? What did you think of it?'

'I thought it quite well-argued.'

'The editor of the *Ranpur Gazette*, an elderly Englishman incidentally, does have quite an effective style. I suppose Nigel told you what he was hoping to achieve in Gopalakand?'

'Yes, he gave me a rough outline.'

'He's been on the telephone this morning and will be back some time later today with the necessary letter from the Resident. In other words his mission was a success. But I haven't told Nawab Sahib yet. I don't intend to do so until after the morning audiences and petitions. He was hoping Conway would encourage him to stand firm on independence, but Nigel has persuaded him not to encourage him. If Nawab Sahib reads that article now it will put his back up. I don't want him with his back up when I tell him that Conway is washing his hands of Mirat and that he should sign the instrument of accession if he so wishes.'

Perron handed Bronowsky the newspaper and said,

'Perhaps you'd better dispose of it. Thank you for warning me. I might have referred to it.'

'It was Miss Layton who warned me you might have been reading it. That is why I came out for a private word. She is a remarkably shrewd and thoughtful young woman. We shall miss her at the palace. Nawab Sahib's daughter is heartbroken and begs her to come back soon. Miss Layton is the only person who has ever succeeded in bringing poor little Shiraz out of her shell. For years I tried. Nawab Sahib tried. I tried to get Ahmed to try. But the influence of the late Begum, her mother, seemed indestructible. Shiraz threatened to go into full purdah, can you believe it? Now she is riding and swimming and wearing modern clothes and even sometimes talking to men. Even Ahmed is showing an interest in her at last. And it is all Sarah's doing. She is with Nawab Sahib now, saying goodbye. He too has become very fond of her. It is a piquant situation. She treats him like a father, but I sometimes think he looks at her and vaguely resents that for the past twenty years I have kept him on such a strait and narrow path. As a young prince, you know, when his father ruled, the Political Department was in two minds about recognizing him as the heir. Their files would reveal some scandalous things about him in his wild youth. Perhaps about me too. Thank God these files are all being destroyed before Patel can get his hands on them.'

'Is Shiraz the Nawab's heir?'

'Oh, no. He has two sons, both older. The younger is in the Indian Air Force, not a pilot, they never succeeded in teaching him to fly, poor boy. The elder is Mohsin, but Mohsin and his wife live mostly in Delhi. He is much involved with business affairs and his wife does not like Mirat at all. She hates coming here. But finally this has had one advantage. She insisted on a swimming-pool being built in the grounds for her to bathe in. It has been very useful to Sarah, in educating Shiraz.'

'The succession is secure, then.'

Bronowsky nodded, but did not otherwise reply. Instead he said, 'Tomorrow I hope that these States Department people will be on their way back to Delhi with their signed bits of paper and that I shall be able to leave the palace and go back across the road to my own home. Then perhaps you will be my guest and in any case come to dinner tomorrow evening, if all goes well. I don't know whether Sarah will be able to come if they are to travel the next day. But I hope Nigel can be there. And Ahmed. Ahmed has promised his father to be in Ranpur for the August fifteen celebrations and I cannot deny him that. Since the Laytons have decided to go back to Pankot he may as well accompany them as far as Ranpur. It is a good opportunity.'

He stood and placed a hand on Perron's shoulder and indicated a double set of doors.

'Nawab Sahib is in there with Sarah. I'm afraid you will not find him very communicative. He is shy with strangers. So do not be offended if I intervene quite quickly and take him through to see his petitioners. The morning audiences are a relic of the past. All the real business is done by members of council and their staffs, but the tradition is important. I shall have to go in with him but Sarah will then look after you and take you back to Nigel's.'

Bronowsky went to an ornate desk, opened a drawer and pushed the *Ranpur Gazette* into it. As he rejoined Perron he said, 'Did you by any chance call on our old friend Aimee when you were in Bombay?'

'No, I didn't. I called on Mr Hapgood though. He sent his regards.'

'Hapgood? Oh, the bank official. But how well I remember that evening at Aimee's. What a terrible disaster you averted – what a terrible mistake I made, taking Miss Layton and poor Ronald there! The previous time I visited her everything was beyond criticism. You made an impression on her, did you know? The next time I saw her, I think in Delhi, she was a bit confused about the precise circumstances but she said, "Where is that British sergeant you brought to one of my parties, who gave me a lovely bottle of whisky, and then took it away with him, the crook?" So, you see? Come. Let us go in.'

*

Extract from Perron's diary, Tuesday August 5.
– to a smaller room, a salon, decorated and furnished in the

Empire style. The Nawab stood at the window indicating something to Sarah (it turned out to be the view of the fishermen on the Izzat Bagh Lake – so-called because an earlier Nawab had declared that the *izzat*, the honour of the ruling house, would be maintained for as long as the lake didn't dry up). Dmitri left me near the door, said something to the Nawab, a small man in comparison with Dmitri. The Nawab came across. I advanced a step or two and bowed. The offer to shake hands was slightly delayed. One sensed that today he distrusted all Englishmen. His long-skirted coat was amazingly shabby. The cuffs were frayed and the material was very thin around the button-holes. (He is a rich man, generous and not mean. His austerities are wholly personal, Sarah tells me.) The face is narrow, lined, quite a deep brown, curiously anonymous. The kind of face you easily forget. But he has the sort of presence you remember, self-containment, suggesting restraint of packed nervous energy and intensity of feeling – suitable in the descendant of men who were feared, before whom Mirat trembled, years ago.

An exchange of compliments. A bleak pause. Dmitri hovering in the background, a gaunt one-eyed guardian, smiling but alert. Then the Nawab offered some samples from his stock of small-talk. I replied in kind. Suddenly he frowned. Perron? he asked. A descendant of the successor to Benoit de Boigne? His ancestors could have had no love for either of them. Relief, when I disclaimed connection. Then the preliminary to courtly dismissal. I must be sure to inform Count Bronowsky of anything necessary to my comfort and to my researches. A friendly, shy, smile. No handshake in parting. He turns to Dmitri as if wondering whether he has omitted anything. One realized his dependence and his current distraction. Before he went he silently pressed both Sarah's hands. Then he and Dmitri went out through another set of doors. A glimpse of a much larger chamber with about a dozen people in it, who bowed deeply; one even making full obeisance.

Sarah and I leave in solemn but not too solemn silence. We run the gauntlet of servants making *namaste* (to her, not to me, I think). Then she drove me back to Nigel's bungalow.

Tippoo was waiting on the verandah. She wouldn't stay for a drink. I didn't press her. She seemed preoccupied.

But before I let her go I said, 'What *did* happen to Ronald?'

She said, 'Don't ask me, Guy. Ask Nigel. Or Dmitri. Or better still, nobody.'

IV

After lunch he slept again. But sleep was intermittent. There was another storm, brief but disturbing, and the rain brought out that smell of damp, of decay. He woke between dozes with a persistent sense of ill-being and was thankful when Tippoo brought in his tea at four o'clock. He thought of starting a letter to Aunt Charlotte, but the room was suddenly intolerable. He dressed and went out to the rear compound to get air and sunshine. There was no sound from Merrick's compound. He inspected the banyan tree. How old would it be? One hundred years at least? So fine a specimen would be especially holy. But its holiness lent no tranquillity to the bungalows in whose compounds it grew.

He found the gate in the compound wall unlocked so went through. Today Merrick's garden looked less well-tended. Overnight the grass seemed to have grown an inch. All the green tattis between the white columns had been rolled up, exposing windows obviously locked and shuttered. One could visualize indoors the shrouded shapes of furniture draped in dust-covers, signs that the occupants had gone and that no one knew when they might be back.

He went towards the house intending to go up on to the verandah but then decided he shouldn't intrude on so much absence, so much impending absence, so much darkness, so much loss. He took the path that skirted the side of the bungalow and came out into the front and stood still, hackles rising.

A van was drawn up. Down the steps from the front verandah two men were carrying a black coffin. The coffin was tilted downwards, resting on their shoulders. When they reached ground level they jog-trotted to the van, then shoved the coffin into the back.

Not a coffin. Merrick's trunk. Another man was bringing down the long sagging sausage of the rolled hall carpet. This went into the truck too. Then the rear flap was put up and fixed. Two of the men got in the back, the other went to the front. Khansamar came down the steps carrying an object that glinted. A picture in a frame. The boy's picture of the old Queen. He handed it to the driver and then went back indoors.

When Perron returned to his own room he paused on the threshold, convinced that in the few seconds it had taken him to open the door someone who had been in there had got away, only just in time.

*

By nine o'clock that night Rowan still hadn't arrived back and Sarah hadn't rung. Tippoo persuaded him not to wait any longer so once again he ate alone. Afterwards he sat on the front verandah with his notebook, his file of newspaper cuttings, a pair of scissors and the day's papers which Tippoo assured him Rowan wouldn't mind him cutting up. A light shone from the clerk's office. He hadn't seen the clerk except on some of the occasions when the telephone rang or the *dak* came, or a despatch rider turned up. Otherwise the little man kept to his room, so far as Perron could tell.

He sat with notebook and files and papers untouched, drinking brandy and soda. He was half-inclined to knock at the clerk's door, invite him to join him, get him to talk about the routine of keeping records for a political agent, or about his life; about anything. Instead he continued drinking alone, watching the moths and insects dance round the dim depressingly yellow verandah lights. The lights were too dim to work by. The light in his own room was better. He didn't want to go back to his room. The room undermined his confidence. The whole bungalow undermined it. Perhaps Mirat undermined it. Perhaps Mirat was a mistake.

He opened the *Ranpur Gazette*, began to read 'Pandora's Box' again but grew tired of it within a paragraph or two. He turned pages, holding the newspaper at an angle to get some light on it. There was no cartoon, but, on the middle pages, boxed, was a piece called 'Alma Mater' by Philoctetes. He folded the newspaper so that he could read this.

'On Sunday when the happy occasion at Government College was over, when the inaugural daïs for the opening of the Chakravarti wing had been stripped of its bunting, of its red carpet and striped awning, the raw timber scaffolding exposed (and already under the destructive hammers of carpenters) I visited the new extension hoping I would pass as someone with business to do there.

'I need not have worried. No one challenged me. The carpenters and the workmen assumed I was a member of the college staff and such members of the staff as I encountered assumed I was connected with the builders.

'Assured of anonymity I had a free run of the college-to-be. Occasionally I faced dangers in the shape either of planks and ladders where walls are still being whitewashed or plastered, or of piles of tins, canvas sheets and tools of humbler trades than will be learned here. But unmolested I visited class and lecture-rooms (a few with window panes already cracked or broken) and found no desks, no chairs, and rectangular spaces where blackboards have yet to be installed. The laboratory looked like the ward of a hospital or clinic from which all the beds had been removed and replaced by long pinewood tables and benches which awaited the decision of someone who might say to what use they should be put.

'The present emptiness was not (for me) diminished by anything the imagination could invent about the future. Accompanied only by my own echoing footsteps it seemed unlikely somehow that in a month or two the desks would be in place and students at their places at the desks, teachers standing on these bare platforms and the as yet invisible blackboards already becoming grey from the wiped-off chalk-marks of demonstrated equations.

'Subdued, I left the building and walked down the asphalt path that connects the new building with the old. A few shade trees have already been planted. The old college buildings from here look serene, weathered. I turn, and try to picture the Chakravarti extension as it will be, ten, twenty, fifty years from now, and am glad really, that few if any of those who will then remember it as the benign mother will have seen it quite

590

as I am seeing it now; raw, uncompromising, so clearly dependent on what as yet unproven teachers and as yet unadmitted students must make of it and give to it before they can take anything lasting away from it.

'I walk home, thinking of another place, of seemingly long endless summers and the shade of different kinds of trees; and then of winters when the branches of the trees were bare, so bare that, recalling them now, it seems inconceivable to me that I looked at them and did not think of the summer just gone, and the spring soon to come, as illusions; as dreams, never fulfilled, never to be fulfilled.'

Philoctetes.

          *

He read the piece again and coming to that final paragraph for the second time found himself moved. The brandy probably. He poured himself another. He got up. His nervous system seemed suddenly awry. He would have to take some action, if it were only to begin packing, or better (because packing meant going into that bedroom), to ring Sarah and tell her he thought he might as well go back with her as far as Ranpur. He went into the hall, consulted the short list of important telephone numbers and asked the operator for 234, the guest house. A servant answered. He asked for Miss Layton and gave his name which was one servants often failed to get right.

After half-a-minute or so, a woman said, 'Is that Mr Perron?' An older woman.

'Yes. Mrs Grace?'

'Yes, hello. I'm afraid Sarah's not here.'

'I'm sorry to be calling so late.'

'Oh, not late really. I don't suppose she'll be long. She's out to dinner. When shall I meet you? I've heard so much about you. Sarah tells me you called on dear old Archie Hapgood. How was he?'

Mrs Grace had a fine contralto voice. He imagined (not without reason) a comfortable-looking bosom, fullish jowls, carefully set hair and once sharp eyes that were now dimmed a little. He liked the sound of her. He told her he thought Archie Hapgood looked well, then said:

'I rang to tell Sarah I'm thinking of going back to Ranpur, and I wondered whether we might make a party of it. There's not a great deal for me to do in Mirat now, and I do have to be back in Delhi by the fifteenth. I suppose the main problem is getting a reservation.'

'It shouldn't be a problem on the day train because nobody needs a sleeper. The trouble is we're going on Thursday. You mustn't cut your visit short, unless it really suits you.'

'It would suit me very well.'

'I'll tell Sarah what you suggest, or leave her a message. How late can she ring you back?'

'No restrictions at this end.'

'Well thank you, Mr Perron. Mr Kasim is coming to Ranpur with us, and perhaps some people called Peabody, but they're not absolutely sure. An extra man would be rather nice. I suppose it's awfully foolish of me but since Colonel Layton went back to Pankot I've been feeling a bit out of my depth.'

There spoke the widow, with one widowed niece, one unmarried niece, a grand-nephew and an ayah, all to look after and feel responsible for. They said goodnight to one another; and having made the decision to go he now felt better. He went back to the verandah to pour himself another drink, and wait for Sarah's call.

*

There was no call but just before midnight a car turned into the compound. When it stopped, Tippoo – who had heard it – was already down there, opening the door. Rowan got out. He was alone. Laura's absence was somehow eloquent. 'Hello, Guy,' he said, coming up, 'I hope you've eaten.'

'Yes, I have. What about you?'

'I've had something at the palace.'

'Well, have a brandy.'

Rowan glanced at the bottle. 'You shouldn't be drinking your own.' The clerk came out of his office. 'Guy, I'll be with you in ten minutes or so. Unless you'd rather go to bed.'

'The last thing.'

Rowan went towards the office, then turned round, 'I nearly forgot. Sarah says she'll ring you in the morning about your Thursday plan.'

Alone, Perron poured himself another brandy and soda. Tippoo came past him with Rowan's suitcase. Ten minutes later he reappeared and said, 'Sahib?' Perron found himself being taken indoors, to a room similar in shape to his own bedroom but on the other side of the hall, and furnished as a study, with a desk, and three easy chairs set round a low table on which there were glasses and a decanter. A connecting door, open, gave a glimpse of a larger room – Nigel's and Laura's bedroom, presumably. Tippoo went in. Presently Nigel called, 'With you in a moment, Guy. Help yourself.'

But he didn't help himself. He was thinking: Odd – I've been here before. And then remembered when and where, and smiled. He looked round the study for the cricket-stump and wondered which of the chairs Rowan would suggest as the best for a slacker at games to kneel on. He was still smiling when Rowan came in. Rowan was smiling too, but at a more recent memory.

'Well, it's done.'

'The Nawab's signed? Congratulations.'

Rowan poured deep amber liquid. 'Soda?'

'To the top.'

They raised glasses, drank; then sat. Settled, Rowan said, 'Well then. I gather you feel you've learnt as much as you need in Mirat.'

'I shouldn't mind having a chat with Dmitri. I gathered that might be possible tomorrow night.'

'But you want to go when the others go, the day after.'

'It would fit in. And I do want to be in Delhi before August fifteen. But I suppose whether I go on Thursday depends on what Sarah and her aunt decide.'

'They'd both welcome you.'

'I gather you've seen Sarah tonight?'

'I looked in at the guest house on my way from the palace. She'd just got back and felt it really was too late to ring you.'

'I'm glad she was able to get out somewhere.'

'She was only over at the women's hospital, saying goodbye to the staff. But they made her stay to supper.'

'In the cantonment?'

'No. The Mirat women's hospital. Just over the other side of the *maidan*, here. She's done a lot of voluntary work for them. Didn't you know?'

'No, I didn't.'

'It used to be a purdah hospital for Muslim women only, but Dmitri got it extended some years ago. She's been very popular with the patients and the nurses. She even got Shiraz to take an interest. The hospital's one of the main reasons she's stayed in Mirat all through the hot weather. If Dmitri had let her she'd have gone out to work at the Biranpur leper colony too. Are you thinking of going all the way up to Pankot with them?'

'Only to Ranpur. I'm rather hoping Ahmed can wangle an interview for me with his father.'

'I'd forgotten your journalistic assignment.'

'It's hardly that.'

'If you're not going back to England from Delhi, you could always come down to Gopalakand. I've left Laura there. I'll be closing down here in the next day or two and joining her. Officially I'm still assistant to the resident in Gopalakand – at least until midnight on August fourteen, when we all become redundant. But Conway won't be going immediately. Laura and I will be there for a week or so as his and the Maharajah's guests, while we decide about the future. Gopalakand might interest you. Just send me a wire at the Residency if you think it would.'

'It might. Thank you. Is it a very tricky situation?'

'Perhaps only tricky for me. The Maharajkumar told me his father's going to sign the instrument of accession too. But he's known Conway a very long time and doesn't want to hurt him by appearing to disregard his advice completely. I think my last few days in the Political Department are going to be spent as pig-in-the-middle. Smoothing things between Conway and the Maharajah. Gopalakand is a Hindu majority state with a Hindu ruler. The only things at stake are the pride of the ruling family and the pride of the Resident. It's much larger than Mirat but self-supporting independence is just as much out of the question. If you do come down everything should be

594

peacefully settled by then, and the Maharajah is very hospitable.'

'Perhaps I'll take you up, then.'

'An old friend of Conway's is coming down too. She's lived in Rawalpindi for years but doesn't want to stay on now that it's becoming part of Pakistan.'

'Who is that?'

'Lady Manners.'

'Have you kept up with her?'

'Not kept up. I visited her a few months ago when we were in that area.'

'Did you tell her you'd heard from Hari?'

'I began to. She asked me not to tell her. It's a subject she doesn't discuss.'

'Why?'

'I think she feels she did what she had to do and that anything else would be an invasion of his privacy and would smack of condescension.'

'You feel that too?'

'I think so.'

'Does she still have the child?'

'Yes.'

'What will happen to it when Lady Manners dies?'

'I imagine she'll be looked after by one of Lady Manners's Indian friends. She's been brought up to think of herself as Indian. She's an enchanting little girl.' Rowan leaned forward and filled their glasses. Perron said:

'How did you meet Laura again?'

'She wrote to me when she got back from prison-camp in Malaya. I'd always kept in touch with her mother. We corresponded for a while. Then we met in Simla. And married.'

'What happened to her first husband?'

'The Japanese killed him. She said it was probably his own fault. He had a bit of a temper. When the Japs first arrived at his rubber estate he put up some sort of show and got knocked about in front of her. They took him to one camp and her to another, of course. Later they sent her his personal effects and a letter of regret informing her that he'd died of fever. She didn't believe it, it goes without saying. She spent some time in Singapore when the war was over, finding out the truth from fellow prisoners of Tony's. Some of the truth. It all went to make up further evidence against a Japanese officer who was tried and hanged as a war criminal.'

'Poor Laura.'

'Yes.' Rowan glanced at him. 'But I don't think her first marriage was much of a success either. I gather she made it clear to you yesterday that ours hasn't been. I don't know why it hasn't. But there you are. She hated it here. That's why I've left her in Gopalakand. She said this bungalow reminded her of the one she and Tony lived in in Malaya. It was one of the things she didn't like about it. So after a week or two we decided she'd better go to the club.'

'*One* of the things she didn't like?'

'It's a bit depressing, isn't it? And I had to leave her on her own a great deal. After three years in a crowded prison-camp she doesn't at all mind being alone, but she needs space and air and light. The Residency at Gopalakand works better for her. This place is very closed in. Damp and dark. I'll be quite glad to get out of it myself. The business of the snake was the last straw. Sarah warned you there'd been one, didn't she? I asked her to.'

'Yes. Was it Laura who found it?'

'Yes, it was.'

'And you who had to kill it?'

'No. I should have hated that. It was Merrick who killed the snake.'

Yes, Perron thought. Merrick was bound to come into the picture. 'What kind of snake?' he asked.

'A young cobra. It was asleep in the bath-tub.'

'The bath-tub? My bath-tub?'

'No. Ours. Through there.' He indicated his bedroom.

'Sarah said it was found under the verandah at the back.'

'I expect she said that to reassure you. No. It was in the bath. Laura happened to go in. She didn't panic. She just came out and shut the door and told Ronald. I was over at the palace, but fortunately Ronald had dropped in. I don't think Tippoo would have been much use. He really *is* terrified of them.'

'How did Ronald kill it?'

The question seemed to put Rowan slightly off his stroke.

'What makes you ask?'

'I imagine he got the last ounce of drama out of it. Unless he'd changed considerably. Which I find difficult to believe. In spite of the funeral oration. And the Last Post. Whose idea was that?'

'Susan's. She said the only time she'd ever seen Ronald moved was at a beating of the retreat in Rajputana. It was a bit embarrassing for us. But the oration was no more than he actually deserved. And he gave Susan a sense of security.'

'Well tell me,' Perron said, 'how he killed the snake.'

*

Does Nigel have a revolver? Merrick had asked. The answer had been, no. *Then I'll have to go next door for a moment,* he said. While he did this Laura went into the compound at the back. She knew the snake had to be killed, but was as much against killing snakes as Nigel was, unless it couldn't be avoided. She walked up and down waiting for the sound of the shot. She visualized, perhaps, the shaft of sunlight in the bathroom slowly and dangerously shifting, leaving the snake in shadow, cooling it, waking it; and wondered whether snakes had thoughts and if so what they thought about. What manner of sleep they slept. What dreams they had. (What dreams do falcons have, under those scarlet hoods? And how different those dreams must be – on the one hand of limitless sky, on the other of endless, endless earth.)

Well here it is, Merrick said. She hadn't heard him approach. She swung round and there he was, a kukri in his good hand, the cobra suspended from the artificial one. At first she thought the cobra was whole but then the head end slipped out of the black glove and fell on the grass, leaving the tail end behind; and Laura cried out and was at once sick, all over her elegant shoes.

*

'He was very contrite,' Rowan said. 'He kept on apologizing. To me, I mean. He said he'd decided he couldn't shoot it because he wasn't sure what the ricochet would do if he missed the snake and hit the tub. In any case he didn't want to puncture the bath.'

If Merrick's story was to be believed he had used his artificial arm as a lure and, when the cobra struck and sank its fangs into the gloved hand, had swung the kukri and cut it neatly into two. A gash in the porcelain was evidence.

'He was taking a risk,' Rowan ended.

'He always did. Had Laura quite liked him up until then?'

'I don't know.'

'I was wondering, you see, as I used to put it, whether you ever felt that he had chosen her.'

'I remembered the phrase.'

'When, exactly?'

'I expect it would be more accurate to say I'd never forgotten it, but I certainly remembered it when Laura and I first got here and found him living alone next door. Susan and the boy were up in the hills.'

'Didn't you know he was in Mirat?'

'Yes, I knew. Sarah and I have always written to one another. I hadn't expected – such close proximity. I didn't tell Laura much about him, just that we'd met. It amused her when he started turning up at odd moments when I happened to be out. It reminded her of the rubber estate, when Tony went down to KL or Singapore and left her alone, and all the local bachelors and grass-widowers homed in on her bungalow, making feeble excuses, or no excuses at all. When you remember what Laura looked like in those days, it's no wonder. But it used to annoy her. She said it made her feel like an object, because if they didn't come to make a pass they just came to stare. Anyway, she made a joke of it at first, of Ronald turning up whenever I was out. She has this idea that she's now physically repulsive. She said Merrick probably thought he was physically repulsive too.'

Rowan stopped. Perron waited. After a while Rowan said, 'But I came home one night and found her in a very odd mood. She started talking to me about her life in prison-camp, and that was something she'd never done. I'd tried to get her to talk about it, but she always shied off. Did you happen to see the scar under her left eye?'

'Yes.'

598

'I ask because with strangers she normally keeps those sunglasses on, even indoors. And you may find this difficult to believe, but I've never found out how she came by it.'

'But she told Ronald.'

Rowan looked away. 'Apparently, yes. I got home and found her in this odd mood. Over dinner she started talking about prison-camp. Then she asked me whether I didn't want to know about the scar. We had a bit of a scene. She asked me why she could talk to Ronald about it but not to me, why Ronald was the only person she'd ever met who could get her to talk as she wanted to talk. Spill out the whole awful bloody business. The only thing I could think of to say – and it came out quite unrehearsed – was that she couldn't talk to me about it because she knew I loved her but had to talk to Ronald because he'd chosen her. As a victim.'

'What did Laura say?'

'Nothing. And we didn't mention Ronald again until a few days later when I got back and found her packing, the day he'd killed the snake. She said she was going back to Gopalakand. That would have been best but I talked her out of it and we decided she should go to the club. As soon as she'd gone the whole situation seemed absurd. There was nothing I could accuse him of. But whenever I saw him he started explaining and apologizing. He wouldn't let it alone. He turned up at the club once or twice, trying to see her, but she says she kept out of his way.'

'But went to the funeral. What was that? A mark of respect or of celebration?'

'She went to the funeral because I asked her to.'

'Why did you do that?'

'The thing was –'

'Yes?'

'To remove anything that didn't fit into the picture.'

'What picture?'

'Of an Englishman who'd earned respect and admiration from most sections of the community.'

'Why did Laura have to fit into that?'

'You know what people are like in places like this. The kind of people who wondered why she'd left the bungalow. It didn't

599

go unnoticed that she wouldn't see him when he called at the club. I had to ask him to stop calling.'

'Did he stop?'

'At once. But he seemed quite hurt. He said he hated misunderstandings. He'd only been anxious to find out why he'd upset her. He implied as well that he hated feeling responsible for any misunderstanding between Laura and me. At the same time –'

'What?'

'I had an idea it didn't worry him and might even please him that people were beginning to link their names.'

'It flattered him to be thought of as the Other Man?'

Rowan glanced at him. 'I see what you mean. I hadn't thought of it in quite such a general way. I just wondered whether he was trying to get his own back on me by making people wonder about Laura and him. I'm positive he knew that Kumar had been privately examined and that I was the one who'd done the examining. Why not? He still had friends in the Inspector-General's department. Someone probably told him.'

'Very probably.'

'Sometimes he actually seemed to be daring me to come out with it. We had a very odd relationship. On the one hand mutual goodwill and respect between a visiting political agent and a police officer who'd done a good job, and on the other this subtle sort of antagonism.'

'How long was he in Singapore?'

'Singapore? He *was* in Singapore. Why?'

'I wondered whether he was ever involved in the case against the Japanese officer who was hanged as a war criminal. The one who murdered Laura's first husband, no doubt among several scores of others.'

'Wouldn't he have said?'

'Not necessarily. But knowing something about the Japanese officer could have been the way he got Laura to talk.'

'It sounds pretty far-fetched.'

'Nigel – for me, nothing was far-fetched with Merrick. I believe he had a photographic memory. He'd only have to look through a file to have a whole situation at his fingertips. And he was quite clever at getting his hands on files. He got his hands on Susan's confidential psychiatric file. Did you know that?'

'No, you've remembered incorrectly. He had an interview with the psychiatrist, that's all. So Sarah said.'

'He did more than that. He saw her confidential file. So when Susan talks about Ronald being the only man she'd ever met who understood her and seemed to know things about her she'd never told anyone inside the family, that's the explanation. He could have tried something like the same technique with Laura, but I imagine she's tougher. What happened to the Red Shadow?'

'The what?'

'That disgusting bazaar Pathan he had trailing round with him in Pankot. The one I kicked up the backside. The one who had his hands on my wallet.'

'I don't know. But Merrick must have got rid of him. He gave up having personal servants when he got married.'

'Why?'

'He was always on the move. They never had a permanent home.'

'He hired and fired as it suited him?'

'No, I think he just accepted what was available. Like Khansamar next door.'

'Who of course is Dmitri's man?'

'Everything here is Dmitri's. All three bungalows. The Dewani Bhavan, this one, and Merrick's. Dmitri lived in this bungalow when he first came to Mirat. He built the Dewani Bhavan round about nineteen twenty-five.'

'Did Merrick ever live here?'

'Yes, I think for a month or two when he first arrived. Before Susan joined him.'

'I imagine he slept in my room.'

'What makes you think that?'

'It has a resonance.' Perron hesitated, and then came out with it. 'What did he do, Nigel? Commit suicide? Cut his wrist and die in the bath?'

'He didn't die in the bath.'

'Nor as a result of a riding accident?'

Rowan said nothing for a while. Then: 'The fall wasn't serious. But he said someone deliberately scared the horse. He was out on the *maidan*. According to Ahmed and Sarah there was no one within half-a-mile, except them.'

'They were all together? What were they doing, hawking?'

'No. Merrick was always trying to scrounge an invitation to watch Ahmed out with Mumtaz. Ahmed's very particular about who gets to watch and who doesn't. He was running out of excuses. They were supposed to go hawking that morning and Merrick was pretty upset when they turned up with horses and no falcon. When they got to the *maidan* he galloped off on his own. They saw him jumping the main nullah. It's pretty wide where he attempted it and he came a cropper. When they got to him the first thing he said was "Did you see the blighter?" He made out that someone who'd been in the nullah had suddenly stood up. Later on he said someone must have thrown a stone. Sarah says there was nothing like that. But Dmitri got rather worried.'

'Why?'

'The last thing he wanted, the last thing any of us wants just at the moment is an attack on an Englishman. It really could have the most tragic consequences. One dead English official, one English official attacked, and that could be it. You'd get some hard-bitten British sergeant in the cantonment belting an Indian and calling all Indians murdering bastards and then who knows what would happen?'

'Perhaps what Merrick wanted to happen.'

'That was rather the conclusion we came to, that he would have liked some of the stops pulled out, some sort of show-down. So it seems would other people.'

'What other people?'

'Whoever it was who arranged his death.'

Perron's heart sank. He had known it, instinctively. Rowan watched him. He said, 'Dmitri and I feel you ought to know. Sarah agrees. And in view of the way you handled an awkward question of Susan's yesterday, she thinks you're to be relied on not to say anything. She's the only member of her family who knows that Ronald was murdered.'

Absurd, really, Perron thought, that he should now feel shocked, outraged on Merrick's behalf. Perhaps he had hated the man too much not to feel guilty now for a violent death. It was as though he had contributed to it.

'Well tell me,' Perron said.

Rowan poured more brandy. This time he topped his own glass up with soda, as well as Perron's. He said, 'After the riding accident he refused to go into hospital but Habbibullah insisted on him going to bed and keeping to his room. He suspected concussion. Ronald was a very bad patient. And of course there was all this business about the imaginary man in the nullah and the imaginary stone. He went on about it whenever I or Sarah or Dmitri visited him. We did that as often as we could. I was the last one of us to see him alive. Sarah asked me to go and talk to him because he'd been on the phone to her saying he was better and asking to be taken out next morning in the jeep and watch Ahmed hawk. He couldn't ride but wanted some fresh air and something interesting to do. So I went across and had a drink with him. He was sitting up in his dressing gown – smoking in that way he had – do you remember? Sticking the cigarette in his artificial hand. He seemed perfectly all right to me. And for once he didn't mention Laura. He talked about getting a job in Calcutta or Bombay, or of offering his services to Pakistan. He was quite frank about not wanting to go home to England. And he thought he stood a better chance of a job among Muslims. He said he'd like to live somewhere like Peshawar, near the old North-West Frontier, where administration was much more a question of off-the-cuff decisions and not of just going by the book. We really got on quite well, rather like the first time we met, on the train to Pankot. He asked me to ring Sarah then and there and fix the morning programme. So I did. I asked her to come round with the jeep at seven. She said she'd have a word with Habbibullah but I didn't tell Merrick that. And I didn't tell him she thought Ahmed wouldn't play. I pretended it was all fixed. He told Khansamar to wake him at six next day. When I got back here I rang Sarah again. She said Habbibullah wouldn't allow it, which was a blessing because Ahmed felt he couldn't refuse any longer. We agreed that she and Ahmed would turn up at seven, but with Habbibullah, and that they'd take it from there. So that's how we left it.

'Tippoo woke me at six and then the phone rang and Tippoo said Khansamar wanted a word, which struck me as odd. Khansamar's one of the best trained servants I've come across, but that's Dmitri's influence. He said something had happened which he couldn't deal with and would I come over right away. So I put on a dressing-gown and went across. When I got to the front of the house Khansamar was sitting on the front steps smoking. There was nothing to suggest anything wrong.

'But then he took me indoors and said, "Sahib is dead. I've locked everything up." He took me into Merrick's bedroom. What I expected was just the sight of Merrick dead in bed but the whole place was an absolute shambles. The mosquito net was ripped to ribbons, the bedsheets were all over the place and stained with blood and Merrick was lying on the floor, dressed in his Pathan clothes, but hacked about with his own ornamental axe and strangled with his own sash. And all over the floor there were chalked cabalistic signs. And someone had scrawled the word Bibighar across Susan's dressing-table mirror with the same brown make-up stick that had been used to daub his face.'

'Did Sarah see this?'

'No. And she doesn't know the details. She turned up with Habbibullah and Ahmed, but we kept her out. Dmitri saw it, so did the Chief of Police in Mirat and the commander of the military police in the cantonment. The station commander was consulted too. The one thing that was agreed was that a murdered Englishman at this stage of affairs is the last thing anybody wants. Particularly when it looks as if the murder was intended to cause disorder and racial conflict.'

'What about the law?'

'Everything is properly recorded, right the way down from Habbibullah's real post-mortem, through the private inquest and the sworn statements of witnesses like myself and Khansamar. And the police and CID haven't been inactive. I doubt that the man or men who murdered Ronald will ever be tracked down though. The operation seems to have been carefully planned and patiently seen through to the end.'

'By whom? Pandit Baba?'

'It was Dmitri's first thought. But the Pandit runs true to form. The CID say that for the past month he's been on a pilgrimage to the Himalayas, and still is.'

'And the Bibighar suspects?'

'Two who're still in Mayapore have been cleared by the police there. One is reported dead of tuberculosis in Benares a year ago, and two more are working as clerks in Calcutta. There's nothing to connect any of them.'

'They got a very rapid clearance.'

'It was a rapid clearance because I gave Dmitri their names. I can still recite them from memory. All Dmitri had to do was get his police chief to liaise with the police in Mayapore.'

'Did he ask how you knew the names?'

'Yes.'

'And you told him you'd examined Kumar?'

'Yes.'

'And what about Kumar. What about Hari?'

'He's still in Ranpur. And also in the clear. Dmitri told me this evening.'

'Not such a rapid clearance.'

'We didn't go through the police in Hari's case. Ahmed got his father's secretary to ask Mrs Gopal to find out what she could through the young man who used to help him. We got the reply today. He's still coaching students. He never leaves Ranpur. He was there the whole of last week. One of his pupils is the youngest son of a Congress minister and he's been at the minister's house every evening for the past month coaching the boy for his matriculation.'

'Things have improved for him, then.'

'A little, I suppose. But it must be a poor enough livelihood.'

'Perhaps he supplements it.'

'How?'

'A bit of free-lance journalism? He used to be a reporter and sub-editor.'

'Perhaps. Incidentally, we now have an address. If you want it.'

'Yes, I'd like his address.'

'I'll get it for you. Then I'll have to go to bed, Guy. I've got to see the States Department people off on the morning train.' He got up, went into the adjoining room, came back and handed Perron a slip of paper with Kumar's address scribbled on it. 'Be careful what you say to Sarah, won't you? She doesn't know the worst details. We had Merrick's bedroom cleared up before she saw it. None of the other servants was allowed to see it either.'

'Presumably they were questioned, though.'

'Yes, but the Chief of Police did that himself, without saying exactly why. Khansamar was put through the hoop too.'

'Where are the other servants?'

'Back at the Dewani Bhavan, where they came from.'

'There must be rumours, surely.'

'Rumours, yes. Too many people had to be involved, and eventually it'll become more or less common knowledge, but the thing has been to counteract the rumours, especially in the cantonment, and keep up the fiction that Merrick died as a result of the riding accident.'

'Who has his clothes? And his arm?'

'The Chief of Police. I must turn in, Guy. If you see Dmitri tomorrow, he can probably answer any questions better than I.'

Perron said goodnight and made to go; then paused.

He said, 'Who was Philoctetes?'

'What?'

'Philoctetes.'

Rowan rubbed his forehead. He looked so tired that Perron was about to leave the question until morning. But then Rowan said, 'The great archer.'

'A great *archer*?'

'Friend of Hercules. One of the heroes of the Trojan war. Sophocles wrote a play about him, but it's one I never read. They had to set him ashore, abandon him on the voyage out. Lemnos, I think.'

'Why?'

'He was hurt in some way. Wounded by one of his own poisoned arrows. Or perhaps he just developed boils and suppurating sores from a vitamin deficiency. Anyway, he stank, and the others couldn't stand the smell. So they set him ashore, and went on.'

'Yes,' Perron said. That fitted. 'Did he ever get to Troy?'

'Eventually. If I remember rightly they decided they needed him after all. What interests you about Philoctetes?'

'I came across the name recently and wondered, that's all.'

606

When he got back to his room he found that Tippoo had brought in all the stuff he'd left on the verandah; the scissors, notebook, the newspapers, and his own bottle of brandy. He had a final drink and read the essay *Alma Mater* once again. That night, fearful of snakes, of ghosts, he cocooned himself in a sheet, within the security of his mosquito-net shrouded bed. He lulled himself to sleep by counting arrows, flying from the bow, at first slowly, well-aimed, and then quicker, until they were flying incredibly fast as the archer stood, holding his ground, intent on survival. Just before he slept he thought: The smell in the room is not after all just Merrick's smell, but also the smell of the archer's wound.

He woke while it was still dark, from a nightmare that had transformed him into a huge butterfly that beat and beat and fragmented its wings against the imprisoning mesh of the net.

V

Extract from Perron's Diary, Wednesday August 6
11 p.m.
An ominous day, ending with the reflection of fires in the night sky above the city. This afternoon, news of the Nawab's accession to India brought out a crowd of Congress supporters who assembled on the *maidan* for speeches and cheers. The police and military kept them away from the palace, and from a convoy of Muslim families making their way in trucks, carts, dhoolies and on foot to the collecting point in the cantonment. Tonight there were repercussions, angry Muslims attacking Hindus. Attack. Counter-attack. The sky glows. Police and military patrol the road outside this bungalow and presumably make forays into the city. They say there will again be no fishing on the Izzat Bagh lake tomorrow.

Beyond the lake you can just see the paler glow of the cantonment bazaar. The *raj* rests quietly in the darkness behind. In bungalows here and there there must be lights and laughter, parties. (The departing Peabodys are giving one.) Here, where I am, a strange feeling of being suspended between these two worlds. On other similar occasions when the situation became difficult, Merrick would be found touring the city, by jeep, or sometimes during daylight on horseback. 'Tonight I miss him,' Dmitri said. He hadn't mentioned Merrick until then. Dmitri and I had champagne. We smoked pink gold-tipped cigarettes. He told me something about St Petersburg (between interruptions, of which there were many). At ten-thirty our meeting ended. The Nawab had sent for him. 'Poor old dear,' Dmitri said. 'He's looked at the sky and wonders what he has done wrong, or what I have ever done right.'

This ominous day began early. She did not ring but arrived with horses shortly after Nigel had gone across to the palace to take the States Department people to the station. They were to travel in the Nawab's salon coach so as (Dmitri said) to give them a taste for princely luxury as a 'frail insurance against any future diminution of it'. Tomorrow we are to travel by ordinary first-class passenger coach. Dmitri has cancelled the arrangement to send us by another of the Nawab's coaches in case after today's troubles it becomes a target for attack by Muslims who feel that the Nawab has let them down. He has got the movement control officer to guarantee a compartment for us. We shall be 9. The old-fashioned first-class compartments seat 8 comfortably and one of the 9 is little Edward and another is the ayah who will probably sit on the luggage. Which leaves only 7 adults: Sarah, Susan, Mrs Grace, the two Peabodys, Ahmed and me. We should be comfortable enough and are due at Ranpur at 7 p.m. The Peabodys are reported upset, though, that they aren't to travel in a palace coach. Dmitri said: 'Don't stand any nonsense with them if they start objecting to the ayah or to Ahmed. Times have changed.' He seems very insistent on this. The number in the compartment won't worry me. It sounds like being a good party. Mrs Grace is fun.

The horses Sarah brought were a pleasant surprise. She was dressed for riding. There was no Ahmed. No Mumtaz. We trotted out to the *maidan* and across to the other side. She showed me (at a distance behind shade trees) the barracks of the Mirat Artillery, the police barracks, and the hospital and told me about the first time she got Shiraz to go with her, how nervous the girl was, how over-awed the staff and the patients were at this manifestation from the Palace: the Nawab's daughter, rumoured to be cross and difficult and haughty. Sarah had broken the ice, in the maternity ward, by picking up a baby she'd become used to handling (whose mother wasn't recovering as quickly as she should) and then placing it in Shiraz's arms. The first contact Shiraz had ever had with a commoner outside the palace. It worked. And of course the mother would never forget it: that the Nawab's daughter had held her son. 'What made you give so much time to this girl?' I asked. 'Her unhappiness,' was all Sarah said. Then she cantered away, towards the open ground beyond the military tents and horse-lines.

Suddenly she cries out and thrashes her reins, left, right, and gallops off, making for the distant city wall, or what is left of it. The gateway alone is intact. I try to catch up but she is by far the better and more confident horseman, and she knows the lie of the nullahs, which I don't. But, behind her as I am, we seem to career together towards that implacable pink stone. Then she suddenly veers and shouts again, loudly, savagely, and races her horse back at a pace I really can't match: thrashing the reins in that way, left, right, as if charging cannon in some desperate enterprise. And there is nothing there except the pale blue sky, the green of the shade trees, the tawny stain of the scrubby earth. I let her go, ease my own horse's pace, watch her; small white-shirted figure, going like a little demon into the distance, leaping the nullahs. I think it was her way of saying goodbye to a place where she has been free and happy. She rides in a wide circle, coming round now and galloping towards me. At first I assume she will ride right up, but just ahead of me she moves in a tight turn and then brings her mount to a canter, a trot, a walk; to a stand. As I reach her she puts it at a sedate walk. We say nothing. It isn't necessary. But as we near the road again, outside my bungalow, she says, 'Come to the guest house and meet Aunt Fenny. We'll have breakfast there.'

Neither of us has mentioned Merrick.

Mrs Grace is a plump rather florid woman (much as one thought). A bit breathless, but very talkative. Susan not up for breakfast. We have ours on the terrace. This is where the Laytons stayed when Susan came to Mirat to marry Teddie

Bingham. I asked about Colonel Layton. Since early in 1946 he has been Colonel Commandant at the Pankot Rifles training depot. A disappointment. He had hoped for the area command. He is handing over now to a man called Chaudhuri, who was only a major a few months ago. The new 1st battalion goes to a Sikh who has been in Pankot for some years, Chatab Singh. For a while there was a problem about the regiment's future. Officially, the Pankot people are predominantly Muslims, as a result of conversion in the days of the Moghuls. The regiment, mixed, but reflecting this predominance, has such a good reputation that Jinnah wanted it and offered it a home near Peshawar. How he thought he could keep it recruited from men who lived in the Pankot hills, one does not know. Some English people in Pankot have raised the question of the silver in the mess and suggest that the new Indian Government should buy all the knives, forks, spoons and trophies, everything of value, and that the proceeds should be shared out among the families of the men who had contributed to their cost. 'So you see we all end up like carpet-sellers in Cairo,' Mrs Grace said. 'John gets hot under the collar when he hears people talking like that.'

Edward comes out. He takes me to see the white peacock. Not the one I saw myself. This one is carved out of marble and is secluded in a secret place among the trees. Fear snakes. When we get back Nigel has arrived from the station, seeing the States Department people off. The Peabodys were seeing off the Rossiters and told Nigel that this evening it would be open house at their bungalow. Mrs Grace said, 'Those awful people. Do we have to travel with them? Can't we rustle up an extra body or two and crowd them out?'

Interesting, this. Universally popular as the English are in India just now, among themselves there emerges this dissension. The old solidarity has gone because the need for it has gone.

*

'But of course,' Bronowsky said, 'now we are all émigrés. Have some more champagne and a cigarette.'

Perron nodded. The servant came to his side and refilled his glass. In the Dewani Bhavan there was the dry dusty scent of potpourri. The lighting was rose-coloured. It glowed on ormulu and gilt chair-arms. In this light Dmitri Bronowsky looked twenty years younger. His lame left leg rested on a gilt and plush footstool. The ebony cane and the black eye-patch accentuated the white of his tropical suit which was faintly tinged by the glow of the lights. He wore a tie of the same pink as the cigarettes.

*

The invitation to dinner had reached Perron at five o'clock. Leaving Rowan working on his written report to the Resident at Gopalakand, it had surprised him to find no other guests. By eight-thirty, after a number of interruptions by messengers and telephone calls, he realized that he and Dmitri were to spend the evening alone. He had hoped for Sarah. As if recognizing a source of disappointment, Bronowsky – leading him into a grand dining-room – said he asked Sarah but that she felt she couldn't leave Susan alone on their last night in Mirat. 'And failing Sarah, I felt we might dine alone. It is a little selfish of me to subject you to my unadulterated company, but not entirely so. If we had another guest or two then I could not tell you the things you have come to Mirat to learn about – how princes rule and live in this country. Anyway, I feel I deserve an evening off myself, with just one sympathetic listener.'

The table was long enough for twenty or thirty guests and the room was lit as if there were that number needing to see what they ate. Perron and Bronowsky sat at one end, where great bowls of flowers gave off heady scents. Bronowsky ate little, seemed to be content with a bite or two of each course and a glass of each of the wines that accompanied them. He talked with skill and good humour. The range of the old wazir's knowledge and experience and the clarity of his memory were remarkable. It struck Perron, too, that he talked vividly because he knew that the opportunities to hold court, while he still had power, were becoming fewer. The last thing Dmitri Bronowsky would ever be was an old and tiresome man living on his memories and boring other people

611

with them. On the day he had to retire, he would probably retire quite happily into himself.

'What is Mirat's future, then?' Perron asked, when the right moment came, between sips of the champagne with which, along with the pêche flambée, the meal was delightfully ending.

'We shall be absorbed into the provincial administration of Ranpur. Our executive and our judiciary will be superseded by those of Ranpur. We shall be ruled from Ranpur and from Delhi. We shall have a deputy commissioner sent down to control us. Some of our younger men will be lucky and secure official appointments. Our revenues will go to Government and Government in turn will accept certain responsibilities for us. Also, and this is so interesting, we shall become a constituency or several constituencies and elect and send members to the legislative assembly. All this I have told and constantly tell Nawab Sahib. I remind him how years ago I foretold it. If either of his sons had political talent, ah then, that would have been one way of maintaining *izzat* under a new dispensation. For in a world where a ruling prince becomes redundant isn't there an opportunity for one of his heirs, someone in his family, to sit not on the *gaddi* but in the assembly, or even in a ministerial chair at the Secretariat?'

'And neither son has political talent?'

'In confidence, my dear Mr Perron, neither talent nor wit. It did not take me long to see that this was and would be so. So. I cast around. And my eye lighted on another member of the house of Kasim. The Ranpur branch. The rebellious political branch.'

'Ahmed?'

'Many people have wondered what I am doing employing the son of Mohammed Ali Kasim who is, by nature, opposed to princes. Many people have wondered what Mr Mohammed Ali Kasim can have been thinking of to allow his younger son to take service in a feudal little state. I do not know what Mr Kasim had in mind. Perhaps he was just pessimistic about the boy in those days. I have always been optimistic. Scratch me a very little and you will find an eternal optimist. Scratch a little deeper and you will no doubt uncover a great intriguer, but I hope a well-intentioned one. Scratch deeper still, never

612

minding the blood, and perhaps you will find an old White Russian of liberal sympathies but intent even now on rescuing his Tsar from the cellar in Ekaterinburg, or failing his Tsar, the little Tsarevich. An English lady in the cantonment who had psychological perceptions once described me so. Your glass is empty, Mr Perron.'

It was refilled.

'It was my intention to arrange, if it could be done without undue pressure, an alliance between the princely Kasims of Mirat and the political Kasims of Ranpur. I had hoped that Ahmed and Shiraz would fall in love one day. They say that when a man falls in love, with a woman, he becomes aware of all his worldly responsibilities. If there is one thing I do most sincerely wish just now it is that Ahmed and Shiraz were man and wife and that marriage had awakened in him all those political instincts he must have inherited from his father, no matter what he says to the contrary. I wish this because just now when Nawab Sahib is in the doldrums, when he summons me at midnight or early in the morning because he cannot sleep or hasn't slept, and stares at me, it would be so nice to say: What are you bothered about? I have always warned you that there may be nothing for your sons to inherit except the remnants of a purely formal dignity, but here is your daughter Shiraz and here is your son-in-law Ahmed, son of a famous and respected Indian politician who still has great influence behind the scenes. When you begged me to come back to India with you because of the little service I had done for you, you said, "I must be a modern state. Make me modern." So, admit it, I have made you modern in every way I can. Moreover you have a son with business interests in Delhi and who has a wife who builds swimming pools and has money in Zurich. You have another son in the air force. Above all you have a son-in-law who may one day represent Mirat in the provincial assembly and, who knows, end as a minister of central government, perhaps even as Prime Minister. Isn't that modern enough for you? Unfortunately, I cannot tell him this because he has no son-in-law. Man can only propose. But given another year or two's grace and perhaps God would have disposed, as I so devoutly wished. For my prince's benefit, you understand, Mr Perron. For my prince. Perhaps a little for myself. As it is I have to go and sit with him, late at night or early morning, and try to prepare him just to face the moment when the States Department people will descend on us again, this time with their scales and abacuses and weights and measures and arithmetical tables, their meticulously devised formula for separating what belongs to the people and what belongs to Nawab Sahib, what is a proper charge on Government and what is a charge on Nawab's personal household, asking how many palaces have you, then, and what are they used for, and who pays for all *this* –'

Bronowsky indicated the room, the table, the silver and the glass and the patient silent servants.

'Who pays, the people or the occupier? And who is Dmitri Bronowsky? Who pays him? How much is he paid? How much pension does he expect from you? How much pension can the people of India afford to pay you so that you can go on paying all these pensions to which you say you are already committed? And I know what Nawab Sahib will say, because he has already begun saying it. He will say, "Dmitri, what have I to do with these people or they with me? What are all these facts and figures and percentages and bureaucratic mumbo-jumbo? If you load my head with all this, how can I hold it up?" Come, let us have coffee.'

As they went Perron said, 'As Mrs Grace said this morning, now we've all got to get used to living like carpet-sellers in Cairo.'

'But of course!' Bronowsky said, delighted. 'Now we are *all* émigrés. Have some more champagne and a cigarette.'

*

The servant came to his side and refilled his glass, offered the open silver box. Dmitri settled his left foot on the stool. He told the servant to leave the champagne in the ice-bucket, to bring in the brandy and then to leave them.

'The thing that holds the members of an emigration together is only their recollection of a mutually shared past, Mr Perron, but they are divided by a deep distrust of one another's present intentions. So there is no creative

614

coherence. And individually they feel guilty of desertion. An emigration is possibly the loneliest experience a man can suffer. In a way it is not a country he has lost but a home, or even just a part of a home, a room perhaps, or something in that room that he has had to leave behind, and which haunts him. I remember a window-seat I used to sit in as a youth, reading Pushkin and teaching myself to smoke scented cigarettes. That window is one I am always knocking at, asking to be let in.'

A steward brought a note. To read it Bronowsky took out a gold rimmed monocle. 'Forgive me, I must leave you for just a moment to attend to this.'

Alone, Perron went out on to the terrace. The garden was flood-lit. At its centre was a fountain whose jets sprayed inward from the rim. In a moment Bronowsky was back. 'There are other illuminations at the front, it seems, not of my devising.'

*

From the front compound they could see the glow of the fires in the city. 'They are burning each other's shops,' Bronowsky said. 'In the past eight months, whenever I saw a sight like this, I was comforted by the thought that Colonel Merrick was coping with it. Tonight I miss him. So perhaps will the police. All I can do is to ensure that what should be done is being done and what shouldn't be isn't. The cost is counted in the morning. Meanwhile one feels a bit like Nero, in need of a fiddle. Perhaps I should send for the court-musicians. But let us go back and finish the champagne.'

They strolled up and down the terrace. The fountain kept changing colour. Perron was struck by the irony of the situation. Here, luxury, elegance. A mile away, everything a man possessed in the world was perhaps going up in smoke.

'Until the war,' Bronowsky was saying, 'there was almost no civil disturbance in Mirat. Such communal dissatisfaction as there was arose from the feeling the educated Hindus had that in spite of all my efforts they were still at a disadvantage, and from the counter-feeling high-ranking Muslims had that Hindus had been encouraged to compete too well. But by and large there was peace, particularly in the rural districts where the things that mattered to people were to enjoy prosperity when it was there to be enjoyed and to feel they could trust their Nawab to look after them when it wasn't. Before the war, Mr Perron, I could tour the state and talk to a Mirati farmer out there in the *mofussil*, a Hindu or a Muslim, and he would prove to have but the vaguest idea of who Gandhi was, or who Jinnah was. For him the world began and ended in his fields, and with his landlord, and with the tax-collectors, and with Nawab Sahib who sat here in Mirat, Lord of the world, Giver of Grain. Out there it is not so very different now but in our towns and in our city they have become affected by what Congress is saying, what the Muslim League is saying, up there in Delhi, in Calcutta and Bombay. This began during the war. Mirat was also affected by the realization that the British *raj* had proved far from invincible in Burma and Malaya and in Europe. On top of that we had all these people who fell foul of the British and scurried to places like this where it was not so easy for your police to get hold of them. It was left to our own. Well, you can pick a man up and send him back where he came from, but you cannot send ideas back, especially if there is an element of truth and justice in them.'

'What led to your applying for help from the States Police?'

'A virtual breakdown in our own police department and a danger of mutiny in our State Armed Force, which consists of one regiment only, the Mirat Artillery. That was last November – but the trouble began earlier when men of the regiment who had been prisoners of the Japanese returned home and it became generally known that some of their comrades had joined the INA and were now prisoners of the *raj*. No one knew at the time quite what to make of this. The prisoners who had stayed loyal came back to a heroes' welcome, naturally. Men of the Nawab's artillery have served in both world wars, in France in 'fourteen-'eighteen. In Malaya this time. The artillery is a Mirati tradition. In the old days they used to make some of those huge old cannon you'll know about from your study of eighteenth-century Indian history and the men from this region have always been adept at gunnery. So. It has always been a proud regiment, too. Unfortunately by the time the men came back, to their heroes' welcome, Congress and the League had already taken the cudgels up on behalf of the INA. Our gunners found themselves in bad odour when they said what they thought of Bose. Some of the most outspoken were beaten up one night in the bazaar, probably by the same people who beat poor Ahmed up when it became known that his father wasn't going to defend Sayed. Perhaps that was a blessing in disguise because it stopped him going into the bazaar to visit what in my youth were called ladies of easy virtue. For a long time afterwards he was faithful only to Mumtaz. But the worst situation arose in the spring of last year, when the officers and men of the Mirat Artillery who had been in the INA came back, the officers cashiered and the men released –'

'At Holi.'

'Ah, yes, at Holi. Almost as stupid a decision as the decision to try the Sikh, the Muslim and the Hindu at the Red Fort.'

'Did the INA men get a heroes' welcome too?'

'It was unofficial, but warmer if anything. There were only two officers and nineteen men. The officers' careers were finished, not that they needed careers, they both came from well-to-do families. The main question was what was to happen to the nineteen gunners. In Mirat, political parties do not officially exist, since the state proscribes them, but there are shadow parties and shadow committees and of course one has always known who belongs to them and who the leaders are and who will therefore emerge presently as the men with local political power in Mirat. The nineteen gunners were being persuaded by both these shadow parties, Congress and League, that they should be reinstated by a grateful Nawab for having tried to help Bose rid the country of the British.'

'Which didn't please the loyal men of the Mirat Artillery?'

'To put it mildly. The cumulative effect of all this purely political propaganda was that on the Muslim League's All-India Direct Action Day, the Mirat Artillery refused duty to stand by in aid of the civil power, and their officers were powerless. The men took a very simple view, Mr Perron. They thought that Direct Action Day was simply a ruse to reinstate the nineteen gunners and they would have nothing to do with it, either way. They sat in their barracks while the civil population ran riot. The Mirat Police were entirely ineffective because they were in sympathy with the League. We had to get aid from the cantonment, British troops, and the officer commanding those troops knew his men were so fed up with India and Indian politics that he dared only issue one man in twelve with live ammunition. I remember standing with Nawab Sahib in one of the upper rooms at the front of the palace and watching the pall of smoke above the city and thinking, My life has been wasted.'

Bronowsky rested against the balustrade, sipped his champagne.

'But one always feels better next day. All the same I have never seen Nawab Sahib so angry. He blamed the poor regiment. He said his grandfather would have had the officers trampled to death by elephants and every mutineer blown from the guns. He raved against Gandhi and Jinnah and then against the Viceroy and the Commander-in-Chief, and then because he knew there was only one head he could effectively roll, he turned on me and accused me of ruining him with all this modernity. It took me a day or two to persuade him that the artillery only needed his personal assurance that the INA gunners would not be reinstated. The police were a graver problem. It took me longer to persuade him that we needed assistance from outside, from the States Police. He felt we could rely entirely on help from the cantonment. But you know, Mr Perron, too much reliance of that kind sours the relationship between city and cantonment. Well. In the end he let me go to Delhi and put the position to them. And so – some weeks later – Ronald.' Bronowsky paused. 'I am a little chilly. It's the fountains. They cool the air amazingly. Let us go in and have brandy.'

*

He had dismissed the servants and served the brandy himself. Now he settled opposite Perron and rested his foot on the stool.

'When I heard who was coming in command of a States Police detachment and in an advisory capacity to the Nawab and myself, it was my instinct to say no, no, no, no, he is a man with too controversial a reputation and the last time he was in Mirat he was subject to the attention of people who seemed determined to persecute him for his behaviour in Mayapore. What are they doing sending him here? What are they doing employing him again in the police? Then I wondered what business that was of mine. And remembered that I had on very first acquaintance found him an interesting and impressive man. Impressive in some ways. You know that he had certain qualities, Mr Perron?'

'I saw only the bad side, I'm afraid.'

'That I think is because in spite of your interest in the past you are a man of the present, as I have always tried not very successfully to be. Merrick without question was a man of the past, so much so that he believed implicitly both in its real virtues and in what he imagined had been its virtues. And you know, in the situation that has existed here in Mirat this past year or so, where few people know what they are doing or why they are doing it, the presence of such a man comes almost as a relief. He treated the whole thing as though it were just a silly quarrel between naughty children. And in a way he was right. He inspired confidence with his impartiality and his absolutely inflexible and unshakable sense of his own authority. It can be a very dangerous combination. But there was one thing about him this time that seemed to me to be new. He struck me now as an inwardly melancholy man. I would never have said that about him before. The only time I saw him, how shall I put it, glow with the old *conviction*, was when he was with the child.'

'Not when he was with his wife?'

'I am no judge, Mr Perron. Unless a man and a woman are obviously and tiresomely publicly wrapped up in one another I find it difficult to judge the degree of warmth between them. That is a warmth I have never enjoyed. One eventually withdraws. Perhaps becomes insensitive. I was, I admit, sensitive to what I thought might be certain tendencies in Merrick when I first met him in Mirat at the time of Susan's first wedding. I wish now that I had been more sensitive to the possibility of these tendencies having become, how shall I say, in no way lessened by his experience of marriage. Even at my age one assumes – well – what it is easiest to assume. So when he first arrived to take up his appointment I said, Are you still being persecuted by people making melodramatic demonstrations, throwing stones and chalking inauspicious signs on your doorstep? We made a joke of it. But he said what he had said in Bombay, that all that had ended. I knew that could be only partly true because Ahmed had told me there was a revival of persecution when he was in Delhi dealing with his brother's and other INA cases. But I decided to take his word for it and there was no reason to suppose that persecution would start up again simply because he was back in Mirat. Unfortunately it did begin again, but in a much subtler way. It may seem a little odd to you, Mr Perron, that whoever wished to persecute him for what he did in Mayapore in nineteen forty-two should have waited so long to bring the operation to its logical conclusion? There must have been many opportunities to kill him in the past five years.'

'It was twenty years before someone assassinated the ex-Governor of the Punjab. Ostensibly for supporting General Dyer over the Jallianwallah Bagh massacres.'

'That's true. Why do you say ostensibly?'

'I shouldn't think the Governor was shot for that at all. It was a conveniently dramatic form of protest against India being dragged into another European war.' Perron smiled. 'I gather from Nigel you have an idea Merrick was a convenient victim too. That killing him was intended to aggravate racial tension as much as anything.'

'Yes.' The old man studied him for a moment or two. 'Not everyone feels the British have earned the immunity you all seem to be currently enjoying. I myself am not entirely convinced that it is fully deserved. But if it's the last thing I do in Mirat, I'll take every step necessary to ensure that this immunity continues, even if it means suppressing evidence and issuing false statements. Do you disapprove?'

'A little.'

'So do I. But I balance my disapproval with the thought of what might be happening now if we had shouted murder, also with the thought that the murder was so subtly planned and executed that the prospect of ever seeing justice done is infinitely remote. Then of course there's the thought of the distress and pain Susan would have been caused by any open

620

investigation. It's a good thing, in her unstable state of mind and health, that she doesn't know in what strange and unsavoury circumstances her husband died.'

'Strange and unsavoury?'

'I don't mean just the manner of death but what made him vulnerable to such a death.'

'Yes, I see. Do his spies come into the picture?'

'Who mentioned spies to you?'

'Susan. She also mentioned Indian clothes. The ones he wore to go out with his spies.'

'Mr Perron, he had no spies. Nor did he ever go out in these clothes. Perhaps in his younger days he used to get up to that romantic sort of trick, colouring his face and disguising himself as a Pathan and going out into the bazaars. And of course in his time he must have employed spies in his department, just as our own police chief employs them. But Ronald and spies and Indian clothes, in Mirat, no, no, these were mere bits of play-acting. Khansamar never believed in the spies. He is a good servant, though, and not given to gossiping. I wish he had been. If I had known about so-called spies then I would have been alerted and I could have warned Khansamar to be more on his guard. And although it would have been a rather delicate thing to do I might have warned Ronald too. He may not have needed a warning, though. It is quite possible that he knew what was going on. In which case his murder might be seen as a form of suicide. Unfortunately I only knew about spies when it was already too late and Khansamar was questioned and told us about these visitors.'

'Visitors as distinct from people coming asking for jobs?'

'Why do you ask that?'

'Susan said people were always coming looking for jobs.'

'That was how it would have seemed to her. Originally that was how it seemed to Khansamar. But with the benefit of hindsight one begins to understand that it was all part of a new subtle form of persecution. At that time, Merrick was living alone, in Nigel's bungalow. The other one was being got ready. According to Khansamar these young fellows began to turn up soon after Merrick arrived. Khansamar turned them all away. He knew they were not Miratis. They span the same tale, of coming long distances to seek work and always offered little chits of references. Khansamar is illiterate. Chits mean nothing to him. Then one day Merrick found him shooing one of them off, a persistent fellow who had come several times. Merrick looked at the boy's references, which may or may not have been genuine, probably not, not that it mattered. Merrick told him there was no work to offer him. But he was back again next day. He stood at the gate and salaamed Merrick whenever he passed in and out until in the end Merrick told Khansamar he was fed up with the sight of him and that he might as well be given a job for a day or two, helping one of the malis repair and lay out the tennis-court in the compound of the bigger bungalow. So this is what Khansamar did. He told the mali to work the boy hard, so hard ·hat he would give up. But he worked so well that in a day or two the tennis court was nearly finished.'

*

Moreover, so the story went, the mali's wife had taken to the boy and had begun to mother him. He was a handsome young fellow and very well-mannered. After working all day in the compound he would make himself useful in the servants' compound. The mali was keen to keep him on but after three days Khansamar went to Merrick and reminded him that the day or two was up. Merrick went to inspect the tennis-court. They were just laying out the lines of lime-wash. Merrick watched for a while, then said, 'He is obviously used to hard work. Put him to cutting all the long grass.'

Khansamar was quite pleased. There was a lot to be done in both compounds. Many odd jobs. And the boy was very respectful to him. When he had cut all the grass in one compound Khansamar set him to work in the other. In the evenings he worked on a new vegetable patch behind the servants' quarters, work which the mali himself had been putting off day after day. On one such evening Khansamar asked him, 'Do you never rest, Aziz?' And the boy said, 'I am alone in the world, father. Work is all I have.'

Old Khansamar had had three wives, ten daughters and no son, ever. It touched him to be called father by a boy like this. He began to give him less strenuous jobs. A week, two weeks, a month went by. Sometimes Merrick would say, 'Well, Khansamar, how is that young fellow of yours? I see you have made something of a carpenter and decorator of him too. What is a farmer's son doing with so many accomplishments? Can he also read and write? If so he can put my books in order, once he has put up the shelves and painted them.'

The answer was, yes, Aziz could read, a little slowly. But every night, now, he read to the servants from the newspapers. He had had to give up school when both his parents died. At an early age, he said, he had left his village to find work in the nearest town. But he had always tried to keep up his reading.

So Aziz was put to the task of finishing the shelves in the bigger bungalow and then of transferring the books from the packing cases and putting them on the shelves in alphabetical order of authors' names.

And one day, when Khansamar was going towards the room where Aziz was working, to tell him it was time for his evening meal, he heard the boy laughing. He looked into the room and saw Aziz sitting on the floor, with his back to the door, reading a book, and turning the pages, turning them rapidly for someone who normally read with difficulty. But, that evening, when Khansamar went to the servants' quarters, he found Aziz stumbling, reading aloud, with difficulty, from the morning newspaper.

*

'You must understand, Mr Perron, that Khansamar had come to regard the boy with affection, as a son almost, and that it was not easy for him to admit to himself that there was something a bit suspicious, that the young man he had seen quickly reading through one of the Sahib's books and laughing was rather a different young man from the one who worked in the compound like a farmer's son. And now he also remembered that when the boy had first scythed the grass he had had to wear rags round his hands the next day and in the evening Khansamar had noticed the blisters, on his palms and fingers. At the time he had merely been touched that Aziz had worked so hard and hadn't complained of his sore hands. But now he was troubled. Troubled by the thought that the boy was not the sort of boy he pretended to be. And that night when he went to bed he couldn't sleep. He found himself tossing and turning and wondering and puzzling. And then something else odd struck him. He realized that since Aziz had turned up looking for a job, and had been employed, no one else had arrived at the gate, waving their little chits and begging to see Colonel Sahib.

'So he got dressed and went to the hut Aziz slept in. The door was bolted on the outside, which meant Aziz was out. It was very late, one or two o'clock in the morning. He went round to the front of the house and found the chaukidar fast asleep on the verandah.'

'Which bungalow was this?'

'The one which Nigel has. The one at which you are staying. The bigger bungalow was nearly ready, but not quite ready. Chaukidar should have been patrolling between the two, but he was fast asleep on the verandah. The front gates were closed but anyone can climb these things. It was simply a peaceful Indian night, Mr Perron, and Khansamar thought, well, Aziz was a strong active young fellow. He was probably in the bazaar, making love to a girl whose husband was away. Reprehensible, but understandable. So Khansamar woke chaukidar up and told him off for sleeping. Then he went back to his quarters but found himself more wide awake than ever, and listening for the sound of Aziz coming back. This, he heard, only a little sound, the sound of the bolt on the door of Aziz's hut being opened. He got up and put on his shawl and went over to the hut and saw there was a light on. So he knocked. When Aziz opened the door Khansamar began saying things like, What foolishness is this? Where have you been? Aziz said he had been at the back relieving himself. So Khansamar said, What, for two hours? Are you ill or something?

'Then he noticed that there were marks on the boy's face and that he had been bathing them. He said, What happened? Did the husband come back? Or have you been brawling in the bazaar? He was talking to him like an angry father who is not really angry. Probably Aziz understood this because he became contrite. He said it was true he had been in the bazaar, but there had been no angry husband and no brawling. He had fallen and grazed himself climbing back in over the locked gate and in the morning he would no doubt have a black eye.

'Khansamar said, Wasn't Chaukidar there to help you over? And Aziz laughed and said Chaukidar was no doubt asleep on the front verandah as usual and that nothing would ever wake him.

'Khansamar did not believe Chaukidar could have gone to sleep again, after being told off, but he realized that with two bungalows to look after it would have been possible for Aziz to slip in over one of the gates, and not be seen. So he just gave the boy a telling off too and warned him that Merrick Sahib might have to be informed.

'When he got up in the morning, which was always before anyone else, to make Colonel Sahib's *chota hazri*, he looked for the chaukidar and asked him whether he had stayed awake and if so whether he had seen anything unusual. The chaukidar said he had certainly stayed awake after being woken but that there had been nothing unusual. Khansamar asked him whether he wouldn't call it unusual to see Aziz climbing over a gate and missing his footing and falling on the gravel so heavily that he had grazed his face badly. Chaukidar agreed that that would be unusual.

'In which case, Khansamar said, chaukidar had neglected to see something unusual, because this was what had happened, and that in the circumstances he could only believe that chaukidar had fallen asleep again, and that this would have to be reported to Colonel Sahib.'

Bronowsky lit another pink cigarette.

'Chaukidar said, I do not advise that. You can accuse me to Colonel Sahib of nodding off for a few moments if you like, but you should not say you know I did because I failed to see Aziz climb over the gate. Colonel Sahib will think you are trying to make trouble for him. For two nights – last night and the night before – Aziz was with Colonel Sahib. I saw Aziz go in through the door of the *gusl-khana* just as I saw him go in the night before. The only difference was that the night before I stayed on watch, expecting to see him come out like a thief, in which case I would have pounced on him. But he came out after some time by the same door, and this time Colonel Sahib was with him, dressed in the clothes he sometimes wears when he is alone. He is at heart a Pathan, and Aziz is a fine sturdy boy. If I were not a dried-up old man I would be tempted myself and it does not surprise me that Colonel Sahib has been tempted because for weeks I have sometimes seen him watching the boy at work in the compound. When he went into the bungalow again last night I thought, It is none of my business, but since Colonel Sahib is not alone in the house I can nod off for a moment.'

Dmitri drew on the cigarette, exhaled, stubbed it out as if already tired of it. He took the ebony cane in both hands and leaned forward, chin resting on the hands that rested on the cane.

'So,' he said, 'Khansamar thought it was no business of his either. But he had seen the mess that had been made of Aziz's face and when he took in Colonel Sahib's *chota hazri* he found him already up, sitting in front of the dressing-table, and wearing his harness. The knuckles of his right hand were grazed. He had beaten the boy with his fist. And at that moment, you know, Khansamar conceived for Merrick a dislike. Not a violent dislike. A cold dislike. Contempt. And of course he wondered why a boy like Aziz submitted to that kind of treatment. Do you wonder, Mr Perron?'

'Tell me why you don't.'

Bronowsky smiled and leant back, swirled his brandy in the glass, sipped and put the glass down.

'I think it is clear he had been so instructed. Instructed to present himself, to stand there at the gate until Merrick had seen him. Also instructed to submit, without complaint, to whatever Merrick did once he had accepted the lure of this terrible attraction, of this terrible temptation which young men like Aziz represented.'

'Instructed by whom?'

'I think not Pandit Baba, don't you agree? If it was the Pandit then he must have studied more than the Bhagavad-Gita. He must also have studied Freud. So I do not think the Pandit. The Pandit has probably long ago been superseded by someone with a more modern and intelligent approach. There are always plenty of gurus waiting in the wings, and many of these young men willing and ready to serve and submit and suffer in the belief that what they do is done for a cause. In their death-photographs they look so pale, so insecure. But not in life. Whoever instructed Aziz, and his predecessors, and those who followed him, had come to know of these tendencies in Merrick. How? Always known? I doubt that. More likely through some later indiscretion or lapse. That he had always been kept track of as a potentially useful instrument goes without saying. And this was the new and subtle form of persecution. Young men like Aziz, turning up, with no instructions I imagine other than to tempt, submit, and not complain, not accuse, perhaps to go, so that they could be replaced, gradually, by young men of steelier temperament, young men capable of taking the ultimate step when the victim was properly lulled.

'But what other instructions the boy who called himself Aziz might have had, one does not know. In the event, Merrick sacked him. He told Khansamar there was no further work for Aziz to do. So Aziz was sent packing. And a week or two later another boy arrived, begging for a job, and coming back day after day, standing at the gate. The same kind of boy. But Merrick resisted the bait. And the boy gave up. Only to be replaced by another. And another. And then Susan and Sarah arrived, with the child and the ayah and the bigger bungalow was occupied. But still they came, these young fellows. Perhaps some of them were genuinely looking for employment. Khansamar thought this was so, because they were not all of them boys like Aziz. But among them, from time to time, there would be one like that.

'And then the tactics changed. Khanasamar did not at first connect the one thing with the other. A young Pathan arrived quite late one night, sometime towards the end of April, when the heat was getting bad but Susan was still here and Merrick was often working late, often slept in a room on the other side of the house. The Pathan insisted on seeing Merrick personally. He said he had an official and confidential message. He was alone with Merrick for only a short while. I wonder what was said? What services were offered? What services implied? In May Susan and the child and ayah went back up to Pankot. A few days after they had gone Merrick told Khansamar that he was expecting a messenger, probably quite late, and that the chaukidar shouldn't lock the gates. The Pathan arrived just before midnight. This time he had a companion. Merrick had them taken to his study, then ten minutes later called for Khansamar and told him that one of these men should be given a bed for the night. The Pathan left and the chaukidar locked the gates after him. The companion who stayed was the younger man. He had a bedroll and said he could sleep anywhere. The verandah would do very well. It was very hot. He would be glad if he could be woken at five o'clock. Khansamar said he was a boy like Aziz but probably better educated. He wore European clothes. He was grateful for the charpoy Khansamar put out on the verandah and for the cup of tea he was given. He said he came from Lahore originally and asked a lot of questions about Mirat, so many that Khansamar said, Why do you ask so many questions? The boy laughed and apologized and said it was a habit got from the kind of work he did. Khansamar asked what kind of work that was and the boy looked surprised and said confidential work for the police, what else?

'Khansamar believed it in one part of his mind but not in another. He didn't worry very much either way. It was the Sahib's affair if he slept with boys when his wife was away, not his. But in the morning when he took the boy some tea he was quite innocently asleep where Khansamar had left him and in half-an-hour he had washed and dressed and gone. Khansamar didn't ask the chaukidar whether the boy had ever left his bed and chaukidar didn't volunteer anything, which might have meant that there was nothing to say or that he had been asleep again – perhaps the latter because Khansamar was sure he smelt the boy's hair-oil on one of the pillows in Merrick's bed when he was making it up.

'And so it continued, Mr Perron, about every two or three weeks, always two young men arriving, one going, one staying. Sometimes the one who had stayed the previous time accompanied the new boy. Sometimes Khansamar had seen neither of them before. None of them was a Mirati and Khansamar never noticed the smell of hair-oil on the pillow again. He questioned chaukidar once who said that yes, on one occasion when he patrolled, the boy's bed on the verandah was empty but that when he waited expecting to see

628

him come out of Merrick's *ghusl-khana* he saw him instead coming back from the compound, as if he had been relieving himself and that when he went over and greeted him the young man acted quite naturally and offered him a cigarette and sat and smoked and talked to him for a while.

'So, one wonders. And one wonders what really was in Merrick's mind, whether there was some reality behind this illusion of spies or whether he had simply agreed with the Pathan to have boys procured for him. And in the latter case one wonders again whether he saw a connection between this arrangement and the older forms of persecution, and deliberately put himself in the way of it. I'm afraid we shall never know, Mr Perron. And in a country as vast as this all these young fellows have just disappeared, as if they never existed.

'But consider it this way. And discard the evidence of the hair-oil on the pillow. The smell of the oil could have been in Khansamar's imagination. He never smelt it again. Not even when the rains came and the boys no longer slept on the verandah but on Merrick's instructions indoors in an empty room, where they were free to go to him at any time. Did they go? Perhaps. But if they went, did anything occur? Or did they just sit there discussing with him the information they had pretended to collect or actually collected for him? Was there any such information? Perhaps. On the night he was murdered the private drawer in his desk was forced open, so something might have been removed. But what? A slowly collected dossier about the subversive activities of real or imaginary political activists in Mirat, or a dossier about the scandalous activities, real or imaginary, of Mirat police officers and Mirati officials? If so, had Merrick ever believed in any of it? When he was going on and on about the man in the nullah and the imaginary stone he never referred to the existence of such dossiers, although he said the chief of police should start investigating what he called subversive elements. So, if he had any dossiers, files containing information collected from these so-called spies, had he believed in any of it, or had he just sat there, listening to these young men, pretending to accept their reports, pretending to need their reports but waiting for them to make it clear what else

629

they were offering, and puzzling them by blandly ignoring every hint, every temptation. You knew him, Mr Perron. Would you say that was possible?'

'I should have thought very possible, but in view of the Aziz business, not very probable.'

'And there I disagree. I think perhaps it was probable precisely because of the Aziz business. I think it likely that what he did with, and to, Aziz revealed something to him about himself that utterly appalled him ...'

'Appalled him?'

'I don't mean the revelation of his latent homosexuality and his sado-masochism. These must have been apparent to him for many many years and every now and again given some form of expression. What I mean by a revelation is revelation of the connection between the homosexuality, the sado-masochism, the sense of social inferiority and the grinding defensive belief in his racial superiority. I believe – although you may not – that Aziz was the first young man he had actually ever made love to, and that this gave him a moment of profound peace, but in the next the kind he knew he couldn't bear, knew he couldn't bear because to admit this peace meant discarding every belief he had. I think he realized that, when he woke up after his first night with the boy. And I think that when the boy turned up the following night he just found himself punished and humiliated. And I believe that when Merrick beat him with his fist he was inviting retaliation. I believe he knew why Aziz had arrived. I am sure that finally, Mr Perron, he sought the occasion of his own death and that he grew impatient for it. He *wanted* there to be a man in the nullah. He wanted there to be a stone thrown at his horse. He wanted what happened to happen. Perhaps he hoped that his murder would be avenged in some splendidly spectacular way, in a kind of Wagnerian climax, the *raj* emerging from the twilight and sweeping down from the hills with flaming swords –'

A steward interrupted, approached, leant close, murmured something to him. Bronowsky nodded. The steward went.

'Nawab Sahib?' Perron asked.

'Yes. He has seen the fires in the city. Forgive me, Mr

Perron. It is a summons I can't disobey. But really it is just that he cannot sleep, and wants company.'

They both rose.

'The car can drop you next door and take me on to the palace,' Bronowsky said.

'It's only a step or two.'

'But the car has to take me anyway. Come.'

Bronowsky led him out on to the terrace, taking the long way round to the front. He placed his left hand on Perron's right shoulder. 'But let me tell you what did happen. Or all that one knows. Which isn't much. There was no apparent difference between all the previous nights of the spies and the fatal night. Two young men turn up. Neither has visited before. One goes. The other stays. Perhaps the one who went did not really go, but came back and stayed hidden, to assist, when the time came. It was a lot for one man to do alone. But all that is a mystery, a little event between midnight and six o'clock in the morning when Khansamar went in with the *chota hazri*. The visitor who was to stay the night had gone. Chaukidar had seen nothing, heard nothing. The fact that he did not see them going does not necessarily mean that he was asleep. When the boys made off they might have gone over the wall at the back. No. The real mystery is what happened in the room. Did Merrick dress himself in those clothes, do you think? Habbibullah says that he was strangled before he was hacked about with the little axe and that he was dressed in the clothes before being hacked. One wonders why this was the chosen night, whether it was because time was running out or because the time was now exactly right for leaving on our doorstep as it were, one dead Englishman.'

Bronowsky stopped, released Perron's shoulder, leant for a moment on his stick. 'I wonder – was the thing done in the old Thuggee way?'

'Not unless the neck was broken and a grave already dug.'

'Ah. I had forgotten that. But it was something else I had in mind – the many days the Thugs sometimes travelled with their chosen victims, to lull suspicion. Isn't there a resemblance between this and the long period of preparation? And then it is said, isn't it, that when it came to it they were mercifully quick. Compassionate, even.'

631

The fountains rose, changed colour, subsided and then murmured on. Bronowsky took Perron's shoulder again and began to walk forward. 'Perhaps it is there, in the compassion, that I have been hoping to see the real resemblance.'

VI

'I hadn't thought that we were to be quite so large a party,' Mrs Peabody said.

She had to raise her voice because the platform was crowded and noisy even where the first-class coaches stood and where the usually sober British were being determinedly cheerful and jolly, seeing off and being seen off. Even Mrs Peabody was smiling so Perron wasn't sure whether she was making a comment or a complaint.

'I expect we'll all fit in easily enough,' he shouted back. Mrs Peabody was thin, but tall, so tall that her greatest problem looked like being lack of head-space rather than of elbow-room. Peabody was the same height and not much better fleshed. It would be like travelling with two bean poles. The Peabodys were, as people put it, 'staying on', but were going to do that in Rawalpindi. So much Perron had gathered. They had an immense amount of luggage whose stowing in the compartment Peabody was overseeing. It had already been going into the compartment when Perron and the party from palace and guest house arrived; and still was. It was a good thing that everyone else was travelling fairly light – as Mrs Grace had pointed out after greeting Mrs Peabody and discovering in answer to her question that, yes, all this stuff *was* going into the compartment because years and years of travelling in India had inspired no confidence in either Peabody, in the luggage vans, even on a daytime trip. For instance one would not, Mrs Peabody pointed out, like to have some of one's things off-loaded by mistake at Premanagar.

After this exchange Mrs Grace had dissociated herself from the Peabodys and their luggage and engaged herself in conversation with Bronowsky and Ahmed while Sarah and Nigel helped Susan and ayah to keep Edward entertained.

This had left Perron under an obligation to make himself pleasant to Mrs Peabody, but it was up-hill work. The Peabodys were working in unison, he inside, she out. Their joint efficiency suggested years of practice. Every few moments she broke off the exchange of small-talk to point a coolie at a piece of luggage, or if she didn't break it off herself Peabody did by coming to the open compartment door and reminding her that such or such a piece ought to be stowed next.

'Well I don't know about fitting in easily,' she said eventually, 'but no doubt we shall manage, since there are only six of us.'

'Eight,' Perron said.

'Dora,' Peabody called from the carriage door. 'We'd better have the guns now.'

'There's still the tiffin-box.'

'I think the guns first, then the tiffin-box.'

'As you wish, Reginald.' She pointed a coolie at canvas-shrouded packages, long and thin enough to be Peabody guns.

'Eight,' she said, not having lost the thread. 'How do you make eight?'

'Eight and a half, actually, if you include both me *and* the little boy.'

'Well naturally one includes you both.'

'Right-o, Dora. Tiffin-box now.'

She pointed a coolie at the tiffin-box. It was a wooden box, of majestic proportions, presumably zinc-lined, with air-holes on one side. Watching it go in Perron thought that at least none of them would starve if the train broke down and the Peabodys unbent sufficiently to share out.

'I still make it only six and a half, unless Captain Rowan is coming to Ranpur instead of joining Laura in Gopalakand. But I think that would still make it only seven and a half. Not that mathematics were ever my strong point. Once the thermoses have gone in we can leave the field clear.' She moved to the compartment door and shouted, 'Reginald? I hope the upper berths are let down. They'll need them to stow *their* few things.'

Perron joined Sarah and Nigel. 'I have a feeling that at least two members of the departing *raj* aren't going to leave without standing by their old rights. Or anyway making a fuss about Ahmed and ayah travelling in a first-class compartment.'

'Oh, for God's sake,' Sarah said.

'The Peabodys?' Nigel asked. 'They'd better start getting used to it. He's making a contract with Pakistan for a couple of years. Actually I don't blame him. He's a brilliant military administrator.'

'Brilliant and only a major? Or hasn't he been quite pukka enough to make it to half-colonel?'

Rowan smiled. 'Originally, no. And she's half-Jewish and very anti-semitic. But she's now the Honourable Dora.'

'The Honourable Dora? What a terrible combination.'

'She's furious that it always gets omitted in newspapers. But it came rather late, when her father was made a law baron. It's never got into the Indian lists.'

'Shall I start stowing our luggage?'

'You mean they've finished?' Sarah asked.

Perron rounded up their own coolies and entered the compartment. It smelt of Peabody's bay rum.

In these old first-class compartments there were no corridors. There was no need of them and one was better without them. Each compartment, coupé or four-berther, had its private lavatory. The compartments were broad enough and the berths long enough to suit the tallest man at full stretch and hold the combined luggage of four long-distance travellers. Normally the luggage could be piled up against what might be called the bulk-head between the sleeping compartment and the lavatory; and there was sufficient space down the centre between the two fixed lower benches to stow ice- and tiffin-boxes without restricting foot room.

But when Perron entered he saw that the Peabodys had commandeered all this space and more. Luggage was piled against the bulkhead, blocking the farther exit and coming within an inch or two of the door to the lavatory. He hoped that the exit at Ranpur was on the same side as the entrance at Mirat. Presumably the Peabodys knew. Stretching from the pile of bulkhead luggage was a line of trunks and cases down the centre of the compartment. Even some of the luggage-space provided by the lowered upper sleeping berths was taken up. He ordered his own party's suitcases to be stowed above, and then remembered Merrick's relics. Were they out on the platform? The answer was at once given – by the appearance in the doorway of a coolie holding one end of the black tin coffin, the battered old trunk, with the stencilled name, Lt.-Col. R. Merrick, DSO, still visible, still eloquent.

'You'd better put it here,' he said, indicating a place that would leave barely sufficient room for people to get from one side of the compartment to another. He hoped the carpet wouldn't come too. But it did. It looked smaller, though. It had been doubled up and tied with string. He had it placed on top of the trunk.

He clambered out, and down on to the platform. The Peabodys were bidding farewell to an elderly servant who was placing garlands round their thin necks. He reported to Sarah. A warning whistle blew. She turned to Bronowsky who took off his rakish little panama hat. Beyond the first-class compartment area the platform had begun to seethe. Perron could hear the mournful voice of the man selling tea. Cha-ay Wall-*ah*, Garam cha-*ay*. Black hands stretched down from open third-class compartments grasping those stretched up to bid goodbye. A woman shrieked.

'Goodbye, my dear,' Bronowsky was saying to Sarah. 'Don't be too long before coming back.' He bent to embrace her.

Perron clasped Nigel's hand. 'I'll wire you,' he said.

'Do. I'll be a better host in Gopalakand. Have a good journey.'

A hand fell on Perron's shoulder. Bronowsky's. The one eye observed him. 'Thank you for coming to Mirat. Here is a little token of your visit.'

He found himself presented with a little package. A book by the feel of it. Then Edward intervened.

'Goodbye, Chief Minister. Thank you for letting us stay at the Nawab's guest house, while daddy's away.'

One by one they entered the compartment. Another blow on the whistle. Distantly the woman shrieked again.

'Mrs Merrick, there is room for your tiffin basket on top of ours,' Mrs Peabody said.

'Please don't worry,' Susan replied. She sat at the far end of the compartment opposite Mrs Peabody, divorced from her by the black tin trunk and the folded carpet. On her lap she held a basket.

'Has your ayah a compartment quite close?'

'Oh, very close, Mrs Peabody. In fact here. Ayah will sit with me, in case I doze off and Edward needs attending to. It's the best thing.'

After a moment Mrs Peabody said, 'Reginald, let me sit at the other end. It is a little close here.' They changed places.

'Are you sure about that basket, Mrs Merrick?' Peabody asked.

'Absolutely sure, Major Peabody.'

Perron, at the doorway, received Edward from Dmitri's arms. 'I don't want to sit down yet, Perron,' the boy said. 'I want to wave from this window.'

'Okay, but let the troops on first.'

Mrs Grace came next. She looked at the compartment and then at the Peabodys and said, 'Good Heavens, it looks as though we're being delivered from Egypt,' and went to sit next to Susan. Sarah kissed Nigel and came up next. She went down and round over the baggage and sat between Major and Mrs Peabody.

'Ayah!' Edward shouted. 'Hurry up! You're going to miss the train.'

Ahmed helped ayah up.

'Come on, ayah,' Mrs Grace said, and patted the seat next to her. '*Baitho.*'

The girl tried to take Edward with her but he resisted. So she went and sat, alert, on the edge of the green leather-upholstered bench. A pretty girl, Perron realized; this morning not covering her face with the edge of her saree. Ahmed came next. He seemed to have no luggage except a small canvas bag.

Another whistle-blow. Ahmed shut the door, turned, lifted Edward up to the open window.

'Goodbye Dmitri!' the child called. 'Goodbye Uncle Nigel!'

Abruptly, the carriage began to glide away. Perron steadied himself against the piled Peabody luggage and bent, peering through the other windows to watch the unfolding tapestry of the departure from Mirat.

I remember (he has said) dark faces taking over from the

636

white faces. I remember the woman who ran trying to keep up with the train.

'Are you really sure about the basket, Mrs Merrick?' Mrs Peabody said. 'Couldn't your ayah look after it?'

Susan didn't reply this time. When Perron had climbed over the luggage and settled himself next to Mrs Peabody, Sarah whispered to him, 'Try to get her to shut up about the basket. It's the urn. Susan won't let anyone else touch it.'

At a suitable moment, when Edward was shouting playfully at ayah, Perron passed the message on. Mrs Peabody opened her mouth, then shut it. Presently she opened her handbag and brought out a little lace handkerchief, moist with eau-de-cologne. She wiped it gently over her dry yellow skin.

They were sitting in this order:

On the bench that ended close to the one unencumbered door – first, Ahmed, then ayah, then Mrs Grace and Susan. The child used this side of the compartment as his roving territory. Opposite Susan sat Peabody, then Sarah, then Perron and Mrs Peabody. At Perron's and Mrs Peabody's end there was almost total luggage block, with Ahmed and ayah visible only from chest height. Ahmed got up and went into the lavatory. Perron heard Mrs Peabody draw in her breath and then slowly exhale. He had the impression that however badly she might need to she would now avoid going to the lavatory for the rest of the day, or get out at the only stop (Premanagar) whether she needed to or not, as a form of insurance against too great a desperation later. She remained tense throughout the few minutes Ahmed was absent, probably counting them, in order to work out whether he was urinating or doing something of a graver nature. When Ahmed came out she continued silent, and Perron began to feel that she was holding *him* responsible for everything, from the overcrowded compartment right down through the urn to the use of the lavatory by natives.

*

'Bang!' Edward shouted. After they had been going for about half-an-hour (and all, one by one, except Perron and the

637

Peabodys had used the lavatory – Perron because he didn't want to go badly enough to feel it worth his while fighting the way over that mound of luggage) Edward had found the perfect use for the piled trunks and cases. He shot them from behind this entrenchment until they were all dead. Except Mrs Peabody, who was resistant to imaginary bullets.

But the 'Bang!' obviously stirred thoughts. 'Do you hunt, Mr Perron?' she asked. These were not the first words she had spoken to him, simply the first she had volunteered.

Perron said he didn't.

'Do you shoot?'

'No. I watched Ahmed hawking the other day.'

'Who?'

'Ahmed. Mr Kasim. Over there.'

'Hawking?'

'With a hawk.'

'Oh. I see. Yes. Really? I don't think I should care for that. It seems to me rather cruel to tame a wild creature. But I like a day out with hounds and a day out with the guns. We hope to get in a few days at Bharatpur before going on up to 'Pindi. You've been to Bharatpur, I suppose? Oh, you should. The jhils there are famous.'

She talked on for a while, about Bharatpur, about Kashmir, about the boundless number of places she and Reginald had been in India. 'We've never been south though, except of course through it to Ooty. There's some good going in Ooty. But the south always depresses me. I never think of it as India at all. We're northern India people by temperament, I suppose. Tell me, what is your regiment?'

Perron admitted that he did not own a regiment and had never served in one except for a few months during the war as a private, after which he had transferred to Intelligence and then to Field Security.

'But you were in India?'

'For a while.'

'In Field Security?'

'Yes. With a man called Bob Chalmers.'

'Chalmers. Chalmers. No, I'm afraid I don't know that name.'

'He's now in pharmaceuticals in Bombay.'

'Really. How interesting. He stayed on, then. Reggie was awfully tempted to go into pharmaceuticals himself, after all one of the few things we can do for this country now is help them fight the battle of disease.'

'And poverty.'

She smiled. 'I sometimes think the poverty is very exaggerated. Most of the Indians one knows could buy one up lock stock and barrel.'

'There are the ones one doesn't know.'

'In the villages, Mr Perron, every peasant woman has her gold bangles. No, no. It is not the poverty. It is the disease. The superstition. The *inertia*.'

'Bang!' Edward said.

Perron died again.

And then so did the train. The luggage juddered from the vibration of the braking. Minnie grabbed the child. They all rocked to and fro for a moment and then steadied themselves. The train came to a halt.

*

'Probably a cow on the line,' Mrs Peabody said. 'Reggie – see what you can see if you can manage to climb over that carpet.'

But Ahmed was already up. He lowered the window of the door and leant out.

'I remember a cow on the line,' Susan said in the dead silence. 'Don't you, Sarah?'

'Yes, I remember.'

'But where? All I remember is the train stopping and daddy saying just what Mrs Peabody just said. "Probably a cow on the line." And there was. But where was it, Sarah?'

'Between Ranpur and Delhi. Nineteen-thirty.'

'Ranpur and Delhi. What lovely names. There's so much poetry in Indian names. Ronnie used to say that. Where is your home at home, Mrs Peabody?'

'We are in Northamptonshire. Just outside Norby.'

'Norby. That's what I mean. And mother says she's found a house in Epsom. It sounds like an aperient.'

'Major Peabody?' Ahmed called out. 'Would you please put

up the windows and close the shutters on your side? Mrs Grace? Please? On yours?'

He was locking the compartment door. Now he pulled the window up and closed the wooden shutter.

'What is it, Ahmed?' Mrs Grace asked.

'Oh, nothing much. Just some kind of silly nuisance. Mr Perron, please, on your side?'

'What's the chap say?' Peabody asked.

'He seems to want the windows closed and the shutters pulled down,' Mrs Peabody said. 'I can't think why. It's hot enough and there's one fan not working.'

Peabody stood up. 'What are you doing? Baking us alive or something?'

Ahmed was helping Mrs Grace to close windows and pull down shutters on the other side of the compartment. Perron started doing the same on the Peabody side.

'What's wrong, Ahmed?' Sarah asked.

'Just some silly people making a nuisance. Don't worry.'

There was nothing to be seen through the windows except a vast hot dry eroded landscape. 'Do you mind?' Perron asked, leaning in behind Mrs Peabody and dealing with her window and shutter.

'Yes I do. I do mind. For heaven's sake!'

'Just shut the windows please and pull down the shutters,' Ahmed repeated. 'Mrs Grace, I think ayah shouldn't sit here. Let her get under the seat just for a while. Come, Minnie.' He got hold of her and forced her gently to the floor. 'Play hide and seek with chokrasahib. Come on, Edward. Look, ayah is hiding.'

Edward shouted, 'Why is she hiding? I don't want to play hide and seek. It's a silly girl's game.'

'No, it isn't silly,' Ahmed insisted. 'Come on, help hide ayah. Pretend bad men are looking for her.'

'Look here, Kasim,' Peabody began – but just then there was a long drawn-out wail, rising in pitch, from up ahead. There was a grumble of voices from the adjacent compartment, then a shout, and the sound of windows and shutters being closed. The wailing continued as an accompaniment now to sudden screams.

They remained, as if transfixed. From under the bench

came a low moan from the little ayah. The boy bent down.
'What's wrong, ayah?' he asked. Ahmed got hold of him and
said, 'Okay, it's only a game. Ayah's pretending to hide from
bad people. Major Peabody, please come to this side and take
ayah's seat so that no one can see her.'

Peabody hesitated, then began to clamber over the luggage.
As he did so something hit the compartment, something soft.
And again. The sound of a hand slapping the side of the
carriage. Behind it all the continuing sound of wailing and
screaming.

'Take the boy,' Ahmed said, and lifted him over into Sarah's
arms. Peabody was still straddled across the luggage.

'Reggie, what are you *doing?*' his wife asked him. He looked
at her as if he thought her a perfect fool but said, 'God knows
what anyone's doing, it must be some kind of damned silly
demonstration,' and completed the movement of stepping
over the luggage, lost his footing and fell against Mrs Grace
and Susan. 'Oh, damn it,' he said and just then people outside
began to pound heavily on the door and the side of the
compartment and then there was a little crack and an
explosion of broken glass and Susan shrieked. Another
explosion; another shattering of glass. She shrieked again. As
if by old instinct, Peabody remained ducked down, forgetting
that the glass couldn't fly in through the lowered shutters. It
was dark in the compartment. Little wires of light lay along
the edges of the wooden louvres. The occupants of the seats
were ducked down too, including Ahmed. Mrs Grace had her
arm round Susan. Sarah held the boy. This was the tableau
Perron saw when after a sudden silence had lasted a few
seconds he looked up and round.

There was a bang on the door. Then a hammering that went
on for some while. When it stopped a man's voice came quite
clearly: 'Come on, Kasim Sahib.' More bangs on the door.
Susan gasped. Mrs Peabody cried out, 'What are they doing,
what are they doing?' Then the voice from outside could be
heard again. 'Come on out. Kasim? Kasim Sahib? Come on.
Or do we have to break in and annoy all the sirs and ladies?
Kasim? Kasim Sahib?' When the voice stopped the hammering on the door began again.

Silence suddenly. Then another shattered window. This

time Edward began to cry. Sarah cradled him. Perron got up – to do what he didn't know: climb over to the door, open the shutter and shout that there was no Kasim there?

But Ahmed had got up too. Because of the noise of Edward crying and Susan shrieking Perron did not clearly hear what Ahmed said, but it sounded like, 'It seems to be me they want.' It could have been, 'Be ready to re-lock the door.' But he smiled, shrugged, and had suddenly unlocked it. As he did so Peabody lunged forward, as if to stop him. But he was too late. Ahmed opened the door and went.

A turbanned head appeared. Peabody must have seen the head at eye-level. Perron saw it from above. The head rose. The man must have been getting purchase on steps and hand-grip. It looked as if he was coming in. He got one hand on the door-handle. In his other was something that looked like a sword but surely couldn't have been. He said, 'Sorry to have disturbed you, sirs and ladies. On to Ranpur, isn't it?' and then let himself fall away, dragging the door shut. Peabody lunged forward again and locked it.

A feeling of terrible relief swept over Perron. At the time it was just relief. It was terrible subsequently; when it sank in that it had been the relief a man feels when his self-protective instinct tells him he has personally survived a passing danger. Perhaps Peabody felt the same relief. And perhaps it was this that presently made him push up the shutter and look out.

Then he lowered it quickly, stood for a moment, staring at the shutter, checked the lock on the door, and turned round and sat on the bench in the place Ahmed had vacated without saying a word.

And as he did so the train began to glide forward – slowly, silkily, smoothly; as if getting stealthily away from a dangerous and incomprehensible situation. Except for Peabody, who had looked out, none of the people in the compartment could quite visualize the scene of this second departure. Later they must all have done so. In Perron's mind it remains so vivid that it sometimes seems to him that he raised a shutter himself and watched as the train drifted away along this stretch of line, on whose embankment bodies lay; some close, some farther off as though they had tried to run away and then been caught and struck down – men, women, youths, young girls, babies; in death looking all the same, like dummies stuffed for some kind of strange fertility festival.

*

It took three-quarters of an hour to get to Premanagar. At first it seemed as if they would cover the entire distance in the semi-darkness of lowered shutters and in total silence apart from the rhythmic clack of wheels hastily putting distance between the living travellers and the abandoned dead; but after five minutes or so Mrs Peabody said, 'Reggie, do you think we might have some light and air? I think otherwise I might be going to faint.'

'Only on your side,' Mrs Grace said. 'Here we have a great deal of trapped broken glass.'

'It was my side I was thinking of. Perhaps you'd help me, Mr Perron, since you're here.'

Perron lent a hand.

'I didn't like that game, Auntie Sarah,' Edward said. 'Is it finished?'

The child's tear-stained face was revealed as the shutters went up. He climbed off Sarah's lap and then up and over the piled luggage. 'You can come out now, ayah,' he shouted. 'We've stopped playing that game. Where's Ahmed? Has he gone to pee again? I want to pee too.' He had to say it several times and then staggered towards the door of the w.c. His unsteadiness suddenly impressed itself on Major Peabody's eye.

'Come on, old chap, then. I'll take you.'

'What's *your* name?' Edward asked as he was taken in.

'Never mind my name,' Peabody said; and shut the door on them both.

Sarah was now leaning forward, both elbows clasped in her hands, her head bowed. Ayah had got up and was standing against the luggage. When the door of the lavatory opened and Edward came out alone she took charge of him and sat with him in the place that had been Ahmed's and then Peabody's and was now anybody's or nobody's. Peabody was in the cubicle for nearly ten minutes. Perhaps he was being sick. He looked very pale when he came out. Finding his new place gone he clambered over the luggage and sat once more in the far corner opposite Susan who still cradled the basket and was still cradled in Mrs Grace's arms.

'Is mummy crying again?' Edward asked.

Nobody answered. But then Sarah said, 'We just let him go. We all of us sat here and let him go.' After that none of them spoke. In this way they came into Premanagar.

*

Before the train actually stopped Peabody got up. Perron got up too. At the door Peabody said in a whisper, 'Keep them in here, Perron. They mustn't come out on to the platform.'

'But I must.'

Peabody said, 'I think not.'

'I'm sorry, Peabody. But I've got to go back to where Ahmed got out.'

Peabody frowned. Perhaps at the use of his surname. 'There's nothing to go back for. He was hacked to pieces.'

Perron didn't really take this in. He said, 'I must get to a phone and ring the palace. We can't just leave it like that. Someone's got to go back.'

From outside, suddenly, as the train came to a halt, came the renewed sound of wailing and shouting. Peabody's breath smelt acid. He said, 'They might turn on us when they take it in. They might decide it's our fault. You'd be better advised to stay here and look after the women. I'm going to find out what's happening.'

'It's all right, Major Peabody,' Sarah called. 'Mr Perron knows what he must do. I'll stand by the door if that's what you want.' She clambered over. Reluctantly Peabody opened the door. An English voice outside exclaimed, 'My God.' Peabody and Perron went down. 'Lock it,' Peabody told Sarah. She said, 'There's no need to lock it now.'

Other English passengers had come down from the adjacent compartments – two of them women. Two Indian officers ran through asking them to make way. Automatically they stood back, as if accepting that this was an Indian affair, not theirs. They stood pale-faced, shocked.

Some of the dead were already being brought out of the

644

third-class carriages. The nearest of these was a purdah-coach and out of this white and black bundles of veiled women were being lowered. Most lay motionless when put down, one or two seemed to be trying to crawl back in. Among the dead from the purdah-coach were the bodies of small children. And beyond the purdah-coach the platform was becoming littered with blood-stained bundles of white cloth, with black limbs sticking out of the cloth. One body lay on the roof of the coach. No one seemed to have noticed it. From some of the windows of the coaches heads and arms hung down. Blood slowly made shapes on the dirty grey concrete of the platform. Ahead, the locomotive suddenly let off steam, as if about to haul the train out again. People began to shout. A wave of panic swept along the platform and then because the train didn't move died away and left only the wailing of those searching among the rows of dead and dying passengers.

*

'I'm sorry,' the MCO said, 'I cannot allow private calls of any nature. I am trying to raise Mirat. The lines may be down. Please go away.'

The MCO was a Sikh. Sikhs, people were saying, had been among the gang that stopped the train and slashed Muslim passengers to death with swords. But if he feared for his own life he didn't show it. He had moved freely up and down the platform. Perron had waylaid him on one of his brief visits to the office where a havildar-clerk was constantly on the telephone.

'If you get Mirat, would you please tell them that Ahmed Kasim, the son of Mohammed Ali Kasim may have to be presumed dead and that the Nawab of Mirat's Chief Minister should be informed?'

'Ahmed Kasim? Ahmed Kasim? Who is Ahmed Kasim?'

'He was travelling with us.'

'Then why is he presumed dead? You are first-class, surely. Please go away. What is one man among so many?'

'Mirat, sir,' the clerk shouted, and handed the phone over.

The MCO grabbed the receiver, at the same time saying, 'Please all of you go away.' He began talking rapidly in a mixture of English and Hindi. Perron was not the only unauthorized visitor. There were about six crowded into the tiny office. But all of them were English – people who were anxious to contact friends left behind in Mirat or waiting for them in Ranpur, friends who some time during the day might hear what had happened and start worrying.

'Let's try the stationmaster,' one of them said.

'He's worse than this chap.'

They had absorbed the shock. The old reactions were already setting back in, but the impulse to take charge had gone. It was the kind of situation that had always been bubbling under the surface trying to break out, the kind that the *raj* had had to try to control. Now the worst had happened.

'God knows how they're going to cope in this place,' one of the officers told Perron as they went back on to the platform. 'Premanagar's always been a dead-alive hole. No proper troops and no pukka hospital.'

The MCO's office was next to the first-class restaurant. The trains always drew up so that the first-class compartments were opposite the places that first-class passengers needed. In this area, then, the platform was an isolated little island, bordered on both sides by the horrors. Perron noticed that armed police had turned up. It was twenty minutes since the train's arrival. He went to the compartment. The door was open. Inside there were only the two Peabodys – he kneeling by an open bag, she lying full length on the bench, hand over her eyes.

'Where are the others?' Perron asked.

'Women's rest room.'

From the bag Peabody was taking a webbing belt and holster. The holster had a revolver in it. Perron got down again and went to the women's rest room. It was crowded. There were several men among the women, looking pale, dignified and protective. At one end of the room he saw Mrs Grace, ayah and Edward, and Susan. He made his way to them, passing from under one area of fanned air to another. 'Where's Sarah?' he asked Mrs Grace.

'She's gone to see what she can do to help. I let her. It's what she wanted.'

Perron pushed his way out again. 'Savages,' a woman was

saying. And a man, 'What do you expect? It's only the beginning. Once we've gone they'll all cut each other's bloody throats. Non-violence. Makes you laugh, doesn't it?' But it didn't make Perron laugh. Once out on the platform he forced his way through a little cordon of armed police into the place where the kind of help Sarah had to offer might be needed. He couldn't see her, so went back again, passing through the area of safety and certainty, out to the other side, through another cordon of police, to another place of horror. Here he saw two Indian nurses, and a stretcher-bearer. A nun. Two nuns. However unpukka the nearest hospital was it had begun to operate. And there were two white women, one elderly, one quite young. A middle-aged Indian in European clothes stopped him. 'Are you a doctor?' 'No,' Perron said. 'I wish to God I were.' And passed on. The two white women were nursing children. The nuns, both Indians, were binding wounds, staunching the flow of blood from terrible looking cuts which revealed the whiteness of the bone, the redness of the flesh under the brown skin. Another middle-aged man, an Englishman this time, looked up and said, 'Are you the doctor?' 'No,' Perron said. The man said, 'Never mind. Water's the problem. Could you help with that? But it's got to come from the tap down there. Not the one for caste-Hindus. But a lot of these wretches are dying of thirst if nothing else.'

It was at the tap 'down there' that he found Sarah. She was on her knees, in the filth and the muck, her skirt wet through, handing up little brass vessels to the man controlling the tap, reaching out for empty ones without looking, placing the filled vessels on the other side. The vessels, mugs, glasses were being brought and taken away by men and women and youths. He knelt by her. 'Come on,' he said, 'let me take over.'

'No,' she said. 'I'm all right doing this. I can't do the other thing. But if you can, please do.'

So Perron picked up one of the brass jugs and turned and went among the dying. Or the dead. It wasn't always easy to tell. He knelt first by an old grey-beard who seemed to be smiling up at him gratefully, joyfully, but who did not respond when he put his hand under the man's neck to try to raise him. The eyes were glazed and the smile was merely a death-smile.

The train had been the 10 a.m. express to Ranpur, its only scheduled stop Premanagar, normally reached at 11.15. The ambush had been laid at a point on the line some miles from the last of three wayside halts, all of which were reached and passed by the express within half an hour of leaving Mirat, and beyond which there was no habitation, nothing but desert, until you reached Premanagar.

As the train came out of a curve on to a straight level embankment, the driver had indeed seen a cow, apparently ruminating. He did not remember seeing more than two or three men asleep on the embankment, but at this point there were a few shade trees growing in the dips on either side, and when he brought the train to a stop he realized there were very many more men. They came up on both sides. Two – armed with swords – climbed on to the footplate. The others began running down the track and climbing into the carriages.

Some passengers said that the attackers were joined by men who had travelled on the train from Mirat and who now produced knives and cudgels and joined the raiders. It must have been one of these men who had noted the compartment Ahmed Kasim got into. Opinions varied about the length of time the train was halted while the men went through it, dragging Muslims out or killing them on the spot. Some said only five minutes, others remembered the slaughter continuing for perhaps half-an-hour. The truth was that it lasted no more than ten or fifteen minutes. At the end of that time, getting a signal, one man released the cow (which had been tethered) and slapped it away to find its own salvation. The two intruders on the footplate ordered the driver to resume his journey and then jumped off. He needed no persuasion. He believed himself lucky to get away with his life and that of his young apprentice. He didn't look back until the locomotive had got up speed. Then he saw men scattering across the rough rocky ground towards a huddle of ruined huts. He saw no vehicles, got no indication of how the men had congregated in this place, or how they hoped to get away. But there probably were vehicles, an old carrier-truck, perhaps, an ancient bus. It was forty-five minutes before the train reached

Premanagar; perhaps another fifteen before the Premanagar authorities had contacted Mirat; perhaps another half-hour before troops, police and medical units from Mirat arrived at the scene of the ambush, having dropped search parties off at the villages served by the wayside halts. At the scene itself there was only the terrible evidence: the dead and the dying. By then, the attackers had had nearly two hours in which to scatter.

By road, the journey from Mirat to Premanagar could be accomplished in one and a half hours, only fifteen minutes longer than the journey by rail. The first contingent of troops and medical staff and armed police from Mirat arrived at about one-thirty in the afternoon, fifteen minutes later than the scheduled time of the express train's normally delayed departure for Ranpur, after a leisurely stop for early first-class restaurant lunches. By then, the deputy commissioner and the district superintendent of police had been on the scene since mid-day. The transfer of dead and wounded to an emergency casualty station set up in the goods-yard area was nearly complete. Some kind of order had been restored. The carriages and the platform were being washed down. The rumour was that the train would leave for Ranpur at about 3 p.m., this time under armed guard, and mightn't be more than an hour or so late reaching its destination that evening. About a dozen of the first-class passengers went into the restaurant. The bar had been in use for some time.

*

Perron's trousers and shirt were spattered with blood. He had lost sight of Sarah. He made his way from the goods-yard back to the platform and the compartment.

Mrs Peabody was still stretched out on the bench. Peabody was bending over the tiffin-box, pouring a drink from a thermos. The carriage was otherwise empty. The garlands which had been presented to the Peabodys in Mirat lay on the floor.

'Have you seen Miss Layton?'

Peabody nodded at the lavatory cubicle. 'She's in there, changing. The others are still in the women's room I suppose.

You'd better change too. Will you have some malted milk? It's very fortifying.'

'No thank you.'

'There's a spare sandwich or two here. Or have you got your own tuck?'

'I don't want anything to eat, thank you.'

'You ought to eat. Especially if you're going back. I've just been having a word with Bob Blake. He'll take you if you still want to.'

'Who's Bob Blake?'

'He's OC the refugee protection force in the cantonment. They got here a little while ago. I told him what happened to Kasim. He's ringing the station commander in Mirat. There can't be anything you can do but you seemed keen, so I told Bob. He knew Kasim slightly. He'll be here to have a word presently, I shouldn't wonder.'

Sarah came out of the cubicle. She carried a hold-all. The dress she had on was creased but unstained. And dry. She glanced at his shirt and trousers. She said:

'Have you had a drink yet?'

Peabody said, 'I offered him one but he didn't want it.'

'I meant a real drink.'

Perron shook his head. 'I don't want a real drink, either.' He felt now as if he was going to be sick. He went down on to the platform. Sarah came down too. She said, 'Sorry to scrounge. Have you a cigarette?'

He got out his case. He found it difficult to open. She tried to steady his hand while he helped her light up, but they were both trembling.

She said, 'Are you really going back?'

'Are you asking me not to? Do you want help in Ranpur?'

'No. No, thank you. I want to go back too. But I can't. I can't let Aunt Fenny cope alone. But they'll soon know at the palace what happened to Ahmed. Someone ought to go back and try to say how it did.'

'Mr Perron?'

Perron turned. A stout, rather red-faced middle-aged English officer had come up. Sarah said, 'Guy, this is Major Blake.' They shook hands. Blake said, 'I'm going back in about fifteen minutes. If you want to come with me can you be ready by then?'

'Yes, I've only got to change.'

'I'm leaving my subaltern in charge of the train, Miss Layton,' Blake explained. 'You'll be quite safe for the rest of the journey. I'm putting on a whole platoon.'

He took Perron's arm, guided him a few steps away and said, 'I've been on to the station commander in Mirat. He told me Count Bronowsky's already phoned him. The news got round fairly fast. I'm afraid the station commander told him that only Muslims in third-class compartments were killed, but that's what he assumed. He's going now to the place where the bodies are being brought in. Is there any possibility that Kasim wasn't killed?'

'I don't think so. He just opened the door and went, Peabody saw the rest.'

'The station commander said that if young Kasim is dead he'd be very grateful if you do come back. Where were you going, Mr Perron, Pankot?'

'Just to Ranpur, then on to Delhi.'

'Any urgency?'

'None.'

'All the same, I'll help you in any way I can to get you away again. Did you see the chalk-mark on the door?'

'Chalk-mark?'

'Miss Layton noticed it a little while ago. Someone had chalked a moon low on the door of your compartment. It must have been done in Mirat by whoever was watching which part of the train Kasim got into. Yours was the only first-class compartment attacked. All they had to do was look for the chalk-mark. Well. I'll send a chap to help you sort out your bags and bring them over.'

Blake went back to Sarah. They spoke for a few moments. Then he touched his cap and went. From the bar there came a sudden roar of laughter. Perron went back into the carriage to get his bags down and change. As he did so he noticed a fresh smear low down on the door, where the chalk-mark had been wiped off.

*

Mrs Grace and Susan, Edward and ayah, were still in the rest room. He didn't want to intrude on them. He said goodbye to Peabody. Mrs Peabody was still prostrate. There was only Sarah to see him off. One coolie had his suitcase, another his hold-all. A lance-naik sent by Blake was in charge of them, waiting to take Perron to the truck, whatever kind of vehicle it was he and Blake would travel in.

'Are these yours, old man?' Peabody called, offering something from the open carriage door: a little package and a canvas bag.

The package was certainly his. Dmitri's gift. Unopened. A book, presumably. Perhaps a translation of the poetry of Pushkin. The canvas bag, for a moment, was unrecognizable. Then was. He came away from the door holding both. Sarah looked away from the bag.

'Shall I see you again?' he asked.

'I don't know.' She was still shivering. 'What is there to see?'

He touched her shoulder. 'A great deal,' he said. Then leant down and kissed her. He let her go. She turned and climbed back into the carriage. He smiled at her, then followed the naik. At the exit he looked back; she was at the carriage door, holding her elbows in that way; watching him. Briefly she released one hand and raised it. And then went in.

*

I'm sure (Sarah has written) that he did say, 'It seems to be me they want.' It's what Guy heard, what I heard, what we heard at the time, and it made sense. And the fact that he smiled encouraged me to think that if he went out to the people who called out to him everything would be all right. This is what it was like at the time. I can't justify it now except by saying that there were so many conflicting claims; how to stop Edward crying, how to stop Susan shrieking, how to explain even to myself just why ayah was hiding under the bench. When he first looked out of the window when the train stopped he must have seen them dragging Muslims out. If we'd been travelling only a week or two later we'd have been prepared for it, because by then the business of stopping trains and slaughtering people had become part of life. No English were ever harmed. And it became quite the ordinary thing to hide Indians, friends and servants, under the seats – Hindus if it was the Muslims who were attacking, Muslims if it was Hindus. And if people hammered on the doors you just told them to go away. But we didn't know that. We weren't prepared for it. I suppose Ahmed was, or saw at once how things were. And whoever wanted to kill him knew he was travelling that day. The massacre itself must have been a retaliation for the killings and burnings the night before in Mirat when Muslims attacked Hindus because Mirat was going under Congress rule. I suppose Ahmed was marked out as a victim not just because he was a Muslim but because the people who killed him didn't want Muslims in the Congress, or didn't trust Muslims in Congress and his father was still in Congress. And perhaps because they knew his brother was a rabid Pakistani and perhaps because on top of that they hadn't forgotten that Ahmed's father hadn't stood by the INA, which made it senseless anyway because Sayed had been INA. But it was all so senseless. Such a damned bloody senseless mess. The kind which Ahmed tried to shut himself off from, the mess the *raj* had never been able to sort out. The only difference between Ahmed and me was that he didn't take the mess seriously and I did. I felt it was our responsibility, our fault that after a hundred years or more it still existed.

Ahmed and I weren't in love. But we loved one another. We recognized in each other the compulsion to break away from what I can only call a *received* life. When I knelt at the tap, filling up those somehow meaningless little brass jugs and lotas and pots, whatever there was, it was driven home to me that what I was doing was just as useless as what he'd just done. I've never hated myself so much as I did then. I felt like throwing the jugs down and saying, Well, get on with it. And I hated Ahmed for not keeping the door locked and telling us he damned well wasn't going to die unless they smashed right through the windows and climbed in with their swords and slaughtered the lot of us, or started a fire under the compartment to smoke us out, so that they could cut us down one by one. All those possibilities must have been in his mind. But when it came to it he didn't let any of it even begin to happen to us. And *I* couldn't stop filling the bloody jars, going through my brave little memsahib act.

I'm sure he smiled just before he went, and I'm sure he said, 'It seems to be me they want.' Major Peabody said he thought he said, 'Make sure you lock it after me.' But I think that's what Major Peabody wanted to hear. Perhaps we all heard only what we wanted to hear. Perhaps there was nothing to hear because he said nothing, but just smiled and went, in which case I suppose that meant he knew there was nothing to say because there wasn't any alternative, because everyone else in the carriage automatically knew what he had to do. It was part of the bloody code. The moment he got into the carriage *he* sub-consciously knew that sub-consciously *we* had cast lots even before there was any question of lots having to be cast to see who would survive and who wouldn't.

No. I don't know what was in the canvas bag. And Guy never looked. A bottle of whisky, perhaps, and a clove or two of garlic.

Coda
Ranagunj airfield (Ranpur). Saturday August 9, 1947.

The tannoy system crackled. An Indian voice speaking in English told the few people sitting on the hard benches of the little airfield lounge that the plane from Mayapore was now landing and that departure for Delhi would be in twenty minutes.

The English officer sitting next to Perron closed *The Reader's Digest* and said, 'How civilized we make it sound. Do you know an extraordinary thing? As far back as December in nineteen forty-five when I flew from Singapore to Rangoon and on to Calcutta on an RAF plane and we landed for fuel in the middle of Burma, the door opened and an erk in white dungarees looked in and said, "You've now landed in Meiktila." '

'Meiktila?'

'Yes. I'd lost quite a lot of good men there scarcely more than six months before in the battle for the airstrip. But here we were, practising for the courteous world of civil aviation. I thought, How quickly the grass grows.'

654

The plane was delayed, delayed by storms. It was nearly midnight. It had rained throughout most of the day. The old Dakota was parked about a hundred yards from the airfield buildings. An immense puddle had to be negotiated by the six or seven people who having taken leave of friends walked ahead of or behind Perron towards the steps leading to the open port. Inside, bucket seats, thinly cushioned, had replaced the old port and starboard benches. About ten passengers were already seated. Passengers from Mayapore. Officers. Officers' wives. A blue-rinsed grey-haired woman who was probably Red Cross. Two beefy-looking fellows in shorts and shirts who might have been Australians but turned out to be English: technicians, perhaps, from the British-Indian Electric Company. Their shirts were black with sweat. They were drinking beer from the bottle.

Perron found a single seat on the port side. He stowed his hand luggage. Sat. Closed his eyes.

Mayapore, Ranpur, Delhi. He wondered how many of the passengers from Mayapore had been in the town in nineteen forty-two, at the time of the Bibighar. Perhaps none. The *raj* had always led a nomadic existence. And these little airfields, relics of the war, now merely hastened their movements from place to place. Some of them were moving out for the last time.

He opened his eyes and stared out of the window at what remained for him of Ranpur: an illuminated puddle. The airfield building. A petrol tanker, now hauling away. Beyond this darkness and this light – after these absurd little marks and portents of human occupation – the adventure. The port engine fired, exploding the silence. The port airscrew began to spin. Little ripples showed on the surface of the puddle, as though the fishermen on the Izzat Bagh lake had cast a net. Another small explosion, on the starboard side. He shut his eyes again. Whenever he travelled by air he prayed just before take-off and just before landing. These were nowadays his only offerings to God. It was inconceivable to him that the prayers could be heard because he felt that if there were a God, God would be praying too, watching these extraordinary machines shudder and flutter their frail way along the tarmac towards the lit runway.

And there was always that moment as the aeroplane squared up and seemed to pause; the moment of dying intention, and then the moment when defiance set in again and the paper-tiger roared and vibrated. It was like being drawn back and then shot in slow motion from a bow, so slowly that sometimes you felt that the pilot's inspiration had run out and left him with nothing but a grinding determination to prove against all evidence that the thing could be done.

The sensation of being no longer ground-borne always came as a shock. The extraordinary thing had again been achieved. Following which, even at night, when there was no visible horizon, there was this sense of exultation.

*

He opened Bronowsky's gift, the book, not of Pushkin poems but Bronowsky's own translations of Gaffur (privately printed, in Bombay, dedicated to the Nawab). From its leaves he took out and read what he had begun writing to Sarah in the airport lounge.

'I'm waiting for a plane that should have come in an hour ago but is delayed by storms. My watch says 1045 so by now you'll be back and have had the message from your father that I rang. I hope Susan will be better soon. Please give her my best wishes. Your father said you'd all be staying at Commandant House for a few weeks because the new Indian commandant's wife isn't joining him yet and he's making other temporary arrangements. But after that? I didn't ask all the questions I wanted to, questions like where are you going when the few weeks are up? Back home? How absurd it is that suddenly there is this question of a roof over one's head. I gathered Susan was only suffering reaction and shock and should be out of hospital in a day or two.

'A false alarm. Someone said the plane had landed. It hadn't. But I shall have to finish this letter in Delhi. I gave your father my address there. I don't know whether I shall go down to Gopalakand as Nigel suggested. Wire me if you want me to come back to Ranpur, or up to Pankot. Your father said you'd had Nigel's telegram, the one he sent from Mirat on Thursday night, finally confirming what was never really in doubt. I tried to ring you that night, and yesterday, but the lines were hopeless. I came up to Ranpur on the night train and got in about 8 a.m. this morning and tried to ring you again from the air force mess where Major Blake arranged for me to put up during the day. He's arranged this flight for me, too. I left Mirat because there was nothing more for me to do there. Ahmed's father arrived there yesterday morning. I met him for a few moments. An impressive man. Hiding his grief.

'When I got back to Mirat from Premanagar last Thursday, and to the place where all the bodies had been taken, Dmitri and Nigel were already there, and had identified and made some of the necessary arrangements. Nigel told me – and perhaps I should tell you – that the only person Dmitri blames is himself for letting Ahmed go on that particular day and for not anticipating that something like that might happen. Before I left last night Dmitri asked me to give you his love, then made us sit down for a moment on a couch and say nothing. It was like a Tchekov play. But shall I ever return to Mirat?'

The letter ended there.

But I thought (he said silently to Sarah, putting the letter away as the lights of Ranpur performed geometrical movements as if they were man-made constellations) I thought – today in Ranpur – of solving once and for all the mystery of Hari, if he is a mystery. Before I came to the airport I went with that little piece of paper on which Nigel had written words and numbers which established an idea of an address, a place where Hari might be found, where he might actually live, exist, eat, perform duties, make love perhaps, follow a life through, be content, be happy, or at least survive and be contacted by strangers, visitors, people carrying messages, and words from Rome. I found the place but it wasn't easy. The taxidriver demanded more money when he reached the street he said led to Hari's. He wanted to go no further. Taxis, he said, did not go into such places. So I paid him off and went on foot. Immediately, I was appalled, and then frightened. I had to remind myself that this was where

657

Hari lived, where he *had* survived. Three or four small beggar boys accompanied me, demanding money. The street was very narrow. Perhaps no Englishman had ever walked down it. To the beggar boys were added a beggar-man and three beggar-women. Other people called out to me from dirty-looking open shops. The smell of animal and human ordure and human sweat was overpowering. I almost turned back. But in the midst of all this squalor a boy of twelve or fourteen confronted me. He was so clean, neat shorts and neat white shirt, anxious to be of service, anxious to speak English to the Englishman. I trusted him. I stopped being frightened. I showed him the piece of paper. He walked ahead, saying: Come, sir, this way, sir. Within a hundred yards or so he turned into a narrow stairway. It led up between two shop fronts to a kind of tenement. The walls of the stairway were stained and greasy. The boy stopped at the second landing. But by now other people were crowding the stairs.

The door the boy and I stood at was bolted outside and padlocked. But there was a card pinned to the jamb on which was typed the name. H. Kumar. The people on the stairs were shouting to the boy. I thought perhaps they were warning him not to disclose anything. I couldn't translate the bazaar dialect. But then the boy said the people were saying that Kumar Sahib was out, visiting a pupil. His aunt was out at the market in the Koti bazaar. She would be back soon. Kumar Sahib would be back later. The boy added: 'Please sir, meanwhile come and have coffee, clean shop. Brahmin shop.'

But I told him I hadn't time. I began to get out a card to give to the boy to give to Hari. But when I looked at the card it seemed like a cruel intrusion. I remembered saying to Hari: What is the difference between *karma* and *dharma*? He didn't know. I had learned the answer long ago. So had Hari. He was living it.

I went down the stairs, passing through that crowd of inquisitive people. Some of them followed us out. The boy eventually gave up pressing his invitation to drink coffee with him and said he would take me to the place where I could find a taxi. We went back through the narrow street, still followed by several youths and men and women. But now that I was out in the open I believed they were only people who wished Hari

658

well, people who merely hoped to keep me there until he got back, so that they could offer me to him as a gift.

But it would have been a cruel gift, wouldn't it? Everything about my presence was cruel. My leaving without a word to him was cruel. When we got to the place where taxis were to be had the boy hailed one. I got out a card again and a pencil, but then wrote nothing on it. I gave the card to the boy. I offered him money. He took the card but refused the money. I told the taxi-driver to take me to the cantonment.

I don't know whether I'm glad that I did what I did or whether I bitterly regret it. In the taxi back I consoled myself with the thought that if ever he needed help he had the card, a little rectangle of pasteboard. I got my wallet out and looked at another of them, imagined him receiving one like it from the boy, in an hour or two, only half-listening to the description the boy would give of the man who had come to visit, the man who had left it, the visitor from another world. I didn't know, I don't know, what harm or good I'd done. Have done. The other thing I had in my wallet was the little essay by Philoctetes which I'd cut out with Nigel's scissors. I'd intended to show it to him, intended to say, You wrote this, didn't you, Hari? I have by heart the passage that comes at the end.

'I walk home, thinking of another place, of seemingly long endless summers and the shade of different kinds of trees, and then of winters when the branches of the trees were so bare, that recalling them now, it seems inconceivable to me that I looked at them and did not think of the summer just gone, and the spring soon to come, as illusions, as dreams, never fulfilled, never to be fulfilled.'

*

Perron replaced the unfinished letter between the pages of the book Dmitri had given him. He stared out of the port. Far below, dim isolated points of light marked the villages of India – the India his countrymen were leaving, the India that was being given up. Along with what else?

He returned his attention to the book, to the poem at the end which was said to be the last Gaffur had ever written;

dictated rather. But by now he had this by heart too. So he
closed the book, shut his eyes, rested his head against the
back of the bucket seat.

*

Everything means something to you; dying flowers,
The different times of year.
The new clothes you wear at the end of Ramadan.
A prince's trust. The way that water flows,
Too impetuous to pause, breaking over
Stones, rushing towards distant objects,
Places you can't see but which you also flow
Outward to.

Today you slept long. When you woke your old blood stirred.
This too meant something. The girl who woke you
Touched your brow.
She called you Lord. You smiled,
Put up a trembling hand. But she had gone,
As seasons go, as a night-flower closes in the day,
As a hawk flies into the sun or as the cheetah runs; as
The deer pauses, sun-dappled in long grass,
But does not stay.

Fleeting moments: these are held a long time in the eye,
The blind eye of the ageing poet,
So that even you, Gaffur, can imagine
In this darkening landscape
The bowman lovingly choosing his arrow,
The hawk outpacing the cheetah,
(The fountain splashing lazily in the courtyard),
The girl running with the deer.

Author's Note and Acknowledgments

A Division of the Spoils is the last in a sequence of four novels about the closing years of British rule in India. The characters were imaginary. So were the events. The framework was as historically accurate as I could make it. Three return visits to India during the time the sequence has taken to write have left me indebted to many people there for information, for help, for hospitality; and I gratefully acknowledge that debt. I am indebted, too, to the Arts Council for an award in 1969.

Above all, I am indebted to seven people who must be named because without their combined encouragement and practical help I doubt that the enterprise could have been brought to a conclusion. Each novel in the sequence has already been dedicated, for reasons that they know, to someone who seemed to be particularly connected with it. I dedicate the sequence as a whole, if I may, to (in New York) Dorothy Olding, John Willey, Larry Hughes and Ivan von Auw, and (in London) David Higham, Roland Gant and Charles Pick.

Facta non verba.

P.S.

The Jewel in the Crown

Paul Scott

India 1942 and everything is in flux. World War II has shown that the British are not invincible and the self-rule lobby is gaining many supporters. Against this background, Daphne Manners, a young English girl, is brutally raped in the Bibighat Gardens. The racism, brutality and hatred launched upon the head of her young Indian lover echo the dreadful violence perpetrated on Daphne and reveal the desperate state of Anglo-Indian relations. The rift that will eventually prise India – the jewel in the Imperial Crown – from colonial rule is beginning to gape wide.

The Day of the Scorpion

Paul Scott

India, August 9th 1942. The morning brings raids and the arrest by British police of Congress Party members. Amongst the prisoners is the distinguished ex-Chief Minister Mohemmed Ali Kasim. Loyal to the party's central vision of a unified free India, his incarceration is a symptom of the growing deterioration of Anglo-Indian relations.

For the long-serving British family, the Laytons, the political and social ramifications are immediate, disturbing and tragic. Some, like Ronald Merrick, believe that true intimacy between the races is impossible; others, such as Sarah Layton struggle to come to terms with their Anglo-Indian past. With growing confusion and bewilderment, the British are forced to confront the violent and often brutal years that lie ahead of them.

arrow books

The Towers of Silence

Paul Scott

It is the last, bitter days of World War II and the British Raj in India is crumbling. Ensconced in the Indian Hill Station of Pankot are the English wives, mothers, daughters and widows of the officers embroiled in the ongoing conflict. With their old beliefs and assumptions under increasing virulent attack, all eyes are upon Captain Merrick and the British military to protect them in this troubled time. But Merrick, though outwardly a consummate professional, is brutal and corrupt, and not even his machinations can stop the change that is swiftly and inevitably approaching, change which is increasingly undermining the old myth of British invincibility.

Staying On

Paul Scott

Winner of the Booker Prize

Tusker and Lucy Smally stayed on in India. Given the chance to return 'home' when Tusker, once a Colonel in the British Army, retired, they chose instead to remain in the small hill town of Pankot, with its eccentric inhabitants and archaic rituals left over from the days of the Empire. Only the tyranny of their landlady, the imposing Mrs Bhoolabhoy, threatens to upset the quiet rhythm of their days.

Both funny and deeply moving, *Staying On* is a unique, engrossing portrait of the end of an empire and of a forty-year love affair.

arrow books